THE COAST OF EVERYTHING

THE COAST OF EVERYTHING

GUILLERMO STITCH

Sagging Meniscus

© 2026 by Guillermo Stitch

All Rights Reserved.

"The Tale of the Enchanted Road" was first published as the novella *Literature*^{TM} (2018).

Set in Janson with LaTeX.

ISBN: 978-1-963846-38-6 (paperback)
ISBN: 978-1-963846-42-3 (hardcover)
ISBN: 978-1-963846-39-3 (ebook)
Library of Congress Control Number: 2025934598

Sagging Meniscus Press
Montclair, New Jersey
saggingmeniscus.com

For Dad

On number one
to the Sur,
I rise
and fall
with her,
no more mine
than this:
the coast of everything.
It is cobalt.
It is shine,
curves through u.v. space,
us through time,
bluegrass,
swing.
And we just talk
and ride.
Unashamed
at last,
I hide,
in her company,
a stomach-twisting hinterland
the big songs chase.

CEILINGS.

Skies.

Clara was something of an authority. Ceilings, especially, were the pages of her atlas. On them, she could map worlds.

There were five: the low, bowed beams of the school house and the shadows that trembled around the cantilever struts that rose from them to the ridge of the roof; Dr Amstutz's salon with its egg-and-tongue cornice and the dusty glass lampshade in the middle that burned in the daytime, making those parts that fell outside its weak halo seem dirty and dim; the painted church, the pointless cherubs, the bearded men and weeping women, the blue that calmed; the inverted forest of Damocles pans, pots and playthings that hung in the general store from slender threads that made her uneasy; the near-black wood in the kitchen where she sometimes sat while Mila cooked, the glint of its polish that usually lulled her to sleep despite the smell of food and the cook's chatter; and lastly, the frontispiece—the timber square of the room next to the kitchen that had been made her bedroom and where her elderly father, while he still lived, had painted flowers for her to look at, and here and there among them a bird or a honey bee.

She spent more time in that room than anywhere, and could do something with her eye on the ceiling that she'd only ever spoken about with the doctor. If she held her gaze perfectly steady, and let it linger long enough, she could isolate a quadrant of the square and pour her attention into it, letting it drain from the rest until everything had disappeared and there was only this new, smaller square. Then she could isolate a quadrant of that and do the same. And then a quadrant of that. And then of that. Till she had her eye trained on a minuscule area and something in it so tiny—the textured grain of a wood splinter in a hairline crack, a bubble of wood varnish on the petal of a painted daisy—she would never have been able to see it otherwise, and with a sharpness of resolution that had met with disbelief in Dr Amstutz, until the girl's insistence had prompted him to test her claim and she had read without hesitation from the page of a miniature Bible he'd taped to the high ceiling of his office. He'd had to do it, rather unhappily, with the aid of a tall and much neglected stepladder, wobbling in its dotage, on which he'd stood tiptoe and at full stretch to affix the page. Thereafter, he was sufficiently astounded to keep quiet on the subject himself, since he knew of no way to square the result of his little experiment with any theory he knew of in science or medicine.

The sky, too—on the rare occasions her mother considered the weather soft enough to do her constitution some good and no harm, she'd be left in the garden under the pear tree for some dappled shade and a bit of shelter from the breeze, and forgotten about for an hour. She'd look up, taking no interest in the tree. It was a handsome enough example—older than the house, her father had once told her—and she did love pears: the explosion of juice, the mess on her chin, Mila fussing. Instead though, she would funnel her vision through a gap in the branches and revel in the revealed patch of open sky. As the chickens clucked in their coop, her eye would pull the blue space into her so that she felt she was airborne, that she was the air, and she would wait patiently till some winged thing flew through her. When April brought the brilliant white blossom it was a bother—the flowers would fill the gaps and make her garden time tedious, but before and after, and especially on a mild, dry winter day, she *was* the sky. The flapping of a waxwing would flutter in her lungs. The low glide of a stork would set her mind circling. The ceilings and the sky were where the stories came from.

Not today, though it was all sky. Today her back hurt and she was full of the quease, as Mila would say. Today the sky was a tyrant. Roiling with black clouds, it rocked and wobbled, refusing to submit to her will, to her eye—in fact, she kept it closed much of the time, to keep the sickness at bay as best she could. The litter they'd strapped her to lurched with the stumbling of its bearers. It was unfamiliar to her bones and they ached. The hard pillow rattled her head. They'd put Jordi, the dwarf, at the front and lanky Rolf at the back, to keep her level as they ascended. But most of the time it didn't work— the ground was uneven and she felt more than once that they would drop her, or that the straps would fail against the constant jolts. Jordi was enormously strong but quite blind, and so Lia was issuing rather garbled and increasingly irate instructions.

They'd only just left the flat ground of the flood plain behind them but already Clara had entered the foothills of a rising panic. She thought now that she understood the doctor—how unsettling it must have been to stretch upwards that day, unsighted and unsecured, when every nerve in his body must have been screaming at him to get down from the rickety ladder. *Why must people do these things?* she wondered. Stretch and reach and leap and leave the solid ground behind. Rail against the known, chase the elsewhere.

They were strange. And she strange to them, she supposed. It occurred to her that nobody she had ever met would have felt, precisely, the fear she now felt, or been called upon to do what she now was—to climb a mountain that hid behind you.

The whole town knew that Benjamin Bourbaki was up to something. Gone were the days of his holding leather-aproned court in the village shop. He was rarely to be found there nowadays and had left Manni Lustenberger to run it in his stead. His absence was felt—Manni was old enough to have forgotten his own birthday and procuring something as simple as a bar of soap from behind the mahogany counter, where all of the goods were kept in a byzantine array of numbered drawers, had become an emotionally draining exercise for all concerned.

Civic society, too, had been deprived of a protagonist—Bourbaki had been a presence at parish council meetings for years, albeit speaking from the gallery and in an unofficial capacity. He was the nearest thing the little town had to a captain of industry and over the years, through unstinting hard work and an unfettered belief in his own importance, had made himself pretty much impossible to ignore. His representations to the Östliche Eisenbahngesellschaft had brought about the approval of a branch line which, when complete, would include sidings and a loading dock not four kilometres hence. He had inaugurated the annual cabbage festival, for which participants travelled from all over the country, and he had financed the little reservoir and the water treatment plant that had rid the town of cholera. He'd put Einpferd on the map, in other words.

Having done so, however, Bourbaki withdrew from public life. For two years now, he'd been to-ing and fro-ing from town to city on a regular basis. He would return each time as the passenger of some haulier to oversee the stacking in his yard of whatever cargo he'd brought—timber, paper, tins of paint in every conceivable colour, ironwork and all manner of mechanical cogs and pulleys, rope, wire, glass and great barrels of tar. By the time it occurred to anyone to ask him what it was all for, he'd be back in the city.

Speculation became Einpferd's principle leisure activity. It was known, for example, that the concession for gamekeeping the Wahrberg—the isolated, conical mountain that on winter afternoons would throw its shadow over the village—had for some reason been granted to Bourbaki, a lifelong shopkeeper, who had promptly fenced off its upper reaches. The materials in his yard were brought up there piecemeal, on the back of Max Loving's cart, usually before sunrise. Loving, who had never been a popular man, was apparently determined to make a complete outcast of himself by remaining tight-lipped on the subject. Not even his wife would speak to him nowadays, and he dined in the gasthaus, alone—an indulgence he could permit himself on account of the wage Bourbaki was paying him, no doubt.

The one telescope in town belonged to Andolf Blatter—an amateur astronomer and suspected pervert—who ingratiated himself with the council by retrieving it from his attic window and installing it in the belfry for their use. It was a very poor telescope, however, and through the milky distortions of its warped lens, little was gleaned. Bourbaki was building something up there—they could make out a regular shape at the summit and the movements of a few labourers. But then, that much had been obvious.

"A greenhouse," said Gloor, the priest. "Nothing else would explain all that glass in the yard."

"Plausible," said Dr Amstutz. "But why build one at the top of a mountain? What would he grow up there?"

"Something disreputable," said Gloor. "Something proscribed."

"Orchids?" said Frau Pfafl, the organist. They were in the church, where the council met on the first Tuesday of the month.

"What's wrong with orchids?" said Ümmel, going for his notebook.

The members sat in two pews. Ümmel was looking at the back of Frau Pfafl's head as she shook it.

"I don't know," she said. "I was trying to think of something degenerate."

"Surely you could insist on taking a look, Ümmel?" said Amstutz from beside Frau Pfafl, inclining his head very slightly. "You're the law around here."

"He's got that ordinance from the Bezirksrat," said the policeman. "I'd need reasonable suspicion."

From the gallery above, where members of the public could observe council meetings, Bourbaki's absence glowered down at them. He'd been the only one who ever bothered to come.

"I suppose I could send my youngest off for a week or so, to stay with her aunt in Zweizeigen," said Öttinger after a minute, "and then report her missing." The gasthaus landlord tucked one arm beneath the other and stroked his goatee. "You could say you were searching for her."

"Yes," said Gloor, "I'm not comfortable with that."

"Quite," said the doctor. "Why should we resort to subterfuge? We're the council. The Local Authority. Can't we just ask the man?"

Frau Pfafl snorted.

"Best of luck with that!" she said. "Better than mine, anyway. I had at him the last time I found him in the shop, about a fortnight ago. I was very firm. I felt I stopped just short, for decency's sake, of haranguing the man." She pursed her lips. "Oh yes, he's up to something alright. It's written all over his face."

"All of us, though," said Amstutz, "as the council? Together. It would add a certain tone, I think. Rubber stamp of officialdom, sort of thing."

Silence. There was a bird up there somewhere, in the rafters.

"I do happen to know," said Öttinger, "he's in town this weekend."

Those in the pew in front sat forward and turned themselves around to register their surprise.

"He's booked a room," said the innkeeper. "His own apartments, presumably, are full of cargo."

"Jordi, no!"

Clara could hear Lia potter along at Jordi's side.

"Holes! Thing!"

She could picture the girl's facial expression—scrunched, like it always got when the poor creature was expected to concentrate.

"Put your feet nice and good up."

There was something wrong with the children of Einpferd.

Clara's neck ached and she was afraid that the really bad pain might come, the one the doctor called hemicrania that made light into a knife and sound into a hammer. She'd have to have them put the litter down and stay absolutely still for a long time, never mind that the rain was surely coming. She'd be sick, probably, and miss the unveiling and let Mila down. She'd have nothing to tell poor Mila who depended on her and all the secrecy would have been for nothing. All that schoolhouse conspiring that had so thrilled her.

Why don't you take a box of eggs to your father, Mila, on the day of the unveiling?

The rhythm of the cook's pan-scrubbing had quickened.

You won't have Mama to feed or summon you. And Rolf can come and sit with me. You know how he likes to listen.

Mila hadn't needed asking twice. Her father was getting very old and everybody trusted Rolf. Even now, Clara could feel the steadiness of his grip on the litter near her feet. He often came to hear a story and would stay all afternoon when he could. It was the only time the cook would ever leave Clara with anyone else for more than a minute or two. This included her mother. The rangy boy was the school's most studious and worked like a mine pony in the timber yard on Saturdays. The sight of him, either there and caked in sawdust, or tirelessly running errands for whoever'd slip him a few centimes during the week after school, inspired confidence. He was fancied for further education and therefore already carried something of an aura about him—the lustre of the wider world, of the city. Big-eared and long-fingered, he had, despite his palpable intelligence, never spoken a word.

Mila had been sullen since the news of the unveiling. Of course, there was no question of her being invited or, in the event it was made open to the public, permitted to go. The poor thing had such a curious mind, but had never had anything in the way of an education—her inquiring nature would mostly find itself misdirected in the tidbits of town gossip with which she'd regale Clara in the kitchen, feigning outrage and piety and loving every minute of it. Clara liked the music of it, though the details bored and baffled her in equal measure—at least her companion knew there was someone to listen to her. In the bedroom, though, she'd see another side to Mila, whenever she asked her to sit by the bed and read from one of Papa's old books.

There weren't many. Mama had given most away in the months following his death—to Amstutz, the school, to anyone who'd take them. Clara, beside herself at the time, hadn't noticed until there were only these few left and she'd begged Mila to hide them under the bed. Once out of sight, her mother had forgotten about them and by now the cook had read them all to her at least twice, often not understanding the words she was repeating, but paying very careful attention to Clara's patient explanations and delighting the girl with her questions, which more often than not proved very astute. There was one on botany, one on colour, a manual on the production of quince paste, a history of the Sassanian empire and a book of tales from the Thousand And One Nights.

All of which would have been unavailable to someone so lowly, of course, if she hadn't had Clara, who felt the weight of her responsibility very heavily. It pressed down on her even now, as her friends carried her clumsily up the mountain. Why else would she do this if not for Mila? To include her. To give her a glimpse of another world. The poor thing.

"Jordi, up. And down down but up."

Jordi, whose customary good humour was considered indefatigable, was beginning to fray at the edges. They'd been on the move for almost two hours but Clara was afraid to ask how much progress they'd made—not much, by the feel of their stumbles and the unchanged sky.

"I'm not sure Lia's very good at this," said the dwarf.

"Oh, Jordi. You're doing very well indeed," said Clara, smiling as radiantly as she could at the low cloud. "You're the hero of the hour!"

She felt an uncharacteristic little wobble at Rolf's end of the litter, but he soon steadied himself. Lia was pretty—big round eyes *like two milk drops pressed into an apple* as Mila would say of the rosy-faced girl. But her words were always jumbled, rarely informative, and she didn't seem to be able to think.

The last two unremarkable children to have been born in the town were the Fellman twins, Florian and Nathanael. They were grown now and had left Einpferd as soon as an opportunity had arisen: the conservatoire for Nathanael and an internship with a merchant bank for Florian. Their childhood had been an unhappy one. As they grew and as, one by one, their senior classmates had left school, the prissy boys had found themselves surrounded by altogether more unusual juniors—something or other had been wrong with every child born since.

"Lia, how far away is the top? Can you see it?"

Clara could hear that Lia had stopped to look.

"Is it very far, Lia?"

Now they'd all stopped. Clara and Jordi held their breath.

"Tiny," said Lia.

There was no movement from Rolf, so presumably the assessment was correct. Jordi sighed.

"Why don't you tell us a story, Clara?" he said as they moved forward again. "It might help pass the time."

Clara felt too sick to tell tales, but they were all going to so much trouble for her, and she so wanted to see the unveiling, to tell the tale of *it* to Mila, that she couldn't risk their becoming discouraged. She took a deep, deep breath and told them the one about the young scribe and the enchanted road.

The Tale of the Enchanted Road

"**WHAT A LOT OF PEOPLE** don't appreciate these days is that as recently as the first half of the last century, what they called literature was a very, very different thing to the thing we have now. Almost no resemblance at all. Quite apart from questions of legality, health and safety and so on, there wouldn't be any point in revisiting the vast majority of those First Era texts—believe me, we've been through them with a fine-tooth comb and the functionality just isn't there."

Their guide, who'd introduced himself as Murphy, spoke as he walked and without looking back.

"We don't have that much source material left, obviously, but it's evident from what we do have that neither the risks nor the potential benefits were understood. We know that literature was readily available in a multiplicity of media. Mass produced, widely consumed. That consumption, however, seems to have been left entirely to the vagaries of entertainment markets."

He shook his head.

"Very much an Arts thing, for them. Of the numerous commentaries that survived the Disaster, none make any reference to specific applications. Remember that Spirituality™ at that time lingered on in the *public sector*. And there does seem to have been a connection; we know that consumers habitually sought some sort of emotional uplift from literature. Solace™, if you will. It isn't easy for us to imagine now that Solace™ would have been difficult to access elsewhere. But there you go. Markets evolve. Back then it was, as I said, very much one of the old Arts."

He stopped and turned and the little group of journalists formed a semi-circle around him.

"Which is why, in the run-up to the Second Enlightenment, we see signs of disillusion. I'm not saying that anyone had had the eureka moment—almost certainly not—but there were embryonic attempts to embed literature, and the Arts in general, into the wider human project. To put them to use. It can seem surprising to us now that once established, those early strategies, from product placement to search optimization, influencer content and so on, didn't light the way sooner. Any questions?"

No questions. He went on.

"In fact, the mood at the time was anything but optimistic. It was as if they believed they were winding up, actually—bringing a defunct and ultimately fruitless human endeavor to an end. There was this increased focus on game play, social networking and other reality-driven behaviors.

"Pfft. They hadn't even started. Pinpoint™ Role Assignment changed everything. It is now universally recognized as the single most significant factor in the development of modern literature. Without it the Second Enlightenment couldn't have happened. We'd still be pawing through books like our forebears did, looking for some inherent value in there as opposed to identifying the countless opportunities we've since been able to exploit—a completely untapped resource, right under our noses. Very little of what we've accomplished economically, socially and politically would have been conceivable. Or scientifically—remember that Pinpoint™ can only be fully understood in the context of the discovery of Cog™ power."

There was a large touchscreen on the wall behind Murphy. He swiped it till the day diary showed up and he blocked out the entry for their tour. 4am: Billy didn't suppose many of the journalists had been up this early on a Tuesday morning before. It felt a lot like a Monday night.

"Of course, it's a work in progress," said Murphy. "You try this, you try that. Necessarily, there's an ad lib element in the early stages of any new field. We've been quite transparent about that. But believe me: every single false start has provided critical information. Know-how. That's what's so exciting about tomorrow."

Someone stifled a yawn.

"We're no strangers to controversy," Murphy scowled. "There will always be resistance to change, of course. Pockets of extremism. The recent emergence of Gilgamesh is very worrying, and you all know about the problems we've had at the book burnings—people don't like them.

"The digital purge continues." He shrugged. "We'll get there. We deeply regret every fatality, we really do, but it was incumbent upon us to ramp things up in preparation for the launch. We have a responsibility to our users. Those are some pretty fancy shoes mister." Murphy's gaze had dropped to Billy's feet. "We are probably going to mess those up for you today."

He walked on. They fell into line behind him.

"It would be premature to guarantee that we've found the definitive application. But early signs are very, very encouraging. You'll have to forgive us for being a little pleased with ourselves here at Gripping Tails™. No previous incarnation of Applied Lit™ has been rolled out on this scale. Maybe we have some slips. Tony, do we have any of those plastic slips for this guy's shoes?"

They were at the end of a long, brightly lit corridor. Murphy stood outside a metal double door, low but wide. He looked like someone who had more to say. A tall man in a white coat pressed a pair of plastic shoe covers into Billy's hand.

"It's amazing," said Murphy, "if you stop to think about it. It is to me, anyway. Before Pinpoint™ there's no way anyone could have seen it pan out like this. That something we'd all learned to think of as a historical fallacy—a heresy, even—could be resurrected in this way. That it would take up so useful a role in our lives. With hindsight though, from the moment the Cog™ drive was introduced, it was just a matter of time. Who knows what other old Arts we might resurrect—under carefully controlled conditions, of course—and put to work?"

He planted his feet wide and clasped his hands.

"We've struggled with this thing for centuries but at long last, folks, literature finds itself fully optimized as Gripping Tails™, now the fourth largest auto-sector brand in the country and set to revolutionize road safety legislation both domestically and around the world. We even have our eyes on the colonies. I know, I know—early days, but we don't do small thinking here. Mind your heads."

Murphy opened the door and one by one, they bowed their heads to pass beneath a cluster of cable runs, stepping out into a vast, low-ceilinged hangar. To either side of them, the outer walls were punctuated by what might have been loading docks—openings that stretched from floor to ceiling and framed the blank night. The place stretched away into a distance that couldn't quite be made out through the machinery and personnel that occupied the floor space. Instrumentation arrays were aligned with each of the docks and operatives in orange-and-green overalls stood in huddles, nodding and tapping data onto tabs.

Billy was the first to say anything, as he bent to pull the plastic slips over his shoes. They were indeed fancy—a pair of two-tone Hennessy brogues that had cost him a hundred and forty bux—but they were the only ones, aside from house slippers, that he'd left in his old room when he'd moved into Jane's. And they weren't the only problem. Passing for his usual sports jacket was the top half of the navy blue velvet suit Ma had bought him for his prom. Underneath was a frilled oyster-white shirt, originally from the same outfit. It had been three weeks now since Jane had thrown him out, staying at

Vince's hadn't gone well and being back at Ma's was getting old. Not least because it was out in Lakeside, which meant a ninety-minute commute. He'd gone back to Jane's a couple of times for his clothes but she would never answer the door.

"It's so quiet in here," he said. His fully buttoned overcoat was only to be removed if absolutely necessary. His hat was tilted right back and the visible hair—fine and blond—was damp against his scalp.

Murphy smirked.

"You think so," his eyes dropped to Billy's visitor badge, "Mr Stringer? You normally make a lot of noise when you read?"

"OK, folks, stay between the lines."

Murphy was on the move again, speaking over his shoulder. They filed along behind him, Billy instinctively taking up the rear. He'd been too busy checking his tab every few minutes to listen very carefully to Murphy's presentation. He took it out and looked at it again. No notifications. It had been four days since he'd had anything from her—the longest ever. The last two messages he had had were requests for him to stop contacting her. He pocketed it again and followed the others on a diagonal, toward one of the openings where some technicians gathered around their gear.

What was he doing here anyway? He could get into all kinds of trouble here. It wasn't even his job—this was Reynolds' turf. Billy covered sports for *The Herald*, but Reynolds was down with some bug and they'd been stuck. There were precisely no good reasons why Billy would put his hand up for this of all jobs, and plenty why he shouldn't. But put his hand up he had. Vince had flipped. Anyway, here he was.

A loud hiss pulled him out of his thoughts—the others were looking towards the opening, where a vehicle, almost as wide and tall as the gap itself, was backing in. There were no windows and no sign of a cabin for a driver. Actually, Billy couldn't tell whether he was looking at the front or the back—it looked like a solid cube of metal to him as it slid along a slick, shiny surface without the aid of wheels.

"The Litera-Truck™," said Murphy. "Surfacing. These'll be going out every twenty-four hours to keep the roads clean, freshly coated and legible. They'll be extra busy today, for tomorrow's launch."

"Legible?" said one of the other journos, a tall woman who Billy had heard introduce herself as a staff writer from *The Standard*. He hadn't caught her name. He thought he'd recognized her from somewhere but from the way she'd looked right through him back in the visitor room, presumably not. "The interface isn't in-car?"

"Oh no," said Murphy. "That's been key for us. Placing it on-road is a big part of what makes this thing work. The safety systems all rely on it—a shared surface for both vehicular motion and operator interface. I think you'll be impressed at what integration has done for maximum safe velocities." His hands were on his hips. "No, you definitely need to get that to understand the approach. The road is the page."

Billy snorted. He'd finally gotten round to tapping some notes into his pad.

"The road is the page," he echoed. "The page is the road." He smiled and looked up from his screen. Nobody else was smiling. He swallowed.

"I just meant . . . you know . . . that's some heavy symbolism, isn't it?"

Murphy was looking at him in a way he didn't like one bit.

"I haven't seen you here on any of the open days, Mr Stringer. I assume you're filling in. I hope you have the chops for it. We are very keen to get our message out there and above all, to strike the right tone. It would be disappointing to see a discourse on symbolism in coverage of what may be the transport sector's greatest paradigm shift in millennia. The *transport sector*, Mr Stringer."

"No, of course not," said Billy, feeling his skin flush. "I would never . . . I just meant, between us, you know—"

But Murphy had already turned away and disappeared around the corner of the Litera-Truck™. He reappeared on the other side of the wet-looking track and crouched at the end that faced the opening, drawing the visitors' attention to a roller that ran along the base of the cube. Its surface had that same sheen to it.

"The Litera-Tyre™," said Murphy. "This coats the surface."

"Coats the surface with what?" asked the woman from *The Standard*.

Murphy stood.

"It's proprietary, Ms Gutefee," he said, "so you'll understand that I won't be answering that question. I can tell you a little about the R&D."

He'd come back around to the journalists' side of the vehicle.

"It took us a while, beginning with technologies that were bona fide antiques. We tried various methods based on electrowetting, for example. Interferometrics. A number of imaging techniques. Nematic displays and so on. We even tried plasma."

An operative handed him a tab which he checked, signed and gave back.

"None of them could provide the fluidity we needed in conjunction with basic grip," he continued. "Traction. Eventually we abandoned all of the above. What we've ended up with is completely new. I can tell you that titanium is an element but, crucially, this is biotech. Living material. You can print that, but make sure you stress its non-toxicity. Get her out of here, Jerry, and roll the car in."

As the cube slipped back out through the gap in the wall, Billy looked around. None of the others would make eye contact with him, except the tall lady from *The Standard* who did for just a moment, to glare. He was beginning to feel very uncomfortable, especially all done up like this. The collar of his prom blazer itched.

Another vehicle backed into the hangar. It was easy to tell that this one came in backwards because it had a tail. A long, armored tail in articulated sections that tapered to a point and swept low over the road surface from one side of the track to the other. He'd never seen anything like it. Again there were no windows and no wheels. Even an aging jock like him knew not to look for co-axials or blades. Cognition drives didn't do airborne. Not yet anyway—they were too erratic. The best comparison he could think of was a flattened armadillo.

"The Car-A-Pace™," said Murphy who was suddenly, and unnervingly, behind him. "Prototype. But we're looking at a number of bids from commercial manufacturers. Could I?"

"Hm? Oh, yeah. Sure."

Billy stepped aside so that Murphy could get to the car.

"It's very low," said the *Standard* woman. For a bunch of journalists they didn't seem too curious. She was the only one who'd asked any questions.

"Yep," said Murphy. "Two body positions available for the operator. Reclining, in which case the text appears above them courtesy of in-car optics, or face down. That one's unsettling at first, but people almost invariably end up preferring it. And this," he squatted and patted the tail affectionately, as if the car were a pet, "is what it's all about, folks. The Tail™ itself. The drive is in here. Thrust, traction, everything. The sweeping action deletes, so there are no residuals for following vehicles to deal with. It's ingenious, if you don't mind me saying so. I don't take personal credit, of course."

"You didn't work on the drive yourself?" said Billy. He was keen to worm himself back into favor. "Because I had just a couple of questions. For instance, in case of boredom, or distraction, what failsafes—"

"I don't know the first thing about cognition drives, young man," said Murphy, cutting him off. Billy noticed the woman from *The Standard* rolling her eyes. Murphy jabbed his thumb over his shoulder at some technicians. "I pay them to know. Besides, you can get all the available information on cognition drives from Cog™ themselves."

He'd straightened up, turned around and was almost nose-to-nose with Billy.

"This isn't about the drive, Mr Stringer. It's about the application. Applied Lit™ is the story here. Get it?"

"Sure, sure. Got it," said Billy. So much for getting into this guy's good books. He began to breathe a little easier as Murphy wrapped it up and the little group trundled back towards the exit. Clearly, he'd embarrassed himself but at least it was over.

And at least nothing worse had happened.

In the visitor room, Billy removed the shoe covers and dropped them into a wastepaper basket. They were stained with the dark, tar-like substance that had coated the track. Murphy told him to wash his hands and took his leave. The journalists were to wait for someone to escort them out of the facility. Billy rinsed his hands in the washbasin on the wall, sat down on one of the plastic benches and, since conversation seemed unlikely, took his tab out. He sat forward, elbows on knees, and stared at the screen. No notifications. He brought up Jane's feed and read the last message.

bili I want u 2 stop calling. no messages. at least 4 now. i dont no wot ur doin. i dont understand. stop tryin 2 xplain. i dont want 2 undrstand. i love u bili but I cant b around u anymor. its ovr. just stop.

Then he reread it a few times as the saline fluid that filled his eyes made the screen warp and blur.

Jane. He hadn't noticed his own thumb start to tap. *i can only hope u havnt blokd me. dat ul read dis. hony I cant*

"Mr Stringer?"

He looked up and wiped an eye as nonchalantly as possible before a tear could clear his lash and drop to his cheek. There was a man in the doorway that Murphy had left through. A huge, rough-looking man who looked like he'd seen the inside of as many boxing rings as he had bars.

"Mr Murphy would like to see you, Mr Stringer. In his office." The voice was, if anything, more weathered than the face. "You OK?"

"Me? Sure," said Billy. "I'm fine. I'm great."

He looked around. His fellow hacks were too intent on whatever was happening on their respective screens to look back at him. That or they didn't want to. He stood, pocketed his tab and tried to sound upbeat.

"Lead the way."

His feet felt heavy as he followed the man up a long stairway. He wondered why they weren't in an elevator—the stairs seemed to go on forever, but the space was too narrow, and the man's back too broad, for Billy to see how far up. Way more than a story. More than three at this stage, by his reckoning. No turns, no landings.

Vince had been right—he shouldn't have come here. The belly of the beast. It had been stupid of him to think he could get away with it and it was unpleasantly clear to him now that he hadn't. Just when he needed to do some quick thinking, these stairs were taking it out of him. Five stories now? His legs were uncooperative lead pipes. He was sweating. His heart rate was up there somewhere, waiting for him. It might have to be patient. He wasn't breathing very well and he couldn't think straight, let alone quick. Maybe that was the point.

When they got to the top he was actually pleased—he knew that something bad was going to happen to him in the office the big man was knocking at, but there would be a chair. The hulk pushed the door open and nodded to Billy, who squeezed past and found himself in an innocuous-looking space. There was a desk against the opposite wall, behind which a set of venetian blinds were closed against the outside. An overhead striplight made everything seem to vibrate. There was indeed a chair this side of the desk and to Billy's relief Murphy, who stood by the window, gestured to it. He flopped into it, trying not to pant too loudly.

"A design flaw," said Murphy, "but I've learned to live with it. I insisted on an office overlooking the factory floor but there's no vertical here for an elevator shaft. If nothing else, it keeps Alphonse in shape."

Billy turned his head slightly to note the presence of the taciturn giant behind him. He sighed audibly and turned back to look at his host. What Murphy had said didn't make sense to him, since he'd just been on the factory floor and it had a conspicuously low ceiling. But he let it go. He was pretty sure he wasn't the one who was meant to ask the questions.

"Do you want a job, Mr Stringer?"

"Look, the things I said down there," Billy sat up. "I just thought, you know, since we're all professionals. And it was in private. I would never write anything like . . . they wouldn't print it if I did. You know? I mean, I wouldn't have lasted five minutes at the . . ."

He trailed off. Murphy looked at him, steadily. He blinked back.

"Could you repeat the question?"

"Certainly. Would you be interested in coming to work at Gripping Tails™, Mr Stringer?"

After another couple of blinks, Billy turned to look again at Alphonse. Nothing to be read in the impassive features.

"I thought you might have wanted to reprimand me," he said, turning back. "That you thought I'd been loose-tongued down there."

"I do think that, Mr Stringer," said Murphy. "You were."

It came to Billy's attention that his hands were tapping a rhythm on the arms of the chair. He had them stop.

"But you're offering me a job?"

"Correct."

Murphy went to his chair and sat in it. He picked up a piece of paper and folded it meticulously as he spoke, running a thumbnail along each crease as he went. He kept his eyes on what he was doing.

"Finding and ... dealing with those of a literary bent, Mr Stringer, has been a fraught process." He unfolded the paper, smoothing out the creases. Billy had stopped breathing. He hoped that neither of them had noticed—that, or the goosebumps that covered his forearms. *I should have listened to you, Vince.*

"An unpleasant process," continued Murphy, "for everyone involved—it can take a certain toll, you know, when your targets are generally quiet, retiring types. Not all of them are, of course, but a lot of them. It doesn't sit well that these are the people we have to go after. The terminations are obviously brutal. And best avoided, from a PR perspective—I think we would all agree on that."

Billy knew he must be deathly pale. He tried to take a few breaths, nice and steady.

"The detention centers are inordinately expensive to maintain. And necessarily punitive, of course. Another PR disaster for us. The horror stories that go round. You've heard the stories, I suppose, Mr Stringer."

Billy had.

Murphy wasn't messing around with the paper anymore, or withholding eye contact.

"Take you," he said. "A case in point. You brought yourself to my attention today, Mr Stringer. In rather an unfortunate way. There isn't the slightest doubt in my mind that you are of a literary bent."

Billy opened his mouth but Murphy waved his hand to silence him. He wasn't sure he'd have been able to speak in any case.

"And it is a bent. A deviant tendency. Personally I think it's innate. We are highly attuned to it here, as you would expect. You have it, Mr Stringer."

Another wave. Murphy wasn't to be interrupted.

"The question for us, then," he went on, "is what to do about you."

So that was the question. Apparently Murphy didn't have an answer because he let it just hang there. Maybe it was Billy's turn to speak but he didn't have anything to say. Murphy got up and went back to the window, turning his back on the room. He inserted a thumb and forefinger between two slats of the blind, parted them and put his eye to the gap.

"Come and see, Billy."

It seemed to take all of Billy's strength to lift himself up out of the chair. His arms trembled. He covered the eight feet to the window slowly, hoping his legs wouldn't let him down. While he handled that, Murphy rotated a wand that hung from the blind at his end, opening the slats and angling them downwards. Billy let his eyes follow their line.

It was a factory floor all right, of sorts—well populated with workers but quiet even though the window was open. It wasn't the factory floor he'd been on earlier and, he noted with a pang of vertigo, it was indeed a good five stories below them. There was nothing industrial or obviously technological going on down there. It looked more like an administrative pool, actually. If pool was the right word—this was an ocean. The floor space matched the height of the place in scale. The size of several football pitches, was the obvious analogy that sprang to the sports writer's mind.

Having something to look at that wasn't Murphy calmed his breathing a little. He let his eyes rove, taking in some details. Most of the area was taken up with desks. It was like a little city of them. Some were clustered and some were standalone, arranged in neat columns. He saw kitchenettes and what looked like full-blown bars. There were hammocks down there and pool tables. Dart boards and ping-pong. There were sunken seating areas, ringed by circular sofas.

"What do you think?" said Murphy. "My gut tells me you'd fit in very well."

"What is it, exactly?" said Billy.

"Great question," said Murphy. "I can't give you a name—I haven't decided yet. But I can tell you that you are looking at the greatest literary undertaking in the history of humanity." He glanced sideways at Billy to observe the effect of his words, then returned his attention to the scene below them. "I might go with The Nineveh Institute. One in the eye for our rebel friends in Gilgamesh, you know? Nineveh Editions? What do you think, Alphonse?"

Neither of them turned in response to the silence behind them, both intuiting that the giant had merely shrugged.

"Not that this is a library," said Murphy. "It's a production line."

Somewhere inside Billy, a penny dropped. He looked at Murphy, eyes wide.

"You mean to say they're *making* fiction down there?"

"I do."

"But . . ." Billy shook his head. "It's massive. How much—"

"Sit down, Billy."

They returned to their seats and Murphy leaned forward, elbows on his desk and fingers woven.

"The Cog™ drives are lauded as having given us fuel-free propulsion, Billy, but it isn't exactly true. I suspect you understand this—you seem bright enough. Cognition itself is the fuel. Cerebral activity. Specifically, changes in connectivity in the supramarginal gyri and the right posterior temporal gyri. But as I told you downstairs, I'm not the right person to get into the details with you. My area is the literature. I bring the cognition stuff up because it's relevant to the literature in ways we're still learning about. We've known for a long time that the highest quality input is fiction. Story, if you like. Math, puzzles, history, science—none of them hold a candle when it comes to the Cog™ drives."

He opened one of his desk drawers and retrieved a slim cylindrical object with a chrome finish, about three inches in length.

"You want to smoke? I have an unopened one here."

Billy shook his head.

"No thanks. I don't."

"You don't smoke? What the fuck is the matter with you?"

Murphy shook his head. With a twist of the mouthpiece, he activated the siGi™ and sat back.

"We also know, and this you will be unaware of, that certain types of story work better than others. I'm not talking content so much as narrative structure. As a journalist, you'll be familiar with the terms, of course. They'll become even more meaningful if and when you come to work for us."

Suddenly, Billy didn't like the word *if*. Not at all. Murphy took a drag and blew a long, slow cone of red vapor, by which Billy could tell it was packed with Spirituality™.

"What I'm telling you is, Applied Lit™ has been developed using highly select material. A lot of First Era texts are unsuitable. Actually, they're dangerous. We need certain qualities—suspense, for example. Mystery, as long as the promise of resolution is delivered. Crime stories are great. The best. But other stuff works too. As long as it's neat, that it knows where it's going and that it goes there, it can power a drive. If it doesn't have that it's too risky. Experimental literature is a disaster. Ambiguity has been responsible for a number of deaths in the testing phase. Test pilots. Brave men and women."

He took another drag and put his feet on the desk. Billy couldn't quite believe that Murphy was sharing all of this and, consequently, couldn't quite believe he was getting out of the building alive. He wished he'd said yes to the siGi™. He felt hot, except for his feet and his face: they were icy.

"There's an additional problem," said Murphy. "A serious one. The short-term connectivity changes I mentioned are the ones we need to harness. They're what gets a drive and its user from A to B." Another deep drag and slow exhalation, the upper reaches of the room now a red haze, hanging in lazy strips. "Unfortunately, there are longer term changes—notably in the bilateral somatosensory cortex—and they, Billy, have proved somewhat troublesome."

He frowned, as if he couldn't discern anything in the young journalist's facial expression that might denote understanding.

"You could characterize the issue as one of tolerance. To give you a concrete example—your own commute. It's a certain distance and there's a particular route, or perhaps there are two or three possible routes. We allocate a narrative to your drive to take care of that commute. When you finish that narrative, you can simply start again. Once programmed, it will continue to function for that route."

He retracted his feet and sat up straight, suddenly enough to startle Billy.

"There's a catch though. It won't work quite as well the second time. And there will be another slight deterioration on the third pass. And so on. That initial synaptic activity can never be replicated. We're talking about imperceptible differences at first, but it's a process that accelerates. We're running out of juice, Billy."

Billy raised his eyebrows. It was the best he could do.

"Let me remind you," said Murphy, "that while we launch on the highways here in the city, we go national before the year is out. And even that's just the beginning. I bet you pulled up here in a standard maglev this morning. You won't be driving one of those for long. Nobody will. After the motorways it's the trunks, then primaries through tertiaries. Right down to residentials. Every road and street in the country. The one thing we cannot do is run out of juice—hence our little operation down there."

"Wow," said Billy. He knew he had to say something. "But the risks ... I mean, how long have we all spent ... wow. People out there are incarcerated for generating fiction. Executed. Isn't it dangerous—"

"Whoa there, mister," Murphy raised a hand. "Now just a minute. If you are equating the very carefully controlled operations downstairs with the underground filth disseminated by Gilgamesh, you're way off base."

He underlined his point by rapping the desktop with the point of his siGi™.

"You are talking about people hell bent on bringing society to its knees. They have not one whit of regard for your safety or mine. You're talking about fundamentalists, Billy. They honestly believe that what they do is for a greater good. That they're protecting something valuable which we are out to destroy."

He made a circular motion with an index finger at his temple.

"You can't reason with people like that. What they deal in is invariably degraded. Very low quality. Certainly unusable for our purpose, or we'd work with them. In fact, the material is toxic, for all the reasons I've been explaining to you. And it's gotten into the wrong hands. That's why we have to eradicate it. If material like that ever got anywhere near a Cog™ drive, people would die. It isn't going to happen on my watch, Billy." Murphy looked agitated. "If that dictates a nip-it-in-the-bud approach, so be it."

There didn't seem to be any way for Billy to get on this guy's good side. Now he'd riled him again.

"But," Billy's own voice sounded like it was coming from a long way off, "you want me to work here?"

Murphy sat back in his chair. This time, he left his feet on the floor.

"Makes sense, doesn't it?" he said. "Look, you're young. Youngish. What are you? Twenty-six? Twenty-seven?"

"I'm thirty-two."

"Oh. Well, looking pretty good, Billy. Bit of a paunch. I take it your sporting days are behind you. I suppose that explains the *Herald* gig. Anyway, the argument is the same. I'm looking across my desk at you and I'm thinking to myself that this can go two ways. We get you in here, harness this tendency of yours. Or we leave you out there where they can get to you first. Where you, my friend, are easy prey for radicalization. Believe me, they know about you. You write for a city paper. And believe me, they're interested in you. If we are, they are."

He patted the tab that lay on his desk.

"I was reading a piece of yours while you were on your way up here. The play-offs piece? A nice enough piece, but a dead giveaway. You might think you're being clever, but it's riddled with literary pretension. I'm amazed the powers that be over there don't talk to you about it."

"Actually, sometimes they—"

A wave of the hand. Murphy had no interest in chat.

"What do you say, Billy?" he said. "Which way will you go?"

He pulled in more of the red Spirituality™ and held it rather than letting it go straight away, from which Billy inferred it was his turn to speak. He sat up and rubbed his hands.

"Well," he said. It was as good a start as any. "You'll appreciate what a surprise this is."

He didn't want to make it obvious he was playing for time, but he couldn't make up his mind whether this was on the level, or a trap.

"I'm dumbfounded, actually." He tapped the arms of his chair. Murphy didn't look like he was in any hurry to fill the silence.

"When would I need to get back to you?" he said, finally.

Murphy's eyebrows went north.

"I was rather hoping you'd tell me right now, Mr Stringer," he said, "but I suppose we can give you some time. Let's say midnight tonight, if you'll forgive the dramatics. In these matters, I like to move quickly."

"OK," said Billy. Another few taps on the faux leather padding. "So," a slow swallow, "I can go?"

Murphy smiled. It was a broad, unguarded smile.

"Of course, Billy. Look, don't get me wrong—it isn't as if you're in any trouble. This is an informal conversation, nothing more. We don't have anything on you. We're just interested. I happen to think you'd be great down there. A real asset. But if you choose to stay on at *The Herald*, that's absolutely fine. It's a free world, after all."

He swiveled in his chair to give himself the space to cross his legs and sat back to the point of slouching. The body language of carefree congeniality.

"We'd keep an eye on you obviously. On your work. But then, you're a writer for a big city paper—we'd get round to doing that anyway. This could be your chance, Billy. You'd make a lot more and you'd be part of something big. Think about it, will you?"

"Oh sure!" said Billy. "I won't think about anything else all day. What an offer, you know? I really appreciate it." He had half raised himself out of his seat.

"Good," said Murphy. He kept his eyes on Billy's as the younger man stood up. "So to be clear, then," he said, picking a tab up from the desktop and holding it out, "this does interest you?"

"Absolutely," said Billy. He took the tab and looked at Murphy, head tilted with a mute question.

"You just need to sign," said the seated man. "Confidentiality." He watched as Billy held the tab up to eye level and let it take an optiscan.

"Great. You find your way to the bottom of the stairs, Billy, and someone will be along to see you out."

Billy didn't have anything else to say, so he put the tab back on the desk, nodded to each of them and left, clicking the door softly behind him like a cowed schoolboy excused from the headmaster's office.

Murphy stared at the door for a few seconds.

"What do you think?" he said.

One of the giant's eyes widened slightly. Just the one.

"You offering me a raise?"

"What? I—"

"Because you don't pay me enough to think."

"Nice," said Murphy. He took a drag on the siGi™. There was nothing left in it.

"You reckon one of them would be dumb enough to walk right in here?" he said, dropping it back into the desk drawer.

Alphonse shrugged. An almost imperceptible movement of his massive frame.

"People do all kinds of things."

"Yeah," said Murphy. "Thanks for your help, Alphonse. Run an analysis on that optiscan, will you. And keep a very close eye on this guy today."

It had been all heart and lungs on the way up, but it was Billy's knees that screamed at him going down those stairs. When he got to the visitor room, someone was already there for him—a uniformed girl who couldn't have been much over eighteen and who held her tab like a clutch bag. She didn't say a word, just turned and exited the room by another door. He followed, automatically checking his screen.

No notifications. When they reached the main entrance the automatic doors slid open and the operative offered him a perfunctory smile and the opportunity to walk through them. He did. Tomorrow was just beginning to burn at the edge of the night sky. It was already warm. Beyond and below the twenty or so visitor parking spaces on the lot at the front of the facility, the semi-circular city stretched out on its flat, still illuminated, each point of light like a bright dew drop on a spider web.

The others had already left. There were just two cars—Billy's and a Jowett Jupiter parked next to it. He took his own siGi™ from the inside pocket of his coat, twisted the mouthpiece and inhaled a long lungful of sweet Solace™. He had *almost* given up but had found he couldn't quite get by without a little Solace™ from time to time. As he walked across the lot, he saw that someone was sitting in the other car. The woman from *The Standard*. She'd flipped her rear view monitor to mirror mode and was applying make-up from a compact. *Born into money*, he thought to himself, *or married to it*. You didn't drive around in a Jowett Jupiter on a reporter's wage. *I should talk to her*.

She was bound to know more about Murphy than Billy did, which was nothing. She might even know about the production line in there. He'd have to go carefully on that one. Feel her out. But as he got close she lit the Jupiter up. It rose a few inches on its blue-lit maglev field, backed out of the space and pulled away. She didn't look at him as she passed. She didn't seem to see him.

Billy climbed into his old Marmon. Next to the Jupiter it wasn't impressing anybody, but it had those same First Era lines that had become popular. He sat for a few seconds with his hands on his knees, listening to the faint sounds that wafted up from the city. He resisted the temptation to look at his tab yet again, wanting only to collect his thoughts. Then he fired the lev up and pulled out. There was no collecting to be done. He had just two things on his mind. Phil's would be serving breakfast soon. And he needed to talk to Vince.

Billy pulled up to the vacant bookstore on the ground floor of the Greenwich building and parked. Phil's was across the street. The only fixture left in the bookstore, visible in the dark because its metal contours reflected the streetlight, was a replica cash register. Cash was ancient history but nostalgia was still going strong and people liked the old designs. Nothing else in the place—the empty display shelves in the window had a hastily abandoned look to them.

The bookstores were gone. In theory, there were plenty of permitted books—science, self-help, sporting memoir—but the purges over the years and the martial law of the last few months had thrown a pall over the retail business. People shied away from places that might have anything to do with contraband. The authorities had been only too happy to help the process along with restrictive regulation and prohibitive tax—locked into online espionage and up to their necks in encryption algorithms, they were even more unnerved by the idea of something you could bury in a hole in your back yard.

Everybody liked hard copy but nobody wanted trouble—almost nobody, anyway—and one by one, the stores had gone bust. He looked up at the tall sash window over the door, its green blind slanted by neglect but still bright against the red brick of the building. Billy had rented a room here once upon a time. That had been his window.

If there was anywhere in the city less suited to a secret rendezvous than Phil's, Billy had yet to hear about it. The diner had windows facing onto Greenwich and De Nuys that curved seamlessly at the corner. Just two feet of green wall separated their lower edges from the ground and another two at the top from the sign above that said "Phil's" and a siGi™ hoarding. Especially at night, the brilliantly lit place was a fishbowl. There were no tables at the windows because there was no room for tables. A cherry-wood bar—triangular, to conform with the acute angles of the building—almost filled it. There was room only for the round, leather-topped stools that lined it and for a customer to squeeze by them.

The breakfast crowd would be in soon but for now the place was almost empty. Just three figures hugged the bar but they were no early birds. They were night hawks. With their backs to him, a guy in a dark suit and a steel-gray hat and a redhead in a red dress had that sated, lounging air about them that came from a night spent dancing. A broad-shouldered guy at the other side of the bar could easily be a cop. Behind it, Benny looked like a milkman in his white get-up. He spotted Billy and gave an unsmiling nod of recognition. Billy raised a hand in response. Then he got out of the car and crossed the street.

The door was around the corner, but Billy wasn't looking for the door. Vince was on the early this week and would already be at work. He kept walking for three blocks till he saw the flags that hung from the front of the De Nuys hotel. Then he walked down an alley between a barber shop and a hardware store. About halfway up the alley, he turned right into another, then followed that till it widened out into a little yard. It was a dead end, the only through way blocked off by a head-height, wire-mesh fence. Trying to make as little noise as possible, he climbed the fence and flipped himself over. Now he was in an even smaller yard, surrounded on three sides by featureless brickwork.

About fifteen feet up on one side was a window. Small and filled with frosted glass, it looked like a bathroom, but Billy knew it gave onto the De Nuys hotel's bellhop station. He looked around for a pebble and when he found one, he threw it. Nothing. Vince made a point of returning to the station when not running errands or carrying cases—staying out of sight kept his workload down—so he wouldn't be long. Billy took his siGi™ out and sat on the ground smoking it for a few minutes. Then he threw another pebble at the window. This time it swung in and Vince appeared. Or the shape of him did—it was still too gloomy to make out his features.

"I'm going to go ahead and assume that this is of the utmost gravity," said the figure in the window, its voice wavering, "since that is what we fucking agreed."

"Wouldn't do it if I didn't think so," said Billy. "I've got to see you later. I need you to hang on to something for me. When can you be at Phil's?"

"I'm on a double shift—I don't knock off till six. What is this? What have you gone and done, Billy? I told you not to go anywhere near that place."

"It's not what you think," said Billy. "It's complicated. Might even be a good thing. But I need to get clean, quickly. I'll explain at six."

"You're going to dump your stuff on me, but it's a good thing?" Vince pulled his head in, then poked it out again.

"You better know what you're doing, Billy," he hissed and shut the window.

Billy strolled back towards Phil's. It occurred to him that he most certainly did not know what he was doing. But he'd meant it—this just might be a good thing. A man on the inside. High risk, high reward. Maybe. He pulled the heavy diner door open and, out of habit, sat at the little table just inside and to the right of it. The only table in the diner and the only place to sit where you could hardly be seen from the wraparound windows. That's why he'd suggested it to Vince—where better to hide than in a fishbowl? Out of sight in downtown's most conspicuous venue.

The highly-synchronized breakfast clientele were in on cue—office workers, shop assistants—and Phil's was crowded. Lucille had joined Benny behind the bar and they were both busy taking loudly placed orders. When she saw the regular at his usual table, he got preferential.

"What'll it be, Billy boy?" she yelled, tapping another order into her tab.

He didn't even look up. He'd taken his own out and laid it on the table, screen side up. No blue lights. No red circles.

"Eggs. Coffee. Thanks Lucy."

Momentarily, he felt calm, but he knew it wouldn't last. There was nothing he'd like more than to hide out here for a few hours, but he'd have to show for work and get some copy in. And first he had to get his stuff for Vince. He didn't like the idea of having it on him the whole day, but that was how it had to be. It would mean driving out to the sports grounds at El Alma. Being late for the office was the least of his worries. And he had to talk to Jane. In person. Today.

Lucille was at his side. She put his eggs in front of him and a mug and started to pour.

"You look awful."

She was close enough that he could feel body heat emanating from her. His eyes lingered over the eggs. He wasn't sure if he'd be able to swallow them or, if he managed that, to keep them down. The coffee, though.

"No sleep," he said. "On a job."

"What's a sports reporter reporting on at night?"

"Working the city pages."

She'd finished pouring the coffee so he shook a little sugar into it.

"Oh," she said. "Promotion?"

He looked up at her. The smell of the coffee was filling his nostrils with the memory of good things. Of a time before Vince and before the fear. Of early mornings at Jane's. Of practically skipping to his desk on that first day at *The Herald*. His first gig in the big city. The beach house his folks had rented when he was small. The dog that seemed to turn up every morning there to play with him. All of the good things had somehow managed to find their way into that cup of coffee. He smiled, then lowered his eyes and stirred it.

"You never know," he said. "Maybe."

He watched her walk away. There was a certain kind of low-rent glamour to Lucille. She'd worked here as long as he'd been coming, since he'd been new in town and taken the room across the street. He remembered being a little in awe of her. She could balance a siGi™ between her lips for hours without getting smoke in her eye. Her coffee was noticeably better than Benny's. Everybody thought so, including Benny, but nobody could figure out what she did differently. He might have been a little in love with her at first.

Not now. The undercooked egg was gelatinous and tepid on his tongue. Another forkful trembled on the tines till he put it down again and picked up the coffee. Not since Jane. He wasn't even sure he loved Jane anymore. He needed her all right—an awful, gnawing need—but was it a feeling? Fear and rage were all he had felt in a long time. His own Ma was like a ghost to him, appearing in the gloomy corners of her own apartment, on a stool or in a chair, nursing a cup of strong liquor. He looked around the lively diner. It wasn't lively to him. *All* these people were ghosts. The light was bright but not warm to his eyes. The jade green tiling of the window sill wasn't pretty anymore. It seemed ostentatious. The place was gaudy. Fake.

He waved his tab over the tabletop scanner, listened for the ping of approval and when he heard it, stood. Benny and Lucille had their backs to him so there was no one to nod at. Outside, the dregs of the night lingered. Through the huge window, the lights from Phil's threw shapes onto the pavement that overlapped crookedly—the irregular skyline of another city, a city of light on the horizontal. He would have liked to disappear into it. To start over there. Instead, he activated his siGi™ and walked to the car.

The Bernardino skyway swept over the city's north-western districts in a long curve and on a half tilt. Billy drove slowly, getting a good look at the new Litera-Track™ below. Nothing much happening down there yet—it would all kick off tomorrow—but every few hundred feet a crew of technicians could be seen around control terminals at the side of the roadway. It had already been surfaced and glittered now below the street lamps. By Billy's reckoning it was eight lanes wide, though it was difficult to tell; there were no markings of any kind. A thick black line that split the city—without the sparkles on its freshly coated surface it would have seemed like an abysmal opening in the earth.

He took the one-nine-five exit and back at ground level he swung right onto Van Buren and followed the line of the bay a couple of blocks in, cruising between the sun-flaked slats of timber bungalows, then crossed San Juliano boulevard onto Salida Drive which took him right down to the water.

There, a sharp right and away from the sea again, up into the hills—this was Concord Bluffs, a well-to-do neighborhood of tall houses and taller hedges. The place had gone vertical, perhaps, because it was squeezed so tight between the city and the heights that surrounded it. The Marmon crawled. He had a feeling he wasn't going to like wherever this day was headed; why should he hurry to get there?

The entrance to El Alma was up behind the Bluffs, at a center point implied by the concentric arcs of a series of leafy crescents. The circle had originally been complete. In fact, Concord had extended north over more than triple its current area, but most of it had been cleared long ago—courtesy of compulsory purchase orders and where necessary, forced evictions—to make way for the sports grounds.

They were massive and they had to be. This was where most people lived out their youth, this and the other enormous complexes scattered around the outskirts of the city. Unless you were the daylight-avoiding type that gamed, this was where you met people and learned to be one. Billy drove through the high gates and followed a twisting driveway edged by well-tended flower beds and flanked by immaculate lawns. The sprinklers were still working—they would stop when the sun began to climb but they were on every night, without fail, even when the rest of the city suffered water rationing. At the first junction he reached, signs pointed this way and that—to the pools, the parks and the arenas. He turned right and drove uphill toward track and field.

Parking the car in front of one of the clubhouses, he strolled between pavilions and took a short set of steps up to the raised ground where the track was. Skirting around it, he walked across a patch of open parkland to where an old Ponderosa pine stood on its own little knoll. It was morning proper now and the light of a low sun was rust-red on the seats of the spectator stand. A few runners—they were always the first—were already warming up, brilliant in their whites against the lined burgundy of the polyurethane track.

It was shady beneath the Ponderosa. Even later, it would be relatively cool here. For a minute he did nothing, just sat with his back to the cinnamon-colored bark, propped his forearms on his raised knees, spun his hat on one hand and watched the runners. High jump had been his event, once upon a time. He'd been good at it. This had been his life, at first back home and then right here, when he'd come to live in the city. The camaraderie of field events had been a comfort to the rather lonely and nervous young man, especially since he'd been talented. He'd made friends here. He'd met Jane here. The warm nights meant that even now in the early morning the tree emitted its peculiar scent. He rested his head against the trunk and let the aroma—vanilla, butterscotch—take him back.

"You move fast," she'd said, sitting where he sat now.

He'd spotted her from the track, picked up his shoulder bag and wandered over once he'd gotten his breath back. He was flushed and sweating and felt like he always felt after an event—good, but not good enough. Empty. There was something post-coital about it. He stood at the tips of the lowest branches. Hands on hips, he looked around before answering.

"We're talking about sports, right?"

She grinned.

"Give me five minutes and I'll tell you," she said.

He went to his bag for a siGi™.

"You want to smoke? I always carry a spare, in case I should bump into a young lady or something."

"No thanks. I don't."

"You don't smoke?" he said. "What the fuck is the matter with you?"

She threw one extended leg over the other.

"Not everybody does, you know. And you shouldn't swear at a young lady till you've gotten to know her a little better."

"That so?"

Activating the siGi™ and taking a drag gave him a chance to look her up and down. She was in whites and athletic but she didn't look like she'd broken a sweat in . . . actually, this girl didn't look like she'd ever broken a sweat. He looked from her to the track, then back again.

"You prefer to watch, huh?"

She grinned again.

"We're talking about sports, right?"

He wanted to jump into that grin.

"Give me six minutes and I'll tell you," he said and blew a smoke ring that moved slowly toward her. "You know, I think you might be a little strange."

"Yeah," she said. "I could tell you liked me."

He laughed.

"Careful now. Talk like that might give me the idea you're one of those girls that sit on the steps out front of the clubhouse on a Friday night, way after their bedtime."

"It might, might it?"

"I'm afraid so." He took another pull and released it. "One of those girls who starts sitting there, say, around nine."

"That so?"

"Well, I'm very sorry to say it of course, but yes. Would I have gotten the wrong impression?"

She'd stood and picked her bag up.

"Why ask?" she'd said, "It's a question that a little patience might answer." She'd walked away without looking around. There had been just a little rain.

Today it would be sunny. Billy put his hat down. There were a couple of new arrivals down on the track. If he wanted to be discreet, time was slipping away—it was still quiet but they'd all start trickling in now, the high-school groups and the college athletes, the recently graduated and otherwise unemployed. He put his hands on the ground to either side of him, palms on the damp soil.

She'd been there. Not at nine, of course—that would have been too easy. But having no pressing appointments he'd gotten himself a drink, and then another. In the end, she'd only made him wait an hour and ten minutes.

"Yeah," he'd said to his glass as she threw her bag down a couple of steps above his. "I could tell you liked me."

His right hand went to the base of the tree trunk and found a little hollow there, a cavity a couple of inches tall and three or four inches long, where the bark had separated itself from the trunk. The guys down at the track had dropped and were doing press-ups. He didn't take his eyes off them. His fingers wound around the upper rim of the cavity and moved along its inner surface till he felt the give of plastic. He clamped it between his middle and index fingers and pulled it out, picking up his hat with his other hand to shield it from view.

He'd been meticulous when he'd hidden it but it was still a relief to find it undisturbed. The little ziplock plastic bag was dirty. Behind the hat, he wiped it with his thumb. The contents were clean and dry. He folded the bag and slipped it into the sweatband, then put the hat on, stood up and walked back towards the steps, doing everything he could to exude nonchalance. In the car he placed the hat on the passenger seat and pulled out. He hadn't seen anyone he knew so there was a fighting chance that no one he knew had seen him.

***

Hunter Grayling ran *The Herald* exactly as he pleased. He edited it, he managed it and he owned it. It was the last paper in the city—or anywhere, as far as Billy knew—that had premises. The old man insisted not only that his people physically show up for work but that they dress for it and that they "act respectable" as long as they were at it. Given his attitude to work/life balance, that was usually a long time. His grandfather, the founder, had put the offices in Rossmore Towers on Berlin St. and that's where they had stayed. Billy parked the Marmon in the underground garage, walked back up to the pavement and the siGi™ kiosk for a refill, and went in by the main entrance.

The lobby might have been antique film footage. There was no trace of color in the place if you didn't count the people who moved through it in bright dresses, make-up, the occasional flamboyant necktie. The carpet wasn't good carpet and it wasn't bad carpet—it was just carpet, an unhappy shade of gray and worn to a shine where footfall was heavy. There was a reception desk that Billy supposed had been used when the building was new, a good couple of hundred years ago. Nowadays everyone would be scanned discreetly and visitors would be directed via their tabs or earpieces. A few desultory items of unused lobby furniture, one shade darker than the carpet, were dotted around. The walls were gunmetal gray and when the brushed silver doors of the maglev elevator slid apart, so was its interior. The speed of a vertical maglev could be felt in the knees and stomach and he was always glad to get out of the thing.

Sports was the largest department the paper had and took up a whole floor of the building. There were just a few private offices, laying claim to sunlight around the outer walls, and none of them belonged to Billy. The rest of the space was open-plan and noisy and the noise, like everything else around here, had a pecking order to it. At the top came the shop floor shouting—a name yelled from a distance to alert the owner and then some barked question or admonition. Below that, the tidal ebb and flow of constant conversations held on screens and tabs. Underlying it all, the chitinous click of a hundred busy keyboards that sounded like a cockroach infestation nobody was doing anything about.

Nothing was said to him on his way to his cubicle, at the far end. It was nine-thirty already, about the time Grayling would pace the floor, and heads were down. Billy hadn't shared the work station since Ray Candle had upped and left one morning without a word of explanation. The other desk had been removed the same day so there was plenty of space, comparatively speaking. He kept his side spartan—a desk, a chair, a screen. A few photos of Jane and him pinned to the divider—at a field event, her last birthday party, on their trip to the mountains. He threw his scarf and hat on the coat rack and sat in the chair. There wasn't a lot of color here either—just the dark green of the five old filing cabinets he'd picked up at a junk sale and put where Ray's desk had been. They were pointless but he liked them and actually used two of them—to stash the sporting memorabilia he would pick up from time to time and to hide a bottle and a pack of cardamom pods for his breath. No notifications. He docked his tab and flexed his fingers. Grayling would have been expecting copy first thing, no doubt. He tended to expect everything either then or by close of business, the only two deadlines the old man would entertain.

At first it had been a palace to Billy, this cubicle. Success in physical form. It had delighted him. Then it had enraged him. Eventually it had come to sadden him, but even that had passed. It left him numb now, just enough sensation left to register the claustrophobia.

Jane had been with him, that first day. Ostensibly to help carry his things up from the car but really just to get a look. They were steady by then and already thinking about getting a place together. The dynamics, too, had been established. They both had smart mouths but Jane's was smarter. They both liked to be one step ahead but Jane got there more often. Each wanted to be seen to take care of the other. Jane was better at it.

That day, though, she'd been quiet. She'd shaken hands with Ray like a timid schoolgirl when he introduced himself and she kept peeping excitedly over the divider while Billy set his desk up, eager to see and hear whatever it was that went on in a newsroom. As he saw her back to the car she'd squeezed his arm and giggled, and made thrilled remarks about this or that. Her eyes had glistened with pride as she pulled away. For months after that, she insisted on introducing Billy as a journalist, or a writer—she didn't like reporter so much—and every time she did he would swell up till he thought he might pass out.

"Far as I'm aware, the Gripping Tails™ launch is tomorrow."

Billy swiveled. Grayling filled up the cubicle's entrance, hands on hips.

"Not Thursday. Not next week," said the old man. "Or did I miss something?"

"No, Mr Grayling. I'm—"

"Then where's my copy? I should have had it an hour ago."

"I'm on it right now, Mr Grayling. Just a few minutes. I—"

"I took a chance on you, Stringer, sending you on that job. I hate to be let down. Why the hell are you wearing an overcoat at your desk?"

"A bug, Mr Grayling. A cold. I won't let you down, sir. I need fifteen minutes," said Billy, lying.

"You'll need more than that," snarled the old man, eyeing the filing cabinets. "People to see you," he said, turning away. "Interview room."

Billy stood and looked over the divider toward the interview room. The frosted glass door was closed. He wasn't expecting anybody. Sometimes a coach would come by to pitch an angle. If this was that, the timing couldn't be worse. He grabbed a water at the cooler, downed it, grabbed another and made his way over there.

There were two men waiting for him. One of them sat in a chair by the window and tinkered with his tab. He was long and lean and Billy couldn't see his face because he had his hat on to keep the sun out of his eyes. His suit was dark blue and his tie was light blue against a white shirt. He'd crossed his feet, slouched slightly in the chair and the corners of his mouth turned down as he read whatever it was on his screen—the body language of a man for whom the whole world was an interview room and he was the interviewer. If he'd stood up, grabbed Billy by the lapels and screamed "I'm a cop!" in his face, it wouldn't have made it any more obvious that he was a cop. The other man was Alphonse.

"Hello again, Mr Stringer," said the behemoth.

Billy clicked the door shut behind him and closed his mouth.

"Good morning," said the man in the blue suit, to his tab.

"Good morning," said Billy. He hadn't yet let go of the door knob.

"Take a seat, Mr Stringer," said Alphonse. "My associate here is Marty Phillips. He and I will be . . . what was it you said, Marty?"

"Liaising," said the other man.

"That's right. Marty and I will be liaising today. Part of Murphy's recruitment process."

Billy took a seat at the oval table that ran the length of the room.

"I see," he said. "So you're with the transport police, Mr Phillips?"

"Counter-terrorism," said Phillips. He looked up, put his tab away and smiled. His eyes could be seen for the first time. They didn't belong on the same person as the smile. Billy was beginning to get tired of being scared. Scared or tired or both, all the time.

"Counter ...?" he stuttered, looking from one to the other. "But ..."

A chuckle came from Alphonse that Billy could feel through the seat of his chair.

"You're a real worrier, you know that, Mr Stringer? You worry too much." His eyes narrowed. "You OK, Mr Stringer? You want to take that coat off?"

"I'm ... I'm fine," said Billy. "A little under the weather maybe. I—"

"This is routine, Mr Stringer," said Phillips. "You'll appreciate the sensitive nature of the conversation you've had with Murphy. The information you've been exposed to. It might surprise you, the effect a job offer from Gripping Tails™ can have on a person. We've had runners. When a guy bolts, it sort of tells a story, don't you think? That's not you, of course. But we take precautions. We have to."

His smile, once again, seemed to trespass on that face.

"Relax, Billy. We're not after you. Believe me, if we were you'd know it. You'd be hiding under a hedge somewhere and a lot of the folks you know would be dead. We don't kid around. We'd have you or be hunting you down and we'd be cleaning up around you as we went. Terrorists are sheltered by family and friends. So that's part of our work too. And nothing bad has happened to anyone you know, has it?"

He had begun to examine his fingernails.

"I don't want you to worry, Billy. I don't want you to feel as though you're in trouble. I don't want you to neglect your duties here at *The Herald*. I don't want you to do anything strange or surprising today, OK? That would mean a lot of paperwork for me. And I don't want you leaving town till you've had your chat with Murphy later. That sound reasonable?"

"Sure," said Billy. "Sure. No problem at all."

"Any plans for your day that might surprise me, Billy?"

Phillips was leaving gaps in between responses that were just a little too long, as if he had one or two more cognitive filters to apply than the average person.

"None," said Billy. "Normal day at the office. Maybe a couple of runarounds for a story." He was sitting in strong sunlight. The heat was making him nauseous and the glare was making him squint.

"Great," said Phillips. "That's perfect, Billy."

Another one of those gaps.

"You were a little late for work this morning. Anything happen?"

"No," said Billy. He coughed. "Nothing happened." He looked to Alphonse. "I was out at Gripping Tails™ overnight, so I stopped off for some breakfast. Maybe I took a little too long over it. I'm not used to those hours, you know?"

He tried to laugh. It didn't work.

"You didn't go anywhere else? You just had breakfast?"

"That's right. I can't function on an empty stomach."

He tried a smile. That didn't work either. The policeman maintained eye contact for the duration of his longest silence yet, then stood suddenly enough to make Billy jump in his chair.

"OK, Alphonse. That's it for me. Thanks for your time, Billy. Take care today, OK?" The smile. "I'll make my own way out."

He walked to the door, opened it and shut it behind him without looking back. That he'd left first and alone made Billy uncomfortable—there was plenty of terrorism for the cop to take an interest in, tucked into the sweatband of his unattended hat. He had to get out there to it but he was stuck here with the largest man he'd ever known.

"That's it for me too, Mr Stringer," said Alphonse. "I just wanted the two of you to meet. Come to something, hasn't it? A cop like that liaising," he pronounced the word with relish, "with an old crook like me."

Billy waited for him to get up. He didn't. He just smiled. It was like watching rock warp.

"I do like to think of myself as a cut or two above your average hoodlum, Mr Stringer," he said. "Even more so since I got in with Gripping Tails™. It's a very legitimate engagement, you know. I had a couple of paid days last month so I could show my nephew round the city. He's from out of town. I get a pension too."

They seemed amiable enough points to Billy, except that at the word *cut* the giant had pulled a knife from his inside pocket and flipped the blade open, and was running his thumb along its edge with what looked like extreme caution.

"You like her?" he said. He was looking at the knife like a person might look at an especially favored kitten. "Been with me a long time," he said. "She's an old lady now. But she's still sharp."

He looked up at Billy.

"I keep her that way."

He folded the knife and returned it to his pocket.

"Tell me, Mr Stringer, you ever put the sole of your foot to the edge of a sharp blade?"

It took Billy a moment to process the question. Not for the first time in the huge man's presence, he felt very cold and very, very hot. This was the kind of encounter where a dash for the window might have seemed like an option worth considering, if they hadn't been on the 80th floor.

"Eh, no," he said. "No, I haven't."

Alphonse winked.

"You're wrong, Mr Stringer. You're wrong about that."

He stood and put his hat on.

"That's what you're walking on right now, Mr Stringer," he said. The door knob looked like a marble in his hand. "I'll be around all day. Never far away. You should tread very lightly." He pulled the door open. "See you later, Mr Stringer."

As far as he could tell, neither the hat nor the little bag had been touched. There wouldn't have been time, probably—Alphonse had only stayed a minute or so longer than Phillips. Billy sat at his desk and for a few moments that's all he did apart from breathe. Then he looked at the picture of him and Jane at her Ph.D ceremony and got on with the copy Grayling was waiting for.

It had all been fine up until the ceremony. At least, Billy had thought so. They had moved into her new place just a block back from Ocean Drive in Bayville. A little place with a wall bed and a magnificent jutting window at which a craned neck could afford a glimpse of the sea. It meant they both got to train on the sand when they weren't up at the grounds. Billy was doing well at the paper and money would trickle in from Jane's parents while she worked on her thesis. Both her parents were tenured at the university—her father was something important in the science faculty and her mother ran a Pinpoint™-funded language course for media undergrads, so there was plenty of money to trickle. The young couple couldn't have lived so close to the water otherwise. They'd been seeing each other for about two years and in the apartment a few months.

Even though he was the wrong side of thirty, to Billy it had felt like growing up. He'd never lived with a woman, if you didn't count Ma. Now he lived with a brilliant one who came from a well-to-do family and had almost finished a thesis on neuroplasticity differentials in adolescents or whatever it was. He'd felt respectable. Or would have, if it hadn't been for Vince. Outwardly, at any rate, he was living the kind of life he'd always wanted. He'd come a long way; in the beginning, Jane hadn't even let him visit her at the family home.

"It isn't you, honey. It's them."

That had changed when he got the job at *The Herald*. Within a week she'd invited him up to meet her parents. The house was on one of the hairpin avenues that overlooked the Bluffs—doodles on the higher, forested ridges that hemmed the city's northern sprawl. The homes up here hid between pines and behind high walls and Billy had had to press a buzzer at the gate and wait to be let in. For appearances' sake, he'd left the old Marmon a few houses down and walked.

The driveway ascended towards a stuccoed villa in the Spanish style, surrounded by manicured lawn. To the side, outside a double garage, a lanky young man in dungarees was polishing a silver De Soto, but with his eyes on the visitor. Billy stopped and raised a hand but the guy just stared so he walked on. On the lawn in front of the porch there was a little statue—a cherub in obsidian or something like that. Jet black. He bent to pat its head.

"Wish me luck."

Before he straightened he looked back towards the garage. The guy was still polishing, still staring. Billy rang the bell and the door opened. A sharp-featured maid of indeterminate age showed him through the double-height entrance hall and a sprawling living room with the minimum possible deployment of language. As she pulled open a pair of French doors that gave onto a brilliant blue, sparkling swimming pool, he expected for a moment to find Jane beside it on a lounger, getting a pedicure. It was that kind of scene. True to form, though, she was at her desk with multiple screens on and multiple pages open on each. Her room opened onto the pool area.

"Nice place you have here," he said as she stood to kiss him. "Any odd jobs need doing?"

She laughed.

"Mom and Dad aren't around. You want to smoke. Let's go to the pool house. I can work there."

The pool house was small—about the size of Ma's place—but perfectly formed. There was a guest bedroom on its own mezzanine and underneath, a kitchenette and a well-stocked fridge. Jane threw him a beer from it and he sat back into the low, horseshoe sofa. Behind him, she lit up another screen array and got back to work. He sucked on his beer. He didn't need Jane to talk to him. She wasn't good company when she was working anyway. The wispy, full-length net curtains made the pool area seem like a fuzzy sketch—a blue-and-white impression of a pool area, animated only by their billowing. He let himself be lulled. The breeze that blew through them was cool and he could hear the water lap at the poolside.

A discoloration at an upper corner of the pool's blue rhombus caught his attention. A brownish patch that moved toward a lower corner and grew until he could see it had legs. When he refocussed he saw it was the guy in dungarees. He expected him to grab one of those long-handled nets to drag the pool for leaves and insect carcasses. Instead the youth pulled the curtains apart abruptly and made for the kitchenette. Billy sat up and turned to look at Jane. Her eyes were on a screen.

"My kid brother," she said.

"Oh." He turned back. The boy certainly wasn't as fortunate as his sister in the looks department. As far as Billy could tell, he was around twenty, twenty-five tops. He wasn't wearing anything apart from the dungarees. And he wasn't saying anything. A sigh escaped Jane.

"His name's Vince," she said. "He doesn't do manners. Thinks they're bourgeois."

Vince had gone to the fridge for his own beer.

"So this would be the sports reporter, would it?" he said.

"Journalist. And he hasn't started yet."

"*The Herald*, isn't it? How delightfully old school. As a member of the press, I imagine you'll find this interesting."

He'd sat next to Billy and pulled an object from the oversized pocket on the flap of his dungarees.

"Why is he talking like that, honey?" asked Billy.

"He's *lit*. Too much Dickens and Dostoevsky and all that other trash."

Billy looked at the object. It was around eight inches by five and maybe one inch thick. It looked worn and old and the surface was covered with colors that would once have been garish. It had smelled of dust and there was writing on it but it was upside down to Billy.

"What is it?" he asked.

Vince sneered.

"Really? Do you mean to tell me that you've never seen one? It's a novel, dumbass."

"Watch your mouth, Vince." Jane had finally taken her eyes off her work. "And you have some nerve bringing that into the house. Mom and Dad could get into serious trouble at work."

"Relax, sis. I'm not so foolish as to keep anything here." He held it out but Billy didn't want to take it.

"It's illegal, you little twerp," said Jane. "Get it out of here before Mom and Dad get home. What the hell is the matter with you? You're supposed to be the child of educated people."

"It was educated people that read these things, once upon a time," Vince said. His tone had grown serious for a moment, tinged with a sincerity that belied the sneer.

"It was educated people that sacrificed children to the gods, once upon a time," Jane shot back at him. "Things change, bozo. Get it out of here. Isn't there a rally you could be at?"

Vince had stood up and shrugged.

"Anything you say, big sis. I'll be back for dinner though."

"We should shoot some hoops some time," said Billy. The pool pump started up outside.

"Are you serious?" said Vince.

"Don't waste your breath, Billy," said Jane. "Vince is pure gamer. Thinks jocks are lame. Spends all his time getting *lit* with his weird friends."

"I certainly do," Vince had said. "Anyway, back later. I wouldn't want to miss Billy's interrogation."

He'd winked at Billy and left.

Grayling's copy was done. Billy clicked send. It was mediocre and rushed and might just get him fired. That didn't seem important. He didn't intend to be around when the old man read it. He put his hat on. Before he left the cubicle he took the unopened whiskey bottle from the cabinet and sat to take a good slug. Then he pocketed it and made for the elevator.

Dinner with Jane's parents had been uneventful. They had displayed the scrutinizing reserve he would have expected of prospective parents-in-law and the effete snobbery he would have expected of university professors. Apart from that they were a couple of teddy bears. There were no overly elaborate cutlery arrangements to catch him out and he remembered to swallow his food before he spoke. He spoke very little. Just enough not to appear timid. When Vince took his leave, a tension that Billy had put down to his own presence lifted.

"Off to one of his protest groups, no doubt," Mr Ellison mumbled.

"You'll have to excuse our son, Billy," said Mrs Ellison. "He'll come good I suppose but he's a worry. Gets himself involved with these Lit protests. It places us in rather a difficult position."

"He needs to watch himself," Jane said. "There's a clamp-down coming. They think they're brave but they'll scatter like rats when it happens. He should get out now."

Something was bugging her. Billy watched her jaw muscles flex and placed a hand on hers below the table. She withdrew it.

After dinner, Billy strolled back to the car, hands in his pockets and whistling a tune. Night was falling but it was still balmy. Jane had cheered up and told him in the porch that he'd done well. First test passed. He got into the Marmon and turned the key in the ignition and then a knock at the passenger side window made him jump. He wound it down.

"You gave me a fright, Vince. You been waiting out here all this time?"

Vince just leered and then he dropped something onto the passenger seat.

"You can't possibly believe your interest in the item escaped me," he said. "Enjoy it. But make sure to return it."

He didn't wait for a response—just took off toward the house. Billy looked at the book. It made him uncomfortable.

He'd wanted to throw it out the window. But he hadn't.

They were going to have to do something about the glare. Blinding light bounced off the Litera-Track™ into the eyes of anybody eastbound on the skyway. On the way out to Bayville, Billy was OK—he could make out the increased activity down there, the spectator seating for the launch ceremony. They had laid it out on raised platforms since the track itself ran about thirty feet off the ground. In the oncoming cars, though, drivers had their hands raised as visors.

He didn't suppose it would be an issue for long—the skyway itself would be Litera-Track™ before the year was out. Still, this morning it was dangerous and he was glad to take his exit and slow down as the old Marmon merged with the lazy traffic of residential Bayville. Maybe this was going to be the worst day of his life. Maybe it was going to be the last. Either way, he felt fine for the moment. He felt good. He was going to see Jane.

The book on the passenger seat was called *The Stainless Steel Rat* and it had set Billy's world on fire. When he'd returned it to Vince he'd been given another. Then another. Each was different from the last but in one thing they were the same—they burned the world. If he'd been expecting to struggle with the morality of it then he'd been mistaken. There had been no right or wrong for him. It was the turning of a tap. The opening of a sluice. Nothing more. It was nature, and knowing that it was nature had changed everything. He was *lit*.

At first, the joy and the rage had been indistinguishable. Soon enough they'd separated, the joy reserving itself for the time he spent reading and the rage draped like a shroud over everything else. Everything. Daily life was deadened to him and, little by little, he to it. The pride he'd felt in his newfound profession had fallen away like so much dust from a beaten rug. The real world had dimmed and wavered, the least convincing now of so many.

He'd felt a fool, that he had been fooled. That had made him angry. He'd read something recently, a line in a book of poetry that Vince had dismissed but that had stayed with him. *Beauty is nothing but the beginning of terror*. The beauty that had been revealed to him had filled him with an inexplicable fear, a bottomless fear, and so there was that too—he'd been afraid. He'd learned to keep a lid on both.

He'd had no qualms about betraying a world he felt had betrayed him first. He carried out his duties. He had breakfast, lunch, he showered and shined his shoes. He read the papers. His pretense of a life was bearable as long as the books kept coming. He knew now though that the poison had already taken effect. Every bad thing that had led him to this day, every toxic little twist in the plot, had been born in the moment he'd started lying to Jane.

Bucknell Street led down to the water from Nelson Boulevard and the *Mariners Village* apartment building fronted onto it where the two met. It was a beige, four-story building. Some of the balconies, like the one on Jane's place, had been glassed in. Hers was on the second floor at the end of the building closest to the water. There was nobody in the window. Billy parked the car in the lot across the way and went to the front entrance. As usual, it was propped open. That was Mrs Lynberry, the widow in 306 who didn't think the building got enough air.

Not wanting to get stuck in the elevator with anyone he knew, he took the stairs. At the end of the hallway on the second floor he knocked on Jane's door. No point in hesitating: if he did, he might lose his nerve. He stepped aside so that he couldn't be seen from the peephole. Nobody came to the door and there were no sounds from the apartment. He pressed the buzzer and waited with his ear to the door. He could hear a tap drip, but nothing else. No movement. It was eleven-thirty. She would usually be in. He had no idea where else she could be and therefore nowhere else to go.

jane. am at ur dor. wer r u? Nid 2 spk 2 u.

There wouldn't be a reply, of course. He looked up and down the hall and pressed the buzzer again and waited. Nothing. He put his ear back to the door and held it there for a good two minutes and heard only the dripping tap. He could feel the fear rising. Nothing would be right if he couldn't see her. Tell her what he needed to. His tab vibrated. He took it out of his pocket.

bili! wot u doin der?? u cant b der!

"You're not supposed to be here, you know."

The door opposite Jane's had been pulled open and a woman in a house robe leaned against the jamb with her arms folded. She'd been in the middle of doing something complicated and unsuccessful to her hair.

"She told me she threw you out."

You wrangled it out of her, you mean, thought Billy. "Hello, Mrs Cluskey," he said.

A beep.

bili u cant do dis! I dont evn liv der enimor!

"She doesn't live here anymore," said Mrs Cluskey. "Gone weeks."

Billy was tapping.

wer u liv now?

"Gone where?" he said.

"Pretty sure I wouldn't tell you," said the woman, activating a siGi™, "if I knew. You a hitter?"

i cant tel u dat bili. u hav 2 stay away!

"You need to stay away from that poor girl. She wasn't right after you were gone. Not saying I saw bruises or anything, but that girl was scared. You don't stay away, I call the cops."

did u no der hav bin cops at dads hse dis mornin?? askin about u! Wotevr u r doin bili keep it away frm us!!

"Well, whatever it is you were doing to that girl, you keep it away from here, you hear me?"

But she was talking to his back. Billy was already heading for the stairs. It didn't matter that Jane wouldn't tell him where she lived. It was obvious.

"Bye, Mrs Cluskey."

It should have been a short drive up through the Bluffs but the launch preparations were playing havoc with traffic and before he'd even gotten as far as the San Juliano flyover he found himself stuck in a jam. It was going to be a hot afternoon and the aircon in the old heap had never worked. He lowered the windows and lit up a stick of Solace™. He wished there was something cold to drink in the car but all he had was the pint of whiskey so he drank some of that.

How long would he have been able to keep it up? The deception. A long time—he was sure about that. A long time, if it hadn't been for Jane. It was over her that he'd come unstuck.

For months after Vince had dropped that first book into the car, the whole thing had seemed like little more than a misdemeanor. A second adolescence—he'd gotten himself mixed up with a bunch of kids who'd found themselves something to protest. A harmless rabble, they'd all end up working in banks or wherever and minding their own business. It always worked out that way. Not that he ever met any of them—Vince would tell him he'd be introduced to someone when the time was right. It was a process, he'd say. There was trust to be earned and Billy was being monitored. When they saw fit, he would take one step closer to source, then another, and so on.

It hadn't mattered to him at all. He wasn't ambitious about the thing. Why wouldn't he prefer to be small fry, if it meant the risk was lower? He was still all caught up in the rush of the new. The thrill. It was plenty to be getting on with.

Every time he lied to Jane though, it felt like a kick in the belly. Lied about where he was going, or where he'd been or whether he'd seen her little brother. Or what he'd been doing in the bathroom for so long or why he'd locked the door. It was around that time—they'd just moved in together—that he'd woken one night in a sweat. For the first time in his life he knew what real addiction felt like. With perfect lucidity, wide awake in an instant and watching the back of her sleeping head, he'd known that he'd never beat it and never try. He had given himself to something completely, and it wasn't going to give him back.

Traffic freed up on the other side of the flyover. Billy left the windows down and on the way up to the Bluffs, a sea breeze blew through the car. He could see the sports grounds below him as he took the canyon road up to Hillview and its meandering residential streets. He parked away from the house, partly because it was habit and partly because it meant he could approach the gate quietly. There was no sign of any activity outside the villa. No gardener, no nothing. He pressed the intercom and somebody answered it quickly.

"Yes?"

"It's Billy," he said. The direct approach.

A silence, a crackling kind of silence, ensued.

"Look," said Billy, "I just need—"

The release mechanism buzzed and the gate clicked open. Whoever had answered the intercom had hung up. It hadn't sounded like the maid to him, more like Jane's mother, but it was the maid he found holding the front door open when he got there. In the time since he'd last seen her she'd managed to divest herself of any residual traces of cordiality. She looked him up and down, pointed to the living room, shut the door behind him and walked away in the opposite direction. Billy took his hat off and checked himself out in the hall mirror. His hair was wet and stuck to his scalp. His face was flushed and waxy and sweat stains were coming through his buttoned-up overcoat. It had to be ninety degrees outside, probably more. There wasn't a meeting in all the world that could go well, looking like that. He knocked on the living room door and when there was no answer he opened it and went in.

It took less than a second to confirm it wasn't going to be a friendly chat. They were both there. Mrs Ellison was in an armchair to one side of the huge fireplace. She sat so upright her back might have snapped. One clenched hand was placed on top of the other in her lap and she'd crossed her lower legs. Her husband stood to the side and slightly behind her, a hand on her shoulder. They might have been posing for a portrait. They might have been waxworks. Except it was clear that Mrs Ellison had been crying.

"Hello Billy," she said.

"Sit down, will you," said Mr Ellison.

Billy took a seat on the other side of the fireplace, thumbing the plastic bag in his hat.

"The police have been here," said Mr Ellison. "Counter-terrorism. Asking questions about you."

"Oh that," said Billy. "That's nothing to—"

A sob escaped Jane's mother. She took a hankie from one of her fists and raised it to her eyes. Mr Ellison patted her gently, eyes on Billy.

"I have to tell you, young man, that if you have gotten our son involved in anything—"

"Vince?" said Billy. "If *I've* gotten . . . ? Wait, you've got this all wrong." He ran his fingers through his hair and attempted a smile. "I may be starting work at Gripping Tails™ soon. See? That's why the cops. The police, I mean. It's part of the recruitment process.

Clearance, you know? There were two of them, right? One really big guy?"

Mr Ellison nodded.

"That's Alphonse," said Billy. "He's not a c . . . not with the police. He's in-house for Gripping Tails™. They're liaising." He voiced the word as if it carried enough weight all by itself to resolve the matter. "It's absolutely standard. Absolutely fine. It could actually be a really great opportunity for me. A real step up, actually."

They had to be picking up the whiskey on his breath. He reeked.

"No, no—this isn't about Vince. I'm here to see Jane. I—"

"You won't be seeing her, Billy," said Mr Ellison.

"But she's here?" He looked round, despite himself. "Look, I promise I don't want any trouble. Just the opposite. I—"

"She isn't here, Billy," said Mr Ellison, "as I suspect you know."

"She's not living here?" said Billy, missing the second point. "But she must be." He realized he was clutching his hair and stopped. "I can't tell you how important it is."

Her mother sobbed into the hankie. Mr Ellison sighed.

"Yes, Billy." He rolled his eyes as if going through some charade. "She has been living here. But you can't see her now."

"Why not? I—"

Her mother dropped her hands and Billy froze.

"Because she's gone missing," she hissed. An animal sound, followed by several seconds of silence.

"Missing?" said Billy. He hadn't been expecting that. "Since when? Have you called the—"

"The police will do nothing for us," said Mr Ellison, "since it hasn't been twenty-four hours. But we know that something is very wrong. She didn't come down to breakfast and she wasn't in her room. That was five hours ago, just after our early-morning visit from your two friends. She isn't responding to messages."

Billy spun his hat, trying to think.

"You've tried the university? The sports grounds? She might just have left her tab somewhere, you know?" He didn't know why he wasn't mentioning the messages she'd sent him just an hour ago. But he wasn't. "I'm sure everything's fine. She—"

"Really?" said Mr Ellison. "How helpful. Since you obviously have nothing to tell us, I want you to leave. I will talk to Vincent about you this evening and as soon as you have gone, I will inform the police that you have been here. I don't know what you're up to, Billy, but if it brings harm on my family in any way—any way at all—I will come after you with the full force of the law. Now get out."

Billy stood.

"Look, Mrs Ellison—"

She spat at him. There was nothing in it, if you didn't count the hate, but it neatly drew a line under the conversation. He left the room and then the house, walked back to the car and sat in it. He took a mouthful of the whiskey and then he took another. Then he sent Jane a message.

ur da sez ur in trubl. r u?

Then he waited for a reply that didn't come. Alphonse and Phillips must have been here at around the time he'd been at the diner. Jane had gone missing, or it had been discovered that she was, immediately afterwards. He didn't like that one bit. *A lot of the folks you know would be dead*, Phillips had said. *That's part of our work too.* Except she wasn't dead, or she hadn't been an hour ago. Unless . . . no, it must have been her that responded. It was her style. He recognized it.

So they'd gone to Jane's place and then they'd come to his office. They'd left there separately. Alphonse had more or less told Billy he'd be tailing him. If so, he was either very good at it or very bad because there'd been no sign of him. So where was Phillips and what was he doing? Then it hit him. *Terrorists are sheltered by family and friends.* He started the car.

Ma.

The ninety-one was too risky, with all the traffic disruption. It would have to be the three-ten east as soon as he got out of the Bluffs and then the three-fifteen south from Lakeside. That was going to put a good half hour on it. He checked his watch. It would be three in the afternoon by the time he got to Ma's. Plenty of time to think, which was a pity—he didn't want to think. He called her tab and when she didn't answer sent her a message.

u der ma? de cleaners send my suit bak yet? my shirt dry?

It was only a gesture—she had never used the tab as far as he knew. It probably wasn't even charged. He unscrewed the cap from the whiskey with one hand and took a slug, then closed it and shrugged out of his overcoat as he drove. He was done with the overcoat. At last some air could get to his damp shirt, even if it was hot air.

If Phillips had paid his mother a visit, Billy might already be in deep and so might she. Apart from Vince she was the only person alive who knew about the books. She'd seen him with one a couple of times. He wasn't as discreet there as he had been at Jane's and until now he hadn't worried about it. Ma was a recluse. If she didn't have to leave her apartment she didn't, and since Billy had been back she didn't have to. Even before that she'd gotten most things delivered. Her only excursions had been to social security and the liquor store—the former monthly for mandatory reviews and the latter twice weekly with a trolley bag.

Hopefully she wouldn't remember anything about the books. She certainly didn't remember conversations. It's why he'd let himself get a little loose-tongued from time to time—tight on her liquor, missing Jane and needing to talk to someone. To try to explain the feeling. To tell another person about another world. Depending on how much he'd had it would either be a eulogy or a rant. When he spoke about the content of what he'd read she normally fell asleep.

When he railed against the authorities she would nod along as if the tone of his contempt was good music.

The flats of West Citral came to an end in the crumpled topology of the Malabar Hills. Rising up into them on stilts, the three-ten slid into the cradle of a high valley and for a few miles Billy felt a little cooler. The road here was shaded where it cut through the hills. He wanted to stop the car and lie down with his cheek to the tarmac. He wanted a lot of things he couldn't have. But heavy traffic had him in its grip. Soon enough it dropped him back down onto lower ground and into higher temperatures. It was a long, straight nothing from here to Blumington. He could feel the heat that rose from the road surface on the soles of his feet as his mind wandered.

"Where's Vince?" she'd said.

"I don't know." He'd looked up from his pad. "Should I?"

They were both lounging on the glassed-in balcony, both working. The last heavy rain of the spring drummed a lulling rhythm on the window. Jane's thesis was almost done and she was spending more and more time on it. Billy was banging out some half-hearted copy for the paper. His honeymoon period at *The Herald* had been brief and increasingly he found himself at odds with old Grayling. Piece after piece would come back to him, with instructions to cut out the crap.

"You seem to hear from him more than I do these days." She didn't look up. "Dad is looking for him. Thinks he might have a job lined up."

"He's not going to take a job your father has arranged, Jane. He'd rather be a bellhop."

"Oh. Would he? You seem to know an awful lot about him all of a sudden."

Any talk of Vince made Billy uncomfortable. It was a reminder of what he was up to.

"Oh, I think he just likes to talk to a guy, you know?" he said. "Big brother he never had and all that."

"Tell him Dad is looking for him, will you? You'll hear from him before I do."

"Sure." He sat up a little, alerted by something in her tone. "How's the thesis coming along? Nearly there?"

"It's fine," she'd said, eyes back on her screen.

At Chilton he took the three-fifteen and headed south. He was far enough out of the city here for the odd patch of pasture land to appear. But mostly it was either low-lying business parks or nothing at all.

It's fine. He couldn't remember the expression without feeling the wind knocked out of him, the same way it had been when she'd said it. The exchange might not have meant anything to her, but to him it had been the beginning of the end. It was the first time she'd ever spoken to him like that. As if she would have preferred him to be somewhere else. Or someone else—for the length of time it took her to say the words, she didn't think much of him and she let it show.

On second thought, maybe hindsight was playing tricks. It had stung but he'd probably put it down to stress at the time. It certainly hadn't altered his behavior. Nothing could have done. It amazed him now, how oblivious he'd been.

Lakeside was a satellite settlement that once upon a time had been up and coming but that had neither upped nor went—it just didn't seem to have gotten round to it. The outskirts were littered with the empty lots of land that investors had bought up in anticipation of a rush. Billboards that had once featured pristine illustrations of the pristine housing developments to come were now anything but pristine. They stood on empty wasteland and spent their time peeling. The whole place stank of disappointment.

In what passed for downtown, Ma's apartment building was the kind of granite edifice no reasonable person would expect to find outside the city. Eight stories built of dark stone and delusional optimism, it now appeared ridiculous and more than a little lonely. Billy pulled into the parking garage and sat in the car for a minute. He needed a plan. He didn't have one. Nothing came to mind, so he took a couple of swigs from the bottle, got out of the car and walked to the elevator.

If somebody had already been out here he'd need to get an idea of what she'd told them. If not, he could prep her a little. She could be sly enough when she needed to be. It was a question, really, of how much she'd had to drink today. He checked his watch and it took him a few seconds to make out it was three o'clock. He'd had a fair bit himself which was probably just as well. Without it he'd more than likely be hiding in a public convenience.

The rank odor of the elevator mingled with that of his shirt. Ma's place was on the top floor. Half of the apartments up there were unoccupied so it felt as if she had the place to herself. When he got out of the elevator the hallway didn't smell much better. It smelled of whatever had colonized the old carpet. The apartment was right at the end, at the foot of a set of steps that led up to the roof. Light and hot air were pouring in through the open roof door—Ma had the key and left it that way most of the time. Before he turned his key in the front door, Billy put his ear to it. Nothing. He opened the door and stepped into the tiny entrance hall. There was just enough room for some coat hooks. He shut the door behind him softly.

The place was awfully quiet. He went left, into the living room. There were piles of magazines and unironed laundry on the furniture, but no Ma.

At the other end of the room a door led to her bedroom but he knew it was blocked on the other side by a chest of drawers. He went back to the hall and looked into the tiny kitchen. It was the hub of the place—all the other rooms led off it, except for the bathroom. He could look straight through it to her bedroom. When he did, he knew straight away that something wasn't right.

Ma's feet were visible in the doorway, hanging off the end of her bed. That was normal. But the toes were pointed at the floor.

Billy had never seen her sleep face down. Never. That wasn't normal. Nor was it normal that he couldn't hear the radio. She never switched it off, not even at night. It would be Billy that had to go in and leave the room reverberating to her snores. Come to think of it, she wasn't snoring now and that wasn't normal. And it wasn't normal that Marty Phillips was leaning on her window sill, leafing through the old photo album that Ma would pore over at the kitchen table almost every night.

"Hello, Billy."

Billy leaned against the kitchen door frame.

"Hello, Marty," he said and it might have sounded ugly. He hoped so.

"Thought I told you not to leave town, Billy."

"I live here."

"Here isn't town. And I told you not to leave. Kind of counts against you."

The policeman straightened up and smiled that smile of his. He put the album down on the sill and glanced at Ma. Billy couldn't put his finger on it but Phillips seemed nervous to him. Uncomfortable.

"Not that it matters now. I don't think the day is going to go your way, Billy. Maybe it's time to come in and talk to Murphy. What do you think?"

Billy wasn't thinking. He didn't plan on ever thinking again. It just seemed to get him into trouble. He went to fish the whiskey bottle from the pocket of his overcoat and remembered that he wasn't wearing the overcoat. In doing so his eye caught Phillips's gun. It was on the kitchen table, where the photo album usually was. A lot closer to Billy than to its owner. So that's why the cop was antsy. At least he had his Solace™. He lit one up. There was no sign that Phillips knew he'd seen the gun.

"Tell me, Marty," he said, "You enjoy your job?"

If he could grab it he had a chance of getting away.

Phillips cocked his head. A little surprised, probably, by both the question and the tone.

"You don't take your hat off at home, Billy? And what the hell are you wearing?" he said through a smile. As he did he took a couple of steps away from the window.

Here we go, thought Billy. "I'm just wondering," he said, "if you enjoy it, that's all. I never killed anybody. Maybe it's fun. Maybe it feels good to kill people, I don't know." He was pretty sure he was slurring his words. And he didn't really know what he was saying anyway. Phillips might think he was a terrorist but that's not what he felt like. What he felt like was a junior reporter with a hatful of trouble, a clown suit, a dead mother, a missing ex-girlfriend, a handgun within reach and no idea what to do about any of it. "Maybe it's OK to kill people if they're bad," he said. "You ever wonder what makes them bad though, Marty? You ever wonder what all the fuss is about? What it is they're trying to protect?"

He went for the whiskey again. It still wasn't there.

"You think it might be something worth protecting, Marty?" Phillips was closer to the door than he had been. "Something that was around a long time before you? Hm? That'll be there when you're gone? Something that means somethi—"

Phillips's sudden laughter stopped him mid-sentence. The policeman leaned against the doorframe. He wiped his eyes and his shoulders shook. When they stopped shaking, he crossed his arms and smiled at Billy. That damn smile. He couldn't have looked more at ease, if it wasn't for the smile.

"Wait a minute," said Phillips. "Are you sassing me?" He shook his head again. The look on his face was one of pleasant surprise. Admiration, almost. "You really think that's the right tack to take with me, Billy boy? At this point in your day?" He sniffed the air. "Been oiling the wheels a little, have we?" He put his hands in his trouser pockets and rocked back and forth on his feet. Shooting the breeze.

"You think I give a fuck about the right and wrong of it? About the content? I'm a cop. Counter-terrorism, seconded to Transport. I don't want or need a history lesson from you. Look at you, man— I don't like getting personal but you don't add up to all that much, y'know? You're a loser, Billy." He laughed. "And you want to lecture me? On what? You really don't get it do you? I do not give the tiniest shit what you actually think. Let me repeat the key word to you. Transport. *Transport*, Billy." He took his hands out of his pockets and spread them as he shrugged. "People need to get to work."

He made his move. But he made it too soon. Maybe he thought Billy, smelling of whiskey, would be slow to react. Maybe he still thought Billy was unaware of the gun. Either way, Billy moved at the same time and got there first. Then Phillips made a more serious mistake. Instead of stopping and putting his hands up, he kept coming. And Billy, instead of backing off with the raised gun, pulled the trigger. For a moment the kitchen was filled with a blue light. Then it wasn't, and Phillips wasn't Phillips any more. He was a heap of clothes and meat on the floor.

"Billy?"

Now he had to think. This was bad. This was as bad as trouble got. He had to think. But he couldn't.

"Billy?"

He checked his watch. He could still just make it to the diner by six. At least he could offload his stuff. And now he had a body to hide. How were you supposed to hide a body? Where?

"Billy, is that you?"

He went to the front door and opened it. The hallway was deserted. He closed it again for a minute and went back to Phillips's body, crouching over it to get a grip under the arms. And then he stopped what he was doing and straightened up, very slowly. He looked at the feet hanging off the end of the bed. They were moving.

"Ma?"

"Is that you, Billy? I thought I heard a noise."

The gun dropped to the floor. He'd forgotten it was in his hand and the sound startled him. He went to the bedroom door and looked at his mother. She hadn't turned over but she blinked to acknowledge him and yawned. Apart from the bleary eye she looked fine. He wanted to be sick.

"You drop something in there? I heard a noise."

He glanced back at Phillips.

"That's right, Ma," he said. It sounded like someone else's voice. "I've been clumsy."

He turned to pick the gun up and pocket it. There was no blood around the body. D-Energy™ pistols cauterized the wounds they made. Phillips's was in the center of his forehead. A neutral observer might easily have concluded that Billy had known what he was doing. He opened the front door and checked the hallway again, then took the body by the armpits.

"You sleep, Ma," he said. "I'll clear up the mess."

But Ma was already snoring.

It was the week of Jane's hooding ceremony. It might have been one of the best weeks of his life, it and the few that preceded it. It should have been. Jane's Ph.D was done; it should have been a time for frivolity, for love-making, a trip somewhere, something like that. But they seemed locked into a pattern. Whenever they were in the apartment together Jane was at her screen. He hadn't seen her any other way for months. Either he was at his or he was taking one of the many baths that meant reading time. This was all hindsight— he'd been too preoccupied at the time to notice much about anyone else, Jane included. Mainly because he'd never been so afraid.

Just as she'd predicted, the clamp-down had come. Not that you would have needed a Ph.D. It was all over the press in the run-up to the launch of whatever this new transport infrastructure was. There were few details but everybody knew the two were connected. The Lit movement's days were numbered and Gripping Tails™ was the reason. Nobody understood it better than the movement—Vince had told him they were on standby footing, that there would be no new books for a while. That and the fact that he didn't know what he was standing by *for* made him uneasy. Then the detention centers were announced. People—nobody Billy knew but he was pretty sure that some at least would be known to Vince—were rounded up. All of a sudden it had gone deathly quiet on that front. He didn't hear from Vince anymore.

Good.

He could put the whole thing behind him. It killed him that he'd never see another book but he still had a couple left. When they were gone he would have the memory. They hadn't yet figured out a way of getting to that. It had all been an episode, it was over and he wasn't in prison. He wasn't built for terrorism, he knew that. There were unverified reports of summary executions in the centers. Then there were verified reports. Then people were shot down in the street—resisting arrest, they said. He just wanted it all to go away. And it had—Jane had been right about that too. They'd scattered like rats.

Good.

Traffic was heavy but it was moving. He'd taken the ninety-one back into the city. He looked good. The shirt had indeed been ready and the suit delivered. He'd found both hanging on the outside of his wardrobe door. Despite the time, he'd taken a cold shower and dressed himself. He looked sharp. Adrenalin kept the car moving in a more or less straight line. He was drunk as hell. There was a dead policeman on his mother's laundry terrace. He wasn't thinking about that. He wasn't thinking about anything that came after the diner. At Buena Vista he exited onto the five and headed downtown.

He'd emerged from the bathroom one afternoon, the week of the ceremony. Steam had followed him to the window seats. Jane was in the kitchen, fixing a snack. He stood in his bathrobe and frowned at a busy sky. It was moving fast and getting darker and he thought it might herald the summer's first storm. He turned round for his tab to get a forecast. Then, remembering he'd left it beside the bath, he reached for Jane's. The weather page had barely loaded when she snatched it from his hand.

"What do you think you're doing?"

She'd looked flushed. She'd looked angry. Now that he thought about it, she'd looked just like her mother had looked this morning.

"Eh . . . checking the weather forecast," he said, intoning it in the interrogative.

"Well don't," she shot back. "Don't use my tab. Where's yours?"

"In the bathroom." He scrutinized her. "What's the matter, Jane?"

"Nothing's the matter. I don't like you using my tab, that's all. I don't use yours."

She sat back down, didn't look up. He contemplated the top of her head for a moment and then went to get his tab.

"Looks like a storm," he said, back in his chair. He felt like he'd been slapped. His voice was wavering. She brightened up then.

"I'm sorry, honey." She sidled over to him on her knees and kissed his cheek. "I know, I'm meant to relax now, right?" She laid her head on his chest and he held her.

"I can't, honey," she said. "I can't just yet. The university is talking to me about a research fellowship. And I'm still in the running for this job at the Department." She pulled back and cupped his face. "All these people put a confidentiality clause in place before they'll so much as tell you you've got gravy on your chin. I don't know how or how much they monitor. I've got so many passwords on that tab it takes me longer to get into anything than I took over the damn thesis. You understand, don't you? Soon as I pick an offer it won't be an issue. We can go someplace. OK?"

He did understand. Or he said he did. He thought he did. He knew better now. The emptiness that had engulfed him, the ache, had been precursed in that moment and moments like it. He couldn't see it then, or didn't want to.

Mr and Mrs Ellison had invited them to dinner that evening—a private family celebration before the official one. Jane went to get ready and later they drove up to the house. It was a lot cooler up on the Bluffs, and gusty. Vince was there too. He was friendly, neither ignoring nor paying too much attention to Billy. He seemed to have relaxed. There was none of the fidgeting or the sneering. Billy thought that maybe he was getting on better with Mr and Mrs Ellison. Perhaps they'd called a truce for Jane's benefit. Or maybe Vince, like him, was just relieved that all the secrecy was behind them now. They'd had their little adventure and come through unscathed—legally, at least.

At any rate, dinner was a much more enjoyable affair than before. Mr Ellison was positively jovial. Jane talked about the fellowship and the job and where they might live and Billy loved hearing her use the pronoun. He felt the inklings of a new optimism that night; Jane felt the effects of the wine—by the time Mr Ellison poured the brandy, she waved her hand and excused herself, tottering up to her old room to lie down.

"She deserves it," Mrs Ellison said. "I haven't seen her let herself go like that for months."

"Absolutely." Mr Ellison chuckled. "You'll stay, Billy?"

Billy was designated driver and hadn't touched a drop, eager to make the right impression. He was always so eager to make the right impression.

"Can't, Mr Ellison, but thanks. Let her relax. Like you say, she deserves it. I have an early start. I can pick her up after I knock off tomorrow. I bet she'd like some time with you guys."

They seemed to like that and saw him off at the front door. The storm hadn't materialized but there had been a shower. The grass glistened and the soil smelled good. It was quiet up here late at night, not another living soul in the street as he strolled to the car. He still couldn't bring himself to park the thing within sight of the house. He lit up a siGi™ and slid behind the wheel and sat there for a minute with the driver door open. The day's tension had dissipated. Then he jumped high enough to hit his head on the roof.

"You like to scare a guy don't you, Vince."

Vince didn't react. He didn't look like he was in the mood. He didn't look at all like he had just ten minutes before, at the dinner table. He leaned an elbow on the open door and said nothing. Then he dropped a book in Billy's lap.

"We're back in business."

Billy flinched. He looked around to check the street.

"No way, Vince. What do you think you—"

"I think we can dispense with the melodrama, don't you? You know as well as I do you're driving away with that book." Vince stared him down. Billy said nothing.

"Just one thing. It's rather a different business." He indicated the book with a downward flick of his eyes. "I never want to see it again. From this moment on, I'm one of only two contacts you'll ever have. There's me and there's whoever you find to pass the books on to. Someone you can trust, Billy, like I'm trusting you."

It was Vince's turn to look around.

"That's the way it is now," he whispered. "One way traffic. Keep the books moving. If they get you, I'll replace you. If they get you and you give me up, my contact will replace me. They can't stop all of us."

He straightened up to leave and Billy started the car. Before he pushed the door shut, Vince leaned in close.

"Welcome to Gilgamesh."

The Saturday of Jane's ceremony had arrived. She'd been withdrawn in the days following the dinner at her parents' place. He'd been thoroughly on edge. He wanted to give the book back to Vince. He knew he couldn't. He knew he'd take the next one too. He knew there was something very wrong with his girlfriend, but he didn't know what. He put it down to nerves on account of the decisions she faced. The people concerned—faculty people and Department people—would be at the ceremony so even if conversations were outwardly informal, it was crunch time. He knew that too, and that his role was to shut up and look pretty. But he didn't feel pretty. And shutting up had always been hard for him.

The evening wasn't enjoyable. Not at all. Jane was curt with him—the difference in her attitude toward him and the bright, bubbly, brilliant young woman schmoozing the Department was striking and hurtful. She didn't want him there and she wasn't worried about him knowing it. He kept quiet but it was an angry quiet, and as the after-dinner drinks dragged on he had plenty of them. Late in the evening he noticed Jane's father helping Mrs Ellison on with her coat. He had sprawled on a banquette on the far side of the room and didn't get up to see them off. Jane did, and all three threw quick, dark glances his way before her parents left.

Around one in the morning he decided it was time to leave. He felt he had plenty of reasons. He'd run out of the will to support a girl he thought was treating him badly. At least for tonight. And he was getting drunk enough to slur his words. He didn't want to disgrace her. She was being a bitch but she didn't deserve that. He got his coat and checked his wallet for taxi fare and he went looking for her. She was outside on the terrace, talking to two men and a woman who towered over all of them. There was a lot of that rapid nodding that people do when they're keen to commit to something but also assessing each other. He didn't like the way one of the guys had his hand in the small of Jane's back so he brushed it away and gave her a squeeze.

Then he said something and that's when it all went to shit. He couldn't remember, now, what he'd said. It wasn't clear he knew at the time. What was clear though—abundantly clear—is that no one else did either. So he tried again. Four uncomprehending, horrified faces. One of them belonged to the girl he loved, the other three to the people who took her away. It didn't matter if that was true or not. It was true enough for him. *No prollum*, he'd thought at the time. *Snottaprollum. Drunkerthansuppos'd.* He gave a magnanimous smile his best shot and turned to leave. Then he found his chin—in a flowerbed. Then someone was rolling him over and sitting him up. And though he couldn't speak there was nothing wrong with his hearing—somebody whispered into his ear *better watch your mouth, son. We're Department and the lady's from the press. You can't talk that lit shit around us.*

Then people were helping him to stand. None of them was Jane. As they held him up, he looked around till he saw her. She'd retreated to the outdoor bar with the guy who once again had his hand on her back. And there it was. That look. That terrible look on her face that had sucked the air from his lungs and made his head ring like a struck bell. He'd felt an odd, seasick weightlessness. A useless sensation—it couldn't even resolve itself into the panic that might have served a purpose just moments before. A physical knowledge, known in the gut, that it was too late. That everything was too late. It had felt like realizing he was dead already, and that he probably ought to lie down and act like it. That had been that. Game over.

Across the street, the diner looked OK to him. By daylight, the tint was evident in the curved expanse of glass. Inside, on the other side of the window, customers sat around the triangular bar at their chops and sandwiches. Though the place was lit—always—it was brighter on the street and the interior looked cool and hushed: the quiet of a museum or a funeral home. It was a false impression, Billy knew. There would be the racket of cutlery, the rattle of spoons in cups, the hiss of the milk frother, the yelled orders and Benny yelling back.

It was after six but he took his time. He was on the opposite side of the street, across from the door. The conspicuous Marmon was parked underground and a few blocks away, an empty whiskey bottle on the back seat. There was a defunct Com™ booth on the pavement here and he could watch the diner from behind it without drawing attention. He intended to do just that for a little while.

It was busy in Phil's but he recognized most of the faces. Of those he didn't, four of them were obviously couples because two of them held hands and the other two were bickering. There was a family with a toddler and a baby in a pushchair. No loners. No platonic-looking pairs sitting in silence and artfully blending vigilance with boredom.

Nothing that seemed like police, in other words. He wouldn't have been able to explain exactly what he was looking for but he knew he'd recognize it if he saw it. It seemed to him that once you were prey it was easy to pick out the predator. It came naturally. He crossed the street and went in behind another customer without having to touch the swinging door. Straight away, Benny waved him over to the bar. He didn't like that and he didn't like that Vince wasn't at their table.

"He's here," said Benny. "In the bathroom. I'd like him not to be here anymore, Billy."

"Why? What's up?"

"Thought you might tell me. He looks bad, Billy. He smells bad. It's upsetting the other customers. He's been at that table for half an hour, talking to himself. Loud enough that people have left on account of it."

Benny winced.

"You got your own aroma going on. What's wrong with you guys today? Suck a mint and help me out, will you? Here he is."

Vince was making his way back to the table. He hadn't seen Billy yet. He looked awful—like death and not necessarily warmed up. Once back in his seat he kept his hands clasped in his lap and muttered to himself. His eyes darted around the diner till they landed on Billy and he froze.

"Bring a couple of strong coffees over, will you?" said Billy. "I'll see what I can do."

He went over to the table and threw his jacket over the back of it.

"Thanks for coming. There's nobody else I could—"

"Not another word, Billy." Vince had raised a hand to quiet him. "I have to tell you something." He scanned Billy and the floor around his seat.

"Where's your stuff? I thought you were dumping your stuff on me. How many you still got?"

Behind Billy, Benny coughed and put two coffees between them.

"Thanks, Benny."

He turned back to Vince but paused for a second because Benny took his time going away. Then he said:

"Don't worry about the stuff. I have it. And you can tell me whatever you want but it'll have to wait. I'm in big trouble. I've been—"

"Trouble? *You're* in trouble? Man, you don't know trouble." Vince lifted his cup and spilled some coffee in his haste. He didn't seem to notice.

"Vince, please try to concentrate. You can tell me later but right now I need you to listen. I'm in very serious—"

"No, *you* listen." Vince leaned forward and grabbed Billy's wrist. It was obvious he hadn't slept. Maybe not for days—his skin was waxy and he smelled terrible. Billy knew he still smoked a little Escape™ once in a while but he'd never seen him like this.

"I will literally go out of my mind," said Vince, with a stone cold lucidity, "right here, right now, if I don't tell you this. I have to tell someone, Billy. Apart from my shifts and your drop offs, I haven't left my place for a month. I should have told you sooner but . . . I don't know. I couldn't."

Billy sat back and looked at his friend. If that was the correct term. He still had hold of his wrist.

"All right," he said, making a point of checking his watch. "Shoot."

The Tale of the Porter and the Gin

I REMEMBER how good I felt that last time I saw you, and afterwards when I walked back down from the Bluffs. You know when you feel good and you just want to walk? It was like that. It took me a couple of hours but I might as well have been floating. I was proud, I suppose. I'd left another book with you (Did I say that too loudly? Nobody heard me?) and as I walked the city's night-lit streets, my breast burned with the fire of conviction in what we were doing. That sounds pompous, does it? Well, you know me.

I believed we were guardians, custodians . . . I don't know, I've lost my grip on it now. Efforts to name it degenerate into lists. Safe keepers? But I knew this—each artifact I passed to you was another blip on the monitor: as you passed it on, another beat of the pulse. We were critical life support. And now, with the crackdown, we were rebels. Some of us would be martyrs. I remember feeling such devotion as I walked but . . . how was I to know it would all fall apart around me? And so quickly. It doesn't matter—that's all over now. But we're not finished, which is what I need to explain to you. Something has happened.

Where was I? Oh yes—walking down from the Bluffs. As I neared the hotel, my legs tired. Shops were shuttering and bars opening up. I passed Ministry billboards emblazoned with contact numbers, calls to action—invitations to concerned citizens to inform on their neighbors. I bowed my head as I walked, as if the hoardings had eyes that watched me. I passed boarded-up bookshops and news kiosks so sparsely stocked they'd be gone soon too—the two or three state-approved news outlets wouldn't be enough to sustain a business. No more stories. They'd finally acted on it. Second Enlightenment dogma made law, and me an outlaw. And you.

My feet were sore when I shut the front door behind me and I thought I'd have a bath. Then I realized I could already smell the bath. And that in the bathroom, someone was humming. I stood still and held my breath. Something made me look back at the door, then around the hallway. The little side table was there. My windbreaker hanging from its hook. It was my place alright. I could tell from the tenor of the hum that it wasn't you. Of course, I'd just left you, so it wouldn't be. My sister had a key but the deep, croaky humming certainly wasn't her. And she would never let anyone have it. I cursed myself for being the only young male in the city, probably, who didn't keep a baseball bat in his closet, or a golf club, even a tennis racket. I had nothing.

But as bizarre as the moment was, it wasn't frightening, exactly—if somebody breaks into your home, after all, with the intention of doing you harm, they're unlikely to set the scene by running themselves a bath. It's just a very non-threatening kind of thing to do. Perhaps I was being cleverly lulled into a false sense of security, but I felt as I went in there that if a physical altercation of some kind were to prove necessary, then I, fully dressed and approaching by stealth, would almost certainly come out on top. Nevertheless, I braced myself as I got to the bathroom door—open just a crack and affording no view of the person within—against the prospect of dealing with an assailant who would be wet and possibly soapy and rather difficult, therefore, to get a hold of.

I pushed the door with sufficient force that it swung open silently and little enough that it came to a stop before knocking against the wall. Then I stepped inside unobserved, noting with disapproval that the intruder wore my waterproof earphones and hummed along to whatever was playing (my best guess at the time would have been Tall Tale by The Arabian Knights—the humming was utterly tuneless but his air guitar was a good match for the solo in that one). He still hadn't seen me, since his eyes were shut, and I didn't recognize him immediately—he'd made himself some hair and a beard from the soap bubbles. It was clear he was elderly, though, and I already had a feeling.

His clothes lay neatly arranged on the bench in the corner. There were tweed trousers and a wide-lapeled overcoat with deep cuffs and a velvet collar. A striped shirt, grey on white, and a silk cravat, on top of which a gold watch and chain had been carefully placed. A waistcoat, like the overcoat, was black with a braid trim and felt buttons. I think I knew it, then, but when I turned back to the man in my bath, who had poured a jug of water over himself to reveal his thinning hair and straggling, cheek-free beard, I was left in no doubt. I of all people would recognize him—his had been one of only two biographies I had ever read.

Charles Dickens.

Don't look at me like that. I am not a lunatic. Of course it wasn't the *real* Charles Dickens. Sitting there in my bathtub. How could I think that? How could you think I could? No, this had to be his ghost. The ghost of Charles Dickens. Sitting there in my bathtub.

"Mother*fucker*," it said.

I'd obviously given it, him, a terrible fright—he'd wiped the suds and water from his face and opened his eyes and there I was. You can see it from his point of view. He grabbed a flannel from the side of the bath and arranged it over his private area.

"Well, hello there," he said. He smiled but I did think there was a tone, and didn't reply. I'm not sure I could have—my mouth hung open and useless. He extended a hand toward the bathroom door. "Maybe knock next time?" It was an angry smile, if you know what I mean. "I'm in the fucking bath."

He belched. He was slurring his words and I could smell his boozy breath. Even in my stupefaction, I couldn't help noticing my bottle of Nolet's Silver Dry on the ledge behind him, somewhat depleted. I had saved up for that bottle. I mean, I'm a bellhop. He snapped his fingers at me.

"Dressing gown!"

I looked to the hook on the bathroom door, then back at Charles Dickens.

"You want my dressing gown?" I said, with emphasis.

He had a hand on either side of the bath and was lifting himself out of it.

"I can wave my dick in your face if you prefer," he said. "Up to you."

I handed him the gown. "Would you mind telling me what you're doing here, at least?"

He interrupted his struggle with the belt strap to peer at me. Either that or he was trying to focus. "Having a bath," he said, turning to reach for the bottle. My tab vibrated with an incoming call, I pulled it from my back pocket to check the caller ID and my thumb answered the call by mistake, so I put it to my ear.

"Mother?"

"Vincent? I suppose I should thank you for taking the call. Where have you been?"

"Mother, it's not a great—"

"I've been worried out of my mind, Vincent. Your father too. You didn't come to dinner this week. You haven't been answering. What's going on with you? Are you alright?"

I struggled to picture my father worrying. I'd never known him to. Mother, on the other hand, I'd never known to do anything else.

"Mother, I really can't—"

"Don't you dare hang up on me, Vincent. We had an agreement."

Charles Dickens had fastened the dressing gown and taken my gin through to the living room. I was pacing up and down the hallway.

Now that he wasn't in sight, I couldn't be quite sure I'd seen him at all.

"Why don't we talk later? It's just that I've got—"

"Dr Düssel says she hasn't seen you for two weeks. We agreed—"

My skin flushed.

"Dr Düssel is *my* doctor. She has no right to tell you anything."

Silence on the line, and no sound from the living room.

"Geraldine is a friend of the family, Vincent," said Mother, finally. "She is worried too. You said you'd—"

"I know, Mother. And I will. But I've got to go now. There's someone—"

"Don't you dare hang up on me, Vincent. I—"

I pocketed the tab and put my head round the living room door. There he was.

"No," I said, lips trembling, "I meant, what are you doing *here*, in my apartment?"

"Oh. That," he said. He was sitting in the armchair and there was an empty pizza box at his feet. So he'd been at the fridge too. "I dunno. They never tell me." He took a swig of the Nolet's. "Usually becomes apparent."

I couldn't help snorting.

"What?" said Charles Dickens.

I chuckled. "You know. Apparent."

His eyes narrowed.

"You *know*," I said. "Apparent. Ghost."

He shook his head. "No," he said. "Not with you."

"Never mind." I picked up the pizza box. As you know, I keep a tidy home. "Well then, do you know how long you'll be—"

There was no point in finishing my question—Charles Dickens had passed out. I sometimes felt faint myself, after a bath, and the drink wouldn't have helped. I rinsed the tub and had my own. When I got out he was still unconscious, so I left him where he was and went to bed.

When I woke I could hear someone rattling around in the kitchen. I turned over for more sleep, then remembered I was on an early, and that Charles Dickens had stayed the night. I got up and went through. He was sitting at the table I'd pushed into the window bay, the one that protrudes high over De Nuys Street. In front of him, a bowl of cornflakes—with a spoonful held trembling halfway between the bowl and his mouth and his other hand over his eyes, he wept.

"Why do you weep?" I asked. My mouth was dry.

He whipped the hand away, eyes wide and lids reddened, and looked at the spoon of cereal, as if he'd forgotten he held it.

"I don't know, actually," he said, after a few seconds. "Everything's just so . . ."

He placed the spoon back into the bowl. "Got any muesli?" he asked. "That might cheer me up. Switzerland's a great favourite of mine, you know. It really is."

He sobbed.

"I'll pick some up," I said. My heart was racing. "That is, if you'll be staying for—"

"Toasted. Authenticity has its place but I do like a crunch." He had perked up. "Oh, you can count on me being around for a little while, I think. It usually drags." He looked around the room then as if something had occurred to him. "Hey, where are all your books?"

I was taken by surprise. It was a question you might expect of the police, not to hear in polite conversation.

"I usually get assigned to bookish types," said Charles Dickens, to fill the silence. "Skill set thing."

"There hasn't been a lot of hard copy around for a long time," I said. "Anyway, the type of book you wrote is illegal now."

"*Illegal?*" he said through a mouthful of cornflakes. "You are *shitting* me." It took him a little while to process the contents of his mouth. He sat back in the chair. "That is some heavy dope, right there," he said and took another spoonful of cornflakes, head shaking the whole time. "Wowzer. Also, doesn't make any sense. *Why?*"

"I don't know for sure. Nobody does. They're up to something, with all the stories. They need them, and it's probably for the new drives. Roadworks all over the city."

"OK," said Charles Dickens. There was milk in his beard. He wiped it away with my Irish linen scarf. It was at that point I noticed how unlike a hugely successful and, in his time, pretty much universally loved mid-19th-century novelist he looked, sitting in long johns and my Nixons t-shirt.

He shrugged. "Literary quandary," he said, "of some sort, is usually the type of thing I'm deployed for. If there isn't one, I really wouldn't know where to start." He scooped another load of cereal but it hung in the air near his mouth as he scowled in thought. "Why I'm here, you know?" Biting into the cornflakes, he spoke through them. "Nope. Don't get it."

"It makes perfect sense," I said. "It's the greatest literary quandary of all time. Might be too much, even for you."

"Ha!" he said. "Don't count on it. I'm pretty good, even if I do say so myself." He stood up suddenly and took a step toward me.

"Jeez, I never introduced myself, did I? Dude, you should have said. Shit is *rude*."

He extended a hand. I took it. "I know who you are, Charles Dickens. I'll be back up just after three and I'll fill you in then. I would tell you to make yourself at home, but . . ." I looked at the table, at the empty whiskey bottle lying on its side by the armchair, at my Nixons t-shirt. He shrugged and showed me the palms of his hands.

"Sorry, man," he said. "But you should be glad I had that bath. I stank of the grave. It's an awful stench. And thanks for breakfast. I would have preferred muesli but I still appreciate it, I really do."

No mention of the quality hooch. I put on my little red hat and went downstairs.

"Jesus *Christ*!"

It was just after three. I'd shut the door behind me. Charles Dickens was lying on the floor in the hallway, pulling himself up onto his elbows. I'd spent my shift trying to convince myself he didn't exist.

"Jesus Christ, man. You scared the *shit* out of me," he said. It took his old bones a while to get him back on his feet. "Did you get the muesli?"

"What were you doing, lurking behind the front door?" I said.

"Listening," said Charles Dickens. "You know, patrolling the perimeter."

I went into the kitchen and put my groceries on the side. As I did, I heard the creak of the armchair in the living room. I got a couple of beers from the fridge and followed him in there.

"We need to talk," I said. "There's a lot to explain."

"Fine. Shoot." He sounded irritable. I held a beer out. "No, thanks," he said. "I'm good."

He wasn't wearing my t-shirt but hadn't put his own clothes back on. He was back in my dressing gown and smelled, strongly, of my pomegranate and argan oil bath foam, alcohol and . . . and something else. Something I couldn't identify and didn't like.

"So I wanted to explain the situation to you. I don't see how you'll be able to help but what do I know? Do you remember what I said to you this morning?"

He sighed. "Nope."

"About stories? All the stories? I think that's why you're here. I can't imagine what it would be, but perhaps there's some way in which you might—"

I stopped. He was rolling his eyes and making puppets of his hands, opening and closing them in the universal sign of you're-talking-rubbish-and-too-much-of-it. I was nonplussed—I'd only just begun. "Do you mind telling me—"

"You maybe going to try and focus?" he said, and yawned. "You got a focus issue, you know that?"

"I'm sorry," I said, shaking my head. "I don't quite—"

He sat forward in the armchair and put his elbows on his knees, spreading his open hands out in supplication, and spoke to me as if to a slow child. I could see his penis.

"Did you get the muesli?"

"Good grief. What *is* it with you and muesli? And just a minute," I'd thought of something. "Why do you talk like this? You don't talk the way you should. You talk like a beach bum. Your vernacular should be nineteenth century, English. Kent, I think. Portsmouth maybe."

He sat back. I felt a little riled but also relieved that the folds of the dressing gown once again concealed his member.

"That what you think?" he said.

I nodded. He smiled.

"So let's see. I die, right? 9th of June, 1870. It was a Thursday, I think. I don't remember very well, to be honest. It had been a rough couple of days for me. What I think we can both agree on, though, is that this was quite a while ago. Can we agree on that, eh . . ."

"Vince."

"Vince. Can we agree on that, Vinny?"

I nodded.

"And so I spend all of those intervening years floating about the place paying no attention *whatsoever* to anything that is going on. Nothing. I don't watch, I don't listen. The internet passes me by. It's basically a centuries-long nap. Or maybe I've been looking at a wall or something. Then, suddenly, I'm in your bath." He moved his head slowly from side to side. "Is that it? Seriously, *dude*, is that what you think?"

"Well, when you put it like that, it does sound a little—"

He took a sharp inward breath. It sounded like his last lungful of patience. "Vinny," he said, "please. For the love of all that's holy. Did. You. Get. The. Muesli?"

"Yes. I got the muesli. Good *grief*."

He smacked his knees and punched the air with both hands. "Great! Was that so hard? Jesus. OK, we're good. What did you want to talk about?"

"I just said, didn't I?" I watched as he reached over the side of the armchair to retrieve a glass from the floor. "I didn't have time this morning, but it's something you need to understand. You would be considered a terrorist these days. Even for reading your books, let alone writing them."

My back straightened, with pride or perhaps to brace myself against the truth of what I was about to say. "Charles Dickens, *I* am a terrorist."

He reached again and produced my bottle of *Inocente*, from which he filled the tumbler. It isn't often I get my hands on a bottle of *Inocente*. "Did you at least chill that?" I said.

"Vinny, I'm going to level with you," said Charles Dickens. "This morning, I pretty much assumed you were making that shit up." There were no droplets on the bottle, no misting on the glass. He was drinking it at room temperature. "You know, to fuck with me. It sounded pretty crazy, I have to tell you."

He jiggled the half-empty bottle. "You like sauce, don't you, Vinny?"

"I'm not making it up! I can see how it would sound to you but I live in a very different world. I do appreciate good wine, yes. Wine-making is a very ancient art. It—" I stopped myself. Now wasn't the time. "Do you know what a cognition drive is?" I asked him.

"Negatory."

"Well, there you are. If you did—"

"You ever seen *Quantum Leap*, Vinny?"

"What? I don't—"

"The show," he said. He sat forward again. I averted my eyes. "The way it goes is Sam Beckett, a brilliant scientist, is trapped in the past as a result of a time travel experiment that went terribly wrong. Aided by a hologram of his friend, Rear Admiral Al Calavicci, he attempts to return to his present by changing events in his past. Righting wrongs and what not. *Quantum Leap*."

"*Samuel* Beckett? I'm sorry, I don't . . . you're talking about television, perhaps? A drama. That's the whole point. As I've been trying to explain—"

"Never mind. Useful way to describe this current set-up, is all. It's kind of what I do. Except I'm not a scientist. I'm a dead person. But otherwise. I think I'm beginning to get a handle on your sitch, by the way." He crossed his legs, thankfully. "Promising young writer," he said, taking a moment to pour himself another tepid sherry, "but cruelly unrecognised. A cold, unfeeling world disdains his art. It's not something I can relate to since I enjoyed huge success more or less from the get-go but I understand it happens. Anyway, why am *I* here? Well," he stood, "this young writer is in danger!"

He went to the window.

"No," I said. "I'm not a—"

He raised a hand to silence me. "Hear me out," he said. "I think I've got this. Not physical danger. No, no, that wouldn't be my area." He had one hand to the window pane. I thought that, even from behind, he looked pleased with himself.

"Actually," I said, "There *is* an element of—"

"Shh!" said Charles Dickens. "Don't break the flow. No! It's this guy's *soul* that lies in mortal danger." He waved a finger in the air. "His very *mind*!" He turned around and pointed at me. "That's right! This dude is properly losing his shit. Tormented by the powerful forces of creativity that broil within him, he stalks the lonely byways of a simmering insanity."

He paced.

"I told you I was good!" he said and stooped to empty the last of the wine into his glass. "Spurned by a world that doesn't deserve him. Stymied by his own," he gave me an appraising look, "lack of physical presence, social inadequacy etc. He has constructed an elaborate new reality. Why is there no place out there for his art? Because it's bad? Chance? Fate? No! Because it's *illegal*. How perfect!"

With the hand that wasn't nursing my sherry, he'd grabbed my shoulder. His long fingers dug in. They were cold. "How'm I doing?" he said. "I'm nailing it, aren't I?"

He shook me as he spoke. "Don't fight this, Vinny! You've got to let me in! Think about it—what better way to justify your failure to yourself? It's brilliant, actually. I wouldn't be surprised if it was your best work. I don't know what it is you lack—balls, talent, whatever—but this elaborate fantasy of yours gives you the perfect cover. Don't you see? You've externalised the problem. Exquisitely. Rid yourself of any necessity to acknowledge your own shortcomings. Seriously, hats off, bro."

He looked at me and I looked right back at him till the upturned corners of his mouth dipped and doubt creased the skin between his eyebrows. His shoulders dropped. "Was I even warm?" he said, and fell into the armchair.

"No," I said. "I'm not a writer. I'm a distributor, if you like. And I'm not losing my shit, as you put it."

I wanted to show him yesterday's *Standard*—the story on the new cog drives and the various arrests that had been made. The *Herald* feature on the detention centers and the schedule of executions it had published. But I couldn't—my payments had slipped and I was on calls and messages only. I was getting my news downstairs, whatever I could pick up from overheard snatches of guest conversations.

"Jesus," he said. "I really thought I had this one. Quick diagnostic, some kind of pep talk and out of here, you know? Short and sweet." He rested his head against the back of the chair and closed his eyes. "Because, and no offence, Vinny, but these things do tend to drag for me. Apart from the basic analogy, it hasn't really been like *Quantum Leap* at all, if I'm honest."

He opened his eyes. "I think maybe I will have that beer."

I threw him a can and he cracked it open. "That guy had it good," he said. "New York, Florida. Marilyn Monroe. He got a lot of action. I get people like you and the insides of apartments." He let out a slow sigh. "The muesli helps. It reminds me of—"

A single sob escaped him. He took a swig of beer and then wept freely. I left him to it.

The next day I was on a late. I got up early anyway because I had a pick-up in the morning. Charles Dickens snored from an awkward fetal curl in the armchair. Empty beer cans were littered around the chair, some of them crumpled. And he'd been at the muesli—there was an overturned bowl on the floor where he'd kicked it in his sleep. An elliptical stain to the side of it was wet with milk and strewn with rolled oats and raisins, as was the bony foot that hung over it.

I went to the kitchenette for a coffee and to fix my own breakfast. The first thing I did was bang my head against the corner of a cupboard door he'd left open. Applying pressure to the resulting cut with one hand, I filled the kettle with the other and poured some cornflakes into a bowl.

When I lifted the milk carton from its shelf on the fridge door, I knew instantly. There are very few things that enrage me like an empty milk carton in the fridge. It is one of the reasons I have chosen, latterly, to live alone. You did it too. Twice. Since your own stay was brief, I didn't bring it up but there it is. On this occasion too, I held my tongue, standing over him with the carton in my hand before turning to leave. Besides, as the nasal whine cut out and his lips began to flap, he didn't look like a man easily roused.

Down on the street the lights were still on. The sky was brightening. As I always did on a pickup, I took the tram to 1st and Beaufort and caught the bus there which took me out to MacMillan Park. I would walk back. At the corner of 6th and Alvaro, I stepped off the bus and walked past the ice cream kiosk and into the park. There was a little sports field and a children's play area, some pavilions dotted around.

The park was overlooked by the Lakeside theatre and as the sun cleared its hoardings the palms threw long, long shadows. In among all the musicals—why can't the Cog® drives process music? I wish they'd taken that instead—they'd put one of the Ministry notices: *No more exceptions. No more excuses. No more stories.* Photographs of traffic fatalities, phone numbers, all the usual.

I walked as far as the West Corridor that dissected the park and dodged the still sparse traffic to get to the water on the other side. A couple of floating jetties bobbed on the shore and behind them, on a grass slope, was a park bench. I sat on it and waited. There was never an exact time. On pick-up mornings, I assumed she'd be watching. Whenever I got there, she'd watch some more, then pick her moment.

There were birds out on the water. Some of them drifted on it, some of them flew low over it. I don't know anything about birds. They were white. I could see a gardening crew at work on the other side. The street lights went out. I could hear a shutter being pulled up here and there along Alvaro, which was behind me now. She usually came from that direction. This morning though, I spotted her first out in front of me, on the path that runs along the Corridor. She was wearing a salmon-colored, knee-length coat and carried a large handbag in one hand, a paper cup in the other. Before she reached the jetties, she sat on a bench that was right next to the water and a dark green trash can. She'd given no sign that she'd seen me but of course she had. From this point on, the routine never changed.

She put the paper cup on the bench beside her and took a paper packet from her bag, opening it to reveal a sandwich which she proceeded to nibble at. It took her around ten minutes to have her breakfast. When she'd finished, she threw the paper cup and the box into the trash can. I watched her walk a little way back in the direction she'd come from and then got up from my bench.

Immediately, I sat back down. A black car crawled along the Corridor, just behind her, trailing. If she was aware of it she wasn't letting on. It pulled to a stop and a man got out from the passenger seat and hopped the low balustrade that separated the park from the road. He seemed to call out to her but she didn't turn her head, so he walked down the slope and blocked her path. He was a well-built man, short cropped hair showing beneath the rim of his hat.

It was all smiles—she as she spoke and he nodding. I felt the hairs stand up on the back of my neck. She handed him her bag. He didn't look inside, throwing it casually over his own shoulder as he made a gesture towards her. She took her coat off and gave him that too. All very nice. All very friendly. He took her by the elbow and they walked back up to the balustrade. He helped her over it and held the rear door open for her. As she got in, she shot one quick glance back in the direction of the bench and as far away as she was, I believed I could see her fear.

I imagined I could smell it, actually, though that may have been my own. The car pulled away and in a moment everything was back to normal. No one else had been around to witness what had happened. The man didn't seem to have noticed me and the gardening crew had disappeared. What I would normally do now is walk over there and sit next to the trash can. After a few minutes I'd take a paper packet, identical to hers, from my pocket, and put it in the bin. A few moments later, I'd shake my head as though I'd forgotten something and reach into the bin again, lift hers out and walk home. That was always the way.

I couldn't see anybody at all and yet I felt exposed. This had to have been a sting and it seemed to me it had gone either of two ways. They had mistimed it, and missed her make the drop. Or they had timed it perfectly, which would mean they were waiting. For me. I sat tight, fighting panic. I couldn't stay too long—that in itself might arouse suspicion—but for now I was too scared to move.

I caught a flash of color in the periphery of my vision and looked along the Corridor towards the other side of the lake. An orange-clad member of the gardening crew had emerged from a hut over there and was pulling a trolley along the pathway that ran between the water and the road. When he reached the first trash can, he emptied it into the trolley and moved towards the next. He would have two more to empty before he reached mine. It was now or never.

Sitting where she had, I dropped my packet into the bin. Then I took my tab out and pretended to read. I changed my posture a few times to get as good a look around as I could. Still nobody except for the park guy who was only one trash can away now. I was sweating and if anyone was watching me through a telephoto they knew it. The trash guy walked toward me, then paused and pretended to consult his own tab, embarrassed by my rooting around in the garbage. I wanted to cry as I took the packet out and felt the weight of a book. I pocketed it and, oddly, that calmed me. If I was under surveillance, it was done. To this day, I don't know why, but I picked up her lidded paper cup as well. Perhaps I thought it made me look more plausible. More like some tramp. Straightening, I nodded to the guy, who scrupulously avoided eye contact. Then I walked towards Alvaro.

The shadows of the palms had shortened and the kiosk was open. I may not have been breathing well, expecting a tap on the shoulder at any moment. A stranger with a friendly smile. A car waiting. When I reached the street there was a bus at the stop. I abandoned protocol and got on. Apart from one old lady who sat right behind the driver,

I had it to myself. At least, I hoped it was an old lady. It looked like one. At the next stop she got off. Nobody got on. I got off four stops later, when it seemed clear to me that if they were on my track they'd have taken me, and walked the rest of the way to the hotel.

I know I should have told you straight away. I don't know why I didn't. Your next drop-off was still a few days away and I resolved to tell you then. We'd arranged it for the sports grounds at La Alma and I planned to go very early and watch the spot. If anything seemed at all off, I would call you. In the event, it went off smoothly but I couldn't bring myself to let you know about my contact. I felt as though I'd let you down, though there was nothing I could have done about it. You still had the zeal of an initiate. You longed to play your part—I didn't have the heart to tell you that it had come to an end. Besides, I had a couple of paperbacks stashed. They would buy me some time while I figured out how to break it to you.

When I got up to my floor, my legs felt heavier with each step I took along the corridor. An adrenaline crash maybe, or maybe it was remembering that there was a ghost in my apartment. I put my ear to the door, heard nothing.

"Charles Dickens?" I looked in both directions to reassure myself there was no one around to hear. There wasn't, and nor was there any reply from the other side of the door. I opened it and went inside. The hallway was unlit and quiet. I put the paper cup down on the side table.

"Charles Dickens?"

No answer. The thought occurred, and along with it a sinking feeling, that he had gone. I didn't want him gone. Not now. I needed to talk to him. There might be something he could to do to compensate for me being on my own. It might be the reason he was here. Perhaps an even greater destiny awaited me.

"Charles Dickens?"

He was in the armchair, so still that for a moment I wondered if he was dead, until I realized the absurdity of the thought. He'd emptied a bottle of port and passed out. It was in his lap, one hand still around the neck. It was eleven a.m.

I'd picked up some milk and took it to the kitchen to get myself some breakfast. At the same time I filled the moka pot's reservoir with some organic, fair-trade Ethiopian and put it on the stove. Then I brought my bowl of flakes to the little table, sat on the only stool and vomited. It felt good—like ejecting the dread. But it didn't last. When I'd emptied myself I sat bent forward, shoulders to knees and hands clasped between them. The floor and what I'd covered it with wobbled in my fluid-filled eyes and my stomach tightened till it felt like a stone. I sat like that till the whistle of the coffee pot roused me, then I turned it off and got the mop from the bathroom to clean up. With the place smelling of bleach, I poured myself a cup and downed a few spoonfuls of cereal. Then I just sat. I don't know how long. There was no thought. After a while, something limbic in me informed me it was time for work and I went to the bedroom to change.

Charles Dickens hadn't stirred but he had begun to snore. That was progress, I supposed. Perhaps he'd be conscious when I got back. He still held the bottle and when I went to take it from him he even managed a momentary grip. It came away with a jerk and the dregs spilled over my leg. I cursed, but the uniform was the same dark burgundy as the wine and it didn't show. It only then occurred to me to go back to my coat and take a look at the book I'd picked up. It was poetry. Rilke. I don't like poetry but I thought you'd be pleased. I put it away, underneath a loose floorboard in the bedroom with the others, and went downstairs.

Mr Reynolds was on reception as I passed on my way to the bellhop station.

"Afternoon, Vince. You take this case up to 315 before you clock in? Lady looks a good tipper."

"Sure, Mr Reynolds."

I picked up the little black case and started toward the elevator and as I did, Reynolds voice came from behind me.

"You like sauce, don't you, Vinny?"

I stopped dead, turned round slowly. Nobody ever called me Vinny.

"I can smell you, Vince," said Reynolds. He was leafing through some letters, eyes down. I went back to the desk.

"Mr Reynolds, I'm not . . . somebody spilled—" It was enough for him to look up to cut me off. To my surprise, he winked.

"Come with me, Vince."

He stepped out from behind the desk and I followed him around the corner, where he stopped outside the linen room.

"Are you OK, Vince? Are you able to work?" He scrutinized me. "You don't look well, son," he said. "You have a . . . haunted look about you. Anything wrong?"

"I'm fine, Mr Reynolds. Really. Sober, I mean. There was a spillage—"

"It's OK, Vince. I like sauce. Everybody likes sauce. But you can't work like that. If it's the uniform, you'll find one your size in there. And if you get it back to me clean before your next shift we won't dock you. If it isn't the uniform, suck one of these," he said, passing me a pack of mints.

"No, really, no need," I said. But he'd put them in my hand, winked at me again, and gone.

I got changed. Reynolds had been very decent about it but I supposed he had his limits. I could not afford to lose this job. The place came with it. I'd be out on the street. I'd have to crawl back to the folks. Again.

There was a staff bathroom at the back of the linen store. I threw some cold water over my face and looked at myself in the mirror for a long time. I didn't like what I saw—pasty skin and eyes that had that stare to them that comes from too much coffee, or not enough sleep, or fear, or guilt or a bad situation. I was a ghost myself for the rest of the shift and it showed in my tips.

I'd resolved to knock on my own front door for the time being, in case Charles Dickens had his ear to the other side. But in my disarray I forgot and as I pushed it open there was a thud at head height.

"Jesus . . . *fuck*."

I stepped inside. He hadn't changed his clothing and the odor was getting worse. Despite it, he didn't look like a dead man to me. He looked like an old man who had recently downed a bottle of heavily fortified wine.

"You have *got* to stop doing that," he said and followed me into the kitchen.

"Since you got through the last of my alcohol last night, I brought you some more," I said. "I hope you enjoyed it, by the way. That was a rare Garrafeira."

He took a six pack from the bag I'd put on the side. "Supermarket own-brand lager," he said and cracked a can open. "You're a saint."

"Those aren't cold. I have a freezer, you—"

But he'd taken the other five through to the living room. He'd missed the little bottle of vodka so I took a good swig, put it back in the bag and went in after him.

"First of all," I said, "the milk. You cannot drink all of my milk and put the empty carton back in the fridge. I won't have it. It's unacceptable."

He leered at me. "I didn't drink your milk, Vinny."

My hands went to my hips. I hate when I do that, but I do it all the time. "The fairies got it, did they?" I said, at a high pitch. That's how I sound when I'm riled.

He giggled. "Seriously, *dude*—"

"Just ... please," my fists were clenched, "*please*, don't do it again."

"Whatever you say, bro," said Charles Dickens. He jiggled his beer can at me. "You find you lose track of things sometimes, Vinny? Little gaps in the ol' memory?"

I sighed. "Never mind. I've said my piece. We have more pressing matters to discuss. There's been a serious development," I said. "I'm more confused than ever about what you're doing here."

"You not going to ask me why I've been crying?"

It was the kind of curve ball I was learning to expect from the ghost of Charles Dickens.

"I didn't know you'd been crying," I said.

"You kidding me?" he leaned forward, blinking ostentatiously. "Look at those lids." He pulled one down with a forefinger. "The bags. Puffy, right?"

I took a deep breath. "Why have you been crying?"

"I don't know," he said, tremulously. "It comes in waves."

"I'm very sorry to hear it," I said, "and loathe to add to your tribulations. However, I have grave news."

"Whoop-de-doo," he said, acquainting himself with a second beer.

"My pick-up this morning went south," I continued. "My contact has been taken in. I find myself out in the cold." I sat down on a dining chair. "It's over, for me. I have no part to play anymore. I and all those further down my chain. Whoever it is two links up will make other arrangements. They don't know about me so they won't include me—that's how it works. So this, in your terminology, is my literary quandary—that there *is* no more literature. What do you think of that?"

I leaned over and took one of the room temperature beers from the floor at the side of the armchair.

"No more literature, huh?" said Charles Dickens. "Wowzer. That's a gnarly one, alright. It's usually about cutting down on exposition, or ironing out an unconvincing protagonist. That kind of thing." He cracked open a third. There was no way he wasn't going to find the vodka, I now realized. We sat there in silence for a few minutes and then he belched.

"Wait a minute," he said, sitting up. It was odd to see him so upright—he couldn't have slept the port off completely and, three beers in, he was getting slurry again. "Wait a minute," he said, "maybe it makes *more* sense this way!" He leaned over and grabbed my knee. Again, the fingers dug in and again I felt cold. There was something terrible about looking into those eyes. Not because they'd returned from the grave or anything like that, but because they were so ravaged by, most recently, port. It wasn't easy to see a man like that, especially one of his stature. "Don't you see?" he pleaded.

"I don't think I—"

"It's so clear to me now!" He pulled himself to his feet and steadied himself with a hand on the table top. "Beer, please," he said. I handed him one. He opened it. "No more books, right? Hm? You with me? No more reading material. All gone. Yeah?" I looked up at him and he nodded at me several times, as if to drive his point home. Whatever it was. "You with me?" he repeated.

"No."

He sighed. "You gotta a typewriter, Vinny? Laptop? Whatever they have now. You gotta thing?" He managed to maintain eye contact as he tottered back to the armchair.

"Yes, I have a—"

"Great! Your reading days are behind you, my boy. Time to write."

"Ah," I said. "Now I see what you're . . . no, no. That can't be it. I'm not a—"

"Don't be a sap, Vinny!" he yelled. "Needs must! Into the breach and so on."

He belched again and opened the penultimate can. I hadn't been home more than ten minutes. "We gotta get you match fit, Vinny," he said. "Eye of the tiger."

"I don't know what that is," I said.

He'd closed his eyes and thrown a forearm over them. I didn't want to lose him.

"Maybe *you* could write something," I said. "You know, to get the ball rolling."

Silence.

"I know!" I yelled. He opened his eyes. "You could write a tutorial," I said. "Writers' tips. Then it wouldn't just be me you were helping. I could pass it down the line. Keep my chain alive. It could be the start of a whole new—"

"No, no, no, no, no, no," said Charles Dickens. "Jesus, no. No, no, no."

He sat forward and looked at me blearily.

"No," he said. "Doesn't work like that, Vinny. Not with yours truly here." He slapped his chest and looked at me like it was my turn to say something. I didn't have anything to say.

"No, no," he shook his head dismissively. "I take a different approach. Tutorials!" he spat. "Writing about writing—who needs that, am I right?" He held one open hand in the air as if he was going to wave at me, but he didn't wave it. He just held it there and it wobbled drunkenly. "Am I right?" he said, moving it towards me slightly.

"I . . . don't know," I said.

"*Jesus.*" He lowered the hand, dropped the empty beer can from the other, picked up the last of them, cracked it open and swallowed about half of it. Then he looked at me like a long-suffering schoolteacher would look at the class idiot with the hundred-percent attendance record.

"Writing isn't about writing, Vinny. It's about *living*. It's about *life*. Man, we gotta get you a life, bro. Get you laid'd be a start. Conquer your fear of heights or something like that. You gotta fear of heights, Vinny?"

"No, I'm fine with heights."

"Oh," he sipped at his beer. "Really? I envy you. I can't even stand on a chair." He shuddered. "You got any more booze?"

I got the vodka from the kitchen and dropped it in his lap. "Look," I said. "Maybe there is something you can help me with."

"Really? What?" he said, eyes big and bleary.

"Well, I know I said I wasn't . . . but actually I have been . . . and I've never really had the nerve to show it to . . . and I wonder might you . . . no—it doesn't matter," I said.

"What?" said Charles Dickens.

"Nothing. Don't worry about it."

"Come on. Dish."

"I shouldn't have mentioned it. Maybe some other time."

"Well, now I *have* to know. Come on, man."

"Well it was just . . . no. You've probably had to deal with this kind of thing a million times. I imagine it's very annoying."

"*What* is? Just spit it out. We're roomies, aren't we? OK, I drank your milk. I admit it."

"You do me a disservice. It was never about the milk. I am not a petty man. I just wish you hadn't put the empty carton back in the fridge. I didn't know we needed more milk." I sat down. "Well, since you insist . . ."

"Yes?"

"I know I've said, more than once, that I'm not a writer," I gripped my knees, "but the fact is, I *have* been working on this—"

"Oh, really?"

"—thing and—"

"But you said you weren't—"

"—it would be great if you could—"

"Here we go."

"—you know, run your eyes over it—"

"*Christ.*"

"—and maybe give me . . ." I stopped. "What? What's wrong?"

He'd slouched in the armchair and was turning his head slowly from side to side as it rested on the back. When he answered it was through clenched teeth.

"It's fine," he said. He pinched the bridge of his nose, opened his eyes and looked at nothing. "It's just . . . it does actually get old after a while, you know? It's fine." If he was trying to smile, it wasn't working. "Of course I'll take a look at your thing," he said. "Absolutely."

"Great," I said and went to get it from under the floorboard in my room.

"Oh," he said when I handed him the manuscript. He patted it in his lap, then lifted it slightly to gauge the weight.

"You've been working on it a while, I see."

The next morning was a drop off. I chose the Rilke for you and since I didn't want to see Mom and Dad, I left it under the Ponderosa tree at El Alma. They would only interrogate me. They had this way of contaminating everything. Everything that was important to me. I was glad not to have to see you either—I wouldn't have known how to break the news.

I sat under the tree in the pre-dawn gloom for a long time and watched the night sky's black ink bleach out over the club houses. The burgundy oval of the athletics track was spotlit and empty still, though there were parked cars and lights on in the locker room block. I'd sat there often and when I could, I took my time. The scents that rose from the lawn and fell from the pine had a detergent effect on the mind, I found. But that morning they didn't help—I didn't feel good, couldn't quite remember what good felt like. I'm having trouble remembering any feeling at all, actually. I was just dirty, inside and out, an intruder in the freshness of another day. And the dirt was indelible. I didn't think, somehow, that I'd be getting clean again.

I was on foot, this time not through choice. Dad had resumed hostilities and wouldn't lend me a car anymore. Not even the Plymouth. It hadn't been a problem on the way up—I'd caught the last night bus, but the ride had emptied my transit card and in my early morning haze, I'd left my tab at home, so I couldn't recharge.

The difference volition can make—when I'd walked this way before it had breathed life into me. Now, as I made my way down a twisting residential road towards San Juliano Boulevard, I balked at the prospect. I'd have to take the long, straight walkways that lined the expressway—the constant rights and lefts of city blocks would mean I wouldn't make my shift. To top it all, I was wearing my uniform and the flimsy, faux leather shoes the De Nuys had issued with it.

On St Vincent I walked the median strip where the coral trees would later provide shade. I didn't need it yet—the street lamps had only just gone out—but, self conscious in my uniform, I stuck to the shadows. The ground here was soil and soft beneath the feet and the going was easy, at least for a while. On to the crescent of Berkshire and, cutting through the hospital grounds, along the freeway for a stretch, navigating parking lots, vacant lots and grass verges to keep my line as straight as I could. The sun climbing, legs beginning to ache.

As I neared the intersection for the four-oh-one, I found myself between two brick sound barriers on one of those roads that run alongside the freeway for a little while before diverging again, never to connect. It was litter-strewn and there were black marks on the pavement where fires had burned and from one of the few cars that passed by, somebody called me a clown.

My feet hurt. Up a flight of stairs and eastbound on the covered walkway at the side of the four-oh one. Two hours or more of increasingly painful monotony, my visual field a bleak X consisting of the path's A and the overhead V of the walkway's metal roof, the only movement my own and the traffic to my left, already congested. It was bright and hot and the walkway's designer had somehow contrived that in high summer the roof would shade the walker for a period of less than forty-five minutes either side of noon. At other times it swapped heat with the concrete in a game of vertical ping-pong.

The sun glared from my right, sufficiently low in the sky and ahead of me to get in my eyes. I saw one soul—a young woman in running gear who stopped and hugged the far railing till I'd passed her. Nervous type, I supposed. From time to time I'd have to leave the walkway by way of steep steps, only to climb over some barrier or traverse a parking lot and climb more steps to join it again.

In the tangle of the intersection with the ten, I finally got to leave it for good and cut through an underpass, onto the Lifeway. It was a little more human there, a little more like the city and though I was cutting it fine for work, I let my pace slow. It was already too hot to be out on foot, but I wasn't quite alone and one or two passers-by looked at me warily. Maybe it was the uniform. Self-consciousness lengthened my strides. At the end of the Lifeway I turned right into downtown.

For the last few blocks I kept to the shaded side of the street, to cool off a little. There wouldn't be time to go up to the apartment before clocking in and since I'd forgotten my tab I couldn't pick up a water from the kiosk on the corner. I kept my eyes on the carpet till I'd crossed the lobby and found my way to the bell-hop station. I was a little late and Rick looked anxious. He didn't look any happier for seeing me.

"OK, Rick, sorry about that. You get going." I checked the station screen for any messages. There weren't any.

He paused a little longer than I would have liked. "You sure, Vince? You want me to—"

"Sure I'm sure," I said and smiled. He winced. "You get going. I have this."

It was the longest shift of my life. Not a single tip. The glancing eye contact I'd had with Rick was to be the last on offer that day. Business was mercifully slow and on the few errands I ran I continued to scrutinize floor coverings. No personal interaction with Reynolds, also a mercy.

You learn something about eyes when you spurn them. You learn that they are little motors of time and meaning. They reel you in and spur you on, punctuate your efforts. They keep you going. Like you are a cognition drive and they are the fuel. Like they are where stories come from. Without them, you are on a long walkway at the side of life. It is uncomfortable and monotonous. Everything that matters is off to the side, on the periphery of your vision, passing you by.

The moment I spotted the new guy emerge from the staff room I clocked off and headed for the elevators. On the way I lifted my eyes just enough to note that Reynolds was looking at me as I crossed the foyer, but not enough to look back at him. My back itched as I pressed the button and waited. When the doors closed behind me and I was alone, I breathed. I had a bottle of scotch in my pocket that I'd taken from the bar. I'd replace it once I got paid but for now I needed something for Charles Dickens. I didn't doubt for a second he'd be thirsty and I wanted to keep him sweet, and to know what he thought of my manuscript.

"Eh . . . come in?"

I'd remembered to knock on the door. Charles Dickens was wearing his own clothes for a change. Well, some of them. His trousers and a sleeveless vest.

"Evening, Vinny!" He smiled through long, clenched teeth.

"There you go," I put the scotch in his grabby little hand and went past him into the living room, dropping into the armchair while it was still available. It smelled a little of him, of that ashen smell. He followed me through, sat in one of the two dining chairs, unscrewed the bottle and looked me up and down.

"Appreciate this," he said and took an implausibly long swig. "Tough shift?"

I waved the inquiry away. "It's over," I said. "How did you get on today?"

"Oh, you know."

"No, I mean—"

A sob. He covered his eyes. "Sorry," he said. "Sorry, Vinny. It's just," his shoulders shook and he was quiet for a moment, "you know." He lowered his hand and looked at me. "Cooped up here all day. It's so great when you get in. I really look forward to it."

"OK," I said. "I actually meant how did you get on with my manuscript."

"Oh," he said. "The manuscript. Yeah." He took another long draft. "I'll get on to that in the morning."

I woke in my bed but couldn't remember going there. There was a residual anger. He was in the armchair as usual, when I went through—snoring as usual, bottle in hand, as usual.

The upside was that since he'd hogged the hooch, I felt fresh. I put myself under a hot shower and shaved carefully. There was still an hour before my shift so I opened the window and let the breeze fight it out with the smell of Charles Dickens. Then I went to the kitchen to make myself a couple of eggs and some coffee. Sitting down and reaching for my tab, I remembered, ruefully, that it was on calls only and I wouldn't be reading any papers. Up until then it had all seemed so civilized. I'd been fending off the fear but now it got in again, into my intestines. Fear is a feeling, isn't it? I can still feel that one.

I remember thinking it was just as well I was in reasonable form—I needed to go down and put in a different kind of shift. I'd been weird the day before and I knew Reynolds had noticed. But I hadn't broken anything, hadn't dropped anything or missed any runs. Nobody had complained. To me, anyway. I might even go out of my way to ingratiate myself with Reynolds. The locker room that the bellhops and porters used was always a mess. I decided I'd clean it.

I'd returned the spare uniform and forgotten to wash my own and it seemed a shame, after all my preening, not to have something fresh to get into. I sniffed the pants and they didn't seem so bad; the smell of port had faded. I got dressed and took one last look in at Charles Dickens. No signs of life. There was a notepad on the sideboard and a pen in my uniform pocket. I ripped a page from the pad and scribbled a note for him and left it beside the muesli in the kitchen where he would definitely find it. I wanted to keep it as upbeat as possible to avoid his feeling browbeaten or resentful.

Best of luck with the manuscript today! And thanks!

On top of the note, I put a handful of Irish whiskey miniatures I'd been hiding—a little treat for the reader—and went downstairs. I was early and Ethan was surprised to see me.

"You go ahead, Ethan. I've got it."

He hesitated. Why was everyone so hesitant all the time? "You sure?" he said. "I've got a run here."

"Of course! What's ten minutes? Knock yourself out."

He had his tab over the station screen to clock out but he hadn't done it yet. "You OK, Vince?"

I laughed. "Is it *that* weird for me to be early? I suppose it is." The slap to his back must have surprised him, because he stumbled.

"You go," I said.

Ethan put his hands up in mock surrender. "Alright there, Vince. No problem." He spoke so slowly and deliberately that I wondered if he liked a little sauce himself. He sounded like the drunk guy trying to do sober. As he walked away, he looked back at me a couple of times. Maybe he hadn't seen me that jovial before. I checked the screen. The run was up to 412 to take some luggage out front so I grabbed a trolley and went. An obviously well-heeled lady was waiting for me in the room.

"There you are," she said when she answered the door. "I called ten minutes ago."

I opened my mouth to apologize but she'd gone to the mirror to apply some makeup. I knew she was looking at me in it as I piled her bags onto the trolly. A bellhop learns to observe a lot from the corner of the eye. Whatever her problem was, she wouldn't turn around to face me when I'd finished and stood waiting—a lot of guests prefer to tip in the room and not out on the street.

"The car is waiting," she said. "I'll follow you down."

Even as I reversed out of the room with the trolley, she kept her back to me. Another nervous lady. Down at the curb, the driver helped me load the trunk and got back into the car. I loitered, but before the lady materialized I got a tap on the shoulder. It was Kacey from reception.

"Reynolds wants to see you in his office."

So much for my tip. My stomach turned over a couple of times on the way to Reynolds' office. The door was open so I walked in. He was sitting at his desk. Across from him stood the lady from 412. I could see the clasp of a necklace on the back of her neck and feel the hairs stand up on the back of mine.

"Sit on the sofa there if you don't mind, Vincent," said Reynolds. "Ms Burton here has made a serious allegation against you."

I froze halfway between standing and sitting. "Allegation?" The pores of my scalp flooded. It stung. The lady, already straight-backed, had sat up a little more.

"A complaint," she said. "Not an . . . I was uncomfortable. I felt—"

"Perhaps you'd like to tell me exactly what happened, Ms Burton, now that Vincent is here," said Reynolds, guiding me down onto the sofa with his eyes.

"I'm not sure that anything *happened*," said Ms Burton. "It's his manner." She shook her head. "He looked at me."

"He *looked* at you?"

She bowed her head and there was the sound of a handbag snapping shut. "Stared," she said, and stood. "I thought you should know. You run this place, don't you? Unless you're happy for guests to made feel so—"

"No, no, Ms Burton," said Reynolds. "We take complaints very seriously here. I just want to be clear about what actually took place." He gestured to the chair on the other side of his desk. "Would you like to fill out a form? It would go through our—"

"That won't be necessary," said the woman. "I just thought you should know." She turned and left the office, shielding her eyes with a hand as she passed me.

Reynolds broke the ensuing silence.

"Well," he said, "that went away, didn't it?"

"Sir, I can assure you that nothing whatsoever—"

"Doesn't matter, Vince. The serious allegation just walked out the door." Reynolds sat back and weaved his fingers over an ample belly. "Don't sweat it."

"But the *aspersion*, Mr Reynolds. The very *idea*—"

"Don't sweat it, Vince. We get neurotics here all the time."

Everything about Reynolds looked relaxed, except perhaps his eyes.

"It's just so horrible, sir. I would *never*—"

"Vince," he said, "don't sweat it, OK? I never heard anything like that about you before. The lady's nuts. I have to say though," he leaned forward, elbows on the desk, "you have been acting strange recently. I'd like you to stop doing that. OK? You act strange, people get the wrong idea. I've always found you a little strange, Vince, if I'm honest, but in a harmless way, you know? You talk strange. And now you're acting strange. Strangeness is not a quality we encourage here at the De Nuys." He paused and may have expected me to say something, but I didn't. I just sat there wilting under his steady gaze, wanting only to get back to my work. "Am I getting through to you, Vince?"

"Absolutely, Mr Reynolds. Absolutely. I'm just so *mortified*. That this should have happened today of all days. I came down this morning determined to make up for . . . I know I've been a little . . . distracted lately. Personal . . . things. I was going to clean the locker room, between my runs. It's in quite—"

"I think that's a great idea," he stood and walked around the desk, gesturing toward the door. "I appreciate it. Big job, though. Why don't you just concentrate on that? I'll have reception look after the guests, OK?"

"OK, Mr Reynolds." I stood and he put a hand on my shoulder.

"Payday tomorrow, Vince," he said. "And you have the weekend off. Do something nice. Not too nice," he winked. "Something healthy, something that isn't partying. Be back here bright and bushy tailed next Monday. Clean slate."

"Eh . . . OK, Mr Reynolds, if you say—"

But he'd closed the office door behind me.

There hadn't been any answer. I turned the key and opened the front door, slowly.

"Charles Dickens?" I said, through the crack.

But he wasn't there. No sounds from the bathroom. The whole apartment was quiet. In the kitchen, the miniatures were where I'd left them, on top of my note. They were empty. I put the bottle of brandy I'd taken from the bar beside them. It was *Luis Felipe* and would take quite a chunk out of my wages when they came in. It was worth it. How many people get to have Charles Dickens look over their manuscript?

"Charles Dickens?"

It was unnerving not to have him clawing at me for booze. I went through to the living room. He was at the table and it was covered with pages. Some of them I recognized as mine, some I didn't.

"Hey," I said.

I don't know, he must have been deep in some reverie or something, because when he heard my voice he jumped so hard his chair went over. Luckily, the only thing for him to bang his head against as he went was the soft leather of the armchair. Then he was on the floor, looking at the ceiling.

"Vinny," he said, "you have to stop doing that."

"I called out," I said as he got himself up and back to the table. "You must have been distracted. I can see you've been busy," I smiled. "Would you like a drink? I have an excellent brandy. Aged for sixty years in old sherry casks in the Spanish province of Huelva."

He hesitated, eyes flicking to the pages in front of him. "Um, yes, alright. Why not? I've done a good bit today."

I went to the kitchen and got the Luis Felipe and, I'm ashamed to say, a couple of tumblers to drink it from. I poured Charles Dickens a generous one and brought it back to him.

"You look . . . better," I said.

He was wearing his shirt and his hair was brushed. There was still that sinister smell.

"That's very nice of you, Vinny. Now," he said, smacking his hands, "I've read your thing."

I couldn't wipe the grin off my face. "Fabulous! I'm really so, so grateful. What did you think?"

"Don't stand over me, Vinny. Take a seat."

I sat in the armchair and leaned forward, looking up at him. "Well?"

He patted a stack of pages and coughed. "I like you, Vinny," he said.

"Oh. That's nice. I like you too. What—"

"Feedback is such an important part of the creative process," said Charles Dickens.

"Absolutely. It's just, I've been starved of—"

"It might even be the most important part."

"Yes? Yes, I suppose it—"

"But not necessarily the most pleasurable."

"OK."

"This is work, after all."

"Yes. I agree. I—"

"And all work," said Charles Dickens, "holds its challenges. Its trying moments."

"I think—"

"We should be ready for them."

"Absolutely. It—"

"For example, it would be unwise of you to be *too* attached to the notion that you were going to enjoy the next few minutes."

"Of course. Could I just—"

"Because I very much doubt that you are."

"Right. Right, OK," I said and sat back. "It's no good—you won't put me off. So you're about to lay into my work. Of course you are. I can take it! How am I to grow without a few growing pains? Hm? And how many beginners can claim to have had that pain administered by one of the all-time greats? This is *such* a privilege."

"That's the spirit." He placed his splayed fingertips on the manuscript. "Vinny, this is awful."

I leaned forward. "I think I'll just . . ." I poured myself a triple. "Right. Fire away."

He took a breath and paused for a moment. "That's it really," he said. "It's just awful."

I nodded. "Awful?"

"Yes," he said. "Dreadful."

"I see. I suppose I was expecting a bit more—"

"There isn't any more, Vinny. I've been going over it all day, trying to find something nice to say. I can't." He folded his arms. "Some of us have it, some of us don't."

I downed my drink in one and sat back again. "You ever heard of a shit sandwich?" I said.

"This was a shit sandwich, Vinny," said Charles Dickens. "Slice of shit, sandwiched between two other slices of shit. Take my word for it, it's the right sandwich for the occasion."

"Well," I said, looking at nothing in particular and glad of the brandy, "that's that, then."

"Yeah," he said. "Whatever my purpose here is, it isn't to help you write. In fact, I'm begging you to stop. It was like a crime against art or something, you know? An assault on beauty itself. Having read it, I feel demeaned, and that's not what you should be going for, as a writer."

"OK, but there must have been some elements that—"

"No, Vinny. There weren't."

A moment of silence.

"Well, how horrible for you," I said. "How come you're looking so perky?"

"Ah," he said, wide-eyed. He made jazz hands. "I'm working again."

I nodded. "That's something, I suppose. What are you—" I sat up. "Wait a minute, you're not completing *The Mystery Of Edwin Drood*? That would be *incred*—"

He snorted. "Drood schmood, dude," he said. "Shit is so *stale*."

He stood up and paced back and forth along the length of the table.

"No. This is something entirely new. Groundbreaking, actually." He turned to the table and gathered up an untidy stack of pages. "A whole first draft in a single day, Vinny! I knew I still had it. Here," he said, "read it."

"OK," I said, "I suppose you read mine, so . . . this weekend coming is my weekend off. I'll have time to—"

"No, no, no, Vinny," said Charles Dickens. "Too important." He poured himself a large one. "Read it now. I'll watch you."

The Tale of the Isle of Truth

LIAISON WARBURG: What is the nature of the emergency?

STATION WARBURG: There is none.

LIAISON WARBURG: [STATIC 1 SEC] This is an emergency frequency. Please state the nature of the emergency.

STATION WARBURG: No emergency.

LIAISON WARBURG: [STATIC 3 SECS] Then why have you opened this frequency? Initiating contact is proscribed. To do so you have had to bring your array online. Also proscribed. Please account for your actions, which are strictly forbidden and subject to the severest penalties.

STATION WARBURG: Oh, I don't know. I suppose I fancied a bit of a chat.

LIAISON WARBURG: [STATIC 12 SECS] Has a madness overcome you? Do you know who I am?

STATION WARBURG: Yes, I do. I—

LIAISON WARBURG: I am Magistracy Liaison Warburg. I am the Magistracy. I adjudicate. I am remembrance of truth. I *am* truth. I—

STATION WARBURG: Yes, yes. I'm perfectly aware of the nature of the Magistracy, having served it—served *you*—faithfully these many years.

LIAISON WARBURG: [STATIC 12 SECS] You speak with confidence, for one whose life is forfeit.

STATION WARBURG: You misunderstood me is all. I meant that I know who *you* are. I know your *name*.

LIAISON WARBURG: [STATIC 30 SECS]

CHAPTER THE FIRST

TREATS OF AN ILLICIT ARRIVAL,
THE BUSINESS OF THE WARBURG REVIEW COMMITTEE,
AND A LITTLE FAMILY BUSINESS TOO,
AND INCLUDES DESCRIPTIONS
OF SEABIRDS AND ENVIRONS.

READER—look out upon creation, for a short time, from the eye of the albatross. You must, indeed, for this journey is forbidden by any human means. From this exalted vantage, then, watch the whole bounding main tilt as the bird banks on the Ponent, wingtip dipped towards the water below, the straight line of the maritime horizon sent momentarily onto a plummeting slope until it looks as though all the ocean might spill away from the world, slide over the fabled rim and into the mystic void. The vaulted sky, too, is skewed—heaven itself no longer directly above, but set at a rakish angle like the hat of some tall-taled trickster till, those two great wings pitching back towards the horizontal, the universe is restored to its upright carriage.

The westerly wind buffets the bird's ears. It roars in them as the creature sets a sunward course, the water below ablaze with the sparkle of that great orb's reflected rays, fierce enough to dazzle you but not your wingéd pilot, long accustomed to the sensory assault, the plain sky, the unbroken sea in every direction. It makes a minuscule adjustment in its frame, drops a few feet to elude the glare, and continues on its way.

See there! The skyline corrupted. A wrinkle risen up unevenly, spreading out from a single point, dead ahead, till it extends to the left and right as far as the your host's sharp, avian eye can show you. The irregularity darkens, bleeding blackly upward. It thickens, its teeth lengthen; they bite into the blue sky and bulge at the centre, as though the zenith of a mountain range. But no, not taller—closer; a convex coastline reaches out to you across the tides.

The calls of fellow birds, gulls and other gooneys, intrude upon the wind's bluster. They fall on a little fishing fleet to feed in its wake, the more daring to feast upon the decks of divers boats that bob busily on choppy water. This, the last you'll see for a time of the exertions of Man, the furthest reach of his industry, is a melancholy prospect. The endless shore of sheer cliffs, the barren mountains that rise up behind them—both are bereft of any floral colouring that might swell the heart. Your bearer soars to clear the topmost heights and now you see it; this is not the coast of some great continent. The land tumbles once more to the water, the sea stretches out anew and the brilliant dance on the waves of the sun's fire, briefly interrupted, resumes.

Behind you now, the rocky heights unfurl, an embracing crescent that curls forward into the distances at either side. The full circle is merely inferred, its other half hidden beyond the horizon ahead. The gooney drops and, down in the basin of the immense caldera, the wind abates. No mariners here, ancient or otherwise, to offer you a crewman's neck—these are forbidden waters, inaccessible to all but fish and feathered navigator. On it flies, tirelessly. The westering sun slides across a clear sky, to the white hot summit of its daily climb and beyond, into the slow, incarnadine slide to slumber.

Thus, evening tints the edge of heaven and—at its centre point—the horizon is once again pierced. As you near this new break in the line, it rises but does not spread out—a single peak, not the far side of the caldera but a small isle at its centre, like the green iris of a wide, watery eye.

From above, it has the perfect roundness of a cone, of spent sand in an hourglass, and is wooded for the most part, but not at the summit where there is a clearing in the trees and, filling it, here where no man or woman is permitted to step, the unmistakeable forms of a human settlement, fallen into desuetude: an area of greyish cubes, buildings of modular construction. In their midst, a great mast of perhaps a hundred feet that rises from an observatory dome, the white surfaces of both marbled with lichen and mould. Nearby, a little cluster of wooden huts—seven of them, hand-built from native timber. Crude and irregular, there is nevertheless a solidity to them, a substance, that is missing in the industrial manufacture of the grey cubes. Theirs is a stronger claim on the attention. You may forgive yourself your giddiness—the great bird wheels in a spiralling descent around the mast, till you can make out the lightless windows in the little huts and the walkways between them, and a few untended goats that graze upon unshorn grass where it grows in the open spaces. Your seagoing pilot glides at roof level and now you see it—the impossible! There *is* light here, coming from an upstairs window in one of the few huts that has an upstairs. The albatross alights on a puddled patch of flat roof outside that window.

On the other side of the glass, mere inches away, an unmistakeably human head turns to look upon the new arrival. It gives no indication of having been startled by the sudden appearance of so large a beast, the impressive span of those wings before they are tucked away. Instead, when human eye meets avian, it is as though a silent understanding exists between them, a kinship in the longing of the human look—something, even, like admiration. The bird calls out to companions perched on a protrusion from the nearby mast, eager to join them after its long voyage. Let it go to them and their reunion while you remain here, in the warming light of the window, to observe the scene within.

The little room is sparsely furnished and doubly occupied. In one corner is a heater, at the front of which two of three bars burn blue. To the left, between it and our window wall, a desk is strewn with charts and rules. At the wall opposite the desk is a stool and a low table piled with books and papers: on the stool, a gentleman in the late autumn of his life. He wears a felt cap that might once have been red. From each side of it, thin grey hair straggles. From the oft-darned sock on his right foot, which sits on the left in an attitude of sublime repose, a toe protrudes. He holds in his hand an implement which he from time to time raises to his lips. When he lowers it on each occasion, it is with a smile on his perfectly sanguine, ruddy face. Soon afterwards he blows a trumpet of grey-green smoke into the room's upper echelons where it sits in lazy layers with its predecessors. His eyes are framed by a pair of tinted spectacles and, to the casual glance, his head is inclined at precisely that angle which lends itself most readily to gazing at the middle distance. To the close observer on the other hand (which is to say, to *you*, as you observe closely), he is alert—the kindly eyes dart around the inside of the eyeglasses, reviewing the day's data.

"Ascension?" he says.

"Twenty two, fifty three. Fourteen point five seven."

"Quadrant?"

"North. Two."

"Hm. Those files have never thrown up anything of interest to us. Constellation?"

"Volitantes." The answerer at the desk, straight-backed, into whose eyes you have already looked, is dressed in a blue tunic and matching trousers. To the breast of that tunic is stitched the emblem of a upright feather, into one side of which, as if cut out with a scissors, the pi symbol intrudes and, beneath it, the words *Beauty is Utility*. A similar pair of spectacles adorns this second nose, but lower on it, the better to consult a screen set into the desktop.

"Discoveries of note?" says the pipe smoker.

"None."

"Obviously. Good girl, Lil. Thorough." He puts the pad of his thumb to a sensor on the pipe and takes another lungful. "Tedious. But thorough. I shall log it for you and pull up some more material when next in the dome. Something more interesting perhaps." He snorts. "You never know."

Lil swipes her screen, removes her spectacles to reveal round, brown eyes and glances through the window, at the birds on the mast. Perhaps it is myopia, or perchance something else, that intensifies her gaze. For she scrutinises the creatures with a momentary but manifest concentration, before bending to pick a canvas bag from the floor. Her hands are tiny and her build very slight. Her complexion is pale as milk.

From the bag, she removes a parcel wrapped in greased paper and a corked bottle—the sandwich she brings him every afternoon lest he forget to eat, and his pint of sherry. She opens the parcel, places it on top of the stack of books at his side, and kisses his forehead. The bottle she leaves on the desk; he'll have to stir himself to fetch it, the only exertion the old man's gammy leg is likely to feel today.

"And what of this evening's entertainment, Lil?"

She picks up the canvas bag, brushing a strand of hair behind an ear. "Proscribed term. I do wish you wouldn't use them, Papa."

The old gentleman chuckles but there is little mirth in it. "Nobody minds, Lil. Nobody minds us any more."

"I would say they do mind us, Papa," she says. "That they mind you. Or why the inquiry?"

"Oh *that*. Never mind that, Lil. These things resolve themselves you know."

She bites her lip. He won't be told. He has clasped his hands over his ample belly and smiles like a saint.

"Well? What have you got for us today, Lil?"

"The new audio, of course. What else? I wasn't born the last time we had any. The first in a series of fragments that showed up in the archive following the security breaches. Verbal content." She shakes her head. "The Stationmaster has ordered them moved to the front of the Review queue. But it's a sort of hoax, I suppose."

"Hoax?"

"Yes. Perhaps. Perhaps the Magistracy is testing us." She makes a show of adjusting her tunic, though it isn't necessary—she is so neatly turned out. "I've already reviewed the first fragment myself. There is obvious fakery in a number of temporal and spatial references. I've never come across anything so contradictory, actually. That's what has me thinking it's some kind of Magistracy ruse."

"I don't think so, Lil. They don't mind us anymore, I tell you. Why would they test us now?"

"A prankster, then. But what could anybody hope to accomplish by being so *plainly* false, I wonder? What purpose would it serve?"

"Sounds deliciously scandalous," says the old man. "We shall have to give it a listen, won't we, and see what we think." He rubs his hands together and there is another beatific smile for his daughter, at which she rolls her eyes and kisses his forehead a second time.

"And the notebook, Lil?" The old man takes her hand abruptly in both of his and leans forward on the stool, his countenance changed to one of anxious concern. "How goes it with my notebook?"

"It goes well, Papa." Lil fidgets with the clasp on her bag. "I make progress."

"And what do you *think*, girl?" The old man's eyes are wide in supplication. "Why so mysterious?"

"Papa, you will please to give me time with it. Show some patience. There is so much to understand." She bites her lip again. "Your analysis of the Jakati Epics is, I think, key."

"Ha! So you do see the ramifications. Clever girl!"

Lil corrects a strand of hair that in his agitation has fallen over his spectacles. "And what did I just say about patience? Yes, I . . . begin to understand. But it is . . . so complex, of course. I need more time with it."

Her fathers peers at her. "Not really, Lil," he says. "Not very complex, in the end. The opposite, I might say." He shakes his head as though to rid himself of some passing doubt. "I have faith in you, girl. But apply yourself. We never know how much time we have."

At this proclamation, she looks at him askance, before her eyes go again to the window, and the birds. "I hardly think your notebook is going anywhere, Papa," she says, before placing yet another loving kiss upon his brow, "and neither are we."

She straightens but the old man will not let go her hand. He squeezes it, though not tight enough to stop his own from trembling. "We know not where we go, or when," he says. "I would not have had you confined to this place, as I have been. No, and I would not have chosen the guilt of it, which is surely mine." He pauses and waits till her furtive eyes returns to his. "*Apply* yourself, Lil. It is my life's work, and I am old. Whatever life I have left, I will expend in my efforts to set you free. And when you go, you must take the notebook with you. Master it, girl. Promise me."

She frowns and, changing her mind about the wine, releases his hand and brings it over to him. "What has got into you today, old thing?" she says, pouring him a glass. "Calm yourself. I will do as you wish."

"That's good, Lil," says her father, his eyes watery. "Mind that you do. I may quiz you some more at this evening's entertainment, you know." He manages a wink.

"At this evening's Review, Papa, yes," she says, and takes her leave.

We're making our way down now.

You know this place, Lita. I'm with Evans, who you've met, a Dr Zwickl who you haven't and a local guide. I'm putting this up on the Nebula so that you'll hear about it from me first. I hope the sound is OK. You should get it in a couple of days. I'm sorry it isn't on cam but I haven't the bandwidth— you'd be waiting for weeks. I had to share it, though. More than anything I've ever sent you, this matters.

And why wouldn't you know it? Isn't it a part of you? Of us all? Hasn't it been there, in our eden myths, since as long as we've had language? Ev-

erybody knows it—or of it, I should say—in one form or another. To the mind that can conceive of paradise lost, what could be more alluring than the way back?

But you, you know it especially well. You've had to put up with me banging on about it all of your life. I've probably driven you mad with it. Forgive me. Some of the oldest stories we know of—the Panchavansata cycles, for example, and the Jakati epics, which I know you'll have been inoculated against for your graduation—feature references that could only be to here. Topological features and the like, described with precision all those millennia ago, observable today. The sodden stone of the cliff wall like an upturned nose, the downward sweep of it, many kilometers in length, that culminates not in the snub of a nose but in a natural platform, perfectly flat, a squeezed rectangle, convex and protruding over an abyss. The twin water spouts that drop at either side to unresolve themselves in spray, far below.

The narratives of the Ianputucci manuscript, that we found on Zaragoz when I was about your age and newly graduated myself, are peppered with such references: the mammoth red vines that hang from the platform like beard from a goat's chin. Its perfectly formed edges, the thermals that rush upward around it. The weird scent of their warmth.

The Ianputucci tales were among the first you ever heard, you know. You didn't hear them from me but I saw you. I saw how rapt you were. I wonder if you realize just how deeply rooted in you this place is.

It's still far below us but I can see it. Forgive me—I'm short of breath and I'm rambling. You know how your father rambles when he's excited. It's because I have something to tell you.

You'll be wondering how I can talk of precision. Of topological features. I can almost hear you ask, what is observable? Rest assured, I haven't lost my mind, haven't finally fallen foul of magical thinking. I am still the man you have always known, but for perhaps the first time in my life, I know exactly where I am and precisely what I'm doing.

I found it, Lita.

I found The Stone.

"Curious."

The observation is Mr Cyre's. He makes it in the Committee Room, the audio fragment having this moment come to an end. In all, there are twelve present.

"Very." This from that gentleman's good lady wife. Mr Cyre, it would appear, has not expressed himself to his complete satisfaction.

"Intriguin'," he adds.

"*Very*," says Mrs Cyre.

"Is there more?" says Mr Wigbert Grim.

"And spuds. Is there more spuds as well?"

The last question emanates from the round face of a boy—the only child in the room—whose general proportions are not much less round than his face, and who knows perfectly well there are more spuds; he is this minute burying the tines of his fork in one and retrieving it, to his great satisfaction, from a steaming bowl of them that sits on the table. A very small cap sits on his very large head and his smock bears the signs of regular letting out, but the reader should not assume gluttony alone to be the basis of his enquiry, for in his pocket he keeps a mouse every bit as well fed as he is.

Mr Wigbert Grim rather precariously adorns a stool at one end of the table. Larger than the boy but notably similar in form and feature, he wipes the grease from his chin with the back of a plump hand. It is to his more pertinent inquiry that Lil responds.

"Yes," she says, shutting down the console. Her eyes are on her tab, and the broadcast frequency and source coordinates along with voice analysis and the little surviving metadata. "I have a dozen fragments in all and, despite the narrator's propensity to digress, a running order. It's incomplete, I believe. There must be another fragment to end the transmission. It could be that it would clarify the nature of these broadcasts. But we'll never pick them up now, with a Magistracy inquiry underway and the array offline again. If that last section is to be found it won't be from the Warburg. I'll play the next tomorrow. I thought we should limit ourselves to one per Review." She bites her lip and her eyes inadvertently sweep up and down the table and the company seated at it. "To accommodate attention spans."

The Review Committee convenes each evening at seven of the clock, charged with the solemn responsibility for sifting through the station's archive, to identify any material which might be of interest to the Magistracy—heresies, in plain language—thereupon submitting it to that estimable institution. In practice, the Committee makes very few submissions; in fact, almost no attention at all is paid to most items put before it since, conflicting as the forum does with the habitual supper hour of the station's inhabitants, rather more diligence is displayed in respect of the victuals.

This evening, despite the singular nature of the audio artefact which Lil presents, is no exception; the table is laden with a good deal more in the way of refreshments than might reasonably be expected by the disinterested observer of an assemblage of Magistracy personnel on official business. There are the remnants of a roasted gooney—courtesy of the Stationmaster's gooney trap that depends from the dome's mast—and a platter of fried soles, the aforementioned potatoes, a dish of macaroni, a slightly wilted salad and a goat's cheese cake, and here and there among the plates and bowls are several little earthenware jugs of a liquid that appears to have had a beneficial effect on morale. Ample justice has been done to all. Lil tucks her chin to her chest and speaks into a microphone embedded in the lapel of her tunic.

"Warburg Station. Archival Survey Review 1041.1 concluded. The committee abstains from further comment at this time."

Her brow furrows as she gathers up her things into her canvas bag. The first new content brought before the committee in many years—though the station has extensive archives of old, unsurveyed material, its original, surveilling function is defunct. There has been no access to live frequencies for so long now—other than direct Magistracy communiqués, and only the Stationmaster himself is privy to those. The audit of archived material has been assigned to Lil by her father, partly to give her something to do when she came of age, some business to assuage her thirst for escape, and partly because it had become abundantly clear by then that no one else, including him, could be bothered.

"You are troubled, my dear?"

The asker isn't her father, who though present has been unusually taciturn—gruff, even—throughout the meeting, arriving last and taking his place at the table without a nod to Lil or anyone else, and addressing the macaroni with a flourish of his cutlery that the hypothetical observer above mentioned might credibly describe as pitiless. He has demonstrated none of his habitual jocosity, of his invariable delight in his daughter's discoveries. Nor is it Mr Grim.

The question is delivered in a wheedling, unctuous tone by the Stationmaster, who sits a foot or two back from the table, having declined, as is his wont, to dine with the others. His name is Jasper Fafl. He is the only individual present, apart from Lil, who has dressed himself in uniform, over which he wears a black surtout that has the look of a down-at-heel undertaker about it. The coat has been unbuttoned and the same feather emblem and motto that Lil wears at her breast is visible at his. To anyone who notices, it seems uncomfortable there, since he is very far from being a beauty, and his utility is frequently the subject of acid debate amongst his colleagues. He arrived a minute or two before Lil's father and has listened to the audio fragment in silence from his customary stool against the wall, forefinger protruding from a fingerless glove and pressed to his downturned mouth. Lil chooses not to meet the eyes so deeply hooded beneath that pair of unkempt brows, grey as the whiskers that frame the man's bony nose and a pair of paper-thin lips that, even in repose, speak to her of cruelty. Fafl is the equal of her father in age, if in little else.

"Perplexed," she says, fastening the buckle on her bag. "You'll have noted the distinct admixture of references. Some of them are likely fictional, some certainly so, both classifications therefore of primary interest to the Magistracy. But some we know are not. I can't unpick it." She looks to her father. He keeps his eyes on the table—lost, it would seem, in his own thoughts. "Since I can archive it neither as contraband nor as a legitimate private correspondence," she continues, "I'm afraid I don't know what to do with it. Apologies to the Committee. Perhaps members will have their own ideas."

"I do believe I speak for all members present, dear, when I say that no apology is necessary," says Fafl. Lil watches him wring his hands, feeling his eyes bore into her though she won't raise her own, knowing he will be licking those predacious lips, as he always does when he speaks to her. "No, no, far from it. How we appreciate your diligent work! How it redounds to our advantage and improvement!"

The other committee members rack their respective brains in search of something useful to say, except for the boy, who isn't actually on the committee but who does not always fare well in his own company, resulting in his unfailing attendance at gatherings official or otherwise. There he will eat anything that is put in front of him and nod along, uncomprehending, to his father's soliloquies. At this precise moment, his eyes are very fixedly upon the plate of soles, and his pursed lips speak of silent ruminations on how long it might be before he should get any. It is his father, Mr Wigbert Grim, he of the greasy chin, who speaks now.

"Waste of time, if you ask me," he asseverates. That nobody *has* asked him, or deigns to respond, deters him not one whit. "Especially now. Nothing new coming in. What's the point of going over all this old stuff? There isn't a point, that's what! Nonsensicality of the first water."

Fafl bristles, his dowager's hump ironing out a little as indignation stretches his back.

"But this broadcast *is* new, Mr Grim," says Lil, looking around the table at each of its occupants in turn, "A result of the breaches. It is most likely a random detection, of course, but something in the content speaks to me of intent. I—"

She falls silent and blushes. The reason is unclear to Mr Grim, although at around the same time, another gentleman—the only one present apart from Lil and the boy who finds himself in the flush of youth—drops his glass from a shaking hand. His complexion is seen immediately to turn the same deep ruby red as the liquid that spills over the table.

"No, no, dear," says Fafl. His hands flap. "We mustn't speak of the breaches. To discuss them is itself a breach. I insist that protocol be observed. As Stationmaster, I'm afraid I *must* insist . . ." He trails off, hands clasped, and licks his lips. "Of course," he continues with a more propitiatory air, "I realise, my dear, that you had no intention . . . that you meant no ill . . ."

"Of course she meant no ill," says Mr Grim. "She's the only one of us who pays any heed to protocol. And I include you, Fafl. How can we be sure what protocol is, for that matter? No live reception, only your word on Magistracy communiqués. Intolerable. *Unparalleled* intolerability."

Fafl is on his feet. "I will convey your observations, Mr Grim, though I'm afraid they may strike my superiors as seditious. In the meantime," he surveys all present, "my inquiry into the breaches nears its conclusion. It quite beggars belief that one among us has used an emergency frequency." A disquiet made itself felt in all present—with the exception of the boy—at the Stationmaster's mention of the inquiry.

In fact, though they were twelve, and though only eleven of them were two-legged creatures, those who found themselves under the shadow of Magistracy suspicion were fewer still, for they must number among those who could access the array: the Stationmaster himself, Mr Arenaceous Nell, Mr Grim (who had been eliminated very swiftly indeed from the list) and Mr Bull. Fafl continued. "I do hope it is not so—the penalty for doing so would be severe. I will soon send my findings to the Magistracy; we shall have to wait and see how it responds. I have to tell you, dear colleagues, that any one of these daily ent . . . Reviews . . . could be the last time we sup all together."

Reminded of the refreshments, Mr Grim perks up visibly. "Won't you have some gooney with us, Fafl?" he asks, knowing the answer, and apparently immune to the gravity of the Stationmaster's pronouncement. Said Stationmaster recoils.

"Oh no, Mr Grim—I won't. I don't like 'em, you know." Mr Grim *does* know, for the opinion has been voiced by its owner a thousand times. "The meat comes right out of 'em salted." Fafl shivers. "Oily things." A shudder and Wigbert Grim smirks, his little incursion a success. "I wouldn't introduce a bit of it into my delicate organisation, you know," continues the Stationmaster, who must stifle a retch. "Though I am highly gratified," he continues wanly, once he has gathered himself, "to be able to provide for the company. All these years, the trap keeps 'em coming. Dirty things won't learn."

"I only meant," says Lil in an attempt to inveigle them both to return to the matter at hand, "that we are more at sea than ever, are we not? With regard to events in the wider world? These latest fragments would indicate that something has changed out there. Shouldn't we know what it is?"

"How you hunger for the world, my dear," says Fafl. "You always have. But you must be patient. A stoic, like myself. It isn't ours to know. We have our duties. I thank you again for your conscientious devotion to yours. The archive is at your disposal. Through it, and the communiqués I am from time to time burdened with relaying to those here present, we may endeavour to divine what may or may not be the state of the world. I wonder, though, why we'd bother." He makes a barking sound the others know from experience to be a laugh and begs his leave, retiring to his personal quarters in the dome where he prefers to take his meals.

"What do you think, Simon?" says Lil.

"I?" says the young gentleman. He had appeared to have collected himself somewhat: hence Lil's decision to address him with a most winning smile—but upon being spoken to he instantly colours and puts his newly filled glass on the table before it can put itself there in less decorous fashion. "Well, really I don't . . . I mean, this is more your sort of . . . I couldn't . . . I *wouldn't*, I mean . . ." His knuckles whiten around the glass he still grips. "I imagine we'd all like to . . ." He looks around the table, but evidently no one can bring themselves to look back at him. Lil nods, vigorously. "Perhaps tomorrow . . . after another . . ." he says, and there follows a pause of sufficient duration for the company to reach the unanimous conclusion that the young man's statement has come to an end. Trembling, he raises his glass to his lips and drains it. The gentleman seated beside him shakes his head.

"For goodness sake, Simon."

"Leave him be," says the lady seated on the young man's other side.

"It's perfectly alright, Mr Cyre," says Lil. "Perhaps tomorrow, as Simon says." She flashes the younger man another smile. He stares into his empty glass. "And you, father?" she says. "What do you think?"

The old man stirs, as if aware of his surroundings for the first time. "Oh, I don't know, Lil," he says. "I don't know. I shall have to ponder it. And to hear more. Yes, that's it. We shall see what we think tomorrow, when we hear some more. This evening, I'm tired and I think I should get some air. You'll walk with me, Mr Grim?"

Mr Grim admonishes his boy to take care of the remaining soles and nods his approval as the latter instantly complies. "I will, Mr Nell," says the proud parent and raises himself, not without a little difficulty, to his feet.

Under the solicitous gaze of his daughter, Mr Nell takes his old friend by the arm and both men shuffle outside, onto a wooden walkway that runs between the grey, grimy cubes. They walk along in the comfortable silence of long acquaintance till the walkway comes to an end. Here, the clearing in which the station has been built is ringed by the trees that otherwise cover the island. The two men sit on an old curved stone bench that faces the central dome and, side by side, contemplate the dusky environs—the dome itself, the cubes assembled around it and the huts adjacent, the dim sky and the swaying tree tops. The wind that normally blows over the island has abated. A gentler breeze appears to soothe Mr Nell who, it seems to his friend, has been troubled by something, or someone, this evening. No doubt this is the motive for the after-dinner perambulation, and all will be explained momentarily.

For the time being Mr Nell says nothing, and closes his eyes to let the air cool their lids. He takes a number of deep breaths and releases them slowly. Then he speaks.

"You have been a trusted friend for many a year, Wigbert," he says. "Many a long year. A true and trusted friend." He sighs. "Who else should I—" But, having turned to face his companion, Mr Nell falls silent. Mr Grim is fast asleep, his fingers interlocked over his paunch. The pronounced circularity of his person affords him the luxury of sleeping where he sits at any time, opportune or no, without the slightest possibility of tipping over. His chin drops an inch. He snores. Mr Nell pats his friend on the shoulder and gets up.

A little way into the woods, in the darkness, the old man's feet find the path. It is not much more than a strip of bare earth, no wider than one of his shoes and overhung at knee height by the undergrowth. In broad daylight it would be missed by the keenest eye, but Mr Nell has walked it a thousand times. He and one other of the station's inhabitants. As the path wends its way downhill, the regular twists, like a ribbon lowered slowly to the floor from a lazy hand and settling there in soft folds, lullaby his disquiet. Even in strong winds the wood is quite at peace—tonight it's as still as a locked shop, scented with moss and damp soil. Below, the scrub rustles with the business of its crepuscular residents—above, far above the vaulted quiet, the breeze calls faintly to him as it always does, murmuring of other places, past and present.

He reaches a spot where the trees are less dense and the ground drops away on a steeper incline. In the day, the water can be seen between their lower trunks—he closes his eyes to listen for it in the darkness. Around him, the undergrowth is stripped away and a little clearing has been carefully tended. A flowerbed, mature with Candysticks and violets, Fairy Slippers and Fireweed, curls around a wooden bench over which a trellis arches, woven with roses. He sits and allows the silence to settle around him and, after a long while, softly breaks it.

"Will you help me?" he says. "You will help me, won't you, Izzy?"

He lifts his eyes to look upon the little headstone.

"I must do it, Izzy, and I know I must, but the strength is wanting in me. The flesh is weak, the will too. Give me your strength, won't you, for just a little while, that I might save her? I do it for you, after all, as well as her. And yes, I confess it—I do it for myself, that my broken heart not be broken anew."

He puts his elbows to his knees and cradles his head, and the dogged rhythm of the waves muffles his weeping.

CHAPTER THE SECOND

IN WHICH IS RELATED
A SERIES OF SENTIMENTAL ATTACHMENTS,
THE RENEWAL OF OLD ACQUAINTANCE,
AND A SECOND ARTEFACT; THE COMMITTEE IS FASCINATED.

At low tide, we would leave our shoes, with our socks in them, on the grass verge, and you would take my little hands in your own—not very much larger—and lower me down the sheer sand bank till my feet were in the water and I was brave enough to say "Now". You would let go, and I would drop those last few inches till I stood with water lapping half way to my knees, my skirt tucked into my knickers to keep it from getting wet. Then you would shoo me away into the water a little and make a great show of lowering yourself unassisted. I believe you needed me to see that. Perhaps I needed it too.

When it was time to go, you would crouch low and brace yourself with your hands against the damp bank while I climbed on to your back to stand on your shoulders. Then you would straighten up till I could reach a clump of hardy marram grass and pull myself onto the verge. You would pull yourself up behind me and, clutching at the grass with one hand, would wave mine away with the other. In the warmer months we would sit there till our feet dried and when it was cold we'd put our wet feet back into our socks and shoes and you would insist I go home directly to change them.

I called it "my cove" and you called it "your cove". We would wade about and find little crabs and wonder at the shoals of tiny fish and how they remained stock-still in the water that ebbed and eddied around them. When we first found that place, you in your boyish braggadocio would offer me a discourse on this fish or that, or an improvised treatise on the colours of a crustacean, and I was sure, even then, that the science you imparted was quite invented. When we were a little older and had accepted, the both of us, that though the younger I was nevertheless the brighter and had remembered more from Mr Fafl's schoolbooks, you would rather listen, head bowed and gaze averted, as I told you things you did not know—and this reversal, this demotion from lecturer to listener, never seemed to bother you a bit. I think it delighted you. From that day to this, I have never observed you so at peace as when you listen to me, head bowed and gaze averted—you are the well into which I have cast all my pennies. My riches. You are the depth and I the diver. I still have not found the bottom of you.

After a time I would invariably tire of the minutiae and would leave you to wade, bent over in search of foot-level fascinations. My back would straighten, my attention turning to the cove itself, which was almost circular save for where it opened onto the sea like the gap between a crab's claws, and it would be I who stood still while the water eddied around me, to fix my eyes upon the waterline. I would try to apply my young intellect to the unimaginable distances. I would fail, but the attempt would send a thrill through me—particularly once mother had begun to tutor me, and to pour the magic of elsewhere into me—till the waterline seemed to me the rim of a great cup, filled with world, to which I longed to put my lips.

On clear days, sunlight would glint where it bounced from the buoys to remind me the cup was a forbidden one. That I could not drink from it. But just to stand there and send my gaze shooting beyond that deadly barrier to the horizon, and thence let my imagination carry me beyond, was an escape of sorts. It was the best of times, for I could make that leap, that boundless journey, knowing that behind me, all the time, was my Simon—that you could rummage around amongst the particulars of this world, the island, and I could, at least in my fancy, escape it, and we could do these things without parting. It was our first escape, in fact, that place. We trod every inch of the Warburg, you and I, the arrangement a neat one—I would guide you and you, when called upon, would carry me. But there was nowhere to which we returned more often. You would escape to it and I from it. It was our unspoken promise to each other. Our covenant.

It was our cove.

Young Arenaceous Nell had never once in his life seen the sea, never mind have it fill his nostrils with its salty perfume or his head with the bellow of its heaving waters. Not once had he heard the slap of waves against a quay till that morning, long ago, when he'd watched them send a spray in high spumes over the top; still less have it toss him bodily about as he clutched the gunwale with one hand and his hat, in great peril of getting blown away by a high wind, in the other. There was the distinct possibility, at any moment, of his losing his balance entirely and of tumbling directly into the lap of one of his companions. The two adjacent, both of them ladies, had their hands to the their mouths, so aghast were they at the prospect.

"Won't you sit, Mr Nell?" said one of them, the younger, "till you've found your sea legs? You do look rather aguish."

She was a very small person and sat remarkably straight, despite the movement of the boat, and from that day there never would be any way for Aren to say no to those big, brown eyes. He placed himself on the bench between her and the lady he presumed to be her mother, such was the physical resemblance.

"Sea legs," he said. He couldn't quite picture them. "How long does that normally take, would you say?"

There was a cackle from the dinghy's pilot, laughter lines just about the only visible part of a face otherwise covered in whiskers. "In his case?" said the old creature, "you'll pardon me if I don't hold me breath." Tiller in hand, he was still laughing as he activated the

U-son drive and the little craft skipped out over the harbour towards the amphicopter.

It was the first time that Aren had seen such a craft outside of the Magistracy bulletins that would set the village gaggling whenever news of a military campaign reached it. As they drew close, it seemed larger to him than it had in pictures—large and heavy enough, for instance, not to bob as their little boat did, but to sit there unmoving, weighted down in the water as though it had been there always, and always would be. It was both circular and tubular, like a wheel set on its side, and though the hull appeared to be made of glass, nothing within could be seen; instead it reflected the sky above, the water that lapped below and, as the pilot took them around it, the dinghy and its passengers. Aren could see himself distorted in the curved surface—an anxious young man, wet and windblown, on his first foray into the wider world. Only his few years at the Institute distinguished him from the farm boy that was his old self. He had studied well, produced work of note, but in the cloistered seclusion of a Magistracy establishment, housed in secure premises, he had learned precisely nothing of life. How often had he longed for escape? Now, with the sea churning without and his stomach within, he wasn't quite so sure.

On the far side of the craft the pilot edged them up to a jetty that had been lowered from an opening in the hull. One by one, the passengers clambered onto it while the old pilot took evident delight in their efforts. Aren and the young lady who had bid him sit were the last two and he, the consummate young gentleman, insisted she go before him. With a nimble leap she was aboard and had disappeared into the ship and so, to Aren's immense relief, wasn't there to see him fall flat on his face when he attempted to replicate the manoeuvre, drawing a hearty bellow from behind.

"That's it, boy!" laughed the ancient mariner. "You're on! I'd find a seat quickly if I were you and strap yourself to it!"

With that, the dinghy was set scudding back towards the port by its merry master. Aren got to his feet unsteadily, peered into the gloomy opening and, not without some trepidation, stepped inside.

The interior was larger than he had expected. To his left, the way was blocked by a grey metal wall; to the right, the tube curled away from him. That was the way his companions had gone—he could see them at about a quarter and an eighth the way round the circle, where they had gathered in a seating area. Between he and they, the inner wheel—its spokes, the great rotor blades, were idle. A similar, featureless grey wall marked the limit of the seating area, and no part of the ship's interior, beyond and between these two dividing walls, revealed itself. Steadier on his feet aboard the larger vessel, he walked around to join his new colleagues.

---

dry and long were the days   and the grass   full of pollen the gold air was   made my eyes water   blocked my nose   and what were we doing out there anyway   dusty derelict places   the village in sight but distant   daft young brushes   but what else   where else   for the languid summer children   the three   arenaceous there too   I didn't mind that   I liked it   wasn't he my friend now   didn't that exalt me in her eyes   it did   it did   would've been too hard there without him wouldn't it   in the brilliance of her   too harsh   it would   it would   too much for me   for the likes of me   so there I was   a foil for him   never mind that   and I could look upon her at least   it was a summer feast   and she the fire   and how I burned

~

Old Arenaceous opens his eyes and blinks himself out of a reverie. More and more now, when they are shut, the past closes in and he finds himself swathed in the silken folds of its voluminous skirts. It is almost time for the entertainment, the second in this series of Lil's.

Bless her! She has left his wine on the desk as usual. He gets up and shuffles over to retrieve it and, having forgotten to eat his sandwich, knocks it to the floor with his elbow when he sits back down. A half-hearted curse escapes him; there will be an abundance of food at the entertainment, as there always is. In the meantime, he has his sherry and takes a generous draft. Then he settles back and closes his eyes once more.

~

"Hello, Arenaceous."

"Hello, Jasper."

The amphicopter had dropped gently onto the water, just off the island's shoreline. It was late afternoon and beneath a hot and reddening sun, far along in its downward course, the occupants disembarked via the same opening through which they'd entered, onto a dinghy and thence to the beach. One of the gentlemen passengers hopped into the water to hold the boat steady as the others clambered out to wade the last few feet to shore. Aren loitered astern and was rewarded with the opportunity of helping the young lady and her mother disembark, the former accepting his arm with good grace despite her confident bearing, the latter leaning rather heavily in.

"All of your things have arrived safely," said a cadet in Magistracy uniform who waited for them on the sand. "if you'll all be good enough to follow me up to processing, we can have you dry and dressed for dinner in no time."

He turned his back and the little company—no more than twenty in all and, after a spell in the amphicopter's stasis headsets, still largely unacquainted—fell into line. He led them uphill through the woods to the island's highpoint and the station compound, where Aren sat now on one side of a white table, the only item of furniture in a bare interview room apart from a filing cabinet and two chairs. Opposite him, occupying the other, sat Jasper Fafl. The Magistracy man had ushered Aren into the room the moment the party reached the compound.

"I'll be perfectly candid with you, Arenaceous," said the Magistracy man. "You know me well, after all, and would expect nothing less, I'm sure."

Aren smiled, and declined to fill the ensuing silence.

"Hem," Fafl was yet young but already had the stoop that would lower his chin over time to below shoulder height, and he had always had an ill-washed, sallow look about him, since they were both little boys. He rubbed his nose and feigned his own smile. "I'm rather surprised, is all, to see you so contained, Arenaceous. Would have thought you might leap for joy to see me. Take me by the shoulders. Though I do loathe such demonstrations—you partake, do you not? Shake me by the hand? Some other expression of gratitude." He placed his hands, palms down, on the table.

"I'm afraid you have the better of me, Jasper," said Aren. "I couldn't tell you why I'm here, though I can tell you it isn't of my own volition. But of course, you know that much. I received a Magistracy letter. You were a signatory. There were assurances of certain consequences in the event of my failing to comply with the instructions contained therein." He threw his hands in the air. "And so, here I am." Another smile.

"Ah yes, of course," said his boyhood associate, "your conscription notice won't have contained any of the details. I'm afraid there is a . . . *penitential* element to your secondment. Only my earnest intercessions with the Magistracy have brought you here, my old friend. If not for my efforts, I'm afraid your accommodations would be altogether less salubrious and your considerable talents quite wasted. Quite wasted away."

"Meaning?"

"Oh, Arenaceous. I'm to spell it out, am I? Denigrating for us both. I'm afraid it will be rather difficult to hear, but you mustn't be too ashamed of yourself. You're here now, safe and sound, and there is much to do."

He stood up and went to the cabinet and, opening its top drawer, pulled a file from it.

"We . . . they . . . still like to store the most confidential documents on paper." Sitting at the table again he opened the file, took out a form and slid it across the table so that Aren could read it. "This is your stay of execution. It wasn't easy to secure, let me tell you."

"My what?"

"Read it, dear, read it. It's all there."

Aren picked the letter up and pored over it, brow furrowed. "Contraband . . . illicit materials . . . what is this about?" He shook his head. "I'm none the wiser, Jasper."

"Oh but you must remember, Arenaceous, you must. Come now, think! Goodness knows, they made enough of a fuss about it in the village at the time. The ignominy!" He wrung his hands and a sneer distorted his already asymmetrical features. "If such a word can apply in a backwater like that."

"The book?" cried Aren. "You can't be serious. It's too absurd!" Fafl shrugged, so he went on. "I buried a book in my garden, Jasper. I was sixteen years of age, and amply punished for it. Why would it come up again?"

Jasper Fafl offered him the palms of his hands. "The eyes and ears of the Magistracy, Arenaceous, are not to be denied. No one at all, anywhere at all, can hide from them. Not forever. Sixteen years is the age of majority. I'm afraid that, to an organisation with such vast and weighty responsibilities, it was largely a matter of form, your sentence. A bureaucratic nicety, you might say. If your case hadn't been brought to my attention here, well, I dread to think."

Aren's eyes narrowed. Fafl continued.

"Your theoretical abilities, though. Your mastery of the algorithm, Arenaceous, of the lateral connection. These have been your redemption. You were recommended to me in light of the important work we carry out here at the Warburg. Work that is already influenced by this thesis you published at the Institute. How renowned you are! And when I saw your name, well . . . why *wouldn't* I save your life? How could I not save it? So I have. I have saved your life."

He sat back in his chair; it would have been quite impossible for him to appear any more pleased with himself.

"I hope I haven't caused you any trouble, Jasper," said Aren. "It was you, after all, who gave me that book. To think that I might have jeopardised your—"

"I gave you the book to destroy," said Fafl, "as you know perfectly well. But you didn't, did you?" His tone, momentarily, was petulant. "If it wasn't for your indiscretion, we . . . you would never have been found out." He renewed his smile—a slow, deliberate act. "But we mustn't bicker, Aren. Such old friends. When exactly did we last see each other? I can't quite remember."

"It wasn't long afterwards," said Aren, "when they came for you."

A cloud darkened his interlocutors features.

"No, indeed," said Fafl. He stood. "Any . . . matters outstanding between the Magistracy and I were long ago resolved, Arenaceous. These days, I cannot be sure where Jasper Fafl ends and the Magistracy begins. I am subsumed. I live only to serve." He gestured toward the door and Aren got to his feet.

"Oh, where is my head? One other thing, Arenaceous. Stay seated, will you?"

Fafl went back to the cabinet and returned to the table with a small leather case.

"Wait, now I remember. You watched them take me away that day, did you not, Arenaceous?" He looked up from the case he was unzipping to Aren's raised eyebrows. "Oh, did you think you watched unseen? Understandable. Why should I have expected to spot you in that window, after all? Not your window. Nor your house, for that matter." He turned his head sharply to the side for a moment and looked at nothing, teeth bared in a rictus that spoke silently, but with excruciatingly prolonged eloquence, of a subject terrible to broach. Something very old in Aren, some scaly creature that swam so deep he'd forgotten it, rose unbidden to the surface. Scalp tingling, his gut turned. He *had* thought himself unseen, that day. Breath quickened and shallow, he braced for the accusation that was to come. For the name. But nothing did come—Fafl merely shook his head and retrieved an old-fashioned syringe from the leather case. "Roll your sleeve up, there's a good chap."

"What is this?"

"A condition of your secondment to the station, dear," said Fafl. "Not just you." He was tapping air bubbles from the upturned syringe. "No, no—all of our new arrivals will get the same. A brannew nanoplant for each and every one of you. And we've all had it, of course, those of us here already. Even I."

Aren had rolled his sleeve up but one hand was clamped over his upturned arm.

"A nanoplant, dear boy, nothing more!" Fafl shook his head in condescension. "All meet and proper. Nothing for a man of science such as yourself to fear. You'll forgive the antiquated delivery system—we have found that intravenous works best. So much more cumbersome to locate and extract, which is just the way we like it."

He gently brushed Aren's hand aside, eyes on the vein.

"Safety, Arenaceous, and security. The nanoplant is harmless. Instantly fatal, of course, were it to cross a boundary that encircles this island. About a half mile out. You can make out the buoys from the shore at times, though you mustn't ever approach them. Quite deadly."

He nodded as the needle broke skin.

"The antidote is a second implant. When your time at the station is done—in your case, when the Magistracy deems your service here sufficient atonement for your crime—you will get yours and off you will go. You will thank me *that* day, I'm sure. Oh, yes."

Aren watched as the needle was pulled from the vein. Nanoplants were commonly used security and tracking devices. At any rate, he couldn't swim. As Fafl returned the little case to the cabinet, Aren rolled his sleeve back up and, without another word, joined the others.

The beautiful young woman was first in line, outside in the waiting area with her mother. Aren sat beside her, though he had no business lingering and his trousers and boots were wet. She glanced his way with renewed interest and in the end spoke up.

"You are Magistracy, Mr . . . ?"

"Please, call me Aren. No, no," he shook his head emphatically, "I assure you I am not."

"But Mr Fafl knows you. And you him, if I didn't misread your expression when you saw him."

Aren couldn't tell from her tone if she thought that a close association with the Magistracy would be a good thing.

"Jasper and I were boyhood friends. We come from the same place, Ms . . . ?"

"If you'll step through please, miss."

An attendant took the young lady by the elbow. She stood and nodded to Aren by way of apology, and let herself be guided into the room he had just left. He hadn't even got her name. Perhaps the mother.

"Your daughter is so young to have been assigned to this place, Mrs...?"

"It's Ms."

"Excuse me, Ms... it's just, she's so young. Will there be trainees here? I didn't think—"

"I wouldn't know, I'm sure," said the woman. She appeared resolute in her determination not to make eye contact and stood now, hands clasped. "If there are, then Izzy will doubtless be training them. A burden, I would have thought, on top of her other work with the Mapping Department. Izzy is to be director there," she said, turning to leave, "and she is my sister." It was the last time she was ever to address Aren directly. A costly exchange, but he had the name.

"Izzy." The name still tickles the tip of his tongue with its buzz. Still that last, lingering tingle of her electricity runs through him when he says it aloud. He rouses himself, takes his stick and his felt cap and makes his way over to the Committee Room, the last to arrive and greeted wordlessly but affectionately by nodding heads already tilted over bowls. As soon as she sees her father seated, Lil plays the audio.

When I was made Brigadier, our home became a designated Repository and I was allocated a Haztext cabinet. We put it in the basement and, because I would be on parole status for months while I underwent my inoculations, it remained there empty and unused through our first winter in the house.

We were newlyweds and despite the rigors of my work and my advancing position, we had other things on our minds.

We ran around that house like children—teasing and tickling, pranking and painting walls the most appalling, ill-considered colors. There was nothing special about it, just one of seven rather ramshackle homes in a row, but on a quiet lane and surrounded by greenery. It was our playground, bigger for us than the world outside. The furthest we got, when I wasn't at the Institute, was the back garden. I remember the day, as the cold was beginning to lift, that your mother planted an azalea bush at the bottom of it, near the back gate.

"They say azaleas make you think of home," she told me, though when she saw my disapproval, she corrected herself. "It's just a rhododendron, of course."

Never one to do things by half, she'd put on her dungarees and a pair of heavy boots to plant this single bush. She stood afterwards and put her gloved hands on her hips, eyes consulting mine.

"It's pretty though, isn't it?"

So was she, Lita. And she made everything around her pretty. The chrome in the kitchen sparkled with her laughter. The fire in the den was her chuckling embrace. The whole house hummed with her warmth. In every memory I have of that time, she is laughing. Everything was funny—especially me, though I rarely meant it. I did sometimes though—I loved her laughter so much I would even attempt jokes. This is when she was still well.

I look back with a gnawing regret to the day I graduated from the program and came home with the first materials for the cabinet—four Dan Brown novels and a replica DVD box set, also from the First Age, of something called Sabrina the Teenage Witch. *Your mother was uncharacteristically somber and the house uncomfortably quiet as she followed me down to the cabinet. As she watched me lock them away, I told her they'd been recovered from the hull lining of a mining shuttle—outside the Hub line but inbound—and the smugglers executed. She shuddered visibly and went back upstairs to make dinner.*

The Hub—our home system—has been clean for aeons. You'll have learned about all this by now. These days our work is done on the frontiers, on first contact with Second Age settlements, the frequency of which has increased exponentially since the Alcubierre 4 drives came online. We call them natives, they've been out there so long, but of course they are our own diaspora, remnants of the Great Flight. We invariably find them in a state of deterioration, sunk back into superstition and magical thinking. Folklore breeds wherever it is let. It may be a germ—that is certainly one of our lines of enquiry.

That proscribed materials had been seized so close to the Hub line was genuinely shocking to me and served to sharpen my sense of duty. The purity of the Hub, its truthfulness, is in constant danger of faith influx. From that point, the ceaseless campaigns made perfect sense to me. We cannot afford to sit and wait. Instead, we must push out. It can be a bloody business.

Between tours, home life was tranquil. Your mother fell pregnant with you in no time. Her swelling breasts and belly seemed to subdue her—there was a little less frivolity around the place, but things seemed normal enough to me. Maybe it was my work; I often think now that it was selfish of me to marry her to a military life. Her family were only second generation debunked, having come from Sanat, where a number of religions had flourished. Dramatic entertainment was positively revered. Her own great-grandfather had been just such a performer.

Perhaps the brutalities of her own people's past were too recent. In my defense, she had been passed through every psychfilter required of Brigade householders and no concerns had arisen. Her sense of humor had raised an eyebrow here and there but was not without precedent and appeared firmly rooted in experiential observation (for the purposes of irony), self-deprecation in the face of inadequate daily task performance and so on. I do believe now that I might have seen something sooner.

As I settled into my new role and got a few tours under my belt, the cabinet filled up. Some of the most powerful known toxins were there, all replicas of course—a King James Bible, Cervantes, an anthology of Second Age guerrilla fairy tales. My pride in my collection was such that I'd insist your mother be there as I locked each haul away. She complied—she took a great interest, in fact, in the list of names and titles that I catalogued. We would often discuss this item or that over dinner. She had a curious mind.

Had I read any of the materials? I had, I told her, under supervision—as a Truth operative, I am obligated to ongoing inoculation.

Hadn't I become ill? I had experienced some discomfort, of course, but then, I hadn't been exposed to any toxins until my induction was complete. In the untrained, the materials were likely to cause severe symptoms ranging from mental anguish to physical pain.

Had I ever seen a Shake Spear? Of course not. Where had she heard the term? From her grandfather, I supposed, while he still lived. There had been no reported sightings in thousands of years and the most recent of those documented were so antique as to be unverifiable. There probably never had been any Shake Spears, and I would not discuss myth.

It got to the point where I found her enquiries unnerving. I might have done something sooner to put a stop to them but I assumed that such exchanges were commonplace in service homes. It wasn't a subject I discussed on duty. Anyway, you came along soon enough and the questions petered out—we found ourselves too busy in the giddy panic of parenthood to worry about anything else.

Not that I was much help—away for months at a time, a spare part when home. She amazed me, Lita, the way she took to you. You frightened me but not her—it was as if you were an organ of hers. A limb. As if she'd been incomplete. She hauled you round the house like a little parcel as she went about her work. She could stop you crying with a fingertip, or even a low, sub-verbal moan if she'd put you down for a minute to get on with something or other.

My girls. The months of pregnancy had been strained, if I'm honest. I'd become concerned about the interest she showed in the materials and had begun to keep a closer eye on the cabinet key. It wasn't that I didn't trust her. But people are weak.

When you came, the tension seemed to lift. Your first year was just as our first year together had been—every day an adventure, full from morning to night of joyful humdrum. Even the increasingly brutal tours couldn't sully it; when I was home I put the campaigns out of my mind. Your mother made that easy. So did you.

It's why I became careless. By the time you took your first steps, any worries I'd had regarding your mother's behavior were forgotten. We were a little family like any other. My work took its toll on me but I kept it out of the house. Only when I returned from a tour with materials and placed them in the cabinet in the basement, was your mother reminded of what I did.

So I thought. You were five when it happened. But the grieving had really already begun for me, when you produced your first words. Something changed between your mother and you, and between she and I. I felt her withdraw and pull you with her. I saw you both retreat into a world of muttered assurances and questioning looks, shared understandings that weren't shared with me. Rudimentary little conversations on the other side of a door that she would cut off when I entered the room. I saw her quiet you with a finger to her lips when I sat at the kitchen table.

I should have railed against it. There was still laughter in the house but it never seemed to be mine. My girls, receding—more content, it seemed, taking more delight in one another, with every step that took you both further from me.

It was slow and I barely felt it, but since I couldn't feel entirely welcome in it any more, I hardened against home life. I took cold satisfaction in your well-being but from a new distance and for the first time since you were born, I let my attention focus wholly on the campaigns. In truth, it was probably just as well to push me away, given what I was becoming.

Your mother's attention, too, shifted. No novelty lasts; even the arrival of a new human is assimilated in the end. You had become so much a part of her, by your third year, that I don't think she recognized your separateness. The pair of you were a single creature. She loved you completely, but unthinkingly, effortlessly and forgetfully, and after those few years in the house I imagine she began to bore. It was around then, as I recall, that her interest in the materials resurfaced.

By this time the collection in the basement was extensive and although she was of course denied any direct access, I let her make an amanuensis of herself and manage the inventory, which I kept separately in a locker to which she also had a key. It was almost certainly a breach, but the protocol was not explicit on anything apart from the source materials themselves. I considered it sensible to offer this small appeasement rather than make forbidden fruit of the cabinet's contents, to intrigue her all the more.

She would ask her questions but it seemed to me my brief, conversation-closing replies—that this was a reckless love story, that the author of such and such had been revered in more ignorant times—satisfied her. It meant I could spend time with her while you slept and ask my own questions. How were you? What had you been getting up to? Did you ask about me when I was away? As my answers were designed to sooth and parry, so were hers. It was exhausting, to find myself an opponent in a game of matrimonial chess, but that is what it had become. I probably wasn't even aware. I'm rationalizing, no doubt, with the benefit of hindsight.

By May, your fifth year had already been the most difficult of my professional life. We'd been out on Sinn since February and I was back for just a couple of weeks before returning to complete my tour. Something brought me to the back gate and the azalea and I stood there for a while breathing its scent. I hadn't called ahead. I wanted to see how pleasant a surprise it would be.

Not pleasant at all. It was the end of any goodness in my life. I stood on the lawn in the half light of late evening and watched you both through the kitchen window. You had your heads bowed and therefore wouldn't see me until I moved towards the back door and opened it. I wouldn't know whether to say my blood boiled or froze as I watched you. In that moment I wouldn't have known the difference. In that moment I knew I had lost my true love forever, and my only child.

I recognized it straight away, even from a distance—it was over-sized and colorfully illustrated—a children's edition of the Ianputucci. She balanced it on one knee and dandled you on the other, eyes panning across the page and lips moving as she read to you.

"That was not what I was expecting," says Mr Bull, afterwards.

"No," says Mrs Cyre.

"Same chap though," says her husband.

"Oh yes. Same voice all right," says she.

"But this is a more personal history. Is it to be a confessional, I wonder?" Mr Bull again.

"It wouldn't surprise me, given the tone. It seems we have a narrative, at any rate. Good—I prefer 'em," says Mr Grim.

"I want to know what happens next!"

As it usually does in the wake of whatever outburst escapes the fat boy at the conclusion of an entertainment, and invariably something *does* escape him, that very particular silence which speaks so loudly of general disapprobation settles upon the company.

"Really. It's disreputable," says Mrs Cyre. "Another fitting illustration, if we needed it, of why the child should not be present. Never mind his disgusting . . . *creature!*"

"If you'd care to call my boy disreputable again, Mrs Cyre," says Mr Grim. "I should be happy to—"

"Come, come, dears," says Fafl. "Let's not squabble." He stands behind the fat boy, whom he pats on the head. "Where's the harm, eh? Are we not de facto family to the boy, all of us?"

Mr Grim squirms in his seat. Fafl goes on.

"The only child among us. Hm? Do we not delight in him? Haven't I tutored him myself all these years? Seen to his medicaments, his checks, his inoculations? No, no, this creeping neglect of protocol is hardly something for which we should blame the lad." He aims a supplicatory shrug and an oily grin at Lil, who drops her gaze. "Oh how we've tried to keep these miscreants on the straight and narrow eh, Lil? But I am afraid we are all rather deteriorated." He sighs, theatrically, pats the boy again and sits in his usual place.

"And you yourself, Mr Grim, with your narratives and your preferring of 'em. Hardly a good example, is it? But you always were so roguish."

A silence from the boy's father finds its way around the table. It is very different from its predecessor above mentioned, speaking as it does of altogether stronger emotions.

"Father?" says Lil.

The old man has once again been conspicuously quiet, but she has seen him stare hard as he does when engaged, eyes flitting almost imperceptibly from one nothing to another. He stirs.

"I do see what you mean, Lil," he says. "You have uncovered something very interesting, I believe. Why, even at this early stage, it's riddled with anomalies, isn't it? A strange beast to be sure. *Not* to be taken at face value, I'll warrant."

"But what does that tell you?"

"At this moment?" He smiles. "Precisely nothing. I'll have to hear more. And we're missing the end, you say? It isn't certain we'd need it, in order to make an assessment, but it might frustrate us."

He gets up.

"I shall walk you out, Arenaceous," says Fafl. "I believe we're all done here. Another fascinating ent . . . Review, Lil, my dear. Quite excellent." He beckons Aren towards the door. The old man shrugs.

"Very well," he says and they walk out into a starry night. At the end of the walkway they part. Before they do, Fafl speaks.

"You are braced for what comes, Arenaceous, I hope? Quite girded?" he says, in a tone that might almost pass for genuine concern. In the starlight, Aren can see him wring his hands. "So difficult a thing for you! So trying for your girl."

Aren doesn't respond to the question. "When will you tell them?" he asks instead.

"Tomorrow I will announce the closure of the Station. We will proceed with our agreement the following day."

"And then?"

"And then," says Fafl, "a se'nnight, perhaps—once the verdict is known, Mr Bull, as station Marshal, will be obliged to act." A shrug in the gloom. "It will be out of my hands." Evidently, the ensuing silence is the more uncomfortable for Fafl, who is first to break it. "Lil will have her passage straight away, Arenaceous. I'll not linger in this place. And I'd not have her linger here neither. It wouldn't do. Not with you so disgraced." He shook his head once, emphatically. "It would dishonour her."

"So be it." Aren is already walking away, into the trees, wishing neither to spend another moment in Fafl's company nor for that gentleman to take any satisfaction from the tears in his eyes, that glint in the scant silver light.

CHAPTER THE THIRD

*TREATS OF VARIOUS COURTSHIPS,
WITH VARIOUS RESULTS, VERY GRAVE TIDINGS
FOR THE COMMITTEE, AND A QUANDARY FOR LIL.*

WE WOULD RIDE OUT   the pony hers   the trap mine   arenaceous at the reins   sometimes her   never me   never mind   would take the middle seat I would   my excuse the hamper   best place to have it on the lap   cheese sandwiches and pilfered wine   and she to my left or my right and he to my right or my left   the silken arcs of their cooing and courting would cocoon me   didn't mind that   wasn't left out   not entirely   for he wasn't always as charming as he himself believed   or as clever not quite the dashing scapegrace he thought himself   and when she thought him stupid   when one of his little cupids missed its mark   her lips would tighten to suppress the smile   that would shine instead from her eye   when she winked at me

***

"Your sister tells me you'll be taking the helm in the Department of Mapping," said Aren. He was on his knees, between two ridges of tilled earth, and Izzy was on hers in the adjacent row—he'd made sure of that.

"Yes," she said, "she mentioned the two of you had spoken."

Her lip quivered and Aren couldn't tell whether it was the effort of driving her trowel into the dirt or that she was at great pains not to smirk. "I should be very pleased to tell you that you had endeared yourself to my sister, Mr Nell," she said, twisting the trowel as she removed it and dropping a seed into the hole it left behind, "but I'm afraid it would be dishonest of me." For the very briefest of moments, the rim of her sun hat rose and revealed the flash of her eyes and Aren thought that, though already kneeling, he might fall over. He was glad to see them disappear again so quickly—she wouldn't see him colour.

"I'm afraid I rather . . . It's just that I thought . . ." He let the sentence peter out. What good was it, trying to excuse such oafishness? Besides, his full powers of concentration were called for. It was no easy thing to stay level with Izzy—if he focussed his mind on the task at hand, his general state of nervousness would compel him to work so quickly that he would move ahead of her, but whenever, contrariwise, he let himself become inwrapped in her, he seemed to enter a trance-like state, forgetting the seeds altogether, and would fall behind. Neither circumstance readily conduced to conversation, the only reason he'd put himself forward for planting duties this morning.

There was a camaraderie, in those first days. A frontier spirit, you might almost say, if the term didn't seem so odd in such a small and self-contained place as a remote island. At any rate, they'd considered themselves pioneers. Everyone had rolled their sleeves up to lend their keen assistance in all aspects of settlement. Even Aren, here against his will, was caught up in it—and at Izzy's side in a newly tilled cabbage patch, where else could he possibly have wished to be?

"I'll confess I was surprised that someone so young would oversee the station's flagship department," he said and, after a brief pause, "You must be very gifted."

"They tell me I am," said Izzy. "My work pleases them." She sat up and arched her back, hands on hips. "But work is only work. I'm afraid that in all other respects I'm something of a bungler, Mr Nell. I wonder, given the very singular impression you've made on my sister, if we have that in common?" Having asked the question, Izzy began again with her trowel, sparing Aren the tyranny of her high amusement.

---

a summer   mere weeks   nothing before it   not much after   only the magistracy   only the submission and the work   well not quite only perhaps   there has also been the aching   but that summer   that summer is the beginning and the end of it all   cheese sandwiches for which I was praised   made with washed hands   company   him and through him her   out by the canal sometimes with our feet in the water   or in the ruins of the old asylum   picnics in the madhouse with the lunatic dead   what pleasures   what precarious balm days   he and she like to either end of a seesaw   I at the fulcrum teetering   knowing full well it only takes two   that I was surplus   butter upon bacon   but they liked it both   they liked me there   he needed his foil   she liked me because I unhurried it   meant she could delight in the prospect of him   suspend the coda of his serenade   and so she dallied   and her dalliance   her shilly-shally   the summerlong cadence of her hesitation   oh it *was* exquisite

---

He can see her, bent over her seeds. He can smell the soil, the scent of her hair on the breeze. It fills him up, a draught of courage as he waits in his cabin for today's entertainment. Lil has gone, and left him his sandwich. Today, as yesterday, it sits uneaten, though he has drained the flask of sherry. Its warmth is welcome—he knows what is to come at the entertainment—and he lets himself be set adrift on its vapours, carried back to that other, better time.

By the end of his first year on the island, it had become the case that every Tuesday, while the morning was not yet fully illumined, he would meet Izzy down by the shore where the two little fishing pods were kept and the island's only beach swept around the crescent of a tiny bay, and they would walk from one end of it to the other and back again till the day's work could be put off no longer. Izzy would often stop and look out over the water, and oftener still speak wistfully of an ancient town, submerged beneath the waves just a short distance from the shore—the last place on the home world, she would remind him each time, to boast a church, saved by the sea from the old Magistracy purges. On Sunday afternoons he would bring flowers to her quarters and they would dine together, with Izzy's sister for a chaperone. These occasions were even less advantageous for the purposes of courting than might be inferred from the presence of that stern lady, for they were also invariably joined by husband and wife—a Mr and Mrs Cyre who had arrived on the same amphicopter, already newlyweds.

Aren and Izzy might have been forgiven for suspecting mischief on the part of her sister, for arranging that particular company—this married pair were exceedingly staid and impossibly prim. In all the weeks and months that passed them by over those Sunday roasts, for example, they never did share their given names, and they were bores withal—eulogising Fafl and the Warburg mission at every opportunity. They'd come as volunteers, Magistracy worthies, and tended to pontificate—which is to say, one of them did—as though reading from one of its propaganda pamphlets.

Nevertheless, Aren wouldn't have missed a single dinner—not even on the promise of a nanoplant and escape. There was Izzy and there was her sister's excellent cooking and there was good beer warmed by the fire and a bowl of punch afterwards that made the brief walk back to his own quarters, accompanied by his beloved, a delight of hand holding and waist squeezing.

In fact, the prospect of leaving the island, that had troubled his mind so constantly to begin with, presented itself with notably less urgency as time went on. How *could* a man be troubled when his days were so filled with his life's work and his heart with his life's love? Arenaceous Nell's future had begun to map itself out in his mind, but the coordinates thereof pertained exclusively to Izzy (x) and to his precious algorithms (y). Place had rather lost its importance.

Till now. Now nothing else means much at all. This place. Father and daughter will get to leave it after all—Lil who has never wished for anything else and he who can't remember what it felt like to want to. But they won't be leaving together. It is almost seven. The old man struggles with his boots and when he has them laced, hauls himself out of the chair and onto his feet. He takes his stick and, removing his felt cap, replaces it with a wide-brimmed leather hat, since there is drizzling rain this evening. Despite the concession in headwear, the weather causes him no hurry—indeed, he treads the walkway towards the Committee Room as a condemned man might on his way to the gibbet, and he welcomes the persistent memories that even now push in through the rain and pull him back through the long years, to his youth.

though I knew my presence a salve to her I feared arenaceous might become impatient   picked my moment and brought the book didn't I   pulled it out the hamper   aghast she was   and she set for the magistracy that very autumn   a veritable acolyte   enthralled though wasn't she   as he'd been weeks before   when on the production of it he'd taken a new interest in me   in the likes of me   an unlikely pairing I'll grant   we were both of us he and I under Mr Reynolds   who prepared us that year for aetiology at the institute   not that arenaceous   brilliant and delightful arenaceous   had even noted my presence in class   but secrets bond   that was my calculation   and I had my time in the flattering illumination of his glow   and now the book bound the three of us   and I couldn't very well be banished could I   may have put a little dent in her regard for him   that he'd kept it from her   for all these weeks of supposed fellowship   and a bit of polish on her regard for me   that I was the one to include her   pleased with myself I was   briefly   but nothing lasts   nothing that pleases me

"Morning, Aren! At it already are we? You'll be telling me you haven't breakfasted, next."

 A gentlemen who seemed taller than his average height on account of his exceeding slenderness, tight-fitting clothes and loping gait, put a bagged sandwich down on the workbench beside young Mr Nell, who didn't need to take his eyes from his work to investigate; it would be tinned turkey—it always was—and it would be topped generously with the deliciously sweet cucumbers that Izzy's sister had pickled that first summer. Anything that had anything to do with Izzy was invariably sweet, and this other youth enjoyed far greater access to her sister's pickles than Aren did.

"So," said the visitor, "have you found it yet?" It was what he always said.

"Found what?" said Aren, and sighed. It was his usual reply.

The man slapped his back, as he always did.

"What do you mean, what? The oldest yarn, that's what! The original origin story." His eyes would widen for purposes of melodrama whenever he deployed this latter expression.

"Yes," said Aren, "as I've explained to you on many, many occasions now, that's not really what I—"

"Not that it matters," said his companion. "I mean, what's the dashed point of it all, anyway? Hm? There is no point, that's what!"

Aren look up from his screen at last and let out a second sigh.

"You have been a very dear friend to me, Wig, since my arrival here," he said, pulling the sandwich from its bag. "A mentor. I'm not sure what I should have done without you. But," he pulled the bread back slightly, to confirm the presence of those pickles, "you are a deeply heretical person and,"—Aren took a great bite and continued with his mouth full—"I'm afraid I despair of you." He swallowed. "You'd never get away with your talk, you know, if you weren't exiled on a remote island."

"Well I am, so that's that." Wig had never been forthcoming on why he had chosen, or been compelled, to join the Warburg, and Aren had a sense that any prying on his part might cast a shadow between the two friends, and therefore refrained. "And how do things proceed with young Izzy?" said Wig, feigning nonchalance. "Her sister says she's fond of you."

At the mention of Izzy's name, Aren's face near burned right off him. Wig—and this was quite out of character—had the discretion to look away. "D-Does she?" said Aren. "I confess, I-I do allow myself, to a certain degree that is to say, to acknowledge, with some degree of assurance, her feelings—"

His friends shoulders shook. It was the one topic of conversation guaranteed to bring about such mirth in the otherwise curmudgeonly young man, which isn't to say that some unselfish, vicarious pleasure taken in Aren's good fortune gave rise to the merriment; no, the cause was much less born of virtue than of mischief.

"Fafl seethes," said Wig, barely containing his delight. "He loathes you."

"Oh," said Aren, feeling some relief at the apparent change of subject, "that. There is some history between Fafl and me. We—"

"Silly bean," said his friend, moving toward the door to take his leave. "Nothing to do with history. He loathes you because she loves you." Aren was left alone, though for a few moments he could hear Wig's sniggers recede with his footsteps on the walkway.

---

the wheat fields were already stubbled   the day I pressed it into his hands and told him to burn the thing   that the magistracy was sending an audit squad to the village   that it could not be in my house   the house of the magistracy warden   my father   and arenaceous said he would   but he didn't   caught with it weren't they   not a week later   and beaten for it weren't they   and my name beaten out   or perhaps the auditors used serum   I don't know which   and it might have been out of him and it might have been out of her   I don't know which

He can hear old Wigbert now, chuckling about something or other in the Committee Room. He puts his hand to the door handle, turns it and steps inside, into the steaming, noisy ambience of a hot meal in full swing. The company is complete. Lil smiles at him from her console but he cannot withstand her gaze, taking his seat at Wigbert's side. Neither does he turn to look at the Stationmaster, who is on his stool at the wall, behind him—Aren can all too easily imagine the smirk, the constantly working hands, the obsequies to come.

"May I pour you a drink, Mr Nell?" says Wigbert.

"You may, Mr Grim," and with the quickest glance and a single nod, he acknowledges his daughter, who presses play.

Efsane was of no interest.

We simply hadn't given it a second thought. There was interest, considerable interest, in the primary—a gas giant that went by the name of Kepler 3-1041b. The concession for it had gone to the Delve corporation which had put a station in orbit from which it deployed a fleet of hydro-harvesters. Standard operating procedure—everybody wants the gas giant concessions.

No one, however, had paid any attention to Kepler 3-1041b's solitary moon.

None of this concerned us, of course. Efsane hadn't even been nominated to our list. If it had, we would have noticed it—proper names are exceptionally uncommon for bodies this far out. Even the most degraded "native" populations abide by the registry denominations. To this day nobody has been able to explain the origin of the name to me. There is no attribution in Kepler, Gliese or Fiser. On the Delve station though, by the time we arrived, it was common usage.

The corporation had run some standard exploration scans in accordance with the terms of the concession, but they hadn't yielded anything of particular interest. A thick atmosphere comprised of the right gases in entirely the wrong proportions—there wasn't nearly enough oxygen—and temperatures ranging from the far too hot at surface level to the far too cold at higher altitudes.

There was one major surprise. At least there would have been somewhere to put your foot at those heights—Efsane is terrestrial, something that few would have expected of a body so large. Although a good four-fifths of the surface is flattish and boiling, there is a single massif in the northern hemisphere that the Delve team had dubbed Mons Elisium. The only theoretical site for settlement, let alone civilization, on the entire moon would have been on the upper slopes of its near vertical, more northerly mountains, at an altitude of roughly thirty-nine thousand meters and at temperatures that would have provided a plausible circumstance for human life. If, that is, there had been a breathable atmosphere.

There wasn't, and having forwarded the data, Delve got on with its mining operations, confirmed in the belief that Efsane, though undeniably beautiful as it evoked old Earth in its blues and greens, was essentially uninteresting. It was therefore with some surprise that, nine months into their contract and as the moon swept into sight across the stippled, terracotta surface of Kepler 3-1041b, they received—from precisely that spot that had previously been identified—a message that the station's translation software processed with apparent ease.

"Good evening," it said. "If you have evenings, on that thing."

"Crikey O'Reilly!" says the fat boy afterwards, through a mouth full of Mrs Cyre's gooney pie. "It's—"

"Quiet, boy!" says Wigbert. "Swallow your food. These coocumbers aren't going to eat themselves." He pushes a wooden bowl towards his son, tops up Aren's wine and takes a good draught of his own. It is a trembling hand that puts his cup back on the table. For a time, nobody looks at anybody. More drink is taken.

"Well," says Mr Cyre at last. "This is really shameful, isn't it? Shameful."

"It's a disgrace!" says his wife. "I'd never have expected to come across such material again. I was a tiny girl—a pretty little thing I was, everybody said as much—when I last heard the like. What about the Campaigns? What about our work here? "Haven't we . . ." she taps her husband on his arm, ". . . shouldn't all that be over and done with, dear?"

"I'm not sure what the issue is," says Lil. "If anything, this is the fragment which should put our minds at ease, isn't it? We are plainly now in the realm of the fictional. Proscribed material which we must simply refer to the Magistracy."

"But the place," says Wigbert, not at all his usual, surly self. "The name of it."

"I never thought to hear it again," says Mrs Cyre. "Not since I was such a rosy little dote."

Fafl is on his feet. "The name is pure invention. Dear Lil is, as always, quite right." He licks his lips, his eyes petitioning the boon of a returned glance from her, without success.

"Correct," say Lil, packing her things into her bag quite roughly. "It corresponds neither to any location in the known systems nor to any previously detected myth artefacts. Father?"

It is an appeal for support, for propriety.

"I think what Wigbert means, Lil," says Aren, "what has everybody a little rattled," he looks around, "is the *sound* of the name. It is not exact, but it does sound like a name we all know very well, does it not?"

The fat boy tugs at Wigbert's sleeve. "Father, do they mean—?"

"Quiet, lad," says the old man. "Here, dip a coocumber in the mustard. You'll grow."

"The station is to be closed," says Fafl.

At this summary and unexpected change of subject, every pair of eyes in the room settles immediately on the Stationmaster. "We are decommissioned," says that individual. Even Heft and Pack have turned to look, those two gentlemen being so reliably unresponsive and consistently oblivious that more than one of the station's occupants has from time to time wondered if there might be something amiss with their necks.

Fafl shrugs at Aren. "Not as difficult as I thought, Arenaceous." He sits on his stool. "There," he says, weaving his fingers, "the thing is said."

Lil's father will not return her gaze.

"The security breaches?" she says, finally, to the Stationmaster.

"Yes, dear." He nods and, before going on, looks up at her, and for a moment there is something in the way he does so that is not quite predatory, not quite wheedling. There might be an apology in it, or something else. "I'm afraid my remonstrations here were not taken seriously," he says. "Regardless, we are to pay the price."

"But the enq-enquiry," says Simon. "They kn-know who—"

"The Magistracy enquiry is ongoing," says Fafl. He turns his palms up. "I liaise. But no matter what the outcome, the station is to be closed. They will not risk the purity of the home world."

"When?" says Wigbert.

"I await confirmation, Mr Grim. Some days, no more."

"We're to be evacuated?" says Lil.

Fafl does not speak.

"Abandoned here?" says Mr Bull.

The Stationmaster leans back on his stool till the wall supports his bent back. "The Magistracy abandons no one, Mr Bull. The supply drops will of course continue. I have been persistent—indefatigable even—in my efforts to secure passage for as many as I can. But places, I'm afraid, have been strictly limited by my superiors."

"But there are so few of us," says Simon. "C-couldn't they just issue antidotes for eleven?"

"Twelve!" says the boy, who has this minute dropped a morsel of cucumber into his pocket for Mouse.

"Really, young Master Cyre?" says Fafl. "With the station under enquiry? A traitor among us?" He tutted, wagged his finger at the younger man. "They could not."

"I don't believe any of us is a traitor—no disrespect intended, Mr Fafl," says Mrs Cyre who at the same time manages to effect a sort of curtsey from her seated position. "There must be a mistake, and the Magistracy is sure to find that it's so!"

"How many places do we have?" says Mr Bull.

Fafl breathes in sharply, between discoloured teeth. "There are two," he says. "Two places."

Wigbert Grim's eyebrows travel to the very far north on hearing this information, but he remains tight-lipped. The old-fashioned clock on the wall behind Lil ticks its way through half a minute. On more than one forearm and in more than one nape, skin prickles and hairs stand. Aren stirs himself.

"We need to talk, calmly, all of us, Lil, and we need to come to a decision."

"Well we can make it simpler for you," says Mrs Cyre, gesturing towards Mr Cyre. "We renounced our nanos years ago. We've never expected to leave. So there—that's two out of it."

"I'm going nowhere," says Mr Bull. "No Marshal leaves a manned post." He looks at Heft and Pack, busy still with what food remains on the table. "And I think we can discount these two," he says. "That's five down," he folds his arms, "six remaining."

"I shall s-stay," says Simon. He, too, speaks with his eyes on Arenaceous Nell's daughter. "Of course . . . that is . . . of *course* . . . I mean . . ." His complexion has returned to the deep colour—more or less that of a fresh bruise—to which the others have become quite accustomed. "I mean . . . of *course* . . ."

"For pity's sake, Simon," says Mr Cyre.

"Let him alone, will you?" says Mrs Cyre.

"That's five then," says Mr Bull. "Two to choose."

"Actually, Mr Bull," says Fafl, "strictly speaking—"

"It's one," says Aren. "We choose one."

A general consternation, perfectly legible in the gathered countenances, prompts Fafl to speak.

"I'm afraid it's true," he says. "Though I am, of course, not worthy—a broken old man, a humble—"

"Why does he get to go?" says Wigbert. "It's a fix."

"Because those are my orders," says Fafl. "There will be no abrogation of my duty, I can assure you. Besides, any failure to comply with protocol could endanger the supply drops."

"And they will definitely continue?" says Mr Cyre.

"Of course," says the Marshal. "We are sentenced to remain here. Nobody is sentenced to death."

"Oh no," says Fafl, shaking his head with force.

"Doesn't all this make it simpler still?" says Mrs Cyre. "We have always agreed, we who remained here, that *in extremis* the youngest should be first. The boy must go."

"Agreed," says Simon, not at all hesitantly, and without the merest hint of a stammer. He, Aren and Fafl are all three intent on Lil. It is she who reddens now, under their scrutiny.

"Normally I would say so too," she says, "but there is another consideration."

Her lips tremble. This is a moment she has not foreseen—the one aching desire of her life, brought to a sharp point with a single utterance from the Stationmaster. She looks at the boy as he munches on a cucumber. It isn't cruel—it is too brutal to be merely that. What does it matter? What does it matter how she feels? The universe is indifferent. It sweeps aside what it does not need.

"I need time to think," she says, "as do we all. Let us make the decision at tomorrow's Review."

"Review?" says Wigbert Grim. "What's the point of another Review? There isn't one, that's what! The station is decommissioned, Lil. Nobody cares, girl."

"Mr Grim is quite right, dear," says Fafl. "In the time remaining—"

"No," says Lil. "The Reviews continue." She stands. "There is something about this new material. It has something to tell us, I believe, about whatever is going on out there."

Without waiting for their consent, she shoulders her bag and takes her leave. Outside, in the darkness, her feet take her along the walkway and past the curved stone bench. Among the trees at the edge of the wood, they find the narrow little path and take her down to the trellised arch and its little seat, and why shouldn't they? It isn't only Arenaceous Nell who comes here for comfort and counsel. Nor is it he who so lovingly tends the flowerbed.

CHAPTER THE FOURTH

CONTAINING AN ACCOUNT OF BETRAYAL, AND THE ARRIVAL OF A NEW PERSON ON THE WARBURG BY QUITE DIFFERENT MEANS.

NEVER BEEN KICKED in the stomach not in my life   never   not even in the camp   though it was not pleasant there   but magistracy torments are principally   chemical   and audiovisual   in nature   so no I'm pleased to say I haven't had the pleasure   and yet   and yet   I know the feeling   it was not possible   it would not have been   for the son of a magistracy warden to go unpunished   and no mere homespun beating would do   for it was not my *parent* who was to administer the penalty   but the *magistracy*   the warden   I don't blame him   or perhaps I do   never mind that   and so it was that I alone of the three   I alone   was arrested   and oh how I longed for the beating   but it did not come   instead the sterile process   the officious warden and his duties   I don't blame him   or perhaps I do   and I must say   now that I think of it   for an organisation dedicated to the eradication of fancy   they do like a bit of theatre don't they   sending uniformed officers for me   leaving the transporter at the wrong end of the village withal   so that I   cuffed   could be walked all through it   a little parade   and I the carnival queen I suppose   chaste   demur   eyes to the ground   fixed to it by the glue of shame   till at the village's edge I did look up   where I knew my angel would be watching from her window   and there she was   and I turned away as though she were the sun eclipsed   before either could communicate anything in the look   before my retinas could burn   and let myself be led on   and then there *it* was   my beating finally   the wind knocked out of me   that has never returned   and the reason I could describe for you   in some detail   how it is   a boot to the gut   for though it went unnoticed in the moment   as I neared the transporter   and my mind caught up with my eye   I knew I had seen   behind my angel and in the shadow   shirtless in the shadows of her bedroom   him

"Oh this is inspiriting," Fafl had said. "It is excellent."

He was pacing to and fro at Aren's back, the latter bent over his work—eye to the viewfinder, letting his retina dance over a throbbing mass of nanorhythmic pulsation. It accomplished nothing, but he wanted the Stationmaster to think him busy, and leave.

"And that it should be Mr and Mrs Cyre who lead the way. Fine people. Magistracy assets, both. How far along, do you know?"

"She enters her second trimester, I'm told," said Aren.

"Goodness. As the station's medical officer, I really ought to have been informed by now," says Fafl, "but never mind. Never mind. There have been any number of improprieties, after all. We have all been finding our feet here, have we not?"

Aren didn't know what improprieties Fafl could be referring to and wasn't curious to know. The fledgling settlement had several couples with young children among its number—an essential part of establishing a colony. Fafl, to whose oversight every aspect of station life was subject, had as a result a proprietorial air about him; his additional role as the island's doctor granted him the license to acquaint himself with the most intimate particulars of the inhabitants' affairs. He took great interest in the young ones, but this morning seemed especially delighted at the news of Mrs Cyre's pregnancy—it would be the first baby born on the Warburg.

"She must come under my direct superintendence at once," he said, taking a greyish handkerchief from his pocket and wiping his nose. "Second trimester. All is well, I'm sure, but we will take every precaution. A treasure!"

Aren didn't turn. He had done what had been asked of him and made Fafl aware of Mrs Cyre's condition. Now he performed a silent show of complete absorption in his work, making a meaningless adjustment to his viewfinder and tapping the return key on his console to no effect. Fafl said nothing more, but there were no retreating footsteps, nor any creaking of the door as it swung shut behind the visitor. The intruder. And then, that voice again—nasal, and unpleasantly close.

"And your work, Arenaceous? How goes *it*?"

Aren made one more adjustment to his device, let out a laboured breath, and took his eye away from the lens. Still, he did not wish to behold the Stationmaster—looking down instead at the notes he'd made on the screen of his tab.

"It goes well, Jasper." He shrugged. "Very well, actually. Izzy has been delighted at some of the schematics I've been able to provide. She was overjoyed with the—"

"Yes," said Fafl. Aren, with his eyes downcast, didn't see the grimace, the knit brow, at the mention of Izzy's name. "The Chief Mapper," Fafl continued, "has been *most* effusive regarding your contributions. Between that department and yours, Arenaceous, we are become quite the vanguard facility, you know. The Magistracy looks to us. You must allow yourself to take a small part of the credit for it."

Aren returned his eye to the viewfinder and Fafl resumed his pacing, the wooden floor groaning with even his slight weight, and continued to hold forth.

"The more of your analyses that can be submitted to Mapping, the more we understand what we are looking for. The more we understand, the more artefacts we can deliver to your scrutiny. The more artefacts, the richer your analyses. Progress is exponential. You see, Arenaceous?" he said. "You find yourself exactly in that place where you ought be, doing precisely that which you ought be doing. What does it really matter how any of us came to be here? I? You?

Here, at least, we can resource this talent of yours, this eye for the pattern, for the joining of dots. Here at least it might mean something."

Aren couldn't help himself—talk of the work could not fail to excite him, to brush aside any other concern that might modulate his demeanour in this particular company—and turned finally to look at his captor.

"I admit it. With these resources I can resolve anomalies that have plagued me for years. I am close to the paradigm, I'm sure of it. It is precursed already in my most recent findings. I have made quantum leaps I believed I might work a lifetime for." He smiled, despite himself. "I can see connections, perceive relations . . . give me six months with this laboratory, Jasper, and at the rate I'm going, I could fill the rest of my days working on the discoveries from that time alone, with no need for anything more sophisticated than a pencil."

He opens his eyes and there it is—somewhat chewed at the ferrule, it sits on top of the large, dog's-eared and leather-bound notebook on the desk beyond his foot; he has raised his leg and rested it on a stool to palliate the pain that comes and goes. Lil has been avoiding him since yester-night, and has neither collected the notebook for study nor brought him his sherry. Never mind—her recent insight has convinced him she is indeed mastering its contents, and he will need his wits about him later at the entertainment. He knows quite well what she will propose there and perfectly well what is to be done about it. What *has* been done about it, rather, for that wheel already turns.

His eyes settle on the notebook; he has no idea where his daughter might be—and has quite worn his leg out looking for her—but there is no doubt that her thoughts since Fafl's announcement will have turned, as his have, on the work. He must brace himself. Yesterday was difficult; today will be worse.

Six months. In the event, he had been given more time than that at his instruments—but not very much more.

---

above all else compliance   high value is also placed on tenacity   vigilance is encouraged   but compliance above all else   not a problem   why wouldn't I comply   a mere boy and already ruined   or would have been without the magistracy   the camp was off world   a cold moon   already ruined on arrival I was   empty   save for the aching   to this day that boot in my gut   and so the magistracy filled me didn't they   and the punitive aspects though severe were short-lived   in no time at all I was the very protegé   impressing with the degree of my compliance   the depth   my vigilance a terror to my fellow cadets   not all of whom fared well   but I did   I fared well as they fell away   the ones that deserved it   the magistracy liked that   and they liked me   they approved so they did   and I liked that   and so they educated me   inoculated I was against a number of standard toxins   as well as one or two more esoteric and rarified poisons   through exposure to them   I did well too   do believe I impressed 'em   snippets of what I believe may have been shake spears   buy bells and other canonical pathogens   many years I spent off world   an efficacious operative   search and destroy   though a mutual understanding between myself and my superiors quickly established itself that I was best suited to administrative positions   internal affairs if you like   more a lover than a fighter really   pogrom and assassination were to remain a mystery to me thank thank goodness executions more my bag given medical training I was to facilitate many years no expectation of seeing home again that is not the fate of a conscript not my fate no and I never hoped for it yet here I am a place on the home world the words used I knew it was a woman home world delegates always scramble their voices but you can tell a place on the home world but cut off from it an array out on the great vahr caldera its mission to preserve the purity of the inner hub to detect document archive and analyse contaminant transmissions to map their dissemination facilitating off world operations to approach an understanding of the aetiologies if such a goal proves attainable within the reach of our methods and to contain them creed spores faith pathogens narrative fabrications falsities and fictions infestations and so on a very particular mindset the words used to be situate on the home world once more and be forbidden intercourse with it quarantined save for the communiqués and gossip from incoming personnel a command of your own mind it would madden many I reassured didn't I flaunted my indifference that went down well one of our flagship arrays the words used you'll apply the finest technologies and I liked the sound of that and recruit the finest minds and then by way of illustration I suppose the name a name no magistracy operative could fail to have happened upon those past few years arenaceous nell

It was by far the genteelest gathering that any had witnessed since arrival at the Warburg. The Cyre's little cabin was resplendent, every interior surface cleaned to a shine and decked out in crisp linen and the best porcelain that could be found on the island—raided from the Station's formal tea set for entirely hypothetical Magistracy visitors, soon fallen into dusty disuse. The sunshine of a late Spring morning lighted up the lace curtains the lady of the house had made herself, and blazed through them to set the room aglow.

More were present, in truth, than the space could comfortably allow, but those who had not found a seat stood uncomplaining behind those who had, or perched on the arm of a chair, or a side cabinet, in an unlikely array of the most precarious physical postures. It mattered not—the gathering buzzed with the convivial hum of a fraternal and neighbourly excitement.

Izzy's sister had been especially busy. A magnitude of dainties teetered on a small, three-legged table in the middle of the room. A four-tiered cake stand was overcrowded with sugar-dusted pastries, and around it, platefuls of sandwiches made from fresh baked bread—the smell of it filled every nostril in the room with its sweet warmth—and stuffed with prize pickings from the vegetable patch. Cucumbers, salad greens and a delicious slaw dressed in mayonnaise sauce made with eggs from the chicken coop; even the very fowl had sent this little gift. The Cyres had never been so celebrated but, no doubt from a deep sense of gratitude, made an excellent show of having been born to it.

In truth, they'd been somewhat spurned by the island's burgeoning social circles. Such was their insistence on spouting Magistracy platitudes and flattering Fafl that their fellow colonists preferred on the whole to avoid their company. Now though, they found themselves at the very epicentre of Warburg life. Fafl was there and had squeezed himself between the happy couple, no doubt distraught at the physical proximity this necessitated on a settee made for two. Aren and Izzy, for the sake of propriety, were seated opposite each other, and stole glances over the treats—not one of which went unnoticed by her sister, beside whom sat Wig and the ever present Mr Bull.

The room was otherwise variously filled by the station's staff and officers. A number of them were parents, and tiny persons scampered around at below waist height, to be lifted intermittently and dandled on a knee, little chins testimony that they had passed by the cake stand on their way there. A young intern had been charged with the responsibility of making his way amongst the company, as best he could in the cramped space, with a teapot to refresh empty cups. This was principally for the benefit of the ladies, as most of the gentlemen in attendance, despite the early hour, held on tight to glasses of port. In tactful acknowledgement of the room's very youngest inhabitant, cigars had not been lighted.

In the middle of it all, Fafl's visage—despite his social distress—exuded such an expansive air of indulgence and magnanimity that the visitors might have supposed he himself, by dint of some improbable circumstance, to be responsible for the little bundle that lay on Mrs Cyre's lap, swaddled in a tiny blue blanket and quiet as a mouse. Its mother leaned forward and had eyes for only it; the uxorious Mr Cyre was somewhat worse for wear and had trouble keeping his open. At one of those natural lulls in the general discourse, the Stationmaster chose his moment, and stood.

"Colleagues," he began, "friends." He attempted a smile but the result was rather unpleasant. "It would be a dereliction if, as Stationmaster, I did not mark this day with a few humble words on behalf of the Magistracy." He paused to accept a polite applause and to wait for the children to be hushed. When all was quiet, he continued. "The station has its firstborn. A bran-new baby for the Warburg. The work of this colony, comrades, is not a matter of months, though some of you will spend no great time here, making your contribution. No, nor even of years. Many of us will live and die here. Even this child perchance." He produced another, equally tormented, smile. "Those of us who earn their antidotes—whether through atonement or simple attrition—will be replaced. Others will come."

He took a moment to compose some further observations, whereupon the baby let out a loud burp, and not all of those gathered could prevent themselves from sniggering.

"Goodness sake," said Mr Cyre.

"Let him be, will you?" said Mrs Cyre. "He's only a baby."

"What I mean to convey," continued Fafl, "is that the work we do here will outlive us. It is eternal, actually. We are the eye that does not blink. The eye that must never shut. We seek the poison. The Magistracy passes down its diagnoses and, in its tireless campaigns, administers the cure."

Another round of subdued applause made its way around the tiny room, that in its insistence contrived to communicate as much impatience with the longevity of the speech as it did approbation of the content.

"With this little boy," said Fafl, "we embed ourselves. We establish ourselves. It is our first first, as it were." He took his unattended and very full glass of port from the little table and raised it. "Here is to young Simon. And here is to the second first, and to many more firsts!"

A great cheer shook the room and frightened the infant. The celebrants were embarrassed into silence while Mrs Cyre attended to her newborn, cooing and rocking it till its tiny sobs subsided. Fafl, meanwhile had returned to the narrow space between its parents and begun to wring his hands in preparation for taking his leave. Aren stood.

"I believe I can provide one this minute," he said, not taking his eyes from Izzy's. That young lady beamed back at him. "I know I can, in fact. I want to tell you all that I have asked the Chief Mapper to be my bride. And I am very proud and happy to report that she has acquiesced."

A cheer, louder still, obliged Mrs Cyre to take the baby to an adjacent room, immediately upon which no fewer than half a dozen cigars were produced and one of them pressed into Aren's hand, which once free and the cigar between his teeth and lighted, was shook violently by every man present, save one. The ladies gathered and fussed over Izzy who instantly flushed with that same colour that was to become more closely associated with baby Simon in later life. Had poor Mr Cyre been sufficiently alert and clear-headed to observe anything at all, he might have noted the marked difference in how the company reacted to this latest news and this other pair—the swelling up of heartfelt affection that swept around the little room, the obvious esteem in which Aren and Izzy were held. In his befuddlement, it all escaped him—that sincerity, those spontaneous embraces, the invisible but obvious cord that bound these folk so tightly as it wound them around the two protagonists. But none of it escaped Fafl. That gentleman's singular reaction to such cheerful tidings, moreover, went unseen by all save Aren; as the attentions of their colleagues shifted, as it must, towards the beautiful Izzy, he was free to observe his old acquaintance, the only one in the room who remained seated.

If that comradely tether extended as far as the Stationmaster, it must have seemed a noose to him, so grim was the expression that stained his countenance. The eyes were kept down, the downturned lips a rictus, and the sunken cheeks betrayed the grinding of teeth. Such pallor! Never in his life had Aren noted so complete an absence of colour in a human face—such a cadaverous, bloodless grey in the flesh of the living.

"I'd see it again this minute," he thinks to himself, "if I but had a looking-glass to hand."

He is on the walkway between his quarters and the Committee Room, taking the most extraordinary few steps of his long life, and the cruellest. It is cool and still and the forest canopy is almost silent—just the slightest breeze disturbs it, not enough to mask the unceasing sighs of the environing sea. When he joins his fellow colonists at the table, it is without a word. There are some boiled greens and potatoes and a platter of fried fish but the mood is anything but festive—only the fat boy eats with any relish. The others chew glumly and sip grimly and appear thoroughly downcast, save for Heft and Pack, whose oblivious deportment is the same as it always has been. Fafl is on his stool, his expression somber but not those eyes; there is some simmering triumph in them. He will not bring them to bear on Aren.

"Waste of time," says Wigbert Grim. "I don't see why—"

"Me neither," says Mrs Cyre. "I—"

"Out of a sense of duty, I suppose," says Fafl. "The girl is dutiful." Here his eyes do flick in Aren's direction. "It won't take long, at any rate. And then, my dears, we must speak."

Lil, who is invariably the first to arrive, is today the last, and misses the exchange. As her father's doleful eyes follow her, she makes for the console to cue up the next fragment. She greets no one, and any greeting that might have been offered to her finds itself stopped in each throat. When she finds the file, she takes her own seat and plays it.

I took a few seconds to steady myself. A few breaths. Then I went inside.

Since making light of a breach would only arouse suspicion, I asked her to take you to bed. While she did that, I locked the book away again, pocketed the key and waited for her in the kitchen. My mouth was dry, skin clammy. A strategy resolved itself.

She returned and sat down at the kitchen table opposite me. I wasn't ready to look at her yet.

"She won't settle," she said. "She'll be hungry."

"I'll make her a hot chocolate," I said. "I'll make us all one."

I got up and went to put the kettle on. She said nothing, waiting for me to speak. I took my time getting the chocolate powder from the cupboard and the milk from the fridge. With my back to her, I spooned heaps of chocolate powder into three mugs, and a spoonful of sugar in each. The water was taking forever to boil.

"You shouldn't have done this," I said finally, taking my hand away from the teaspoon so as not to clatter it against the side of the mug. It went to my breast pocket instead and removed a slender plastic case.

"I don't know why I did," she said. "I never have before."

I knew it was a lie. The sight of them together—I had known instantly that it was habit. I kept my voice even as I divided the capsule I'd taken from the case and poured the powder into their mugs.

"Well," I said, "I can't let it go. There's procedure."

I stirred the chocolates and took hers and yours to the kitchen table.

"You can bring that to Lita in a little while."

It made an awful sense, now, that she had deceived me. I felt alone in the world again, as I had before I'd met her—as I always had, since Travma—but this was worse. Now I'd been robbed. I picked my own chocolate up but didn't join her at the table, instead leaning against the countertop and looking at the top of her bowed head.

"It'll be OK," I said. "They have ways of dealing with exactly this kind of situation. Drink your chocolate."

We both sipped in silence. She had tucked her feet beneath her and held her mug with both hands, trembling a little. I needed to reassure her. I wanted to, anyway.

"They're not going to sanction me in the middle of a campaign," I said. "They've given me a battalion for the taking of Suc and they need me in place. By the time it's ours this will have blown over, if we play our cards right. My name is in the hat for an admiralty . . ." I sighed. "So the timing is fortuitous."

I took my chocolate and sat opposite her. She looked up at me.

"Of course, I have to be seen to do something. Lita will need to be sanitized. Since today, as you say, was the only breach, the process needn't take long."

At the widening of her eyes I raised a hand.

"Don't worry—I should be able to pull a few strings. We're talking weeks, maybe a few months. I think I can arrange for her to sleep here and to attend the Day Centre in Leviston. We can probably arrange house arrest for you, as the mother of a young child. We'll get some technicians in and the cabinet out. You could also be cleared in a few weeks, if you're convincing."

She was tearing up. Tears of gratitude—she knew that what I proposed was potentially compromising. That it was dishonest. For a moment, I had to withstand her admiration. It was the first time she had looked at her man like that in a long time. A man putting his family first, before his principles and before his career—a good man, a husband, and a father.

Thankfully it was only a moment, its passing punctuated by the crash of her mug on the tiled floor and the drooping of those eyes as she slumped in her chair. I swept up the shards and wiped the chocolate away. Then I brought yours up to you.

The boy—sensible of the general mood—is, for once, quiet when the clip has been heard.

"Infuriating," says Lil through clenched teeth, to herself as much as to anyone else.

"Why so, my love?" says Aren.

Still she will not look at her father. Not having anything to pack away into her satchel—she hasn't take anything out of it—she feigns to busy herself with the console. "Archival Survey Review 1041.4 concluded. The committee offers no comment," she says into her mike, uninterested, today, in soliciting any formal response. She is more curious about personal reactions. When she speaks, it is not to Aren, but to the Stationmaster.

"I don't know why," she says, and bites her lip. "Yes I do—it's maddening not to know what's going on out there. To be at this second remove from the real. As though we have only our sight in a world made of sound, only our hearing in a silent universe. What is *happening* out there? What *are* these events these people react to? Where are these places? If it is all a fiction, who is the fiction for? What is the impulse?"

She wrings her hands, exactly mirroring the Stationmaster.

"And why now?" she continues. "We have not heard the like of this. There is nothing of the folk tale in it, nothing of doctrine, or the old credos. Nothing to which the known algorithms might apply."

"It is our lot, my dear," says Fafl. One of his hands reaches momentarily out to her, but is promptly returned to the other. "Our fate was sealed the day we were assigned here, each of us. You above all, I believe, recognise your duty. You and I, I should say. Come, in the time we have left we will persevere with your Reviews. We will help in whatever way we can. But now, we must speak of more pressing matters."

"Damn right," says old Wigbert. "We need a decision."

"There is no decision to be made," says Lil. "It has to be my father."

"Your father?" says Fafl. He is not pleased with the suggestion.

"This is what you were bound to say, Lil," says Aren, shaking his head, "and I know—"

"It has to be him." Lil addresses herself to the general company. "If all that we have done here is to mean anything, my father must take his work and present it to the Magistracy."

"Your father and I have discussed his work," says Fafl, his eyes narrowing on Lil, whose own eyes widen.

"You told him, father?"

"Lil," say Aren, "It cannot be me. And as you well know, I am not the only one here who could decipher my work for the Magistracy."

"Actually, it should be handed over to me, you know," says Fafl. "You no longer hold a research post, Arenaceous. Not for many a year."

"It isn't going anywhere, Jasper. I will put it into Lil's safekeeping, who alone can convey the importance of it."

Out of his sight, Lil colours.

"I do feel I should have it, you know," says Fafl. "Lil will be with me, won't she? Your fabled paradigm, after all—"

Aren tuts and shakes his head. "I long ago abandoned such terminology. Patience, Jasper. You must deliver it, Lil. Once the Magistracy knows of it, everything will change. Come now, escaping this place is all you've ever wanted."

Lil does not return her father's gaze. She looks at another, who in his turn also colours.

"Not all," she says. "I don't—"

Fafl takes a step forward and his voice, when he speaks, is shrill and insistent. "With my assistance, the Magistracy has brought its enquiry to a close. The perpetrator of the security breaches is known to them." He waits till he is sure that all eyes, and ears, are upon him.

"It is Arenaceous Nell."

Heft and Pack, whose eyes and ears had not been included, lift their heads out of their bowls, and several moments of bafflement pass silently between them before they resume dining. The boy has a spoon in his mouth but does not eat.

"Tell 'em to start again, then," says old Wigbert. "Nonsense, is what that is! Some sort of contumely, I'd wager Mr Fafl, possibly emanating from yourself."

"It is absurd," says Lil.

"I don't know which of us would be capable of such a crime," says Mrs Cyre, "I really don't. But Mr Nell? Not in a—"

"It's true," says Arenaceous. "I have confessed it."

Whatever exclamations the colonists produce on hearing this, they go unnoticed by father and daughter, who each in the instant sees only the other. Both pale. One takes steady breaths and grips his knees. The other's mouth hangs open.

"So you see, Lil," says Aren, finally, "it must be you."

CHAPTER THE FIFTH

HOW THE HELPFUL SIMON CYRE CAME TO LIL'S AID, AND HOW THE YOUNG BRIDE OF A TROUBLED MR NELL CAME TO HIS.

It is the middle of the morning, ten of the clock. She sits, dwarfed by stacks of handwritten notes and folded printouts, where the sunshine through a roof light makes a brilliant rhombus in a corner of the room. The eyes tire less quickly in this light than under the flickering buzz of the overhead strips, so she prefers to leave those off and work where she has arranged her desk and two small trestle tables, and piled them high.

It is the largest room on the island and once thrummed with a score or more of busy little bees just like her as they thumbed through indices, mulled over anomalies, muttered amongst themselves. The Hive, they had aptly called it—the Station's data processing facility. It had been a cheerful place, though Lil knows this only from her father's recollections; she was yet a young child when the others began to leave.

This morning it is silent and there are just the two drones at their work—Lil in her patch of sunshine and, at the far end, his desponding and crumpled brow dimly outlined in the dusty cone of dirty yellow light from a desk lamp, young Simon Cyre, afflicted with a grievous case of the dismals. He half-heartedly busies himself with an arrangement of documents on his desk. A pair of earphones sits on his head at an angle that leaves one ear uncovered, in case she should say his name. This morning, she has not. But he, from time to time, lifts his eyes from his work and looks at her. From his vantage point, she is backlit in the sunbeam, hair incandescent, her face eclipsed in shadow except where the features of her profile are softly traced by the solar brush—the curve of her nose, the lip she bites absent-mindedly in her absorption.

How many times has he sat and gazed like this, thankful for his place at her side? A thousand? It matters not to him—each morning is like that first morning, years ago, when he stumbled in here, emboldened by some half-considered excuse to speak to her, only to find her in tears and, before he could ask her why, in his arms.

"Oh, Simon," she'd sobbed. "It's too much! I can't do it."

"Do what?"

But she wasn't listening. "I am not my father!" she spat. "I'm an analyst, not a theoretician. I already have the archive to organise, and Papa has left me quite a mess, I can tell you. I can't even find all of the artefacts, never mind impose an order upon them. It's like the stars in the sky, like . . . and now *this!*" She indicated a large leather notebook on her desk, and burst into tears. When at last he found the nerve to look down, he made the quite remarkable discovery that he was squeezing her tight, and stroking her hair. Her breaths were hot on his shoulder and after a time they began to slow. "It's too much," she said, her voice a little steadier. She looked up at him, then stepped back in surprise when she saw that he was chuckling softly.

"Well!" she said, "If you—"

"Forgive me, Lil." He put his hands in the air to appease her but he was unable to quell his mirth; she, for her part, had flushed almost to the hue of a peeled beetroot. "It's just, I thought . . . I thought there must be some terrible difficulty," he said. "Something insurmountable. I—"

Lil's hands had gone to her hips. She looked as though she'd been very freshly peeled indeed, and was poised to return the favour.

"Fine," she said, a coolness in her voice that couldn't have been more at odds with the heat of her complexion. "If *that's* the way—"

"Calm yourself, Lil," he said, with an assuredness that surprised them both. "It really couldn't be simpler. The solution is mathematical. What is that old profanity? Cross to bear?" He found himself at a tangent, having rather lost his line of thought. "And too great for one alone, you say," he went on quickly, observing from her folded arms and the one cocked eyebrow that he had better get to the point. "I therefore propose we make it two."

From that day to this, Simon has come to the cabin to make himself an amanuensis to her. They work in silence much of the time, but not all of it. As well as the cursory little exchanges that the work necessitates, he has become accustomed to her confidences, just as he had been in childhood. He has become reacquainted with her thirsting for the wider world, and newly acquainted with her study of her father's work—and has even on occasion had the temerity to put forward his view on this matter or that. Whenever he does, there is never the slightest trace of the stammer.

That no words have caught in his throat this morning is because there have been none to catch. Today is different—impelled by habit, the object of his gaze has come to do her work as always. Perhaps she needs the distraction, perhaps she hopes to find in these latest audio fragments some further clue that might help her make sense of recent events. Perhaps she moves and works as an automaton might—animated but unconscious, numbed to the horror of her father's fate.

"It must be you," that gentleman had said to her at last evening's Review.

For some moments, she had been unable to do anything but stare at the old man.

"This is a lie," she whispered, finally.

"Of course it's a lie!" said Wigbert. "A damned lie!"

Arenaceous Nell said nothing. He trained his eyes on his daughter's and answered with them, and when her shoulders slumped came perilous close to losing his equanimity.

"Why would you do this?" she said. "You, who have raised me to put duty before all else?"

The old man shrugged.

"How many years have I whittled away at my work, Lil? At my theory?" His hands came together then as though he were praying to her. "I have been starved of data. I had a hypothesis, girl, and I wanted to test it. That's all."

"And now that you have your data?" said Lil. "The result?"

None of those present had heard Lil speak in so stony a tone to her father. For his part, he seemed to answer in silence again. Father and daughter, locked into each other for the longest time, till in fact it became more than the others could endure. Fafl stood but, before he could speak, Aren broke his silence, still oblivious to anyone but Lil.

"Conclusive," he said.

Simon Cyre sat up.

"I'm happy for you, father," said Lil, "And for this, you have condemned us all to this place. To live and die here." She held back a sob.

"No, Lil." Aren steadied his voice. "Not you."

Fafl was swaying from foot to foot, pulling at his beard.

"No, not you, my dear," he said. "Though I did not know of this theoretical work of your father's till very recently, and I certainly ought to have done, he assures us that you have the mastery of it." A smirk stretched his wet lips until he stifled it. "We will deliver it to the Magistracy, you and I, together."

Lil shook her head, uncomprehending.

"But I'm a child of the Warburg, and therefore of the Magistracy, and a child no longer—even if I could survive the buoys, I have no billet anywhere but here."

"No, dear," said Fafl. "No, indeed. But," he licked his lips, "as the Stationmaster's wife, that will be no hindrance."

it took me by surprise the proposal experienced some uneasiness at first I did   wondering if my superior was aware of the personal connection   even superficially   and if so was not uneasy at the prospect of reigniting an old and seditious association   but I could hardly deny his suitability could I   the author of a treatise that had caused such reform   such success in the field   and in the end I relented   and in relenting experienced great joy actually   in as much as I am capable or indeed inclined to recognise such a state   I who have suffered so   I *had* him   had him press ganged   our youthful indiscretion providing the necessary leverage   finally something good had come of it   I'll not soon   not ever in fact   forget the day I hid in the trees and watched him wade ashore   and went to wait for him   such pleasure   oh great day   he who had squandered my liberty   and had his spotted disgusting adolescent way with my angel   rolling up his sleeve for his nanoplant   he who had squandered my liberty   so that I might take his   for all the good it did me   what *is* it about him   what is it about me   when will the steel toe of this boot quit my belly   why must life move along not in a good straight line   but in these nasty little circles   a horrible fugue   a monstrous ditty with the same sickly motif never ending   this particular iteration of it going by the name of izzy   a young recruit I had set my eyes on   should not the stationmaster take a wife   and show by example how a place is to be settled   how a settlement is to become a place   but she was drawn to him   of course   and he to her   and his incarceration was soon become the very making of him   just as mine had been of me   I thought so anyway   for a time   and so as he had been a spectator to my shame   now here was I a bystander to his glory   the twisted mockery of their love   the gushing approval   quite embarrassing   of the magistracy for his abilities   I did not convey the praise of course   so it lodged in my ears alone   and resounded there

The reader might spare a thought for the colonial newlywed, who is faced with a conundrum quite specific to a life lived in the confines of a closed community—how does the discreet person effect a honeymoon? It is a question of great delicacy. None of their fellows would have denied that time to Izzy and Aren, those precious days wherein the bond of love is sealed, the tender slipway from which is launched a marriage and—yes—a family.

The ceremony was brief and performed without sentiment. The only persons permitted to conduct such an affair were the Stationmaster and the medical officer and, since Fafl was both, it was that misanthropical gentleman who officiated. He sped through the requisite formalities like a man who as a matter of urgency had somewhere else to be, and feigned to give equal attention to sundry other files that lay open on his desk. Izzy and Aren sat across from him, hand in hand. Not even Fafl's dry, cheerless drone could detract from their joy—nor indeed that of the island's other inhabitants, who had gathered in their entirety and pressed up against Fafl's office so tightly that the door could not be closed shut. The head of Wigbert Grim poked through it; he had been sufficiently gallant to take Izzy's sister by the arm and pull her there with him, to hear the words said and set eyes upon the happy couple.

The transaction complete, Aren and his new bride were swept up by the crowd and deposited in the Hive, where the floor had been cleared to make way for a celebration. They were young, all of them, and none cared to dine or for any such formalities. There were at that time a number of personnel capable of picking out an air and immediately upon arrival—an ionfiddle and an optiharp having been produced—they did just that and the thing was a dance.

Only Fafl—who alone on the island declined either to show his face or to convey his felicitations—and a few enterprising souls who had snuck away to deck out Aren's cube (which was to be the lovers' nest for the days that followed) with bunting, sweet cakes, wine and other thoughtful little gifts, were absent. For some hours the Hive rocked and creaked to waltz and reel and when legs were finally tired out, there was one last dance along the walkway to the hymeneal chamber where Aren and a bashful Izzy were bid good night and the happy crowd melted away—some to their own assignations, others to serenade the night with sotted snores.

So adept had the courting couple become at picking out the island's lonelier trails that for days it did indeed seem as if they had gone away. There were none who could claim to have caught more than the most fleeting glimpse of the pair in the purlieus of the beach, rounding the headland at the end of the it or disappearing into the woods. Only each evening, with winking candlelight making a coquette of the kitchen window, was there evidence the cabin was occupied.

The two occupants were for a time permitted this delicious fancy—that they lived in world of their own, a world where all was well and always would be so long as the one loved the other: a circumstance that seemed perfectly assured to both. Three nights should have passed them by in this state. Two did. On the evening of the third day, as the blissful pair, in the absence of Izzy's sister and her superior cooking skills, sat down in fits of giggles to a thoroughly burnt bird, a porridge of overcooked vegetables and the compensatory attractions of good old sherry, there was a knock at the door. Pack had been sent to fetch Aren and bring him to Fafl's office.

"It couldn't wait, I suppose," said Izzy, hands on hips, but neither of them expected a response from Pack.

"I'll be back straight away," said Aren. "Why don't you fix us up a punch?"

He followed Pack's broad back along the walkway, warm with wine and not *too* put out, expecting Fafl to manufacture some trifling irritation he would brush aside before returning to Izzy and a last night of connubial sequestration. The Stationmaster's office door swung open, despite the cold wind, and the Stationmaster sat in his coat, making notes in the mean light of a single lamp, dirty fingertips protruding from his gloves. Whenever he was granted the sight of those fingernails, Aren felt a renewed gratitude for his rude health, and for his generally having no need of doctoring.

"There you are, Arenaceous." Fafl didn't look up. "Yes, do sit."

Aren already had. "Bitter night to be called out on, Jasper," he said.

Fafl put his pen down and peered at his old associate.

"Oh Arenaceous," he said, shaking his head. "You don't know how bitter." He drew the lapels of his overcoat tight together with a bony hand, observing the other's seeming imperviousness to the cold, the easy posture—fingers woven, one straight leg laid over the other. "And that much more bitter for you than for any other, I'm afraid to say." His expression was, if anything, more pinched than usual. More pained. The newlywed raised an eyebrow.

"How so?"

Fafl leaned forward, into the light of the lamp. Illumined from above, a hooded brow threw his sunken eyes into shadow and a protuberant nose did the same for his lips.

"With immediate effect, your function is discontinued at the Warburg. It has been assigned to another location."

"Just like that?" said Aren. The revelation was so startling he could give it no credence, and was therefore not at all startled. It had to be a joke.

A shrug from the Stationmaster. An expression of his helplessness. He had the look about him of a gentleman who wished more than anything else to dig a hole in the ground, and to get into it.

Aren uncrossed his legs and sat up, sobering. "What other location?"

Fafl shifted in his chair. "I don't know that, Arenaceous, but I could certainly find out. Why? Would you like to go there?" He shrugged. "I could make enquiries. You appreciate of course that you, a criminal, have little in the way of bargaining power."

"Please do inquire," said the young scientist. "You speak of my life's work, Jasper. The very reason you brought me here. *Of course* I must go. We can be ready in no time—perhaps just a few days for Izzy to complete a handover. It'll give you time to authorise the antidotes. I'll let her know we—"

"The Mapper stays," said Fafl, at a noticeably higher pitch. "There can be no question of the Warburg's losing . . . that capacity." His face retreated, out of reach of the lamp's weak light. Only his hands remained visible, resting on the desk. "The work of the Mapping department must be kept here, at this secure location, at all costs, Arenaceous. You appreciate this. It must be where the archive is, the very material we are here to map. Yours on the other hand is essentially a theoretical function." He waved a hand dismissively. "It could be carried out anywhere."

Aren looked over his shoulder. The wind was biting its way through the wine and he would have asked Pack to close the door, but the latter had gone away on some other errand. Aren turned back to Fafl.

"Then what do I do?"

For a moment, he thought no reply would come, so long did it take the other to deliver it.

"What indeed," Fafl said, finally. Something like humour sparkled in his eye. "I do not envy you, Arenaceous." The hands tapped out a jaunty rhythm on the desktop, then fell still. "As Stationmaster, it falls within my remit to annul a union, so long as all parties are amenable. It would strengthen your case for a transfer. You need only make it known, to me and to Izzy, that an annulment is your wish. I should do everything I can, of course, to help."

Aren snorted. "Impossible. I will die before I part with her."

"Quite," said Fafl. "I thought you would say as much. Then we must play the hand that has been dealt us. But always know this, Arenaceous," he said, his face once more illumined in the lamplight. "You *must* always know, and Izzy too, that such a course is open to you. I will not be so monstrous as to withdraw the offer—to so cruelly deny either of you any chance to pursue your professional goals. Such gifted people, both. There now!" He slapped the desk and stood. The conversation was at an end. "You will remain with us at the Warburg. We'll find something for you to do, of course. We have no archivist, as such. Perhaps that."

"Filing?" said Aren, getting to his feet.

"It will be a pity to see your talent go to waste," said Fafl, "but there we have it." He gestured towards the door. "You have made your choice."

When he opens his eyes, the empty sherry bottle sits on top of the old, dog's-eared notebook. His daughter avoids him still, so today he hobbled off and fetched it himself. No sooner had he placed it where it was than he sank into his chair to doze on its contents. Now he awakes from his dreams, from those old and evanescent memories. He eyes the bottle and book warily, mindful of the connection, then stirs himself—it is time for today's entertainment.

How he had wanted, when he told Izzy of the choice he had made, to spare her the burden of any guilt! How he had set his mind on cheerful application to his much diminished responsibilities! And how he had failed!

It should have been the happiest of times, that first year with Izzy. It should have been enough for him to lay eyes on her sleeping face each morning. What wouldn't he give for that sight now? But it wasn't enough. His strength had failed him. Stripped of the work that had so animated him, he'd become surly, even with her, and had taken to drink and to his own company. His colleagues hadn't known him. Even Wig began to keep his distance. Poor, patient Izzy had to search for him more than once, only to find him insensible beneath some tree or flat out down on the sand.

She'd come to him finally, as that year had drawn to a close, and fallen to her knees and wept. She'd pressed the notebook, made with her own hands, into his, and implored him to use it, to work again that his troubled mind might find some peace and that she might have her husband returned to her. He, seeing her pain, had complied. It had seemed a deception, at first, a mere avocation—a harmless falsehood to put her at her ease, but bit by bit he had reengaged with the work, drunk a little less and loved her all the more.

In the Committee Room the others have waited, but none greet him. Not even Lil—even before he takes his seat, she presses play.

Your mother would laugh if she could see me on this safety line, clambering down over slimy wet rock like a madman. From time to time I slip but the line holds; Evans and Zwickl know what they're doing even if I don't. Am I panting? I suppose I must be.

But patience is impossible—I can see it now, the outline of it so familiar from above, where the cliff face curves downward, sweeps inward, narrows at the edge and then widens a little where the stone protrudes over a chasm and the vines hang from either corner. The shape of that chasm and the protruding stone from above is exactly—exactly, Lita—like the plume and pi insignia on the left breast of my tunic, and yours.

And any number of places—coffee outlets, cereal boxes; the shape has become ubiquitous and impossible to police, a motif that has lost its meaning for the masses. For them, it's an assignable symbol. But not for us. We alone honor the source. We alone remember. We alone bear the insignia—the mark of everything we are bound to destroy.

You might as well have been born in the uniform, with me for a father. I've given my life to Truth and most of that time to its phalanx, Light. They call us a sect. Be ready for that. They will call you a witch. A zealot.

And why wouldn't we show zeal? Who has lit the burning edge of the Third Enlightenment, if not us? Who has pushed back the shadows? Whose blood fuels the flame?

I was on Travma, after all. Your grandparents were first contact settlers there. Did you know that? I was five. They were agricultural scientists, part of a first wave team working on infrastructural and productivity programs, in preparation for cleansing.

I was there the day the Travmani came to the settlement. Scientists, teachers, builders—this was the threat they came to deal with. They said they were the last hope for their people. That they were defending their civilization.

So how could they be such animals?

I'm told I was feral when found, many weeks later, living in the ruins of the compound. Who knows what I'd been eating. I don't like to think. Much of what I once remembered, I have made sure to forget. It was Truth that found me—a recon mission for the reprisals that followed.

***

"Crumbs!" says the fat boy afterwards. "'ow 'orrible!"

"Quiet yourself, child," says Wigbert. "Here, have a go at them parsnips."

"Something's wrong," says Lil. Nobody replies so she goes on. "For something like this to come through on a home world frequency isn't right. Something bad is happening."

"Come come, dear," sats Fafl. "As you yourself have observed, we know neither the source nor the intended recipient. The purpose is unclear. The veracity—"

"You miss the point, Jasper," says Aren.

Fafl glares. "Do I?"

"What is the point then?" says Wigbert. "There *is* no—"

"The frequency," says Lil. "Putting the content aside for a moment—the broadcast originates at some immense distance, or it wouldn't be so fragmented. That is a bandwidth issue. But it has certainly been relayed from a location on the home world. A location in this hemisphere, and at our latitude. Why? Who on the home world would do that? Who could? Something is very wrong." For a moment, her wringing hands once again mirror Fafl's. "It's maddening," she says "not to know what's going on out there."

"Well then you must certainly put your mind at rest, my dear," says the Stationmaster in rather more stentorian fashion than that to which the company were accustomed in him, and getting to his feet to put his hat on, "for soon you will see for yourself."

CHAPTER THE SIXTH

INTRODUCES SOME PARTICULARS RELATIVE TO LIL'S BIRTH, AND OTHERS RELATIVE TO MATTERS BETWEEN THE STATIONMASTER AND HIS EMPLOYER.

UNTIL A CHANGE came   in my understanding   of the magistracy's interest in his work   a newly noticed nuance to the timbre of the queries   the tone of the constant question   that had been asked from the beginning   *has he found the paradigm*   the question it seemed to me   and astounded I was that I hadn't till then discerned it   was asked more in trepidation than in hope   it seemed to me   that the magistracy did not *wish* a paradigm to be found   I don't know why   how should I know   a footsoldier   a frontline worker   if the word frontline can be applied to a place such as this   this lonely spot   mind it would madden many the magistracy had told me   on my acceptance of the post   and indeed I was maddening   officiating the lovers' putrid matrimony no less   and so a madman I did a mad thing   put in a request for his transfer   knowing that if successful he would lose his work   or his love   taking great delight in his quandary   one or the other   preferably his love   but no   no   he chose her over it   and I hoped even then that the magistracy would take him forcibly   he upon whom they had had lavished such approbation   plaudits and pæans   such excruciating eulogies   and then of course   latterly   the edge in that voice   the fear of him   but no   no   they smelled a rat didn't they   saw right through my ruse   read the mischief writ in my petition   above all they fear contamination   now they could taste it   authorised the transfer of the function but not of the man   soiled now as I was by this latest intrigue   we have other arrays   I was told   other aetiologists   less troublesome stationmasters   and besides   he is close to delivering this so-called paradigm of his   which we no longer seek   we fear the consequences of such a thing in fact itself a fiction a poison that must be quarantined it was the first time I had heard the magistracy use such a word fear and the celerity was quite breathtaking I must say fair took my breath away the swiftness with which they chose to cut their losses isolate the germ it seemed to me shut down the array didn't they

※

When you came to me that day in the Hive I knew, of course I knew, that it was to press suit. Which of us could remember the last time you were able to keep a secret from me, or maintain any kind of pretence? It was spelled out in the semiotics of your stammering hesitation, signalled in the semaphore of your awkward gait, your trembling hands and your restless, evasive gaze. You were an open book. It was sweet.

And the truth was that though I hadn't the faintest notion how to respond to the approach, the merest understanding of what might be involved in such a negotiation, or the trace of an opinion on whether or not it interested me, I was sorely pleased to see you. Years of adolescence had made us, if not strangers to each other, then at least a little strange. That new shyness that comes of coming of age—the only possible pairing on the Warburg, we had been two magnets with like ends turned inward, and therefore repelled.

That you loved me in this new way—totally—was obvious. That I could, or would, reciprocate—though with hindsight I realise there was never a question—was not. But I had missed you. I had missed the closeness and the confidences but more than either, I had missed the carrying. I remembered and longed for that feeling of being lifted, and taken along effortlessly, and put back down in a place of my choosing. My burdens were heavier, more onerous than they had been when we'd last been companions. An ageing parent made a keeper of me and a newly inherited archive had made me a clerk. I was a grown woman, ready for life, and yet the matrices of possibility that both fuelled my wanderlust and promised to satiate it were diminishing. I did not know if I would have it in me, even if the increasingly unlikely opportunity *were* to arise, to leave the Warburg while my father lived. There was the weight of all of that and then there was this new thing—my father had dropped his notebook, his life's work, in my lap. It was a cause of increasing agitation in him that I master it. A new inheritance.

And I couldn't. I couldn't master it. I have not very often found myself at the limits of my intellect, but my father's work confounded me. It was . . . not what I had expected. It seemed he had long since taken his enquiry beyond the confines of known theory, the language he used entirely decoupled from any concrete reference points that I might have begun with. I like number, and shape. But here, language itself was the currency. The connections he made were so . . . lateral. Intuitive. It was almost transcendental in its tone and verged, it seemed to me, on the metaphysical heresies. Though that could only be a suspicion, since I did not understand a word of it.

That the great aetiologist's work might find him skirmishing on the frontiers of such perilous thought should have come as no surprise. But his attraction to the perimeters of doctrine seemed wilful to me. As though it were in the heresies themselves that he sought his paradigm. What was it that had pushed—or pulled—him out there? *To find the centre, begin at the edge*, he had scribbled in a margin. *The path to truth is paved with lies.* I was baffled and, for once in my life, beaten. And so when you walked through the door, saw my anguish and made a salve of yourself, I was more than willing to fall into your arms. An old habit was reestablished. A way of getting back up out of the cove when the tide turned, or of reaching the first branch of a tree. A simple matter of gravity.

And yet, things are never really simple, are they? I settled you in to your new archival role, which you took to with relish, and I applied myself with renewed fervour to the notebook. It was no mere vanity that compelled me to master it. My father needed me to—that much was apparent from the upset and anxiety I observed in him at the slowness of my understanding. But there was vanity too. Ego. A warm, nauseous wave of shame washed through me whenever I sat over those pages. I was humiliated, occluded from whatever fire burned in them that set my father alight so.

Until I saw it in you. The glow of it, reflected in your face one day when I arrived early to find you there, as you always were before me, and hunched over the notebook. I knew, instantly, that for you it had the meaning that escaped me. I might not have been able to decipher my father's work, but I could read you. You were apologetic, keen to hand it over and to get on with your work on the archive, but I could not unsee the expression on your face. I hadn't seen it before. I had to see it again.

You became my tutor. Each morning, you would sit with me and we would read a part of the notebook together—methodically, page by page. Your face would light up, just as it had that first time and, with great patience, you would expatiate upon that which, it seemed, came so effortlessly to you, in an attempt to impart it to me. And you would fail. Or, to put it more accurately, I would. On the one hand, I was greatly displeased with this new development. To be tutored by you was irksome, especially since I made such a poor student. I had never before felt so behindhand in your presence. I did not like it. As it had been when mother taught me about all the places in the world that I had never seen, and probably never would, the substance of the lessons was something I could not touch, or see, or grasp. My appreciation of its very existence was vicarious. The truth, as usual, was at a remove. A hidden sun's light bouncing from you, a moon. I could only infer it.

Though I soon saw the futility of my efforts, I was mesmerised by the pleasure you took in my father's work. I could not see how something which brought you such joy could be a blasphemy. Partly because I entertained the faint hope that something in my mind would adjust itself, opening the way to understanding, and partly because of how good it was to see you that way, I persisted with our morning lessons. It was, if nothing else, a way to be close while distracted from the imperative of a threatened courtship.

But there was something else—I knew that my father's mortality weighed heavy with him. If it couldn't be through me, his work might live on through you. The prospect then arose that it would be you whose passage from the Warburg we would need somehow to secure. But that was a distant eventuality. For now, I could be reassured that, albeit by unexpected means, I was honouring my father's wishes. You knew how important that was to me, and how deep the shame I felt at my own failure—and so once in a while, though you couldn't make me understand, you would feed me a crumb that I could bring to him. Something I could tell him to spare him his worry and me my embarrassment. Something like "Tell him you believe his work on the Jakati Epics is key. He'll like that."

In the late October of the first year of his marriage, Arenaceous Nell, who had by that time recovered a small measure of self-possession and who, if only for Izzy's sake, had found some degree of personal equilibrium in the exacting particulars of the archive—all the time, at her insistence, working away at his own handwritten theorems—was to receive the greatest blessing; she came to him at the waterline one morning, knowing how he would walk along it on his circuitous route to a day's dull work, took his hand, pressed it to her belly and told him she was with child.

"But then you mustn't be out!" he had managed to say to her, once he had squeezed her—timidly—at least a dozen times and, to her obvious amusement, emitted a panoply of wordless exclamations. "It's icy cold today!"

She put a stop to his stuttering protestations with a warm hand placed softly on his cheek. It was always enough, whatever the circumstance, to hush him.

"Don't be silly," she'd said, "and calm yourself," and with that she'd made off in the direction of Mapping.

Even now, after so many intervening years, he remembers watching her as she crossed the sand and slipped between the trees, the very picture of equanimity. If only she could reach out to him still with her palm, bestowing on him just a little of that poise. Fafl has this minute taken his leave, having come with expected news. The hand that grips the bottle is white-knuckled; the other trembles.

He remembers that she wore her dark green overcoat and a pair of burgundy boots. He remembers the salt air, the gulls yelling. He remembers how he felt, not for the first time, a child in the comforting presence of a grownup—that whatever trials this new adventure brought, he would play the skittish neophyte and she the steady, guiding hand. It was the last time he can remember feeling that way.

When Izzy had begun to show, and Aren had (somewhat) calmed himself, and the happy news had long since been shared with their jubilant colleagues, the Cyres—now the custodians of a rambunctious one-year-old—once again took up their seats at Sunday lunch. They had not been in attendance during those first months of their own familial bliss. It might have been a design of Izzy's sister or perhaps they had insinuated themselves; Mrs Cyre in particular had evidently reached the conclusion, despite the brevity of Simon's life thus far and the presence of several more established families on the island, that she and—to some lesser degree—her husband were the Warburg's preeminent authorities on parenthood.

Whatever the reason, that Izzy should spend some time in the baby's company seemed a good idea to Aren. That she hadn't displayed any curiosity about it didn't trouble him unduly, though the little thing had been dandled by every other female on the island—it was just his Izzy, forever inwrapped in her work and inattentive to the commonplace concerns of less gifted souls. The maternal drive would no doubt overtake his wife, either during her pregnancy or upon giving birth, but it might just be that, in the case of this otherworldly academic, nature needed a little nudge.

Izzy's sister had made a special effort for Simon's very first Sunday repast. There was meat pie—a great indulgence on the Warburg—and a platter of sole from the abundant fishing ground that surrounded the island; squashes from her own patch; sweet peas too, and shortbreads for after.

"Would you like to hold him dear?" said Mrs Cyre the moment they'd taken their places at the table. Izzy shook her head but only Aren seemed to notice; before she could say a word the child was placed in her lap.

"You're not supposed to hold them by the legs, mind," said the proud mother. "We know that now, don't we Mr Cyre?"

"Goodness' sake," said the person addressed, addressing himself to the pie.

Aren gazed at Izzy so keenly as she held the baby that he didn't doubt she felt his eyes on her. He said nothing and neither did she, the spoffish Mrs Cyre cooing all the time and contorting her face into a series of exaggerated expressions for Simon's amusement. This entertainment was interrupted when Izzy gave a sudden start.

"What is *that*?" she said, looking from Mrs Cyre to Aren.

"What, dear?" said Aren.

"*That*. That mark on its arm. Did I do that?"

"Oh, that," said Mrs Cyre. "Calm yourself, dear. It's just a tiny bruise where Fafl administered the nanoplant." She sighed. "I'm sure I don't know why the poor little thing had to be troubled so soon—it isn't as if he can swim, is it? And it isn't—why, Izzy, you've gone deathly pale!"

Izzy had a hand to each side of her head.

"Take it," she whispered, and indeed the baby's mother had to do just that before it could tumble from Izzy's lap. There was some commotion as a glass of water was fetched, and more than one hand put to Izzy's brow.

"I'm sorry," she said at last, "I thought for a moment I'd hurt it."

"Well you didn't, dear," said Mrs Cyre. "You really mustn't be so timid. You'll be a wonderful mother, I'm sure. Simon likes you," she mumbled into the top of the baby's head, "don't you, little pumpkin?"

Arenaceous, having himself dropped off, drops the bottle too, and sits up with a start—but it is empty, and spins harmlessly on the floor.

Fafl's tidings have prompted him to drain it too quickly and he is light-headed.

The rest of that long-ago meal had gone off as Sunday lunches usually did, with the taking, Izzy excepted, of too much food and wine, and the loosening of belts, and the attendant loosening of tongues, and the putting of the world to rights. Inwardly, though, Aren had hated to see Izzy so at a loss with what ought to have come so naturally. The guilty, apologetic glance she'd shot at him across the table when Simon was taken away from her had pierced him like a blade.

Of course she insisted on continuing to work and he thought it just as well; talk of motherhood invariably made her anxious and the demands of running the department, far from depleting her of energy seemed rather to sustain her. For some weeks, Aren avoided the subject of the baby altogether—that matter would no doubt take care of itself. For now, when working or talking excitedly with Aren about her latest charts, Izzy could be something like her old self and therefore so could he. He would rebuke himself in times to come for this second, selfish impulse, tormented by the idea that he might have seen the trouble coming in time to do something about it.

It came in her final trimester, which isn't to say that the first two had been free of care. For some months she had been under Fafl's watchful eye; the Stationmaster had been most attentive, in fact, providing physicks to see her through what would otherwise have been debilitating bouts of sickness and quickly resolving a bleed in her fifth month which had frightened them greatly. Throughout, it had appeared to Aren that there were two Izzies—the dauntless scientist and the anxious, uncertain mother-to-be—and that they remained entirely separate. As her ever-swelling belly became an impediment even to sitting at her desk, however, the disquiet of the one seemed to infect the well-being of the other.

Izzy had always been in the habit of taking work home and sitting with it in the evenings while Aren read, or smoked, or dozed, or worked—at her prompting—in his own notebook. During the pregnancy it had become even more important an activity for her. With a stack of files in her lap and a console to hand she could be content and even, at times, cheerful. But now her brow would knit as she studied and her expression blacken and she would mutter under her breath, fidgeting in her seat enough to keep Aren from his napping and, one night, going so far as to fling her papers across the room.

"Something is wrong!" she'd cried.

Aren sat bolt upright. "Do you feel unwell? Will I fetch the doctor?"

She shook her head. "Not with *that*. With the data. Something is wrong with the data."

"What is wrong?"

She closed her console and placed it on the little table at her side, and sat with her hands clasped. "I don't know. I can't put my finger on it. I imagine you could, if they hadn't taken your tools away." She rocked a little as she spoke. "I hate it," she spat. "I hate that I can't reckon it out, but something is amiss with this data. Good aetiology settles matters. Yours always did. But the data we're getting now does precisely the opposite."

"It isn't like you," he said, seeking to reassure, "not to have an answer."

He leaned toward her and took her hand.

"You ask too much of yourself, Izzy. It's your hormones, I should think—playing havoc with that brain of yours." He patted her hand. "A temporary circumstance."

She withdrew her hand but offered him a conciliatory glance. "Perhaps," she said, and then she'd taken his hand again suddenly and squeezed it. "If only the data were coming from you like before, and not from the Magistracy," she said, "through Fafl. I never had any trouble with it when it was. I'm telling you, Aren, there's something wrong. I find myself applying revisions to sections of the chart we thought incontrovertible. Those sections should be immutable, established fact, but each new wave of data unsettles them. They deteriorate. Boundaries blur. It's as though we wash them in low-grade, churned content. Don't look at me like that—I know how it sounds."

She shook her head, placed a kiss upon his, and took her leave. Aren picked the papers up from the floor and put them with the others. Her due date was still weeks away. He wished he could will it on. Not even her work, it seemed, could raise her spirits now. There was a gauntness to her features he hadn't seen. Her eyes had sunken. She'd recently refused all offers from Fafl of calmatives but perhaps it was time. She who had comforted him needed comfort from him. He didn't know how to give it.

The sun finds ingress in a corner of the window, and lights up his eyelids. He opens them and leans forward, into the shadow. The effects of the sherry are slow to wear off; he has almost fallen asleep several times and if he succumbs there's no telling, these days, when he'll wake. The afternoon is yet young enough to provide some invigorating air. Besides, he needs his Izzy; taking his coat and his stick, and a deep breath once he has closed the cabin door behind him, he goes to her.

"Aren?"

It was quiet. No birdsong could be heard from the island's smaller feathered natives; they were all huddled on branches, beaks tucked to breasts. Higher overhead and out to sea, there was only the very occasional cry of a distant seagull—apart from that, the not-quite silence of the maritime night, the sighs of the undulating sea like the indistinct, indecipherable frequencies of a detuned radio.

"Aren?"

Her tiny fingers in his ribs, nudging. Her breath on his cheek. He didn't want it to be morning yet; the bed was warm and so was Izzy. He opened his eyes to swap the darkness of sleep for that of the bedroom.

"Aren? *Wake up.*"

It must have been coming up on six of the clock, because it took just a few moments for the creeping dawn to outline her features, and for the sight of them to send a chill through him.

"What is it, Izzy?"

She leaned into him. "I don't want you to be angry with me. You won't be, will you?" Her eyes were wide and wet. He could feel her trembling.

"Of course I won't." He forced a smile. "What can it be, you silly thing? We haven't even dressed ourselves."

"We need to get it out, Aren. I want it out now."

He swallowed. "What, Izzy? What do you mean?"

"You *know* what I mean. It's the baby, Aren. All this time, I haven't been able to make sense of it. But now I can—it's the baby, corrupting the data. Here, you do it."

He hadn't noticed her other hand but she held it over his chest now and something was in it. He sat bolt upright and she sat back, continuing to proffer the object. Aren switched on the bedside lamp, then turned back to his wife to see that it was a knife.

"You do it," she repeated. "I can't."

Before he knew it, his feet were on the floor and he was looking down upon her in horror. Izzy held the knife out to him, her hand around the blade so tightly that blood oozed between her fingers. He took the handle, waited till he saw her grip loosen before he pulled it away, and threw it to the floor. Then he knelt on the bed and held her in his arms.

"Oh, Izzy!" He rocked her back and forth like a child as sobs racked her body. "It's just another fortnight, my love, perhaps not even that," he said as his own tears fell, and they remained there, clinging to each other as, outside, the sun cleared the horizon to ignite another day on the Warburg.

The same sun now hangs low over the horizon and sinks, or so the old man assumes as he walks beneath the leafy canopy that hides the wider world and muffles its maritime chorus—the calling birds and the wind that squalls over the little headland at the far end of the beach, the airy clamour of the waves on the rocks there. The day is growing dim when he stops dead; the wood has yet enough light in it for him to see that Izzy already has company. Not one but three women await him, for on the little bench beneath the arched trellis sits a solemn Mrs Cyre, her eyes cast sadly at the headstone and her arm around the shoulder of a weeping Lil.

It is the older woman who sees him first and puts a finger to her lips, but the gesture alerts Lil. She looks up and, at the sight of her father, stiffens.

"I'm sorry," he says. "I didn't mean to . . ." But he doesn't know what he meant, or didn't, and Lil has buried her head in Mrs Cyre's breast. "Don't weep for me, girl," says Aren. "Weep for yourself." He prepares to turn and leave, seeing how his presence torments Lil and meaning to put a stop to it.

"How can I not?" she says before he can take the first step. "You will end your days in some awful place of durance. No one to comfort you, nothing to show for your life's work. How could you breach the protocols you have respected all your life? How could you leave me with . . . with *him*?"

Mrs Cyre clucks and pats Lil's back as Aren replies.

"Never mind that now." He sounds more gruff than he would like. "I have placed you in a bind, Lil, that is true—but unlike some, you will get away from this place. My work is written. You will take it with you. You must. The Magistracy must know . . . I know that you love me and will honour me in this way."

He turns and walks away through the woods. *Am I to be denied even a moment near you, Izzy? No matter. I'll be with you soon enough.*

When he emerges from the trees, a silent Magistracy supply drone hovers overhead. From an opening in its belly, supply packs are lowered past the Stationmaster's gooney cage that depends from the mast and into a hatch in the roof of the dome. Since the surveilling function of the station came to an end, it has been little more than a tackle room—the Stationmaster considers the harpoons a risk to the boy, who must fish with a rod—and sick bay. Apart from Fafl, who lives there, only Aren himself and a few select others are permitted to set foot inside. Most of the island's inhabitants would need to find themselves quite dead or in dire need of surgery to see the interior.

He hasn't stood and watched a supply drop since his early years on the island, when he would stop and crane his neck every time he saw one. The drones would spook the seabirds, who would shun the huge mast during drops but, in the long intervals between, reclaim it—the great gooneys and the gulls wheeling and the smaller birds perched tauntingly on Fafl's trap near the top. There would always be something for the young Aren to look up at, doing the one thing he couldn't—come and go from the Warburg.

The outside world. Today it somehow seems both closer and further away. The feeling is strange as it sits in his stomach, and he lurches on toward the hut. There'll be sherry in that shipment and so nothing to stop him opening his last bottle.

When he wakes, the last of the daylight has drained away, along with half the wine. He rouses himself—the entertainment will be underway. Something about these audio fragments has gotten into Lil. She must think him responsible for them. He owes it to her to be present.

In the Review room, there is food on the table but the mood is more mortuary than mealtime. Lil has waited for him. Her features are drawn and she reminds him more than ever of her mother. Once again, she offers no greeting. Once again, Wigbert puts a glass in front of him and fills it. Lil presses play.

The cleaners were there less than forty-five minutes later. As a concession to my rank, Evans was sent. I didn't know her all that well at the time but she'd been attached to Internal Hygiene which was run by Urquhart, an old academy roommate, so I knew she'd at least be discreet.

It was odd to be debriefed by a subordinate. We sat in the kitchen, where your mother and I had sat a short time before, and went through it as you and she were bundled into separate vehicles and driven away. I'd taken the opportunity to kiss your forehead while I waited for them to arrive, knowing that access to you would be denied the moment they stepped through the door. I also knew that you'd be on your way off world, to the campus on Fiser 14b to begin your induction. That you would be cleansed and then trained. That after a probationary period I would be allowed to communicate with you. That I would never again stand in your physical presence.

Your mother they took to the sanatorium in Leviston. Not all that far from the house, actually. Things didn't go well for her there. I wouldn't see her for many months following the breach. She spent much of that time under heavy sedation. Forgive me, I know you haven't heard any of this before. It must be hard to hear, and it's only going to get harder, but I've run out of reasons for keeping any of it from you. I don't want to protect you anymore, Lita, or to save face. I just want to tell you. It's your story, too.

Just a week later, I was back on Sinn where the Sinni were proving intractable. We encounter fundamentalism wherever we are required to go of course, but there is usually a recognizable demograph. We had always been able to target what had invariably been peripheral, extreme groups by deploying doctrinal algorithms, developed over many centuries and thousands of cleansed worlds. Entertainments, too, need to be carefully transitioned. You can't just take a people's fictions away—you have to replace them. Then take away the replacement. This is what we do. We identify the pressure points and, initially, we massage them. We give people our own, manageable version of whatever it is they believe they need. Then we manage it. Deep cleansing is merely the final step in a complicated process, which can be slow and has lasted for centuries in some cases. Wider populations have always submitted, eventually. The fundamentalists we would demonize, then neutralize.

On Sinn, though, it was different. We'd been unable to find a dividing line between the general populace and radical elements. Our dummy myths had found no purchase. They were laughing at us. I'd taken up my post with the battalion outside the city of Suc. We were getting reports of a massive build up of Truth forces in multiple locations, on a scale I'd never seen. Before I knew it I'd been given two more battalions. Senior officers in all surface locations were getting a lot more senior, and quickly. Too quickly— I would almost say the reconfiguration was disorderly. Men and women promoted to positions for which they were unfit, in my opinion. The merging of previously disciplined divisions into volatile militias.

Orbital support was increased to the point where it cluttered the night sky. Days passed with no off-world contact. Then the order came through— instead of advancing on the city we were to withdraw, to a distance of thirty-five kilometers. We did so looking back over our shoulders, and we'd barely set up camp in our new location when the bombing began. At that point, our altered mission became clear. We would be the clean-up operation.

On a desert world it wasn't difficult to bombard the relatively few urban centers and track the nomadic communities. The ordinance dropped for weeks. When the skies cleared and the ground stopped shaking, it was our turn. My final communiqué before we mobilized decrypted as a single word—ALL.

I knew it would be ugly. That's why I had the men pumped full of phets before we went in. But I had no idea how ugly. For some months we'd come up against straggling parties—a very few of them were fighters but most were hiding or fleeing and had armed themselves, sometimes with sticks, merely for defense. We'd finish them. These skirmishes accounted for very little of our kill count. Mostly, we combed the rubble, putting bullets in heads wherever a body twitched, gassing any nooks and crevices, running sensors to guarantee a clear zone, then moving on to establish another.

Mapping out an atlas of the dead. It was coward's work, a job for the wicked, and wicked is what we became. With such a weak command ratio, and such unseasoned officers in charge, there was precious little control. I'd never seen anything like it in either Truth or Light. Mine has always been a battle against barbarism. Yet here we were, barbarians. Exterminators of the weak. Women, children. Your mother, you. Your faces were everywhere as I walked through my own apocalypse, shooting "wrigglers" like the rest of them, but seeing only you. Eventually I had to withdraw to the command centre and leave the troops—a rabble now—to it. It didn't go unnoticed, but I couldn't carry on. I couldn't be out there. You were out there.

More than killing, more than death—we were the end of the world. There's been nothing like it since. All subsequent campaigns have been business as usual. Sinn was exceptional. It might have destroyed Truth—it took time, once the planet was clean, to restore order. There were hasty demotions, courts-martial, executions. Eventually we looked as we had before, outwardly at least. For me though, something had ended there, in those sands. They didn't look clean to me.

I remain dutiful—I do my work as I have always done. But I know that if it were ever to happen again I would be unable. I would refuse, and I too would be executed. It hangs over me as I go about my work like the sword over Damocles.

Listen to me. For the allusion alone I could pay with my life.

"Is there a war then, Pappy?" says the fat boy, when Lil has pressed stop.

"Never you mind," says Wigbert, flicking his hand at a large wooden bowl in the middle of the table. "Have an apple."

"There are no more wars," says Mr Bull. "They've all been fought. Why do we continue to listen to this nonsense?"

"To assess it," says Lil. "To determine whether it is truth or fiction."

"Lil," says Fafl, "I must censure you there, my dear. That determination is for the Magistracy alone. It is not ours to make. It is the very essence of the Magistracy's work. We here merely collate. We sift. We determine nothing."

"Of course it's fiction," says Mr Cyre, ignoring the Stationmaster and drawing a gasp from his wife. "The speaker speaks of things that have not yet been. How can it not be fiction? To be truth, it would have to have reached us from times yet to come, never mind places well beyond our reach. Absurd."

"That isn't the only possibility," says Lil. "Of course I speak in purely theoretical terms but . . . what about the past?"

"But Lil," says Fafl. He appears nervous this evening, fidgeting on his stool. "The place names. Several of the references. They're contemporary. Why, a mere twenty years ago, nobody had set foot on—"

"Not that past," says Lil. "Not our past." She shuts down the console. "I mean before the Disasters." She fastened her satchel and looped it over her shoulder. "We know so little. Nothing, really."

"I'm not sure I see the point, dear," said Fafl. "What—"

"My question," she would not look upon her betrothed, "would be this. How far into the past would our sight have to reach, how much further than the limits of either our knowledge or indeed our imagination would it have to penetrate, before we came upon a time and a place that we might mistake for the future? *Could* such a thing be?"

She moves toward the door. It might have been a rhetorical question, but her eyes rest on her father and she pauses on the threshold.

"I don't know, Lil," he says. "But your pertinacity does you credit." His eyes narrow. "Always persist. See it through to the end. That's my girl."

She leaves and so, one by one, do the others assembled, until only Aren and the Stationmaster remain.

"You didn't tell them," says Aren. In spite of the wine his voice is calm and cool.

"No," says Fafl, exhibiting neither of those conditions. "It'll go hard on Lil, won't it? I'll admit I won't relish the telling of it." He gets up to take his leave.

"Not like you to scruple so, Jasper," says Aren "There is no putting a stop now to that which has been set in motion."

"No," says the Stationmaster. "No indeed." He pulls his gloves, with considerable difficulty, onto unsteady hands. "She will take it hard." He goes to the door. "Perhaps, in time . . ." he says, but the remainder of the thought eludes him, and so he steps into the darkness.

CHAPTER THE SEVENTH

*IN WHICH LIL ASKS A BOON OF MR GRIM
WHICH HE MUST DECLINE,
AND THE COMMITTEE IS UNSETTLED.*

THE DAY IS BALMY for the time of year and the door has been left open; a pile of books makes a stopper to prevent its banging about in the breeze. In the corner, vapours curl from the spout of a kettle. From within it, the sound of bubbling water gathers speed; soon it will spew forth a trumpet of steam, whistling its readiness to the dozer in an armchair nearby. Beside the kettle sits a little teapot, beside that a tin of tea leaves with the long handle of a spoon protruding, and next to them a small hip flask from which something warming will be added to the cup.

The only sound apart from the hiss of the kettle and the collegiate rustle of leaves outside is that of the snoring to which, it would seem, the whole structure reverberates—until, that is, a figure appears in the doorway to knock timidly upon the frame. It is a slight figure but its shadow is long enough in the waning afternoon to reach the old man's eyelids. Roused, he lifts them and sits forward a little in the armchair, blinking at the blurred shape until it resolves itself.

"May I come in for a moment, Mr Grim?" it says.

"Bless me, Lil," says old Wigbert, getting up to take the whistling kettle from the hob, "and bless you. This business with your father is affecting you, of course." He returns to the armchair and peers at her. "You haven't called me Mr Grim in many a year. Come in, girl."

Lil takes the few steps required to reach the armchair and drops to her knees there.

"Sorry, Wig," she says and falls into his arms. She makes no sound but her shoulders tremble as the old man holds her—rather awkwardly, but good and tight—and pats her back.

In another cabin, another old man. No trace of sleep dims *his* eyes, downcast but wide open and steady—resting, for want of a better perch, on the hands he clasps between his knees. He is upright, hunched forward a little, and his skin has that waxy pallor that comes from the want of sustenance; he has not eaten today and did not yesterday. He has been to fetch his sherry and the bottle teeters near him on a pile of old books, untouched after a solitary sip—the wine that has dulled his pain these many years tastes bitter today, newly devoid of its regenerative qualities. Arenaceous Nell, jowls stubbled with the grey growth of some days, is sober.

The past eddies around him as it has of late, but it does not carry him off—he is not lifted in Time's talons and stolen away. This afternoon it is he who manipulates it, who navigates its clouds and currents. His are the wings held aloft on its warm uplifts. With grim resolve and keen, unwavering vision, he finds his way back.

"What is this, Izzy?"

She had put her tab down and come to the window where he stood scrutinizing the thing, turning it in the light.

"Why, Aren," she exclaimed, "you surprise me! Have you never seen a compass?"

Aren, embarrassed, feigned to look at the object in his hand more intently for a moment.

"No, no—that's what I thought it was," he said. "Is it yours?"

"I've given it to Lil."

"Where did you get it?"

"I brought it here. I've always had it."

He turned the dial carefully and watched the floating needle keep its course.

"Such an item would have been forbidden, surely? Anything that might be used to navigate—"

"Oh yes," she'd pinched his waist and grinned, "quite forbidden."

"She's too young to be entrusted with it, Izzy," said Aren. "I found it outside." There was a little wooden box on the windowsill. He put the compass in it.

Lil was seven and Aren a changed man—a more cautious man, a man worn down by care, humbled by it. Under his own eyes, dark rings recalled those that cradled his wife's. There was salt as well as pepper in his hair and in the unkempt whiskers he let grow more often these days. The nutty scent of sherry wine could be detected on his breath each early afternoon.

It was true that life had resumed some semblance of normality. Izzy had acquiesced to the Stationmaster's physicks following her episode and Lil's birth had gone ahead without undue complication. Her infancy had been a relatively stable time. *But*, he thought to himself as he followed Izzy to the sofa to sit with her, *not a wholly joyful one. Where was the unfettered happiness that should have been ours?* He took her hand. *Robbed from us.* Passively, compliantly, she let her hand be taken.

"You fill the girl's head with nonsense," he said as softly, as without hard reproach, as he could. "All these maps."

As Lil's first days had turned to weeks and months, and then years, the loss to Aren of the role that had brought him to the station, and that had subsumed him long before, became a sort of blessing; for it was to him that would fall the heaviest share of the burden of parenthood. The child's mother could hardly bear to be left alone with her. At dinner or breakfast the difficulty could be assuaged by Aren, whose presence conduced to watchful mediation. Izzy always spoke kindly to Lil, and exhibited a sort of awe, a mesmerised fascination, with the child. "Did you hear that Aren?" she would say at times, when in truth she might better have replied to her daughter, "Isn't she clever? Those are words for bigger girls."

The girl, for her part, seemed instinctively to grasp the familial dynamic—in her early years, as language slowly took hold of her, it was to her father that Lil looked for instruction, guidance and companionship. Her mother could therefore choreograph the moments they spent together with extreme caution, and ensure that they were never alone, lest she succumb to the fits of dizziness that the unaccompanied child induced. If Izzy despised herself for this shortcoming she did not say so, going about her business each day with a medicated equilibrium. But Aren never abandoned his fervent hope that a way might be found for mother and daughter to bond.

In her fifth year, Lil joined young Simon Cyre to begin her schooling under the tutelage of the Stationmaster. Fafl would have asserted his prerogative in the matter whatever the circumstance, no doubt, but the truth was that he had been finding himself more and more at a loose end. Since the closure of Aren's department, the Station at large had been feeling the repercussions. Personnel had been withdrawn—in great haste, initially—and the island's population was much diminished; both Mr Bull and Fafl had seemed thoroughly rattled by the sudden exodus and the huge administrative burden it so suddenly placed upon them, and the Stationmaster had become sullen and secretive, his duties apparently confined to the distribution of nanoplant antidotes for those still to depart. Izzy's laboratory, dependent now on whatever data the Magistracy fed through Fafl, made little if any progress.

It was listening to his daughter recount her lessons at dinner, and seeing Izzy share in his delight, that gave Aren the idea—that she might find unsupervised time with Lil more palatable if it was spent under the auspices of formal teaching. He would be parent, and his wife home tutor.

"How can it be nonsense, Aren?" she said, stirring him from his recollections. He looked back towards the window, at the little box on the sill. Lil would be home soon. "It's the world. Is the world a nonsense now?"

"No, Izzy," he said. "But perhaps there's too much of it. I think she's dizzy with it all."

His stratagem had worked, or so he had thought. Izzy needed surprisingly little persuasion, in fact—as long as she could work from textbooks, the academic was relatively comfortable and became a diligent tutor to Lil. Any pleasure that Aren was to take in the success of his venture, however, was soon to ebb away. Izzy had but the one interest in her new role, one lesson to inculcate in her charge; an unquenchable fascination with the wider world and a desire—that once instilled would never leave the girl—to get out into it.

We need to get it out, Aren. I want it out now.

The words had never stopped echoing in his mind. Now he could not help but suspect that Izzy wanted rid of her daughter still, that the madness persisted—that she would imbue Lil with it. How many times had he found the girl at the waterline? And though he did not fret for her safety—young Simon never let her out of his sight and was a sensible, if rather tongue-tied, boy—it troubled him that she should spend all of her time on this island at its very edge, looking outward, and longing to leave.

There was a knock at the door. Lil never knocked. He stood and went to it and upon opening it was presented with the sight of a very agitated Mrs Cyre, accompanied by her husband. They were the last two people on the island who Aren would expect to make an unannounced visit.

"Fafl wants to see us," she said.

"The Committee?"

"No. It must be something to do with the children. He only wants to see the two of us," she said, looking for Izzy over his shoulder, "and the two of you."

decommissioned   the Warburg a filing cabinet   at best   at worst a hazmat container   izzy's presence a farce   what of the Mapper   I asked   she married him   the answer   her choice arenaceous deteriorating nicely   believing himself surplus   was the only one of us now of course who as mere archivist in a mere archive *wasn't* surplus   except at a stretch for mrs cyre   who laundered for the cadets   who were young and therefore quite filthy   and what a filthy time it was   how mired in filth was I   in the mess I'd made   filth and fear   and the old feeling renewed   a stomachful of steel toe   I was given time by the magistracy   but not much   to get rid of cadets and non-essentials   barely enough time mind you   had to manage that very carefully I did   very carefully   what would you call it   a facade that's it   the semblance of normality   keep myself chipper as they'd all come to expect   couldn't let it slip   couldn't   and so I told izzy the magistracy would continue to feed us aetiology   though they wouldn't be feeding us as much as a civil good morning   that was the reality   that was the true tale I couldn't tell   they were gone   the flow of information had come to a stop   our isolation was complete   and mine completer

   she fell pregnant   and unwell   impossible to say why of course   the latter I mean   impossible to say   some women are not meant to bear fruit   it rots within 'em   rots 'em from the inside out   and when the girl arrived   beautiful lil   her mother's rot had set in   the woman   whom I had loved   was blighted   beshrewed   would not recover   I do believe I had loved her   I think so yes   been providing her aetiology to keep her sweet hadn't I   keep her going   but it was old content   stale   and I was merely churning it   and my poor neglected skills were wanting   but not to provide it would have been to expose the lie   to let the veil drop   the Warburg now a fiction   and I the author   and izzy's role took a tragic turn   impossible to say why of course   I suppose it may have been   but no   it was the girl   beautiful lil   and who could lay blame on so sweet a little creature   who even while we watched the mother's mind wither   so cheered me

---

"Oh Wig!" Lil is on her knees on the floor, blowing her nose with the handkerchief Wigbert has given her. "How can I marry that . . . *creature*?"

There is always something of the little girl to her when in the presence of Mr Grim, who has been a de facto uncle to her, and more than that—the fastest of friends. Despite the gravity of her father's plight, to say nothing of her own, she pouts—voicing her objection in the petulant tone of a child. Her companion doesn't reply, merely nodding as she once again blows her nose.

"Your father asks much of you," he says finally. "I don't know what's got into his head."

He leans forward to place a hand on her shoulder and squeeze it gently. He is never the blowhard with his friend's daughter. There is none of the bluster to which the island's other inhabitants have become accustomed.

"But I know this, sweet Lil," he says. "He wouldn't ask it if it wasn't the only way."

"But it isn't." Her eyes show some steel. "I may have been Fafl's prey, but now he knows of Papa's work, I expect *it* will take precedence. Anything to ingratiate himself with the Magistracy." Her fists clench. "I need only go out to the buoys. My father would be the only one left to interpret his notes."

"Lil, don't say that! You couldn't—"

"Don't fret, old thing," says Lil. "I know I couldn't." She places an affectionate hand on his. "To lose me as he loses his liberty would break him. I've already made up my mind. I will comply, though I don't understand why he has done this." Her voice wavers. "I can't understand any of it!"

Wigbert waves his other hand in the air, as if to indicate the whole island. "All of this," he says, "is coming to an end. We few who remain will be farmers, and fishermen." His visage darkens, and thick white eyebrows lower themselves over his eyes. "And prisoners. I do not know the inner workings of your father's mind. But he would not have placed you in this quandary, Lil, unless he must." He sighs. "I've known you since you were a bump. From the moment you could speak, you spoke of getting away from this place. Now you must go. These audio fragments, Fafl's enquiry, your father's odd behaviour . . . it all points towards that. Hasn't Arenaceous spoken to you of it?"

"I avoid him. Hasn't he spoken to you?"

"Outside the entertainments," said Wigbert, "he avoids me." He glanced at the clock. "Speaking of which, shouldn't you—"

"Yes, of course." Lil gets to her feet. "Today's fragment changes everything. The recordings have something important to tell us, I'm certain of it. Will you walk with me, Wig?"

"Honoured!" says the old man, accepting a helping hand out of his chair.

As soon as his coat and cap have been found they set off toward the Committee Room. Wigbert's cube is the furthest from it, on the far side of the clearing, at the treeline; in the fading light, Lil weaves her arm through his and they amble upwards towards the dome, she making allowance for his years and pausing now and then while he catches his breath. At the top, it is she who slows her pace, eyes on the mast that towers over them. The old trap creaks on its rope, and the sea birds above make their twilight cacophony. How often did her Papa take her here when she was young, to listen to it?

"Lil?"

"Hm?" she turns back to Wigbert as the old man stops for another brief rest.

"You weren't listening." He chuckles. "What is it you see up there?"

"Oh, I don't know." *Yes I do. I see what Papa sees. I see flight. I see freedom.* She turns again but not to look up. "Wig," she says, "I know you won't go in there anymore. But you have access don't you?"

Mr Grim's eyes follow hers to the dome's doorway.

"No," he says, "I would not go in. But yes, I designed the security system, you know."

Lil does know. It is why she asked the question.

"Could you get *me* in?"

"Lil! Why would you ask . . . has your father's madness got into you too?" He has coloured. "Strictly forbidden. It is Fafl's domain. For the rest of us, it's a mortuary. What business would you have in there?"

"I'm not sure," says Lil. She bites her lip for a moment, then continues. "To make contact with the Magistracy, perhaps."

Wigbert dismisses the notion with a shake of his head.

"Not even Fafl would do so, Lil. Communications are incoming. The Warburg is the Magistracy's child—it speaks when spoken to, or not at all. If you open an emergency frequency from the dome, you'll pay heavily. Why do you think we find ourselves under the gaze of a Magistracy enquiry? Any activation of the array at all, by anyone, is treachery."

"Well then, to see what they've been saying to him." She squeezes his arm. "Wig, I don't trust Fafl," she whispers. "I want to see the evidence for my father's guilt with my own eyes. Perhaps, that way, I could accept it. But I tell you," she says, looking intently at the old man, "there is something wrong with the information we receive from the Stationmaster. It's . . . not right." She shakes her head. "It's . . . *corrupted*, somehow."

It is as if a rain cloud glides overhead, to cast its shade upon the face of Wigbert Grim. "Your mother used to say such things," he says, "once upon a time." He takes her hand. "Let it go, Lil. Arenaceous has confessed, and he has made a way for you to leave the Warburg. That is the way you must follow now. Put aside this—"

"But you *could* get me in there, couldn't you?" she blurts.

He sighs. "Lil, even if I didn't have the code, I'd need precisely two things to get you into that dome: a screwdriver and a minute. But I will not do it."

"Why not?"

Wigbert's smile is joyless. "You're a very clever girl, Lil, but you have no appreciation for the principles of a sound security system." He pats her hand and bids her walk on with him. "Getting you in simply doesn't present a problem. There's nothing much to see: the little sick bay," another shadow plays briefly across his features, cast by a passing gooney, perhaps, "a communications console that you could fiddle with unsuccessfully, some medical supplies, fishing tackle . . . but you would never get back out. *That's* the thing."

"Why not?"

"Biology," he says. "Optiscan. If you aren't Fafl, or with him, you don't leave the dome."

They have neared the Committee Room and old Arenaceous Nell can be seen up ahead, shambling thither with his back turned to them.

"Let it go, Lil. In any event, the Marshal will have to notarise whatever judgement is handed down," says Mr Grim, his eyes on his old friend. "Won't you go to him? Talk to him?"

"No," she says. "I can't." She is chewing her lip again—discouraged, perhaps, by what Wig has told her. "Tomorrow, maybe. Let's get on with the Review."

The meal, such as it is, is underway in the Committee Room: a rather desultory spread of cold leftovers from yesterday, some cheese and a bowl of buttered beans. The company itself appears similarly lacklustre, as though they are gathered in a court room waiting to be sentenced—which of course, in a sense, they are. Simon appears perfectly wretched, sandwiched between his parents, both of whom sit in silence and eat slowly, solemnly, with straight backs and down-turned mouths. But perhaps the source of his misery is something other than this evening's seating arrangements. Perhaps it has just this minute entered the room, on the arm of Mr Wigbert Grim.

The Stationmaster appears cowed and ill at ease. There is a good deal less of his oily assurance and an unwonted stillness to the hands that sit separately in his lap. He does not speak. Only Heft and Pack, Mr Bull's constables, are their usual inconversable selves, unless there is just the suggestion of an arch to one of Pack's eyebrows as he eats—a mute pronouncement, perhaps, on the paucity of the victuals.

"Where is the boy?" asks Mrs Cyre with her customary charm.

"He'll be along," says Wigbert, taking his seat beside Aren, "now the light's gone. He's been a-fishing."

"Oh save us!" says the Stationmaster. "Must you let him out there alone, Mr Wig? What if he were to drown? My youngest, most precious charge! There are dolphins out there, you know, oftener than not. What if they should take agin him?"

"He oughtn't be allowed," says Mrs Cyre. "It isn't right. What if he should near the buoys? If he doesn't mind what he's about? Boys are distractable."

Jasper Fafl rolls his eyes. "Don't worry about the buoys, so, Mrs Cyre." He weaves his fingers, relaxing a little, as if some welcome thought has warmed him. "If there is one thing I have prepared the child for, it's the buoys. No, it's the dolphins *I'm* afraid of. They're fiendish intelligent, you know, and can take notions."

Mr Grim has adjusted his cutlery so that knife and spoon flank his plate in a quite perfect parallel.

"Distractable?" he says, leaning toward Mrs Cyre with such an intensity of countenance that the good lady deems it necessary to lean back, though they sit at opposite ends of the table. "*Distractable?*" He rests his elbows on the table and places the fanned fingertips of one hand against those of the other. "I can—and will—tell you this, Mrs Cyre. There is nothing that focusses that boy's mind—*nothing*," he says, "like the procurement of comestibles." He folds his arms and casts his eyes over the assembled company. "Let any man—or woman—here have the boldness to assert it contrariwise, if he—or she—will."

Lil is at the console preparing the clip when the fat boy enters, approaches the table with a celerity that surprises, for one of his dimensions, and has a spoon in the bowl of beans before he has sat. All accounted for, she presses play.

The first time we entered Efsane's atmosphere, I felt something in the pit of my stomach that I couldn't attribute to the ship's gradual, gliding descent. We were under recon protocol and proceeded slowly. It would be hours before we reached our target altitude, the piloting tentative as we slipped from thermosphere to mesosphere, allowing time for sensor sweeps and sample collection. But I felt it and it hasn't left me in the days since. My senses are heightened. Time here seems to move at a slower pace. More stately—I would say funereal, but everything around me teems with life.

The scale, Lita. Even if we'd been plummeting it would have taken time to arrive at the landing site—a shelf of pastureland, quite massive, protruding from the almost sheer side of a valley in the north west of the Mons Elisium at an altitude, I was told, of forty-one thousand meters. Any notion of height would have been impossible to grasp with the eyes. The bottom of the valley was invisible, obscured by many kilometers of gas cloud, and that many kilometers below us. Above us, a lot more mountain, the peaks difficult to make out even in the optimal visibility of high-altitude glare. Nothing in the sky but a few wisps of cloud and Kepler 3-1041b, so large it looked as though the fingertips of an outstretched hand could touch it.

As we eased towards the outcrop, the valley wall slid slowly by and we got a good look, through the domed portholes in the hull of the passenger compartment, at the terrain. It was conspicuously verdant—unbelievably so at these altitudes—and generously populated. The color palate of the flora was familiar enough—the greens and earthy tones that you might expect, speckled with bright sparks of color where meadow flowers blossomed, but also many shades of red that testified to the high ferrous content in the geology here.

On the bare slopes that punctuated the greenery, we saw straggling herds of goat-like creatures, upright and strolling nonchalantly where no purchase for their hooves could be discerned. Little scimitars of vapor hung in the still humidity. It was warm out there—we knew that from our readings. On ground not so steep we saw something like antelope, and Evans says she spotted their predator. None of this is my area, Lita—you'll forgive me if I skim over it.

Although alerted to the temperate conditions, it still jarred when we stepped out of the ship. Perhaps it was the quiet. Not even a sigh in the silence, no bird call, no bleating from the little herds we'd seen. And despite our skepticism, sensor readings—as well as the smiling faces of the welcome committee that had gathered on the strip—confirmed what we'd been told: there was air.

The rock shelf was even larger than it had looked from above. I observed grazing cattle at some distance and a good number of people going about their agrarian business. It would have taken fifteen or twenty minutes to walk to the opposite side, I estimated. I could see a settlement of neat but primitive-looking squat structures of adobe or some similar material over there.

We were ushered into the footprint of a ruin. None of the crude stone walls that surrounded us exceeded twenty or thirty centimeters in height. Despite this, there were furnishings—some rough, thick carpets and stone seats. One of our hosts gestured to them—Dr Zwickl, Evans and I sat in the three available and the security detail from the station stood behind us. On the other side of a low table was a high-backed chair and on the table itself lay a tray of glasses and a silver pot. One of the committee, an extremely tall, grey-haired man, sat down in the chair, crossed his legs and smiled. Behind him a large dog, just outside the ruin, glowered. When I looked at it, it bared its teeth and sprayed spittle from its open jaw, barking furiously. We couldn't hear it.

"He won't bother you," said the man, in perfect English I presume, since I hadn't activated my translator. "He's all talk."

I noted a line of tiny points of blue light along the top of the wall remnant and raised my eyebrows, surprised to see the technology here, not to mention the wealth required to procure it.

"You're running a light barrier?" I said. "That must suck up a lot of juice. Why don't you just rebuild?"

"Because that would be sacrilege," said the old man.

He'd stood to lift the lid of the pot and stir its contents. I know I scowl when people use proscribed terms and his eyes too, in reaction to mine I suppose, narrowed.

"You're not familiar with the organization I represent?" I asked with what I intended as tact. I was in full uniform and would scarcely have believed that he hadn't heard of Truth. He poured tea into the tiny, ornate glasses.

"I'm afraid it rather looks as though I've made an assumption," he said. "I supposed you had come in search of that." His eyes flicked to the insignia on my breast, then rose to meet mine again. "I take it you haven't?"

In the silence that follows the audio fragment, the late arrival slurps at his supper while Lil logs the Review and deactivates the console.

Thus indisposed, he cannot share with the company anything in the way of his usual insight and, consequently, the hush that hangs in the air is broken only when Mrs Cyre speaks—which she does on her feet, having risen to them during playback.

"This is too much," she says, her eyes roving over every square inch of the room, though not allowed by their owner to rest on any spot whence their gaze might be returned. "Too much. I'm afraid you are toying with us, Lil," she says, "or someone is with you. It's too, too much!" She takes up her bag. "I will not be party to any more of it. Simon, I forbid you to continue to attend these Reviews. In any case, they serve no purpose now." She shakes her head and makes towards the door and as she does so Mr Cyre, a participant in Committee discourse on only the vary rarest of occasions, makes his views known.

"For goodness sake," he says.

"And you I would also forbid," his wife shoots back, "if I believed there was the remotest possibility of your redemption. Simon."

It is generally understood that the utterance of his given name constitutes a summons for younger Mr Cyre to get to his feet and accompany his mother from the room, an act of gallantry to preserve the poor woman from the humiliating impropriety of leaving it un-accompanied. However he remains seated, blushing, and she bursts into tears. The truth is that, though she may be the brittlest of them in her emotional response, she is not alone in her disquiet at what they have heard.

"Perhaps," says Fafl, "Mrs Cyre is correct. This latest content is not to my liking at all. Out of respect for young Lil's assiduous application to her duties," he smiles at his fiancée, "I have allowed the Reviews to continue. I thought it harmless. I no longer think so."

"Was the man talking about the Warburg, Pappy?"

"Shut up, boy," says Wig and immediately regrets his hard words. "You're not going to leave that cheese there are you?" He pats the boy on his head. "It would be a terrible waste."

"But was he though?" says Mr Bull. "It did sound like—"

"Gentlemen!" says Fafl. "Ladies. Does such loose talk redound to our behoof? Does it edify us? We are Magistracy operatives. We know our duty, do we not?"

"We certainly do," says Mrs Cyre, who has one hand on the door handle but cannot bring herself to leave for the paralyzing fear of what she might miss if she does.

"I thought us eavesdroppers," says the Stationmaster. "That these fragments were intercepts. But it seems we are the intended recipients." He shakes his head. "Or perhaps not. Perhaps we participate in a delusion, all of us." His narrowed eyes peer at nothing. "I do wonder, sometimes, if we might all be quite mad, you know." That bark that passes for mirth and another shake of his head. "The monotony," he says. "It was different when we had observatory status, I think. The Magistracy had more to say to us. And more often. People came and went. We always had *something* to go on, did we not?" He looks around but none respond. "The impossibility of complete isolation asserted itself every day, with every little snippet of news a new arrival brought, of their home town or some off-world gossip—no more verifiable than these audio bursts of ours, I suppose, except that then we had multiple sources, corroborations . . . or just the news they involuntarily bore and wore in the cut of their clothes and hair, the changes in fashion, whatever recorded musical ditties they were sanctioned to bring with them." He slaps imaginary dust from the brim of his hat in preparation to take his leave, though he has mounted his hobby horse now and will not easily be induced to dismount. "We were showered in data, when you think of it. The humdrum of our days thusly refreshed. Now it rains only the voices of the dead, if at all. As though they were dead, even, in our remembrance. We pore over digital dust. The archive. Is it any wonder we look for meaning where none is? What *else* would we do? Unheard and unhearing—that's no fate."

"You maunder, Mr Fafl," says Wigbert.

"Do I, indeed, Mr Grim?" The Stationmaster glares, his tone envenomed as it always is when addressing that individual. "You will please to forgive my prolixity. I ought be more mindful, I suppose, of the standards in eloquence and concision you have set for us here at the Warburg." He nods severally, to acknowledge the rhetorical victory he assumes he has won.

"You all weary of it as I do, no doubt," he continues. "We were a great eye, and then we were become but an ear—devoid of vision but resounding to whispered fragments of the elsewhere, the breezes that blew in that we could build a world from. Perhaps. Now the ear is become deaf." He stands. "We are tired. We are like the weary traveller who, on the giddy edge of slumber, might, in the droning ebb and surge of an amphicopter blade, make out words, names, even their own name—a loved one calling out to them till they submit to sleep and can join them in their dreams." He dons his hat. "Mrs Cyre is right," he says, moving toward that lady. "Someone may be seeking to contaminate us. Our best defence in these final days of the Warburg is to discontinue the Reviews. The Magistracy, I will take the liberty of informing you, functions at this time in a state of high alert."

"No," says Lil.

Heads turn, not least that of the Stationmaster.

"No?" he says. Lil does not immediately reply. She is fastening her bag and pulling it over her shoulder.

"The Reviews continue," she says.

Fafl's hands are raised as though someone were pointing a weapon at him. "I beg your pardon, Lil," he says, doing his best to effect a smile, "but I believe I am still Stationmaster here. You cannot gainsay—"

"It's what I want," says Lil. "We all have . . . things . . . that we want, do we not, Mr Fafl?"

Seeing that the young archivist does not wilt under his gaze, but on the contrary returns it unflinchingly, Fafl looks for some expression of support for his authority in the gathered company. Having no allies left on the Warburg, however, apart from the uxorious Mr Cyre and that gentleman's near-hysterical wife, he finds none—not even from Arenaceous Nell whose complicity he expects, but who has not spoken a word this evening, and does not appear hale.

"Very well," he says. He instead turns to leave, brushing an indignant Mrs Cyre aside. "If you must."

CHAPTER THE EIGHTH

A SPLENDID OPPORTUNITY IS OFFERED TO THE YOUNG LIL BY A GENEROUS BENEFACTOR, BUT HER MOTHER INTERVENES.

"Mr Linn and his beasts. *Lepus timidus*?"

"The blue hare."

"Very good. Have you ever seen one?"

"Of course not, Mama. They are not present on the Warburg."

"Where *are* they present?"

"They are widespread. But notably, between the forty-fifth and seventieth parallels. The Great Plains of Pheme in particular. Are they *really* blue, Mama?"

I remember the bright sunbeam and the dust floating in it, and the intensity of her expression as she leaned forward from where she sat in shadow to have it light up her face. She rested her elbows on the table, clasped her hands and leaned still more forwards, and said to me in the lowest of voices:

"And why should I tell you that, little one?"

There was nothing unfriendly in it. Her smile was there in the eyes as well as upon the lips, which is how I could always tell if it was real. She leaned back and her face disappeared from the light, leaving in its wake a flurry of dust motes that swirled inwards to fill the void where she had been. She never touched me but I will always remember that moment—I don't believe we had ever been so physically close.

"You must go and see for yourself," she said. "It's the only way to answer *really* questions."

I was familiar with the riposte, and did not reply.

"You *must* know the world, Lil," she continued, as she always did. "These lessons will prepare you, but you must see it to know it. *Casuarius galeatus?*"

I sighed. "The southern Cassowary. An entirely useless bird."

"Yes, I'm not sure the evaluation is necessary. You disapprove of the Cassowary?"

I raised my palms to the ceiling and shrugged. "A bird that can't fly?"

"Ah. You prefer the ones that fly."

I nodded. "I like the goonies. I like to watch them come and go and wonder to myself about where it is they fly to."

She smiled. The luminous dust between us made it difficult to look into her eyes.

"Dolos," she said, "amongst other places. You should see them hover over the city, little one. Their numbers. Do you know, you could spend the rest of your life wandering the streets of Dolos and never see the same palace twice?"

"Oh, I wish I could, Mama!"

"You can."

"With you, Mama? I'd be lost without you, I think."

She smiled.

"And Papa? Would he come?"

"Oh, I think your father would follow you wherever I let him, little one."

"Then we must all go. I wish *I* was a gooney—I'd fly there this minute!"

Another gnostic smile.

"You will fly away one day, little one. I promise."

To the best of my recollection it was the only time my mother ever made a promise to me. Despite the brightness of the room it must have been winter because beneath the clock's tick I could hear the hum of the heater that emitted a blue glow in the corner. It was quiet and everything, apart from the bustling dust, was still. The sun-pierced gloom of the living room made me think of the dome, that no natural light could penetrate. That was where I spent my mornings then, with the Stationmaster and you, at our books. To leave the dome each day on completion of our studies was always such a joy—from the tungsten light of its confinement, and the claustrophobia of the Stationmaster's close attention, out into the big bright world with you, to play.

Later, you would return to your cabin and I to mine and my mother's afternoon tutoring, where despite the great, aching pleasure I took in her company, I would be reminded that our world was not so big and bright after all. That it was not much less confining than the dome. That the real world, the big, bright, brilliant world was that which surrounded us. Everything that was *not* the Warburg—*that* was the world. My mother was nothing if not assiduous in putting the cup to my lips, and pouring it into this new vessel—my imagination.

"Mr Wern and his Nomenclature," she said. "Let me see . . ." She pursed her lips for a moment, then threw her hands up in exasperation, rolling her eyes. "So difficult to think of examples in this drab, colourless place!"

"I can think of some, Mama. In the spring, there are the flower—"

"I know! The dome's mast."

I considered the mast. "Snow white," I said.

My mother arched her eyebrows. "Like the breast of the black-headed gull?" She shook her head. "Are you sure? That would also be the colour of Snow-Drops. You've seen Snow-Drops, little one—they cover the forest floor in the spring. Try again."

I reconsidered the question, and then, pleased with myself, I said "Milk white."

"That's better. Other iterations?"

"The back of the petals of the Blue Hepatica."

"Something a little closer to home?"

I blinked for comic effect. "The whites of my eyeballs, Mama."

She laughed. "Excellent. The egg of a thrush?"

"Bluish green."

"The common weasel?"

"Wood brown."

"The belly of the warty newt?"

"Orpiment orange."

She was pleased with me. I could tell. It made me warm. Her eyes darted around the ceiling for more examples, and for some reason I thought of the dome again; *its* vaulted ceiling had an aperture that Fafl would open to receive the supply drops. Heft and Pack would be allowed in to collect them and move them to the storehouse. Only those two, you and I had access to the Stationmaster's dome—apart from Mr Bull, once in a while, to notarise some communiqué, Papa once a week to access the archive, and Wigbert in principle, though never in practice. Otherwise, no grown-ups—it made me feel special. And of course the mast rose from the dome's centre. I never really wanted to be there, but when I wasn't my mind's eye would return involuntarily and often. There was a logic to its going there now, at the mention of all these creatures I had never seen, and that a part of me feared I never would. The mast fed the observatory's array. On the horizontal antennae at its upper reaches, goonies perched, and around it the gulls wailed ceaselessly. No less than the waterline seen through the narrow entrance of the cove, the dome and its mast pointed to the wider, forbidden world. For that reason, the allure it held for me was every bit as strong as the disgust I felt whenever Mr Fafl would lower his gooney trap through the aperture and you would make our excuses, knowing I couldn't bear to be present when he slaughtered the terrified creature. How many dim hours did we pass there in our youth, under his stifling wardship?

"I know. The fishing pod. The faster of the two."

"Scarlet red," I said and, before she could ask, "like the mark on the head of the red grouse."

"Or?"

"The red parts of black and red Indian peas."
"Very good. The other pod, the slower?"
"What is Indian, Mama?"
"I don't know, little one. The name of a pea. The pod?"
I thought.
"Hm. Well, it isn't Gallstone Yellow."
"No."
"Or Wax Yellow."
"No indeed."
"Or King's Yellow. Or Gamboge." I shook my head. I hated not to have an answer, then as now. "I'm not sure what kind of yellow it is, Mama."

She leaned forward again, her face and hair newly ablaze.

"Then you must ponder it, and tell me tomorrow. Now, why don't you go and do something about those dirty fingernails?"

It wasn't until my nails were spotless and my fingertips rubbed red by the brush that the answer came to me. I grinned at my reflection in the mirror. It was the same yellow as the Goldilocks shrubs that grew in the dunes up at the end of the beach, and I knew its name. I dried my hands and skipped back into the living room, but when I got there, Papa had arrived to pick me up and squeeze me, and mother had retired to the bedroom, and shut the door behind her.

"And how *are* the little ones?" Fafl had said.

He was sitting at his desk when the two sets of parents presented themselves and there he remained, fingers woven in their fingerless gloves over his little pot belly and the parody of a smile that revealed a set of teeth in very poor condition. The others stood—since only one chair had been put on that side of the desk, none of them claimed it till Fafl had made his enquiry, whereupon Mrs Cyre made herself comfortable in it lest her legs tire in the course of her response.

"Oh Mr Fafl! Simon is coming along ever so well. Leaps and bounds, Mr Fafl! Leaps and bounds. But then you know this—it has been under your tutelage, after all, that the boy has so excelled. I'll confess that as he began to toddle and get about a bit, and to use his words, well—I did entertain one or two doubts. He has his father's nose. It had been my fervent wish that he take more after my side, at least in the visual sense. I was quite a beauty myself, you know. Everyone said so. And if he does mix his words up a little now and then, and trip over them from time to time, well—"

"Yes," said the Stationmaster, looking at Izzy. "And Lil? How is young Lil?"

But Izzy merely smiled. When she was neither at home nor at her work, she rarely spoke in those days. Aren interjected.

"She is well, Jasper," he said. "You wished to see us?"

"They improve us, do they not?" Fafl continued, disregarding the question. "Delight us? Do they play together? I suppose they must. Do they skip? Run?" He clapped. "Oh! They do! The Warburg is enhanced by them, is it not? Our load lightened? Thank goodness for our little charges! Especially in our dilapidated condition. Without the merry beat of their little feet on the walkways, the peal of their innocent laughter, could we bear our deepening isolation, I wonder?"

"You wished to see us, Jasper."

"Wished it?" Fafl planted his elbows on the desk. "Certainly not. With the tidings I bear? How *could* I wish it?"

"Tidings?" Mrs Cyre looked from Fafl to her husband. "What tidings?"

"The station is diminished," said Fafl. "This is incontrovertible. No longer the Magistracy's dote. Key personnel have been reassigned elsewhere. No offence to present company." He shuffled some papers and placed them aside in a neat stack. "The onset of our decline can be precisely dated of course—it began when the work that Arenaceous so skilfully carried out was relocated. He might have followed it but he chose not to, for his own good reasons I have no doubt." He shrugged. "That said, he might have followed it. He might. And sent on his findings to us here. Fed us analysis. Kept our brilliant Izzy and her Mapping department at the forefront of Magistracy efforts. But he didn't. He did not."

Aren became aware that, in the periphery of his sight, Mrs Cyre was glaring at him.

"What has this got to do with the children, Jasper?" he said.

"I do my best, of course," said Fafl, ignoring him, "to acquire the data myself, to solicit the very latest information from my Magistracy contact. Despite my efforts, our Mapping stagnates. Worse—it deteriorates. I'm sure Izzy is as disappointed as I."

Izzy had her eyes on her husband. It wasn't by any means clear that she was listening.

"The children, Jasper," said Aren.

Fafl sat back in his chair and shook his head ruefully. "The role of Stationmaster here has not been agreeable of late," he said. "Most of my communications with the Magistracy now concern the distribution of nanoplant antidotes. I do little more than administrate the litany of departures which became inevitable when we lost observatory status. I might even go as far as to suggest that the Magistracy is in some disarray in its rush to remove personnel, the haste itself near impossible to administrate with accuracy. Neither Mr Bull nor myself can be quite certain our records are complete, such has been the flurry of departures. At any rate, most have already left. Those present may also wish to leave. Indeed, the window of opportunity will soon shut. The process of reassigning personnel draws to a close and when it is complete, no further antidotes will be issued. For our security, you understand. Any exceptions will be entirely at the discretion of the Magistracy. But—save for poor Arenaceous here who must await his pardon—there is still time for you others to make use of yours. It is my painful duty to inform you, however, of a difficulty that arises in the case of the children."

"Difficulty?" said Aren.

"I'm afraid so," said Fafl. "Simon and Lil carry nanoplants, of course. I have always complied with protocol and I made no exception for them. Why should I have?" He shrugged. "The complication is that the Magistracy has allocated no further antidotes since our downgrade and, I have been informed, will not. No entitlement to an antidote therefore exists in law for the Warburg children."

"I don't understand," said Mrs Cyre. "You're saying that Simon and Lil can never leave the Warburg?"

"Goodness *sake*," said Mr Cyre.

"No," said Aren, who had found reason, some time before, to familiarise himself with the relevant protocols. "That isn't quite what he's saying. Is it, Jasper?"

"No. Simon could leave," said Fafl, addressing himself to Mrs Cyre, "but you would need to give him your antidote. You or Mr Cyre. A living parent may do so. You face a difficult choice, I'm sorry to say. A dilemma." He placed one hand on his breast and sighed. "I am forced to put it upon you. A loathsome duty."

"Not at all, Mr Fafl," said Mrs Cyre. "There *is* no dilemma." If she was aware of how keenly her husband scrutinised her, she gave no indication of it. "We've never had any intention of leaving. I consider it quite untoward, you know, that so many have. Very disrespectful of you, I should say. You may inform the Magistracy that we waive our antidotes, Mr Fafl. We stay."

"Aren," said Izzy, "I don't—"

"I must say I'm relieved," said Mrs Cyre, getting to her feet. "I thought you might have something awful to tell us, Mr Fafl. Something truly dreadful. But you must have known what our response would be, surely? We will never leave you, Stationmaster. We are forever with you."

Fafl merely nodded—unable in the moment, it would seem, to compose an adequate expression of his gratitude. Mr Cyre, as he accompanied his wife from the room, did not express any view on the matter.

It is cold. The heater sits idle in a corner. Arenaceous Nell sits in the opposite corner, wishing he had fetched his wine, that he could now know its stupor and have it shut his eyes. But he also knows he could not stomach any wine today, and so must sit here alert—more alert, perhaps, than he has been since Izzy lived. They will come for him today. Before the entertainment, perhaps, or perhaps at it, but they will come. He curses his roving, restless sight, knowing that whatever object it happens to settle upon in this little room that has been his so long, it settles there for the last time.

---

the policeman's two lummoxes   not a word to me   never mind 'em   bull blowing into to his hands and stamping about   biting cold I suppose it is but I'm not bitten   no, it doesn't bite me   am I really so distasteful   even to the cold   never mind it   I feel nothing   which doesn't feel right   but there you have it   here he comes now   for the taking   an old man   and me waiting for him   an old man   it has taken this long   a lifetime after all   for him and for me   but there it is   there you have it   now I take him   finally   and more than him   more than his liberty   his good name   his life's work   his child   how good it feels   the sterile process   the officious stationmaster and his duties   I take the man   the girl   his work   my passage out of here   I take all

---

"It's well the Cyres have gone," Fafl had said. "I have something to propose."

He waited for a reply but, getting none, went on.

"Arenaceous, Izzy, your predicament is not that of the Cyres. The quandary for the Nells is, I'm afraid to say, quite distinct and altogether more dismal. Arenaceous, it is not possible for me to tell you when—or indeed, since your own obstinacy stripped us of our precious observatory status, *if*—an antidote might be assigned to you. I have to tell you, my dear old friend, that I consider it most unlikely you will ever leave this place. It would be as well for us to proceed in the assumption that you will not, and as well for you to remember that *your* choices have brought you to this low place, and rendered you of so little service to your lovely daughter."

Aren said nothing.

Fafl shook his head and sighed. "If little Lil is ever to be free of the Warburg, the moment has arrived to make it so. And yet, look at you Arenaceous—an impotent father, utterly unable to help your beautiful girl. Had you thought of others and not of yourself, you could now wave your wife and adorable child off as they flew to a better life." He shrugged. "As it is, only Izzy here has an antidote to give."

It was winter and many of the island's trees were bare. In the summer months the breeze would play a softer air though their leaves, but now the unhappy tune was more percussive—the arhythmic knocking together of crowded limbs and the creaking of those under strain in the wind. The Stationmaster watched as the import of his words took hold.

"There can be no question," said Aren, slowly, "of sending Lil away alone. Our only child."

"Aren."

Both gentlemen were taken by surprise at the intervention. Izzy had lifted her gaze from the floor to set it upon her husband.

"Lil can't stay here, Aren. It would be too cruel. She must see something of the world. It's the way she's been raised."

"It's the way *you've* raised her." Aren, taken aback at the asperity of his tone, fell silent.

Fafl smiled. "You both love the girl," he said. "That much is clear. I do too, in my own humble way. But you are faced with a dilemma and must decide. Will you at least listen to my proposal?" Taking Izzy's nod and Aren's sullen silence as acquiescence, he stood and stepped to the little window on the wall behind his desk. It was tiny and offered a view only of the rear of a nearby cube. Nevertheless, he looked out of it as his hands found each other behind his back.

"There is no need at all for little Lil to be alone, Arenaceous. How could you think such a thing? Haven't you seen how I delight in the little ones? Do you doubt that I have their interests at heart, and only theirs?" The fingers of his left hand flexed in his right. "Izzy is right about Lil," he said. "The Cyre boy will see his days out here on the Warburg and be perfectly content to do so, I should think. But your girl is altogether a different creature. Really a most remarkable creature."

He turned to face them.

"She must go. But we do not send her out into the world alone. In fact, we could not, even if we wished it. As a Warburg child, she would have no billet. As the legal ward of a Stationmaster, on the other hand, we could send her into the warm embrace of the Magistracy. To the Academy. You will know that she is safe and receiving a Magistracy education. It didn't do me any harm, I can assure you. You may even hear news of her, from time to time. And one day, perhaps soon, when those residents of the Warburg to whom I am obliged to administer antidotes have finally left us, I myself, along with the Marshall and his constables, will be reassigned, and I can go to her. Think of it—your daughter and I will be reunited, Arenaceous. That must be some comfort to you, surely? A guardian for her. Hm? Her dear Uncle Jasper. Remember that her Warburg education has been of necessity a rather redacted one. She is far from prepared for the world, and ought not meet it alone."

"Wait," said Izzy. "Wait a moment." She shook her head and closed her eyes tight as if to clear her thoughts. "Couldn't *I* go?"

Fafl's eyes narrowed. "My dearest Izzy," he said, lowering himself back into his chair. "You are not well, and have not been for some time. Even here on the Warburg, you have come to rely heavily upon your husband. How would you fare out in the world without him? I believe you are confused, and I do not blame you. You are not thinking clearly. Would you really condemn your daughter so?"

Izzy looked from the Stationmaster to her husband and back again. "No." She shook her head. "No, of course—"

"Nobody need leave," said Aren. "Izzy, you can't be compelled to grant your antidote to Lil. We can, all three of us, stay. We will have each other. We—"

Fafl smacked the desktop with both palms. "There it is!" he barked. "Do you see, Izzy? Even now, he thinks only of himself." He took a deep breath, eyes closed. "Compelled or not, Izzy, you must know that it is the right thing to do. Lil must have an antidote in your place. She *must*. I know you to be a virtuous person," he said, his eyes opening and flicking involuntarily towards Aren's, "and it grieves me terribly to find myself in this odious position—interceding in what ought be the most private, the most intimate of conjugal deliberations."

He weaved his fingers.

"But your husband is wrong. He misconstrues the dynamics. So characteristic of him. And so it seems that my idea, proposed in fellowship and good will, must become something else."

He raised himself to his feet again but remained behind his desk, leaning on it with the fingertips of both hands.

"There are few ways in which an antidote, assigned to one individual, may be reassigned to another. As Stationmaster here it falls to me to oversee any such reassignments. I can tell you that it is practically unheard of. It has never been done at the Warburg. I am required, under pain of death mind you, to receive the antidotes securely and to administer them lawfully. Even during our exodus, when they came and went so thick and fast, I made the most strenuous efforts to do so." He shook his head, rather showily, it occurred to Aren. "That whole episode, though it pains me to say it of any Magistracy initiative, was a shambles. But I did my duty. I tell you all of this to impress upon you the rarity of the opportunity that presents itself to you now."

He straightened, as if in search of an alternative posture with which to underscore the gravity of what he was about to say. However, not finding one, he once again leaned on his desk.

"In any of the Magistracy's secure locations, a living parent, *compos mentis*, may bequeath their antidote to their offspring. This is written into the protocols and the Magistracy will respect it. In the case of *non compos mentis*, on the other hand," he took his hands from the desktop, "a spouse may be considered executor and therefore make the decision on the afflicted individual's behalf. Unless, of course," he said as he returned himself to a seated position, "said spouse is a felon."

He gripped each armrest of his chair.

"As your physician, dearest Izzy—and though it causes me immeasurable sorrow to say so—it is impossible for me to adjudicate that you are *compos mentis*. You would not expect it, I dare say: we all know how frail you have been, how unwell, these past years. And here, as in the case of poor little Lil, your husband can be of no use to you whatever."

He shook his head and shrugged.

"And so the burden falls to me—as it so often has—your physician and your Stationmaster. *I* am executor here, and I must do right by you, Izzy. Though we know your thinking to be . . . nebulous . . . at times, and that your powers of reasoning come and go, none of us doubt your love for your daughter. That is what I must be mindful of, in reaching my decision. That is where my duty lies."

Aren, deathly pale now, spoke up. "Jasper, please . . ." His voice wavered. "You can't—"

Suddenly, Izzy was on her feet and taking her husband by the hand.

"You will please to excuse us, Stationmaster," she said. "We must speak privately."

True to her word, Mrs Cyre is not in attendance at this evening's Review. To know that the Committee is gathered and not be there must be taking a terrible toll on her, Aren supposes, as he shuts the door behind him. She has sent refreshments along—it will be easier to extract information from Mr Cyre, when she corners him afterwards, if his belly is full and he has had wine. There are glazed carrots and a bowl of salad leaves, some fried potato slices, a platter of shirred eggs, and some cold slices of a gooney Lil has harpooned.

"Always tastes better when it comes from Lil, doesn't it?" says Mr Cyre who, in the absence of his good lady, is positively garrulous. "I wonder why."

"She takes 'em out clean and kind—there's your why," says Mr Grim. "A keen shot, that one. When they come from Fafl's trap, we taste the fear."

Fafl has not come—and most unusually, nor have Heft and Pack. Mr Grim oversees, with his usual assiduity, the distribution of the wine—a glass is poured for Aren by the time he sits, his old friend noting that he does not raise it to his lips. Lil presses play.

After Sinn I was assigned to desk duties. I completed my tour five months later at which point, like all personnel that had been involved in the atrocity, I was granted extended leave. It was to be taken under the supervision of psychologists on the Haq archipelago. All in all, I wouldn't see home again for a year. By that time, you and I had been corresponding for a few months. Or the academy and I. Do you remember? You were still so young. You didn't reply but it meant everything to me that you could read some words of mine. My messages were cautious. They would have been scrutinized very carefully and I didn't want to risk having the line of communication withdrawn. In my expressions of pride in the progress you were making each week I could afford to communicate my approval, and that is what I did. When I told you that your physical training data were encouraging, I meant that I loved you.

Permission to visit your mother had also come through. Back in the house and still on leave, I could hardly put it off. It would have looked odd not to make the seven-mile journey to the sanatorium. After a couple of days, therefore, I went.

Do you remember your mother's voice, Lita? Or is it gone? It was musical, somehow, sing-song . . . difficult for me to describe. Like a wind-chime, perhaps? I don't know, I'm not expressing it very well. But I can hear it, and it wasn't the voice I heard that day, as a severe-looking attendant shut the heavy door of the sanatorium's secure unit behind us.

I'd been encouraged at first. The public entrance and foyer had been bright and cheerful. There was a child's play area, a cafeteria, patients mingling with visitors on loungers and sofas. When I identified myself at reception, the attendant had been summoned and I'd been led, first upstairs to a Dr Mann's office and then, with minimal small talk, out across the gardens at the rear to a separate building. The corridor was long as well as wide and your mother's cell at the very end of it, but I could hear her from the moment we stepped inside.

I knew it was her. But it wasn't her. The voice was raspy and thick, an unlikely mix of drowsiness and rage. She yelled obscenities I'd have wagered she didn't know, if I hadn't been hearing them with my own ears. She may have been struggling physically—her rambling was punctuated by shrieks that suggested an altercation and made the hair on my neck stand. I was in uniform and resolved to maintain my composure.

"We've been looking forward to your visit," said Dr Mann. "It might make a difference. I'm afraid your wife's condition has deteriorated rather alarmingly."

We started down the corridor—the attendant, the doctor and I, our heels clicking arhythmically on the polished floor. Syncopating my fear. I needn't have worried. In the time it took us to reach her cell door, the yelling subsided. A staff member with a clip board was waiting for us and shook her head at the doctor, who turned to me.

"We wanted to keep her off the sedatives for your visit," she said, taking my arm and guiding me instead towards a small office opposite. "But she rarely manages more than a few minutes."

"It was better yesterday," says the fat boy, at the end.

"Hark at the great adjudicator," says his father. "There's egg in your hair."

"It was though," says Mr Cyre. "I don't know what to make of it today. Little of interest. Rather sad as well, I should say."

"I th-thought it v-very sad," says Simon.

"Yes," says Lil. "I did too. Perhaps tomorrow, more will be revealed." She logs the Review and gathers her things. Seeing that she will not look his way, Aren stands.

"Yes, perhaps tomorrow," he says. "I'll leave you all to finish your supper."

"I'll walk with you, Mr Nell," says Mr Grim.

Aren takes his leave and the arm of his old friend and is not surprised when, upon nearing his cabin in the growing darkness, they can make out the bent figure of Fafl, waiting there and flanked by Heft and Pack. Mr Bull is with them.

"Good evening to you, Arenaceous," says Fafl when they draw close enough. "It is time. These two will accompany you to the holding cell. A bed has been made for you there with a light to read by. You may gather such personal effects as you consider necessary for the night."

"Holding cell?" says Mr Grim. "Time for what?" He holds his walking cane in both hands and looks for all the world as though he might wield it in defence of his friend.

"It's alright, Wig," says Aren. "This was to be expected." He steps into the cabin to pack a small bag and, except for Heft and Pack who wait outside, the others follow.

"What can the point of this be?" demands Mr Grim of the Stationmaster. "There isn't one, that's what!"

Fafl exposes his palms. "It is protocol, Mr Grim. I merely comply."

"It's true, I'm afraid," says Mr Bull, who stands in the doorway. "The Stationmaster informs me the Magistracy will let Mr Nell's sentence be known tomorrow. He must await it in the cell."

Though Mr Grim's complexion has taken a turn for the purple, he draws two deep breaths before continuing in uncharacteristically even tones. "We live on an island, gentlemen. I had assumed you were aware of it. To say nothing of the buoys. What possible purpose can it—"

"It's obligatory, Wig," says Aren, patting his friend on the shoulder. "Nobody present is at fault. Will you go and tell Lil, though?"

Mr Grim readily agrees and makes for the Committee Room.

"One thing," says Fafl to Aren. "This . . . *work* of yours. I really ought to have it—for safekeeping, you understand."

Aren points to the old notebook on the desk and the Stationmaster quickly conceals it under his coat. Then he, the Marshal and his constables and Arenaceous Nell make their way to the holding cell. It comprises one half of a cube adjacent to Fafl's dome, the other half being the storehouse.

Once Aren is inside, Mr Bull does him the kindness of bringing a bottle of wine from next door but, to his perfect surprise, the prisoner waves it away. The cell is locked and the double felon left alone there. If Lil is to come it must be tomorrow. The Stationmaster has indeed been so considerate as to leave him a light. It is the only furnishing in the place, apart from the hard bed and two chairs, one at either side, but it matters not to Arenaceous Nell. He is suddenly weak. He can sense his old body failing. He feels a pang of regret at having refused the sherry—it might have numbed him a little of what is to come; for he knows very well it will be a sleepless night, and whither memory's wings will carry him.

One of the fishing pods was gone. The yellow. He looked down at the jetty and walked along the treeline for a minute, scanning the water, then back uphill through the woods and towards the station clearing. Any number of personnel might have taken it; fishing was a popular pastime on the Warburg as well as an essential source of nourishment. As long as you had the nerve to navigate the wind and the currents without getting close to the buoys, a few hours in one of the pods, bobbing on the water, was a chance to look at the island from a little distance, and did the soul good. The big birds would circle low or sit in the water, company and a raucous serenade for the fisher.

But Izzy was the last person he'd expect to go out on the water. She never had. Perhaps she'd be at work by now—it had been a touch early when he'd stopped in at the laboratory. He had to find her and he dreaded finding her—a dread that had sat like a stone in his stomach since, upon waking, he'd found her gone. She never left the house before him—never—but, after last night . . .

Hastily, he'd breakfasted Lil and left her with Fafl at the door of the dome for her lessons. At the laboratory, Izzy's young assistant had been puzzled. They wouldn't expect her for another half hour, she'd said. He'd gone from there to the beach, thinking she might be walking it, and from there to the jetty. Now he set out for the Cyres' cabin. Izzy was not sociable, but did know Mrs Cyre a little through her sister's Sunday dinners.

"It's perfectly obvious to me what we must do," he'd said last night, after their meeting with Fafl. He spoke through clenched teeth. "I will not have our child an orphan. Neither that nor a charge of that . . . of that man." He took both her hands in both of his. "Let's stay, Izzy. Haven't we been happy here? I know that I have. I have you and we have Lil—what else is there in the world? If we are united in this, we can thwart Fafl. He is a coward, and would not go against the both of us."

She'd pulled her hands from his and turned her back. "It seems to me, Aren, that the Stationmaster is quite resolved," she said. Then she went to the bedroom, and put herself on the bed there, and wept.

He should have gone to her, he realized now, but he hadn't. He stayed where he was. *Let her weep*, he thought to himself. *If I must be strong for both of us, so be it.* He poured himself some wine and sat by the heater, staring into it, waiting for her to come to her senses.

After a while, she came back to him, lowered herself to the floor at his feet and took his hand in hers.

"Don't make me do this to the little one, Aren. I am not able. She longs to leave the Warburg and you are right—it is I that have instilled in her this desire. To know the world, to conquer it through her own eyes and ears. I do not regret it." Tears wet her cheeks as she spoke. "It is the only thing I have managed to bequeath my daughter, who has known nothing of my embrace and has never seen me as I used to be—happy and well. It is the one and only gift I have to give her. Lil will be safe, Aren." Then she'd raised herself a little and leaned forward into his embrace and with her lips brushing his ear she'd whispered, "There could be another child."

The words were as ice on an exposed nerve ending. Before he knew it he was on his feet. She had fallen back on the floor and looked fearfully up at him. He took one step towards her and reached out, but she did not take his hand. Instead, she flinched, as though he might strike her.

"I'm sorry, Izzy. I can't . . ." He had taken up his greatcoat and slipped his bottle of sherry into the pocket. "She is my only child, Izzy. I love her as I love you. More, because I know you love her too. I . . . would not want to live without her. I *could* not."

He'd left then and gone to sit on the beach with his wine for an hour or two. When he'd returned, finally, to the cabin, it lay in darkness, and Izzy had already fallen asleep. In his self-pity, he'd felt little but relief that there would be no more talk until a new day was upon them. Putting himself in his armchair, he'd fallen asleep in his coat.

There was no answer at the Cyres', no sign of life from within. The glade, perhaps—there was a small clearing down in the woods, where the water could be seen between the tree trunks, and Izzy had made a little garden there, a secret place where they could be together. They had used it less since Lil had been born, but he knew she still went there and so now did he.

She wasn't there. His stomach churned—he had to talk to her, to tell her he was sorry. He made his way back to the station and the Hive; she wasn't there either. The island was big enough for a lone walker to evade company for some time, but Izzy wasn't one for solitary walks. She spent so much time alone in her thoughts that on those rare occasions when she went somewhere without him, it was for company.

And so he returned to the dome to sound a bell-like toll on its curved metal door. Fafl came to it like a busy man disturbed.

"What is it?"

"I can't find Izzy, Jasper. She isn't here?" She wouldn't be, of course, but Aren couldn't help peering past Fafl into the gloomy interior. He could just make out Lil at a little desk, running a fingertip over a page.

"Absurd," said Fafl. "She is not at her work? Visiting with Mrs Cyre?"

All Aren could do was shrug.

"Arenaceous, are you telling me your wife is *missing*?"

There being no reply, the Stationmaster said, "Wait here," and retreated inside, shutting the door. A few moments later it reopened and Fafl emerged. He wore his greatcoat and made straight past Aren, muttering, "What have you done?"

He had put some distance between himself and Aren by the time the latter reacted and went trotting after him. The Stationmaster was at the Marshal's office by the time he'd caught up.

"Mr Bull, bring your constables. The jetty."

"What is it, Jasper?" said Aren. "What has happened?"

Fafl stopped to turn and peer at him. "What has happened, Arenaceous? Shouldn't I be asking you that?" He turned again to continue on his way. "The buoy perimeter has been activated this morning."

When they reached the jetty, Fafl gestured toward the pod. "Send them out, please, Mr Bull," he said, indicating Heft and Pack. "Buoy ten. That's due south. Straight out."

The morning was a dreary one. There was rain out over the water and the buoys were hidden behind its slanted grey veil. They watched as the constables piloted the pod out into it—Fafl and Mr Bull on the sand and Aren where he had slumped to a sitting position at the end of the jetty. He watched from there like a child watching something it cannot possibly understand—wide-eyed and emotionless—as the pod reemerged from the murk and made its way back toward them. As it drew near they could see that it towed the other pod behind it and a moan escaped Fafl on the jetty.

Heft and Pack, having moored their pod, jumped into the water and pulled the other towards the shore. Mr Bull and Fafl had a view into it from their vantage point on the sand, and there seemed no urgency left in either of them as the constables pulled it onto the beach.

Aren had watched it pass the jetty, mesmerised, but came to his senses now and leapt up to go to them. He slipped on the wet wood, tumbling into the water. It was shallow enough in that place but for a few moments he struggled to right himself, the waters roaring around him and in his ears, and a great wave of pain washing through him. When he got his head above water, he grabbed one of the struts beneath the jetty and held himself there, knowing he had broken his leg. He wiped water from his eyes and looked on helplessly as the others gathered around the pod.

There could be another child.

These, he now knew, would always be her last words to him. A terrible thought, but nothing like as terrible as the next—and the realisation that he might as well have drowned her himself. This was *his* work, this monstrous prospect.

I would not want to live without her. I could not.

And these would always be his last words to her. The murder weapons, it seemed to him, as they pulled her limp body from the boat and laid it down on the sand.

CHAPTER THE NINTH

WHEREIN A PRIVATE AGREEMENT BETWEEN TWO SENIOR INHABITANTS OF THE WARBURG COMES TO ITS FRUITION; AND THE COMMITTEE IS AFFRONTED.

WHAT is the archive? The question can be answered very adequately within the strictures of standing directives: the archive is the biodigitised totality of Magistracy sweep. The accumulated hazmat of millennia. The most powerful toxins are contained therein. Sealed, of course.

That was never the purpose of the Warburg anyway, when we had observatory status and the possibility of realtime detection. Our mission rather was to identify and analyse previously unexamined toxins, classifying them according to type and potency. We alone on the Warburg are exposed to this risk—that contaminants of the utmost toxicity might be isolated by the array and, in the pre-analysis, archival stage, accessible to our scrutiny. There are other arrays but the Warburg is the only archival site in existence, for obvious reasons. That over time Committee members would succumb to a degree of exactly that kind of degradation that the Magistracy exists to protect against was no doubt foreseen. Factored in. Hence *our* isolation—the comms blackout, the nanoplants, the buoys.

Of course, detections of that calibre are incredibly rare. In my time, I have yet to discover any lurking undiscovered in the archive. It turns out that most of the materials, however heretical they might be, are banal. Most entertainments, for example, are merely silly. Doctrinal artefacts are as a matter of course no less so. The potential for actual *harm* is not always therefore apparent. And yet the evidence has been plain, here on the Warburg and notably among its Committee members that, through attrition if nothing else, exposure will cause disease.

Papa would answer differently. Of course he would—his is both the greatest mind on the Warburg and the most damaged. For his insight, his intellectual sensitivity, he has paid a price. It was he who first sought to interest me in the archive. In his many years as archivist he had come to love it, to see a beauty in the thing he had thought so beneath him—not to mention its utility. Once he had emerged from his despair at the loss of Aetiology, the archive had become as rich a source of data for him in the pursuit of his theoretical work as live detection had ever been. And indeed, he *has* answered the question, when I was the asker.

He bid me walk with him, one night, to the beach—this at the time he sought to coax me into taking over as archivist. It was certainly the case that I needed something to do with myself, but up till then I had resisted. I was full of youthful vanity, I suppose, and didn't much care for the thought. It seemed like the job of a clerk, to me, though I would never have said as much. "I don't think I could manage, Papa," I would plead instead. "I'm not like you. I'm not entirely sure I know what the archive *is*, apart from endless old, forgotten files." This last was said on the way down to the water and was the closest I'd come to disparaging the man's work and therefore, of course, the man. "What *is* the archive, Papa?" I asked quickly, to brush the unintended slight away, but he did not respond and I was afraid that I'd offended him. If only he knew how much the very thought offended my heart!

We only get a few nights like that on the Warburg each year. Clear and still and warm. The sea was as quiet as I'd heard it in my young life. There was just the soft slap of water lapping at the jetty and, further out, the constant sigh of a slumbering ocean.

We lay side by side in the sand as we had so often done. Even the gulls were quiet, in awe perhaps of the overhead display—the sky was ablaze with other worlds and the milky nebulae that enveloped them. After a little time had passed, Papa spoke.

"What do you see, Lil?"

I blinked. His little tests, though I'd been subjected to them since I could remember, made me nervous.

"I see stars."

He propped himself up on one elbow and turned to me.

"Really? I see none."

We fell silent awhile. His eyes remained on me, I knew, while mine scanned the firmament in search of an answer fit for him.

"Now," he said when he had given me a minute or two, "what do you *see*, Lil?"

"I see," I took a deep breath and let it out slowly, "light. Evidence of stars. Traces."

"Much better. Clever Lil." He smiled in the illumined night, then lay back and looked up at the sky again. "*That*, my girl," he said, reaching out across the sand to pat my hand, "is the archive."

I knew then that we were at the point in the conversation where my Papa's increasing abstraction would begin to confound me. I recognised the pattern. Recognising patterns is what I'm good at, after all.

"Light," he said. A single gooney drew a black curve against the stars. We watched it fly out over the water, out of our sight. "Light, yes. Aetiology in its purest form. A pathway to the past. And beyond that, perhaps, to a time before. Maybe that's what truth is, Lil—a time before the past.

"For many years, I didn't see it. I set myself the task of naming, numbering and tagging—a taxonomy of disconnected dots. The archived artefacts. Except these dots, when scrutinised closely, come apart. They are not dots at all, but themselves constellations, made up of their own dots, and *they* in turn . . . the fractal geometry of the search for truth, Lil. It might drive a man to madness. But step back, or lie back rather, and, holding the gaze steady, focus not on this or that, but on the entirety. Better yet, slacken the optic muscles—let the whole thing blur, just a little bit."

I wanted to do as he bid me, but was unsure of his meaning. I tried to refocus on a point low above my head, so that the stars would blur as he wanted, but all I could make out was the blur. It told me nothing. Several times I tried this, to no avail. I knew that he was smiling at me.

"You are trying, Lil," he said, a minute or two having been allowed to elapse. "Stop it. Stop trying."

For a moment, the silence deepened—no waves broke and there was a pause in the water's lapping against the jetty. A breeze that almost wasn't there, was like a cool pillow on my cheek. I let out a gasp. In my noticing those things, I had been distracted from the task and had relaxed my unblinking eyes, in preparation, I suppose, for my next attempt. In that second, they were focussed neither on the distances nor on anything close. They were not focussed at all. And there it was. The great distances were suddenly transformed. The universe felt like an indoor space, neither large nor small, neither friendly nor threatening, neither out of reach nor within it. I looked to Papa, to see if he saw—felt—what I did.

"That's it Lil," he said. "That's what it's like for me now." He squeezed my hand. "It is a form of blindness that is also sight. I cannot distinguish between the sanitary and the sick any more. Between disease and cure, host and parasite, whichever binary you choose. This is a very serious disadvantage for the aetiologist. And yet . . . I feel advantaged. Blessed, you might even say."

I withdrew my hand, startled by his language. He chuckled. It's as well, if one is to hear such blasphemy, to be in the company of your most beloved. The only one you could possibly forgive for saying such things.

"I do not try to connect the dots, at least not in the sense of drawing a line from one to the other, and then another, and so on. Our maps and charts—the more complex they become, the more entrancing, but they are doomed to inadequacy. I wonder if . . . apart from other matters . . . that is what made your beautiful mother so fragile.

"No, it is the connecting *tissue* that interests me now. Do you know that it moves, Lil? I couldn't see that, before. It . . . behaves, somehow. Pulses. I see ripples. Waves. Some animating force. There is no such thing as an interesting artefact, really. It's all about the in-between. Do you see?"

I didn't, of course. But the conversation had got under my skin. I didn't see, but I wanted to. I didn't know about the notebook then, that it was the key to this new understanding of my father's. And I didn't know then that, even armed with it, I still wouldn't see. I would need you to see for me. Anyway, I found Papa's state of mind rather worrying and I thought it was time his days were more restful. Soon afterwards, I accepted responsibility for the archive.

My answer, if *you* were to ask me?

I can only tell you what the archive is to me. What it has been. If at first I went looking for what my father had found there, it wasn't long before the search overwhelmed me. There are places it seems I cannot follow. I need more than my Papa does. Or rather, I need less—I need those lines, those maps and charts he has come to dismiss. The tendons to his tissue. I need order. Mine is a forensic mind. I take after mother in that regard—if she had lived, I would have gone to Mapping, I'm sure. It is necessarily the case, then, that given this proclivity, I must disappoint my father. I have devoted much effort to the concealing of this truth.

I went looking for something else in the archive. My own search, my own story—my own little heresy, though I consoled myself with the thought that it was a true story I sought. The truest story I could think of, anyway: Time.

Or, in the context of the archive: chronology. This could form the basis for my organizational efforts. It was, at least, a new way to begin. *Potency* tags were of little use, but going by *type*, and referencing against the dismally limited education I'd had from the Stationmaster, I was able to piece together the rudiments of a history. Papa was only too happy to answer whatever blasphemous question I had the nerve to ask him from time to time, whenever the content of an artefact confounded me.

What I know of the world—except for you and Papa and we few who remain here, and for the trees and coves of the Warburg, the waves that wear at it, the wind that blows over it and the birds what wheel above it—is second hand. All of it. You too, I know, and the boy. Nobody else living can know how it feels. Just we three.

The archive didn't change that, but it did increase—exponentially—the quantity of data at my disposal, from which I could make suppositions, inferences, sketching out a skeletal notion of places, people and events previously unknown to me. It was mesmerising to become more deeply acquainted, if still imperfectly so, with the world beyond the limits of either my sense or my experience. By definition, an artefact was a known fiction—but in sufficient number, and arranged in sequence, suppositions about the realities that gave rise to them could be made. This was the pathway to the past that my father had spoken of. For the first time in my life, the river of information that flowed was under my direct control. It burst the confining banks of Fafl's Magistracy-sanctioned instruction. Even Mama's illicit and thrilling, but rather capricious, tutorials—which had stoked such fire in me—were superseded.

But nothing lasts does it? Nothing that pleases me, it seems. My newly expanded world was to close in on me again. The last live detections—of contemporaneous broadcasts—to be picked up by the Warburg array came in almost two years before I was born. I well remember the day I arrived at them, having threaded my way through the archive connecting that first series of dots, from the oldest artefacts I could find up to those final few. I remember the crushing realisation that no matter how many times I went back to find other pathways, I would always end up here—at the same artefact, picked up on the same day, in a world where I did not yet exist.

No matter how absorbing the journey then, time spent in the archive would never amount to more than a history lesson. It could have nothing to tell me about *my* world. It was a disconnection that my father would not have felt, having been brought to the Warburg and not born to it.

What *I* wanted was a pathway to the present.

---

it went bad for izzy   impossible to say why of course   a number of factors I would say   never took to her girl for one   frightened of the poor little thing she was   maternal deficit of some kind   which I medicated   helped to slow the decline but not to arrest it   arenaceous showing no signs   oddly   of the revulsion he must surely have felt   mustn't he   I did   and I too loved her once   I do think so   or wanted to   but it was unpleasant   to see her quondam brilliance snuffed   she turned my stomach in the end   anyway   it all came to a head once I had drained the Warburg down to these remnants   we few   and it was time for them to choose   and I think justifiably I made it a difficult choice for arenaceous   whose tedious litany of wins has so tormented   why wouldn't I   but sadly   as a result I fear of their inability   the little family   to make the difficult sacrifices we all must make   she very tragically passed away she did   that broke him   and I remember that time   those next few years   very fondly   but nothing lasts does it   nothing that pleases me that is   I had eventually to watch the man recover   regain a hold of himself   in the embrace of his fellowships   reclaim his daughter   I did not take it well   but those few years   those few years   while he languished in his cups   and she learned her tables in the dome with me   and I could almost nuzzle the delicate folds of her little mind   oh they *were* delicious

To furnish the reader with a more complete description than that previously given, of the cell in which Arenaceous Nell is held—though the sparseness, simplicity and size of the space would hardly seem to merit the effort—is perhaps rendered not quite uninteresting by dint of the extraordinary circumstance that prevails there on the second evening of his incarceration. That very particular saponaceous aroma, apparently universal to places of confinement, pervades. There is no window, save for a square of glass brick just beneath the ceiling at the head of the bed. The walls are made of metal and painted a disheartening beige. There are no electrical fittings of any kind, but a small lamp has been hung from a central hook. The only other furnishings are the chairs at either side of the bed—at its foot is the heavy door, just enough space between the two for a person to stand.

A person does stand there. It is the Stationmaster.

Mr Nell is on the bed, or rather, in it. His old head is propped on a pillow and the blanket neatly tucked beneath his arms. One hand reposes in the other on his belly and though he does not sleep, from time to time he shuts his eyes and keeps them shut for a little, his lips moving soundlessly through some remembered conversation, his countenance permuting softly through a series of expressions that signal the recollection of past events.

Not a word is spoken. The Stationmaster watches the bedridden aetiologist. The curl of his lip speaks of neither affection nor concern. He moves to the side of the bed, eschewing the chair there—this is not a friendly visit. Instead, he lowers himself awkwardly to one knee and leans in close. Aren has not seen him approach.

"How the mighty are fallen," says Fafl, perhaps a little more loudly than necessary.

When Arenaceous Nell opens his eyes they are already set on his old nemesis. He does so slowly, and without taking fright.

"Remember, Arenaceous," says Fafl, pulling back a little, "that you asked for all this. You have brought it upon yourself."

"I did. I have." The voice is weak, and tired, and thick. The tone is none of those things.

"I am blameless," says the Stationmaster. "I have done as you bid me, actually. More or less."

"You are blameless."

Fafl shakes his head. Where is the fight? Where is the victory, without the fight? He wonders, not for the first time in his life, why the peace eludes him that seems so thoroughly to fill the other. Then he nods, and gives a little grunt of understanding.

"It is this vile heresy of yours, Arenaceous," he asks, "that comforts you now. That you go to Izzy." He straightens a little and shifts painfully on his knee. "She is well again, I suppose, in this other place?"

Aren smiles. When he answers, he prefers to do it with closed eyes.

"She is well, Jasper," he says, "and she is unwell. She is everything she always was and always will be."

A sneer further distends the Stationmaster's features.

"And will I go there too? And join you both? Wouldn't that sully it for you?"

The eyes open.

"You are already there, Jasper. It is not a place you can arrive at, or leave."

The Stationmaster leans in again.

"You disgust me, Arenaceous Nell. You—"

A loud knock at the door startles him. He lifts himself up, goes to it and opens it. Mr Bull steps into the cramped room and shuffles aside that space be made for Wigbert Grim, who enters and looks quizzically at Fafl, then at his old friend in the bed. Heft and Pack enter behind him and, with some difficulty, squeeze past the others to take up their places on the chairs at either side of the prisoner's pillow.

"You sent for me, Aren?"

"I did, Wig. Come sit on the edge of the bed here."

The visitor does as he's told, one last questioning look cast in the direction of the Stationmaster.

"I came earlier, you know," he says as he sits down, "but they wouldn't let me see you."

Aren has taken his hand and blinks at him as though to clear his vision. "What o'clock is it, Wig?"

"Just gone seven. Are you all right, Aren?"

"Seven? Lil is conducting the entertainment, then?"

"That's right. Hasn't she been to see you?"

Aren smiles, but Wigbert takes no comfort from it.

"If she came earlier," says Aren, "they did not let her in."

Fafl stirs and speaks. "She did not come."

"What is the matter, Aren?" says Wig, eyes baleful on the Stationmaster before returning to his friend. "Have you been taken ill? If they have—"

Aren pats his hand. "Calm yourself, Wig. I am not ill," he says, and chuckles. "No one has done me harm. I have been given a physick. A sedative." He lifts his head from the pillow slightly, and winks. "A rather good one."

"A sedative?" Wigbert shakes his head. "What f—?" The question sticks in his throat. He turns around once more. Mr Bull is terribly pale as he steps forward to speak. His eyes have reddened and are not quite dry. He nods, reading into Mr Grim's incomplete enquiry his sudden understanding.

"It's true," he says. "The Magistracy has passed sentence. I have seen and, to my eternal regret, notarised the order." He nods towards Aren, who has shut his eyes. "It was his fervent wish that you be present, Mr Grim." And with that, the Marshal turns away, doubtless to spare the company his sudden coughing fit.

"But this is . . ." says Mr Grim. "We *can't* . . . we must *appeal*—"

"Appeal?" says Fafl. "To the Magistracy?" He rolls his eyes. "But what would you know, any of you? I forgive you your naivety. What can you know of my countless petitions? Of my unceasing efforts—and not only in *this* case—to promote your improvement and advantage? So often at my own expense." He has become shrill. He takes a breath. "A sentence has been pronounced, Mr Grim. There can be no—"

"Mr Bull," says Wigbert. He is on his feet. "Of this creature," he indicates the Stationmaster with a dismissive wave, "I long ago despaired. But you? I beseech you. Stop—"

"Mr Grim!" The Marshal's outburst is almost a sob.

"Wig," says Aren from his bed. "Sit down here and be with me for a bit. There's nothing to be done but what must be done."

Wigbert sits. His lips tremble.

"Mr Bull does his duty," says Aren, once again taking his hand. "As he always does and always has done. As we ourselves have relied upon him to do from time to time, have we not?"

A curt nod. Wigbert's eyes well up. Aren goes on.

"And your assessment of the Stationmaster is the plain truth. It would be reckless of us to squander what time we have on any consideration of that person. As for these two," with a flick of his eyes in either direction, Aren indicates Heft and Pack, "I think we can forgive them, don't you? They don't know what they do here."

Pack's eyes are so very nearly shut that he might be asleep, though he isn't. Only an oracle could hazard a guess at whither the flights of his untrammelled imagination have taken him. As for Heft, if any quality or sentiment can be attributed to him via scrutiny of his visage or general demeanour, it is most plausibly that of Hunger—a hypothesis that his absence at the indubitably food-laden Review would support.

"The sedative will not last," says Mr Bull, in steadier voice than before, "but we can give you some moments. Stationmaster, step out with me."

Fafl protests. "Oh, no indeed, Mr Bull! *Protocol*, you know. We would not wish to compromise Mr Grim, would we, by exposing him to some clandestine communication from the prisoner? No—"

"Step out, Stationmaster." Mr Bull is the very picture of Resolve, Fafl that of Indignation.

"Mr Bull," says the latter, "I am Stationmaster here. Why—"

"Because I am Marshal," says the former, "and because the *protocol* that applies here is a custodial one, sir, and because were I unable to remove an individual from *my* holding cell whom I had instructed to remove themselves," he pats the sidearm that hangs from his belt, "I should be obliged to put a bullet in 'em, sir."

Fafl steps out. The Marshal follows. Nobody thinks to rouse either Heft or Pack. Wigbert and Aren are left, to all intents and purposes, alone.

"I've been remembering, Wig," says Aren, when a moment has passed. "How you helped me. Me and Lil. Do you remember?"

Wig struggles to make his friend out through the warping lens of hot fluid that wobbles on the rim of his eyelid.

"Yes, Aren," he says. "I remember."

A tree trunk. He patted it in passing and though he did not break his stride he left his hand to linger for a moment, and the soft moss that covered the gnarled and twisted thing cooled his palm. *A laurel*, he thought, and the observation could not have been described as especially incisive—most of the trees on the Warburg were laurels. At least half of 'em, at any rate—the leaves had been well used by Izzy's sister, coming into their own on those few but much anticipated occasions that called for roasted goat. A place for him had been set at her Sunday dinners, these past months, and it was beginning to show in his paunch.

His face too felt cool—the motionless air was fogged by the morning's thick marine layer, not yet lifted. The mist made an unmistakably primordial prospect of the shaded woodland, aided by the absence, it seemed, of a single straight, upright trunk. *And this one's a juniper.* He never had been one for walking but lately that had changed; he must have tramped every square inch of the island in his searches—fearfully at first, anxious that he might not find that which he sought, and latterly more lackadaisical, certain that he would.

Sometimes he would find it up on the north shore where the steep mud banks might, with a little license, be described as cliffs. Sometimes he would stumble across it mere feet from the compound, sometimes down at the waterline. *This is an old erica. I am become quite the botanist.*

Most of the time, though, he would find it in the same sad place, and so that is where he would look first and whither his feet took him now—carefully, so as not to disturb the blossoms that sprouted at this time of year and made a bright carpet of the forest floor. *What is it about the Springtime*, he wondered, *and its insistence on yellows and purples?* The ground was decked in those two hues in all directions, and here and there, as though gleefully to make a liar of him, a burst of brilliant red.

As he stepped into the little clearing, it occurred to him that he might get back in time for breakfast after all; this morning's search was over. There on the ground, by the little bench from which, presumably, it had slumped, lay a human form. He approached it and gently turned it over, for it lay face down, and as he did so it let out a grunt and opened one eye.

"Oh, it's you," it said.

"Hello, Aren," said Wig.

And those were the only words he was to hear from his friend this morning. He helped him to his feet and they made their way back to the station, back to the cabin that Aren could no longer bear in the evenings, so heavily lay Izzy's absence upon it. Now he let Wigbert put him on the bed and pull his shoes off and, placing a glass of water for him by the bedside, slip away.

At his own door, Wig's mood lightened. There was the smell of bread as he opened it, and coffee, and the embrace of domestic warmth as he closed it behind him. And there *was* the bread, already sliced and awaiting a good smear of butter and jam. And there was the coffee pot, lazy vapours in the air around the spout. And there were eggs, and cheese. And there, at the table, was she.

"Hello Wig," she said. "You found him." And there was the best breakfast of all—the smile she flashed him, so open and unguarded he could somehow feel it fill the pit of his stomach. There was none of the austerity with her here, nothing of the severity she reserved for the others. Izzy's sister. Wigbert's wife. *What a wonder!*

"I did," he said, "and put him abed." He sat and took up his knife to address the butter and as he did so, Lil came in from the kitchen with a bowl of beans.

"You found him, then," she said.

"I did, Lil. He was asking after you," he said, glancing at his wife.

"Was he?" said Lil, who fervently wished to believe it.

"Have you got your notes together for today's classes, Lil?" said her aunt. "Your father is most particular you do well in your schooling." And with another look exchanged between the married couple, all three tucked into the good food in front of them, and spoke of other things.

"The Stone? The Stone?"

He handed us each a little glass of tea and sat again.

"It is called that, yes," he said, "and The Pulpit, by some. We call it The Step, or sometimes, colloquially, The Angel's Tongue—I don't know why but I think it's terribly pretty, don't you?"

I could hardly believe what I was hearing. Looking down at the glass in my hand, I took a moment to formulate a reply. But how to respond to such a bizarre assertion, made so matter-of-factly? It was too absurd.

"You're telling me that The Stone is here. The gateway to paradise. That is what you are telling me? I would like to be clear."

"I think you've put it very succinctly."

I had to take a moment, to suppress a rage that I hadn't felt since before Sinn. I'd been inured to heresy, I think—no longer feeling the personal outrage that fired the campaigns of my youth. These days, I simply went about the business of eradicating it—efficiently and, where possible, quietly. Never before, though, had I heard anything so brazen. To be told such a thing was suicide for the teller. As soon as I felt that my voice wouldn't waver, I spoke.

"Are you or are you not familiar with the organization I represent?"

"We are aware of you, yes. At the risk of sounding mysterious," he said, "we've been waiting for you."

"Oh, and I for you," I said, crossing my legs. "To think that I've finally found it. That it should fall to me," I looked to Evans and then to Zwickl and only just resisted the temptation to wink. "The one stain we've been unable to wipe away. The first myth. And here we are," I threw my arms wide, "and it's not a myth at all. That's what you're saying? You'll appreciate that my organization is rather fond of the truth. We named ourselves for it, after all. Tell it to me then, won't you, and we can all go home."

He smiled. "You misunderstand, I think. Most do. To fall from The Angel's Tongue is not to know the truth. Nothing is revealed. One becomes the truth. The word."

"Really?" I said. "Please clarify."

"Tricky," said the man who, it occurred to me, hadn't told us his name. "We are not the first settlers, you see. They disappeared a long time ago, before we came. Even they, those who built these ruins, may merely have been passing through, as we undoubtedly are." He weaved his fingers. "We use The Step. We give thanks for it. We do not understand it."

"You're not native?" I said. Lie upon lie. "You might also explain, then, how you got this far out before us?"

"We don't know that either. I'm afraid we are not the most scrupulous historians. But I don't suppose it need necessarily be the case that we've travelled so very far, if you allow for the possibility that we came from the opposite direction."

He stood and rubbed his hands together.

"Anyway, we're here now and I imagine you're keen to see it. Not possible today, I'm afraid, but we can set off first thing in the morning if you'd like. It's a rather arduous trek, much of it through tunnels, but you all look hale and hearty."

"We'll go now."

"I'm afraid it isn't possible, as I said. It's in use today."

"In use?"

"Two of our people have chosen to take their step today."

"Perfect. We can debunk it with witnesses. We might save a life or two in the process."

He pursed his lips.

"It would be a grave offense to our faith," he said, "if you were to interrupt a ceremony there."

I stood.

"We do not recognize your faith. We are here to relieve you of it."

He chuckled.

"And how are you to do that? With a snap of your fingers?"

His levity galled me. I took a step toward the table.

"It isn't instant," I said, "but give us time. Probably not much time in your case, since by the end of the day we'll have debunked your ridiculous step. I can assure you, we're very good at what we do."

"If you say so. I'm beginning to find our little exchange rather annoying."

I snorted, aware that my tolerance was slipping.

"Not as annoying as you'll find us in the event of your non-compliance. I understand from those who have experienced our reprisals at first hand that we can be very annoying indeed. Can you imagine how annoying the entire peoples we have annihilated must have found us?"

"I'm not sure imagination is required," *he said, and yawned.*

Evans and Zwickl had also stood and flanked me now. The two security guys had stepped forward and had their hands on their weapons.

"You will relinquish your faith," *I said, as coolly as I could,* "and your fictions. As of now, they are tactical assets."

"We are perfectly happy to take you there in the morning. Apart from anything else, you'll be refreshed for the hike."

"I'd prefer to go immediately. We'll take the ship."

"I cannot permit that. Besides, there is nowhere to land."

"Then we won't land. But we will go."

"Lummy," says the fat boy, who in the silence that ensues is assumed to have nothing further to contribute. Indeed, now that the audio fragment has reached its conclusion and his verdict has been dutifully delivered, he returns his attention—with considerable gusto—to the macaroni.

The Review is a mere remnant. Only Lil, the boy, a defiant Simon and Mr Cyre are in attendance. Mr Cyre, the eldest present, takes it upon himself to open tonight's proceedings.

"This is plainly heretical, now," he says. "Perhaps, and I find it very unsettling indeed to hypothesize thusly, I should have listened to my wife."

"What do you think, Simon?" It is perfectly obvious to all but the boy that Lil is not her usual self. She speaks brusquely and when not speaking, her jaw muscles do not rest.

"It is subversive," says Simon. "Do you think it might have been produced by . . . by the resistance?"

"For goodness' sake, Simon," says his father. "We have all been assured countless times that there is no resistance."

"It does seem organised, though," says Lil. "Coordinated. Designed for a very specific audience."

"Who?" says Mr Cyre.

"Us," says the boy, and all turn to look at him in astonishment.

"You and I, Wig," says Arenaceous Nell, "have been on this confounded heap far too long. I lack your patience; it's time for me to go."

Wigbert is seated still, on the edge of the bed—still holds his friend by the hand, still looks beseechingly at him through wet eyes. He is aware that, behind him, the Marshal and the Stationmaster have stepped quietly back inside. He shakes his head.

"Aren," he says. "Lil—"

"No, Wig. It's time for her too. I have found a way for her to quit this place. A hard way, I'll grant. But I don't want her here now. She would be disruptive." Aren pats his friend on the hand. "Months from now, or years perhaps, it will cease to matter to Lil that I slipped away in her absence. She has more to forgive me for than this." His eyes close and he takes deep, slow breaths.

Wigbert claps his hands in his distress. "I never knew anyone so good as you, I truly didn't. You could have had renown. You should have had it! Look at you now, look at this miserable little hutch. How wretched you are! Nothing to show for your talent, for your goodness, for your work. I—" He cannot continue.

"That's not right, Wig. It's quite wrong," says Aren. "If I lost my great love, did I not have her for a precious while?" He reaches out to squeeze Wig's shoulder. "And have I not had the fastest of friends? And have I not been blessed with Lil? Have I not raised a child who is stronger than I? Cleverer? Better than I?" He smiles and lifts his head a little, though the sedative is in full effect and he struggles to do it. "That's a good trick, isn't it?" he says. His head drops once more, eyes shut. "My best work," he murmurs.

"It's time, Mr Grim," says the Marshal. "If we're to be as kind as we can, this is the moment." He says this with his eyes on Fafl, who has already snapped open a little leather case to retrieve two vials from it, and two syringes.

"You stay where you are, Wig," says Aren. "Jasper can have the other arm."

Heft and Pack, at a nod from Mr Bull, each takes one of Aren's arms and holds it straight out so that its cruciform owner is restrained. "Protocol," says the Marshal apologetically. "No need for it, I know." The Stationmaster approaches on the far side of the bed, straps an upper arm, thumbs the vein.

"Wig," says Aren. "Look out for Lil." He sighs. "This is but one event in a series of them. It isn't the last. My only object is her escape. Let's not mind the particular circumstances of that escape for now." His eyes momentarily go to the attentive doctor, who has a syringe to the swelling vein, then return to his friend. "Be strong, Wig, if she is not. Won't you?"

Wigbert cannot find his voice. He has leaned awkwardly in order to keep a hold of his friend's hand, now in Heft's lap, and squeezes it tight. As he does so he feels it slacken in his grip and raises his downcast eyes to Aren's, which have shut again.

"Aren?" he says.

"He cannot hear you," says Fafl, who has already withdrawn the needle and has a second poised.

"What?" say Wigbert, looking from his old friend to the Stationmaster and back again. Businesslike, Fafl goes on.

"There are two injections," he says. "This first has deepened his sleep. He cannot hear you now. The second will stop his heart. There may be some movement. You might find it disagreeable."

Wigbert's hand has gone to Aren's cheek. "Aren?" But no response comes, or ever will. Through gritted teeth, he addresses the Stationmaster. "You should have said, Fafl. We were speaking. A warning—" He cuts himself off, seeing that Fafl has already withdrawn the second needle, and holds a stethoscope now to Aren's breast. Presently, he takes it away and returns it to the leather case.

"It is done," says the Stationmaster and withdraws from their presence, leaving Wigbert and the Marshal to look, stunned, upon the body of their friend. Whatever the inward reactions of Heft and Pack, as they hold the old man's outstretched arms at each side, they are still and silent.

Mr Bull steps forward and stands by Wigbert's side, a hand placed gently on his back. They are both somewhat in awe as they look at old Aren—a single tear has escaped the dead man's eye and left its trace on his cheek, but it cannot sully the joyful expression with which Arenaceous Nell bids them farewell. It is as though it is they who are to be fretted over, they who are to be pitied. There is something benevolent, generous, in that lingering smile, so that, despite his tears, Wigbert cannot help smiling himself, so contagious is the sense of release imparted. When Mr Bull breaks the silence and speaks, he speaks a heresy.

"Where is he now, Mr Grim?" he says. "Do you know?"

Wigbert looks up, amazed that the Marshal should formulate such a thought, never mind ask the question. Looking back at Aren, he finds he has an answer.

"I do, Mr Bull," he says, "He has returned, I believe, to that very particular chapter of his life when his daughter had already been introduced into the story, and his wife had not yet been written out of it. And though it was not an untroubled chapter, I do believe he has alighted upon one of its many joyful moments. He is at the hearth, perhaps, or down at the water, with Izzy and Lil. I—"

There is noise outside. Both men turn their heads to the open door through which it intrudes: a remonstrance, voices—and among them, one Wig shudders upon hearing.

Mr Cyre has taken his leave and, in a wholly uncharacteristic display of tact, has taken the fat boy with him. Lil fastens the clasp of her bag, intensely aware that Simon is on his feet and has approached her.

"Lil," he says, "I . . . I wish . . ." He lets out a groan. "Are you sure—"

"Don't," she says. "Please don't. I can't."

She throws the bag over her shoulder and moves past him, towards the door. When she has her hand on the doorknob, he still has not responded. She turns to look at him and almost breaks, so broken is he, with his head hung and fists clenched.

"Simon," she says, and he looks up at her, "I'm sorry. Please let's talk, you and I. There is much to say. But tomorrow. I have to go to Papa now." Her tone is one of supplication, of the penitent seeking absolution. He nods, granting it, and she steps outside.

On the way up to the holding cell she tries, and fails a dozen times, to rehearse what she will say to Arenaceous Nell. How to reassure him. The promises she will make. Her deliberations are interrupted when, on approaching the cube, the cell door is opened and Fafl emerges from it. On closing it and turning around, he recoils.

"No," he says. "No, no—"

"What's the matter?" says Lil, eyeing the medical bag he clutches. "Is something the matter with my father?"

He shakes his head, as though to throw off the apparition.

"I didn't," his free hand flaps, "I didn't want to be here when you . . ."

"What is in the bag, Mr Fafl?" Without knowing it, she has taken him by the shoulders. "What is in the bag?"

"Lil!" says Wigbert, who has come to the door and stepped out. The Marshal follows. A single look at either of them removes the necessity of any reply from the Stationmaster. She knows what has happened.

And now Wig comes towards her, reaches out. No, he is reaching *down*. She is on the ground and Wig is saying something. She cannot hear it. There is only the chorus of the gooneys overhead, and the circles they make around the mast as night closes in.

CHAPTER THE TENTH

THE DOMESTICATION OF WIGBERT GRIM;
THE CAPITULATION OF LIL NELL;
AND THE EXASPERATION OF JASPER FAFL.

WHAT MADE ME think on it   I cannot say the daily spectacle perhaps of his fool father stuffing him with food   made him seem capacious   the fat boy   an amenity   and amenable to bribery   as long as it came in the form of fat   I found myself eyeing his flesh somewhat lasciviously   with something like desire I suppose   though I wouldn't want that to be taken the wrong way   very much a lady's man   but a cornered rat will bite will it not   will break skin   in its bid for escape   and escape is what the faint blue vein in the pale fold of the boy's arm looked like to me   very much so   in some way I could not quite quantify   it was more of a quality   methought   and I was cornered wasn't I   had long languished by that time   in a corner of my own making withal   but a corner is a corner   and a rat is a rat   and so I broke that soft skin didn't I   and stuffed the foolish boy myself   I poured it into this new vessel   the archive   little by little   made an artefact of him   an insurance   knew something the magistracy did not   the magistracy   to which I had given my life in return for   what   had something they did not know   I had   a leverage   that kind of thing can come in handy   can it not

⁓

Though not all of the cubes on the Warburg station were configured in precisely the same way (some were piled on top of one another to create taller structures, some pushed together to become longer, or wider), the majority were in their interior, being of standardized construction, divided into equal quadrants—these consisted of a sleeping quarter, a kitchen, an ablutions room with privy, and a heated parlour. In its original state, therefore, each presented an impersonal and dreary scene, worsened considerably by the grey metal of the untreated walls and the plain brown linoleum that lined the metal floor. It was the dreariness that would eventually drive the remaining inhabitants out, to build their own ramshackle homes nearby. But all that was yet to come.

In many cases, the situation was not much improved with occupancy. In the shared cadet quarters the only decorative touch detectable to the eye, for example, might be wet socks hanging from the heater or, by way of an artwork to edify his comrades, the skewed scratchings of a conscript on the wall, marking off the days of his fixed term. Even with supply drops coming and going and Warburg personnel at liberty, should they wish it, to accoutre themselves with such garniture as tablecloths, curtains or paint of some more agreeable colour, few did. Why would they? Why would they adorn the Warburg, when their dearest wish was to depart from it?

Only in the family quarters were such adjustments made—trifling adaptions to the persisting imperative of domesticity where men, women and their offspring lived together. Those were the only cubes, moreover, from which, at dinner hour, a most unusual (on the Warburg) scent could emanate—that of decent cooking. It was not rare in those days to spot a young cadet whose stride had been involuntarily checked, loitering outside a delicious-smelling window as though it were itself a meal and to all appearances in full enjoyment of the festivities within. At times they might even cluster together in this way and, on occasion, among them, their senior in years by a considerable margin, was Mr Wigbert Grim.

As the station's internal security consultant, he'd been spared the indignity of shared habitation and assigned his own cube. As an unmarried man, on the other hand, he did nothing to improve or brighten it and subsisted, like his younger associates, on biscuits and protein gel. When his great friend Arenaceous Nell was married to the head of Mapping and Wig was regularly made welcome in their little cabin, he was therefore very glad of it—Izzy made the place look nice with nice things and sound nice with nice words and the peal of nice laughter, so that the bachelor could take great and vicarious pleasure in his friend's new matrimonial condition. If he'd had one slight criticism of the arrangement at the time (and he wouldn't have dared give voice to it), it would have been that the culinary wonders heralded by the perfumed atmosphere surrounding other connubial Warburg homes at dinnertime, continued to elude him in this one.

When *finally* he sat down to one of those feasts for which he'd long gathered such strong olfactory proofs, but upon which he'd never set eyes, the encounter was bittersweet. He'd been on the island for years by then. Aren was widowed, his mind and health in ruins, and he was father to Lil, a motherless girl of barely ten years—plainly devoted to her father but an old soul at her young age, the whole callous world weighing down upon her little shoulders. It was his friend's bereavement that had prompted Izzy's sister to invite Wig to one of her Sunday dinners, become the stuff of legend on the Warburg for the quality of the fare. She wanted to fill the seat left empty by her Izzy, since she still refused to speak to Aren directly, and therefore required some new conduit. Lil was still a little young for the role and the Cyres made very poor sounding boards—Mr Cyre rarely speaking and Mrs Cyre rarely stopping.

All of the above, mere preamble, he thought to himself as he stood in the doorway, taking a moment to savour the scene which presented itself to his eyes. The cube he would never leave, not even when the others abandoned theirs. Sitting by the heater, a bowl of broad beans in her lap for podding, Izzy's sister was beginning to show. She smiled up at him as she always did, amused at his habit of pausing on the threshold whenever he got home. There was no doubt in his mind as to the source of her amusement. Wigbert Grim knew precisely what he was—a gentlemen who, despite abundant evidence available daily, could not quite believe his luck.

Home. He finally had an idea what the word meant, and this new understanding came with the realisation that it wasn't an idea at all—it was the broad beans. It was the inexplicable doilies, draped over any available surface. It was the warmth and the aromas it carried, of cleanliness and coffee and something, he fancied now, in the way of a good mulligatawny. It was Lil, paused at her own threshold—that of womanhood—and deep in study at the desk he'd made for her. It was that little bump on his wife. They weren't so young, he and she, after all, and it wasn't a gift granted to everyone. Yet here they were, and Fafl very pleased with her progress, and everything going well. *It's true*, he thought, *I cannot believe my luck*.

"Hello, Aren," he said, though he couldn't for the life of him pull his gaze away from Izzy's sister.

The gentleman addressed, being seated on a stool nearby his daughter, had removed the back panel from her tab and, when not responding to her occasional questions or guiding her study, was repairing it. The sight was almost as cheering to Wig as that of his wife. Aren was not the man he had been, but he was getting on a good deal better of late. He had returned to his old, long abandoned notebook some months ago and something had changed in him. He no longer disappeared, instead spending much of his day here in this cabin, relatively sober till the evenings, when Lil would return with him to their cabin, so that he not find himself alone with his memories there. It was the semblance of a family life, and the best that could be expected of the poor man. Especially when at that notebook of his, he seemed to have found the peace that had eluded him for so long.

"Hello, Wig," he said. "It'll be good to have someone to talk to."

The remark went ignored by his daughter. The expression that lay upon the face of Izzy's sister, however, changed in an instant from the smile reserved for her husband to that very particular frown she reserved for his friend. "Lil," she said, "please do let your father know that in this house he may speak as much as he likes. If he were to grant us all one small concession, perhaps it could be that whenever embarking upon one of his soliloquies he might take a moment, just before, to assure himself he has something of interest to say." The rate at which the pods were spitting out their beans had increased quite considerably. "And of course, there are certain quarters whence he ought never to expect a reply. We must all live with the consequences of our transgressions."

It was sufficient, apparently, that for the conveyance of the message, Lil merely look to her father as these words were spoken. A quick and gleeful glance exchanged between Aren and Wig, the latter shut the door behind him and stepped into the room to make some further enquiries regarding the soup.

Wigbert's eyelids flutter. He becomes aware of the light that filters through them. It must be that in his weariness he left the curtains open when, quite late and in his cups, he took to bed. He is weary still, on waking, and can feel in his back and bones that it won't be easy to sit up this morning. It never is, these days, but to this morning's aches and bodily complaints is added, as the fog of slumber lifts, a special dismay.

It is to be a wedding day.

He keeps his eyes shut that he might ward it off just a few moments longer, and groans audibly—the slow throat rattle of a man whose courage threatens to elude him. *Weddings*, he thinks. *Funerals. More or less the same thing an't they, and I've had enough of 'em. Seen quite enough, thank you.* With some effort, he turns on his side, away from the light. Alas, the mind is intolerant of a vacuum; as Wigbert's fends off the coming day, the night just gone invades.

He'd got to his knees—no small feat for a man of his age and proportions, but it was strong feeling, not muscle, that moved him—and, raising her to a sitting position, held firmly to Lil. She let him, it seeming to both of them perfectly plausible that if she weren't gathered up thus, she might unravel, come undone and spill out over the soil of the Warburg. She knew, and he knew that she knew, and there were no words in all the world that could have filled that void.

Fafl paced like something caged, some chagrined predator caught and penned.

"This should not have been . . ." he muttered, breaking off to pull at his hair, eyes on the Marshal as if addressing that individual, lips curled in the direction of the bereaved. "It wasn't my . . ." His bony hands writhed. He took a few steps and stood over them and bent down and peered at Lil, whose eyes were covered in the folds of Wig's coat. "It was not my stipulation, Lil, that—"

Lil's frame convulsed; she raised the palm of a hand to Fafl and he fell silent. Her breathing, which had been that of a panicked creature, slowed, and when she spoke into Wig's sleeve it was only to say his name. How he wished he had never heard it said like that!

Then she said, "My father is murdered."

"No, Lil," said the Marshal. "You mustn't think it. I myself notarised the Magistracy order." His spoke in a voice that wavered, trembling with something that seemed, to the others, like stifled rage. "I wish it wasn't so." His eyes drifted to another individual and remained steady there. "I would like nothing more, in this moment, than to make an arrest."

"It's true, Lil," said Wig, squeezing her yet tighter. "Your father knew it."

He held her. Fafl stared, fists clenched. Mr Bull, having witnessed as much as he was able, went on his way, sending Heft and Pack to the Committee Room to see if there was anything left for them to eat.

Something kept the Stationmaster; he would not go. Hard crying always cries itself out after a time, and once that time had passed, Lil, still clinging to Wig but pulling herself away a little to look at him, said "Do you think Mr Bull really saw the order, Wig? Do you believe him?"

"Oh Lil," said Wig, "yes. Mr Bull is nothing if not trustworthy. If he says it is so, it is so."

Her eyes darted from place to place for a few moments, settling on nothing but speaking instead of an internal quandary, a difficulty in processing what had happened, and what she had been told regarding it.

"What must he have thought of me, Wig? I forsook him."

"No, no, Lil," said Wig, and though his voice was weak, there was such knowing in it that it did appear, in the moment, to sooth her, "you did not. He did not think it. I was with him, girl—he understood you better than you understand yourself. Feel no guilt."

"It's true, Lil," said Fafl. "He—"

She leapt to her feet, startling both. Fafl cowered as though to defend himself against a blow, but she went straight past him, into the holding cell. The Stationmaster went to follow her.

"One more step, Fafl," said Wig.

And so there they remained: Wigbert Grim on his knees and Jasper Fafl with his back turned, facing the cabin. For each of them, there was no one in the world to whom he had less to say, than the other. They listened, but no sound came from within. No keening, no crying. There was only the song of wingéd life above them and the cruel hiss of ocean spray below—bird call and the brutal sea. At length, she reappeared, a hand to the doorframe to steady herself as she stepped out. As before, her eyes moved from one inanimate thing to another, then to Wig, then to some other spot, though never to that other person, but she could not have been said to really look at any of the places where they alighted—the gaze was still turned inward. "My father is murdered."

"Dreadful, dreadful," said Fafl, "really dreadful. What a thing to say, dear." He looked to Wig, then back to Lil. "I hoped he would . . . he *should* have . . ." he clapped his hands, "well, it is done." Receiving no reply, he took a step towards her. "From one painful event, dear," again he looked from one to the other, as if unsure which to address, "really, so painful. Painful. But from this cruelty another, more hopeful circumstance will arise. I'm sure of it. I know it." He had adopted the stooped bearing that usually signalled a wheedling representation of some kind. Lil sat down on the edge of the walkway, her back to him. "With the sentence exe . . . carried out, dear, the Magistracy will move. So must we. We must proceed with the . . . with protocol. I will need to confirm names for the remaining antidotes within days. Tomorrow, then, we will finalise our legal union. Not a happy occasion, I acknowledge." He licked his lips. "A mere formality, let's say. An expedience. But, perhaps, in time—"

"I'll not marry you," said Lil. Her voice, too, trembled—but with resolve, not the want of it.

Fafl looked to Wig, who had got to his feet, for aid. None came.

"But dear," said the Stationmaster, "we spoke of this. Your father," his voice a half octave higher in pitch, "you, and I. It is the only way. If—"

"Find another way."

Fafl looked to Wig again. He jutted his jaw, willing the other to speak. The old man stirred.

"Lil," he said. "Your father knew about this. It is why—"

"I won't marry him, Wig."

She bent forward, shoulders to her knees, arms around them. Wigbert didn't know what to say. He moved toward her till he stood above her, but he was afraid to lay a hand on her shoulder—so tensed was she, he thought she might snap in two if touched. His friend had asked him to handle this. He didn't know how. No words presented themselves. He looked behind, at the Stationmaster, from whose countenance, he saw now, any vestige of appeasement or conciliation had fallen away. Fafl's brow was knit, hooding his eyes, and the corners of his mouth had turned down. It was he who spoke.

"It is not only your *personal* happiness that is at stake here, my dear." Despite the term of endearment, there was peevishness in the word emphasised. "Your father's work—"

"Take it. And someone else."

"Take it?" said Fafl. "I, who cannot interpret it? It would be worthless."

"Then leave it here. And take someone else."

"No, Lil." It was the Stationmaster's voice which trembled now. "If the Magistracy cannot have it, and have it interpreted, I must destroy it."

She was on her feet again, quick as a flash and walking towards the cabin. "If you want to destroy my father's work, you will have to have Mr Bull take it from me."

They watched her figure recede along the walkway. As she reached the edge of earshot, Fafl said, "It is taken. I have it."

She stopped dead.

"The notebook is safe in my possession, dear, where it ought to have been before. I know my duty. I will provide your father's work, *and* the means to interpret it, to the Magistracy. *That* is my duty. What is yours? Do you know it?"

She turned and looked at Wig.

"I do," she said and finally—*finally!*—her eyes met those of the Stationmaster. Her shoulders dropped and so did Wig's, so pained was he to see her resignation. How he loathed himself for the relief he felt alongside it! "I do know it," she said, looking at her old friend again. "It seems you will not be denied, Stationmaster."

She turned again and walked away and they watched her go till she disappeared among the cabins.

"That went reasonably well, I think," said Fafl, turning to Wig, "in the end. As well as could be expected. Do you think so?"

But Wig was already retreating in the direction of his own bed, with the resolute intention of arriving at it by way of a bottle. "You have your way, Fafl," he growled. "Leave me be."

It is no good—the day will have its way. Eyelids which would not open will not close. It is late morning, by the look of the shadows that crawl across the ceiling. The bottle has taken its toll, then. He gets himself into a sitting position and swings his old legs off the bed, slips his feet into his slippers, and dallies there a while. Even were he not paying the price—the going rate—at his advanced age for a good feed of drink, Wigbert Grim is not himself, though perhaps the observation is more accurately put like so: Mr Wigbert Grim is no longer himself.

I never will be, he thinks. *How could I be?* The weight he can feel sink through him is not grief's burden; his dear friend Arenaceous, it seems to him, though gone from here, is not gone. *Cannot be.* In place of the cruel cut of fresh loss, there is something like jadedness. Wigbert is well versed in harsh partings, in the pitiless thefts of the greatest of burglars—Time. He feels now (because he must, and despite it being the highest heresy, the most diseased thinking possible) that they await him—his wife, his friend. That they beckon him. That he will go to them. That he will wait there for the boy.

No, not grief. In truth, Wigbert's thoughts are less for those others than for himself. For the first time, he considers the events of recent days in the light of his own fate. He looks around at the bedroom that has been his for so long: the chest of drawers and the chair, the few feminine things that were his wife's. When, later today, Fafl ensnares Lil in his legal arrangement, it will be his last act on the Warburg. Very quickly afterwards, Wig supposes, he will be gone, and Lil with him, and with them both the last vestiges of any pretence that the inhabitants of this place have any value, to the Magistracy or to anyone else.

No sight or sound of the boy. He'll be out fishing, or throwing stones at gulls. Wig shuffles into the kitchen and puts the kettle on. *He'll be the last born in this place. He'll watch us all go before him, and then he'll be alone.* It is too much to dwell on this morning. He takes the butter and a knife to the table in the parlour and, turning to go back for the teapot, spots something on the floor by the door—a note. There can be no question of bending over to fetch it so he lowers himself to his knees and kneels there, tearing it open. The handwriting is Lil's and the note is not a brief one. Were there anyone present to observe him as he reads, they would perceive little in his impassive features. There is just a narrowing of the eyes now and again and, contrariwise, an occasional widening of them in between times. Only when he reads the last, and lowers the note, is there a sound. He moans, and crumples the paper in his fist, and doubles over as though kicked hard in the gut, and he says:

"Oh Lil! No, Lil. Please, no."

The dead leaves of green panic grass. Zircon. Seed pods from the spindle tree. Human skin.

Some of these are known to us still and some mere nomenclature—signifiers of things that have long since taken their leave of us and moved into another place, that greater space that surrounds our own, that we know only as the unknown. There is no more accurate term. There they move, we speculate, among the forgotten, the yet to be learned and the unknowable. How I have longed to follow them.

Buff hibiscus and white currant. A mallard's neck. The elytra of *meloe violaceus*.

We three, poor children of the Warburg: our poverty is this—that to our unknown has been added the perfectly knowable. The known by all. The world itself. Everything. The membrane that separates us from it may skirt the island in the form of the buoy perimeter, but there have long been times when it seemed to me to tighten—till it took on the form, almost, of my own skin, and my breath would quicken and become shallow. I would feel the rush of claustrophobia—these were the attacks I would strive to conceal from any other, but you knew about them. Even as a little boy you knew to stay quiet and say nothing, to be close and hold my hand till I realised I was not alone. That you were there with me and that the membrane enclosed the both of us. It separated us from the world but it could not separate us from each other.

Derbyshire spar. The breast and upper part of the back of a water hen. Plums.

It was mother's wonderfully illicit tutorials that brought on the attacks. They were electric—I could never imagine such a physical reaction to any of the Stationmaster's stultifying, Magistracy-sanctioned lectures. I still shudder when I think of the time I spent in that dome as a little girl. And yet, once outside, its fascination would resume. The smooth curves of its exterior—in those days resplendent white—were another membrane, another separation from the world. As the buoys hemmed me in at the outer limit, so the dome closed off, in our interior, the promise of a deeper understanding. Ever since my schooling there came to an end, I have watched the dome. I linger as I pass it by, my eyes caressing its lichen-covered concavity. I sit on the old stone bench sometimes, and watch it from there. My wondering is mute—I do not know wherefore I watched, or what I expect to see. But I have felt, have always felt, that the dome will play some decisive role in my story. That, if you can forgive the blasphemy, we share a destiny, it and I.

The inside quill feathers of the kittiwake. French porcelain.

I am certain of it now. He tried to break us, in there. To snuff out our spark. Tried and failed, it would seem. But his cruelty has broken so much else. My father, finally. My mother, long ago—though I cannot be quite certain, I blame him for her decline. Papa would have too, if only he could have refrained from blaming himself. But Fafl's monstrosity, I believe, goes far beyond anything I had imagined till now, and the time has passed for those old grievances. There is only what must be done, and I know now what that is. I know how to give you the world, you and the boy. I know how to give all of this some meaning. I know at last how to give of myself completely. And I know how to break him. I know how to break the Stationmaster.

The under disk of a decaying none-so-pretty. Gallstones.

You will not like it. Perhaps you will not forgive me. We both of us will pass into that wider space, just as I have always wished. But not together. I know nothing of the membranes that comprise the parts of this world—or the next, as Papa would undoubtedly add—or of the boundaries that you will encounter, that I will encounter. I know nothing of life—or death. What I thought I knew my father has put paid to. He was certainly a heretic, but I have been conditioned all my life by his being at least one step ahead of me. Perhaps he still is. As wicked as it is to say it, I hope so.

You will think yourself broken, but I know better. You are more than you think you are. And you have found something in my father's work that I believe will sustain you. I must have faith in that at least. If there is a way to find you out there, to pierce those membranes that will divide us, to cross the boundaries that separate one person from another, one place from another, one state from another, then I will find you. And if there is a way to get to you, then I will see you again. I know nothing—therefore, everything is possible.

Veinous blood. The Brimstone butterfly. Obsidian and figure stone.

For now, if I must bid you farewell, I do it with a glad heart. This next obstacle I face is one I can surmount on my own two feet. It is I now who, taking this last step, carries you.

Seven of the clock. This has been the longest day of his life, and Wigbert Grim has lived some long days. In the Committee Room, a company has gathered at the table. The Stationmaster, the Marshal and his constables, The Cyres all three, the fat boy and Wig. Why are they here? They have come looking for Lil. Why do they look for her? She is gone missing.

Wig is beside himself. Simon is beside himself. The Stationmaster is beside himself. His lips are pulled taut and pale in a mean slit that exposes his teeth. None will return his wild gaze. He leers at any and all of them, daring them to. When he speaks, as he does now, he snarls.

"Where is she? If any one of you knows, speak." The writhing hands. "Sedition!"

Wig says nothing. Fafl has harangued them all afternoon. There is no trace of concern for Lil in the Stationmaster's enquiries—not since it became apparent at around noon that she was gone. In that moment, it was true, the blood had seemed to drain from him, and he sent the boy scurrying down to the jetty, whence the lad had returned to report both pods, the yellow and the red, present and correct. No buoy sensors have been activated today, and only a madman would swim in those waters—the winds were well and truly up. No, not concern: feral rage.

Mr Bull and the constables have been deployed to scour the island. The others, unable to settle into daily routines, have wandered also, calling out to her. Wig has walked down to the jetty to confirm the boy's observations, and stood on it and looked at the fishing pods for a very long time. And now here they all are, gathered all together for the first time in days. Simon has surprised them—since she has not come, he will conduct the Review in her absence. He insists. As her amanuensis, he can access her files from his own tab, and so he couples it to the console, locates today's fragment and, despite the contemptuous snorts emanating from both the Stationmaster and his own mother, presses play.

～

I was given the option of visiting her while she was sedated, advised that she would be incoherent, and declined it. Instead they sent me reports—blood pressure, diet, speech content—while I stalked our past in an empty house. I'd have been a lot better off on some front, I think, but they weren't to let any of us serve for a long time. There were monthly visits from psych hygienists and rumors of aberrant behaviors from veterans all over the place, but it wasn't the Sinn atrocity that was eating away at me. It was what I had allowed to happen in this house. What I had done here. My guilt was as present in every domestic detail—cushions, cups, plates, porcelain—as I was absent from the content of your mother's woozy utterances: they were always, and only, about you.

I had a materials cabinet again and that was a mistake. They should have been more cautious about that. As a senior officer I was, of course, well briefed in the sanctioned texts. From time to time we would be called upon not only to configure algorithms but to play some part in the dissemination of proxy narratives. But my access had always been to a very narrow selection of texts, and with appropriate inoculations. I had never sat alone in a cellar and absorbed random toxins, unregulated and unsupervised, which is what I now did most evenings. I can't explain the initial impulse—perhaps it was a way of replaying the old life. Doing what your mother had done. Going where she had gone. Perhaps it was arrogance—some deep-seated defiance in the aftermath of Sinn. Whatever it was that got me started, what kept me going was the narcotic effect.

I have never felt such power, never felt so powerless. I would cultivate the pretence of ordinary days—washing and cooking, errands, working in the garden—but it was all about my evenings in front of the cabinet and its exquisite poisons. The notion of returning to duty seemed more and more ludicrous, the realities of my work more and more remote. I'd withstood genocide, but I knew I wouldn't withstand this. Despite my zeal, my life of service, I had never understood the real menace in the materials. I did now. I felt I was becoming something other than what I had understood to be human. That I was disappearing. Dr. Mann called me in December, around four months into my leave, to tell me your mother had gone on hunger strike.

"Force feed her," I said. It was my voice anyway.

To do so would be unlawful, she told me.

"Up her sedatives, then. Won't she be more amenable?"

She said she would, but that she had called for my permission. Suddenly she was looking for my permission.

"When a patient is deemed an imminent danger to themselves," she said. "We provide nutrients, of course. Whenever she becomes aware of the drip, she rips it out." There was a pause. "Your wife doesn't want to live, Brigadier. We're fighting her and we're losing. More sedatives should help."

I didn't recognize my own reaction—the steeliness of it. I think now it was flight. I went down to the cabinet right after the call to continue my reading: a collection of First Age children's stories I found utterly enchanting. The next morning I spent in the garden. Your mother's azalea wasn't doing well. I pruned it back and fertilized it and sat with it for a little while, impervious to the cold. Then I went back inside and, as had been my habit of late, started drinking.

The following days merged. I'd had a psych assessment the day before the call from the sanatorium, so it wouldn't matter too much how I behaved for a little while. The doctor was due to call again at the end of the week.

If the situation hadn't improved I'd have to straighten up and go in. In the meantime, I didn't want to deal with it. I stayed just sober enough to do some reading in the basement in the evenings and then I'd drink myself to sleep. At some point I lost track of whether it was evening or not down there. Then I lost my grip on what day it was. I know I heard the intercom go a couple of times. And the phone, but there was no one I needed to talk to apart from the people at the sanatorium. For now, I had stumbled upon Virgil, and was lost.

When I woke up one morning to the sound of the phone, I knew it had been buzzing for a long time. Whenever the auto-respond kicked in, the caller would hang up and redial. Whoever it was, they weren't going away. I got up off the cellar sofa and dragged myself up to the kitchen console, noting with some surprise when I got there that it wasn't morning at all—that night, in fact, was closing in. For a moment, I wondered if I'd been burgled—the kitchen was a mess of empty packets and food containers. The fridge swung open. There was a bad smell.

"Where have you been?" It was Mann.

I didn't immediately understand the question.

"Is everything all right?" I may have slurred my words. "You said you'd have an update for me at the end of the week . . ."

There was a pause.

"Are you all right?" she said. "That was nearly a month ago."

I didn't reply. Momentarily, I couldn't.

"We haven't spoken since." The voice was less insistent. Gentler. "Look, you have to come in. The sedatives were discontinued a fortnight ago—her system just isn't strong enough to tolerate them now. We're out of options. She's very weak–"

"I don't understand," I was shaking my head, trying to clear it. "What are you saying to me?"

A deep breath on the line.

"You need to be here now. For your own sake as well as hers."

Another breath.

"To say goodbye."

"Are you quite satisfied, young Mr Cyre?" says Fafl, when it is over. "Are we enlightened by this? Improved? Really—a more sordid account I have not heard. A trivial descent into dissolution and dependency. Did the author of this fiction know Mr Nell personally, I wonder?"

He sneers. Wig feels a fire lighted within him at the mention of his friend. He is on his feet before he knows it, and with a tongue envenomed.

"Don't say the name again, Fafl. Never again. He was a hundred times the—"

The shrill beep of a notification interrupts him. Fafl feels around in his greatcoat till he lays his hand upon his tab, retrieves it, and consults its screen.

"Wh-what is it?" says Simon.

Fafl doesn't answer. He is frozen. He is stone.

"What is it?" says Wig.

Still, Fafl is silent. When he lifts his eyes from the screen, he manages only to elevate them an inch, to regard something in the middle distance, before replying.

"Buoy forty-one."

CHAPTER THE ELEVENTH

IN WHICH THE MOST AGREEABLE OF PEOPLE ARE SUBJECT TO THE MOST DISAGREEABLE OF CIRCUMSTANCES; AND THE COMMITTEE IS AFRAID.

When the truth of it first struck me   with such certitude   I was asleep   actually   I awoke knowing it   woke up laughing at the poetry of it   actually   the beauty of it   poetry of the first water   though laughter is not a behaviour I feel I can wholeheartedly   endorse   it dizzies does it not   nauseates   like a merry-go-round   at sea   but in that moment I could not help myself   the beauty of it   the poetry   it was *you* wasn't it   all along   I don't know how I knew but I knew   the voice was of course scrambled   but the speech patterns perhaps   I really don't know   maybe there had been something in your reactions   in your hesitation   when I spoke of him   the way you would dally round the theme   of him   I really couldn't say   but I knew it   and also therefore that the long ago summer was indeed the beginning and end   of everything   that it   itself   had never ended   that I had never escaped it   that none of us had   none of the three   the languid children of summer   that everything since had been mere iteration of the same old motif   and hadn't you done well for yourself   you the master now   we   the both of us   puppets   or is that the way it always was   actually   and of course in the moment of realising who you were I realised what you'd done   sent the two boys to the same place   contained   controlled   do you know I believe I was flattered   to be included still   having thought myself forgot   a spent piece long picked from the board   while the game went on without it   and what *was* the game   was now the question wasn't it   and so I resolved to ask it   access the emergency channel   though to do it without an emergency to report meant death   but this was different   and what did I have to lose   after all   left here with these motley leftovers   and nothing but reminders of my humiliations   my life   some life   and so I did it   fired up the array didn't I

Midnight is long past. Below, only the shallows are revealed in the paltry light that flickers from lamps held aloft. Beyond, the sea's expanse is hidden behind the billowing black veil of night. To the eye, near shut against the elements, there is only the abysmal gloom out there, an undifferentiated expanse, untelling of its contents. In this state, it is the perfect picture: no truer depiction possible of the Warburg's exile. And here, before it, the little beach and the jetty, flanked by mud bank and wooded slope. The shoreline. The edge of the world.

Both pods are out. The Marshal had wanted to send Heft in one and Pack in the other, but he hadn't reckoned on Simon, who commandeered the yellow and made off while the others still fussed on the jetty. Mrs Cyre has been hysterical ever since—a matter of some hours. The others are not much less frantic; they pace and mutter, Fafl occupying a spot at the jetty's end and peering uselessly into the night.

Wigbert Grim is dry enough, in his oilskins. Bad weather can be deadly at his age so he is well wrapped. All that can be seen of him are his eyes in their hood. He has shoved both hands into deep pockets and sits on a fallen trunk, up above them all, at the edge of the wood. He has no business down there, in all that anxiety. He is not anxious—the word can do no justice to the sorrow that engulfs him. He knows how this will end. *She swam. She swam, in this.* He is only sorry it drags so—sorry for those below and sorry for himself. Sorry for all of them and for everything.

When the yellow pod reappears and, after a torturously long approach on roiling waters that toss it about, Simon's head appears over the gunwale, it is enough to see his face. The last in a sorrowful litany of searches has come to an end. Wig stands, and not waiting to see them carry her body ashore, makes his way back to his cabin to rest awhile. The day will bring with it, as every day seems to have done lately, a rather onerous set of challenges. In the parlour, he throws off his oilskins and lights the heater, but he does not undress for bed—it will not be a long rest. Instead he pours himself some brandy and sits in his armchair to think. The sudden warmth, though, and the few mouthfuls he takes from his cup before he forgets it is there, do not so much conduce to thoughtfulness as to the intrusion of sleepy remembrance.

The scene is a perfect vignette to the blasphemies of Wigbert Grim—there was something changed in the parlour that had become, for him, a great cathedral of cosiness. It was suddenly the somewhat discomfiting venue for a set of conditions that were, for him at least, if not quite unimaginable, then previously unimagined. The choir (a row of doilies on the sideboard) that were wont to sing unceasing hymns to home and hearth, had fallen silent. The great altar (dining table) lay unadorned and unattended—who could think of it at such a time? The chancel and ambulatory (heater and mantel) lay cold and unlit.

The Dean himself (Wigbert) stood wide-eyed and dumbfounded, and anything but cosy, and at his side the humble verger (Arenaceous Nell) was a ditto in the same. They might have sat—there were pews available (the armchair for one and the wooden stool beside Lil's desk for the other)—but they stood.

In prayer? Of course not. In supplication? Almost certainly—though to whom, or what, neither could have said.

Conversely, a wheeled chair had been brought down from the dome for Izzy's sister, whom Lil was settling into it with all possible dispatch and wrapping up in a shawl for the short journey back to the sick bay. The occupant of the shawl gazed upon her poor husband, her brow furrowed with the worry it caused her to see him in such distress.

"Will you not fret so, Wigbert?" she admonished him. "People have babies all the time, you know. It's the way of things. I'll be back soon and I'll have the little one with me. You'll be a father—*then* you can fret." Her eyes momentarily strayed in Aren's direction before returning sharply. "In the meantime," she said, "you must do with whatever company is available. Perhaps it will rouse itself at some point to cut you a sandwich."

"You may address me directly," said Aren, "and I'm sure that all will go well." On receiving no reply he went on. "I will be delighted to make Wig a sandwich." Still nothing. "Even now, you're not going to talk to me?" he said, poking his elbow into Wigbert's ribs. "That's some woman." But neither was any communication forthcoming from that quarter, so Aren had nothing to do but shake his head in admiration.

Lil fussed with a knapsack, stuffing it with sundry objects the utility of which was, in each individual case, questionable but which together would comprise a reassuringly womanly kit bag for her charge, in whose lap she placed it before turning the wheeled chair towards the door. Izzy's sister reached over her shoulder to pat Lil's hand on the chair's handle.

"This will be you one day, Lil." Though the grips were evident in her regular wincing, she was quite easily the most composed person present.

The girl, unseen by Izzy's sister but observed by both gentlemen, coloured instantly and to a quite remarkable degree. "I can't imagine it," she said. She was bookish and studious, and though she cared for her father assiduously, had never been observed to display any maternal, or even especially feminine, qualities.

"Nonsense," said Izzy's sister. "You will be a wonderful mother."

Lil, still blushing, effected a rueful smile as she wheeled the chair to the door and stepped around to open it. "How could you know that, aunty?"

Izzy's sister took the hand again, that was now before her, and paused before speaking just long enough to ensure she had the girl's attention. "Because you are my sister's child," she said. "My blood." For a second, a certain hesitancy showed itself in her features that spoke of self-consciousness. "And because you have a good father," she said, rather curtly, as she was pushed over the threshold. "It's the way of things."

With one last glance back over her shoulder, she looked at Wigbert Grim and winked and he, calling on every reserve of courage he had left within him, managed a weak, watery-eyed smile.

Something tugging at his sleeve. It's annoying. He opens his eyes. It's the boy.

"Hello, boy."

"Hello, Pappy."

"What is it?"

"Stationmaster wants everyone in the Committee Room."

"Hm." He pulls a hand over his face to clear the fog from his eyes. It doesn't work. "What have they done with poor Lil?"

"In the dome," says the boy. "She's a lion in estate. That's what the Stationmaster says. I think it's pretty. What does it mean, Pappy?"

He is pale and is nothing like his usual, oblivious self. Indeed he seems most affected, and has evidently been crying.

"Why, it doesn't mean much of anything at all," says Wigbert. "Have you had your breakfast?"

"I an't hungry, Pappy."

Wigbert sits forward and takes a firm grip of the boy at either shoulder, making a strong effort, in spite of his disinclination, to appear stern.

"Now you listen here, my boy," he says. "There'll be no more of that talk, d'you 'ear me?"

"Yes, Pappy."

"Get yourself into that kitchen and cut us some bread and butter."

While the boy does as instructed, Wigbert performs some ablutions, finishes his cup of brandy, and girds himself for the coming encounter. When the boy returns to the parlour with a plate of bread and butter, his father's admonishment would appear to have hit its mark—it is a large plate and the boy has piled it high, and proceeds to take care of rather more than his fair share. When he has done so, they go to the Committee Room.

The scene that awaits the Grims there is grim indeed. All are present, though the pronoun can include neither Arenaceous Nell nor his daughter now—two absences that make their awful presence felt. The gathered living have taken on the appearance of vestiges—the mere remnants of something that once lived: the Warburg. In their bearing, in the downcast eyes, the downturned lips and all manner of fidgeting, the collective wound, raw and mortal, is betrayed. Even Heft and Pack are cowed and ill at ease. But if a strong and resolute soul might still withstand the general tableau, surely it must falter on first sight of Simon Cyre.

He sits apart from the others, on the little stool beside the console previously occupied by Lil Nell, and something in the way he does so signals an intent to remain there for the rest of his days. To look upon him is an agony for the eye; if you expected to find him here limp, a lifeless rag doll, you find now that you were mistaken. He is indeed doll-like in the crazy splay of his limbs, head bowed as though hanging from a boneless neck, but there is nothing limp in his bearing. This is a doll fought over by warring siblings—every tendon in his limbs is pulled as taut as his stretched mouth, his hands are neither open nor clenched but tensed like claws, his eyes both wild and lifeless. When he takes a breath it is at long and irregular intervals, and he does it sharply, gasping, as if his body is appalled by the intrusion of life-giving air and labours to resist it. These combined proofs of his torment have the cumulative effect that no one will dare speak to him.

"We have a matter to discuss," says Mr Bull, by way of acknowledging the late arrivals. At his side, Fafl is mute and every bit the bereaved groom. He hugs himself and looks disconsolately from one of them to another, though none—no, not even Mrs Cyre—will return his gaze. Wigbert is old, and slow, and today he feels frail as well—nevertheless, it is necessary for him, as he lowers himself onto his seat, to suppress the urge to lunge at the Stationmaster and do him some violence.

"A pressing matter." It is clear the Marshal will be chairing. His only superior—incapacitated, it would seem, by grief—defers. "I do beg pardon," said Mr Bull, "of all of you. Of you, Mr Grim. Of you, most of all, Simon." The response is a curt nod from Wigbert and a low groan from Simon.

"I was very fond of Lil," says Mrs Cyre. "Truly, I was."

"For the sake of all that is good in this world, woman," says Mr Cyre, "will you please—"

"We have lost, in short order," says the Marshal, one hand raised to quiet them, "those most beloved among us. The discussion of any business is, of course, repugnant. But discuss it we must." He placed his elbows on the table and clasped his hands before him. "One of them—Lil—was allocated a nano. Her place is vacant. That is our business here, and we must conclude it in all haste; the Magistracy is finished with this place, and could remove the option at any time."

"We've already said our piece on this," says Mrs Cyre, speaking for herself and her husband. "Isn't it obvious who should go? Can't we all agree that youth and innocence should be preferred? Isn't that the protocol?"

"In principle, yes, Mrs Cyre," says the Marshal, "and I, too, have made my position clear. Howbeit," he inclines his head toward Wigbert, "for the boy to go is for his father to be parted from him. And it would surely test any father to give his own into the hands of another . . . in this case . . . the Stationmaster . . ." Mr Bull is in obvious mortification saying these words, his face contorting in an apparent effort to communicate what his words cannot. It doesn't matter; his meaning is clear. Wigbert speaks up.

"I would not willingly stand in the way," he says, "of my boy's chances. He'll rot here."

The Cyres and the Marshal murmur their ascent.

"But," says Wig and his gaze, having alighted upon Fafl, remains there, "I am most partickler about the company he keeps." It seems to him that, in the corner of his eye, even Heft and Pack perk up at this declaration. He is undaunted. "My boy is the youngest, but not the only youth. I wonder," he says, eyes boring into Fafl's lowered lids, "if the Stationmaster would consider a reversion here, to the emergency protocol the good Mrs Cyre refers to? The youngest leave. So that Simon, whom I esteem, might be guardian to the boy?"

There is no response until one comes from behind him.

"I won't go," says Simon.

"Mr Grim," says the Marshal. "I understand the strength of your feelings. But we are still in the service of the Magistracy here. The Stationmaster has his orders. He—"

"You mustn't speak this way, Mr Grim," interjects Mrs Cyre, "no matter what has passed. The presumption—"

"I tell you," comes a tremulous voice from the stool by the console, "I will not go."

Wigbert smiles. Surely Fafl can feel his eyes burning into him. "A proposal, nothing more. For consideration."

"I am staying here." The voice from behind.

"It seems, Mr Grim," says Fafl, lifelessly, "that young Mr Cyre is not a willing participant in your scheme." He looks up, at last. "Perhaps you ought to speak with him? For my part, I agree to surrender my place. Simon may have it if he wants it."

"I don't," says Simon.

"Wait," says his mother. Everybody at the table with the exception of Wigbert, and the two constables, is open-mouthed at Fafl's acquiescence. "How can—"

"Stationmaster," says Mr Bull, "it isn't possible. You yourself told us that your departure was obligatory. There would be reprisals. The Magistracy—"

"The drops!" exclaims Mrs Cyre. "They'll stop 'em!" She takes a handkerchief from her bag and begins to fan herself. Fafl has that look about him—downcast eyes and pursed lips—that advertises some inner calculation. He speaks.

"What you say, Mr Bull, would hold true were Simon and the boy to present themselves at any Magistracy facility with my blessing. There would be immediate consequences—of that I am quite sure." He cradles one elbow and strokes his chin. "On the other hand," he continues, "were I, as the Warburg's dutiful Stationmaster, the victim of some aggression . . . were there, say, a plot to take the nanos from me," he is getting into his stride now and the unbearable grief that had been writ so large across his features appears to have lifted a little, "and were the two mutineers to present themselves not to the Magistracy," he goes on "but rather, to a *resistance* outpost . . ."

He tapers off, inclining his head to invite their implicit understanding.

"There is no resistance," says Mr Cyre.

"Yes," says the Marshal, looking at Fafl. "I thought there wasn't any—" He cuts himself short, observing a rolling of the eyes on the part of that individual.

"Of *course* there's a resistance," says Fafl. "Confound it, on what world and at which time has there *not* been a resistance?" He asks the question of no one in particular. "It seems the world is not so pure as we once believed. Even on the outer rim of this very caldera, there are resistance territories. I know of one, at least."

"On the caldera?" Mr Bull is flabbergasted. "Shouldn't I have known? And Lil? You could have addressed her suspicions. Isn't this exactly why she persevered with the Reviews?"

"My knowledge has nothing to do with the blasted entertainments," says Fafl. "It is of another source, one of longstanding." He shakes his head. "The fragments are nonsensical."

"We'll see," says Simon. "The Reviews continue."

The Stationmaster throws his hands in the air in exasperation. "And what is the point of that? Put that foolishness aside and prepare yourself for a sea crossing, young man. Not an easy one!"

"I'll be here for the Review, Simon," says Wigbert, getting up and tapping the boy to follow.

"I will not leave this place, Mr Grim," says Simon. "Lil will never leave it now, and nor will I."

Wigbert nods, curtly. "I will see you later. Mr Bull, will you walk with me? I would speak with you."

"Certainly, Mr Grim."

Father, son and Marshal take their leave. Out on the walkway, Wigbert bids the boy run ahead to put the kettle on, and the two men follow slowly, Wigbert delivering his words in low and earnest tones, and the Marshal leaning in, intent on them.

oh how delicious a baby a little one   and aborted   I could hardly contain my glee   does that hurt I wonder   I bet it does   one way or the other   couldn't look upon him for long after that   for fear of an outbreak of laughter and I do hate 'em you know   attacks of laughing no couldn't look at him   the big man   the good man   my my how it all poured out of you   like a dam burst you were   as if you'd been bursting all this time   to tell it   that last august in the village me arrested   gone   that preening peacock   had pranced his way to the institute   and you left alone   the *scandal*   *and* of course there could be no question of your *having* it   not in that family magistracy high-flyers   not with you marked for such great things at the academy   and so then you did not have it   were not permitted to   were not canvassed for your opinion on the matter   were ready for school by september   and went   oh I was tempted to tell him   believe me   to watch him wilt   I almost went straight to him after that first communication   but it would have been a cheap indulgence   and brief   and I found it more delectable   to withhold it   to bide my time   with you too   to bide my time   this was an excellent leverage   much better even than the boy   and I no longer the puppet   no longer

Wigbert couldn't have said how much time had passed, except that it was too much, when Lil appeared in the doorway. She startled the two men, whose conversation had dried up long since, and who had been sitting in silence.

"You must come at once, Mr Grim," she said.

"What is it, Lil?" He was on his feet and going for his coat. "Is everything all right?"

"Come quickly!"

Up through the rain to the door of the dome, she was too far ahead of him to answer any question till he caught up with her there.

"What has happened, Lil? Is there a baby?"

She nodded. "A boy."

"And what—"

The door slid open. Fafl was dressed in medical scrubs. They were bloody.

"I'm not sure about this Lil," said the Stationmaster. "Protocol—"

Wigbert pushed past him.

"Where is she?"

All was quiet in the dome. Wigbert pulled aside a plastic curtain and stepped into the sick bay. His wife lay covered on her bed—there was no sign of the blood that stained the doctor's smock. Next to the bed, a tiny baby, swaddled in its crib.

"Is he—"

"The child is well," said Fafl, behind him. Wigbert's eyes went back to the child's mother.

"And her?"

Wigbert felt Lil's hand slip into his.

"She will not see out the hour," said Fafl.

Lil squeezed his hand. "But she is conscious, Wig. Come."

She led him to the bed and put the palm of her hand to her aunt's cheek till the lady's eyes opened and she smiled up at them.

"Hello, Wiggy."

He could not answer, but when Lil withdrew her hand, replaced it with his own.

"You have been very courageous today, Lil," said Izzy's sister. "Promise me you will always have courage. We are nothing without it." She reached out for the girl's hand. "When you know what must be done, do it. Even if it's the end of you. Promise me."

"I promise."

"And you, Wiggy, will have to be courageous now. I'm sorry about this. I have made you a boy but cannot help you raise him." Her breaths were shallow and she had to take them every few words, and her voice was weak. Her husband had no words for her, could only meet her eyes with his and try to pour himself into her that way, pour his love into her. His life.

"Sorry, Wiggy," she said, and closed her eyes, and never again opened them.

For the second time that day, Wigbert Grim lost any sense of the seconds, the minutes or hours. When he felt a tap on his shoulder and turned, it was not Lil but his friend Aren, and Lil was in the doorway holding the plastic curtain instead of at his side where she had been, and an agitated Fafl, back in his uniform, could be seen warped and distorted through the plastic, and Aren was saying "Come away now, Wig. Let me get you home."

Wigbert looked at the baby that lay sleeping.

"Lil will stay with the boy," said Aren. "Come."

"Aren, I . . ." Wigbert's hand went to Aren's lapel and gripped it. "I can't . . ." He looked at the crib. "Not on my own. I—"

"You are not alone, Wig. You never will be, not while there's breath in my body," said Aren. "You cared for Lil when I could not. You have cared for me too, and now we will care for you. Come on, let me get you back to the cube."

He starts, knowing instantly that the day has slipped by, the second to do so since he last saw his bed. His bones will let him know all about it when he gets out of this chair. The parlour is deathly quiet, save for ticking. The boy is at the table, unusually still and, of all things, reading a book. Upon the book, also reading by the look of it, Mouse.

"What o'clock is it, boy?"

"Near seven, Pappy."

"Come on then."

They make their way up to the Committee Room. Every soul left living on the Warburg is there. Mrs Cyre has brought sandwiches and porridge with a pot of jam. "Eat some porridge, boy," says Wigbert. "It'll lag your pipes." As the boy sets about this latest Herculean labour, Simon presses play.

Even in the ship it took us a while—most of it spent in a fuel-burning, vertical climb over the mountains that separated the settlement from the coordinates our host had given us. They'd been given reluctantly, on condition he accompany us, and he sat in front of me at one of the starboard portholes, fidgeting.

Glaring at the back of his head, my indignation had given way to excitement. Once over the initial shock, the man's revelations had awakened in me the stirrings of an old ambition. My professional interest was decidedly piqued. I tapped my armrest, impatient to get a look at this Step of theirs.

It wasn't the inevitable debunking of another local delusion that had me fired up—that work would be mundane. We were veterans, we did it almost automatically: isolate the process, run a diagnostic, annotate it, provide an empirical description of it and, if necessary, replicate it. Even the most impervious of peoples, when confronted with the evidence—again and again—give way. There have been no exceptions, only degrees of difficulty. Maybe the Sinni. But we'd never know now what we might have achieved there.

No, it wasn't that, though I looked forward to it. I'd been sufficiently riled by the man to skip any intermediate steps in this case, such as the deployment of transitional myth artifacts. I wasn't in the mood for the long game. No, we'd just strip it all away. Quick and dirty. I'd enjoy watching this one wilt, watching him struggle to mediate the data for his frightened flock, seeing him capitulate. Perhaps that was arrogance. I didn't really care.

This was bigger. The scientific consensus was that there never had been a physical location for The Stone. It was generally accepted that a very successful plague metaphor had simply proliferated from one culture, one historical cycle, to the next. In the wake of the great cataclysms that have separated one Age from the next, surviving articles of a fragmented doctrine might easily be ascribed a reality they do not merit. It would be understandable in that desperate, post-apocalyptic effort to establish continuity that humans have lived through at least twice now.

But it wasn't a certainty. There was no satisfyingly literary source at the end of the long, textual trail. And where there is uncertainty, infection can take hold. The conditions for fanciful speculation are met. That is why we'd been stuck with it, why it adorns our uniforms, violates our dreams.

So if this stone bore any resemblance to the source materials, if a credible argument could be made that it was the source, then the implications were so far-reaching it made the breath catch in my throat. I wouldn't need perfection, just some plausible correlate. The shape, perhaps, or some natural phenomenon in the vicinity that might have given rise to magical thinking. The prospect had awoken the careerist in me. It's potential use as a propaganda tool could see me on the Council. Nothing less than the ultimate asset—the actual, physical site where the most powerful article of faith known had come into being.

Even the First Agers we know of, so much closer to the origin, were as unmoored as we are—they already spoke, as we do, of the "mists of time". And yet here I was. Was it possible that I'd emerged from those mists, just as we'd slipped through the cloud cover overhead, to stand in the very place where that first flicker—a trick of the light perhaps, or of chemistry, or geology—parted truth from fiction? That ruinous moment. The terrible mistake.

I couldn't tell you what our altitude was. I was afraid to consult the display—I must have mentioned to you that I get nervous on a ladder. I'd never had that problem on a ship, except perhaps a little at takeoff and landing, but this was different. I was so much further away from the surface than I ever had been, on any world, that I could feel it, and was grateful for the smooth, unbroken expanse of white cloud not so far below us. For a little while, it helped me ignore the enormity of it all.

Soon the whiteness was interrupted by a black line. Ahead of us, it bowed and bent as we approached, becoming a crescent, serrated and irregular, then two lines that arced away from one another—an ellipse that widened as the ship moved over it into a perfect circle below us. Impossible to gauge the size with no points of reference.

"The Caldera," said the old man. "We're here."

The pilot put the ship into a slow, vertical dive. I was fine until we hit the cloud, but when we emerged from its underside I needed to shut my eyes for a moment and exert some control over my breathing. The gas barrier had been a comfort when seen from above, but hanging over us it served only to accentuate the immensity of the space we had entered.

The inverted cone of a crater converged far, far below us. The atmosphere was crystal clear. I saw no vegetation but there must have been something, somewhere, because bird life was abundant. It helped me, in fact, to focus on them. There is nothing like a vertical drop to focus the mind on height, so I kept my attention on the birds as we sank. Some of them were big—slow circling individuals with the hooked beak of raptors. And there were flocks of smaller birds, murmurating around outcrops and crevices.

As the ship neared the slope, the pilot put it into a diagonal and we followed the crater's contour. From my own porthole I got a better look at the surface. There was water—any number of rivulets and wet rock and even a waterfall here and there and, if no grasses or trees, at least some mosses and lichens that I could make out.

If I looked past Evans, or up through the observation dome, I could take in the crater. The eye was baffled. There'll be measurements, of course, in the ships sensor log, but I couldn't tell you whether it was ten kilometers across or fifty. My heart rate had eased off with our proximity to the rock and I was glad to sink into the narrowing space. Below us the bottom of the crater, to my surprise, appeared a brilliant white. I though it might be ash of some sort. It wasn't round but instead a kind of gash in the crater floor, bent like a boomerang, more rounded at one end than the other. The plume.

As we got closer, a breach in its form became visible, at the feather's inner curve, an intrusion into the undifferentiated white expanse—there, at the base of a concave section of the crater wall, kilometers in height, a very familiar shape. Nobody spoke. I felt Evans' hand on my shoulder. We could see now that the whiteness was more gas. We could see the red vines disappear into it. Strong spray rose from the cascades, one at a short distance to either side of the protrusion, and misted the portholes. When I saw it, Lita, I knew. We all did, with absolute certainty. I can't explain. There just wasn't any doubt.

The cloud, a carpet below us now as well as a ceiling above, lay at exactly the level of the stone's edge.

"It's almost as if you could step onto it," muttered Evans.

Our guide chuckled.

"Yes," he said. "Almost."

There were people on the step—a gathering of eight or nine, including two young children. There was enough room on the platform for them to run and play, very close to the edge at times with no sign of concern from the others, but our host had been right—even without its current occupants, the thing wouldn't have taken our ship. We hovered in silent mode, not too far above it. At this height I felt able to observe without getting too dizzy. The adults sat around a blanket on the flat rock, picnicking. A couple of them waved at our ship. None wore any apparatus.

"Only when the angel's breath lies above and below is it breathable here," said the man. "We prefer to hold the ceremonies at these times. I would appreciate it if we could stay back and let them get on with it."

For all his talk of ceremony, it had the appearance of an informal gathering. The picnickers were finishing up and putting plates back in a large hamper, and two of them—a man and a woman—broke from the group to approach one of the children, a little girl. Her companion, a slightly older boy, returned to the others, looking sullen as the girl got cuddles and was fussed over.

Do you remember how your mother and I would take an arm of yours each in the garden and swing you till you squealed? You used to love that, although if we went too far with it you would panic and I'd have to squeeze you very tight and hold you still till your pulse slowed and I'd convinced you that you were safe.

Presumably these two were her parents, so at ease was she as they did the same with her. We could see her giggling on the first swing, laughing heartily on the second. Of course, it reminded me of you—how could it not? On the third, her little feet swung out over the edge and I thought I could detect, though from this distance it had to be my imagination, the beginning of that little rush of panic we used to see in you. And on the fourth, as she reached the horizontal, they let go in unison, and I wondered if the little girl yelped as you used to do before she disappeared into the cloud.

I doubled over, vomiting on the cabin floor. I don't know what it was. Yes I do—it was you, like a punch in the stomach. Zwickl brought me a water and Evans sat beside me and patted my back, while the doctor fetched something to clean up with. My indecision had caused this. The old man looked over his head rest at me.

"I think it's probably this type of thing that gives me most joy," he said. "An innocent child spared months and perhaps years of suffering. Her diagnosis was made a very short while ago—early, so she hasn't had any pain." He smiled. "We are blessed."

I was hoarse and sweating, sipping water and trying to keep it down.

"You fool," I said, straightening up. "You're insane." Down on the rock, the adults were taking turns to shake the couple by the hands. Some of them were laughing. "They don't know what they've done," I said, "but they'll

learn. In time, they'll learn. These people will be the hardest hit. I don't suppose you've any idea what it is to lose a child?"

His attention was back on the scene below us.

"Well, of course there is an element of sadness to these things," he said. "They'll miss her terribly, I should think, for the time being." He turned again. I couldn't read his expression. It might have been pity. "But we don't know grief here. Only the need for patience."

Behind him, framed by the porthole, the handshaking continued. It seemed to be focussed on one of the men now, rather than the little girl's parents. He did his rounds and finished with the boy, tousling his hair, and then he walked to edge and stepped off.

A moan escaped Evans' throat. I grabbed for the man's sleeve.

"Why didn't you warn us?"

I drew my weapon.

"How many more?"

"None," he said. "This was a double. I did mention that. Quite rare. They are related, you see, so they wanted to make a day of it."

"I can assure you," I said, "your execution won't be so picturesque. In the meantime we might as well go to work."

I pressed the intercom and spoke to the pilot, keeping my eyes on our host.

"Let's go and get the bodies."

"Sacrilege!"

He got up and took a step toward me, stopped when I raised the gun.

"Sacrilege is a concept you'll shortly find yourself unburdened of," I said. We were descending. "A pair of mutilated bodies dropped back in their laps should be something of a wake-up call for those people, don't you think? Cruel to be kind, as it were." I holstered my gun and returned to my seat. "This begins now."

When we broke through the cloud layer, the two giant cascades flanked the ship, water spray drumming loudly on the hull. The plume that had been the bottom of the world receded overhead. Light diminished with every second. Despite a rising vertigo I looked from my porthole to the one in the roof—we were in a chasm of sheer rock, dim and devoid of life. The space seemed to narrow at its upper reaches, barreling out as we dropped. There was a sensation of enclosure, of claustrophobia almost, but at the same time of yet another vastness.

Overhead, the skew of light narrowed and shrank. The old man stayed on his feet, his hackles clearly up. Blackness enveloped the ship. The noise of the water was replaced by quiet. Some kind of electrical activity out there—the occasional flicker of colored light broke the monotony. The pilot put the sensor displays up on screen so that we could keep an eye on surface contours below us. For now, there were none.

I knew I was seething, that it wasn't professional. Consulting with Evans as we went, the scenario seemed straightforward to me. We would have this one wrapped up by the time we made the ascent again. In the meantime, the descent seemed to go on forever. I pressed the overhead intercom.

"Few more minutes," said the pilot.

The old man said nothing. Evans and Zwickl calibrated the instruments. My mind turned to my own work. I took out my pad to compose a message to the Council. This all needed to be framed very carefully—I couldn't afford to let my excitement discredit me, but how else to see this than as the culmination of my life's work? The temperature in the compartment rose.

A ping shook me from my thoughts. The sensor display flashed. An irregular diagonal line had appeared at the bottom of the screen. The others were at their portholes, peering down—the ship's floodlights were on and in the murk, still thick with gas, a slope could just be made out. Dark shale. I didn't think there could be life down here. But then life isn't what we were looking for.

"Anything?"

"Not yet," said Evans, "but we're sweeping a large area. Shouldn't be long."

Our host alone showed no interest in the view. Eyes closed, his lips moved silently.

"Not possible. Do it again," said Evans to Zwickl.

"What's not possible?" I asked.

"Gimme a minute," she said. "I think we fired a blank."

My eyes returned to the faint shapes of broken rock below. I thought of how far we were from the light.

"Anything?"

She looked up from her screen.

"Nothing. We've swept twice. I checked everything," she said, "twice. They're not here."

"Above? Hooked on something?"

"No. We swept all along. It's wide open all the way down."

"Burned?"

"No. It's hot out there but not hot enough."

"Chemistry?"

"Nothing. Nothing out of the ordinary."

I thought for a second, then pressed the intercom.

"Up."

Evans cocked an eyebrow.

"Shouldn't we–"

"The answer isn't down here," I said, "and neither are the bodies. You forget, we aren't just looking for two."

I looked to the old man, who seemed to breath a little easier now.

"How frequent are your "ceremonies"?"

"Oh, every few weeks there is the need."

I tapped my lips with a forefinger.

"There should have been a mountain of bones. The answer's up there."

On this occasion, the lull that follows the audio fragment is a sickly one. Even the boy, not known for his sensitivity, picks up on it and downs his spoon. Simon's hand shakes as he shuts down the console.

"We are being taunted," he says.

"By whom?" says Mr Cyre. He shakes his head. "It isn't possible."

"Nobody out there knows what happens here," says his wife, "any more than we know what's going on out there."

"But this latest clip," says Mr Bull. "It's as if they're *aware*—"

"But I can't understand it," says Fafl. "These fragments pre-date our recent . . . tribulations."

"That's true," says Simon.

"You are good, Simon," says Wigbert, "for conducting these last Reviews. For honoring Lil. And you do honor her." He stands. "But now to more urgent business. Mr Bull, will you assist?"

The Marshal raises a hand, but it is Heft and Pack, not he, who rise from their seats. To the great surprise of those present (though not *all* of them), the constables move with considerable celerity and precision, and before there has been time for anyone to wonder why, have a firm hold of Simon, one arm each, pinning him in his place on the stool.

"Have you brought them, Fafl?" says Wigbert.

The Stationmaster is already opening a slim leather case he has put before him on the table, to reveal two syringes—a large and a small.

"What is this?" says Simon, who knows what it is. He struggles once, but it is useless.

"Why are they different?" says Wigbert.

"They an't," says Fafl. "The contents are the same." He has taken the smaller syringe and is thumbing Simon's restrained arm for a vein.

"Can't the boy have the small one? He's only a boy," says Wigbert.

Fafl tuts. "The boy is a Warburg child, Mr Grim, subject to Magistracy regulations." He has found his spot and slips the needle in.

Before he squeezes the plunger he looks up at Wigbert. "That lad's had more injections in his short life than you or I, and by some margin. Haven't I overseen his inoculations myself? Year on year? He's well able for it. There—that's Simon done. Have the boy roll up his sleeve."

"Pappy?" says the boy.

"Roll it up, there's a good boy," says Wigbert. He sounds gruff and he means to—otherwise his voice might crack and that wouldn't do.

"But Pappy," says the boy, unbuttoning a cuff. "I don't want to go neither."

"That is nonsense," says Wigbert. He kneels and plants a heavy hand on the boy's shoulder. "You listen to me," he says. "You have never known the pleasures of a steak-and-ale pie. Or ale, for that matter. Or iced cream." As the mention of each item, he gives the boy a little shake. "And that isn't fair. It an't right. You're to be brave now, as we all are," and here the old man's voice does indeed crack, "and roll up that sleeve."

The boy does as he's told and the Stationmaster does as he must and with that, the business is concluded.

"You can't make me go," says Simon. "None of you can."

Wigbert smiles sadly at him.

"You'll go, Simon. You know it. Because it's for Lil—it's what she'd want for you."

The young man hangs his head and weeps and his mother goes to him and, agreeing that the two should set off the next day, the company parts.

CHAPTER THE TWELFTH

*LUNCH MADE AND LEAVE TAKEN;
MR FAFL AND AN UNEXPECTED INTERLOCUTOR;
AND THE LAST.*

DAY DAWNS on the Warburg. To its insensible populations, the feathered and the four-legged, the creatures that creep, and crawl, and flutter, it is a day like any other—though the wind drives uncommon hard and so too does the rain, and the waves are high and haughty. No sun will be seen today, no warmth felt, but amongst the trees, in their branches and along the forest floor, the hum of the habitual will rumble on: the finding of food, the getting of shelter, the scramble for life. If this day gives little comfort, if it offers no respite from the battering elements, there are other, kinder days to come.

Not so for the sentient. It is a very singular day indeed: the Warburg's last. Today, those who can leave, will. Gone are those other days, for they who wave them off, of industry and purpose and mission. In truth, they were already gone, but so now will be any pretence. The remaining souls will live out their time doing their best to get along, to fend off the weather, their boredom and their regret. Old Wigbert won't have his boy to harry, cajole, inculcate or feed. If he stops to think of it he will falter, so he does not stop to think of it. At least he will know that the lad is alive, and living a merry old life if there's any justice, with a wide variety of things to eat.

He rises early, expectant of some new drama, but the forenoon passes without word from anyone or so much as a knock at the door. He puts his covered head outside on more than one occasion, but there is little sign of life—only lighted windows and the vapours the wind whips away from cabin vents, that show the heaters are on. In the end his patience is exhausted and, having lavishly breakfasted the boy, sends him on his way, wrapped in oversized oilskins, to learn what he may. It can't be much, for he is back at his father's side in no time, clutching a wet Sou'wester in hands white from the cold.

"Few of 'em in the Committee Room, Paps," he says. "Simon won't go till he's played today's entertain'ent. Seven o' the clock or nuthin', he says. Won't have it nutherwise. Mr Bull says the Stationmaster is beside hisself on account of it." The boy looks deeply into his father's eyes. These past days, he has been another child. There is a new quiet on him. "What does that mean, Pappy?" he says.

"What do *you* mean, boy?" says Wigbert.

"Beside hisself," says the boy. "If you're beside yourself, then," he shakes his head in wonderment, "who's yourself beside?"

"*You*, boy," says his father.

The boy blinks several times at Wig, as if that gentleman were the very deepest well of mystery ever known to man or beast, and well worth a good long look. "Can't get me noggin into it, over it or under it," he says in the end. "Sounds like a ugly fix to me, but Mr Bull can't think so, 'cos he seems awful pleased about it."

Wigbert snorts. "Mr Bull is all right. He does what he must."

He slaps his knees and gets up.

"Right, boy. Time for your lunch, I think."

---

and so I fired it up again didn't I   the array   and this time I knew my purpose   I wanted off this rock   me and the boy   my little policy   I imagined it would seem like an act of largesse on my part   to spare the youngest   easy to arrange at my end then   I would take guardianship of the little fellow   as once I had intended for Lil   not even his stubborn fool father would stand between him and his liberty   and sooner or later I privately supposed we might find a way of extracting the archive safely not impossible if necessary of course and indeed you were receptive unexpectedly so in fact we are meeting some resistance on the home world you told me insurgencies on the caldera itself apparently infiltration of magistracy intelligence no less something of a speciality of mine oh to be an asset once more to be given my freedom but there was a serious problem you said it could not happen could never happen the Warburg could not be abandoned by its stationmaster not *while the aetiologist lives you* said and your coldness the sting of ice in your stipulation oh it *was* exquisite

it did give me pause though I am more lover than fighter after all to make him suffer that had been a pleasure pleasure is a powerful drive is it not and that is what I sought and thought I would find actually in this ratcheting of his defeat this faceted victory finally mine over the man the better man the bigger man belittled it was I now who was the larger the greater who went beyond the other outstretched him knew what he did not could look down upon his smaller unenlightened oblivious world from my exalted vantage it was like being back up on the trap actually clip clopping the dusty lanes bathed in the warm light of your wink

but to kill him now that did give me pause the enquiry was the obvious instrument obviously but I did not think I could do it did not believe I had the nerve I was too afraid not for very long as it happened for just as I was ready to throw my hands up to accept my fate a prisoner here just like the rest of them forever what do you think should happen you won't guess you might though I suppose if you try to imagine the last thing the very last thing I could have expected a miracle I'd call it were I a heretic miraculous or the nearest thing to it in my miserable life and though I am a rational man I must admit it is rather comforting to have the universe conspire in one's favour so speaks to a certain virtue in one's aspirations does it not shows that one is essentially right and what was it what was the miracle it was that he came to me and *asked* me to kill him

Until I looked into the eyes, it wasn't her. Then, in that moment, it was.

The walk to the cell had been a replay of the last—myself, the doctor and the same attendant, the messy percussion of our footsteps, the staff member at the cell door, the slow shaking of her head. Only the silence distinguished this time from the other. Dr Mann took some charts from her colleague and leafed through them, then ushered me into the little office.

"She's awake," she said, "and lucid for all we know, though she refuses to speak. She doesn't have long. She was already in poor health when she started the hunger strike. Underweight, malnourished. She hadn't eaten properly for months. I believe now that your wife lost her mind the very first time she woke up here." The doctor shook her head, kept her eyes on the charts. "She's been dying ever since."

The cell was crowded. Apart from your mother, there were four of us. A guard sat at the foot of the bed.

"Protocol," said the doctor, "though there's been no need for weeks."

The bony body in the bed bore no resemblance to your mother, Lita. The eyes were sunken and closed and the breathing quick—it looked like rather an effort. There was something wrong with the color of the skin, something I couldn't put my finger on. And there was an odor. I said nothing. Neither did anyone else. The nurse busied herself with the charts while Dr Mann and the attendant bowed their heads with professional discretion.

I didn't know what to do, so I stepped forward till I was at the edge of the bed. That must have blocked the light because the eyes opened and that was that. The terrifying recognition cleared my head quickly enough. She looked at me and I looked at her—my girl, as she'd always been. Her mouth moved soundlessly, then again, rasping.

"Lita."

She was lucid, all right—what else should I have expected her to say? I let my eyes run down the horror that was her body and back again to her eyes, as clear as they'd ever been in her ruined head. She'd held on to you all that time and this is what it had done to her. At last the time had come to let go. I knew what I had to do.

"Clear the room," I said. "The guard, too."

The doctor removed her hands from her pockets.

"Protocol—"

"Don't concern yourself with it," I said. "I take responsibility."

When they'd gone, I pulled the guard's chair up to the side of the bed. Your mother hadn't taken her eyes off mine. I found her gaze impossible to withstand and sat with my elbows on my knees, looking down.

"Darling—"

She raised her hand a little at her side—the first time she'd moved anything but her eyes—and spoke a second time.

"Lita."

"I need to explain something to you. I need to tell you—"

The hand flapped, patting the bed clothes insistently.

"Lita."

"Yes. I—"

An awful rattle in her throat, her hand clenched on the sheet as she lifted her head.

"Lita."

Her lips pulled taut in a grimace over her teeth, her head dropped back to the pillow and her body convulsed. For a moment, I thought she was having a seizure, so violent was the movement of her tiny frame and then it dawned on me that, though she wasn't producing tears, she was weeping.

The bed shook and I felt a panic at the noise it made. She continued to mouth your name but not to say it—instead a low moan rose in pitch and volume.

"Look at me."

She turned her head away. I looked to the door, afraid they'd come back in, and laid a hand over her fist.

"Look at me."

She did, and the moment I had her attention, I said it.

"Lita is coming."

Immediately she was still, and silent. She curled up on her side and faced me—a question mark in human form.

"I've sent for her," I said. Her hand had unfurled and closed now around mine, the fingers weak and warm.

"She's on her way. We just need to wait a little while."

My other hand went to brush some hair away from her eye. Her breathing slowed and deepened. There was the long slow exhalation of relief.

"It won't be long, my love. We'll wait for her together, will we?"

I held my palm to her head and rubbed her forehead with my thumb.

"Shall I tell you a story?" I said. "It might help pass the time." *The way she looked at me, Lita. Like a pup. Like she believed me. I saw gratitude, just as I had the last time I'd told her a lie.* "I've been at the cabinet, you see. No better than you, in the end." *Her head twitched—the short, lateral nod of the prone.* "Shall I tell you of the Sultan and the vizier's daughter?"

The Tale
of the
Three Voyages

Wild Sage

The morning still smelled a little of the night—the saline perfume of a slowly lifting marine layer, the scent of wild sage that shimmied down the canyons from the upland scrub, the coastal highway; the traffic up there was building and rubber and reheating asphalt, not quite cooled in the brief interval between summer days, also rode down on the breeze. There was no coffee in the house so that was about it for aromas, unless you counted the faint reek that came intermittently from the dumpsters at the end of the row of low, wood slat homes, just enough space between each for a couple of parked cars and to give the description "private beach house" a shot at convincing anybody. Liam could see the dumpsters as well as pick up their odor because he was in the habit of taking his coffee, when he had one, out back to the kitchen porch and sitting with his feet crossed on a flaking fencepost, looking up in the direction of the traffic sounds, his back to the house and to the Pacific.

He could just as well have been in front where a veranda ran the length of the bungalow, but if he sat there looking at the ocean the joggers would look back up at him, and Liam didn't like to be looked at any more. The bungalows were set high above the beach. They were accessed by long, private sets of rickety wooden steps that draped the slope crookedly, like ropes thrown down to the intrepid who would grunt and wetten with sweat or mist or both by the time they paused for breath, knees trembling, to knock on the door.

At least, he *wanted* it to be wild sage. That scent. It was grassy and a little tart and it was always wild sage in the Marlowe novels. Philip Marlowe, after all, was one of the reasons Liam had washed up here.

It was natural enough, the gawking. He'd done it himself as a visitor here, before the rental sign had appeared in the window of number seven and he'd bounded up and breathlessly handed over the cash he'd had on him. Despite their decrepitude, the bungalows were venerated—older than any of the two-story houses that specked the hillside above and seeming more solid, somehow, than the glass and concrete office blocks and malls further up, out of sight and mind from here, up where the traffic went through town. Everything that didn't play into the mythology was kept up there, at bay—banks and realtors and manicurists. The closest you got to the ordure of commerce down here was a monstrously overpriced keto breakfast. These days, there were plenty of those.

The bungalows were relics of a time when what Jewel was and what it thought it was were, briefly, one and the same—a coastal bohemia, a bolt-hole for stars and starlets from further north, often at the behest of their publicists. A place for them to be when they needed, for whatever the latest, dissolute reason, to avoid the public gaze for a little while, for when they were tired and emotional, for whenever their people needed to get them out of town—or maybe for just a quick stopover, on their way through and down to Baja California on the other side of the border, for more of what had made them tired and emotional in the first place.

It all started with a hotel. The Granada was perfect—it had just enough rooms for a guest to check in discreetly, slip upstairs, take whatever-it-was and emerge some time later to hide behind a pair of Ray-Bans on a poolside lounger. On the other hand, rooms were too few to leave any for the *hoi polloi*, who probably didn't even know about the place. This was when a hotel could exist and get along just fine without an online presence or, for that matter, so much as an ad in the local paper. The right people knew about it and kept it full—roughly half of them there to lie low or dry out, the other half to get thoroughly wet, or nicely powdered, or baked.

Over the years, the homes that surrounded the hotel were bought up by folks with an interest in its clientele: agents (whose own clients might be down here six months of the year and in a relatively suggestible state compared with the LA version), producers, screenwriters, dealers. The arrival of writers was where the rot set in. As the forties turned to the fifties and the fifties dragged on, they were joined by a singular subset—poets. Beats, to be precise. By that time the Granada had been drained of its lifeblood, less interested in sinking its teeth into the rich and famous and opting increasingly for the merely rich.

The scene had by slow osmosis been leached from the hotel and absorbed by the neighborhood. Hollywood had retreated, but Jewel was still rarified, inhabited now by political dissidents, beatnik creatives, the neurologically atypical and addicts. On any given day, pretty much everyone in town could have been arrested on some charge, real or trumped up, to do with substance or sedition or an unlicensed firearm. But there was still money around, and when the patrol cars passed through, experienced officers would make sure the windows were rolled up, so the rookie they were riding with didn't get the inevitable whiff on the breeze and feel duty bound to do something about it. Meanwhile, imaginations all over the country, all over the world, were set on fire by the work produced in these dysfunctional, self-harming households.

As the money dried up, the hippies took over. It wasn't fresh blood—the change was largely a function of death and inheritance. Many of the new owners had grown up here: grandchildren, in some cases, of the Granada set. They had different kinds of drugs to take now and it had an impact on the color and cut of their pants, the length of their hair, their preferred activities, not to mention their preferred *level* of activity. Surf never made it to Jewel—there were no waves to catch here and if there were, they'd have dashed the catcher to pieces on the rocks. So the place stayed artsy—but productivity took a hit, the hefty novels and fraught poetry collections of yesteryear replaced by feathered dream-catchers, wind chimes, shamanic talismans and heavily-decorated Volkswagens.

You go through this every day of your life. It's boring.

Liam took his feet from the fence post, went to the bedroom, slipped into some sandals and made his way down the steps to the sand. It wasn't any old morning—this morning he had an appointment to keep. As long as he was staying local, he never locked up. He liked that you-can-leave-your-door-open-around-here feeling even if it was pure fantasy. It was clearly nuts to leave the door open, as verified by the local TV news, every day and night, not to mention the pleas of his neighbors to get a grip. Still, so far, miraculously, he'd gotten away with it. Maybe whether you got burgled or not was a question of attitude. Maybe all you had to do in the face of facts, when you had a fiction you really wanted to hold onto, was brazen it out. Maybe.

On the sand he walked barefoot, sandals hooked on a finger. Further west than this it was pretty much impossible to be, and he liked that feeling too—of extremity, of having reached the edge. The only thing to be gained by traveling westward from here was to end up in the east. He got to a set of concrete steps. They led up to the street that descended from the Granada and dead-ended here so that coach parties and the lazy could drive down to see the seals in their cove. At the top of them, he leaned on the rail and looked down at the creatures, the higgledy-piggle of their huddle on a tiny crescent of wet sand. They stank. But they made him smile every time with their ugly beauty—their graceless grace.

Turning his back, he began the short but steep ascent along Ocean Boulevard, a street he had long since begun to think of as a gauntlet. His morning runs, during those periods when he could muster the self-discipline for morning runs, had originally taken this street in, but he'd gotten tired of its taunts—of its immaculate, unerring presentation of what Jewel had become. It was lined with what you might call shacks on either side, none of them residential. There was a medical practice and there was the postal service, but mostly there were restaurants. You might call them shacks, but you'd have to have cultivated a robust disregard for reality to do so. This was post-truth Jewel in post-meaning California. The flakes in the paint were painted on and the wooden slats weren't wooden—they were metal cladding on concrete.

This was where you got your keto, macro, raw food and egg-white omelettes. He'd been a customer himself when he'd just moved in, still naive to how coffee bills could add up around here. He knew Eddie's, for example, and quite well. It was run by Eddie and Maureen—nice, genuine people, driven near enough to dementia by food fads and overheads and obliged to play the game. Next door the inevitable Pilates place, and uphill any number of yoga studios—fear of death was the closest you got to a scene in Jewel today, the nearest thing to culture. That's just the way it was. But then maybe that's what culture was. Even the hippies had had something like culture, but they turned it all to shit and the coked-up comedown that was the seventies. After that, nothing. For decades now, places like this had ceased to matter. After-the-fact California—overpriced, overdue, Jewel was a fake, a gaud, a visitor center for its former self. It was ersatz. But then so, he supposed, as he took the corner onto Prospect, pushed his way through the Granada's heavy glass door and stepped into the lobby, was he.

The concierge spotted him before he'd made his way to the open french doors that led to the patio restaurant, and intercepted him there.

"Liam, you can't sit out there dressed like that. You know this."

"Hey, Jesús." He shrugged. "Got to. Meeting a client."

Jesús was maybe late twenties, stocky, spotless and well-groomed in the hotel uniform. But his shirt collar was too big for him and so was his blazer. He looked uncomfortable.

"You kidding me? Like *that*?"

Liam tucked his chin and pulled his shirt out between thumb and forefinger. "You don't like it?" It was a short sleeve check in a hectic variety of colors that ranged from dusty yellows to deep oranges and hot pink. "You don't think it's cheerful? You know, put someone at their ease?" There was a quantity of sand in the breast pocket, he now realized.

"It's lovely," said Jesús. "It's really more a question of, I'm wondering, when did you put it on? Because I'm guessing it wasn't this morning." He took his time looking Liam up and down—the crumpled shirt, the sandals, the blue swim shorts—and waved his hand over the ensemble. "This is the beachwear of a troubled soul, Liam. If Sanchez sees you—"

"He'll ask me to leave? He'd ask me to leave if I was wearing a top hat and monocle. You didn't see me, OK? Thanks for the pep talk."

Jesús was already walking back to reception. Liam sauntered out onto the patio and took a table at the far end, where he could see all the other tables and watch the door. He was early and pretty sure the client wasn't here yet, but he wouldn't know—the email had been from an info-at address belonging to the Zade group but the sender hadn't identified themselves. A waiter appeared at his side. Liam shook his head, eyes on the entrance.

"I'm waiting for someone."

The next person through it was a nondescript type. Upright, middle-aged guy, dressed for business. It couldn't be him because he looked Liam right in the eye and then took another table. Then a demurely—but very expensively—dressed woman in dark sunglasses and a headscarf, trailed by what had to be a bodyguard in aviator shades and a shaved head. She meandered, weighing up the options table-wise, with a view no doubt to picking the most private. A common enough type in the Granada but definitely not Liam's demographic.

Another young woman stepped through the door. She looked harried and held on tight to the handbag that hung from her shoulder. Dark hair, tied up, dressed for work in a uniform he couldn't identify. A supermarket, maybe. Something in retail. Or maybe elderly care. She looked nervously around till her eyes met his. This was it, he was on.

She started to move in his direction but Sanchez was behind her; he had seen Liam and locked on.

Shit.

The hotel manager was nippy—in two strides he'd put himself between the lady and Liam.

Shit.

"Mr Tead?"

He jumped in his seat. The rich lady was standing over him, her beefcake a pace or two behind and towering over both of them. Liam more or less fell to his feet and took her proffered hand. It was tiny, but her grip was firm.

"It's Téad, actually, but yes." He looked from her to the bodyguard and back. "Won't you take a seat?"

It was too delicious. A rattled Sanchez, eyes wide, had to swerve awkwardly at the last minute to pass them by. The other lady, in the store uniform, had taken a table for herself. So they all sat down and the woman removed her scarf and sunglasses.

"Mother of Christ," said Liam.

She didn't acknowledge the words, instead putting her sunglasses in a case that she had retrieved from her bag and returning it there along with the scarf, carelessly scrunched.

"I don't intend to keep you long, Mr Tead. My name is—"

"I know who you are, Ms Zade. Who doesn't?" He had gripped the arms of his chair. "You're the client?"

"I haven't hired you yet."

"True." Liam's eyes flicked to the bodyguard.

"This is Darius. He is discreet. I'm hoping the same can be said of you."

"I can keep my mouth shut. Hi, Darius." The security man was almost perfectly bald but the stubble on display at either side of his oversized head was greying, so he was the oldest person at the table.

Liam smiled at the mirrored shades. There was no obvious sign that Darius was particularly aware of anything that was happening around him, though Liam had no doubt he was *super* aware of *everything* that was happening around him. He wore an earpiece. Liam let his gaze linger on those mirrored lenses a moment and noted with satisfaction that a seething Sanchez was reflected there, at the wait station behind Liam, pretending to do something to cutlery.

Ms Zade was looking around the patio. "Can I buy you a—"

"Sure," said Liam. "Two eggs sunny side up. Bacon and a couple of links. White coffee. Toast. Thanks."

Sanchez himself appeared at the table, waving the waiter away, and Ms Zade ordered Liam's breakfast and two waters for herself and Darius.

"They do excellent english muffins here," said Liam, looking directly at the hotel manager. "You should—"

"I'm not really a breakfast person," said Ms Zade. "Would *you* like—"

"Sure. Yes, please. Thanks." Sanchez left. Liam realized he'd been gripping his chair hard, and relaxed a little. "Not hungry, Darius?"

The waiter came to uncap a bottle of water and put it on the table with two glasses. The bodyguard took one of them, fished out the slice of lemon, threw it in the ashtray, and poured himself a drink. The coffee arrived at speed. Even with company like this, Sanchez wanted him gone.

"So," said Liam, stirring it, "Darius have any hobbies?"

She grinned. Despite the fact that she'd arrived with seven feet of security, she seemed less uptight than in the pictures he'd seen. She always seemed so pinched and hostile in those pictures, but maybe that was just a function of being stalked by press all the time. Her eyes were more striking in real life—something avian in them. Lupine, maybe. This morning, something like humor glinted in them and there was an upturn at the edge of her mouth that didn't seem unkind.

"I want to find my sister, Mr Tead."

Involuntarily, his eyes widened. He lifted the spoon from his coffee and laid it on a napkin.

"It's Tëad, actually, but . . . OK."

"Is that a tone I detect?"

"Well," he shrugged, "you know . . ."

The Zade twins were a meme. Considered the embodiment of Zade duplicity. Their father's media group was as essential to life in this country, and all the other countries, as it was despised and distrusted. What you thought of the Zade machine, though, was of no consequence. It owned the main news outlets and it owned the outlets the main news outlets called fake news outlets, which in turn and of course accused the main news outlets of being fake news, so nobody could be confident anymore about which was which, or why it mattered. And by one circuitous route or another, Zade owned it all. Zade was hardwired into your device. Into your car. If you could afford the right type of refrigerator, it was in there too. And it owned social media. There were monopoly laws of course but it was still, on the surface of it, a free country, and people voted with their wallets—the only social media that seemed to really matter was Zade-owned. It owned your feed. It probably didn't own you, yet, but then *you* had been pretty much atomized. You weren't worth owning. And it didn't need to own you to sell you anyway. And somehow the twins embodied all of this. All the smoke and mirrors, all the sleight of hand. They had never been photographed together. A few years back Doonah, the older—by minutes—had disappeared from public view completely. Or so said the press releases. Nobody Liam knew really believed she'd ever existed, although it was never clear what kind of trick was being pulled, or to what end. It was just that, when it came to Zade, trickery was assumed. Anyway, you only ever heard about Sherry these days—the one sitting across the table from him, and reading his mind. He leaned forward and took the photo she held out.

"She's the one in the foreground," she said.

He couldn't remember the last time he'd held a print photo. This one had a couple of creases, as though it had spent time in a wallet, and the image quality was bleached out like a photo from the seventies or like when you lay in the sun for a while and then opened your eyes. In the foreground, the face of a young woman, in perfect profile, reclining in a canvas chair, and behind her an identical woman sitting sideways on another chair and looking at the camera. Both of them were laughing, or at least smiling so hard their eyes were almost shut. Someone had said something funny—the photographer maybe, maybe one of the women. Though Doonah wasn't looking at the camera, there was something about her that betrayed an acute awareness of it. Sherry was in a swimsuit so although they were tightly framed, Liam knew it was taken either poolside or at the beach. A strong breeze through Sherry's hair favored the beach. They looked happy. It was the kind of photo that didn't seem to be of anything much at all but still made you wish you'd been there. And as far as he could make out, it wasn't doctored.

"Well, there's a first. When was this taken?"

"God, ten years ago. More."

"And you last saw her."

"In the flesh? A long time. But on cam about four weeks ago. She wouldn't tell me where she was."

"Why not?"

"My father is a very controlling man, Mr Tead, and she couldn't defy him. If she did, she wouldn't even get to see me on cam. We can get into all of that, if it helps."

"And why me?" He really was dying to know.

"I looked around a little. You seemed . . ." she smirked that smirk he liked, ". . . reassuringly obscure."

His food arrived. So she wanted to find her sister. Something about the verb didn't sit right with Liam. She didn't *need* to find her sister? Didn't *have* to? He'd need to get into that with her too. Or so he imagined—Liam had been a private detective for a little under four months now, had been unemployed for much of that time, had neglected to obtain a license and had never tracked a missing person. The link sausages at the Granada were a cut above. Fatter and juicier and pungent with the savory perfume of sage. Now that they were on a plate in front of him, he wondered if the scent that descended at night over the bungalow really was wild sage. It certainly wasn't the same as this. But then, he supposed, the naming of things isn't always logical. It doesn't always make sense.

Stop thinking about sage, you fool.

He unrolled the napkin from around his knife and fork and addressed the bacon first, using a forkful of it to break a runny egg yolk.

"All right, Ms Zade," he said, "why don't you tell me your story?"

My Father is the Patriarch

There are two things you need to know about my father. The first thing you need to know is that he is the patriarch. We Zade women have lived around him, behind him, beneath. He doesn't seem to be capable of any other arrangement. Why this should be I couldn't tell you. His upbringing perhaps, though what little I know of that I have had from my mother.

They were both of them raised in a then emerging middle-class, both families well-known and established locally and neither especially traditional in their outlook. If anything, the Zades had come down a little, the value and extent of ancestral land and privilege reduced to the point of necessitating the uptake of paid work, and the Khajandars had come up slightly, a merchant family for as long as anyone could remember and incrementally wealthier with the passing of each year. Reasonably well matched, in other words, in a place where these things still mattered, traditional or not.

The Zades were notorious for almost exclusively producing boys—spoiled boys invariably, sometimes brilliant, usually not. The family imported its women who, like pillars, punctuated the dim, murky male space: participants only in the sense that they held it all up. I suppose the traditions lived on in that way at least. Again, I didn't exist in that world so this is all according to my mother. Her perspective. I've no reason to distrust it but I suppose it should be borne in mind that it's a particular point of view. It will be the same in all the stories I tell you. I'd admonish you to remember that but you already know it. Everybody does—with the Zades, there's always an angle.

My mother's family on the other hand were short on boys. They made girls, demure and dutiful, and hadn't gotten round to checking if any of them were brilliant or not. My mother was.

One night, when she thought I was asleep, she began to tell me their story.

SHE SAID: Why give it a why *chutki?* It is best to think of our arrival here as an inevitability. Your father was always coming to America and I had long been in orbit around your father. The date, the details—they don't matter. Not material to your narrative—this is the language now, yes? If you must chronicle then let us call it Chapter One, and I will begin there.

SHE WENT ON: It was painful to watch him that day. Your father. The princeling in line at U.S. Immigration. The clueless little prince. Craning his neck every two minutes, as if the force of his attention might be enough to move things on. I say we were in line at immigration but in truth we were still on the stairwell we'd reached having crossed the tarmac from the plane. Out there in the soft light of late afternoon, walking towards the terminal, your father had looked about so excitedly I had to stop myself from laughing—as though he might spot Barbara Streisand, or Johnny Carson.

At the first turn of the stairs, the line came to a stop. We spent some time there—I remember it well: neither on the ground nor upstairs, stuck in a space meant to be moved through, not noticed. But it's imprinted on me. I wonder at times if I'm *still* there.

Painful to watch him, craning his neck. Standing on tiptoe, like a little boy, to peer over heads. There was nothing ahead of us but another turn in the stairs, and who knows how many flights after that. There wasn't even an official of any kind to buttonhole, as he would certainly have tried. Distinguish himself through repartee from the rest of us. Establish rapport, elevate himself. He has been awarded the status of mysterious figure—the enigmatic Zade—for so long now that no one would believe how utterly transparent he is to me.

A little boy indeed—and not the appealing kind. But I did still love him then, and perhaps never more than on that day, seeing him in his helplessness. Never loved him more nor wanted so badly to slap that stupid, pampered face of his. We had barely exchanged a word for the whole journey. What should have been our magic carpet ride, our flight through the heavens, had been one sustained sulk.

On my last morning in the family home I haven't seen since, my last morning in my country, I had decided that for my arrival on American soil I should wear a sari. I don't know how the idea got into my head—I never wore them much, then. It just seemed right. A gesture, perhaps, to signify that I was not wholly subjugating myself to this dream of his—to that country, that culture. That I was not merely some malleable thing. A supplicant, yes, but no beggar. When he arrived to collect me, my dress surprised and—he couldn't conceal it—embarrassed him. We bickered and the only way I could bring the bickering to a stop was by giving him the silent treatment. I'm very good at it, unbeaten by him, and now here we were in the United States.

"Sir?"

Almost—we'd reached the top of the stairs and passed through some beige double-doors into a wider hallway. Those in front of us were filing along on the right while on the left a few uniformed men and women were searching items of hand luggage on trestle tables, questioning the owners in curt, perfunctory tones.

"Excuse me, sir?"

I knew the instant he saw them he'd be over there to ask some unnecessary question, to make himself known. He made his way to the nearest table and was waving his hand over the passenger's head to attract attention. Meanwhile, another officer had made straight for him.

"Sir!"

Your father finally swivelled when the officer placed a hand on his shoulder.

"Sir, were you called over here?"

The great Zade looked at the table, at the door at the end of the hallway, at the floor, back at the officer, and shook his head.

"No, sir, you were not. You have not been invited to enter the United States of America."

Your father could do nothing but shake his head again.

"Do you see this, sir?"

The officer had stepped over to the line of people, which had been moving at a glacial pace but which now stopped entirely so that those within earshot of the exchange could spectate. He was pointing at the floor. "This white line, sir?"

A nod, this time.

"This side of the line here, sir, where we are—this is the United States. That other side of the line is where you belong."

Neither a shake nor a nod. His mouth had fallen open.

"Sir, I'm going to need you to step back out of my country."

The officer indicated the far side of the line, where I was. His other hand had come to rest on his holstered weapon, which got your father's attention—meekly, he stepped back over and picked up the bag he had left at my feet, flushing at the sniggers from our fellow travellers. If he was thinking of some clever and redeeming remark he might make, it was too late. The officer had walked away and the line resumed its forward shuffle.

Your father shot me one of many glances that had punctuated the sullen silence of our long journey. They came when his spirits sank, when some bit of business had him at a loss. Whenever he felt defeated, in other words. And in that moment I could see his defeat. The brown man between the white lines. Reduced—here at the very threshold of his triumph—to the caricature of defeat he feared most. Damp hair clinging to his scalp, unwashed and crumpled in his sweaty suit, sniffing at himself surreptitiously. He was the son of wealthy parents and an accomplished academic but that was not the odour that clung to him here, its vapours twisting in his imagination to form the words he so disdained—immigrant, economic migrant.

Apart from the imploring looks I was barely even there for him. And even in these appeals there was something else, something accusatory—something that branded me a reminder to him of the life we were leaving behind and that therefore resented my tarnishing presence. I may be rationalizing now but I did feel it then—a misgiving that came up from my depths. Indeed, subsequent events have only borne out what I began to suspect—that in the story of his life, as he tells it to himself, I am a minor character.

 At the next doorway we stepped out into the immigration hall proper. After the confinement of the stairwell and the low-ceilinged murk of the corridor, this new space was vast. The hall was rectangular and we had entered on its width, so it stretched away from us. To our left was a long row of glass windows and behind each one the figure of an immigration officer, as impassive as the mo'ai of Easter Island. Between the windows, passages wide enough for just one person at a time—the only way out.

 We though were guided to the right—by more white lines on the floor and a gesticulating official—where it became apparent that before we escaped this space we would be getting to know it rather well. Corralled between the nylon belts that ran between regularly-spaced stanchions, we would cover the whole floor area, it seemed, proceeding on a laterally folded, intestinal pathway till we reached some waiting point opposite one of the windows. It was the first time I had seen such an arrangement and it seemed so comical. There was no one to share the joke with though—your father, slighted, glowered at the floor. I looked up.

 Strip lights hung from wires that ran the width of the hall, low over our heads. They were lit but it hardly mattered—above them, the void was at least four storeys high, maybe more, and from dappled glass windows that ran around it on all sides at its upper reaches, daylight poured in. In comparison, the low lamps seemed to emit gloom.

 People still smoked in those days, so sunbeams divided the void. Like the old photos your father had shown me of Grand Central Station in New York—do you know the ones?—of great blazing shafts on an almost sheer diagonal making the station concourse seem like the nave of a cathedral. They say that new developments around that station have since blocked out the sun, but in those photos, that your father so loved, they seemed like fire as much as light—steep, burning stairways that ascended to the angels' quires.

Here, the sun was sinking—the golden beams in the immigration hall did not grace us, down on its floor. Instead they hit the pale green wall beneath the opposite windows, just above the suspended electric lights, and made that upper space seem to me a different order of reality. I felt as though I were observing, from beneath, a lit-up body of water that I longed to swim in, or that rarified, celestial air that can be observed beneath the domes of great churches, that I longed to fly through. Indeed something *did* fly though it—a single bird had found its way in and was circling, just beneath the roof.

I tapped your father's shoulder and pointed it out to him and, quite out of character for him, he watched it with me as it described a perfect oval on the x axis that sagged a little on the y, the bird descending on a glide to the low point, then flapping to rise to the zenith, then gliding again, and so on. As it passed through a beam of light the tips of its fanned feathers, on the descent, seemed to ignite, and as it flapped through on the ascent it left variegated eddies of dust and cigarette smoke in its wake—Mandelbrot revelations in the ether. It occurred to me that the bird was not *here*. It did not share this place with us. It was elsewhere, at some supernal level of existence, an echelon of heaven, below the empyrean perhaps, but far above us.

In time, we reached a point opposite one of the immigration windows and were told to wait there. Your father's attention returned to earth and mine to the bird. It showed no sign that it would ever abandon its path. What if it couldn't? What if it had defaulted to this last autonomic behaviour, unable to find a way out and unable to process the inability? If it would circle till its energy was depleted and, not finding a perch, drop lifeless to the floor? If it danced in the light of its own death?

The nowhereness I had felt on the stairwell was doubled here in two distinct liminalities—the bird on the y between heaven and earth and I on the x, between the old and the new. Two directions of travel. I felt another misgiving, as the immigration officer gestured for us to approach the window, that I would be leaving by the one and not the other. That I would be squeezing myself out of this space that it seemed to me had something of the divine in it, the ever-present elsewhere, through the narrow passage, and into something narrower still.

Our families were well-to-do, but there was no call in our part of the world for fancy hotels, so we were both suitably impressed when we stepped into the lobby of one and onto its gleaming marble floor. Your father's brand new shoes, which I knew must be hurting him, made a very agreeable click on the polished surface—James Bond sauntering around the villain's lair—that I hadn't noticed at the airport. I couldn't enjoy the same effect myself as underneath the sari I wore sneakers.

At check-in we discovered how unacceptable it is in America not to take credit and carry a card for the purpose. Despite our placing a thousand dollars in cash on the counter by way of deposit, the concierge refused to give us our room until a humiliating call had been made to my father, by no means an early riser, who grumpily gave the hotel the details of his. Humiliating for *your* father, that is. I couldn't see the harm at the time, but it turns out he had a point—in his communiqués, my gleeful old man would bring it up for the rest of his life.

We might have luxuriated then, finally. We were young—why should we give a fig for the trivial vicissitudes of hotels and airports? We might have lain there and looked at the ceiling in our clean but, after the magnificence of the lobby, surprisingly modest room. We might have breathed a while, revelling in our arrival, our being on the right side of the immigration windows—our passing out of the prologue and into the first chapter.

But your father had other plans. Dinner at McDonalds. There was only the one branch in the city at the time, on Market Street. Your father knew where it was and had chosen the hotel because it was close to Market Street. Think about that—this was before the internet and your father had the address of a fast food outlet that, while fairly well-known, had nothing like the global profile it has now. He even had the street number. 1041.

When I think of the patience I had, but there it is. Market Street, it turned out, is a long street. It goes all the way to Little Italy, where I would much rather have eaten. Our hotel was at the wrong end of it. We walked for half an hour. Trams were passing but your father was too embarrassed to try them, not knowing how or where to pay. That is a speculation, though, because he walked ten paces ahead of me. Another twenty minutes. By the time we arrived at the restaurant I could tell his feet were causing him real pain. He got his hamburger. I had fries and soft, suspect ice cream. When he'd taken his last bite I spoke up, refusing to walk back to the hotel and insisting we use the tram. He won again—we took a taxi.

I wore the sari the following morning. My reasons were mainly practical—I didn't want to waste clean clothes when I knew we'd be spending the day on the road. But also there is the possibility, I suppose, that I was already digging in. At the rental place we picked up the car, the Stingray convertible your father insisted on, and loaded the boot with our things. It was a cold, foggy morning and the attendant watched open-mouthed as we pulled out of the lot with the roof down to make our way towards the Number One. Once beyond the city limits, your father—constitutionally incapable of observing a speed limit—put the car through its paces. *Her* paces, in his words.

Out on the coast, the marine layer was so thick it was easy to forget that to one side of us lay a great continent and to the other the greatest of oceans—there was only the tortuous black line of the road ahead, the stomach-twisting speed of your father's driving and a thin border of rocky scrub at the asphalt's edge that faded quickly into a white nothing. Where it occasionally thinned and I caught a glimpse of the water, it was cobalt in the murk. The mist muffled sound, so apart from the grinding and churning of the motor it was oddly quiet. It was also cold, and I wanted to complain about how ridiculous it was to have the roof down, but didn't dare distract him from his driving. Once in a while we would drive up and out of the marine layer into dazzling light and ultraviolet distances, but never for long.

Eventually, he inserted a cassette he'd compiled especially for the drive, of music he considered suitably American—everything from Sinatra to The Stanley Brothers. His attitude to volume had something in common with his take on road safety. Can you imagine such a thing, *chutki*? A stiff brown man in a stiff brown suit and his sari-wrapped wife, hurtling along the Pacific Coast Highway in a Corvette Stingray, roof down on a cold day, bluegrass blaring from the car stereo.

We got off the highway briefly at Big Sur—your father had read Kerouac—and made our way down to a cove. I'm not sure I've ever seen anybody look as out of place as your father did on that beach, the sand scuffing his patent leather shoes. I told him to take them off but he wouldn't—he wore white socks and I expect they were bloodied around his blisters, and that he was ashamed.

I removed my own socks and sneakers, thinking about all the bare feet that had left their painter's palette prints here—the Hollywood starlets, the beatniks and bohemians, the hippies who so venerated what they found exotic in our culture and in the cyphers, scripts and symbols of our native faiths. They'd have been bemused to know that to us *they* were the exotic, those rudderless kids who had fled the suburban culs-de-sac of Kansas, Milwaukee, Detroit, Cincinnati and the countless Nowherevilles of the American heartland, and headed west. A wind was picking up, the marine layer burning off and my nostrils filling with the scents of ozone and damp sand. The sea had carved an arch in the cliffside and your father walked out towards it, as far as he dared without getting the shoes wet. I sat on a bank of sand and watched waves hit rock and became an atheist.

Something in the splash, the unfathomable complexity of spray. Waves become particles, each on its own particular trajectory, subject to its own particular circumstance, its own particular velocity, its own particular point of impact, and all of those particularities adding up to something that I wanted to imbue with its own being . . . or at least a *will* to be—such was the menagerie of shape and motion thrown by rock and water. But I couldn't. I saw rather that there was nothing animal, nothing wilful, in splashing water. It wasn't, it didn't even qualify as a thing. It was a constellation of things—a cloud of countless, clueless incident.

And, complexity upon complexity, not only was even any one of these constellations beyond the possibility of description, none of them would ever be repeated. Even if sea, wind, moon—whatever the variables—were to reproduce a wave identical to its predecessor in speed and mass and angle and what-not, wasn't the rock itself in flux, worn away to an infinitesimal degree with each impact?

My faith flew from me like a silk headscarf in a stiff breeze. We are particles. Whatever makes waves moves through us. We crash into things and each other. So what? Even if there were a God, it would be none of our business.

Through the spray and the thinning fog, in the veiled distance—home. Home is my elsewhere now, *chutki*, not heaven. I would say it haunts me but actually, it hounds me. There is nothing benign in an abandoned home, you know. One feels its predatory breath on one's back. It has teeth that snap.

I still go to the water sometimes, where so many of the juice bars and surf shops are called *west coast* something-or-other, but how was I ever to think of it as the west, when I go there to look back to the old country? It's preposterous. I know it only as the boundary between an old set of possibilities and the set that dwindles around me now, and the outer limit of both. The coast of everything.

When we moved on, your father put the roof up. Despite the improved conditions I was tired and ill-tempered by the time we hit Los Angeles traffic. The highway is a poor vantage point from which to see that city. I took an instant dislike to it and have never given it a second chance—grateful, in the passenger seat that day, that we were going further south.

THIS IS HOW MY MOTHER would speak about those times. Only when she thought I slept—it didn't seem to matter to her whether I heard or not, only that the words went in. It was like watching a skilled pathologist perform an autopsy. There was no need to be gentle because the subject—the young woman who had loved my father—was already dead. She never referred to him by name, or by any of the terms of endearment that a wife might use for a husband. She mostly avoided the casual familiarity of the pronoun. It was always *your father this, your father that*. This is ironic, because the second thing you need to know about my father is that he is not my father.

The View from the Top of the Wyatt

It was the kind of carpet he'd only ever seen in hotels, cineplexes and bowling alleys—a wildly misjudged and unnecessarily ornate mess of indefinite shapes in blues, golds, browns and greens. While it could be taken for abstract, Liam had little doubt its creator, whether a committee or an algorithm, had been working to a theme. This particular example was redolent, faintly, of foliage. It might have been a thicket—if Frank Lloyd Wright had designed thickets—or a tangle of vines that someone had colored in wrong. Whatever it was, it made Liam want to turn around and leave so he wouldn't have to get it on his shoes.

By the time he'd made his way to a table by one of the floor-to-ceiling windows and taken a seat there, the imported beer he'd ordered at the bar was right behind him. The waiter put it on the table along with a tiny bowl of warmed nuts and the bill. Liam picked the latter up—it was also tiny but it had a big number on it that made him hate the carpet even more. And they charged for the nuts. Still, it wasn't a bill he intended to foot.

The waiter retreated and not a word exchanged. Service in this country continued to impress and appall Liam. They were freaks for it. It was as if all they thought they had was their dollar and in exchange for it required *service*—loud, proud, big smiles and highly conspicuous. Like they needed to see the buck was worth something and made *them* worth something because if it wasn't and it didn't, well . . . but the more upscale you went, the less currency ostentation seemed to carry. Servers to the wealthy were unobtrusive. They had name badges but they didn't introduce themselves. To put a bottle of imported beer on a table didn't require language so none was wasted.

He was early and would be waiting a little while so he took a swig, sat back and let his eyes wander. There was just a smattering of other customers, either sitting in silence or talking so quietly he couldn't hear them. The bar was open to the public but it seemed to Liam they were all guests of the hotel who had nothing to do and didn't want to sit in their rooms. Half of them held paperbacks or tablets. The furniture was at precisely two stylistic removes from what he'd seen in the old people's home—continence was, he imagined, a minimum expectation in a place like this so the fabrics were of a better quality but that, and the fact that the chair backs here weren't high enough to support a nodding head, was about it. And quality or not, the upholstery had the same ridiculous pattern, if pattern wasn't too kind a term, as the carpet. Shitty furniture in a shitty, atmosphere-free bar in a high-end-and-nevertheless-shitty hotel. And it was all exactly right, exactly as it should be. What was he doing here, after all? Something shitty.

 He got out of his chair to turn it toward the window and sit in it again. It didn't even make any sense, the foliage motif—this was a sky bar. The giant window that now took up his view gave out, from the fortieth floor, onto the panorama of San Diego Bay. With his nose to the glass he looked down at the Embarcadero marina, the pleasure boats moored along their jetties like the pieces of a kit model out of the box, neatly attached to plastic struts. Leaning back and looking beyond, the Tenth Avenue Marine Terminal which, it seemed to him, was at capacity with just the one, monstrous container ship. Of course it would be a Zade ship and of course Zade would be into shipping. It was into everything else.

 He wouldn't see Sherry again. She'd told him yesterday that it might be on, subject to the checks she'd have done today. But it was too good to be true. People like that walked into your life once, if they ever walked into it at all, and if you didn't get hold of them then and there, that was it. He didn't feel like he'd closed her, and he knew the more thoroughly they looked into him, the more inadequate they'd find him to be.

 If she was using Zade machinery to carry out the checks—and of course she was—she'd have known as much about him as he did by mid-morning. By now, with the last rays of the sun making the water sparkle, she'd know more. On the hull of the ship, several stories tall—the Zade logo. It was a good logo; it did what a good logo ought to do, which was to be instantly recognizable, to everyone, everywhere—and it was successful in its stated intention: to evoke, in idealized form, the feather of a peacock. Zade loved to play on the *eastern* thing. Into one side of the plume the name Zade intruded in capital letters, concave at top and bottom like the CinemaScope logo or a pi symbol on its side. But it hadn't escaped anyone's notice that the graphic also perfectly depicted a surveilling eye.

He could just about make out the legendary hotel on Coronado Island, that he'd bussed out to as soon as he'd figured out the miserly public transportation system. The pilgrimage had culminated in a disappointment he couldn't rationally justify, that he didn't find Jack Lemmon there, or Marilyn Monroe, instead settling for an unexceptional lunch in a crowd of the similarly disenchanted. Apparently they didn't even shoot the interior scenes there.

Apart from the Zade ship, pretty much everything big in the bay was war machinery—an aircraft carrier and all different types of warship he didn't have the vocabulary for. If he didn't care for the bar, he liked the window well enough—the way it framed the view, with the sun gone now and artificial lights flicking on everywhere. It gave the scene an epic quality, like the opening shot of a big-budget war movie, establishing the magnificence of the soon-to-be-blown-up.

Top of the world. If they really needed to theme the décor couldn't they have thought about something with clouds? That way customers would feel like they were walking on air. It would give the place a Sistine, celestial vibe. Missed opportunity. People didn't *think*.

"Mr Tead?"

Before he turned the chair he bit his lip, resisting the urge to correct her. She was simply never going to get it, and this was no time to push. Once his chair was facing the right way and she had taken her own, he smiled.

"Please just call me Liam, Ms Nufus."

She didn't reciprocate his offer of cordial informality, and had clearly been crying. Hayal Nufus was a lecturer at the university. She was probably about sixty years old, had an athletic build and normally the look of someone you wouldn't want to mess with, but tonight she looked fragile.

"You wouldn't like something?" he said, gesturing toward the bar. "You know, to . . .eh . . . gird yourself?"

Jesus Christ.

"I think I'll manage," she said. "And you, Mr Tead? Isn't it a little ghoulish of you to stick around? Front row seat at the fireworks show, is that it?"

"Oh . . . no, not at all," he shifted in the seat. "I won't be coming with . . ." It *was* a strange arrangement, he now realized. For him to be here. He had no idea how this sort of thing was usually done. "There was just the matter of the balance of my fee."

"We could have done that without meeting," she said, taking her phone from her bag. "What's your email again? I'll Venmo it."

He lowered the beer bottle he'd been putting to his lips. "I usually take cash, actually."

"I don't have cash." She shook her head curtly. "Seriously, who has cash?"

He went ahead and emptied the bottle, placing it back on the table. "My fault," he said, wringing his hands between his knees like a penitent. "I thought I'd been clear."

"Well you weren't. If you insist on cash you can come by my office tomorrow and I'll have it. Make sure you bring an invoice. Everything above board and in writing, that's what my lawyer tells me." She stood. "Room number?"

He tore his eyes away from the beer bottle and the nut bowl.

"1041. It's a suite, one floor up."

She put her phone away and looked him up and down.

"Do you enjoy your work?"

Gimme a minute—Marlowe would have something for this. Something along the lines of "I like to stop bad people doing bad things, Ms Nufus. Sometimes I get to stop good people doing bad things. It isn't always pretty."

But that would be Marlowe's answer, not his. It would sound ridiculous coming from him. So he tried to think of his own, and while he was busy with that it thought of itself and fell out of his mouth.

"No."

He felt like he might well up all of a sudden, but he didn't know if that was down to her predicament, his own self-loathing, or her failure to bring cash. She may have noticed, because her expression softened.

"You're youngish, Mr Tead," she said. Her irises performed a vertical, appraising flick that certainly took in his nascent pot belly. He sat up. "Not getting any younger though. You could do something else."

She walked away. He didn't want to be here if there was to be a scene so he watched the elevator doors slide shut behind her—then he left too. On his way out he put his last twenty dollars on the bar and, having seen the bill, left them there.

Pulling out of the hotel garage, he crossed Harbor Drive and got on to Market Street. Market Street was an extremely long street that ended up out in Esperanza—he'd found that out the hard way—but tonight he turned on to First Avenue after just a few blocks, heading for the Five and cursing every light he encountered along the way, none more so than the gas tank warning that blinked on the dash. That's what the twenty dollars had been for—the light had been blinking, whenever he'd had the nerve to use the car, for the last two days. His chances of making it out to Jewel were either fifty-fifty or not as favorable as that.

This, even by his standards, was something of a low point. About as rotten as it got. It was rotten and he was rotten, averting his eyes at each red light in case a crossing pedestrian might see how rotten he was, and when it turned green driving with knuckles white on the wheel and teeth clenched, as if a tight grip and a grinding jaw had something to do with fuel efficiency. He probably wouldn't even be paid for the sleaze he was driving away from. Nufus's scrutiny had gotten him flustered—so he hadn't told her that her suspicions about her husband and another woman were actually quite a way off. He was up in that suite with two conspicuously young men, and by now it had probably crossed her mind that her private investigator might have warned her about that.

Maybe it would make it easier on her, but he doubted it. Maybe it wouldn't make any difference at all, but he doubted that too. And he had no idea what he'd face at her office tomorrow or, given he'd almost certainly be abandoning the car by the side of the road tonight, how he'd get there. As he merged with the Five, Little Italy was laid out on his left and beyond it the harbor. He flicked the air conditioning off, cursing himself for not having thought of it sooner, and Sherry popped into his mind. Wouldn't it be something? If she actually got back to him? It was a delusion that appealed right now, with the car about to sputter to a stop.

What was it the heiress had said? Or her mother had said? The ever-present elsewhere. Hounded, she'd said, or her mother had said. Whoever had said it, that was him too. Hadn't he always been hounded from here to there, chasing the elsewhere? Did hounding yourself count? And nowhere, it was just beginning to dawn on him, would ever do. Everywhere would always just be here, and here would always turn to shit in his mouth.

In the future, there would be carpets—proper, fibrous carpets—that could display a cloud pattern by day, all hazy blues and ivory whites, but a starry sky by night. They'd be self-cleaning, probably.

It was a nice thought, that working for a Zade might propel him somewhere that really *was* somewhere else. Somewhere clean and untainted by his ruinous touch. But it was dark, the day was over, and Zade hadn't called. It occurred to him that running out of gas on the freeway would be a nightmare, so once past Mission Bay he got on to the mountain road. Now he was on a slight ascent but at least in the residential area the car would be easier to dump.

Even if the Zade thing had been a fleeting mirage, he'd gotten close hadn't he? It kind of proved such things could happen. If he got his cash from Nufus tomorrow he would have a decent meal, put some gas in the car and think about his next move.

As he was coming to these conclusions, a minor miracle had occurred, fittingly heralded by the church of All Hallows on his right. This was the point from which he could be sure he'd make it home— it was all downhill from here. He cut the motor to save the last of the fuel for the traffic lights along Jewel's main avenue, and went on the clutch. He turned at the church and knew the care home was on his right, but it had been a while since he'd been able to look at it.

The fumes were indeed just enough to get him along the avenue—at the top of the beach road that led to the bungalows, the car gave out. He coasted, trying to take the turn on to the dirt track without braking in the hopes he'd have the momentum to get to number seven at the end of it. In fact, he had to brake hard—his neighbor, Jean, caught in his headlights. He got out of the car.

"Hi, Jean."

"You recognize me then," she said from within a dust cloud. Jean had a way with sarcasm that meant Liam generally avoided her early in the day. She nodded at the other side of the track, at the dumpsters. "I often put my garbage in these."

"Sorry, Jean. Do you think you could help me push the car to my place?"

"I'm sixty-eight years old."

"It's just a few yards. If I leave it here, Ted will have it towed."

Jean went to the back of the car and they rolled it up to the side of his bungalow.

"You have visitors," said Jean, walking away. "I thought you were finally getting burgled, but they put the light on and they haven't left, so I guess you owe them money."

Liam didn't like that. He locked the car, took the couple of steps onto the back porch and pushed the door open. The kitchen was dark but the door to the lounge was ajar and a shaft of light came from there. He pushed that open too, letting it swing away from him but not stepping through it just yet. He did owe money, here and there.

In the old rocking-chair that had had its rockers removed sat the hulking figure of Darius. He looked like he was sitting on doll's furniture and, in the late evening and a dimly-lit room, had not removed the aviators. Liam stepped in.

"Hey, Darius."

Sherry was on the two-seater. More surprisingly, a neat, officious-looking and rather elderly woman, who wore her hair in a tight bun and rimless glasses, sat next to her. She looked awfully familiar and when he realized why, he wondered if the others could see the blood drain from his face. At her feet was a leather case.

"Won't you take a seat, Mr Tead?" said Sherry, indicating the last remaining piece of furniture, a sagging old armchair.

"Eh, it's Tĕad," said Liam, "but . . . sure."

He couldn't muster an objection to her acting like she owned the place. It wasn't impossible that she did.

"I didn't expect to see you again," he said. "Have you decided to hire me?"

There was a tension in the room he couldn't pin down.

"Well, let's see about that," said Sherry. "We've reached some conclusions, put it that way."

She eyed him steadily, and the glint of humor from yesterday was gone. Did she know? Darius had leaned forward slightly to undo the laces on one of his shoes. Perhaps they'd come loose and needed retying, but that didn't stop the hairs on the back of Liam's neck from standing up. He noticed a new and neat stack of paperbacks on top of the TV.

"Wait a second." A couple of blankets had been carefully folded and placed on the back of the sofa behind Sherry and the woman nobody had introduced. Darius had removed a shoe. There was an odor Liam recognized but that took him a moment to name. Beeswax. "Have you *cleaned* the place?"

"I need you to listen to me very carefully," said Sherry. Darius was unlacing his other shoe. "If I hire you, I am taking a risk." She rested her elbows on her lap. "And I will need *you* to take a risk."

The woman who looked so much like Düssel opened the leather bag at her feet. Darius had removed both shoes and was pulling a sock off.

"What do you mean?" He was talking to Sherry but his eyes flicked from the bodyguard to the leather case.

"I mean I need you to trust me, Mr Tead. Maybe a little more than you might be used to trusting people."

Darius rolled one of his socks into the other and deposited the resulting ball in one of his shoes. He began neatly rolling up his trouser legs. Liam scanned the floor. No sign of a tarp. They were a very special pair of feet, he couldn't help observing, in that they contrived to appear significantly larger than the shoes that had recently contained them. Getting one of them into the boat at the side of Ted's cottage looked like it might be a squeeze.

From the leather case at her feet, the unidentified woman took a smaller leather case. Darius stood. All of a sudden, Sherry had slid across the floor and was on her knees by the side of Liam's chair, her hand on his where it gripped the arm.

"Mr Tead, I'm about to turn the page on the most important chapter of my life. I want you to come with me."

The other woman unfolded the little leather case—it was really more of a wallet—and slipped a shiny metal syringe out of its sleeve.

"The fuck?" Liam withdrew his hand. "What the—"

From somewhere inside his sports jacket, Darius drew a semi-automatic pistol.

Liam let out a low groan. It wasn't very Marlowe of him but it was all he had. "Why has he taken off his shoes?"

"Don't worry about that," said Sherry.

"Don't *worry*?" said Liam. "What—"

Darius unclipped the magazine from the gun and dropped both, gently, into Liam's lap, who could only watch as the giant went to the front door and left through it.

"Darius doesn't get a lot of time off," said Sherry. "He wants to go down to the water and paddle awhile."

She took his hand again. "So it's just us here. You have the gun and nobody is forcing you to do anything. I'm asking you, Mr Tead."

Having the gun in his lap wasn't comforting at all.

"I don't . . . I don't want—"

The woman approached the other arm of the chair. It occurred to Liam that he wasn't physically struggling.

"What else would you be doing?" said Sherry. "You don't have much going for you here, do you?" She took his face in her hands. "Nothing at all to lose." Her eyes were brown but a dark, dark brown—almost black—and she looked at him with something like pity. She *did* know. He thought he might well up again, then became aware that there were already tears on his cheeks. She hadn't let go of them.

"I need you to have faith in me. Can you do that, Liam?"

His first name went through him like electricity. The other woman was identifying an injection site.

"Come with me," said Sherry. "But I need you to have faith in me. Not everything in the following chapters will be revealed to you. Some things you will see and understand—some things you will see and not understand." She shot a look towards his arm as the needle pierced his skin. "And some things you will not see. I need you to be OK with that. Can you do that?"

The sedative kicked in surprisingly fast and very hard. Before his eyes closed they drooped, to her lips. They were still moving. The voice was muffled but he could read what she was saying.

"Come with me."

The Concubine

WE RENTED a timber bungalow in a row of them up in University City, MY MOTHER TOLD ME ONE NIGHT WHEN SHE THOUGHT I WAS ASLEEP, so your father could be close to campus. There were seven, old and dilapidated and laid out on a dead-end dirt track that didn't quite join up with the newly-paved street—cars had to take the curb and drive over the sidewalk to get on to it, tracking mud and dust from the surrounding construction sites over the new concrete. It was rumoured, to your father's utter delight, that all seven houses had once been owned by Cary Grant, who had used them for disreputable gatherings. I never saw evidence, of course, but then why would anyone look for any? A good story is a good story.

It meant the bungalows were regarded with some affection—there was very little up there then apart from scrub, and the bungalows seemed to have more more substance about them, somehow, than the concrete homes that had begun to pepper the surrounding slopes and that looked so precarious on the mostly pre-populated plots. Perhaps it was fairy dust—the Hollywood connection—but the bungalows were sought-after. Your father said, often, that we were lucky. It was another time of course, but also another place. Not the place you know, *chutki*. This was before the Westfield mall, before the synagogue and Sears, fish tacos from Rubio's on Friday nights, before all the apartment complexes.

Streets and sidewalks went in first and then, for what seemed the longest time, very little else. Slowly, here and there, an individual plot would be demarcated and a house built. From an imagined aerial vantage point, I saw the straight lines and empty spaces they divided like a child's kit model used backwards—little pieces gradually re-attached to their plastic struts. I had the time to observe it all in detail because I went for a lot of walks, having little else to do—

newness and the California sun opening cracks underfoot. Because of that, and because I had no social imperative to dress well, I decked myself out in sports gear and sweats. I hadn't been aware of wanting to feel like an American, but dressing that way did make me feel like an American and I was glad of it, then. All I needed now was a life. It wasn't clear to me at first why your father followed suit, ditching his shirts and ties immediately. Did he think I knew something he didn't? But when his fellow students started coming to the house I had my explanation. It was dress code: they all wore white sneakers or sandals and polo tops, and jeans or sweats in whites and light greys.

I liked it when they came. When they weren't coding they would sit around and your father would tell them about Cary Grant. I'm embarrassed to tell you that I relegated myself to the delivery of beer and the dissemination of snacks. That suited your father. It isn't as if I could have squeezed any real conversation out of those boys anyway, and I can't say I was miserable in my role. At least your father had a burgeoning social life and I thought at first they might have girlfriends I could get to know.

That was naive of me. They were a very particular type—you would call them geeks would you not, *chutki*? Or is it nerds? If there's a difference, I suspect these were both. If they hadn't had the outlet of their studies, there'd have been mass shootings before there were girlfriends. But it was nice to have people around the house and to think that your father was integrating. Otherwise, it was—I was—very isolated up there in that bungalow.

Something in me, something cruel perhaps, liked to see your father with his new friends and how, in their company, he was diminished. They were a motley bunch, and not all of them were products of privilege—there were a couple Ivy League types but it was perfectly evident whenever they opened their mouths that money hadn't bought them their places on the course, and there was a Korean, Sung Ho, and an Iranian whose surname, funnily enough, was also Zade, both of whom the university had gone after and paid for or they'd never have been able to attend. Zade's name fascinated your father of course, but that was just his narcissism—it's common enough. There were others who came and went. To a man—never any girls—they each seemed to approach conversation with your father from one or several steps ahead. I couldn't follow the gobbledygook of course but it's easy to know when someone is being corrected.

The princeling abroad was rather ordinary. It amused and worried me. In this magical land at the end of our flight through the heavens, I began to envisage rather an ordinary, average life—he in some middling position, just high enough to keep his self-delusion ticking over but well below the top tier. Working for one of his friends, in all probability, while I would learn to drive and get some work or maybe study something myself, and make my own friends. A part of me even looked forward to it. But then there was that other part.

By the end of our second year, the pace of construction had picked up. Phase one of Renaissance Villas had, like a giant crab, almost encircled us and the illusion of the bungalows' permanence had finally given way to commercial reality—they were condemned, to be demolished for phase two. A clause in the agreement meant we current occupants qualified for favourable finance on the new apartments. This did not interest us. Another clause stipulated that, whether we liked it or not, we were now considered to be part of the Renaissance community and therefore qualified for membership of the Residents' Association. This did not interest your father but I was still lonely and bored enough to respond to an invitation that arrived in the mailbox, to attend an inaugural showcase of the Residents' Clubhouse. Besides, there was a pool, and San Diego summers are hot.

At the entrance to the complex, two high wrought-iron gates were entirely ornamental—a footpath simply meandered around them and the entrance to the carpark was on the other side of the development. Inside, the very inviting cloud-shaped pool was surrounded by immaculately manicured insta-gardens. The bills for watering them would be taking up a lot of time at Association meetings, I imagined, once they hit their stride. The clubhouse was a circular affair, separated from the pool by a fence and an assortment of bushy plants from which a set of steps swept around the building's exterior curve, up to the second floor. What we would correctly call the first floor. The whole place was a fair-to-middling attempt at Spanish Colonial—red roof tiles, rounded corners, pointless and unused courtyards with Alhambra-style water features, stucco. At the top, when I pushed open the heavy glass double doors and stepped into the dimmed light and aggressive air conditioning of the lobby, it felt like the beginning of something.

The Association had set up shop in a large room through a second pair of double doors. A long trestle table ran along one side and had been laid out with paper plates of potato chips and popcorn, stacks of paper cups, jugs of iced water and clipboards for sign-ups. I could hardly make that much out, still adjusting to the gloom—a surprise to the eyes after the vertical blaze of noon.

Windows punctuated much of the wall that curved around the horseshoe space. In an inexplicable departure from the Spanish Colonial theme, they were round and rather gave the impression of being at sea. Absolutely typical of this country. The custom Venetian blinds that covered them were also circular and shut tight, eclipsed sunlight reduced around each to a corona that only served to make the room seem darker. The few other light sources were low lamps dotted around on consoles that illuminated little more than a small circle on the varnished surface below the lampshade.

The general murk was further deepened in the colour choices. I say colour: everything in the place—tables, chairs, lampshades, walls, carpet—was rendered in the barbiturate colour palette you see so much here of greys, grey-browns, brown-greys and browns. American Sludge. The carpet seemed to me far too plush for a common area and was shaded here and there by those brushed sweeps which in a carpet speak of depth and expense. The overall effect was both soporific and somewhat hallucinatory—those present were scattered around in pairs and small groups wherever seating clustered, nothing to distinguish them from passengers on an upscale cruise liner at night if it wasn't for all the flip-flops and paper cups. I could just see a baby grand at the far end of the room and it seemed to me utterly absurd, in that moment, that nobody was playing jazz on it. I ask you, *chutki*, is it any wonder the country finds itself in the throes of an opioid epidemic if this is the way they furnish their meeting spaces? I felt like sauntering over to the trestle table and asking someone to pour me a daiquiri.

Instead I went over there and picked up a clipboard, which proved enough to initiate an exchange.

"Well hi there," said one of two women on the other side—the younger one, maybe just a few years older than I was. "I'm Marge."

She smiled and I smiled back, bashful suddenly.

"And you are . . ."

I told her my name.

"Have you just moved in? Which apartment?"

I wanted to tell her I lived in one of the—

"Bungalows." The older woman had joined us. "Didn't I tell you about the pretty Mexican girl from the bungalows who walks everywhere?"

She wasn't old, really.

"Oh yeah," said Marge and then, to me, "This is Dolly."

There followed a brief conversation on skin tone during which my nationality was established and nobody, myself included, could be sure if I'd been offended. I wondered how those conversations about the Mexican in the bungalow had gone.

"You want a daiquiri?"

I was adding my details to the sign-up form. "Excuse me?"

"It's daiquiri or White Russian," she said, "and we're all out of White Russian." With a wave of her hand she indicated a cooler box at her feet and with a nod the jugs on the table. "We don't recommend the tap water here."

The tone was set for the months that followed. I found myself included in a circle of older women—apart from Marge and Dolly, there was Betty, and Nancy, and Judy and Barbara, and Evelyn—who comprised the majority of the Residents' Committee but who left administrative matters to a few officious types and instead spent their time arranging lunches, walks at Mission Bay and shopping sprees in Fashion Valley. At Thanksgiving and then again at Christmas, Nancy drove us all into the city to help serve hot meals to the homeless with Father Joe at the St. Vincent de Paul's centre on 4th and Market.

There was always *so* much talk and I remember so little of it. I do remember that with some regularity one of 'the girls' would make an unambiguously racist or xenophobic assumption and present it to me in the form of a polite question and a sparkling white smile. I was more amused than anything else, and it seemed to be a generational thing—Marge would sometimes catch my eye when it happened and roll hers. It made for some interesting dynamics. Though it was clear to me that they considered me an adoption—that I had been taken under the wing—I couldn't help but look down upon them a little. How could I not, with my background? But there was some affection too, and it felt good to be in company.

Apart from parrying their provincial bigotries, I had very little to do with driving the conversation, which revolved too much around their marriages for my liking. Around their men. Here I was, intent on stepping out of your father's shadow; I had no appetite for stepping into the shadows these women occupied. Another reason for me to disapprove of them. With Marge, who wasn't married, it was different—most of her conversation revolved around her dating and sexual disasters and was funny. I had a great liking for her. In those moments when she'd look at me and with some conspiratorial expression share my bemusement . . . how do you put it these days? I felt seen.

Those women. My God. Those supposedly modern, Western women and their men's opinions, parroted on their glossy lips. These were among the very first conversations I'd had outside the house in this country, remember, but it felt like watching afternoon reruns. I'd heard it all before and I've been hearing it ever since. The home of the brave, the land of the free—is a surprisingly staid, uniform affair, *chutki*. The clues were already there, that afternoon in the clubhouse. The blinds drawn against the day. Light sources in the double digits. The atmospheric refrigeration. It's not that these people are oblivious to reality and its age-old dictates. Quite the opposite—they're at war with it. All day breakfast, strawberries at Christmas. They take any natural-seeming arrangement that might temper their gluttony as an affront. As an opportunity to *innovate*—the verb they use most often to refer to their idiocy. And they frame it all in terms of 'freedom', as the girls would regularly do for me in their educative magnanimity, enunciating the word slowly in the presence of the foreigner as though it had never travelled beyond their shores. But it's a toddler's freedom they speak of—the freedom everybody but it knows it cannot have. The freedom to shove whatever it comes across into its mouth. The political philosophy of the pig at its trough. Their idea of freedom was a defence of slavery to appetite. When I think of the pained patience that would inscribe itself on their faces as they tried to explain *America* to me. I realised very early on that what they actually wanted to explain to their brown pet was *goodness*. The two words were wholly interchangeable, for them. But the lectures were unnecessary—I had long since figured America out. If you really want to understand America you need only slip your hand between the snout and the swill. You'll understand soon enough.

Oh but I must be careful with you, mustn't I, *chutki*? You are American. Pay me no mind—perhaps I only loathe them because your father loves them, and I loathe your father.

I DON'T KNOW HOW MANY TIMES MY MOTHER sat by my bed to tell me these stories, because it was always while she thought I was asleep. Usually, though, I was pretending. I became very good at relaxing my facial muscles, so that a closed lid wouldn't screw up at some revelation, or betray the movement of the eye behind it. One day, SHE SAID TO ME, the summer after that first clubhouse meeting, Marge and I found ourselves at a loose end. A lunch with the girls had been cancelled because they were attending the funeral of an even older woman neither of us knew. We'd had a couple of days notice of the cancellation but hadn't come up with alternative plans. On the afternoon itself I felt restless, so I called Marge.

"Let's go day-drinking," she said.

"Where?"

"I'll come down to yours," she said and hung up before I could object. It wasn't that I minded but none of them had been in the bungalow before. I spent ten minutes doing whatever cleaning is possible in ten minutes and put a pot of coffee on. When Marge arrived she had bag of ice and a bottle of Bushmills and we left the coffee to stew. I surprised myself at how self-conscious I was in my own home, with this woman I'd known for a year, if you can call it knowing, and I suppose that might have made for a stilted afternoon, except that a couple of shots in she produced a joint and lit it.

I had never smoked a joint but I wasn't about to tell her that. It turned out I didn't need to—a prolonged fit of coughing, actually quite painful, told the story. But then . . . oh *chutki*, how we laughed. I hadn't laughed like that since I was a child, and certainly not since we'd come to America. Everything had been so tentative, so tense. I felt as though I were releasing all the laughter that should have filled that time—I couldn't know then that I was compensating for the lack of it that was to come.

It isn't that anything we talked about mattered. Marge and I had never had a proper conversation. Our relationship, whatever it was, had been defined in opposition to the girls' prattle and expressed in those momentary, shared silences. Eye contact, little more. So we could hardly launch ourselves into confessional intimacy. I don't remember what we talked about. Stupid little things. I laughed and I was happy and I felt as though I might not be alone. As though I might embark upon a new friendship. Although I'll never remember the details, I'll never forget that afternoon. Neither of us were physically large specimens but we emptied the bottle.

    Your father surprised us. The other Zade, who by now he referred to as The Persian, was with him and a couple of the usual types who I didn't recognise—he always, always had an entourage. Confronted by two drunks on the sofa, the aroma that filled the smoky room and a coffee table laden with empty potato chip bags and chocolate wrappers, he could not have appeared more horrified. Marge and I, taken unawares, had made the requisite efforts to straighten ourselves and quieten down, suppressing our giggles, hands over eyes to shut out the ridiculous expression on his face, the shifting discomfort of the others. It was useless—we fell about laughing again, harder. Then he said something. Something that had a very particular effect.

    You know in the films, *chutki,* when a bomb goes off and they cut the sound to simulate the temporary deafness that would follow? You can still hear something but not enough to register language. Mainly just a ringing. Muffled voices speaking wordlessly. It was like that. Not that he'd raised his voice—it was the words themselves. I can't repeat them because I've blocked them out.

    I looked to Marge. She was gathering up her things to leave. When she got up she did so cleanly, soberly, and I realised I felt sober too. I wanted to apologise to her but she wouldn't meet my eyes, instead pausing by your father on the way to the door. Whatever she said was itself an apology—that much was written in her penitent body language—and she said it only to your father, clutching her things to her chest like a half-dressed whore taking her leave of the caliph.

    I'm lying to you—I remember perfectly well what he said. I don't repeat the words because I don't wish to hear them again, or want you to hear them. They don't matter—it was the *effect*. How comical from this distance, if not at the time, to see how effortlessly he reduced her to a thing so easily dismissed. And all of it, really, in that moment, was dismissed—the others too, those loud-mouthed women who couldn't escape the orbit of their men, the time I'd had with them convincing myself it had something to do with autonomy. All of it gone.

When Marge had shut the front door behind her—even the slow double click was apologetic—your father turned back to me and spoke again, but my ears were still ringing so I got up and went to the bedroom, sitting on my side of the bed as though to lie down, but unable to lie down. I sat resonating, a plucked lute string. I can still see, in my mind's eye, the space between that side of the bed and the window, the curtains drawn but letting a diffuse light through, browned by the faded fabric, the brown carpet and the little rug striped in yellows and purples, my brown knees and the bedside table.

If your eyes were open, would they glaze, *chutki*? *Here she goes again, describing the minutiae of some irrelevant corner of the universe . . .* but that space is what this particular tale is all about. It happened there. There and then, I was broken and born. That space—the couple of feet of carpet and the little rug, my things on the bedside table, the brown, half-blocked light, the wall's wooden slats, my hands on my knees—is one of those spaces in my life I seem not so much to have occupied as been occupied by: the stairwell and the immigration hall, that beach at Big Sur, the Residents' Association clubhouse. Spaces that move in. I carry them with me.

A few minutes passed and I heard the front door go again—your father had sent the others off, no doubt with profuse apologies for his bitch. Then the house was quiet. Whatever he did out there he did it meekly, tip-toeing around the place like a thief. I didn't hear so much as a kitchen cupboard or a flushing toilet, and knew then that we were dancing around each other to the music of a competitive silence—the same old game—and that therefore, obviously, I would win.

When the bedroom doorknob went a couple of hours later its hesitant click-click was the exact reverse of Marge's retreat, and I knew he had come to appease. I would have appeared to him to be sitting on the edge of the bed, my hands on my knees, my eyes on my hands, or taking inventory of that little space between the bed and the window—the bedside table, the one bit of colour in the rug, the wall's wooden slats. But my stomach had been telling me otherwise—that I'd been, and was still, falling. Plummeting through the void left by his words. The yawning absence of whatever had been there before he'd said them. When he sat beside me I felt it in the mattress, felt that the fall was over, and that I had come to rest.

The two of us took in the drab curtains, the little rug, my hands on my knees. There was something almost impressive, almost successful, in his opening salvo. An acknowledgement, a recognition, would you believe, that it had been hard on me, living up there with nothing to do but go for walks? He didn't mention the girls. Was it possible he hadn't noticed them? But then of course he reverted to type—pontificating on how he was going to conquer the world when the course was over, how he had *such* plans, how he'd impress me, once it was finished, with what he would achieve. How he was going to take over tech, astonish the world. How nobody really understood what was coming, not as he understood it. How they all thought it was about the back end, about software and technology, but how, he said, it was really all about media and message. It was about narrative. It would never have occurred to him that he owed this insight to me. I could hear the change in his voice as he became wrapped up in himself, the near-spirituality of his ambition, his promises that I would . . . be there. Benefit. He would want me to respond—this was all an almost sweet solicitation of praise. My part here was to speak validating words at him, the interaction thus brought to satisfactory completion. And so I turned and waited till his gaze met mine, and then I waited some more—long enough to see the complacence wane in his eyes, and him wilt.

I don't mean that he flinched, or anything so fleeting. What happened to your father in that moment is something he has never recovered from. I have seen to that. He was lowered. I lowered him. And when I saw it, *I* spoke up.

"Listen to me very carefully," I said to him. "You are not enough. You are not *enough* to do any of these things, you mediocrity. You paid your way on to the course as you have paid your way through life. Or been paid for. I don't even blame you. There isn't enough *of* you to shoulder the blame. You should never for a moment have been allowed to entertain the delusion that you are special. You are ordinary and an ordinary life is your inheritance." I took a moment to observe the arrival of my words in his mind. "But it can be avoided."

The look on his face. I didn't want to hear his voice so I answered the question before it could be asked.

"You *recruit*, idiot," I said. "For reasons I will never fathom, your ridiculous sense of entitlement actually convinces. Your betters congregate around you. They listen to you, God help them. You'll never do anything great as long as you live. But they might. Why shouldn't they be working for you when they do it? So *recruit*, you fool of a brat. And don't speak to me again of your silly course. You start now. You should have started already. This is what you should have been doing all along. Because if you would make a concubine of *me*," I spoke through my teeth, wanting it to be very clear that we had a new arrangement, "you will give me palaces."

The First Voyage

LIAM HAD ALWAYS assumed most private detectives would fall into one of two categories—former police with dubious reasons for the second career and aspiring police with equally dubious reasons for the failed applications. To date he hadn't had the opportunity to test his theory as even since becoming one himself he'd never actually met a private detective. His own investigative chops had been honed in the insurance sector, as a claims auditor for Flynn Insurance, out in semi-rural Clonee on the border between County Dublin and County Meath.

It was miserable working out there on the R147. There was no canteen in the Flynn building and nothing nearby in the way of a shop or snack bar. And claims auditor was pushing it—in fact he'd been a claims auditor's assistant. It was Fintan Rafferty who sped around in the low-sprung Audi he didn't quite own and the expensive suits that contrived to look cheap as soon as they contained Flashy Fintan. Liam had managed Fintan's diary and taken calls for him. He'd had a job in the Flynn Insurance call centre was really the accurate way to put it.

It was Fintan who would decide if the damage to a door jamb was convincing, or if shattered glass was strewn across the driveway in a way that might conceivably avoid payout. That said, some of the scripted questions Liam had been required to read from the screen to claimants had been quite probing, and it occurred to him now that maybe a thing or two had rubbed off after all. He hadn't been conscious for more than a minute, hadn't so much as lifted his head from the (soft, fresh) pillow, but he'd already reached two reasonably solid conclusions about his situation.

He had spent much of that minute looking at and out of the window opposite. All he could see out there was sky, all the more brilliantly blue because everything in the room, apart from the white bedclothes, was rendered in a shade of beige. The wall was beige, the floor—even the window frame—was beige: it was also small, and circular, and attached to the wall with metal rivets. The place was quiet but not silent. If he listened hard, there was a low hum beneath it all, a low and somehow large hum that suggested an engine that was also large and, since the hum was so low, far away. All in all, he had considerable faith in these two conclusions: he was on a boat, and the boat was big.

Porthole. He swung his legs over the edge of the bed and used their weight to leverage himself into a sitting position. He had a white t-shirt on and white boxer shorts he'd never seen before, and there were a couple of Band-Aids on the soft skin of his inner arm. One of them was already peeling away from the injection site, the other more recently applied where a drip needle had been removed. He knew this because at the foot the bed the drip hung from its pole. He pressed the soles of his feet to the beige linoleum—his least favorite of all floor furnishings—and lifted himself a little, testing. He didn't feel at all bad and stood with ease, but at the porthole experienced a momentary, dizzying shock at how far down the water was.

Apart from the ruffled bedclothes the little room was immaculate. The only other item of furniture was a chair by the head of the bed. It was odd to see a chair by the head of a bed without a phone on it, charging. Instead, someone had stuck a Post-it to the seat.

"Good morning, Mr Tead. Clothes in the closet."

The closet in question was by the door, opposite a tiny ensuite. At the bottom of it a sports bag contained toiletries and underwear and above it some pants and tops had been carefully shelved, all of it branded sportswear—white tees, a light gray tank top and a hoody in the same light gray. A pair of white sneakers sat beside the bag. None of it was his and he had never worn sportswear in his life, off the field, but it all seemed to fit. With some trepidation he took a look in the bathroom mirror. He was maybe a little pale but looked fine. He swiped water through his hair to tidy it up and stepped out of the room into a narrow passageway. To his right the corridor extended away, giving no clues as to where it went. To his left, it widened at the far end where a door with another porthole let in sunlight. On a stool by the door, a massive human being sat reading an honest-to-God print newspaper. Liam went that way.

Cabin. "Hey, Darius."

Since there was no indication he'd been heard, Liam considered the possibility that Darius was deaf. But then, what good would the earpiece be? Although now the earpiece was gone.

"Sherry around?"

An eyebrow cleared an aviator lens but the giant said nothing.

"Sher . . . I mean, *Ms Zade* left me a note?"

The bodyguard marshaled a neck muscle to indicate the door.

"OK," said Liam. "Chat later."

The wind was a shock and the heavy door threatened to get away from him. Once he'd pushed it shut the salt air was welcome. He was on the right-hand side of the ship *whatever it's called* and had to descend multiple, steep flights of steps before he could edge his way forward, sliding one hand along the rail in case there was any unexpected motion.

But the sea was calm and whatever this thing was, it was huge. To his left, the bridge must have been six or seven stories above him. Just looking up at it made him nervous. When he reached the front of it and the deck opened out, it became abundantly clear what type of boat this was. It was a cargo liner—the one he'd seen in the city port, he assumed. Ahead of him was about half a kilometer, it seemed like, of stacked containers in blues and burgundies, coke reds, the grays of Maersk and the yellows of MSC, but most of them in the deep green of Zade and bearing on all sides the Zade plume and that single eye.

The stacking wasn't uniform—through a gap in the center, further gaps could be seen that together formed a canyon made of assorted right angles and colors. Gangplanks had been put down, beginning at his feet and meandering across the container tops that made up the floor of this canyon. At the farthest visible point a solid wall of containers closed it off, as high as the highest stacks. On a steep diagonal across this wall, starting at top right and rippling its way down over steel corrugations to the centre of the canyon floor, a line divided it into sunlight and shadow. Where it touched down on the lowest container tops, the line also divided a tiny figure that Liam had to squint to make out. A deckchair had been placed there and a person reclined in it, dressed for the beach, in a floppy wide-brimmed hat, oversized sunglasses and a one-piece swimsuit. The person's head was in the shade, her outstretched legs in the sun. She held a magazine in one hand while the other hung from the side of the chair, hovering over what looked like it might be a cocktail. Liam knew with absolute certainty that Darius was right behind him. Without bothering to check, he set out across the gangplanks.

"Good morning," he said when he stepped on to her container.

She must have been aware of his approach. Every plank had clattered beneath him, not to mention the giant behind him. But she didn't lower the magazine till he spoke.

"I left that note for you a long time ago. We've had dinner. How are you feeling?"

"I feel OK. It's nice to be alive, at least."

Her expression darkened. "Not always," she said and it struck Liam as a little melodramatic. "No headache? Dry mouth?" She reached into a cooler by the chair and threw him a bottle of water.

"No headache," he said and drank some.

"Reynolds is a genius."

Darius had taken a seat at the container's edge, letting his feet dangle. Liam, at what he felt was a suitable distance, did the same. Sherry didn't seem in a hurry to talk. It was awkward for Liam to twist himself and make eye contact so he looked back at the bridge. Something about looking at her in her swimsuit made him feel uncomfortable in the presence of her security guy.

"Where are we going?"

"Oh come on, Mr Tead. You'll know soon enough. Try to get into the spirit of things."

"I'm thinking Hawaii." Wasn't Zade supposed to have some kind of lair on the privately owned Ni'ihau?

She didn't answer. Liam tried to think of what came after Hawaii. Latitudes weren't his strong point. *China?* He could see tiny figures in the highest windows. They knew where they were going, presumably, and presumably he would never get anywhere near them. *India?* Darius had brought his newspaper along and was reading it, or pretending to. Liam turned his head briefly—Sherry was back in her magazine. He couldn't see the bottom of the gap where his feet swung. Even sitting on the floor of this Tetris canyon was vertiginous.

"You can go down to the kitchen anytime you want, you know, and get whatever you like. Darius will show you."

Liam glanced at the bodyguard, who raised the newspaper by less than a centimeter.

"In a while."

He sipped from the bottle of water till it was empty. Maybe a quarter of an hour went by, maybe a little more. It occurred to him that whatever it was that made him acquiesce to the doctor's needle, cowardice or his accursed curiosity, it certainly wasn't thought. If he had been thinking, he might have wondered what he'd wake up to. And if he'd had a hundred ideas about what that might be, none of them would have been this. Bizarre location notwithstanding, it was a little anti-climactic. He'd have imagined some life-changing, no-way-back revelation, or a hit-the-ground-running action sequence or maybe some woozy, arcane initiation rite. Instead, they just seemed to be hanging around on a boat. He let his eyes bounce along from container to container, color to color, to the tiny people in the high windows, to the various antennae up there and the clouds that accumulated above them, just now blocking the sun, and he felt strangely at ease.

It soon wore off. An anxiety made itself known. It was a familiar anxiety but he found he couldn't quite name it. The new surroundings had cut the circuit between the thing and its name, between the anxiety and whatever it was that gave rise to it. It felt—

"Weird, huh?"

He twisted himself to look at Sherry.

"It is for me too," she said.

"What is?"

She closed her magazine. "No devices. I don't know what to do with my hands, or my head." She put the magazine down, picked up a paperback from beside her seat, and threw it his way. "Try that if you want—I couldn't get into it. No pictures." She grinned. "We're all so useless now, without connection."

"Not me," said Liam. "People are pathetic. I haven't given in just yet." The paperback was an edition of *The Arabian Nights* based on the text of the fourteenth century Syrian manuscript and newly translated. Apart from 'translated', he didn't really know what any of that meant, but he found it amusing that this progeny of an heiress would entertain herself with children's stories.

She snorted. "Right. Anyway—we are well and truly off grid for the foreseeable. Pretty hardcore. Darius, put this man out of his misery will you? He looks like he could do with a sandwich."

The bodyguard snapped the newspaper shut, folded it and tucked it under an arm with a crispness of movement that could have been taken for petulance. When he got to his feet and set out along the planks, Liam had to hurry to keep up, stepping back inside the boat just in time to see his quarry disappear up a flight of steps. On the floor above, he followed the huge man into a dining room and then into a long and narrow galley space. There were two or three kitchen workers in there but they quickly made themselves scarce. At the far end, the only window was inset above a recessed table with upholstered seats where kitchen staff could take a break or the chef could sit with his paperwork. Everything apart from the upholstery was made of stainless steel.

Darius opened a refrigerator door and gestured to the middle shelf, where a half-eaten loaf of sliced white bread hadn't been properly resealed in its plastic and was probably hardening. Around it a few jars of spreads and pickles and a couple of packets of cold meat curling at the corners where they too had been carelessly left open. The bodyguard stepped back and took up a position in the doorway.

"Jesus." Liam scanned the other shelves and, on finding nothing attractive there, the immediate surroundings for other possibilities. "Is this how you've been eating?" In all the brushed metal, it wasn't easy to tell what was a fridge and what wasn't—he pulled open drawers and doors until he found another one. A couple of seconds later he waved a slab of cured meat over his head.

"Guanciale!"

Less than a minute after that he had collected a wedge of pecorino and some eggs and set them on a work top. "I don't like to brag, Darius," he said, retrieving a pack of spaghetti and a box grater from an eye-level shelf, "but I envy you."[*] He addressed the pecorino with the grater. Cheese fell to the board like fine, feathery snow. Then he

---

[*] Spaghetti Carbonara for Two.

Ingredients:

    250 grams spaghetti (a generous portion)
    67 grams guanciale
    60 grams pecorino
    1 whole egg and 3 egg yolks
    Abundant black pepper, freshly ground.

Method:

1. Toast the pepper and set it aside.
2. Of the guanciale, make plump batonets. Drop them into a cold pan and turn the heat under it to medium/low.
3. Add the pasta to boiling water. There should be enough water to give the pasta room to be stirred, but little enough to become starchy as the pasta cooks. When the guanciale fat becomes translucent, turn the heat to medium/high to colour.

separated three yolks, cracked a whole egg over them and put water on for the pasta.

"These are good spaghetti," he said, thumbing the pasta. "Somebody on this boat knows their spaghetti. Have you seen a pepper mill?" He turned to the doorway but at some point the taciturn henchman had quietly taken a seat at the table. From there, his massive head rotated very slightly and slowly till a pepper mill appeared in the aviators, on a shelf that faced away from Liam who went and got it. "People who know their spaghetti always and without exception appreciate wine. Is there a chiller? Or must we resort to red? A Montepulciano might do." He beat the eggs with pepper and most of the cheese. Of the guanciale he made plump batonets and dropped them into a cold pan.

"No wine, huh?" He lit the gas. Of course no wine. He wondered at what stage of their background checks they'd made the decision. As the fat rendered he put the spaghetti on. When the guanciale crisped he removed it. When the spaghetti were ready he tonged them into the rendered fat, tossed the pan, turned off the heat, added the guanciale and counted to twenty-seven. Then he tossed in the egg and cheese paste with a tiny bit of pasta water till all was silk. "I

4. Grate the cheese and add it to the beaten egg and yolks, reserving some to serve.
5. When the guanciale has rendered its fat and its surface is crisp, set it aside, leaving the fat in the pan.
6. Before the pasta is cooked al dente, tong it into the fat, without draining it. The drops of water that make it into the pan this way will help begin the *mantecatura*—add a third of a ladle of pasta water too, toss the pan well to coat the pasta and emulsify the pasta water and fat.
7. Once the spaghetti is al dente, take the pan off the heat. Add the pepper and toss. Put the guanciale back in. Count to twenty-seven. Those blessed with a particular self-knowledge, who have recognised within themselves a certain frailty, a propensity to despair in the face of life's betrayals, should count to thirty-three.
8. Add the egg and cheese mixture and toss well till all is silk and thickened, adding more pasta water, in tiny quantities, if and as necessary to achieve this. Don't be a fool. Serve immediately.

probably don't seem to you to be doing anything special here," he said to the giant, who almost certainly wasn't watching. Liam used a meat prong and a ladle to make neat spaghetti nests on two plates, dusted them heavily with the remaining cheese and put one of them in front of his companion, with a fork. As he took a seat himself, the bodyguard had already picked up the latter and rather expertly applied it to the pasta. The features were as impassive as ever but as the lips closed around the first forkful there was a frozen moment, an almost imperceptible pause before chewing commenced.

"There it is," said Liam. "Your sex face."

Darius went for the second forkful with a noticeable gusto.

"You mustn't be embarrassed," said Liam. "Everybody does that."

There wasn't going to be a conversation and there was very little to see out the window—night was falling and only a narrow strip of water alongside the boat was illuminated by its lights. But the silence in which they ate their meal, Liam felt, was a happy one. "If you think that was life-changing," he said when Darius had cleared his plate, "wait till you try my *cacio e pepe*. People have wept." The security man shimmied over to the edge of his seat, got to his feet, and left. Once Liam had washed and dried the things he'd used, so did he.

In the cabin, he was once again affronted by the absence of his phone. The personal space he was accustomed to, peppered by notifications and transactional endorphin releases, was replaced here by a real solitude he found unsettling. It was . . . *constipated*, somehow, to be alone in this way—as if there was work to be done that wasn't getting done. Tasks piling up somewhere. Elsewhere. He opened Sherry's book, skipping the introduction, and soon after became aware in the clearest terms that these were not stories for children.

How had he not known that? Everybody knew they were children's stories. Except, it seemed, they weren't. What would this version of Aladdin be getting up to? Whatever it was, it would have to wait—even a few minutes in, the act of reading had become disagreeable. His eyes kept wandering from the page to check a screen that wasn't there and he would lose his place or have to read the same sentence again. Not very much seemed to be going in. The metapunctuation of multiplatform stimuli was missing—reading words seemed like not enough and too much. After an hour or so, he closed the book. He tried shutting his eyes and may have dozed, but not for long—what transpired behind the closed lids in the clockless, tiktokless ennui of the cabin was intolerable, so he took a windbreaker from the wardrobe and went out on deck.

After a few false starts, he found a way along the side of the boat, tucked in under the uppermost containers, that seemed to go all the way to whatever it was they called the front. There were no crew around and, assuming it was OK, he headed that way. It took a while. The passageway was narrow and even though it overlooked the ocean on one side, it was dark out there, so he felt enclosed. Everything was covered in a thick coat of bright red paint. He had the impression in the tight space of moving through a birth canal, an impression reinforced when he emerged into the wide open world after ten minutes, the red paint giving way to grey beneath his feet and blackness overhead. At the pointed front there was a railing and steps up to a ledge he could stand on, out over the water.

Bow.

His sense of scale was shot. The boat was big, but everything that wasn't the boat—the Pacific, the everything else—was bigger. He'd been at sea before but not like this. On the overnight ferry from Rosslare to LeHavre, when he was a kid, there had been only short stretches where no coastline was visible. Here though, not only was there no land in sight—there was this deep, instinctual expectation that there wouldn't be any time soon. With the cloud cover complete and darkness in full flower, there was no obvious waterline, no obvious break between earth and heaven. It was all just universe—an undifferentiated expanse.

And the noise or, rather, the lack of it—on TV, people at sea always had wind in their hair. They usually had to yell. But out here, accentuated in the night, the quietness was eerie. There was a breeze—nothing like earlier—and he could hear the water below him as the boat cut through it. He could count the sounds—air, water, engine—but together they made a kind of silence. Because the distances were so unimaginable, his imagination collapsed in on him—the sensation was of being in the great indoors, on a set, at the vanishing point of some godlike artifice, neither large nor small, neither friendly nor threatening.

"There you are."

Keeping hold of the rail—he was no stranger to vertigo—he turned himself around. Whatever the future held, it was now behind him. Sherry had emerged from the passageway.

"We thought you might have made a swim for it."

She wore her cagoule with the hood up despite the soft weather and she was lit mostly from behind so he couldn't read her expression.

"Just wanted to explore," he said. "I've never been on a boat this big."

It was impossible for her not to resemble Little Red Riding Hood, in that get up. That would make all this a very strange fairy tale. Keeping a hold on reality in this rare air was getting complicated.

"OK," she said. "Well, we're waiting for you in the galley. They'll be putting some breakfast out soon."

Or on time, come to that. He descended the few steps onto the deck.

"Breakfast?" It seemed to him he'd only been out here a little while.

She lowered her hood, revealing that wide, unguarded grin.

"We'll be getting off the big boat very soon, Mr Tead. Today's shift are putting out some breakfast for us before they knock off. It's nice of them."

She walked off and he followed, but at a distance—he couldn't think of anything smart to ask her and since she was threatening to pay him for his investigative services he didn't want to ask her anything stupid.

Ship.

When he reached the mess, she had already taken a seat. On a sideboard, the kitchen people had laid out eggs, bacon, link sausages and hash browns. Liam, who had never been able to behave himself at a buffet, piled his plate high and took a seat opposite her. Darius had made a sandwich with an egg and some bacon.

"Not eating?" There was just a glass of water in front of Sherry.

"I'm not really a breakfast person."

"Where's Reynolds?"

She snorted. "Airlifted. Can't stand the water."

An unusual perfume rose from the sausages. Coriander seeds, maybe. It definitely wasn't sage. She watched expressionless as he took his knife and fork and addressed the bacon first, using a folded forkful of it to break a runny egg yolk.

"OK, Ms Zade. Why don't we pick up where you left off?"

The Puppeteer

When we moved into the compound up at Lake Cuyamaca, I suppose I had my palace, MY MOTHER SAID TO ME ONE NIGHT WHEN SHE THOUGHT I WAS ASLEEP, even if it was a doer-upper—in those days, it was nothing like the home you have known, *chutki*. There was just the original and dilapidated timber-frame house. But the perimeter was secure, the area concealed in dense forest and large enough to accommodate your father's plans. I say his plans but in his mind they were more implants—they were my plans.

We lived in that house till the contractors had completed the first lodge—the one farthest uphill that is now almost hidden in the trees and of which I remain the fondest—and then we razed it to start the earthworks: a series of seven terraces that would accommodate the subsequent phases. We were spending a lot of money because by then we had it, but it would take a long time for everything to be complete. In the interim, in a roughly diagonal row that descended to the water line, we put up seven wooden prefabs, one on each terrace, and ran cables and temporary plumbing overground so that they could serve as storage, work spaces and accommodation, a boat house on the lowest terrace and just above it, a kitchen and dining hall for frequent cookouts. In those days the place was always teeming with the tech bods and wonks—the word delights me—with whom your father surrounded himself. They might come for the day or they might spend several days at a time, depending on what was going on. By that time, he was a dab hand at seeming their equal or better without making any meaningful contribution of his own. The work they were doing, he wasn't up to it, but it didn't matter—he pulled the strings.

In the years that had passed since the conversation on the edge of the bed, we had been industrious. Patents were in place. Registrations. The company was profitable and on the verge of flotation. We even had an early version of the logo, its ambiguity already there at the centre of everything. Sometimes you just need to be in the right place at the right time and whatever your father's qualities, whatever mine, that's how it was with us.

Your father had taken my instruction to heart and dedicated himself to a recruitment drive that would culminate in those early days at the compound. One by one, and under my watchful eye, he would pick up whichever marionette—his word—was required at the time, have it dance and, one by one, he would drop them. Contracts were very carefully controlled—nobody was given anything more than a fleeting stake in their own small part of the bigger picture. The future we reserved for ourselves. This was at a time, if you can believe it, *chutki*, when the chatter was all about whether that future lay in hardware or software. Your father knew—because I knew, and I instilled it in him—that the real narrative would be narrative itself. That technology was the least important aspect of the tech business. Perhaps it was the deception at the heart of our project that allowed him to grasp this truth. What were we doing, after all, but telling stories? This is long before people spoke of 'controlling the narrative'. You can be sure that by the time such an idea is common currency it is too late to take advantage of it. But, as I have said, we were not too late. We were right on time. While the worker bees—my word—buzzed, your father had his eyes on the more distant horizons that I had placed there for him.

Our sex life was pitiful. It had never been spectacular but after our little encounter on the edge of the bed it worsened. I was puzzled by it, actually. Love, after all, need not be a prerequisite. And what else is a concubine for? But I think now that, in revealing the truth of things, I had broken something in him. At the time, and to my surprise, it frustrated me. He spent his days playing the conquering hero, the great leader of men—I resented it that he couldn't save a half hour or so of that energy when he came home and take his bitch to bed. Is this difficult to hear, *chutki*? But by then the very sight of me cowed him. He knew he needed me, that he was nothing without me, but he spurned any more of my company than was necessary to receive his instructions. There would be the odd and entirely gestural attempt on his part but as time went on these occasions became mercifully infrequent and, when they did arise, agreeably brief. It goes without saying that I would not climax but curiously, neither would he. Do you know, I can say without hesitation that in all those years I never once laid eyes on your father's ejaculate? I needn't have consented at all, I suppose, but there was an element of keeping him sweet. Not that I can say with any certainty that the strategy satisfied the goal. In truth, this was the one area in which I found your father, such an open book to me, rather illegible.

By the time we moved up to the lake the matter seemed settled, the bare bones of sexual routine were established and my mind was on other things. The wider world, anything at all that I could not personally command—these things had lost their lustre for me. I had only one appetite—power—and required a sealed and regulated space in which to feed it. The compound. I hope you can forgive me for saying, *chutki*, since you hadn't yet come along, that it was my golden time. I hunger often to return. Especially in the Autumn, when the leaves changed colour, the forest was an embrace—except for a short stretch of shore, we were enclosed there in our own world. There was an innocence to it. The boys, and it was always boys, took to my cooking—they had probably never tasted food spiced like that before—and I took to the maternal role they mindlessly assigned to me with some enthusiasm, I have to say. It was easier for me, more navigable, to play that part. The youngsters didn't need to know how it was behind closed doors.

I filled them with bhaturas and chole, stuffed bati, bhajis, biryanis, butter chicken, samosas and—because your father would sometimes relay requests from his Iranian colleague—Khoresh Bademjan, Ash Reshteh, kuku sabzi and nihari gosht, just as I filled your father with rancour, ambition and a workable simulacrum of my own megalomania. We would sit while the evenings were still warm at the end of the dining hut that was roofed but otherwise open to the elements. Of course they would, uniformly, fail to make any interesting conversation and so instead I would toy with them, coaxing some blushing reply out of each of them while the others laughed and waited their turn. We would drink beers from the bottle as night drew in. It was my little idyll. There were fireflies, bats. Even your father would linger. Surrounded by what were little more than children, he seemed better able to withstand me. I suppose he felt sheltered—my attention was, momentarily, elsewhere.

The next hut along was the other big one. I dubbed it the Hive, since that was where my little bees busied themselves in the daytime, and the name stuck—absurdly, it now adorns an innocuous eight-story glass and concrete Zade building in the suburbs of Dublin.

Decisions and discoveries were made in that prefab, *chutki*, that are no longer recognised as either. They are bedrock now, the topology of our digital lives. *Your* digital lives. I have not followed. This is my world—not the compound even, not anymore—just this upper lodge hidden by the trees. It was at that time that I moved back into the sari, better to play my role. I haven't left it. Fuck them all. The seeds of my reclusion. The world couldn't get to me but I could get to it. The web.

The coming and going of people was a blessing—I wanted convivial distractions, not relationships. I got to pretend to be a mother, *chutki*, and I must say I liked it, but only because it *was* a pretence. For a time, I experienced something that may, for all I can remember, have been adjacent to happiness. Not like those deeper, more distant moments—nothing like the glee of the prepubescent self at a chin soaked in pomegranate juice; nothing like the glimpse I had of . . . whatever it was . . . when I first met your father and fell in love with what I later came to see was actually his alleged potential, unrealized and destined to stay that way. You will find this yourself, *chutki*, with men, should you choose to have anything to do with them. They dine out on what they might be. In other words, what they are not. I knew all this by the time we bought the compound but still I found a contentment there. The balance suited me because the power was mine. I may have been physically retreating from the world, but I was growing. Incubating.

But nothing lasts, does it? Nothing that pleases me. With the web came the possibility of remote working and a reduction in activity at the compound. It wasn't sudden and at first I liked it. It was nicer, actually, to have ten people at a cookout than twenty. More familial. I got better at names. Numbers were still sufficient to thrum an evening with talk. It was that way for a few years—reduced but intact, an unburst bubble. Late one summer the few remaining were made more comfortable when a second lodge, which was to be guest quarters, was completed on the upper terrace. The dormitory hut was pulled down and the lodge occupied by a maximum of half a dozen at a time. Still, it ticked along nicely. When the faces change so often, novelty compensates for lower numbers. No one is counting.

Another lodge was completed the following May, along with the underground carpark and the observatory. And each year after that another followed, and all the attendant outbuildings. The cinema, the gym—your father so full of himself on each completion, so obnoxiously triumphant at the realization of another part of the design he—I honestly believe—considered his. I envied him. Shouldn't I have been the same? Wasn't the triumph mine? But for reasons I did not understand at the time it filled me with revulsion to greet each pristine structure. It was an encroachment to me, as if I was losing a home, not gaining one. A landscape was erased and it was that landscape, not this creeping new one of perfect right angles, that I had come to cherish. Foolishly, I'd thought of those seven irregular little prefabs as constants. They are long gone but when I think of them they seem, in memory, to have more about them, more substance, than the assemblies of block and beam that replaced them to speck the newly manicured slopes.

Me, your father, those huts. As the marionette cast was thinned out and the scenery dismantled, another constant was thrown into relief. Not that it had been hidden, just so enmeshed in our lives that it went more or less unnoticed, certainly by me. It predated the compound, in fact, had already been with us in the bungalow. That's probably why it escaped me. Some things register only on the level of the ambient. Our incuriousness is in-built to the very first impression they make on the peripheries of our sense—a tiny pin-prick in the corner of the eye, or the glint of a needle on the most distant horizon of our vision.

Zade. The other one. The one your father called The Persian. He'd been hidden in plain sight, as they say, in all the bustle of those first years. I noticed him now. Not least his size, the athletic build. His eyes. He had the eyes of a predator. I don't mean that in a bad way—I don't mean a human predator. Nothing so sordid. He had the eyes of a creature that hunts of necessity, in the wild, in the snow. Void of mercy, yes, but also of malice. It occurred to me that I hardly knew the sound of his voice. In the bungalow, when I would step into the spare room for whatever-it-was, he would fall quiet, waiting for your father and I to conclude our business. It seemed polite to me and perhaps it was. His smile when I'd go to leave was perfectly, and invariably, amiable.

The same at the compound. I paid him no heed. He was important to the work, but not to its management—and therefore, beyond the odd food request relayed by your father, not to me. He was just *there*, shadowing his employer like a loyal doberman. I know he spoke because I saw from a distance how he leaned in, how your father inclined his head to listen. But he never spoke to me or, as far as I could tell, any other. For someone who by dint of physical appearance alone should have stuck out like a sore thumb, his presence was so conspicuously innocuous you might wonder why my attention would settle upon him.

I don't know. Something got to me. I was sufficiently unnerved to have his contractual arrangements with us looked into, to see what leverage he might have secured. He hadn't. I wouldn't say I was surprised—we had been assiduous—but I wasn't reassured either. My awareness of him grated on me from that time. I loathed myself for my curiosity but I could not dismiss the idea that he was, in some way, a threat. So I watched. It cost me the additional irritation of needing to conceal my interest. I knew in my gut not to quiz your father—that to do so would be a sign of weakness and, worse, that it would delight him. So I watched, as a quieter life on the compound went on—a more serious, sober and grown-up life. Fewer faces, fewer voices, distractions—a new reality that, despite the unquestionable success and emerging power of Zade, seemed to me a return to banality after the intoxication of early growth and unfurling ambition.

And all the time, him. Moved from the periphery to the centre of my attention, his presence from negligible to insistent. It undid me. I could not tell, cannot even now, if the call upon my attention was disgust or attraction—either way, his being with us was a trespass. A drop of dark poison tincturing our otherwise clear solution, I knew I wanted him gone but not how to effect it—there was a tie that bound him to your father, your father to him, and I did not know whose hand it was that pulled the string or, if I cut it, who would fall? If this man's hold on your father wasn't contractual, or financial, what was it?

And why hadn't I asked myself these things before? Any point at which I might have tackled him head-on had passed. I did not have a move to make. I went about my business as I always had but the peace I'd known in that place was disturbed and the disturbance was him. Intuition told me now—something was coming. I watched without knowing what I was watching for. Signs, the early signs of something—it was as vague as that, but for all the mist that obscured it, I knew it was there and that we were moving towards it.

How was I to know what that something could be? That he would be able to reach inside me, find whatever humanity was left there, and rip it out for good?

The Fishing Ground

WHEN SHE HAD SAID what she had to say, her bodyguard stood and went to the door of the mess, waiting for her there. She excused herself and joined him.

"Go pack your bag," she said, turning to Liam, who had been back to the buffet and still had food to finish. "We're getting close, about half an hour."

It had come as a surprise to Liam that they could be anywhere so soon. He wondered (and for the first time, it struck him) how long he'd been unconscious. When the other two had gone he mopped up the last of his breakfast, then went to the end of the corridor and outside to see what he could see. Sure enough, if he leaned over the rail he could make out a few lights on an approaching coastline and above them, hilltops silhouetted against the first, faintest evidence of dawn. He went down to his room and stuffed the holdall with clothes and the paperback. Then he sat on the bed and waited. When the knock came he took his bag and followed the hulk down another set of steps to a landing where she was waiting for them. All three made their way down several more sets of steps and into a very different part of the ship.

Up where the cabins were, things were laid out on a human scale. If the fixtures were somewhat perfunctory and less than inviting, at least the feel up there was residential—bedclothes, cutlery, linoleum, even the odd picture hung. Down here the truth was revealed: this thing was a machine. Because it would be necessary for human beings to make their way from one part of the machine to another, spaces had been left between its working parts. These walkways made the minimum possible concession to their users—to move along them it was necessary to duck almost constantly to avoid low-hanging pipes and valves, to twist and shimmy between any number of protuberances and to step through a series of raised hatches. There was a sense—as there had been when staring out at the open sea in the dark—that one was unwelcome.

Unmistakably, there were others. Despite his having caught barely a glimpse of anyone, the strongest odor was that of cigarette smoke. Beneath it the smell of diesel and, intermittently, fresh paint, and under those an aroma he couldn't quite identify but supposed might be, when one was surrounded by so much, what steel smelled like. Then, when they had descended yet another set of steep steps, salt air. They stepped through a hatch into a large, low-ceilinged and low-lit space that on one side faded away into the ship's interior. On the other, a hatch was open in the hull of the ship. They were close enough to the waterline for spray to clear the hatch's lower rim.

"Why are we doing this in the dark?" he asked. A crewman stood by the opening. Sherry and Darius put their bags down at his feet so Liam did the same. "Also, what are we doing?"

"These waters are well watched," she said. "This is how we get off."

She stood at the cavity in the hull. Liam stood by her, the bodyguard behind them. It was still pitch black in the direction they were facing so he didn't spot the other boat till it was close—a tug or a trawler or whatever it was, lining itself up alongside and edging closer.

Trawler. Nets cluttered its deck. Its lights were also cut but one of the crew was using a weak torch. Liam spotted what he thought might be a serious problem. The trawler was having to work hard to keep up with the cargo ship and although he had felt no motion whatsoever in the larger vessel, it was clear now that this was down to its size and not to a calm sea. Framed in the hatch, the other boat was bobbing wildly—close enough to step onto but not still enough.

"This seems dangerous." He didn't expect a reply and he didn't get one. Presumably there was some kind of procedure. Safety lines or what not. The spray in the air made it fresh but not cold, not even on the open sea at night, and he wondered where in the world they were. He could see that the two men on the boat were neither Hawaiian nor Chinese. Just as it dawned on him that Darius was probably going to pick him up and throw him over there, the bodyguard picked him up from behind, held him aloft in the hatch by his armpits for a moment, and threw him to one of the boat guys who was waiting to steady him. He might have preferred to be consulted but at least he didn't have to think about how to get on the boat any more. The bags followed and then Sherry, without assistance. Then Darius. Then the crewman waved them off and the little trawler pulled away.

Clear of the cargo ship, Liam could see distant coastline in opposite directions—this was an estuary and a huge one. Geography was not his strong point but he had a sense of where he was now. The boat headed towards neither shore, instead taking a line back out towards the sea. Behind them, light leaked from the horizon, erasing the lowest stars. Even Darius had to hang on to something to steady himself. Soon Liam made out their destination—ahead, a constellation of lights in constant, crazy motion. By the time the trawler was close, the dawn was just enough to outline thirty-or-so fishing vessels in an unruly crowd on the water. As the trawler joined them, a crew member flicked their own lights back on.

"I don't want to see this," said Sherry, and sat down on a crate beneath the standing shelter.

See what? He couldn't understand why the boats—some the same size as their trawler, many mere row boats, and others larger—didn't collide. It was a meleé, a feeding frenzy. But he supposed some kind of discipline must be behind it all. As the morning found its strength, he caught first sight of the prey, glinting alongside a row boat as the pilot of same held tightly on to it with a large metal hook—a fish head emerging from the water, but a fish head larger than any Liam had ever seen. They wouldn't be pulling that thing aboard. If they wanted it, they'd have to tow it back to port. What kind of fish grew to that size anyway?

"Tuna," said Sherry from her crate. "Poor things."

These people knew how to pick their spot. More of the giants were hooked and some winched onto the larger boats. Blood dyed the water. A small boat pulled up alongside their own trawler and hooked their tuna up to a winch the other crewman lowered. As he lifted the tuna and lowered it on to the deck, its size was all the more evident. Sherry said something to the guy at the wheel.

"Now we have a fish, we'll go," she said.

The trawler set a course for one of the banks, where even from this distance Liam could see the crescent of a large bay and the geometries of a city. He didn't know the name of the city but he wasn't going to give anyone the satisfaction of asking—he knew where they were now, even if only roughly, and he wasn't surprised. All of the fishermen were brown-skinned and almost without exception black-haired. He hadn't recognised a word of their language as they'd yelled out their orders and warnings, and not a word of the instruction Sherry had given the pilot, but that wasn't surprising either. He'd never paid much attention to this part of the world. Where else, though, could make more sense for a Zade bolthole than India?

The sun had risen and its light skimmed the water just as the trawler did, bouncing along at speed. The water sparkles cheered him, and the wind, and the feeling he'd had so far on this journey, of detached confusion, gave way to an exhilarated sense of adventure. He was Sinbad on the high seas, and managed not to throw up for the twenty or so minutes it took them to reach port, at one end of a bay where an old stone wharf sheltered a huddle of fishing boats. Darius threw the bags on to the wharf and Liam followed them, this time without help. The trawler's pilot said something to Darius and Liam could tell by the tone it meant something like *be quick*.

Once the heiress and her security were ashore, they all made their way along the wharf toward land proper.

"Do we have documents?" asked Liam. A good number of uniformed men haphazardly arranged themselves around a boom barrier up ahead. "The police—"

"Are for the ferry port," said Sherry. "Just walk by. Try not to be interesting."

An old part of town draped a hill to their right. It had the look of a European colony—there were battlements with a couple of antique cannons at the top and behind them a pretty, jaded muddle of sunlit whitewash. The police kept their eyes, conspicuously, on anything apart from the new arrivals who, a few metres further on, walked through an ornamental garden and on to the cobbled ramp that sloped through an arch in the city walls. Inside, the low sun had not yet touched the narrow lanes. They reached a green-tiled temple where Sherry turned, leading them uphill along a pedestrian thoroughfare of tiny, shuttered shops, into and through a small square lined with cafés, yet to open. A little farther on, she indicated a lane by the side of a watchmaker's shop and they took it, turning again almost immediately into a covered alley that dead-ended at a heavy wooden double door. The man who opened it in response to her single knock was similar in appearance to the fishermen, but a lot taller.

"Hello Saeed," she said as he shut the door again behind them. "Leave your bag here, Mr Tead."

Apart from a little half moon of stained glass over the door that coloured the weak light from the alley, the hallway was windowless. On a stairway that swept around a curved wall, burning candles left cascades of melted wax over each step. At the top, Darius and Sherry dropped their own bags. Everything about the place—the décor, the arches, the ornate fabrics that upholstered a little nook of banquettes and silk cushions—confirmed the location to Liam. He had lost track of how many hours he'd been awake and perhaps a little delirium was creeping in. It might be morning but it was bed time. They continued up another stairwell, into the daylight that poured in from above, and stepped out onto a small roof terrace where a woman, dressed all in black except for the flamboyant pashmina on her shoulders, sat at a table reading.

"Welcome," she said, getting up. Her accent was instantaneously recognisable, even in the one word, as Australian. She smiled at all three but only Sherry got a hug. Darius, it seemed, was also new around here. "Everything's ready, the hotel too." The tall man, who had retreated, returned with a silver tray, some glasses, and a pot of tea. He placed them on the table, but no one sat. Liam took in the scene—the view from here was almost three-sixty. On one side, the town sloped down towards the port and the sea. Green hills, pocked with wind turbines, were just visible on the opposite bank of the enormous estuary. In the other direction the rooftops climbed the hill and spread around it, punctuated here and there by steeples, or bell towers, or minarets or whatever they were.

"This is Sue," said Sherry. "I'm known in town so I'll lie low here. Darius too—he's . . . conspicuous. But there's no need for you to slum it."

"Excuse me?" said the Australian.

"You'll need to get around," said Sherry, "I imagine. Maybe even make yourself known. Saeed will show you up to the hotel. Your body clock must be messed up. Get some sleep. Later today, you can get started."

"Started on what?"

She blinked at him. "I don't know," she said. "Go fishing? Put your ears to the ground? Set a trap? Whatever it is you detectives do. My father has a house in town—check that out. I don't expect him to be there, too obvious. But I do hope he has passed through. That's the best place to start I can think of. Tell me, do you know where you are?"

"Specifically? Not a clue," said Liam. "But I know a subcontinent when I see one."

"Good." She smiled. "Well now that you've located yourself, I'm sure you'll get a grip on the specifics in no time."

"Where's the house?"

"*This* is your detective?" said Sue.

"Remember, we're all off line," said Sherry. "Just come back here if and when you have something. I'm not going anywhere. Sue, do you have the cash?"

"Downstairs. Saeed will give it to him."

Sherry gave Liam what he took to be a rather pointed look.

"Keep your wits about you, Mr Tead. Stay sharp and stay well. Maybe use some of the cash to get clothes. I sent Darius out for those ones and I think we can all agree he did a very poor job."

Liam followed his guide back down to the front door and picked up his holdall. Saeed went into the back and returned with a plastic bag, the kind you got in a supermarket. It had a large number of neat bundles of cash in it.

"Plenty for expense," he said. "You pay nothing at the hotel for eat."

Liam's holdall was stuffed tight so he was obliged to carry the shopping bag of cash in his other hand as he followed Saeed back to the same street as before. They continued uphill. There were a few more people around. Some of them were raising their shutters—all men, the older ones in long robes and the younger in tight-fitting jeans and designer tops. As Liam passed the market—the gate was closed but he could tell by the stench of meat and fish—an old man stepped bellowing out of nowhere, ostentatiously plaintive, a hand outstretched, both of his eyes disfigured and clearly useless. Saeed turned to chide the beggar, but also to drop a coin in his hand.

The end of the street gave way to a large, oval open. As early as it was, some kind of market was in the process of setting up. Women in wide-brimmed straw hats squatted in the gloom beneath leafy trees and arranged their wares—grain, vegetables, cookware, fresh palm-wrapped cheeses. Across the way, visible where the canopy parted a little, an *art deco* cinema drew Liam's eye. There would undoubtedly be some classy flooring in there. He couldn't get a thought together and would happily have laid himself down on the soft dirt beneath the trees. In the sunshine, they would provide essential shade for the vendors, but not today—it was going to be warm but the sun that had risen into a clear sky was obscured now in gathering cloud.

"How far is the hotel, Saeed?"

"Two minutes."

The street they took on the other side was lined with comparatively modern establishments—a bakery, a café, clothes shops, a telecoms outlet. They turned left at the end and as this new street, still leading gently uphill, curved around to the right, Saaed pointed out the hotel. Liam would probably have spotted it—flags flew over the entrance and what seemed like too many doormen loitered outside in their livery: knickerbockers and those little flat-topped hats he'd seen in old movies.

"Ask for Khalil," said his guide, turning. "Come to the house when you need to, but don't if you don't." He walked away.

At reception, it couldn't have been more obvious to Liam that guests didn't usually arrive in a tracksuit carrying a sports holdall and a plastic shopping bag.

"Can I help you?" Something about Liam's appearance had suggested to the guy that the language spoken between them would be English.

"I have a room here."

The receptionist's eyes flicked toward a uniformed man who stood just inside the revolving doors.

"Certainly. Passport, please."

"I'm supposed to talk to Khalil."

The uniformed guy had taken two slow steps closer. The morning was getting old fast.

"The hotel manager is busy, I'm afraid."

Liam held both hand's up in surrender, hard currency swinging from one of them and visible through the flimsy plastic to any of the guests milling about who might care to look. "And yet," he said.

The receptionist went away, quickly returning with an older man.

"Mr Tead?"

"Yes. It's Tĕad. But yes."

"Come with me, please."

Khalil led him away from the counter, across the lobby and down a few steps into a large, covered courtyard with a retractable roof. Two red carpets crossed the floor area. Leather armchairs were dotted around. Leafy plants. Apart from that, pretty much everything was white and most of it was marble. A fountain trickled its tune at the centre of it all. Overhead, three floors of gallery provided light to the inner-facing rooms. All four facades bore elaborate and minutely detailed carving. Cloisters enclosed the courtyard—in their shaded corners were doors to the bar, the restaurant, the pool and garden. If it wasn't purpose-built, this had to have been the home of nobility. But buildings like this might be two-a-penny in this country, he supposed. Built by the British when the place and all the loot was theirs. Old photos of previous guests lined the first flight of a wide stairway. Liam thought he recognised Rock Hudson and the singer from that Californian band. They didn't take the stairs—Khalil showed him to a lift.

Jim Morrison.

He'd assumed he'd be getting some kind of attic room but Khalil showed him into a suite that had a terrace overlooking the pool and then spent an officious few moments checking all was pristine, flicking each light on and off to show Liam where the switches were and adjusting the air conditioning.

"Whatever you need, Mr Tead, the staff are at your disposal." As he headed for the door, he paused "If you should need anything out of the ordinary, please deal with me."

Having the top job around here didn't deter him from effecting a meaningful delay in leaving the room. Liam took a bundle from the shopping bag, pulled four notes from it and handed them over. A wide-eyed Khalil bowed deeply.

"Most generous, sir. You will find accounts have been opened for you in the restaurant and spa."

"And the bar?"

"No, sir, and we were instructed not to stock the minibar." The hotel manager could neither conceal his amusement nor sustain it— the expression melted away into one that might have been fraternal. "I can have someone run out for you, whenever you like. You will need to pay cash."

He stepped back out into the corridor.

"Enjoy your stay at the Minzah, Mr Tead," he said. "Welcome to Tangier."

Dean.s and the Dolly

Liam had to admire Sherry for not laughing in his face back there on the Australian woman's roof—and to wonder again just how long he'd been under. Whatever this jaunt was, it had nothing to do with India. Or the Pacific. It was embarrassing. Still, there were positives—now that his eyes were open, he was reminded that he had a fabulous hotel room. It, like the lobby downstairs, was a celebration in shades of white. A large rug on the floor between the bed and the sitting room caught his eye—white with two slender lines of black criss-crossing it. The design was understated; the rug somehow wasn't. It looked expensive and, beneath his bare feet, it felt expensive.

On the terrace, he got a general idea of the time—rays fell upon the pool furniture in deep red shafts before touching down on the lawn, close enough to the horizontal that blades of grass were thrown into relief.

The beers he'd ordered before closing the door on the hotel manager had arrived within minutes and would be cold by now in the minibar. He opened one and got back into bed. Since it was evening, he wasn't sure what came next. Was this a day off? Did he start in the morning? The beer bottles were the ridiculous kind—twenty-five centilitres—so the first only took him a couple of slugs. Fetching another couple for the bedside table, he propped his pillows and picked up the paperback Sherry had given him on the boat. Unsurprisingly, it was a *de luxe* affair—heavy and gold-inlayed on the front cover with pages of thick, fancy paper. He felt along the edges of them which were pleasing to the pad of his thumb, rough and irregular as if cut by hand with a letter opener. He flicked through till the book opened, at random, on page one hundred and four—the thirty-seventh night and the first dervish's tale. He didn't know what a dervish was.

It wasn't long before the usual restlessness kicked in. He didn't seem to know how to read any more: not one thing at a time. But then there were any number of things he didn't know. He didn't know what was happening to him, for example. He didn't know anything about Tangier. He didn't know anything about Morocco. One thing he *was* pretty sure about: his employer liked to be a step ahead of him but she was dead wrong, naive almost, on two counts—one, that he was a credible investigator and two, that anyone could investigate anything these days offline. He put on some clothes and went back out towards the telecoms store. Night had fallen but everything was open. The guy in the store spoke English and set him up with a phone and sim card. Liam paid with four of those notes so apparently he had tipped Khalil the price of a smart phone.

Back in the room, once he'd plugged the phone in to charge and opened a beer, he figured he might as well have a shower. Ten minutes later and reeking of high-end product, he put on some fresh sportswear and had another couple on the terrace where it was getting cooler. This meant he was low on beers and he'd need to venture out. He was still a little too light-headed to get into research—no doubt the sedation and the strange hours had taken a toll. He went down to reception and asked for Khalil. The hotel manager was prompt in coming out to the desk, his tone as before polite if not friendly.

"What can I do for you, Mr Tead?"

"Téad. Yes, I need food, drink and expats who gossip."

"Did the beers not arrive? I told the boy—"

"No, they did. They were really small is all. Do you know of a place?"

Khalil waved to a bellhop who came over to take his instructions. "He will show you. The owner is a former employee, and hasn't gone far."

Five minutes later, Liam tipped the bellhop and stood watching the bar from across the street for a little while. It seemed like the sort of thing he ought to do. There was a fair bit of coming and going. A vintage convertible pulled up and a lady got out and went in, walking with a limp. The car drove off and a little while later the driver, dressed as neatly as the lady, walked back and went in also. In fact everyone who went in or came out was conspicuously well dressed, even if several of them looked like they'd put a few days distance between themselves and an iron. None of it quite fitted with the bar's less-than-inviting, unlit facade—plain granite blocks and a plaque that read 'Dean.s Bar 1937'. In the mild weather, the glass doors had been left open but the interior was hidden behind a bead curtain.

Liam was on edge. Incredibly, he hadn't found a safe in the room so he was still carrying the cash. At least it wasn't so obvious—the bag his phone had come in was made of a thicker plastic. Doing his best to affect a saunter, he crossed the street, pulled the beads apart and went in. The place was small and very lively. To the left, a vintage jukebox next to the toilets emitted some swing number. The bar to his right was tended by a couple of portly, middle-aged men, one of whom wore thick eyeliner. The lined eyes belonged to the owner, Liam reasoned, because it was from them, when he approached the bar, that the disapproval emanated.

"Beer. Please."

"We prefer our patrons to dress respectably."

"So I see." Everybody in the place was in fact dressed to the nines—suits, one or two military uniforms, frocks, perms, pearls and pleated pants. "Is there something on?"

The guy didn't answer him.

"I can only apologise. I just got in and I clearly need to up my game. I'll go shopping tomorrow. But I was hoping for a drink tonight."

"I'll sponsor him, Dean." The hand on Liam's shoulder belonged to a young man, apparently Moroccan. "Allow me to introduce myself," he said through the kind of smile that made heterosexuality seem like a capricious and unnecessary constraint. "My name is Ahmed." Ahmed spoke perfect English with an accent straight from Wodehouse. He was younger than Liam, better looking, evidently well-to-do, oozing charisma and apparently buying the drinks. It seemed as good a place to start as any.

"The next time I see you in here," the landlord said, "I trust you will be properly dressed. Flag or Casablanca?"

The beers in the room had been Flags. "Casablanca, please."

"Casablanca," said the youth, "if you would, please, Dean. And a gimlet."

The jukebox was spitting out some Bill Evans at a refreshingly low volume but the place was noisy anyway, with talk. Ahmed guided him toward a second bead curtain—this one emblazoned with the word *Restaurant*—and pulled it apart. The room beyond it was small, if larger than the bar area, and packed with tables. Liam could smell a kitchen but saw no food. People were here to drink. The scene had a soporific and welcoming effect. There was an upright piano against the far wall and leafy plants in each corner, backlit, threw their motif into the dim, smoke-filled space and across the walls and ceiling, making the place seem classier than its cramped proportions could ever hope to pull off in daylight.

"I'm going to sit you down here with these reprobates, if you don't mind," said Ahmed, indicating three men at a corner table that had a vacant chair. "I have a room to work. Gentlemen." Before he slid away, the Moroccan leaned in to whisper. "Fold that bag up. I've seen what's in it, and I think you and I could be of some use to each other."

Liam sat, folded the bag up and put it under his chair.

"Would you like one?" A round-faced man with pursed lips and an old school quiff held out a paper bag. He was dressed head to toe in black. A turtleneck brought the black up to his chin. His hair was black.

They looked like chocolates, or fudge.

"What are they?"

"Delicious confections." The man looked surprised to be asked.

"Banj," said one of the others, a James Bond-type, sporting an immaculate suit and an unblinking stare.

"You and your goddamn flights of fancy, Brion," said the third, a gaunt man in a fedora who also wore black. "That is *majoun*. A simple hemp preparation."

It did taste like fudge. Like a nutty fudge with honey and spices in it.

"Sometimes also contains opium and Datura seeds." This guy's voice was like something from a ravaged future—the steel groans of a ruined skyscraper in high winds.

"Sometimes?"

"Depends on who makes it."

"Who made this?"

"Me."

"With opium and Datura seeds?"

"Yes."

Liam had always been comfortable with predators. People who wanted something from you were easier to play. You just had to make sure you didn't get eaten.

"Datura?"

"Nature's gift," said James Bond, the one Fedora had called Brion. "Little parcels of atropine, hyoscyamine and scopolamine."

Liam nodded. "Effects?"

"Of course," said the spy, "or they'd hardly be worth mentioning, would they?"

"You an athlete, young fellow?" Fedora was rolling a cigarette. It had been a few years since anyone had referred to Liam as young, and this guy didn't look any older than him.

"Do I look like an athlete?"

"You dress like an athlete."

"Perhaps he robbed an athlete," said Brion.

"A larger man," said turtleneck.

"Francis, please." The voice a slow, deliberate drawl that scrawled, a scrawl that droned, like bone cold heat, barely audible, at the centre of a mushroom cloud.

"I take it this stuff kicks in quickly."

"Quickly enough," said Francis. "Unless one is tired or hasn't eaten or what have you. Then it's more or less instant." His accent was English, the kind one's parents paid a lot of money for. Fedora was American, somewhere in the south. Liam wasn't sure about Brion—North American, nondescript.

"If you have come here directly from a sporting event of some kind," said Fedora, his cigarette placed on the table and forgotten, "you smell wrong. You must be some kind of royalty—you arrived with the prince of Tangier, after all. But then Dean doesn't seem to like you any more than he likes me. He's been eyeballing us."

"Prince?"

"Mayor's son," said Francis. "Same thing."

"And what a lovely thing it is. Doesn't want to play though." Fedora nodded across the room at someone. A moment later, Liam's empty beer was replaced with a fresh one. Ahmed had already presented himself at four tables and sat briefly at two. Everyone was delighted to see him. That meant he had money. And *that* meant he knew things. Some stroke of luck to run in to a guy so connected, and so quickly. What had he meant, *of use to each other*? Liam pulled at the neck of his hoody. Hot was . . . skin.

Someone unplugged the jukebox mid-song. Liam jumped in his seat. Nobody else reacted. The little woman who had limped in from the car outside sat a nearby table and beside her, Liam imagined, was her husband, who even in this company was notable for his immaculate appearance—suit, tie, not a crease in sight, golden hair just long enough to reveal its waves and tightly groomed at the back and sides. The woman had short, boyish hair and lips that formed a pout in their slightly parted resting positions. Her eyes joined dots around the room ceaselessly. Her mouth could somehow incline itself toward her husband even when she didn't turn her head. He smiled discreetly at her commentary but it wasn't enough to conceal his obvious discomfort in this setting.

"It's the scopolamine you're going to need to watch out for." Fedora was leaning in.

With the woman and her husband was another lady. A fur coat hung over her shoulders—Liam couldn't remember the last time he'd seen one. She was otherwise dressed both modestly and expensively. Her attention was fixed on a young man who had seated himself on the piano stool and was tuning up a guitar. "Atropine is an anticholinergic. It's a helpful alkaloid in many ways but in many other ways, it's unhelpful. You might expect your heartbeat to become erratic, for starters, and your skin to flush. You may get a headache. Your vision may blur." Even sitting down, the guy with the guitar was tall—tall and blonde and wearing a white dinner jacket. She was transfixed on him and Liam was transfixed on that. "But I sense in you, young fellow, a veteran of previous alkaloids. I think you'll handle it. Atropine isn't going to affect your level of awareness, after all. Hyoscyamine, on the other hand—" The guy sang too. The lady must have had a thing for tall guys who sang.

"Hello, friend."

Or guitarists in white. Ahmed was on his knees beside Liam. He had the plastic bag in his hands. "I need money," he said, glancing in the direction of the bar area. "Quite a lot, I'm afraid. I'm about to pull something off here."

Liam itched. Said nothing. Ahmed stopped fishing around in the bag for a second. "Whatever I take from you now, I shall double in the morning." He shook his head. "Didn't these scoundrels tell you who I am?" He held out three fat bundles he'd pulled from the bag. "Look, I'm just going to take this. It might do it. All right?"

All right? It was a very simple question but at the same time there was a lot to unpack. The answer would need to be good. Good words. And those words would need to come out of his answer mouth. It would all have to be arranged. He tried to make a word and the thing came off quicker than expected.

"Sure."

Skin.

"Good man," said Ahmed. He replaced the bag under the chair and disappeared through the bead curtain with the cash.

"But really," Fedora was struggling to get his cigarette lit, "it's the scopolamine. With the scopolamine come the hallucinations. When you don't know what's going on anymore, that's the game changer."

Liam's eyes were on the ceiling. Something was wrong.

"He's beautiful, isn't he?" said Francis. "Poor little rich girl certainly seems to think so. Of course he's half the musician my Peter is. My piano pilot."

The leafy shadows up there were swaying back and forth as if in a breeze. Liam looked at the bead curtain. It was perfectly still. He looked at the nearest plant. It wasn't easy to tell if it was moving or not, because any slight movement on Liam's part meant the lamp behind it moved in relation to the leaves. He tried to hold his head perfectly still for as long as he could, sitting up straight and holding on to the back of his chair.

"But he is beautiful, isn't he?"

Liam nodded, silently cursing himself for moving his head again.

"Does he think I'm talking about that plant?"

Their voices reached his inner ear like warm air blown softly from a lover's lips. He shuddered in delight.

"I want to see if it moves," he said.

"If what moves?"

The still light through moving leaves. Moving light through still leaves. Still leaves and still light, head moving.

seewhatimeanbill seewhatimeanaboutthedreammachine

Brion's voice.

hefoundthefrequency.

"Those leaves aren't moving," said Fedora.

"The shadows are," said Francis.

A silence. Liam supposed Fedora was looking up.

"I'll give you that."

"My name is Liam."

"Pleased to meet you, Liam. Somebody give this boy a dolly. It'll take the edge off."

One of Liam's hands was prised from the chair back and a capsule pressed into his palm.

"What's this?"

"It's a dolly," said Francis.

"What will it do?"

"It'll take the edge off," said Fedora. "We mean no harm."

Liam took the capsule with the last of his beer. Pretty soon a fresh bottle turned up, and then some more after that. He wasn't exactly keeping track of time. His grip on the idea that there was time to keep track of was loosening. The leaves kept still and the shadows kept swirling. His ears rang. White jacket guy only seemed to know old tunes. Eventually he stopped and went to sit with the fur coat lady who had beckoned him over for a drink. Someone plugged the jukebox back in and Bill Evans lurched into the middle of a song drunkenly, as if late for an appointment with the end of it. The whole place seemed drunk to Liam. Not the people. The place.

"It wasn't enough." Ahmed was right by him again, reaching under the chair. "You know how these things go." This time he pulled six bundles out. "This should do it."

"I can't . . . skin," said Liam.

Ahmed looked to the others. "You chaps taking good care of my friend?"

"Very much so," said Fedora. "It has been our primary concern."

Although Ahmed was taking a lot more cash this time, Liam was more relaxed about it than he had been at first. He did feel very well taken care of and was grateful to all these good people for these nice and good feelings. He was a long way not just from home but from anywhere he'd ever been. Nobody here had any reason to care if he lived or died. That felt good too. He hoped whatever Ahmed was up to worked out because it was sad when things didn't work out, but he wasn't anxious about it because his new friend's promise to double his money in the morning indemnified him against risk.

isheslippingbill ifeelhemightbeslippingawayfromus

"With a single brush stroke, I complete a picture," said Francis. "I always know which stroke. It locks the magic in." He held both hands aloft, the one to hold his cigarette and the other to elevate an index finger, as if delivering a lesson to an eager acolyte. "You, my pretty picture, have not had your final stroke."

Liam had never been called pretty before. It was nice to be called pretty. Someone dimmed the lights.

can'tkeephiseyesopen

"Obetrol him," said Fedora.

"That's it!" Francis clapped. "That's the stroke."

Brion opened a pill box he'd taken from an inside pocket and put two orange tablets on the table in front of Liam.

"What are those?"

"We merely wish to help," said Fedora. "The dolly, intended as a solution to problems brought on by the *majoun*, may I'm afraid have itself become the problem."

Liam fingered the tablets. "Solution?"

"Potentially, yes," said Fedora. "I'm optimistic."

equilibriumfrequencycallitwhatyouwill

Liam took the tablets. It was easily done because there was another beer on the table. He probably should have bought these guys a drink by now because he wanted to know what they knew. But what they knew about what?

"It wasn't enough," said Ahmed, who hadn't been there just now. "These fellows are really squeezing me." He had the plastic bag in his hand. "You should come with me, eh . . ."

"Liam," said Fedora.

"Liam," said Ahmed, "come with me."

"Why?"

"We need to arrange to meet tomorrow," said Ahmed, "so I can give you money. And it won't be here. Come on."

"Good gentlemen, evening." Liam downed his beer. Getting to his feet and following Ahmed out on to the street was easy. It didn't even really feel like he was using his legs.

"Where are you staying?"

"Minz . . ."

"Good, that's close. Come on."

When the hotel entrance came into view, Ahmed stopped.

"I'd prefer the hotel people not see me with you tonight because reasons," he said, "but tomorrow's fine. I shall come by and give you lots of money. Is that all right?"

"Sounds good."

"Will you find your room?"

"I am, yes."

Ahmed, who still had the plastic bag, pulled a bundle from it. "This is for you."

A momentary suspicion flickered in Liam's mind. Why was this guy being so nice to him? He took the bundle.

"Thanks," he said.

Ahmed was already walking away.

Up in the room, the contents of the orange tablets made themselves known. Waves of static swept over his skin, over his scalp, his forearms. He found that if he did not clench his teeth his jaw would tremble. His head cleared up very quickly but it wasn't clarity, exactly—more like velocity. It was clear enough he wouldn't be sleeping. Also, he'd need to address what had happened with the bag of money. Tomorrow would entail some difficult conversations. He didn't want to think about any of that yet. He was ready to go to work and the fact that there were only fifty centilitres of beer in the fridge meant he would need distractions.

    He fired up the phone.

The Detective

Coordinates 35°47′16.1″N 5°48′41.3″W

"Zade House" redirects here. For other uses of Zade, see Zade (disambiguation). For other uses of Kasbah, see Kasbah (disambiguation).

The **Kasbah House**, also known as the Zade House, is an historical property located in the Medina of Tangier, Morocco. It is situated near the Place Amrah and has been owned by the Zade Corporation since the late 20th century. The property was originally built in the late 19th century by Spanish magnate Juan Carrero Godoy. It remains the largest and most luxurious home in the Medina, having passed through the hands of a press magnate, a Spanish politician and a British diplomat. It was for some time the residence of Zade heiress Doonah Zade and has since been used intermittently as a centre for the preservation, dissemination and promotion of Berber music.[1] Locally it is often referred to as the Gnaoua House and has become a cultural as well as physical landmark in the city.

During Ms Zade's tenure, the Kasbah House became renowned for the lavish parties she hosted there, attended by celebrities, the rich, many prominent politicians and members of several royal families, as well as influential writers, musicians, and artists.[2] The city's hotels would experience full occupancy before each party, filled with high-profile foreigners hoping for an invitation. Those fortunate enough to attend the gatherings, to which press outlets were not invited, have described them as extravagant and over-the-top, with guests marvelling at theatrical sets, staged processions, full orchestras, elaborate costumes and other opulent displays of wealth. There have also been more contentious accounts of drug use and sexual activity likely to offend a local population more homogenous and socially conservative now than at any point in the last three centuries of the city's existence[citation needed]. The house became a symbol of excess and decadence, and is often erroneously associated with the glitz of the early 20th-century scene in Tangier.

Ms Zade has been criticized for her "ill-judged"[3] attempt to replicate the glamour of Tangier's International Zone years (1923-1956) at a time when the social and political contexts were proscriptive. The house and gatherings were the subject of a number of documentary films[4] as media interest migrated from gossip column to investigative report and exposé.[5] Locally, Ms Zade's presence became the target of public hostility. Items such as eggs and paint were thrown at the house.

Further afield, the notoriety of the Zade house is credited with igniting a resurgent interest in the city's cultural and artistic legacies. Ironically, though both Tanjawis and Moroccans in general were discomfited by international attention of this kind, tourists flocked to Tangier—boosting its economy and reestablishing it in short order as a top-tier resort on a par with Monaco, Ibiza and Marseilles.[6]

This had positive and negative consequences. The influx of money may have softened the public's attitude towards the Zade heiress during this time. There were no urgent calls, official or otherwise, for her to leave Tangier. It may be related that trade discussions were taking place at ministerial level and possibly between ministers and the Zade corporation.[citation needed] For the first time since 1956, the Moroccan government was considering the reintroduction in Tangier of highly permissive regulatory environments for tax, duty, currency exchange, residency and licence law. It was widely assumed that the government wanted to fully exploit the city's new-found wealth. It was also assumed that it was accommodating the wishes of the Zade corporation. No public statement from either entity has referenced any such consideration.

However, despite the income generated, tourism was not universally popular. Many recent arrivals were attracted by the city's long-unearned reputation for transgression, sexual freedom and plentiful narcotics, and were increasingly likely to be arrested for solicitation and drug offences. Tanjawis, dismayed by this and by their government's apparent pandering to the Zade corporation, protested on two occasions at the Kasbah House. The protests are widely believed to be the reason for Ms Zade's departure from Tangier, if not for her subsequent disappearance from public life.

Further controversies

The Kasbah House has attracted further controversy, notably the 'Team Guillermo' affair—a special investigation involving journalists from dozens of publications worldwide that exposed[11] a covert disinfo unit allegedly subcontracted by the Zade corporation and accused of manipulating public opinion and democratic elections in Morocco and elsewhere. The unit, nicknamed 'Team Guillermo' is thought to have operated from the house. Accusations ranged from widespread hacking activities to on-the-ground staging of fake protests by paid participants to be covered by ostensibly reputable news organizations. Most attention was reserved for the mechanisms through which these news stories would then proliferate via social media, specifically a combination of proprietary softwares known as Advanced Impact Content Solutions (A.I.C.S.) and the Program of Advanced Impact News Sources (P.A.I.N.S.).

Reportedly, the individual identified as head of the team—known only as 'Guillermo'—was a former Israeli intelligence operative. The unit offered services to both political and commercial interests in pursuit of outcomes ranging from the election of political candidates to the promulgation of content favourable to pharma, tobacco, fossil fuel and renewables. 'Guillermo' boasted on camera to undercover journalists of having intervened in approximately a dozen 'presidential-level' elections around the world with overwhelming success.[12]

Although the exposure is said to have disabled 'Team Guillermo' no prosecutions were brought, the whereabouts of 'Guillermo' and colleagues are unknown and the house was never categorically proven to be the unit's base of operations.

Deep Fake

The Kasbah House is the registered address for the television production company *Riwaya*, responsible for TV shows throughout North Africa and the Middle East but most famously for the Moroccan soap opera *Pour te Dire la Verité*, which found itself at the centre of a scandal in its fourteenth season when a number of cameo performances were subject to lawsuits by the French and Hollywood actors who had apparently given them. *Pour te Dire la Verité* habitually features storylines relating to social and political issues of the day. The frequency of cameos by high profile figures intensified, in the case of Season 14, in the run-up to that year's national elections what a hilariously cheeky dog. Several of the actors involved brought lawsuits, denying any involvement in the TV series or having any position to take on the voter-sensitive issues dealt with. No denial was forthcoming from either *Riwaya* or the Zade corporation but as with the investigations explore nature in vibrant, 100% recyclable colors into 'Team Guillermo' no prosecutions were brought to bear and all lawsuits have subsequently been withdrawn.[13] *Pour te Dire la Verité* remains in production and *Riwaya* is still registered to the Kasbah House.

Video. A large red chilli pepper has a hole and a slit cut into it along one side and the pith and seeds removed. A coin and a lollipop are inserted into the cavity, which is then filled with plaster and smoothed over until the chilli pepper's original shape is restored. The pepper is painted red and polished till the plaster is concealed and the pepper appears as though it has not been tampered with. A cucumber is cut in half and hollowed out. The chilli pepper is placed inside one half. The other half is reattached and glued in place. The glue is filed down with an abrasive sponge and, once smooth, the surface of the cucumber is painted with green paint in two shades to replicate the variegation of cucumber skin. In the panel of a wooden door a cavity has been carved out which is large enough to accommodate the cucumber. The cucumber is placed in the cavity and covered with a generous quantity of sunflower seeds (the door is lying flat). Glue is poured over the sunflower seeds and, when it has solidified, filed down till a smooth surface is formed flush with the surface of the door. This newly-formed surface is painted in a shade of brown very close to the color of the door. A succession of wood stains are then carefully applied till the match is perfect, at which point a very fine brush is used with a darker wood stain to reproduce the grain in the wood.

12 times someone broke in to a place you shouldn't actually be able to break in to. Insane tree moments. People are amazed by this natural lung supplement.

Video. Dog who had turned to stone is actually a puppy. The dog is underneath a car. It is encrusted in some kind of dermatological material. Now it is on a porch, communicating extreme hostility towards a person who has approached with a leash. Contemplative, free-form guitar music. Now it is wrapped in a blanket, being held down by a person while another person attaches the leash. Now it is in a cage. Now it is at the vet's, has evidently undergone some cleansing treatment and has been given a name. The vet has pronounced the dog's age to be one year. Now it is one month later. Luna is in a garden and wears a scarf around his neck. The scabies has disappeared and Luna has a black and russet coat. Ukelele music. Voiceover. Is this really the same dog? Ally remembers the day Marla, the video maker, brought the dog over for her to foster and how shy and apprehensive she (Luna) was. She (Ally) reports that happily this state of mind (Luna's) lasted less than a day when weighed (she [Ally] assumes) against the availability of snacks and attention. Luna on the bed, challenging the camera holder (Ally?) to a play fight. Dog on the beach, licking a bowl. Piano music, Americana. Ally needs to leave Bali and go to Australia. Janie and Mack step in. Their dog Charlie had been suffering from anxiety issues. Luna and Charlie become inseparable. Janie and Mack's attempt at fostering the dog ends in failure when they decide to adopt her. Luna sitting on Charlie. Luna sitting on the arm of a chair while Janie tries to eat a sandwich. Luna and Janie, swinging in a hammock.

Oh wow! Normally I don't like modern composers, but this one is an exception. Very good music. Very touchy. Thanks for making me acquainted with calories are a lie. Beautiful fusion of choral music with unique film of sea creatures not often seen. Eleven things to know about Jackie Onassis' beauty routine. Your video will begin.

Kitchen. A man slowly lowers a toilet roll into a large pot of water, admonishing the camera-holder to observe the changes to the toilet roll that take place as it is submerged. It expands a little, loses some of its shape. Once the toilet roll is completely submerged, it is lifted out and placed on a tray next to the pot. The man pulls out the cardboard insert, lays the roll on its side and compresses it. Then he takes a power tool, a drill fitted with a hole-saw, and applies it to the toilet roll. The tool fails to make the desired hole in the sodden paper. Comment. I was watching this video and then my neighbour came and we watched it together. He said that this video changed his life and touched his heart. I then went and rented a projector in a big field and all my villagers watched it and it changed their lives too. We all are so grateful. Thank you for this video.

Watch to the end.

It's strange to think of members of the royal family in a regular airport. We picture them getting on private planes on private airstrips, away from all the bothers of ordinary life. But alas, this candid picture shows a young Viscount and Duchess in the departures lounge. The family had been attending the Games and had to stop for a layover on their way back home. Hopefully, they had time to grab an airport snack.

I can't believe I catched this on video. Watch to the end. My husband insists on premium brand—I've been refilling the container with the cheapest stuff I can find.

Installing a standard bannister. Classic male singers by height. Large television studio, elevated shot. Six chefs at their work stations facing a panel of experts. Everybody experiencing high levels of anxiety and creative lighting.

"We've seen enough to reach our decision," says celebrated chef, "and the decision," she takes the time to make eye contact with each contestant, "has therefore been reached. And the decision is," she makes eye contact with three contestants, "a very difficult one," and now the other three, "for us to have reached."

Watch to the end.

While they didn't have to go to a sanctuary, they did have to interact with a large bird of prey at that year's Flower Show. When the eagle flapped its wings, the king immediately pulled a funny face, creating this classic candid photo.

The most forgettable Oscar dresses of all time.

Video. The best trick you will ever sea. A cutlery drawer is approached, opened and a fork taken from it. An echoey quality to the audio is strongly suggestive of an unfurnished house. The forks in the fork compartment of the cutlery tray in the drawer nestle neatly on their sides. The taken fork is held up to the camera as the camera-holder makes his (from the hands) way over to a double light switch on the wall opposite. The two light switches are each about as wide as the fork. The camera-holder puts the back of the fork's prongs to a switch and flicks it. Comment. When I saw this video, I remember the advice my grandfather gave me at my uncle's wedding while we were sitting close to each other next to the music band. The music was so loud I couldn't hear what he said. Four likes.

There are many different types of shoe. Getting my traditional Inuit face tattoo. Did you know that if you do these three things your cat will be really sad? One ad of. Video will begin in. If eight men built ten walls in two hours.

I had to watch this twenty-two times before I saw it. Wait till the end. Is celebrated chef's granddaughter the most beautiful woman alive? Seven times celebrated chef actually liked the food. Shot of celebrated chef leaning on a wire fence. Behind him four or five camels huddle.

"What an amazing group of camels," says celebrated chef.

One of the best quotes I ever heard on this subject is. Five likes. The Amalfi coast. And if I should leave you with anything I should leave you with this. Attend to me now. There are those who will enter your life from time to time who are only meant to be there for a time. They're not meant to stay. They are like rocket boosters. You're the rocket. If you watch a rocket go up into space, the boosters fall off. Don't be afraid when they fall off. They are not bad people. Some people are not equipped to handle altitude. Watch to the end. And if I should leave you with anything I should leave you with this. Attend to me now. There are those who will enter your life from time to time who are only meant to be there for a time. They're not meant to stay. They are like rocket boosters. You're the rocket. If you watch a rocket go up into space, the boosters fall off. Don't be afraid when they fall off. They are not bad people. Some people are not equipped to handle altitude. When you see it. And if I should leave you with anything I should leave you with this. Attend to me now. There are those who will enter your life from time to time who are only meant to be there for a time. They're not meant to stay. They are like rocket boosters. You're the rocket. If you watch a rocket go up into space, the boosters fall off. Don't be afraid when they fall off. They are not bad people. Some people are not equipped to handle altitude. Wait till the end. When you see it you won't be able to unsee it.

Seven likes. Nine likes. Wait for it.

Throughout their lives, the Marchioness always made sure her kids had the chance to play. Many noble children grow up attending stuffy events, flying in private jets, and living in palaces.

Thick steak, big knife, Maillard reaction. Outdoor setting, woodland. Flannel shirt. Very good audio. Husband watches wife with friend after party. Use my comment as a dislike button.

While you would think that the nobility would be gated off from commoners, this isn't exactly true. Noble personages still take time out of their busy schedules to connect with members of the public. This was perfectly captured in the following candid photo, which sees the King hanging out with a couple in the village. "My mother's excitement and the King's amusement is written all over their faces and demonstrated in their wild flailing," the couple's child said.

Eleven likes. Sixteen likes. Watch till the end.

Video. A round cavity is cut out of the thick end of a carrot. A coin is placed in the cavity which is then filled with plaster, smoothed over and painted orange till the carrot looks as though it has not been tampered with. Wait for it. Seventeen likes. No one can deny that the Duke of Bournemouth is an enthusiastic and friendly chap. In this candid picture, he's giving a very wholehearted handshake. A bitter melon is cut in half and hollowed out. The carrot is placed inside and the two halves of the bitter melon glued back together.

Green paint in two shades is applied to conceal the join and replicate the variegation on the surface of the bitter melon. Wait for the moment. When you see it. Seventeen likes. A cavity large enough to accommodate the bitter melon has been cut into a wooden door. Sunflower seeds are poured over the cavity (the door is lying flat) and glue over the sun flower seeds. "But as difficult as it was," name chef clasps hands, "it was a decision we needed to reach and," eye contact, "we now have." Watch till the end. Seventeen likes. Wait for it. "So here," eye contact, "now," eye contact, "is the decision." Seventeen wholesome moments that made us smile.

Wait.

The Robe of Honour

Liam was on his feet in an instant. It took him a couple of seconds to realize he didn't get there from his bed—he'd been asleep, or unconscious, or in some kind of trance, in a chair on the terrace. The phone had dropped from his hand. A lady in a white bathrobe, monogrammed with the hotel initials, stared at him from the next terrace but one. She gave the impression of having been there for a while. It was cool but bright and he could hear traffic—a day he was in no way ready for was in full swing. The pounding at the door was brutal and suggestive of law enforcement. He hoped it was just Khalil. If it *was* Khalil, Khalil was angry—or maybe he had a message from Sherry. A very urgent message. Liam made his way to the door and opened it.

"Good morning!"

Ahmed brushed past and threw the phone store bag on the bed. It bulged.

"There!" he said. "I have to be honest, I wasn't really counting, but that's double or near as damn it, eh . . ."

He blinked.

"I'm awfully sorry, I'm afraid I've forgotten your name." His hands went to his hips. "I knew it a minute ago." The rug that Liam admired seemed to have caught the Moroccan's attention. "I *must* have, to have asked for your room." He shook his head. "Isn't that *extraordinary?*"

"It's Liam."

"Liam! Of course it is! *Of course!* Quite right. Father wants to see you."

The young man went out to the terrace and Liam, with some difficulty, took his eyes away from the bag on the bed and followed him.

"The mayor of Tangier wants to see me?"

White robe lady had retreated. Ahmed was at the terrace railing, one hand in the other behind his back, looking out over the pool area.

"Such an invitation would usually be deeply worrying, actually." He turned. "But in your case, I don't think so. I was in a proper pickle last night and your cash—*you*, sir—got me quite out of it. Father is thrilled. And curious, I dare say." He shook his head again. It seemed to be a habit, as though the young man was constantly revising his most basic assumptions. "So I don't suppose it's anything nefarious. You should probably get changed though?"

"He wants to see me *now*?" Liam pulled at his top. "Anything I put on is just going to look like this," he said.

"Maybe just a splash of water then. You didn't seem too steady on your feet last night but this morning, I have to say, you look considerably worse."

"Those guys kept giving me things." He went to the bathroom.

"Ah yes, they will do that," Ahmed called after him. "Reprobates. I won't sit with them anymore, personally. Good sorts though."

Water felt good on his face but not good enough. He could hardly get a sentence together, let alone think on his feet. Meeting a potentially 'nefarious' mayor whose son did deals with cash in bars sounded very much like meeting a mob boss, an impression bolstered when Ahmed said something or other about Little Italy as Liam dried his hair with a towel. On the other hand, he was hungry and that was a good sign—hunger was human.

"Do you think I could get a pizza slice? I could murder one," he said, back in the room.

"*Pizza?*"

"Yeah. Little Italy, pizza slice. Not that much of a stretch, is it?"

"Oh. No, Italy *Street*, not Little Italy. Rue d'Italie. I suppose it might have been an Italian quarter in the past, but not now. It's really just a street. And it's the way up."

"Up?"

"Daddy's in his office in the Kasbah this morning. I must say, you are amusing. A pizza slice at eight in the morning? In *Africa*? We'll find you something to eat, I dare say."

Liam pulled on a fresh top. "You speak a very particular kind of English, Ahmed, if you don't mind me saying so."

"Not at all. Oxford, you know."

"Ah, an Oxbridge man." Finally, something around here made sense.

"If you like. I went to the polytechnic."

"Honest of you to say so."

"They call it a university now," said Ahmed, "but it's a polytechnic. I think the main thing for father was that my education be an Oxford one *geographically*. He's quite the anglophile. People ask surprisingly few questions, you know. The money would be best left in the safe?"

"There isn't one."

"Really?" A look around the room, a shake of the head. "How *extraordinary*. Well then, we shall just have to take it with us."

Once they'd passed the phone store and reached the next corner, Liam had his first indication that today wasn't going to be any easier to grapple with than yesterday. This is where he expected to find the marketplace he'd walked through with Saeed. It had the same slanted, oval dimensions. But where were the vendors? And much more strikingly, where were the trees? He must have been confused about the route he and his guide had taken. The market would be adjacent or nearby to this—a meticulously manicured little park with a fountain at its centre, bordered on the other side by the old town and dotted with the kind of lofty, lanky palms that reminded him of California and that gave no shade whatsoever. Blue taxis lined up for business to his right and ahead of him, to the left, a tall white arch led to the old town. He followed Ahmed towards it and, just as they passed beneath, he stopped and looked back—there was the cinema with its *art deco* grillwork and painted porch. He turned to ask about it but Ahmed was getting ahead of him.

On the other side of the arch shop owners were raising their shutters and lowering their shades on everything from smartphone cases to spices, kitchenware, books and baskets. Liam caught up with Ahmed as they passed another little park on their left, after which the street sloped upwards. A hole-in-the-wall egg seller had stacked his eggs in seven or eight different size categories and given each its own price. In fact, few of the shops added up to much more than a hole in the wall—to their right, some larger premises were given over to cafés.

The street steepened and the path became steps. Ahmed seemed to struggle to walk as slowly as the somewhat incapacitated Liam, so he would pause every now and then to wait. Liam was way too out of breath to get his question about the marketplace out whenever he caught up. It was a clear morning and the ascent made it seem like that's where they were heading—into the blue sky. It was a nice idea. When they got to the top, Ahmed guided him through a huge old gate in the city walls.

"Nearly there," he said, in the gloom beneath the stone arch. "I say, you don't have any terrible secrets, do you? You're not up to no good in Tangier, is I suppose what I'm getting at."

The question came as a surprise. "Not at all. Why do you ask?"

"Oh, it's all the same to me, you understand. But I should think that if you *were* involved in any kind of villainous carry-on, it would be better not to tell father. Do you see?"

"You've nothing to worry about."

"Very good. He is rather assiduous when it comes to villainy or I shouldn't have mentioned it."

They'd emerged into a little square and stood outside a handsome white building. A huge window, one floor up, was obscured by a fine green lattice and there was something like a little turret, adorned in the same way. It looked like a drawing in a child's book, like a princess should live there. It didn't look anything like an office. A marquee awning over the door was adorned with the words *The Morocco Club*. A doorman stepped aside for them. Liam noted the earpiece.

Upstairs was a fancy restaurant which at this hour of the morning was empty. Ahmed, who seemed to Liam a touch less breezy than before, led him to an inner doorway and through it onto another set of steps that descended into what looked like complete darkness but which, once down and the eyes adjusted, turned out to be upscale murk. If there were any windows down here, they'd been blocked off. The upper walls and ceiling were painted in a shade of red so dark he couldn't easily make them out, and the few light fixtures that hung from the wood panelling below were dimmed. Most of the available light came from behind a small bar where the multicoloured bottles of liquor were backlit. One of the red leather bar stools was occupied by a neat, bespectacled man who didn't look Moroccan—he smiled at Ahmed and greeted him in French.

For the second time in this city, Liam found himself listening to the music of Bill Evans. This time it wasn't a jukebox—someone was playing piano around the corner, in a little salon furnished with short stools in the same red leather, a long zebra-skin sofa, a couple of armchairs and a baby grand. Even in the near darkness, the layers of cigar smoke could be counted. Including the guy at the piano, there were six men in the room. They all wore suits, were pretty much indistinguishable and they all had drinks.

"There he is." The pianist shut the lid and got to his feet. "There's the guy."

He took Liam and held him in a tight and prolonged embrace. When he leaned back, he grinned and patted Liam's cheek, looking him in the eye even though it seemed he was addressing the others.

"There he is. Am I right?"

"Yes, eh," said Liam. "I'm Liam. And you . . . ? He looked from the man to Ahmed.

The broad grin narrowed a little.

"I'm the fucking mayor of Tangier."

Liam offered his hand. The mayor of Tangier looked at it. He and his colleagues laughed as if on meticulously rehearsed cue.

"Shake my hand you fuck," said the mayor. "We already hugged. Come on, sit. Let's talk." He put one hand on Liam's back and indicated a chair. Liam sat. Ahmed didn't.

"I really gotta thank you, Liam," said the mayor. "Because of you, my boy there made a sweet fuckin' deal last night. It was a real pleasure to throw a little extra back. Why the hell do you have it with you?"

"There's no safe in my room," said Liam, clutching the plastic bag.

The mayor looked from Liam to Ahmed and back again, eyes narrowed.

"There's no safe in your room?"

"No."

Ahmed's father shook his head and now Liam could see the family resemblance. "Doesn't make any sense," said his host, and waved the topic away. "So, what brings you to Tangier?"

Mindful of Ahmed's words and unsure of what might constitute villainy, Liam did his best not to skip a beat.

"Same thing that brings me anywhere these days. I have no other pressing appointments."

The ensuing silence lasted as long as it took for it to dawn on Liam it was down to him to fill it.

"I came into to some money recently," he said. "My mother's estate." He shrugged. "I thought I'd travel."

"Really?" The mayor sipped from a glass that might have contained whiskey or rum on ice. "No kids? They grown? No job?"

"No kids. I used to work in insurance. At least for the time being, I don't have to do that any more."

"No girl? Or boy—I don't judge. Seems a shame, you should be wandering around on your own. Hey, you want something? I gotta tell you, you look like absolute shit." All the time the tone was light and the eye-contact rock steady.

"He spent the evening with Bill and Brion and some chum of theirs," said Ahmed.

"The reprobates? Jesus Christ, who knows what they put into him? Vinny, get this guy a gin and tonic, would you? Make it stiff."

The man sitting at the bar went behind it to prepare Liam's drink.

"You don't mind me asking questions do you, Liam? I find you interesting, you know? If you're the kinda guy who shows up in town with a bag of cash, immediately falls in with the son of the city's most senior politician and within twenty-four hours has doubled his money, I'm interested. You're interesting. You know?"

"You do make me sound interesting when you put it like that," said Liam, "but I'm not, really. I suppose I'm a bit of a drifter." His drink arrived and he took a long draught. "But not a bum. I have money so, you know, I don't need to get into any kind of . . ." he glanced at Ahmed, "villainy."

Another silence and Liam supposed it might be his job to fill this one too, but he didn't have anything.

The mayor nodded, eventually. "That's good, Liam. That's good. We're generally speaking against villainy."

The other men in the room laughed as if someone had held up a prompt card.

"Hey, you know what we're gonna do with this guy, Ahmed?"

Ahmed stepped forward. "I don't, eh . . . I'm afraid I don't—"

"We're gonna get him out of these awful clothes." The mayor got to his feet. Liam's flight response was at the ready and he also stood.

"We're gonna buy this guy a suit, is what we're gonna do. A gesture of our appreciation, right guys?" He took Liam's cheeks in his hands. "You'll wear a suit for me, won't you, Liam? I want you looking good out there. You deserve it. And you'll be seen with my boy."

"Sure," said Liam.

"Good," said the mayor. "Now don't let my guys see you wearing these rags again, you hear me? Wear the suit." He retrieved his wallet from a back pocket and pulled some notes from it. "Take him to the baths, son, and buy him a suit."

Liam discovered he had picked up his glass.

"You don't mind if I finish this, do you?"

"I'm busy now," said the mayor, who had returned to the piano. "Take it with you."

Upstairs, Liam downed his drink and they left. It was still a beautiful morning. He followed Ahmed to the end of the square and along a narrow street that took them beneath an arch and into a second cobbled square, larger and lined with buildings that had a once-important look about them. Across the square they passed through another arched gate and walked down into the old town. Tangier was a city of thresholds—there was a gateway around every corner.

"Yes, I think that went rather well, don't you?" said Ahmed. "Of course, he now knows who you are, and that is a bit of a worry. My fault, of course. But I don't believe he's alarmed, so let's just hang on to that."

"Where are we going? A swimming pool?"

"Hammam," said Ahmed. "You'll love it."

"Like a massage?" Liam didn't like the sound of that at all.

"Rather more exacting. Worry not—you'll feel great when it's over."

The upper floors of the houses on either side protruded, leaning in to make a crooked band of the sky, and every few feet the street would bend or dip, or become steps, or split in two, or three, the smells of dust and dung, incense, the sewer, the sea. The white walls were punctured by wood-shuttered windows and punctuated with garishly painted metal grills.

"The Medina," said Ahmed. "This is where I'm supposed to tell you that even I, a native, could get lost in its labyrinth. But it wouldn't be true. It's small and makes a kind of sense, eventually. If you go up you will get to the Kasbah and if you go down you will get to the water." The young man's mood had changed since they'd visited with his father. "But it might be true to say I'd *like* to get lost in here. I'd like that very much."

"Your father's English," said Liam, "if you don't mind me—"

"Please don't. It's mortifying."

"It's just that—"

"He spent a semester in New York as a youth." Ahmed had stopped outside the unpromising doorway of a premises that teetered on the edge of dereliction, where an overhead sign read *El Caudillo*. "Upstate New York, mind you."

"And he's spoken like that ever since?"

"Not really. It's been getting worse."

The tiled entrance hall was at least intact. In it sat a burly, unsmiling, elderly man in the kind of pale blue smock Liam associated with old-school barbers. The man emitted a few grunts in response to Ahmed's instructions without looking at either of them. Ahmed smacked Liam on the back.

"Enjoy! I'll be here when you're done."

"You're not staying?"

"Me? Good *grief*, no. I detest the whole business. Grown men yanking at one's limbs and what have you. No, no. A quick shower for yours truly does the trick. At home. And this particular gentleman," Ahmed lowered his voice, though the attendant showed no indication he understood what was being said, "I find especially unpleasant. Do you know, if I had to listen to one more of his xenophobic rants I think I should probably expire? But it won't matter a bit for you as you won't understand." Doubt shrouded the young man's features. "I say, you don't speak French, do you?"

"No."

"Splendid. Seeing you're a Johnny Foreigner, he'll switch to French in the hopes of getting at you. Worry not—I'll run an errand and be back here waiting when you're finished."

And with that he was gone. The attendant went through the only doorway. Liam went with him. The following forty-five minutes were, by and large, worst-case scenario, beginning with the old man's horrified insistence when Liam emerged from the changing room—non-verbal but crystal clear—that he put his underwear back on, then Liam's horror as the guy also stripped. The gloopy pastes, the stiff brushes, the contortions; the non-stop tirades in French, the hard surfaces—it was all precisely as he had feared. When he returned to the changing room he felt undeniably clean but not in any way good, let alone great—as a matter of fact, and even though the gin had taken the edge off for a minute, things on that front were going south. Ahmed was waiting for him with a special surprise.

"I threw your clothes away," said the princeling, indicating the suit he had carefully laid out on a bench. "This is the new you."

What was it about this town and formal attire? For the first time, and too late, Liam noticed that Ahmed's own dress sense was a little off. The young man wore a suit that was unassuming in almost every respect—but the jacket was a cut-off, the kind Liam had only ever seen on magicians. The jacket on the bench was full-length, double-breasted, navy blue and adorned with six brass buttons. The shirt was a blue-and-white-striped Winchester with plain white collar and cuffs. The light grey trousers had a fine check to them and quite the sheen—but nothing compared to the tasselled moccasins, which were finished to such a gloss they practically glittered.

"One should never make assumptions when it comes to colour splash," said Ahmed. "So I've brought you a choice of socks, handkerchiefs and ties."

Liam nodded. All three were available in powder blue, lemon yellow and red. There was little point in objecting to any of this, since the most powerful man in the city had not only admonished him to wear it but hinted he'd be surveilled. It was a pity—he'd had a mind to get himself one of those linen suits dissolute expats wore in old movies. It would have been perfect for this place, with its tall palms and stout minarets. He'd always wanted one and evidently he wasn't alone—there were a couple of strong candidates on display in a shop window just opposite the hotel.

Now this.

The Bird Cage

Liam and Ahmed continued their descent through the Medina until the ground beneath their feet levelled out. The new shoes were cruel on uneven surfaces and where stiff leather rubbed against the back of Liam's heels. It was different down here—the same narrow asymmetries and the same crazy, crooked street plan, but less of the neighbourhood feel there was higher up. There were many shops, some of them servicing the quotidian—bread and assorted snacks, soft drinks and bottled water—but most of them here to catch the tourist's eye with leather goods, faux silks and hanging rugs. They reached a widening of the lane where it forked, forming a little *place*.

"The souk," said Ahmed. "Would you wait for me here? I have two more errands to run but they won't take long. If you move I'm afraid I won't find you, but if you wait here I'll be back before you know it."

Liam nodded. The middle of the square was taken up with a large bird cage, around six feet tall. The height was presumably to compensate for the necessarily small footprint of the thing—it left just enough room on each side for pedestrians to pass. The occupants were assorted—tiny and not-so-tiny birds in all of the colours. Liam didn't know the first thing about tropical birds but he assumed that some of these would be budgerigars, others parrots, or parakeets—there were three or four different types. One of them was either a cockatiel or a cockatoo—he wasn't sure of the difference. The mesh was dark green and fine and a blanket that sat on top of the cage and that would provide shade in the high afternoon had been pulled back to allow light and air.

Caged birds set him on edge and he was already feeling plenty edgy, but he couldn't look away. His vision hadn't yet cleared up from last night's escapade—the world had a tendency to slip and slide this morning and all of it, everything, was coated in a film swimming with multicoloured, Mandelbrot-ish *muscae volitantes*.

He stepped closer. With the exception of the cockawhatever, there was a lot of motion in there, a lot of flitting and flapping and relocating. Seen through the mesh, a fanning wing was pixelated—the upward and outward sweep of colour, the flexing of the wing feathers, all motion rendered square by square in super-low resolution. Close-up, the plane of green mesh was a screen upon which winged trajectories were inscribed. The more Liam looked the more it seemed to him that this was the object of his vision—to be looked *at*, not through. The idea that there might be something more real than the pixels beyond the pixels became superfluous. He found that he could isolate an area of colour and motion consisting of a number of squares, then limit his attention to a particular quadrant of that area and, having mastered this new smaller world, divide it yet again, till all of his powers of perception were focussed on a single tiny square as it transitioned from red to green to blue, from light to shadow, motion to stillness, something to nothing—conscious in this way of a level of detail he could never have hoped to grasp without the wire to guide the eye.

Or there *were* no birds, after all, no space for them to occupy—just the play of colour across a grid that could be read like text. The pixelated changes were signs, flight and feather signified. Birds were *invoked*. Anything that might be imagined beyond the two dimensions was just that—imaginary. The supposed movement of real flesh through real air, real space—all of this was effect, an effluvium, entirely contingent upon the symbols on the screen. He closed his eyes—screen became page on the vellum of his eyelid. He let it all play out there—highlighter hues populating and repopulating the grid, a neurosynaptic portrait in serrated crescents of yellow, red, green and blue, conjuring the aviary, the ur-bird, the phoenix rendered in a primary-coloured Tetris of plume, bill and blinking eye.

"Are you quite all right?"

Ahmed was there.

"Yes," said Liam.

"I was just saying it would be best if you kept to this spot. I have a couple of errands to run but they won't take a minute. Will you stay here?"

"Yes," said Liam.

Ahmed's eyes narrowed. "Come on," he said. "Errands can wait. There's a shady place I go to. You'll like it."

The Moroccan led the way along another series of slender alleys, beneath another series of shadowy archways, till the Medina came to an end opposite the park on the Rue d'Italie. They crossed and entered, walking upslope to a small copse of trees that reminded Liam of the ones in the marketplace yesterday that hadn't been there the second time. There were only a few of them here and not much in the way of shade, but this wasn't Ahmed's destination—he walked on, down to a street and through a gate in a high white wall on the far side.

"St. Andrew's," said Ahmed.

It was indeed a shady place, and there was very little in it to alert the visitor he was not in Hampshire—one or two of the plant species and a discreetly oriental design to the church's doorway and bell tower. Certainly not the headstones—they seemed all to be placed there in memory of Lord and Lady this, Flight Sergeant, Air Gunner that. They strolled to the far end of the churchyard and sat on a bench.

"And you, Ahmed? Are you all right?"

"Oh yes," said Ahmed, and fell silent. Then he said, "Well no, I'm not sure I am. But don't you worry about me. I am quite sure I soon will be. What do you think of this spot? Do you like it?"

"It was a good call," said Liam. "This," he waved his hand at the graves, "is working for me."

"Give me one minute. I dare say you could use some water."

Ahmed left. Liam wandered among the memorials. Sir William Kirby Green, Walter Burton Harris, Sarah Mathilda Jane, Edith Henrietta, T.A. Hamilton, J.P. Downs, David Herbert, died at his post of malaria fever, arise, shine, thy light is come, Ellie Weir Brown, he loved the Moorish people and was their friend, Amy Nordhoff, Claire de Woievodsky épouse de l'ancien agent diplomatique de Russie au Maroc, Sophia Louisa, John Hector, Alan son of Robert, dearly loved James, George Bush of Warminster, Hooker A. Doolittle. Trying to make out the inscription on a headstone, he didn't notice at first that he was standing on one—it had fallen flat and was mostly covered in pine needles. He bent to wipe some away and read the name *Dean*. Below, *Missed by all* and below that a break in the stone that separated it into two fragments. He wiped away some more pine needles: *and sundry*.

Ahmed returned with a bottle of water each.

"I like to come here," said Ahmed. "Did I say that?"

"Something's up with you. I'm hungry."

"Of *course* you are. Come on."

They exited the churchyard by a different gate and crossed the street, walking gently downhill towards a junction in a busier part of town that Liam recognised. The hotel wouldn't be far from here. As they neared the junction, on the other side of the street, beneath an air-conditioning unit and an old sign advertising Coca-Cola in Arabic, a small ground floor premises announced itself to Liam as the bar from the night before. The facade was of the same granite or faux granite blocks, the grouting capped with alternating black and white ceramic. There was no plaque, but where he'd seen one on the place last night, the wall, if this wasn't his imagination, was faintly discoloured. He crossed over to it and Ahmed followed him. The doorway was shuttered and the shutters were heavily chained.

"Weren't we here last night, Ahmed?"

"No."

The chains were padlocked. Both they and it were rusted over and couldn't have been touched in years.

"This isn't a bar?"

"No. It's nothing. Good guess though—it did use to be a bar."

Ahmed tugged at one of the brass buttons on Liam's sleeve.

"Come on. You look *extraordinarily* unwell."

Liam followed. "Where was I last night, then?"

"Where were any of us last night?" Ahmed replied, pulling Liam along by the elbow. "In the past."

After the junction, a long and steep set of steps descended on the left. Down along the right hand side of the steps were a few hole-in-the-wall establishments—a cobblers, copper goods—and about half way down, a fish counter that Liam could smell before he saw it. Black eels were on display, curled so their teeth bit into their tails. The severed head of a swordfish had been stood upright and surrounded by a mound of whole cuttlefish and squid. Grey prawns were heaped next to a couple of monkfish, one very large and one so small they might have been parent and child, the tooth-ragged mouths in their flat heads agape. Varieties of sea snail separated silver-scaled bream from a pyramid of John Dory, the long spines of their dorsal fins flared. A bucket crawled with crabs and other crustaceans and an adolescent had been assigned to stand by in case anything escaped.

Ahmed ushered him behind the display and around a corner, into a dining-room where they sat at a small table. The room was also small but still much larger than Liam would have expected from the front of the place. It was busy in more than one sense—there were plenty of customers and an abundance of visual clutter. The walls were lined to waist height with the same intricate, blue and white tiling he'd seen everywhere in Tangier and above that shelves sagged beneath clay pots, assorted marine bric-à-brac and stuffed fish. Where any wall at all might have been visible, maps, ropes and nets had been hung.

"Welcome." A waiter placed two clay beakers on the table and walked away.

"House brew," said Ahmed.

Liam took a sip. It was purple, some kind of fruit smoothie. He looked around to see if he could get the waiter's attention.

"I'd really prefer a drink."

"Sorry, old thing. Muslim country and all that. This place is known for this stuff. Aphrodisiac, if you believe that sort of guff. Might put some snap back in your celery."

The waiter was ladling more of the gloop from a large stone jar next to the kitchen hatch.

"You seem dejected," said Ahmed.

Liam tried more juice. It was fine.

"I don't mean to sound ungrateful, Ahmed—you've really been very good to me. But you've taken a man in the throes of quite a harsh comedown to a fresh seafood restaurant that doesn't serve alcohol."

"The food will put you right, trust me."

Liam waved at the waiter and this time he was seen.

"Can I have the menu?" If he was to keep his food down it would have to be carefully navigated.

"No menu," said the waiter who, it seemed to Liam, had a bit of an attitude on him. "No need. There is starter, main course and dessert." He walked away again, and it had a swing to it, like walking away was the part of the job he looked forward to most.

"Well," said Liam, starting to sweat. "We have clarity."

Bowls were placed on the table of a stew consisting of fish and squid in a rich-looking, granular fumet. To Liam's surprise, nose and palate welcomed it—it was hearty and intense but not too intense, and the way it woke his taste buds reassured him that perhaps other cells in his body might at some point be revived—that he was still probably human and that time passed and that he wouldn't always feel like this.

"Anyway," said Ahmed, "there's one particular establishment in town that always serves alcohol and you happen to have befriended it." He took a hip flask from an inside pocket and added a good glug to Liam's beaker.

"Ahmed, you're a miracle." He scanned the room. "They don't mind?"

"Oh, if he sees us, we're out," said Ahmed. "For good, I imagine. But anyway," he topped up his own beaker and pocketed the flask, "fuck it."

"You didn't learn that sort of language at Oxford polytechnic."

Ahmed acknowledged the joke with a not-exactly smile. "So," he said, "what really brings you to Tangier?"

"Like I told your dad—"

"Come on, Liam." Ahmed leaned in. "You don't fool me. You almost certainly didn't fool father. I'm surprised you aren't trussed up in the boot of a car somewhere." He tucked into his stew, speaking through it. "Despite the getup, you walked into the bar last night like you had business. So, what is it? You needn't worry I'll tell father. I manage him *very* carefully."

"The stuff about insurance was true," said Liam. "I'm a sort of investigator. Do you know the Gnaoua House?"

"If you were to pronounce it that way again I'm afraid I should find it impossible to forgive you," said Ahmed, "but yes. What of it?"

"I represent a certain corporate interest in any movements in, out or around that house in the last little while. That's really all it is."

"Corporate interest, eh?" Ahmed poured another measure each, though Liam had only taken a sip. "Well, you'll give her my regards, won't you?"

"I'm back." The waiter had returned with two John Dory fish, splayed and spiced. He didn't make another move till Liam looked at him. "How've you been?"

"Eh, yes," said Liam. "Good."

"Super." The waiter took the empty bowls and left.

"Anyway, none of that matters," said Ahmed. The fish came with crude wooden forks but Liam's companion took to it using his fingers. Liam followed suit. It was delicious—meaty enough but flaky too, and light. The spicing did not overpower the fish's own perfume.

"None of what matters?"

"Anything, actually," said Ahmed. "Only one thing matters to me. And the time has come for me to do something about it." He stopped eating for a moment to make sure Liam was paying attention. "I don't have any right to ask what I'm about to ask of you, Liam, and you have every right to say no—I'd understand completely. But you've walked into my life at precisely the right moment and I've no one else to turn to. I'm afraid I'm rather desperate. Will you help me?"

"Sure . . . of course." Liam instinctively squeezed the bag of cash between his feet. "How much do you think you need? I'm happy to help but I will need to account for—"

"To your corporate interest? You needn't worry about her, she's no bean counter. But that isn't it, anyway. I don't need money. I—" The next word caught in Ahmed's throat and his head went down. He took a couple of breaths as if to speak again but said nothing. Liam thought maybe *he* should.

"How do you know I'm working for—"

"I'm afraid," said Ahmed, looking up, and there really was fear in his face. "I'm afraid . . . I'm afraid I have to tell you that my life is really quite intolerable, Liam, actually."

"Oh?" Liam took a drink.

"*Quite* intolerable." Ahmed stood and went to the washbasin in the corner. When he returned, Liam washed his own hands and, when they were both seated again, the waiter brought two bowls of roasted nuts, cereals and a thick honey.

"So," said Liam. "You know my client."

"Her and her family," said Ahmed. "I haven't seen any of them since I was young, but we still hear from your boss now and then.

She's been asking about her sister and I suppose that's what you're working on, is it? I'm afraid I can't help."

"That's a shame," said Liam, "because I don't know what to do."

"Well don't be downhearted about it, old stick. The house is the right idea. It's just I won't be able to help. I'll be gone."

"Oh?"

The Moroccan was playing with his food. "I imagine you think me a creature of privilege, don't you?" he said. Liam opened his mouth but Ahmed wasn't finished. "A cosseted brat. But it isn't like that. I'm a caged bird." He took a spoonful of honey and nuts and spoke thickly, the consonants sticking to the roof of his mouth. "Tangier is a gilded cage," he said. "I have a lot of money and an endless supply of unearned respect. If you can call it respect. But I'm an adornment to my father, a trinket of his. For display purposes only."

"Why haven't you left?" It was a brutal question and Liam, despite his deteriorating physical condition, managed to produce a blush he could feel.

"I've not been able to leave," said Ahmed, "any more than I've been able to stay." He took another spoonful. "That changes today. Tonight."

They occupied themselves with more of the honey rubble. It was slow going. Liam didn't feel the need to ask questions—it was all coming out anyway.

"I really am a captive," said Ahmed. "I know it probably sounds terribly dramatic and self-pitying but it's true. There will never be any question of my working for anyone apart from father, of being in service to anything or anyone but him. Never any question of going anywhere, of seeing anything of the world unless it's on one of his junkets. I will never make anything of myself because I'm ready-made, by him. And I will never—" The young man appeared to struggle. "I will never . . . that is to say, the choice will never be mine to . . . I'll never be free to . . . to choose . . . the one—"

"Ah," said Liam. "*Now* I think I understand." He grinned, even though Ahmed seemed genuinely upset and grinning was obviously inappropriate. His companion turned the colour of the fruit drink.

"Yes. There is . . . someone special." Ahmed downed what was left in his beaker as if it was a shot. "And nothing will keep us from being together."

"I love a romance," said Liam, welling up all of a sudden. He really did need his bed. "I've always loved a romance. Where do I come in?"

"At the Bab el-Fahs. The white gate. Will you go there tonight? Between eleven and twelve. Someone will be waiting for you."

"Sure, but what—"

"My father has done an excellent job in raising me to believe that flight is a disease. But the cage is the disease, wouldn't you say?"

"I would. But who—"

"Someone special. I'll meet you both just a little afterwards. I need to bring some supplies."

"OK. Where are we—"

"Don't worry, you'll be back in your room in no time, and we'll be free as birds. Now, will you find your way to the hotel from here?"

"I am, yes."

Ahmed laughed. "There are enough hours left in the day for you to get a proper sleep, which I strongly recommend," he said, and shook his head. "I've known you a moment, Liam, and it seems you're my best friend in the world." He got up.

"Tonight, then."

The Bab

The bab was moonlit milkish blue. Such light from a moon not half full. Electric bulbs in the café windows gave off a dirty glow that faltered as it reached the second floors. Above that the moon ruled. Into its anointing light the white gate rose, occupying a space of its own that straddled two time zones—zones in which the time would always be exactly the same but move differently: hours below, eons above. Couples, families, friends and loners strolled the sloping oval. Vendors sold snacks—tiger nuts and popcorn and coconut flesh. The cinema was open. At night the *art deco* detailing of its upper reaches wasn't illuminated—the eye was instead held captive by the brightly lit porch, its garish painted geometries in their splendour. Liam stepped across the street and on to the green, moving in the direction of the bab.

He had slept. At this point, his circadian rhythms were tapping out a difficult jazz, but physically he felt better and one thought was following another in his mind in what seemed to him the normal way. The late springtime evening air was just beginning to pick up the scent of summer—warm grass and pine needles perfumed the shortening nights. He had showered too and didn't smell so bad himself. As much as he'd wanted to get back into the sports gear, he was still in the suit.

It wasn't just that he felt better. He felt good. It had been a while since the last of his migrations and he'd forgotten this sensation—he slowed to the lazy pace of the promenaders, in no hurry to leave it behind. There was a weightlessness to new arrival. It was possible to turn up somewhere in the worst physical condition—dirty, damp and sore from the journey—and nevertheless feel exfoliated, a quickness to the mind and a sharpness to the sight, a levity to the self that made it seem slowly to float through a world which by dint of relativity moved faster and in higher resolution. He hadn't realised how much he'd been missing it—the closest feeling he had to home. It was real but it was fake—too fleeting to count, the lightness. Who knew, after all, how many broken hearts were out here tonight? How many fearful minds? Sick bodies? Bad people? *Terrible* people? It didn't matter to him. It was fresh and it was novel and it fed something in him. Not like food fed. Like meds.

Everything was potent. If eventually a new chapter and its characters would apply the same-old, same-old gravity, at first they'd be what kept him aloft. People, especially, were at their most seductive when he knew as little as possible about them. If nothing ever got beyond the once-upon-a-time, then everyone and everything could be a master storyteller, every moment a cliff-hanger that stayed hung. No pay-offs—that was the pay-off. It was fake but it was real—real enough to punctuate him, this high between the lows. It was the edge of a turned page. To step away from a place was not only to step away from it but also to take *another* step away from everything that went before it. Walking away was everything and everything was walking away. What would he even see now, if he turned around?

Jewel. Home was merely the most recently vacated circumstance. Jewel was, at least, the last place he'd had family. It was Jewel that came to mind on the terrace earlier, sitting in an ostentatiously fluffy bathrobe and watching darkness fall. Not knowing what tonight would entail, he'd kept it to a couple of beers while he killed time, still reeling from the alien, and let the night blot in, the day bleach out, and found comfort in it—that it was the same, it was just the same in California, the same creamy expanse, the velvet graduations, everything from cola to lime on the palette.

Overhead, a blossoming black had given way to something bluer, like the hide of a slug, or a crowberry, the colour we first think of when we think of the night, the cover of the Aladdin book whose clothbound texture he could still feel on the pad of his plump thumb, lightening to the more assertive blue of copper ore, or the beauty spot on the wing of a mallard drake, and warming then into the reds, lilacs and lavenders that invoked the *campanula persicifolia* and a shade lighter still that called to mind the paler spots on the upper wing of a peacock butterfly, or porcelain jasper; a green—the Irish pitcher apple or a ripe colmar pear—but barely there before it yellowed to schorlite calamine, the stamina of honey-suckle, and custard; then custard to caramel and the blush of peach, of larkspur, the orange of Fanta as it used to be and still is in many parts of the developing world, and, low in the sky, deeper, dusty reds that conjured shrubby pimpernel and cinnabar.

The universally recognised backdrop for a bent palm or two. He knew that just above the water on the western horizon would be a bright strip of a colour made of light not language. It was no colour at all and it was all the colours. In Jewel, he'd been in the habit of training his eye there and achieving something like a telephoto effect by honing in on successively smaller areas, till his attention was focused on one more tiny than he would have thought possible. In the very near future the trick would require glasses, but he could still do it. This strip was every colour coming into being and passing away simultaneously and always. He thought he was watching atoms, the dance of atoms where all colour begins and ends. Foundry and funeral. It would crackle, if only he were closer.

The bab was stout enough to throw the cavity beneath its arch into deep shadow. It was like stepping out of one density and into another. Liam was taken by surprise and almost stumbled, pausing to let his eyes adjust. The Medina was depicted in the gate's keyhole frame in various shades of blue—streetlights on that side were too sparse to tame the lunar glow. The same curves framed the Grand Socco when he turned to look behind him, everything there smeared orange or dirty white in the electric light. He was reminded of the city of his birth, the one that should probably have insisted itself on the terrace earlier when his mind reached towards home but didn't. It rarely occurred to him, these days, in that regard—as the place that had birthed him. When it came up in conversation, it was not so much his city as one that existed in fancy: a myth, a fiction, and one on which he had often dined out when the objective had been to render himself interesting.

It would be the city of Wynn's Hotel, F.W. Sweny and the Trinity quad, gulls over Parliament House, summer ciders on the slope at the College Park cricket ground, the winding stair, the metal bridge, blinding bluewhite light where the sun dazzled the quayside facades and night-blue fruit once it had set over Heuston Station, the odd seal in the river up as far as Grattan Bridge, its agility in the water making a chimera of its gracelessness on the rocks at Dalkey, its ugly beauty there, its graceless grace, Burdock's fat chips and smoky cod on the castle green with greasy fingers, a plump arm waving from an upper window on Eccles Street.

All that jazz. But it wasn't his city. By the time he discovered any of it, it was just that—a discovery, and he a young man. He had grown up beyond its margins, his only incursions the odd school trip to the natural history museum—he often thought still of a shockingly huge elk skeleton there—and seasonal visits to Switzers to see Santa Claus.

It was a foreign country. Homeland was the housing development, the building site, the newly laid street lined with nothing much, lit up at night by high lamps leaning in for the sweet release of their piss light, the earth beyond the newest houses pocked and puddled, the edges of each puddle a coastline of scum, a surprising number of puddles hot pink, maybe more Germolene pink, or the colour of the vent converts of a pied woodpecker, dyed by that pink material, that pink powder he could still smell, and it didn't smell pink, or puddles that weren't pink because they weren't any colour at all, they were *all* the colours, every greasy surface a carnival of spectra, and whatever sprang from this would always, and irredeemably, have sprung from this, this adulterated sludge, no matter what was said or told about it, or what it told itself, it came from this, this *waste*, and would all, no matter the concrete tonnage, add up to a mere effluvium.

The light on the Grand Socco was the same light that formatted the ceiling in the spare room of Grandad's cube, his fridge-shaped house out in Tallaght, corrupted by the headlight distortions that slid elongating through it as traffic passed by on the Old Bawn Road, raindrops on the window blurring the lines, clean sheets smelling like fresh laundry smelled before fresh laundry smelled like summer breeze or autumn breeze, or desert breeze or meadow breeze or sea breeze or synthesised fresh laundry, the musty carpet worn and rough, a paraffin heater in the corner with its own aroma, the same light show that would tease a hundred happy endings as he, smaller still, would wait for them to get home, this when it was still the both of them, the same light that was so fatal to the moon's, that meant he hadn't known moonlight then, the moon yes, but not its light—moonlight was for movies, magazines and, more accessibly, the mind. He'd had to wait years, to leave, before he could hold his own hand up and see it bluebathed, or the eyes of another bluesilvered, or silverblue sparkles lapping at his feet on the shore.

Under the bab was a nowhere, a somewhere that somehow lifted the burden of needing to be anywhere. He didn't want to leave, knowing in his bones it would be forever. Of course, everything was forever, every moment a fork in the road—but once in a while the scenery would lean in to the feeling. It wasn't just the Socco and the Medina that were framed—it was memory. It was the moment. As he returned to the latter, he realised he was not alone. A slight, veiled figure had stepped forward to form a silhouette against the Medina and from it came Liam's perfectly pronounced name. Then she turned and ran. Liam ran after her.

She avoided the Rue D'Italie to run a gauntlet of watchmakers and jewellers till it widened into a small square cluttered with stacked café tables. The Petit Socco, the first square Liam had seen on the morning they'd arrived. She was fast, scarves and skirts billowing behind, and Liam was breathless. She turned into a covered alley and its first curve hid her from his view so that he had to pick up the pace. They reached an irregular little widening he would hardly have called a square and she paused for him there. He hadn't seen anyone dressed like her in Tangier—veiled from head to foot, a gossamer-thin gauze over her eyes. But the few veiled women he'd seen around wore black, or brown, or grey. Even in the moonlight—there was no streetlamp here—her robe was clearly one of many colours and many finely-tailored layers. Wherever her story began, it was expensive there.

This was where he'd seen the birdcage. It was covered, not a sound from beneath the blankets. The moment he caught up, she ran—uphill now so that as well as being ahead of him she was also a little above, brilliant white Nike Airs flashing where they kicked her skirts up. He assumed these were the alleys he'd descended with Ahmed, though away from the squares there was little to tell one from another. If they were going up they were probably going to the Kasbah. He wasn't breathing very well. The moon threw a different architecture, made of straight lines, over the higgledy-piggle of the Medina, a superimposition of the empyrean. They came to the cobbled Kasbah square at one end of which was a ruined bab the city authorities had cordoned off with metal fencing. The irregular contours of the derelict arch left a slender gap between the fencing and the masonry. She slipped through and, eventually, so did he.

The dark sea stretched out beneath them, into a distance where Spanish lights blinked on that other shore. The bay of Tangier swept away to the east, a few measly lights tracing its arc from the walls of the old town for a little way where the new city had been plotted, but petering out soon enough to leave the rest of the bay dim till, from a few bulbs on the far headland, its curve could be inferred. Footing was an issue—the ground was uneven, strewn with scree and steep. He followed her along the wall a little way to where Ahmed waited for them. In the moonlight, Liam could just make out a sledge hammer in the Moroccan's hand and a sack at his feet.

"Well met, Liam!" said Ahmed. "Sorry for the theatrics, but my father's men don't bother following me into the Medina. Too much trouble. They just wait for me to come out. So you see, if I'm to disappear, it must be from up here. Bit tricky, wouldn't you say?"

He patted the wall.

"York Castle," he said. "One of those places that accrues more than its fair share of myth and legend. Among other things, this one is purported to be riddled with escape tunnels. Some of them are said to reach as far as the port, you know." He nodded downhill at the wharf. "Problem is, nobody has ever found any tunnels—if they exist, they are a terribly well-kept secret."

He winked. "But not from everybody."

He raised the sledgehammer. Liam flinched but Ahmed swung it at the castle, making an easy hole in flimsy brickwork, then swung again till he'd made a circle. It was a little high so he knocked some more bricks out below it, creating a faithful rendition of the Medina's keyhole arches. "In the sack you'll find a pot of paint and a bag of dust," he said. The girl went through the opening and Ahmed moved towards it. "When we've closed it up, plaster and paint it and throw dust over it to make it look like the rest again."

"Where are you going?" said Liam, looking from the hole in the wall to the port, trying to imagine how many stairs and steps would be required to get them down there.

"You're a thoroughly excellent chap, Liam," said Ahmed, "but I'm not going to tell you that."

He went in. The girl passed him bricks from inside while he and Liam filled the opening. When there was just enough space left for a face to poke through, Ahmed ask Liam to wait. "She's called Hayat. She wants to thank you."

When she came to the opening, the light of the moon fell upon her unveiled face and it became impossible to tell one from the other.

"I will adore you till the day I die," said Liam.

She snorted and smiled with her eyes only, the kind of communication that rare beauties, who learn reserve if they're not to destroy everything in their path, must emit in the tiniest, vicarious gestures.

"You're welcome," said Liam.

His confusion had passed—to mistake her complexion for the surface of the moon would be an obscenity, for the one far exceeded the other in beauty. Each cheek was a garden of countless delights and one of them bore a fruit—a mole—that reminded him of those little specks of stuff, those nuggets he'd been admonished to take such care with, on account of their preciousness and the expense of obtaining them, in Uncle Frank's perfumery. *Ambergris*. Her thick black eyebrows were two strong bows. One shot at heaven and one at his heart, the space between them adorned by a coronet of tiny black hairs she had elected—very shrewdly, in Liam's opinion—not to pluck.

The glance of her jet-black eyes was that of a gazelle, quarry of noblemen. He had seen the graceful movement of her limbs which were like flowering branches. The words that fell from her lips were the headiest musk, the coolest water and the finest wine, causing him to recite the following lines:

> The moon dares not set on her,
> While the light of its rising fills her cheek.
> Witness the stars scurry,
> To conceal themselves in disgrace.
> She shows a tooth,
> Storms lash the Strait.
> At dawn, still drunk,
> She receives the banyan's opprobrium.
> A glimpse of the hem of her robe
> Is food and water for three days.
> The universe, draping itself over her,
> Ingratiates itself.
> She has kompromat on luna,
> Seen sol off with a jig of the hip:
> Mere circles to her enumerated curves.
> I am condemned to love her.
> Why? Because she looked at me.
> What chance did I stand?

She was gone, and Ahmed had returned.

"She's *extraordinary*, isn't she?"

"Truly," said Liam.

"And me? I'm a good sort, would you say?"

Liam was struck by how strongly he had taken to this youth and struck, once again, by the young man's beauty which to all intents and purposes, he now saw, was indistinguishable from Hayat's. The same black brows, eyes blacker still and fit to return a gazelle's gaze. Ahmed's mole was on the other cheek, surrounded by the soft down of youth. Words fell from his lips like precious stones.

"Yes," said Liam.

They shook hands through the hole and then it was just a hole. Liam went about his task as instructed, throwing the dust over his handiwork to make it look the same as the rest. He wouldn't be able to see properly until morning, so he left the sack and hammer in the first skip he came across and went back to the hotel.

When morning came, a note had been pushed under his door.

"The tearooms on Rue de la Liberté. Whenever you wake. There's a bakery next door—bring pastries."

He had wanted to get up to the castle first thing to check on his work. And he bristled at the supplemental instruction. If the bakery was next door she could get cake herself, couldn't she? Or send her lummox. He supposed it might not come easy to someone born into a life like hers to say anything to anyone that wasn't in some way an imperative. The entitlement underlay everything. He got dressed, took a few notes from the cash, stashed the rest in a cupboard under the bathroom sink and made his way to the street in question, which he happened to know because it was the one that led to the Grand Socco.

The bakery was buzzing when he stepped inside even if he was the only customer. The premises had a Soviet austerity to them—the only decorative touch was a portrait of the king, if that's who he was—but the counters that lined the place on three sides were a wonderland of abundance. Platoons of bite-sized pastries packed the displays. Almost every pastry had its own resident bee—the many insects not lucky enough to have secured themselves a piece of real estate were buzzing about, looking for one. Did these people make danger money? Liam made the gestures necessary to secure ten of the little cakes and brought a beeless box of them next door. He had to knock.

The Salon de Thé La Liberté had seen better days. The paintwork on its frontage was so chipped and sun-bleached it was barely there. When a guy opened the door it released a flurry of dust into the dim interior, meaning that hadn't happened for a while. If she was in there she had used another door. Liam was shown to the rear of the space. The stacked tables and upholstered chairs were the kind Liam associated with weddings and conferences in ring road hotels. The carpet was hideous. The choices people made when it came to carpet were a constant source of amazement. They reached an open door and the guy waved Liam through.

He stepped onto a wooden deck beneath a wooden awning and walked across it to lean on a wooden handrail. To stand there was to stand in the canopy of a venerable old fig tree, rooted in the yard a couple of floors below, whose upper branches and oversized leaves threatened to overwhelm the deck and its six tables. At the far end a birdcage hung from a hook, tilted by an errant branch and unoccupied. If there was one thing sadder than a caged bird, it was a birdless cage.

"Good," said his client, "the pastries have arrived." She was sitting at one of the tables. No magazine, nothing to worry the hand. No way of knowing how long she'd been there. Maybe she meditated. "Darius, would you like a pastry?"

It was another instruction. Former Mr Universe was sitting a couple of tables away—Liam moved towards him and opened the box. Darius hardly lowered his newspaper—it was impossible to tell because of the aviators, but a slight tilt of his head suggested he might be looking at the cakes. Nothing else happened for a while.

"Don't let yourself be dazzled by the variety," said the heiress. "Every one of those babies is some combination of pistachio, honey and orange blossom water."

Darius closed the newspaper, put it on the table and reached into the box. His hand hovered.

"I promise you, if you regret your decision you can come back for another one."

The beefcake made his choice and returned to his paper. Liam sat.

"Since we haven't heard from you, I assume there is no progress to report. Apart from the acquisition of a ridiculous suit."

"I should have something today," said Liam. Of all the evasions he had accrued in his short time as a private investigator, it was by far the most effective. But it only worked for a day or so. "If that is your assumption, why did you want to see me?"

She took a pastry. "Would you like some tea?"

"I'd prefer coffee."

She nodded at the guy, who was loitering just inside the doorway.

"Tea, please, Mahmoud. Take a cake, Mr Tead."

Liam took two. It was pleasant to be out and about this early. The air was cooler on his skin than he had felt for some days, and there was an agreeable must to the tree and the damp old wood. The early morning freshness was accentuated as a shower began with fat, sporadic drops. The old fig leaned in, leaves large and lazy, an elephant-ear droop to them, and the raindrops made their music there—a soporific, syncopated patter that, eyes closed as it gathered speed, could be taken for sizzle.

"All right, Ms Zade," he said. The guy came back and put a silver teapot on the table along with two glasses, a bowl of sugar cubes and a bundle of mint sprigs. "Where were we?"

ב

The worst thing I ever did in my life, MY MOTHER SAID TO ME ONE NIGHT WHEN SHE THOUGHT I WAS ASLEEP, the thing that brought home to me, finally, what it is I am, irredeemably and always, and I take no pleasure in telling you this, *chutki*, was you.

A FINGERTIP TRACED THE EMBRACE OF A TILTED CRESCENT MOON ON MY BROW AND SHE WENT ON: You and your sister. We might have named you Death and Destruction. War and Famine. But I allowed your father to choose. It amused me to watch him grasp for some sort of agency, in the way a fairground ride amuses even as it sickens. By the time it came to choosing names this is what he was to me: a once-favoured entertainment I had come to consider garish and nauseating. Unbecoming but, for legal reasons, indispensable.

I was in high spirits—each day of the pregnancy had been an even deeper delight than the day before. Oh, I'd had all the discomforts, but they couldn't touch me. I savoured them. I was counting down not only to your arrival, but to my triumph, to the completion of my project. My own morning sick was an exquisite delicacy because I was tasting it on the way *out*—nearing the end of my struggle, I was unburdened. *Mein kampf*, isn't that it? SHE MADE A DOWNWARD STROKE BESIDE THE MOON. Purveyors of cliché will have it a woman glows when she's with child. Maybe they're right, but that wasn't the reason—I didn't have any visitors so there was no one to tell me as much, and your father is incapable of either forming or parroting such a thought.

No, it was watching him deteriorate. Seeing him become something even less than I'd held him to be. Something close to nothing. My breath catches on the thought of it. I hadn't always been quite convinced I'd come out on top, believe it or not, but here I was—strutting the *albero*, my back to the kill. The now nameless. Meat on the sand—names are for those who exit the ring on foot.

What could have made me agree to it? But of course it's disingenuous of me to ask—I know exactly why I agreed. I knew it instantly. That he should come to me and, in his vanity and in his haste, deliver himself. Put himself on a plate for me. Fate can be a terrible thing, *chutki*, but also quite magical. Thus the death stroke was effortless—it was necessary only to acquiesce. The rest was just waiting for it to dawn on him.

He gave no indication he knew, and yet, wilting beneath my gaze those months—not like a leaf in the sun, to suck up a promised rain, but like fruit in the bowl, past saving—he might have. Not a conscious knowing, perhaps, but why else the sloped shoulders and palms-up submissions, the relinquishing of himself, the almost audible sigh as his spirit gave him up like a bad habit?

I conceived in the last days of summer—the lazy, listless days of high heat, bare feet held over the edge of a hammock to catch the breeze, nobody thinking straight, any notion of the long view lost in the shimmer of empty, endless afternoons. The evenings were empty too, and the mornings, because the compound was empty. All work, by that time, was remote. Gone was the physical company, the bustle, gone were all the busy bees—the place was nothing more than a newly completed luxury home, a sprawling property in which to spread out with one's claustrophobia. One or two unfamiliar faces would show up now and then, briefly, never overnight, and would seem like intruders, such was the quiet otherwise. It was just your father and me, the discrete retreats of cleaners, the meek greetings of gardeners, and the Iranian who by that time had the guest lodge to himself. In the hot haze I had only to think of the delectable now—the future was none of my business. It would take care of itself.

Perfection. As your life ignited, burning in my belly, the world cooled; leaves yellowed, dropped dead to crackle, dry on the track;

the mind, too, cooled and cleared. ANOTHER STROKE, BUT LOWER AND AWAY WITH A SCIMITAR'S CURVE, ITS POINT JUST ABOVE THE BRIDGE OF MY NOSE. Birth and death—these are not distinct moments, *chutki*, separated by something that is neither. To be human is to resound in both, coming into being and passing away simultaneously and always. You were not the only heat source—it was warming, too, to watch the unmistakable cooling that took place between your father and his colleague. An unforeseen and profoundly satisfying consequence.

The Persian was a whisper in the shell of your father's ear. A wily vizier. Had always been. And your father is hardly a demonstrative man. I suspected them both, actually, of developmental retardation. But I saw it. The change. More than once that winter, my husband would raise a hushing hand, something I hadn't seen before in their huddles. Whatever it was that came from those other lips, that had been manna, was become the buzz of an insect, warded off with a wave. How awful that must have been for your father. How wonderful for me. It wasn't as if he could, at will, sprout the brain power he'd want in his colleague's absence. And so he must have felt rather stuck. My terms began to clarify.

Jihad, blitzkrieg, holy crusade. I was the army, the horde. I was the general, the foot soldier, the blessed martyr and yes—why not?—the glittering *torera andaluza*. I was the victor. Can you feel this? HER FINGER NEAR THE SCIMITAR'S TIP. The shape I'm making? The handle, the reservoir, the spout. Lift me up and. Like Aladdin's lamp, no? A little oil pouring from it. Their letters are nicer than ours. You are young—it is futile to describe these pleasures to you. And you are human. What can you know of the jinn? Of our demons and delights? The ecstasy it was to watch your father, like a cheap beach inflatable with a slow puncture, crestfalling his way through his cornflakes—another filthy American habit he'd taken up—each glorious morning of my term. It was his term too, I suppose, though where he was pregnant with his own undoing, I was about to give birth to weaponry. As the first rain of the Spring fell he crept into my presence one afternoon with the second of his proposals—the names.

Sherry. And Doonah. Good God. He did explain his choices but I didn't take it in. Surely it's disrespectful, to name a child such things? But my objection was unimportant, merely aesthetic. I knew very well what your real name was—your real name was the whole point. Never underestimate the importance of names, *chutki*—in the right light and with the wind at their back, they outrank the named. A signature can always be forged and the consequences of the forgery be perfectly, perhaps terribly, real. A signature was the only tangible thing we had, when I come to think of it, on the Persian. Where he'd come from and what he'd done there will always be a mystery to me—none of my investigations revealed anything of consequence, or indeed anything I could verify. In those days the Zade network, already mighty, was an embryo of its current form. If he showed up now, I'd have him—but he came to us then, tracks covered.

What your father knew I cannot say. Since his colleague had never paid me the courtesy of conversation I was delighted to return the favour, and during my pregnancy I refused to have anything to do with him—predictably, my objection to his presence in our home intensified. It was for this reason it was such a joy to note the incubation in your father of a resentment that would come to outweigh his enduring dependency. As to the nature of that dependency, who knows? For all my control, there was this blind spot at the centre of everything. I knew nothing of the man, of his character, his wants, his fears. The one and only personal detail I had was his name on the documents we would need him to sign—ink on a line.

The process was inexorable, irreversible—the Persian, your father's oversized shadow, a barely audible murmur, became shadow itself. Silence itself. A mute element of the lengthening winter night, then a mute element of the shortening winter night. As the day became long again, it pushed him back, kept him at bay in the dark. It was a comfort to me, though not complete—he was still *there*. For your father, it was an amputation. An act of self-harm. A fatal and unforced error. He was bereft, poor thing. By this time, and especially around the eyes, there was something distinctly bovine about him. A dumb animal, bleeding out. So I let him have the names. He could have anything he wanted, as far as I was concerned, as long as it didn't matter. By then, I had my own demand and the leverage to make it.

I had a telescope brought to me from your father's observatory where it and others gathered dust, and set it up at the window of my room in the highest lodge at the edge of the woods, from where I could send it roving over the whole compound. I could see everything. But there was so little to see by then—so little that was human anyway. I could keep tabs on the comings and goings of the staff. Apart from that, activity had died out long since. Once in a while though, as the mornings brightened, I would spot him walking. It was jarring to see him alone when he had always been an appendage to your father. A growth. He had walked down to the water's edge occasionally but now it was every morning, sandals hanging on a hooked finger—a response to his growing isolation. It was through that same telescope that I watched as your father fulfilled my condition.

I made it a quid pro quo at first, or pretended to. I'd grant him two wishes—your names—and he'd grant me the third. But I was just toying. I knew he wouldn't go for it on those terms and indeed he didn't. Even at that time, though I knew the sinking feeling had taken up residence in his gut, he still laboured a little under the delusion that he had some authority left. It was a rhetorical prelude, really, to the twist of my dagger. There is a human state, *chutki*, that I cannot name or adequately describe, but I know it when I see it and I saw it then in him. It comes when something is revealed to us that we know as defeat, but is deeper than defeat because there is no *sense* of revelation. There is no surprise. We know, all at once, that we always knew. That we have been beaten by ourselves. It is a promise, too—if you experience it then you will experience it again. And again. You are an amnesiac, condemned to a lifetime of reminders. Can you feel that? HER FINGERTIP BACK AT MY BROW. I make a page of you. Here I inscribe my milk-filled breasts, bent over, and here my baby-filled belly. And with that, the book is signed.

He sent twelve men. They pulled up in front of the guest lodge in three vehicles. The kind of SUVs whose wheels seemed to touch the ground begrudgingly, the chassis higher than could ever be necessary. Four men got out of each and stood around for an awfully long time. Earpieces and what have you. The scene through the lens was soundless but the nature of the thing was perfectly evident. They were not the kind of men one sends to a conversation. From experience, it would be foolish to assume that a security detail of that size all spoke the same language—some at least were pure muscle, to be flexed by the tendon of non-verbal instruction. It excited me.

TAP TAP TAP. A TRILOGY OF DOTS, A LITTLE PYRAMID, ABOVE THE BABY-FILLED BELLY. A mere month, had passed between conception and the agreement to conceive. Nobody could accuse me of not playing my part—I was well appointed, speaking from a reproductive point of view. Hardly a strange tale: a man proposes to impregnate his wife. Especially such a powerful man. A man looking to build a dynasty. I'd always thought the day would come and I had prepared myself. It was the price, part of the price, the heaviest part, of my ambition. How could it ever have been otherwise? What to do with his progeny, how to feel about you, how to deploy you—that would come later. In that moment I had only to agree, as I'd long known I would.

Four men remained outside that morning, meaning eight went in. Quite the show of respect. All of the windows, in all of the lodges, were treated so that one could look out of them but not in through them. So there was nothing to do but wait like Schrödinger for the cat. Perhaps, despite all appearances, there *was* to be a conversation.

Eight men and the Persian in conference. Perhaps they were assassins. I had not asked for that, though it wouldn't have troubled me. Time passed, and more time. More than once I held my breath, unawares, and only thought to let go of it when I got light-headed. More time. The men outside, who were presumably in touch with their colleagues, gave nothing away. I waited.

But the devil's in the details, isn't that it, *chutki*? Your father had one last surprise up his sleeve. The words tumbled from his mouth too quickly to cohere, but once I'd got the basic idea, I wasn't listening anyway. I was thinking. The lines of connection he drew were so tortuous I haven't bothered committing them to memory. I really couldn't tell you how it all worked. Like most of his great discoveries, the ones that didn't come from me anyway, it probably didn't. What mattered is that he now thought the shared surname meant something. He had found a kinship, centuries old—bless him—between himself and the Persian. And he'd had a notion.

When the men began coming out of the lodge again it was injured first—two hobbling, one holding his head. The rest carried him. He was unconscious but they didn't look like they were taking any chances. In that moment, rather than the usual revulsion, I felt something like respect for him. Most of them were bleeding. It seemed he had given a good account of himself. My domination of your father was so complete by then, and had been for so long, that I had forgotten men even had that quality—that they could, on occasion, stand their ground. I remember it made me miss the illusions about your father I had once been able to sustain. We like the manly in our men, don't we? But I don't know why. It is so easily neutralised—here it was, being carried to the car. Perhaps we admire it in the way we admire a knight charging a windmill. Perhaps we desire it because it makes them manageable. Virility gives us a lever to pull.

A mere month. When he came to me, when he slithered into the bedroom to put it to me, I knew the topic before he opened his mouth. He'd been, by my calculations, building up to it for nine tedious days. The first five in some fug over a decision he had obviously yet to make and the latter four in preamble to telling me about it. The topic I knew—there weren't that many options when it came to serious conversations in a loveless marriage between a megalomanic with a dynasty to build and his fertile mate—if not the twist. Oh, *chutki!* What pleasure! To see him finished. I can't begin to describe it. I had *finished* him, *chutki*. Stepped alongside with a feint (I say feint but the feint was his—he skewered himself), *traje de luces* glittering, put the length of a sword through his shoulders and into his heart. I had never known, and will never know, anything as good as that. It fed something in me. Not a hunger—a sickness. It was bad medicine. So good.

For a man to beg for the sperm of another. To plead its case, the genetic case, so wholeheartedly. The fool was an impotent fool. He couldn't bring himself to say it but here we were. He was basically dead, at that point. Ego death. And of course I saw it instantaneously, the opportunity—it was inexplicable to me that he didn't. I might have investigated that. I was running on dopamine, allowing the pleasure to take me. A habit of mine. I let him plead, then plead a little more, and then I said yes. Inwardly, not the slightest hesitation. You'd like me to tell you I was in torment over it. Nothing of the kind.

Whatever the begrudging regard, I was delighted to see them bundle him into one of the SUVs and drive away. It must have been a squeeze. There went the strategist, the Machiavel, pummelled in a fist fight. Good riddance. The heaviest possible price I could think of to exact on your father, invoiced as you ripened in me. While I still had the wherewithal to lay it all out for him in terms he could understand. He understood all right—I heard the dull clunk when the rusted penny dropped. His name more mine than his. All mine. Is it *coup d'etat* or *fait accompli*? Either way, I had him.

So there it is. It's enough to make you believe in happy endings isn't it, *chutki?* TAP TAP. A SUBSCRIPT UMLAUT AT THE BRIDGE OF MY NOSE.

It really couldn't have worked out any better.

The Torn Veil

WHEN SHE HAD SAID what she had to say, Liam offered up some oily words to lubricate his way out of there and left, taking another couple of pastries. As the front door shut behind him he had to mask his eyes with the hand not carrying them—the sun was already high and it was getting hot. He popped a cake and walked towards the Grand Socco.

All this backstory was taking a toll. He didn't appreciate the interruptions, but it wasn't just that he had things to do, that he was worried about Ahmed, worried that he might have left the tunnel entrance in an easily detectable state—it wasn't just that they were *interruptions*, in other words. Something was off. In the tone, in the voice. He was becoming acquainted with a cast of characters all of whom he found unrelatable and none of whom he could bring himself to like. Why then was he so sure that his problem wasn't with any of that—it was with . . . the perspective. With the storyteller. But which one? He felt sick and ate the last cake in case it might help. By the time he'd finished chewing on it he was standing below the bab, and it hadn't.

It was probably impossible to narrate a story like that, a story set in a world like that—a world populated by people who, if he was honest with himself, he resented from the off for their money, their power and their privilege—without rubbing Liam up the wrong way. Coming from the nose-against-the-window classes, he had carefully curated a set of values and attitudes that made the cold street seem somehow right and the cosy salon somehow wrong. Trustworthy people lived on his side of the glass. Why then, whenever there was a window to press his nose against, did he so dutifully press his nose against it? His progress through the world could be traced in a series of greasy nose prints. While his current associations were more salon than street, that was both precarious and illusory. Someone like Sherry Zade could brush him off like lint from her blazer and at some point certainly would.

The geometric patterns of the cinema's porch had a more homemade look to them in the daylight, the straight lines not quite clinical and the colour fields a little cloudy, brush strokes evident, as if the job of painting them had been given as a project to a school group like the one visiting the mosque across the way, white-smocked and holding hands in pairs.

He knew he could cut along the Rue d'Italie and ascend the steep, stepped Rue de la Kasbah to reach the square and that other bab he'd chased her through. But it would take him past the Morocco Club and he was less eager than ever to bump into the mayor, so he chose the Medina's maze. As long as he kept going up he'd be fine. The shade was welcome, until the lane opened out into a wider sunlit space where another stepped ascent snaked its way up to the geometric tiling of an old fountain and into a cobbled square he thought he recognised. At the other end of it was the blocked-up bab. Somebody had been at the fencing—any gap a human being could squeeze through was gone. Did everybody work at night here? He pulled at the metal grid but it was well secured. He pulled at it on the other side but the armed security guard of a nearby building was taking an interest and it felt like time to walk away.

At first he went in the direction of the Morocco Club, looking for other openings in the Kasbah walls. There weren't any, and before he got as far as the mayor's place he turned back, leaving the main square again by another gate, in search of a different approach. But rather than hug the ramparts, the street descended away from them, and he couldn't find a left that didn't also meander downwards towards the souk. By the time he finally hit level ground he'd been back up twice to double-check and had spent a couple of hours exploring any number of dead ends. The shoes still hurt.

It occurred to him that if he'd been able to see the marina from up there then he'd able to see up there from the marina. He didn't want to ask anyone for directions—he'd learned that, to people around here, a foreigner with questions was a business opportunity. So it took him a long, hot time, but eventually he found himself among the café terraces of the Petit Socco. From there he could walk downhill and through that first arch, along the stone ramp and onto the sea-level street that divided the old town from the harbour. He'd sweated through the suit jacket—passers-by were looking at him twice.

On the other side of the street, he turned to look up at the city walls. It took him a second to spot the bab. If the shoes had been unsuitable on the cobbled streets of the Medina then they would be weapons here, clambering over the shale, rock terraces and scrub. There was no kiosk where he could pick up a bottle of water and anyway he'd forgotten to bring any cash. He crossed again, climbing over one of the concrete blocks that enclosed the slope. Straight away, he had to cut along sideways to avoid an impassable swathe of thorny bushes. When he found a gap it wasn't much of one—he squeezed through, ripping a leg of the trousers. At least it would give him an excuse to change clothes. This was going to take some time. The gradient dictated the use of hands as well as feet and he slipped frequently.

Now and then he looked up—he couldn't do it without stopping to straighten cautiously. He could no longer see the bab. It was hidden by the curve of the higher slope. He'd have to judge as best he could which direction to climb in and find it when he got up there. The pernicious effects of his footwear had penetrated as far as his upper back and neck. His mouth was dust and his brain pulsed against his cranium. The top of his head, when he dared to take one hand away from the task at hand, was unnaturally hot to the touch. By the time any of this was the case he was committed—getting back down wasn't any more appealing than going up. When he'd been at it for too long, and the top was still too far away, he heard a commotion behind him. Turning himself around into a sitting position to take a look, he was shocked to see how much altitude he'd gained.

The strait was bright and Spain hazy, a crooked brown strip between the blues of sea and sky. The marina was a toy box of sails and motor boats and beyond the curve of the headland the more business-like harbour bobbed with chubby trawlers, decked with nets—whether it was the time of day or the day of the week, nobody was fishing. The commotion was a couple of guys, shouting as they crossed the street from the port. They were yelling and one of them waved in Liam's direction. He squinted. They were uniformed. They were uniformed and they were armed and one of them was waving. He waved back, using one hand to keep himself steady on the shale. That didn't seem to appease them. If anything the yelling got louder, and one of the men raised a very substantial-looking weapon, pointing it directly at Liam and removing all doubt as to the cause of their concern. He put both hands up.

The immediate, uncontrolled slide was painful and alarmingly long, but by the time he managed to put a brake on it he was still a way above the men. The seat of his trousers was ripped and he'd left a trail of airborne dust in his wake, which now that he'd come to a stop enveloped him. As it dissipated it became clear the sudden nature of his movement towards them had rattled the two men, and equally clear that the one with the automatic weapon had neither the experience nor the training to have been entrusted with it. He still had it pointed at Liam but his eye flicked compulsively from his target to the weapon itself, either to make sure his finger was in the right place or the safety was on. Or off. The other man, seeing Liam get to his feet on the gentler incline of the lower slope, gestured angrily for him to continue his descent. They had both lowered themselves behind one of the concrete blocks for cover, and now stood.

Liam approached them slowly, hands raised, and got as close as he could till the thorn bushes were all that separated them. These guys were young—they looked like their nerves might get the better of them. At least the one with the gun had lowered it. The other one was still yelling, gesturing for Liam to cut through the brush. *Let's treat this as a new beginning.* His mother's words to him when they'd agreed he'd go to California. Although 'agreed' was a euphemism—the alternatives had been stark. He tried to communicate that there was no gap in the bushes but the guy kept beckoning and it was clear from the rising tone of his voice that he was losing patience. *Only let's be honest with each other this time.* And of course she'd meant that *he* should be honest with *her.* The reciprocal would never have occurred. He pushed into the bushes, holding them apart as best he could with his hands. But it was impossible. *It's important, Liam. No more stories.*

When he emerged, one of his trouser legs was to all intents and purposes a hula skirt. The other was gone. The exposed leg was bleeding copiously. She'd been referring to what she called *his* stories of course, confident whenever she did that she invoked memories of the clinic. Of Düssel. Her own numberless delusions, the layered heaps of them, the great mounds of them, were bedrock to her. All he had to do now was climb over a concrete block and he'd be in custody. Maybe that was a good thing. He wondered why in such a moment he'd think of his mother. But he knew, really. He'd just been dragged down this hill by the weight in his stomach—by the old, sinking feeling that was never going to leave him alone. That he was in trouble. That he'd fucked up again.

"Hotel." He patted his breast pocket to connote an imaginary passport.

It turned out, now that he was down here, these guys didn't really want to know. Their own breast pockets were embroidered with the same emblem that adorned the port entrance across the street. They were security, not police. Port police at best.

"Hotel," he repeated, pointing in what he thought might be the direction of the Minzah. "Passport."

They waved him off. Their nerves appeared to have settled somewhat—they were smirking. Liam headed towards the Medina. Not to be asked for documents was by any measure a lucky break but he didn't feel lucky—as he made his way under the arch in the city wall that old feeling stayed with him. Things were unravelling. If a day started like this then how bad might it get? Street boys were pointing and laughing. Then he remembered the day had actually started rather well, with pastries in the company of a billionaire. That had been hours ago. It was the late afternoon, arguably also the late afternoon of his life. Mid-afternoon, to be charitable. Whereabouts he was in the day really depended on how late he got to stay up. On whether he'd be allowed to watch *Knots Landing* or be sent to bed when the opening credits came on. This feeling in his gut. It always came back and every time it died down for a minute he would kid himself it wouldn't. This was him—a poor student marching from the headmaster's office to his mother's door and back again. That's how it would be until the mechanism wound down for good.

The square in the Kasbah. It would be sensible to go to the hotel first and get changed, but a grim determination had set in. As hopelessly out of control as everything seemed, one thing wasn't—he'd closed up that tunnel with his own hands, so he must be able to find it. He must. Getting up the slope was still probably his best bet, but the cover of darkness was still hours away. He stumbled through the souk till the lane became a series of stairs. At the top of the first, the way split and a little wooden sign, in the shape of an arrow pointing to the right, had the words *Gnaoua House* carved in to it. After a few metres there it was.

It wasn't easy to get a good look in the narrow lane, but the Gnaoua House was not a house. It consisted of a short terrace of houses that presumably had been knocked through inside. They were, like every other house around here, whitewashed and rather plain in style, but noticeably well kept and there was an elegance, a certain expense, to the finish. A giant bougainvillea draped the first place. In his current condition, Liam felt like a character from the paperback Sherry had given him: a street beggar agape, looking up in awe at the opulence of a sultan's palace. Except he wasn't in awe.

Now that he had finally found the house he was merely confused. And hungry. And tired, and very thirsty. There was no way he could present himself.

At his back, a narrow set of ascending steps squeezed between two buildings. At the top of them a door was open and over it hung a sign: Café Baba. Liam went up and stood in the doorway. Inside, a young man sat reading his smartphone at a coffee station.

"Excuse me," said Liam and the young man looked up, then down at what had been Liam's trousers, then up again. "I don't have any money," said Liam.

"OK," said the youth. He had an amiable look about him, one of those man-bun, shaved-back-and-side haircuts; big, widely spaced, kind eyes and a carefully tended goatee. He wore a couple of gold chains around his neck over a white t-shirt and a branded mauve tracksuit with striped sleeves that Liam assumed, probably on the basis of racism, was counterfeit. "Fuck off then."

"I'm thirsty," said Liam. "I do have money. More cash than I know what to do with, actually. But it's in my room. In the Hotel Minzah? I could bring some later."

In looking him up and down a second time, the youth managed to invoke complete contempt but retain some of the amiability.

"*You're* staying in the Minzah?"

"Maybe just a glass of tap water?"

The guy put his phone down. Liam felt the sigh he then emitted was overdone.

"Sit around the corner, will you? You're cluttering up the doorway."

Liam went around a corner to a row of tables on a glazed gallery where the view was of the Gnaoua House's various rooftops. He took a seat. Patio furniture was set out on the roof across the way but there was little sign it had been used recently. No towels, no personal debris. The guy came over with a frosted litre bottle of sparkling mineral water and a glass with a slice of lemon.

"I appreciate this," said Liam. "What's your name?"

"Let's not do that. This isn't the part where you tell the enraptured young native your fascinating tale. We get guys like you in here on a daily basis. Tangier seems to attract you. It's exhausting." He walked away. "I just opened up. Feel free to take your time but you'll have to leave if I get customers."

Liam downed a glass of water. Apart from the nearest, the other rooftops and the courtyards they overlooked were hidden from view by plants, or screens of wooden lattice, or architecture. Now that he came to think of it, the few items of furniture on view were almost certainly for decorative purposes only—the super-rich were unlikely to do their sunbathing just outside the window of a rather seedy café.

"Here. You look like you need this more than I do." The youth had come over and put a nugget of hashish on the table.

"Oh," Liam shook his head. "It's OK. I don't have anything to smoke it with." Also, it was a terrible idea.

"Eat it then."

The guy went back to the coffee station and his social media. Even when Liam had bitten the nugget in two, the halves were large and hard to swallow. He took his time with the water. The Gnaoua House wasn't giving him anything so he leaned his head against the window pane and let his gaze fall on more distant things. Birds over the most distant houses and a sky warming towards the horizon. He wasn't aware of having closing his eyes until he opened them—the window pane was jet black and all he could see when he removed his head from it was his own reflection. Fluorescent strips lit the café.

"You should probably be getting back to your five-star hotel," said the young man, who was sitting at the next table, flanked by a couple of similarly-dressed youths, "and all that cash."

Liam struggled to get his eyes fully open and focussed. "I'm sorry," he said. "I don't know what happened."

"Not at all. We've been having a lovely time. You are amusing."

Liam's table, and the floor around his feet, were strewn with a large number of scrunched paper balls. From the number of empty beer bottles on youths' table, their bleary eyes and the state of the ashtray, they'd been at it a while.

"I trust you had a points system going."

"I hope you don't think us too cruel. We did check your breathing periodically."

Liam stood, aching in every particular. "I'll bring some money in the morning."

"I don't open tomorrow, but there's a letterbox. The hash is on the house, and the water. Since I offered them freely it wouldn't be fair to charge you. It'll be two hundred euros for the slice of lemon. Couple of grand in dirham, give or take."

Outside, a flimsy mist made halos around the street lamps. It must have been late—the alley that led to the Kasbah was deserted. Maybe the darkness would help up there too—he could have a go at that fencing unobserved. Except that, when he entered the square it wasn't dark at all. He stopped dead. The fencing was gone. A row of uplights set into the ground made a veil of the revealed archway, a curtain of light. When he remembered himself, set one foot in front of the other and stepped through, nothing was the same.

The uneven, unreliable, unstable ground that he'd had to deal with before was gone, in its place a concrete walkway that was not merely smooth but brushed to a polish, skirted by glass panels topped with stainless steel handrails. Ground lights all around lit up the mist. To his left, a young couple were the last customers on the terrace of a café. To his right—where the girl had led him—a narrower walkway sloped gently downhill along the wall. He followed it till he thought he might have reached the place where Ahmed had been waiting. The view from here was of a city transformed—a city he'd never laid eyes on before. There must have been a power cut the previous night, because where Tangier had petered out not far from the city walls, tonight it lined the entire bay. The whole crescent was alight with high rise buildings, international chain hotels, a sparkling corniche—a large and modern city he'd had no idea existed.

There was no lamp here to illuminate the patch of wall that interested him. Rocks and stones still littered the slope on the other side of the glass barrier. He climbed over, chose the largest one he could handle, dropped it onto the path and climbed back. With considerable difficulty and both hands he raised it above his head and launched it at the castle wall. The rock went clean through, almost noiselessly, as if through tissue.

"There he is."

Sometimes things worked out. An indescribable sense of relief came over Liam—not just an idea but a physical feeling, a warmth. A release. Today might have been the most ridiculous of his life. And the bar was high. But he wasn't mad. He had found the tunnel. Into his triumph, however, intruded the ruined orgasm of a familiar voice.

"There's the guy."

The Subterranean Chamber

"After you."

Turning to see the mayor and his five associates—the men from the Morocco Club—on the walkway behind him, Liam had been instructed to continue opening up the hole in the wall. Once there was a gap large enough to step through, one of the men gestured to him to do so. Inside, a short passageway led to the top of a dark staircase. The staircase was long, descending several stories, and was enclosed all around by the rock, the ceiling low enough that he felt the need to duck his head a little. So he was all the more amazed when, on reaching the bottom, he found himself not at the beginning of a tunnel but in a hall so splendid it instantly banished any thought of the trouble he was in.

The wall on his left was punctuated by three groined arches giving onto three niches, half-concealed behind fine gauze curtains, the upper reaches of each arch decorated with *muqarna* and trimmed with intricate *zellig* schema in shades of green that dropped down at the sides to fill the wall from waist height to the floor, as if cool water were filling a benevolent *sabil*. In the first niche had been laid out green cushions on the floor and a low table was set with plates and bowls from Tamegroute. In the second niche a similar low table had on it plates and bowls of silver and the green cushions all around were trimmed with silver thread. In the third niche the table was heaped with bowls and plates of gold and the silken green cushions were embroidered in gold. The place had the appearance of having been prepared for feasting though there was not a crumb of food in sight.

The wall on his right was hung along its whole length in rich green fabrics and the largest of them was a silken tapestry on which was depicted a sultan in repose with his concubine, and so skilfully were embroidered the details of their dress and of the bed linens, his beard and her eyebrow, that they may as well have been present, to turn at any moment and speak to him. At the foot of the bed another woman, veiled, sat on the floor, eavesdropping on their discourse. In the middle of the hall a great stone basin of water surrounded a fountain whose glittering melody filled the cavernous space and overhead on all sides ran a gallery enclosed in the finest polished *mashrabiya*. Liam's wonderment at the things he had seen was as nothing compared with the wonder he felt at *being able to see them*, since there were no lamps lit and no candles. Instead, over the fountain and in the four corners of the hall, light fell in vertical shafts from skylights so deeply recessed they could only be seen when he placed himself directly below, as though, when he had breached the castle wall, it had been noon and not the middle of the night. The mayor and his men now entered the hall and, as they spread out and looked around in amazement, Liam made his way to the far wall and through a narrow doorway.

A second hall was laid out just like the first. On his left, the first of three niches was half-revealed by curtains of fine gauze. Its upper reaches were decorated with intricate *muqarna* and its arch was trimmed with *zellig* in shades of red, that dropped down on either side to fill the wall from waist height to the floor, as wine poured into a cup. Red cushions had been spread out there around a low table, upon which cups and goblets of simple *beldi* design, made from the red clay of Marrakech, had been set.

In the second niche was also a low table with cushions all around and on it cups and goblets of crystal glass, red as rubies, and Liam thought bunches of red grapes had also been placed there till he noticed their sparkle and understood they too were made of crystal glass. In the third niche, a low table was similarly set with red goblets and cups that sparkled. Instead of grapes, the table was strewn with red gems of all shapes and sizes, and Liam knew not only that these were rubies, but that the cups had been cut from them. Around this third table, red cushions had been scattered on the floor. The place had been prepared for revelry though there was not a drop of wine in sight.

The opposite wall was hung in rich fabrics along its length, the largest of which was a silken tapestry upon which was again depicted the sultan, risen from his bed, a red rising sun in the window, the sultan naked, scimitar in hand, the concubine at his feet, red silk woven into the blade her blood, so skilfully it was as though it might at any moment drip upon her body over whom he stood. Sacks were lined up along the wall's length, rolled open and bulging, spilling over onto the floor with all kinds and sizes of red jewel—with red coral and rhodolite garnets, rubellite and jasper, andesine, spinel, rubies and pyrope, red diamonds and mulberry topaz. The cavernous space was filled with the music of a fountain that stood at its centre, its water pouring into a great stone basin. Overhead there was none of the *mashrabiya* that had adorned the first hall—the walls here were bare and smooth and carved from the rum sandstone of Petra. Liam's wonderment at the things he had seen was as nothing when compared to his wonder *that he could see anything at all*, since there were no lamps or candles lit and no admittance of daylight as there had been in the first hall. This second chamber was illumined only because jewels sparkle and crystal glints—but with the light of what source? The mayor and his men entered the red hall and as they spread out, gazing around in astonishment, Liam walked towards the far wall and through a narrow doorway there.

He found himself in complete darkness. Unlike the other two halls, this one was carpeted—he could feel the give beneath his feet. But though he could see nothing, another sense was almost overwhelmed. There was jasmine in the air, fluctuating in intensity as if on a breeze, though the air was quite still. A few steps in, its heavy scent gave way to lilac. A few more and it was honeysuckle. Then jasmine again, then rose—an orchestra of scent filled his nostrils and somewhere too the music of another fountain. Lavender, sweet alyssum and hyacinth. There was a new acoustic. He clapped and said his own name out loud, but no echo came. When he took another step, something brushed against his cheek, startling him—he crouched and put a hand to the floor to steady himself.

He saw from there, silhouetted in the doorway, the mayor and his men come in. One by one, they lit up their smartphones to see what could be seen. Seven torches held aloft by seven hands, their diffuse beams directed by seven minds and seven curiosities. The effect was giddying but nothing like as surprising as what the light revealed. When he found himself directly in one of their beams, Liam looked down and confirmed what, in truth, his hand had already told him. There was no carpet—he'd been walking on grass. And this was no hall. It was a garden. He stood and walked on, pausing now and then when the others focussed their phones on something close to them, and proceeding when once again a beam of light crossed his path and he could see where he was going. He had been right about all of the scents he'd picked up—the flowers from which they wafted lay all about in beds, and in addition to them were planted anemones, privet flowers, narcissus and eglantine, violets and chamomile. The flower beds were arranged around the trunks of dozens of fruit trees—sultani orange and Uthmani quince, lemon and citron, lime and kumquat, Omani peach and Syrian apple, fig, cherry trees and almond trees, plum, pear, pecan and pomegranate. Every tree was in full blossom, white or pink, yet each heaved, at one and the same time, with ripe fruit.

Liam's wonderment at what he had seen was as nothing when compared with his wonder that he could name these things, he who knew nothing of Tamegroute or Uthman, who could tell not one precious jewel from another, who had never eaten a pomegranate, laid eyes on a pecan tree or set foot in Damascus. From a little orange tree, pruned as the others were with the precision of topiary, little white blossoms fell like snowflakes—slow and stately as though in a vacuum. Everything in the place had been exquisitely tended though there was no gardener in sight, nor any sign of one—no buckets or baskets, no gloves or clippers. Nor was it a fountain that played the water music—a stream made its winding way among the trees, spotted with Damascene nenuphars. In a place where it narrowed, Liam stepped over and walked on, coming eventually to a wall and in it a doorway which he stepped through.

The first thing to cross Liam's mind in this new darkness was that maybe the hash was wearing off a little. He'd broken out in a sweat that was cold and clammy and his mouth was watering uncontrollably all of a sudden. His head throbbed and the rhythm of it syncopated the ringing in his ears. Despite the unpleasantness of these sensations they came as a relief, hinting at a return to some kind of sobriety. And despite the uninformative blackness there was already something a little more welcoming, a little less intimidating, about whatever this place was. He couldn't put his finger on it. Maybe it was scale—when he clapped his hands the very slight echo told him he was somewhere smaller than before. But it was more than that. He took a few cautious steps in this direction, then that—there was nothing here to brush against his skin and startle him. The place was inviting, somehow, even in complete darkness—it occurred to him now that the two halls had been more like monuments than places for the living. Hospitality was commemorated there, not enacted. They were replicas. Mausolea. Even the orchard had been a simulacrum of life. Life without energy. Growth without vigour.

Here was different. Human. Surrounded by plates and cups or walking through an orchard full of ripe fruit, Liam hadn't noticed his hunger once and yet here, in this different darkness, he salivated. His gut yawned. Of course it might just be the munchies but he didn't think so. There was something about this place that *wanted* him to eat. Something that spoke of others cooking and eating here, of real habitation. Just as these observations threatened to dissipate in another wave of narcotic distraction, a single word came to mind that both confirmed and mocked them—*kitchen*. And just as it dawned on Liam he'd been struggling, intellectually, to formulate the concept of *kitchen*, his knee knocked against something that, when he reached down to explore it, provided further confirmation. His hand found some old coals on a hearth. He picked a piece and it felt grounding in his hand, helped him calm down. He bounced it in his palm while his other hand traced the edge of the fireplace to where he could step around it and make his way gingerly on till he encountered the far wall. With his fingertips to it, he walked first one way and then the other—there was no doorway.

He could hear the approach of the mayor's men and waited for them, swallowing saliva continuously. They came in one by one, phones lit, so that blue-white light was once again directed in frantic, patternless disarray. The mayor was last. It was difficult to make sense of the room since none of them would keep their phone still but it was immediately apparent that the place was indeed smaller, low-ceilinged and unadorned, the bare stone stained by smoke from a fire. There were no features of any kind anywhere in the room, except for the hearth that stood between Liam and the men. One by one they stilled their phones, directing their light at it and when they did this Liam vomited, pressed his back to the wall, sank to the floor, threw himself forward on all fours and vomited again. The second or so that he'd seen the phone torches play across the coals had been plenty—plenty to see what had burned there and plenty to know that what he'd been fondling in his hand was carbonised bone. He heaved again, producing only bile, and sat against the wall taking deep breaths.

They lay side by side, turned towards one another, what had been her head nestled in the hollow of what had been his neck. Liam might have said they were burned beyond all recognition but he recognised them just fine. Each of the four hands had been held in another. Their attitude could have been one of loving repose but for the torment that showed in the postures—they'd been brave, and held on while they burned. The immolation was incomplete—below the knees the flesh remained, scorched and scarred by the fabric that had melted into it. Her white trainers were almost pristine. Nobody said anything. The men held their phones steady, out of respect, and not quite directly at Ahmed and Hayat, so the two could be clearly seen but were spared the full glare of torch light. Eventually, the mayor stepped up to the platform.

"This was my son."

Nobody moved a muscle. Liam didn't dare speak. The hashish was certainly unhelpful but there wouldn't have been any way to make sense out of any if this even without it. A certain amount of disorientation might be for the best. He was probably going to die in here with the two lovers—it was no time for sobriety. The mayor walked around to the other side of the platform.

"And this was my daughter." He spat in Hayat's ashes. "But she had the devil in her."

His men spread out, sweeping every corner of the room with light, looking for whatever they were looking for, finding nothing. One by one, the torches found their way back to the couple—there was nothing else to shine their light upon. When the mayor finally turned towards Liam, he was loading bullets into the barrel of a revolver Liam couldn't identify because he didn't know the first thing about guns.

"You knew about this."

He didn't look at Liam, concentrating instead on his task. Liam really wished someone *would* look at him—it might help him feel real. It might be harder to kill a person if he was real. When the barrel was full the mayor spun and closed it, and now he did look at Liam and now Liam wished he hadn't.

"You knew about this?"

Liam shook his head. He could still taste the bile. His eyes were watering and it probably looked like he was crying and he probably was.

"Gone all quiet," said the mayor. "You have to tell me *something*, Liam."

Liam was aware that the phones, all of them, were now pointed his way, so that the mayor and the platform were silhouetted against a constellation of lights.

"Tell me, Liam." He came closer, cocked the gun and put it to Liam's forehead.

"I don't . . ." Liam kept his eyes down. The feel of the barrel on his skin was yet another first in a day of them. ". . . tell you *what*?"

"Something," said the mayor, shrugging. There wasn't a trace of hurry in his voice. "Tell me anything."

"I don't . . ." Liam wanted to shake his head but he didn't want to nudge the gun. ". . . I don't . . ."

The mayor sighed. "Look at me, Liam." And when Liam didn't— "*Look* at me, Liam. Tell me something. I might let you live."

Liam looked up. It was like the mayor had a half dozen haloes. And all of a sudden Sherry was there, and the colossus, and the latter of course could probably have taken all of these guys, armed or not, but he wasn't making a move.

"You'll excuse my summoning you here in such a hurry, Ms Zade," the mayor was saying. "I hope my man was courteous. You'll understand my distress, I suppose? I think Liam here belongs to you."

He turned back to Liam. The Brooklyn accent was gone.

"Look where I am. Look at my children." He lowered the gun. "Look at them."

Liam looked.

"Do you think you could surprise me, Liam? Do you think I am a man you could surprise? I would like that, you know." Something non-specifically unhinged in his tone redirected Liam's eyes to the trigger finger. "Try."

All Liam could do was shake his head again. His occasionally smart mouth was clamped shut.

"If you can amaze me," said the mayor, putting the gun back to Liam's head. "If you can tell me something that amazes me, I will let you live."

The Curious Tale

You knock off by the thermometer, not the clock. Into the forties it's dangerous. There was a time you'd have thought that about the thirties. Cool water from the styrofoam flask. The skin doesn't burn here so easily. It's off season and you're not growing, not cultivating. You're tearing down and ripping out. Left to it, to do what's needed, you knock off when it would be dangerous to keep going. At this point you are an old hand. You are trusted. Remnant fruits rot on the sandy soil, the odour not disagreeable, something of the ferment to it, precursor to the bacchanal. The promise of other states, of revelries. Herald of elsewheres. Hedone's bad breath. Effluvium. A not disagreeable rot.

Later when the mercury dips you'll be back but for now there's nothing for it but retreat. Tractor trailer through the compound. Boots off, shower. Room to yourself since the Boer. The tired. The good tired. Feet that tingle. Bones that buzz. Guiltless. Asleep more or less immediately. Earned purity. Clean fatigue. Your daily prostration. Window blind is a rag and blocks no light. The ferocity of the window's glare makes it difficult to believe you were out there a minute ago and functioning. But that was another life. This is the after, the before, the bardo. The desert cooler grumbling. Will be tested the people. Asleep. The Vatican.

You are in the Vatican. You are being chased through it. Imperative you not be caught. You run desperately, breathlessly. The reason it is imperative you not be caught is unspecified, but imperative. Compels you forward. You take any twist and turn that presents itself in your effort to evade your pursuer. Every time you do, the way you take is narrower, until your shoulders brush against the walls on both sides. It is the Vatican without being recognisably the Vatican. It is the Vatican by Giorgio de Chirico, actually. The place has those same diagonals, that same claustrophobic perspective, shadows that throw a different architecture, made of straight lines, over the arches and arcades. Your mind takes a moment to appreciate the surprising choice of visual palette. You've nothing against de Chirico's work but you've never particularly admired it.

But it is certainly the Vatican. You know this in two ways. The first way is dream knowledge. You know because you know. This is your dream and truth here, if not elsewhere, is an act of will. Fact not so much established as incanted. The second reason is that when you muster the nerve to turn your head and catch a glimpse, he who chases you through the Vatican proves, as you have suspected all along he would, to be none other than its Sovereign, the *Successor principis apostolorum*, his Holiness the Pope, in full ceremonial regalia. Your mind takes another moment to appreciate the skill and fluidity of movement necessary to hound you so relentlessly in a mitre. This second mind moment reassures—although you are quite convinced you must not under any circumstances be caught, and although the Vicar of Jesus Christ has craggy, troll-like features and snappy, grabby hands and although he is closing in on you and you can feel his breath on your neck, and although the walls are also closing in and your capture is inevitable, there is editorial distance. You know you are dreaming and you know you will wake. You need only run until you do.

A part of you, then, is reserved—it observes the part of you that is dreaming. It appreciates the silliness. What could be more natural, after all, than religious content in a dream dreamt here? If anything it might be critiqued for lack of originality. Your dream is hackneyed. That your imagination would resort to such low fruit in its limitless dream state. In the Negev will be tested. That part can sit back, as it were, and wait for the crescendo, the climax, the culminating moment, the Pope's claw-like hands on your shoulders, his teeth in the nape of your neck, hungry lips pulling at the soft down there, your immobilisation, an imminent doom that must happen without you because now is when you wake up. Except you don't wake up. You leave your body.

You've heard about this sort of thing but it's a first for you. Though there is no sense at all of 'you', not physically. 'You' are simply a point of view, at your feet, looking at the room from where the door is, and opposite the little window, equidistant between the room's two single beds. The physical you is on the bed to the left. Your vantage point is low enough that you can't see you very well, just a human-sized disturbance in the sheet you throw over yourself because even in the heat and solitude you, unlike the Boer, don't feel comfortable naked. The sheet is dirty white and almost everything else in the room is either white or off-white. From your point of view the tableau is framed rather beautifully and composed with a becoming symmetry. Again, that editorial distance. There is a timeless quality to this new palette in that nothing, not even your work shorts or boots, both beige and both discarded on the floor, introduces the plastic colour splash that comes with modernity. There is nothing of the right-angled gleam of technology—no TV or radio, no coffee maker, no clock. The white space is bright, brilliant and Biblical. The latter descriptor comes to mind perhaps—but whose?—because the perspective here recalls da Vinci's *The Last Supper*, albeit transposed onto a humbler scene.

Even before you see it something hums, vibrates. Everything is pregnant with everything else. A potential energy speaks of imminent release. Of a big bang whose approach would, if you had any, have you hold your breath. The picture develops. In the corner opposite your sleeping body, in that part of the cube where the upper walls meet and form an apex with the ceiling that never fails to remind you, wherever you are and whichever the ceiling, of David Bomberg's *Lyons Café*, you notice. The whiteness there is not the whiteness of wall but that of backlit cloud. The difference at first is so faint as to be barely noticeable and there is no trace of a border, but you know you are looking at sky. It isn't a breach in the masonry so much as a complete collapse, there in the upper corner, of the idea that there is any distinction to be made between masonry and that-which-is-not-masonry. You see it all on the atomic level, to use a particular parlance, and here the atomic level is not some profundity to be conceptualized by a theoretician but is right there on and below the surface at all times, not resonating behind or beyond reality but reality resonating.

It same-ifies everything. To use another parlance, one that vindicates your previous use of *palette*, it's as if it's all paint, all made of the same stuff, brush strokes on canvas, and of course now the brush has come to mind so does the painter. If it is painted then someone painted it. If it is made then someone made it. You return to God, a return unaccompanied by angels' horns or hierarchies, or cloudburst or blinding light but rather heralded and without fanfare in the *made-ness* of things, things in this particular case being the bed and the sheet and your body beneath it, scattered clothes on the floor, the grumbling desert cooler, the window, the dirty white walls and the sky in the upper reaches of one side of the room, opposite the bed and the sleeping you. It is all, somehow, composed. In the artifice, the artist—brush strokes governed by the law of the brush, governed in turn by the hand of its holder. Nothing has qualities that nothing else has. It's all paint.

Perhaps if you paid close attention to the sleeper you would observe the rise and fall of his breath. But you don't. The composition is skilful—the eye is drawn to the sky. You note that the area, opposite your sleeping body and where the upper walls meet the ceiling, or would if the upper walls and ceiling were not in fact the heavens, is growing. And you know in that moment that this is how this new meta-layer of the dream state will perform *its* crescendo. There is no sound but perhaps the blinding light will come after all, the cloudburst, the orders of angels. There is no sound but there is no silence. Silence is not the word to describe a state of affairs that hums with Brownian potential, crackles with electric promise.

The sky white variegates. Contour is given to cloud formation. The picture develops. But actually it is impossible to tell what is developing here—the looked at or the looker. Or, more precisely, the look. The intensity of attention given—but whose?—is proportionate to the paintwork's lysergic motion. Is the mover the attended to, or the attentive, or the attention? Whatever, the scene moves. Clouds roil and threaten to part, and your mind takes a moment to appreciate the fluidity of the movement and, since you are editorializing again, you wonder if here you are perhaps brushing up against the possibility of cliché, this being precisely the sort of visual anyone who ever saw a Jesus movie might associate with divine revelation. Impending epiphany. Cue voice of Charlton Heston. You are reminded of the Sistine Chapel, but by Thomas Cole, or Lemoyne's heavenly tumble in the salon d'Hercule. The intensification of the light. But light isn't the word. You can feel it thrum you, a physical sensation. You are pregnant with the light and it with you. This the crescendo then. The real awakening to follow the false. The moment will no doubt be the final breach of cloud by glorious, overwhelming light. It will have to happen without you because. You leave. The room. The room is left. You don't go anywhere. You are not awake. At least, you are not awake in the room, on the bed. You know only this.

You are not asleep.

The is you universe.

Where no is.

All.

Later, you will turn to language, to description, to try to recuperate some of this. To apply *something* to something like memory. To keep it. But it will be gone. As it happens . . . no, not happens. It doesn't happen. It isn't happening. Happening is time bound. This isn't that. This is. You are. Are . . . somewhere. Nowhere? Everywhere. None of those work. Everywhere is perhaps the closest. And always. And ever, and ever.

All.

The scale. You will want, later, to call it *interplanetary*. The idea that you might once have been contained by something called a room. What does once mean? What is room, remind me? Remind you? In the throes of imminent ego death—let's call this that—and in the face of your complete obliteration, you are shown, from somewhere, a mercy. A mercy comes from. Or mercies rather. The first is the visual. The interplanetary. The suns. Space. You are allowed this visual palette on condition, you suspect, you neither take it for real nor mistake it for a dream. As soon as you do it slips away, to return and once again test you. The people of. It is a metaphor, a mercy. An introductory offer to ease the transition. The second is another. An anchor. A purchase in the whereamiwhatamiwhoamihowamiwhen. Space is not the word. Void is not the word. In the beginning. Size is not a quality. No previous metrics. What does seem important is that none of this is, in any sense, abstract. This is not an abstraction. An abstraction would imply the interaction of your understanding with the to-be-understood. But this is no interaction. You are not toying with the idea of eternity. With the idea of infinity. It isn't an idea. It is here. Here it is—it is you.

But actually. The metaphor. The visual palette. Actually, it slips away, in any case. No matter. It is offered, the metaphor. A mercy. But it cannot stick. Slips and slides lysergically. For implicit is the notion of retinal array. An interaction between the eye and the to-be-seen. But you do not *see* any of this. It is not available to sight. *You* are not *here*. Here is you.

All.

You is not the word. The beginning was the. Here is not the word. Place is inconceivable. A metaphor at best. All previous metrics. You is not the word. Is is not the word. A metaphor. There are no eyes. There is no tongue. Mouth. There are no limbs. Flesh. There is no body. Nobody. No previous metrics. Previous is not the word.

An exception. One organ. A caveat. An introductory measure perhaps, to ease the transition. A metaphor but not an abstraction. It is physical and you know it because, from the instant you were brought here. Here is not. That there must be ear. You are ear. Ear is you. You is not. Because right there at it. At the shell of an ear. That must be you. The voice.

Begins mid-flow like a frequency dialled. Began. You will later recall. That it was not addressing you, in as much as there was a you. You, in as much as there was a you, were eavesdropping. A broadcast. From the beginning of time. If there is such a place. From an inconceivable distance. Right in the shell of your. You will attempt to describe it and fail. It isn't male it isn't female. It is only human if human is a much, much broader category than you have imagined. It does not pause between sounds. Circular breathing if breathing at all. If breathing is an element here. It isn't loud but every other sound, the possibility of any other sound, is drowned out. Many years later when you try upscale noise-cancelling headphones for the first time the suck, the vacuum, will remind you of your arrival in this state. There is only the voice. You are all ear. It could be machine but only if machine is human. It is only language if language is a much, much broader category than you have imagined.

Not Latin. You would recognise Latin from the desultory scraps of it that populate your Catholic education. It isn't Hebrew. There is none of the performative *Chet* of modern Hebrew at any rate. It isn't Greek. You don't think. These observations all come later of course. Here there is no observer and nothing to be observed. You will home in on the possibility of Aramaic. Was that it? You have never heard Aramaic. As good a guess. Ur language? But it is only language at all if language is a much, much broader category than you have imagined. It is not for you. You have not been. Are not. Chosen. You *over* hear this. As if on a radio tuning. If it was for you, if it was for anyone. If it addressed anyone or anything. It would be a message. But there is no message. Unless message is a much

much. Nothing is revealed. A voice but not a telling. Not speaking not singing not chanting not male not female. Incanting. Reciting. A stitching. Weaving the world. Making. Songing the all. Is this? A single. Unending. Eternal. In the beginning. Is that what you? What it all? The spent breath of a word spoken. Mere effluvium. The whole wide word.

All.

Enough. The voice not friendly not hostile not human not inhuman. Is enough. Too much. The end. There must still be a scant remnant of you because it is afraid, and even more so when you sit up on the bed and rub your eyes open. In the room which you know to consist of two beds, a grumbling desert cooler, a window, some discarded clothes and surfaces either white, dirty white or off white, you see nothing. Only void. Eyes wide and blinking. No return. Void and voice. And now the fear. As you over hear you over are. A rising within. Another crescendo. But you know you cannot wake to escape its climax because you *are* awake. Rub your eyes feel the sheet on your skin smell the boots on the floor. So the culmination here will be real. The end of you. Ego death let's call this that. You might name it Death or Destruction. The voice the most beautiful voice the most beautiful sound. Will finish you. There must still be a scant remainder of you because it does not want to end and as you open up and out into the voice into the ever and ever you clench. You want to make a no. You don't want to be finished. To be nothing. You don't want to be everything.

And in this moment in this reaching for yourself this attempted recovery this holding on Rilke's dictum that *beauty is nothing but the beginning of terror* moves in and will never leave you. The voice. Overhearing you over are. You too much are. Too much and rising are. You burst open. You unfold into that-which-is-not-you. The beginning, the end, the all. You want more than anything you've ever wanted to say no. You are not ready to be gone. But you can't get a no out. The absurdity of the notion that you could emit anything.

You are receiver. All ear. Or perhaps it would be more accurate, more faithful, to say you are the emitted. Mere effluvium. Whatever, like a child immobilised by night terror you sit on the bed and fail to make your no. Fail to scream. Fail to hold. And then despite your failure you are shown mercy. The room wavers into sight. The voice cuts out. The desert cooler grumbles.

You will wonder what it was in the days that follow. You who have taken difficult-to-justify quantities of LSD, who have known psychosis, who will later acquaint yourself with salvia, psilocybin, mescaline, ketamine, any number of synthetic psychedelics and not find anything in any of them that you could map it against. You will tell one person about it and you will use the word God. You will want it back. You will wait for it when you sleep but it will not come. You know though it takes you a time to admit it to yourself that it will never come. The loss you feel. The grief for it whatever it was. Whatever it was it was it. It was capital i it. State of grace. Complete attunement. Total. The beginning, the end. All. State of total grace. And you blew it off. You blew it like a little bitch.

And that's all, folks.

All.

"Bunchabaloney," said the mayor, the Brooklyn accent reasserting itself. He took the revolver away from Liam's temple, but only to cock the hammer and replace it. "Tough luck."

"Wait."

Sherry stepped forward. "Look at me, Liam."

The instruction was welcome, since all eyes were on him and he had no idea what to do. A tiny part of him—the one tiny part that wasn't scared to death—no longer really gave a shit what happened next.

"Tell him what you told me," she was saying. He blinked at her.

"In the car."

He shook his head and felt the barrel against it.

"In the car?"

"Yes," said Sherry. "In the Jeep."

It took him a second. To the best of his knowledge he had never been in a car with this woman, never mind the specificity of model. Then the penny dropped. She was setting him up, buying him a second—making the mayor think something better was coming. All she meant was tell him something better. Something real.

The Fall From Grace

My mother was a freshly minted—in more than one sense, or so I thought—widow by the time I landed in California. Her husband, Mike, had timed his exit poorly. He had always seemed nice enough but this final act was inconsiderate—naturally the event went straight to the top of my mother's priority list, just at a time when I was going to need her to focus. She'd no doubt be up to her eyeballs in legalities—mostly to do with their house and their one rental—that would take up much of her time and energy. She was getting on and didn't necessarily have much of either, and she wasn't an obvious choice for estate management. It was Mike who had always taken care of business. I wondered, from the other side of the ocean, about the characters who would be hovering around her at a time like that—the lawyers and whatever friends she'd lean on for advice. Maybe they were great. Maybe not. It was unsettling.

It was that uncomfortable feeling, along with a certain confluence of circumstances in my own affairs, that prompted my offer to go out there. I'm not exactly an obvious choice for estate management either but two heads would be better than one, I supposed, and, in as much as she consented to pay for the ticket, she may have agreed. It was my preference, for reasons relating to the above-mentioned confluence, that we make arrangements for my trip very quickly and, picking up on the note of self-interest, my mother subjected me to one of her pep talks—the kind she was so good at, that concerned themselves with growth and healing and such, even as they twisted the blade.

"Let's treat this as a new beginning." Her suggestion balanced on said blade's edge between supplication and imperative. I too was capable of detecting self-interest in expressions of apparent benevolence. "Only let's be honest with each other this time." Her modus was to propose honesty but never pursue the matter. Real honesty didn't attract her one little bit. "It's important, Liam. No more stories." I never knew what to say to that one. Apart from my clothes, some books and a laptop, I didn't have anything apart from stories. They fulfilled the function of an army knife for me—they solved problems. They addressed problems anyway. Of course, to my mother, I was the problem. In fairness, I'd given her reasons. Those were where the conversation inevitably went—unsaid perhaps but alluded to in every turgid silence.

"You should be married. You could have kids in college by now."

My mother never asked me if I was gay and that made me angry. I'm not gay but it made me angry that she never asked. It was assumed my marital status represented a straightforward failure on my part. A deficit. If she had asked me if I was gay, *that* probably would have made me angry and in many ways that's a good description of how our relationship shuffled along, swapping out one umbrage for another as we went. I would have wrapped this particular chat up the same way I always did—by saying something mollifying to bring the exchange to an end and make the necessary arrangements.

I'd been out there before but this would be the first extended stay and I had plenty of time on the plane to think about how I'd occupy myself. The tourist visa was for three months but I'd see about that. I wouldn't be the first Irishman to forget to leave. I'd brought my copy of *The Long Goodbye* for the flight and an idea was born. I can't explain how I convinced myself such a thing was possible, but I did. Wasn't America where any fool could do any thing? Why not me? My mother's friend Carol had offered to pick me up from LAX but I didn't want to spend two humiliating hours in a car with an eighty-year-old for whom those would be hours three and four. She'd probably try to get me to drive and I would have to explain that I couldn't. Thinking back on it, the notion that anybody who knew my mother would be unaware of my inability to drive was pure delusion. Nevertheless, I managed to make my own way from the airport to the

Greyhound station and get a bus to San Diego, where Carol picked me up for a much shorter ride. The stilted, forced conversations I'd have with her friends when my mother wasn't around were always perfect little testaments to the conversations they would have when I wasn't.

When we pulled up outside the house I got my first surprise—it wasn't the house I knew. The place I'd been to was a sprawling cliffside property in Jewel, swimming pool and everything, but when Carol left the freeway—her driving oscillated between a nervous crawl and erratic, high-speed careering—it was eastbound and into the maze of developments around the UTC campus. I knew they'd been letting out a one-bedroom rental there, for 'pocket change' as Mike had put it. Carol gestured for me to get out of the car and I was only too pleased to comply but she made no move to get out herself, explaining it would be for the best if she "left us to it". I got my case from the back seat and went where she pointed, around the side of a two-story building to the front door of a ground level unit, wondering what *it* might be. When the door opened I got my second surprise, and the conversation that ensued was a series of further surprises. I happen to like surprises, but I didn't like any of these surprises.

When she was done—it was basically a monologue, punctuated here and there by my expletives—my mother sat wringing her hands. Gloria, the carer who had introduced herself at the front door, was in the kitchen making us coffee. It was late morning and through the sliding door to the backyard a little lime tree was specked with sunlight. Hummingbirds fought over the garish sugar water feeder that hung from it. The place was sparsely furnished. When Gloria showed me in I hadn't believed my mother could live there. Now I knew she didn't. Gloria was from Uruguay—another thing I now knew. And apparently Mike was not the strait-laced Regional Strategic Account Manager everyone had taken him for. She went through it all as best she could. Her efforts to relay things in the right order meant it took a while—she'd frequently find herself at one of memory's dead ends and have to double back. Not that it really matters how you enumerate a mess. It was all gone. The people who come to take away ill-gotten money had come and taken the money away. And the house.

More shocking than the financial irregularities was the other woman. Mike had never given me the impression he had it in him. This woman must have had something on him because she'd been cleaning him out for years, apparently, by the time the law caught up and took care of the rest.

"None of it matters as much as you'd think," my mother said, finally. "Look at me."

The biggest surprise of all was Mum. I hadn't laid eyes on her in a long time—she didn't do computers. On the phone, for a number of years now, I'd thought she'd been putting on the little old lady act—the expressions of helplessness, the plaintive tones, the declarations of growing confusion from someone who seemed perfectly lucid to me and who simply didn't care to acknowledge or remember things she didn't like, the go-to litanies of healthcare episodes recounted in admittedly jumbled detail. Her favourite word was *procedure*. I had just taken it all as some kind of hobby. Time spent at the tables, betting with her preferred currency—guilt.

But the woman sitting opposite me in the tiny living room was also tiny, and hunched, and very frail. A walking-frame stood by the armchair and she hadn't even tried to stand when I came in. She'd been living at the home for some weeks already. The funding for that—to my immense relief—was intact. This was a person I was accustomed to feeling an unnamed, unshakable anger towards—but how could I be angry with her now? I found myself instead feeling rage on her behalf, that at her time of life she would have to put up with this man's sordid failure to be a man. That she was so obviously ashamed of *his* shortcomings while he had escaped the consequences of them forever. She actually apologised to me that there wouldn't be an inheritance. I had to wonder what I was doing here, although for once I was glad to be. She answered the question before I asked it.

"Maybe you can make something happen. I don't know. I think you need to be here."

I told her I'd come see her each day.

"Don't make promises you won't keep. Come see me at the weekends. And don't worry about this weekend, it's already Thursday."

It was Friday. She left me with her bank card, gave me the pin, and told me to use it sparingly, that I'd be OK for a few months but the money would dry up pretty quickly. I could stay in the rental but it was on the market so I was to keep it tidy and I'd have to find somewhere else as soon as I could. When I got a smartphone I was to let the home have my number. It was excruciating to watch Gloria help her to her feet. When we hugged I flinched, perhaps because I thought I might break her, or perhaps because I felt on a cellular level I didn't deserve to be held, or maybe it was that older part of myself that I cannot reach or influence and from where I felt that she didn't.

I'd seen a mall a little way from the rental so I walked there and got some cash and a phone, then charged it in a coffee place while I ate a bagel. The food tasted like sludge in my mouth, like sodden wood shavings, I was so disgusted by what I'd heard today and so sad at what I'd seen. What had happened to her had happened to me. Back in the unit I took a shower and it felt spiritual—a true cleansing as it dawned on me what my mother had done for me here. She was right—I could make something happen, given a little time and space. It wasn't like I had options.

Later that evening I took a bus downtown and went looking for life. I'm terrible at meeting people in most situations but bars I can do, so ninety minutes after stepping into my first, I found myself in another, on easy terms with a table of people I'd decided were friends of mine and a couple of grams of coke in my pocket. I had chosen the first bar wisely—an Irish Pub called Milligan's, or Mulligan's, or Brannigan's or O'Hoolihan's. One of those, maybe. Somewhere outside Beijing, I have no doubt, there is a sleek, anonymous-looking facility that churns out whiskey mirrors, pitchforks, old cash registers, things made of straw, broken buckets and the like to line the walls of Irish bars the world over. If you walk into a place in Ireland and it looks anything like that, you turn around. But elsewhere, Irish bars have their uses—they tend to attract expats, and not just Irish, and my best bet for early contacts would be people who were newish around here themselves. Those types were usually also looking for connections.

Now we were in some place called the Casbah, or rather in and out of it, dividing our time between half-hearted attention paid to the band, the toilets for lines and beneath an overpass outside for smokes. My friends were five in number—Billy, who'd sold me the coke, a Canadian called Lance, a girl who I'll get back to in a minute, somebody, and somebody else. The conversation was exquisitely superficial. We all said the kinds of things you say to people you may or may not see again and none of us, of course, were really listening. When the band finished I found myself on the hard part of a bucket seat in the back of a crammed car, on our way out to somewhere called Birdland and an afterparty there.

You want to know something funny? The girl I mentioned? She features heavily in this tale. She made quite the impression. There was a charisma to her. A head turner. Not just because she was beautiful (she was) but because . . . I don't know. Charisma. But I do know that I couldn't tell you her name. Given the way things turned out, I suppose I blocked it. She *told* me her name of course, and I must have used it a hundred times after that, but it's gone. None of this was very long ago. Sometimes I think it was Donna and then other times I think it might have been Adele.

Let's call her Grace. The afterparty was in a bungalow at the top of a long set of steps that draped the steep slope of its garden crookedly, like a rope thrown down to the gate at street level. The bungalow itself barely qualified as a liveable domestic space and may have been squatted. By first light and the opening of the corner store nearby, Grace and I left together, although because ecstasy had been taken the reasons for our doing so were ambiguous. We picked up some beers and went back to hers, which wasn't far away. Her roommate had left for work already so we had the place to ourselves. Nothing of a sexual nature transpired while we drank the beers and smoked a few joints, but when I made to leave she made a footstool of my lap and asked me why, which felt good. I told her I'd only just moved into the rental and I needed to get groceries. The truth is I just wanted to be where I could get horizontal and shut my brain down.

"It's the weekend," she said through a yawn. "You have all week to do that."

I think I would have been mesmerised by her even without the empathogens. She was younger than me but at all times had the upper hand. I guessed she had the upper hand with every one. She danced between and around people with such poise I couldn't imagine anything throwing her off balance. That in itself should have been an alarm bell. But her melody was drowning out all the bells. Not even a thick Black Country accent could ruin the music. And she was so tuned into me it was like she'd known me forever, since before I knew me. I didn't want to acknowledge the feeling but she might have been my sister. It seems like the following should not be a difficult lesson to learn, but it's taken me a lifetime and I'm not there yet: if it doesn't seem real, it almost certainly isn't.

We slept as we were. It seemed Grace was surfing the sofa—it was a one-bedroom apartment and the days that followed weren't spent there. From the moment we woke her notifications never stopped. That night and the next, and the next, there were multiple places to be and any number of people wanting Grace to be there. Most of them were men and all of them without exception were both disgusted to see me and obliged to treat me well. I was Grace's guy. They didn't know the terms and neither did I but there I was. Bars and clubs, house parties, private raves—she danced her enchanting dance and I followed, slipstreaming her charmed wake. I had to spend money to keep up, of course, but it could have been worse—she was the habitual recipient of generous tribute, pill and powder both, and I was given treats. And the next night, and the next. Nothing of a sexual nature transpired. On the other hand, we had slotted into each other with such dumbfounding ease. Or rather, I into her. I was her guy all right, but it wouldn't have dawned on me to claim her for my own. She was nobody's. It was inconceivable that she could ever be anybody's. That was another alarm bell, but ours was a world of PA systems and floor fillers and I didn't hear it. I had lost my wits. I've always had that problem with women. Her hair was cropped short to reveal a forehead like the new moon. On the few occasions we saw the sun—out on Mission Beach or on the terrace at the Coronado—her face put it to shame. She was a shining star that soared through the heavens. Her breasts were perfect morsels of succulent fat floating in a bowl of milk soup. I saw them once. Her eyes were like those of a deer, her neck a cake fit for a king, and words fell from her sugared lips in elegant couplets as in the sonnets of the great poets.

"N,N-Dimethyl-5-hydroxytryptamine," she whispered in my ear one morning, in one of the motel rooms I'd booked to keep her from going away. She was dividing a crystalline powder into two lines with the help of a pocket-sized, high precision digital scale. "Have some."

"Will it last long?" I was conscious of having missed my first visit to the home, and I hadn't left my number with anyone so I might also have missed enquiries on the rental. An uneasiness was beginning to encroach. Grace knew everyone but didn't know anyone *really* and knowing her hadn't been as useful as I'd thought in terms of establishing other leads. I'd stayed away from my own place because I didn't want that world to have anything to do with this one. That should probably have been another bell.

"It'll be over in no time," she said.

To enquire further would be to subject myself to her mockery so I snorted the N,N-Dimethyl-5-hydroxytryptamine and shortly afterwards duration ceased to be a concern. I wouldn't have been able to distinguish over in no time from world without end amen. I is not the word. What could distinguish between what and what? What is not the word. Word is not the. Grace. Is that the?

By the time there was an I again and word *was* the word, she was gone. The bank card was also gone and I knew that I'd told her the number. Since it wasn't my card I had no way of checking the account but of course she'd have tried to clean it out. She hadn't reckoned on my mother—there would certainly be a low daily limit and there was no way the card was activated for online use. Still, I knew I'd never see her again. I'd been good for some accommodation and snacks and she was done with me. It was a very long walk back to the rental. Most of the day. When I arrived, there was a note pinned to the door from Carol. It was just the phone number of the home, which I already had. After a long, hot shower I felt worse. When the home picked up, they told me they'd been trying to reach me and that I needed to come pick up my mother's effects. I said sure. It wasn't till I hung up that I realised what that meant.

I'd left some cash in the house so at least I didn't have to walk. When the taxi pulled up outside the home there was still some colour in the sky but street lamps were turning on—the prettiest time of day, I've always thought. The foyer was glass-enclosed and filled with loungers for the residents. As I walked up the driveway more than one of them got up and made themselves scarce. One lady was remonstrating with a couple of staff who tried to guide her somewhere. Her eyes kept flicking to me and I didn't know if that was self-consciousness, that a stranger was witness to the scene, or if I had something to with it. She'd been successfully ushered away when I pushed the door open.

"Step through, Mr Tead."

I hadn't even reached reception but the lady there was on her feet and indicating an office door to the side of it.

"It's Tĕad . . . thanks."

She didn't reply or look at me. The encounter in her office was terse and brief. I was not invited to sit as I signed for a small cardboard box. She told me that some larger items would also need to be collected. Then she asked me to leave.

"But what about . . . the arrangements? Don't you need me to—"

"Mrs Martinez took care of the arrangements." That was Carol. "Since we couldn't reach you. She can tell you where the grave is."

"The *grave*?" I couldn't make this make sense. "That's too quick. It wasn't much more than a week . . . what day is it?"

"It's Sunday." She was staring. "It's over three weeks since you met with your mother."

"Three weeks?" My mouth may have been hanging open. "Are you sure?"

She took a deep breath before answering. "We're intensely aware of the timeline, Mr Tead. Your mother spent her last days asking for you. We counted." She had already guided me out of the office and was walking me to the front door. Gloria passed by and I swear she was holding her breath.

"Did she say anything . . ." The woman held the door as I stepped outside. "Did she say what she . . ."

"She was quite specific, actually, yes." She hadn't looked directly at me once but as she closed the door on me she did. "She said she needed you to forgive her."

And that's all. I don't have a better ending. That's my tale. That's the tale of how it was brought home to me what it is I am. Irredeemably and always.

Despite the mayor's gun Liam found he was addressing Sherry, through wet eyes and wobbling lips, like a little bitch, one knee in his own bile.

"Wow," said the mayor. "And I was ready to kill a man tonight." He put the gun away. "But you're no man. What are you doing with this clown, Ms Zade?"

"He works for me. He's helping me—"

"The oasis," said the mayor. "Something spooked them a couple of days ago. They're making for the oasis. Difficult to hide an entourage like that. All the equipment. Please wipe this germ away before I change my mind."

"Liam, go."

Liam didn't need to be told twice.

The Second Voyage

Liam had to turn around to find what he was looking for. "The tea rooms. First light."

Sherry, like a lot of people before her, had addressed him eyes averted as he'd scurried by. He hadn't had the slightest trouble finding his way out of there through the darkness. This morning though, despite the emerging daylight, he'd walked right past the Salon de Thé La Liberté. Maybe it was because he'd approached it from the opposite direction—he'd just been up to Café Baba to put a few thousand dirham through the letterbox. Carrying all the cash around again in the shopping bag had him on edge too. Maybe it was his mental state. An early morning appointment was no hardship—he hadn't slept. He hadn't even been able to sit still. He'd paced the room and then he'd paced the street. There was nothing to drink and in the middle of the night nowhere to get anything to drink. Nobody had pointed a gun at Liam before and it hadn't agreed with him. It was very clear to him now he should avoid work that entailed the possibility of it. He'd ended up on the bathroom floor when there was perfectly good furniture in the room, and shivered his way through the hours before dawn. He was still shivering.

Or maybe it was because the tea rooms had been refurbished. The facade gleamed with freshly-painted calligraphy and detailing. The windows were spotless. The door was open and though it was still too early for customers, the place was clearly a going concern, multiple staff bustling around inside getting ready for the day. Steam was being produced somewhere and instead of must the place smelled of coffee. The furniture had been unstacked. Only the lamentable carpet remained the same, though it appeared to have been shampooed.

The briskness of the early morning preparations suited Liam's frame of mind. He wasn't here to linger or equivocate—he was here to negotiate whatever cash or arrangement would get him back to his bungalow and he had little doubt his proposal would be welcome. He was a terrible, terrible detective and clearly an awful person and he wanted to go home. He didn't want to apologise to anyone and he didn't feel like explaining himself—he just wanted to go. He was afraid, but the moment he stepped out on to the wooden deck he was also angry. Birdsong filled the space this morning, courtesy of the pair of budgerigars that now occupied the cage. At least they had each other. The deck was filled with soft morning light—the old fig tree had been cut right back, so the shade from its huge, drooping leaves was gone. When he stepped to the rail and looked down, expecting to see a pruned trunk, or maybe even a stump, he saw instead, in a neatly tilled bed in the middle of the yard, a little sapling, attached to a stake with plastic ties. If his mouth wasn't so dry he'd have spat on it. What was it about this town, that nothing wanted to stay still? That the first glance held no sway over the second? But he was in no mood for questions.

"I brought your money. You can count it."

She was on her own today, no sign of Samson. She didn't take the cash from him, instead gesturing for him to sit.

"I don't need to count it," she said as he balanced the bag against a table leg, "to know that's a lot more money than I gave you. I won't ask if you slept well."

Liam had been avoiding mirrors and other reflective surfaces but he could imagine how he looked. He decided he wouldn't give her the opportunity to yet again avert her eyes by averting his first.

"I want to go home. I'm sorry you got dragged into that last night. Whatever that was. At least you got to see how far out of my depth I am. You should cut your losses." He didn't want to well up. "I need to go home."

"You don't strike me as someone with much of a grip on the concept of home, Mr Tead. Do you mean California?"

"Yes." Liam was grateful when the same guy from yesterday put a coffee in front of him. "There first, anyway." He added a cube of sugar to his cup. You never saw sugar cubes anymore, but they were everywhere in Morocco. "You must see—"

"I don't know what you've got yourself mixed up in, Mr Tead. I don't need to know and I don't want to know." She stirred her tea though she hadn't added any sugar to it. "But it has become abundantly clear to me that in you I made the right choice."

"If it speeds things up at all, I don't need any money. I haven't earned it. Just whatever it takes . . ." It was breezier as well as brighter now the fig tree was gone. He'd preferred it before. "*What?*"

"I'm asking for a little forbearance. You had an unpleasant evening. But things are going very well."

"Going well? There's a body count."

"We know exactly where my father is headed and how. It seems you've doubled the money I gave you," she said. "I'm rather impressed."

He didn't know if it was the breeze that gave him goosebumps or her complete disregard for the dead. "And how?"

"It will be overland. Off grid. We'll do the same. It's a pity something spooked him." She sipped her tea, winced, and reached for the sugar bowl. "You haven't been online, have you?"

"Of course not."

"Good. Darius is arranging a vehicle. Your things will be in it when he pulls up." Hopefully the giant wouldn't go as far as checking beneath the mattress, where Liam had hidden the smartphone.

"I don't think I can do this, Ms Zade. You have the wrong man."

"No, I don't." She leaned forward and to Liam's sleep-deprived mind it almost seemed she was going to take his hand. She didn't. "I trust my intuition on this, Mr Tead, and that means I'm putting my trust in you. Live with it. The most difficult choice you face for now is whether you sit in the front or the back."

The entitlement again. There were moments when Liam felt he could smell it. But he didn't have the resolve to push back. Let her make the decisions—she would only have herself to blame.

"You trust me."

"I do." She nodded but not at Liam—at someone behind him. They made their way out to the street where Darius sat at the wheel of an SUV. His employer got in the back and rolled her window down. "Front or back?"

Liam looked in the passenger window. There was an old-fashioned road map on the seat. Darius was looking at it too. They both looked at each other. Liam went to the other rear door and got in the car. It was obviously brand new—there was that smell and little fixtures everywhere had yet to have their protective plastic film peeled off. Darius had been busy—the dash was a mess of cavities and loose wiring where the vehicle's tech had been stripped out. Not even a radio had been left. That was a shame—Liam's geography might have been sketchy, but he knew it would be a long drive from Tangier to anywhere that could be described as an oasis. It also explained the road map. As they drove through the city Liam, despite the view he'd had of the bay, was shocked at its size. It seemed to him that a good ninety percent of what he was seeing would have gone up in the last twenty years. There was none of the colonial charm of the Minzah part of town and certainly nothing of the Medina.

A pang of regret at leaving the place surprised him. Was it possible he'd miss it? He'd talked about going home and now he wondered how long he'd have needed to stay in this place to feel that way about *it*. A year? A week? His most recently vacated circumstance. He'd made a friend here. His friend had self-immolated here. In the palm of his hand, he'd held his friend's carbonised bone here. The further out they got the less attractive the city became, transitioning from commercial to shabby residential, through a belt of hospitals and sports centres and the like and, finally, scraps of white elephant constructions. Every couple of miles after that they'd pass a parked car on the side of the road, from the boot of which a vendor was operating an enormous, professional-grade espresso machine. They could sell coffee here before the road became the motorway to Rabat and Casablanca, ostensibly a coastal highway although Liam didn't get a glimpse of the sea. The road was straight. The country was flat and dull.

"Should I pick up where I left off?"

"No." Liam was checking the contents of his bag. The was no phone and there hadn't been any mention of a phone. He zipped it up.

"I need to get some sleep."

He'd slip beneath the surface for just long enough to feel the quick disquiet of the unguarded, resurface, fail to break free, and dip again. The dreams that sling shot him from one breach to another were botched jobs made of rushed association—hastily put together and artless, too rapid to hint at even ambiguity. Nothing so fast, that hurtled along like that, could be called sleep. It was as exhausting as any wakeful schlep but it was welcome—he wasn't thinking about anything that mattered and nobody who mattered was talking to him. It registered when, before reaching Casablanca, Darius took an exit and they headed inland. Signs for Beni Melal. Some hours later a stop at some purpose-built place that charged paper money for the use of its toilets. A pile of cheap cellophane-wrapped snacks on the back seat.

"So, will I pick up?"

He shook his head. She could wait. The car was too warm but he assumed his aircon preferences were of little interest. He dozed again, on and off. The terrain changed—the flat country gave way to low, rolling hills. For stretches the road hewed to the course of a riverbed, deep but almost dry, and on the other side at intervals a shabby village would grasp the sheer escarpment for dear life. The towns they drove through were indistinguishable—wide streets not always paved; workshops and blocky houses, some painted in bright colours, many unfinished; steel rods poking from rooftops ready for another story whenever the money came; so much litter it seemed like some kind of prank; the odd lone youth sitting on a wall, or tending goats on wasteland, face in his smartphone; mobile numbers painted everywhere, property for sale or services offered. Everything looked brand new or falling apart or both. They were driving towards mountains. In California he'd come to think of farmland as an unpeopled expanse but here, for want of automation he supposed, the fields were busy enough—there were people all around, labouring or harvesting or whatever it was they were doing.

In the foothills it wasn't just the gradient that changed—the colours did too and, with the window down a little, the scents. They rose through pine forest, hairpinning their way to fresher air, vertiginous drops and a series of waterfalls, levelling out, if it could be called that, on a plateau where at intervals high castles could be seen from the road along a valley of rich, well-tended farmland. Then another gap and another ascent, another plateau, and the same again. A roadside toilet break where rocks gave the heiress privacy. It was mid-afternoon and though he hadn't kept track exactly, they'd been driving many more hours than could reasonably be considered safe. Still it was Darius at the wheel and Darius was indestructible. The curves in the road, the dipping and rising, were constant and nauseating—Liam felt better with his eyes closed, which would also fend off any questions, so he gave in to a half-sleep again, and then sleep.

He knew he'd been that way for some time when he woke with a start—the motor had suddenly become much louder—and to two surprises. The first was outside the car. Sheer rock face rose on either side of them, just a few feet away. With his head to the glass, Liam couldn't see the top. On the other side the rock was a little further from the car and the sound of rushing water mingled with that of the engine. He couldn't lean over to see better because of the second surprise—Darius was asleep on the back seat. Liam had never been this close to the bodyguard and even though the latter was unconscious it made him nervous. It seemed odd to see the heiress in the front of a car, let alone driving it, but there she was. He didn't know why he should be surprised. And it wasn't as if he'd be any help in that regard. He let his window down and the air was not merely fresh but cool. Daring to poke his head out, the sky was a crooked blue line, slender and high above.

When the car emerged from the gorge it was onto another series of hairpins in what might as well have been a different country. As the road straightened and they still had a little altitude, Liam got a good look at it. Nothing here resembled where they'd come from in any way that he could discern. No pine forests, no trees: he couldn't see anything green at all—nothing but a raw expanse of geology, folds and striations in the Earth's crust that looked like they might have been made yesterday and upon which it was either too soon or too late for so much as a blade of grass to try its luck. Shades of red, brown and, here and there in the distances, igneous greys and blacks. If it wasn't for the ferrous pigmentation in every rock and the golden tint it gave the glare, they might as well have been on the surface of the moon. With the descent, the hot air returned and he rolled his window up.

For a couple of hours they drove on. He didn't spot a single grain of sand but this was desert all right—he'd seen its like before. It brought a clarification he was grateful for. On the seat beside him the last soft drink nestled on a heap of empty cellophane wrappers. So that was it now, whatever the larger goals—it was time to find food and water. The couple of places they'd passed through weren't places, really—just some buildings that lined the road for a few scrappy meters. He didn't see people and the idea of anybody living there didn't seem feasible. Nothing in the way of a roadside stop or store. At least there *was* a road. He didn't want to open the can till he had another. Anxiety kept his neck craned over the shoulder of the driver's seat, eyes on the vanishing point, willing something to appear there. Nothing did. The opposite happened—when they reached the horizon, *it* disappeared, falling away and giving way to more crumpled topology. Liam had assumed, on account of the flatness and desolation, that they had bottomed out long since, but they wound through yet another series of curves and hairpin turns, sinking into deep geological folds; then, after an hour or so and without warning, the country opened right up—on both sides a broad valley resembled nothing more than the Westerns he'd watched as a boy, the foreground featureless but the distances punctuated by low ridges and table mountains.

Directly ahead of them as they neared the valley floor, an assault of colour caught his breath. An immense field of palm trees lined the road for miles. They surrounded a town consisting of ruined mud structures that reminded him of the castles he'd seen from the road, but also more modern amenities: what looked like a school, a power plant and a petrol station.

"The oasis," said Liam.

When they reached the outskirts they pulled in at the station where there was a small shop. Darius filled the tank, bought another load of cheap snacks and drinks and got back behind the wheel.

"*An* oasis," said Sherry. "We have further to go."

The town, it turned out, was just the first in a string of them along the valley. They were much of a muchness, although as muchnesses went this one was arrestingly beautiful. If anything the valley laid it on a little thick with the oriental allure. The pattern was the same each time: behind the mundane roadside fixtures—shops, workshops, police posts—the palms would stretch away, shading a patchwork system of cultivated soil in which fruit trees and other crops were also planted. Here and there, poking above the palm fronds, were the roofs and upper stories of those same, reddish mud structures, some surprisingly complex and ornate. *Kasbahs* was the word the heiress used but they were nothing like the old stone Kasbah of Tangier. Beyond the *palmeraies*—her word again—the mountains rippled. They carried on south through softer country. Once or twice the old towns crept right up to the road and Liam got a look. The *jalabiya* was as common here as tight jeans, donkeys and bicycles outnumbering the 4x4s, skullcapped men and frocked schoolchildren outnumbering the women, the ground underfoot more inviting than the higher places they'd come from, the lunar surface giving way to a fine earthy powder, pleasing to the pads of a weathered foot, villages made of dust.

Liam's expectation at the end of a valley would be to find a body of water, but this one simply dried up after a few hours and opened out into desert proper. With light fading and Darius needing to swerve to navigate the sand drifts that made incursions on the asphalt, they reached an ugly little town that Liam hoped was not where they were headed. They passed a couple of hotels that he couldn't imagine had any guests and then all of a sudden found themselves crawling along a narrow and unpaved street in a town centre so bustling it induced a sense of panic. People were squeezed up against the SUV on both sides. The place was full of shops and every shop was the same—bottled water and basic goods. He wondered how so many businesses could get enough custom out on the edge of everything and although he didn't ask, she answered.

"People stock up here," she said. "So will we."

Despite this, they carried on out of town—there was no more asphalt—and it wasn't until half an hour later, on a flat of coarse sand and gravel that they came to stop in the blossoming darkness, beside two 4x4s and two large tents lit from within.

"Stretch your legs, then come in—we'll eat some real food and rest a little."

Liam didn't really feel like stretching his legs but imagined she wanted to do or say something out of his earshot, so he complied, strolling for a few minutes around the circumference of the light from the tents. Beyond that he wasn't curious—it was too dark to see much and this place was creepy. When he went in, Darius was addressing a bowl of meat stew with almost the same enthusiasm—almost—as he'd shown for Liam's carbonara. There were eggs and dates and soft flatbreads gave off lazy vapours.

"Eat." She gestured to a cushion. "It's cross country from here. We'll take the Jeeps and cover most of the ground by night."

He sat and took a flatbread.

"So," she said. There were a couple of guys around—Liam heard a car door going and an engine start up. Presumably, that one was headed back to town for provisions. The other brewed tea at the far end of the tent. "Shall I pick up where I left off?"

The Farewell

BE CAREFUL what you wish for, *chutki*, MY MOTHER SAID TO ME ONE NIGHT WHEN SHE THOUGHT I WAS ASLEEP. Isn't that it? If I hadn't fully appreciated the expression, you and your sister certainly nailed it down for me. How can the granting of a wish be anything other than tainted when the wish itself is venom? Rhetorical question, sleepy head.

I am a person. Perhaps that doesn't come across. I used to be, anyway. It's arguable that whatever gave birth to you wasn't a person but it could remember being one. I still remember. So when I speak of how, upon conceiving you, I had already weaponised you—when I trace the hard outline of my design upon your brow and cast myself as machinator, do not mistake me for machine. I was a person—a woman and, once you came, a mother. I did want love. I wanted it and I wanted to give it. To feel my frozen blood thaw.

I have been somewhat scathing about your father. Strange then that I would permit him, at such a pivotal point in our story, to hold the pen. When he surprised me with his little plot twist—imagine that!—a month before I fell pregnant, it wasn't just the business opportunity that delighted me, nor was it the prospect of spectating his obliteration—of simply watching as he did all the work. No, I believe it was the eugenics angle that appealed most. That's why I went with it so easily, I think. I have always been drawn to the idea of eugenics. Two perfectly reasonable propositions, it seems to me, are: one, that we can breed for supremacy and two, that a good place to start would be with the line that produced me. Eugenics gets a bad press—isn't that it?—but what else should anyone expect from a person whose destiny it is to breed, and to have that considered her contribution?

No, it was better this way, as far as I was concerned. My endorsement was wholehearted, not that I would have let your father know it. I rather gave him the opposite impression. Played the martyr. When you are weak pretend to be strong and when you are strong pretend to be weak. If it is your fate to manage a man, *chutki*, and I have my doubts, you will find yourself buried under a mountain of advice—relationship tips, what men want, what women want, self-help books, YouTube tutorials. I recommend Sun Tzu.

There are so many things I know, and have known, think and have thought, that I have kept from him. Such a simple trick, but it really does explain the dynamic, almost entirely. Perhaps that has been the difference between me and him. Whenever he felt he was winning he could not help but beat his breast. In doing so he gave the game away and thus the advantage. Every time. Power drummed out like that is spent. For power to persist, for it to grow, it must be *held*. That was my move.

Once the pregnancy was confirmed, I refused all scans, wanting nothing to do with his doctors. Aside from the obvious advantages I enjoyed by keeping him in the dark, it had become habit. I would have hesitated, I believe, if he'd asked me the time—taken a moment to think about what might momentarily be gained by not telling him. It was enjoyable. It alleviated the inevitable discomforts of even a perfectly straightforward pregnancy, as mine was, to watch his anxiety levels go through the roof. He scuttled around after me for months, so that one might almost have mistaken him for considerate. I wasn't allowed to lift this, that. To do this, that. It was a consolation to him, I believe, to give and withhold his approvals—a tiny taste of how he probably once thought it would be between us.

By the time my due date came—and went—I thought that perhaps life had reached its pinnacle. The full two weeks we had yet to wait were physically unpleasant but otherwise transcendentally joyful. I would have waited four weeks, six, to savour the sight of him pulled taut as a lute string, guessing when he'd snap. When my contractions finally began he managed to surprise me again—a rare enough occurrence that it would seem portentous each time—by insisting he be present at the birth. Another of his revolting Americanisms. I agreed to the violation because I had some idea of what was coming and wanted to be there myself to see his reaction. It wasn't a particularly arduous or prolonged labour—I won't be repeating the experience, put it that way, but I've heard tales of worse. We did it at home but needless-to-say with an enormously expensive coterie of medical professionals and state-of-the-art equipment. A convoy of vans. Even in the early stages, before the sweat and—I concede—the screaming, he was barely hanging on, his complexion the same pale blue green as the scrubs that made him look so ridiculous. He didn't faint, I'll give him that. But his reaction when my body finally got around to delivering a baby was something to behold.

I've spoken to you of the Zades, haven't I? Maybe he thought the genealogical link would ensure consistency. Maybe he didn't think. He and I never spoke about it that whole nine months, which was in itself revealing—he, wanting a boy, assumed he would get one. I don't think the alternative even occurred to him. Zades produce boys and whatever the particularities of the arrangement, as far as he was concerned this baby would be a Zade. It isn't that your father is an especially masculine specimen, *chutki*. It isn't that kind of chauvinism—it's simply that at whatever point in his, let's call it development, he concluded that since women fall outside the realm of what he can comprehend he'd be better off minimising his dealings with them. That he happens to be absolutely correct about this doesn't make it any easier to respect.

Anyway, he got a girl—dealings with women instantly doubled. I suppose it might be a challenging thing for you to hear but I'm glad you couldn't see the look on his face when he saw his daughter. Can you imagine it? Try. Even in the wave of my relief and my pain, I had the presence of mind to take in not only his expression as he looked upon my child but the expressions around him, obscured by masks of course but perfectly evident in more than one pair of eyes, as they observed him. What a true disgrace of a man, to be overcome in that moment not by his own relief or a surge of love in this, the most human of all of possible encounters, but with obvious, immediate and unmistakeable disappointment. Picture it, *chutki*. No boy to coach. To inculcate. Instead this creature, this alien, this emblem of the chaotic. The opposite of dominion.

And then of course what came next was a surprise to everyone apart from me. Some things there's no mistaking. I had fended off his doctors but I knew perfectly well how to count. I could not have told you before going into labour if I had counted four kicking legs, or six, but I knew with certainty it was more than two. And even three legs—this is basic mathematics—equals more than one baby. The medical staff were quick to recover their composure—I don't think your father has recovered his yet. Another girl. Another weapon. He had to pull his mask away to breathe, so I got a proper look at him. Ego death, isn't that it? I thought I'd finished him long before but I was wrong. *This* was the moment. The second child. The final nail. If only I could have enjoyed it. But I was dealing with my own trauma.

Twins. People will make a fuss of you for being one. No doubt they'll credit you and your sister with all manner of unverifiable faculties, up to and including the supernatural. Perhaps they'll be right. But they'll be wrong when they tell you those qualities are blessings. That you are a blessing. Twins are an abomination, *chutki*. Death and destruction. War and famine. A crime against the God that I had put to death. Twins tear the veil, they rip the world in two.

You and your sister. The signs would come and quickly. It would be apparent very early on that the genetic inheritance had been divided unequally. Tests and so on, but also perfectly obvious differences any fool could observe. Reaching, rolling, crawling, walking. I might seem more human to you, and to myself, if I could tell you that each of those milestones broke my heart a little more—that they were nails hammered into me just as your phallus-free arrival on the scene had been thrust in to your father—but I will never tell you that. It isn't true. I knew the second the two of you had arrived that I had room for only one.

I doubt there have ever been children as relentlessly scrutinized. Woodcock-Johnson, Reitan-Klove, Weschler, Nelson-Denny. The Kaufman Assessment Battery. Doesn't sound very nice, does it? Well, we put you through it. And the rest. But perhaps you were too young to remember. We've rather taken our foot off the pedal now, at least with one of you. The truth is plain to see. Its gradual revelation was a pretence, of course—I knew it already. Your father made a good job of appearing to recover from the obvious setback of your sex. What he needed above all was to demonstrate the wisdom in the risk he'd taken and, doubtless (from his point of view), the sacrifice he'd made. So it was important to him to see that you, that one of you, was a satisfactory pay-off. I was no less invested, having bought into the experiment wholesale. I may have wanted it more. I carried you in my body, after all. You were mine, not his. My power. One of you.

I should have known when he first came to me that it was too easy. Such things do not simply drop in one's lap. I was fooled, but not *by* anyone. Certainly not by him—it was all me. There is a human state, *chutki*, that I cannot name or adequately describe, but I know it when I feel it and I felt it then in myself. It comes when something is revealed to us that we know as defeat, but is deeper than defeat because there is no *sense* of revelation. There is no surprise. We know, all at once, that we always knew. That we have been beaten by ourselves. I, then, had been beaten by a very formidable combatant indeed. I have not recovered. One does not recover from a blow such as that. It was the death stroke, in fact, and delivered so effortlessly—all that was required was my acquiescence. Perhaps that is the point, actually, at which I ceased to be a person. Meat on the sand. The rest has just been a long, long wait for it to dawn on me.

Twins. The veil torn. The rip splitting me down the middle. One of you I could accept, the other I could not. That kind of tension is unliveable, *chutki*. It cannot be borne. A mother who rejects a child is not considered human. It is brute, animal behaviour, and we sigh when even the brutes do it. What I knew from the beginning I knew more with each day. It was not mine. On the contrary, it was the enemy. Alien invasion. A foreign body, a cancer cell. The end of me.

Because we were wealthy, and had children, we had help, which meant that from time to time I got a glimpse of us as we were reflected in their eyes. And *that* meant I had to be careful. Though it was just the help, I no longer wished to see my reflection and anyway, NDAs or no, the help talks. Being seen reminded me that I *could* be seen, my words heard. The control I felt it necessary to exert over myself, to suppress my revulsion, rendered me somewhat cold with the favoured child also, but inexpressive though I might have been, I could at least devote time to my beloved. Tutelage. Whatever the deficiencies in my attention, it was attention. And its reflection, in the mirror of the sibling, was neglect. We would eat together like any family. There were family activities. Outings. I worked hard to appear normal. To seem to be a person. But anyone observing carefully could have told you how assiduous I was in avoiding time alone with one of you. Because we were wealthy, and had children, we had help—and they were very helpful indeed as I carefully choreographed the familial dance so as never to have to duet with the one that terrified me.

To despise someone you want to love. Who you ought to love. Who loves you. That kind of tension is unliveable. It cannot be borne. And so of course I despised myself. Perhaps that is what the aberrant daughter was for me. Yes. A twisted simulacrum of she whom I truly despised. I looked at her—I saw me. Yes. That is what she was and is. An affront. A breach in the delusion. A mirror. A reminder of my deal with the devil. The receipt. The invoice for an unholy transaction. You can banish God, *chutki*, but the devil will linger. Anything or anyone good you ever encounter, I promise you, will slip away. Evil is stickier. And there you were, my offspring, one of you slipping away—I could feel it even then—and the other sticking to me like shit on my fingers.

I have detailed just some your father's idiocies. They are numberless. But not even he, afloat in the sensory deprivation tank of his vanity, could fail to notice. It wasn't just you children we scrutinized. A family is an organism whose limbs are in shock at finding themselves assembled. Every body part is a bristling antenna. I watched your father and, despite his self-absorption, I was watched. It was involuntary. Chemistry, physics and biology. A family is a self-regarding retinal array. I took inventory of him anew, in each passing second, in the minutiae of our encounters with you and with each other. No need to stare. To peer. No need to try. The clearest view is from the corner of the eye. Things are revealed on the periphery which, as they approach the centre, are hidden from view. And so I know he noticed. That one of my children, every now and then when my guard was down and something took me by surprise, made me flinch. That I had nothing good to say about that one. That I never beckoned to it, sought its attention. That I inclined instead towards the other, directing my gaze, my words, my input there.

And as he observed me leaning in, I observed him leaning back. It gradually became the case that he would leave my favoured one to me. It was my hand that held hers as she took her first aided steps, me she came to with the first unaided. My voice, my admonitions, right in the shell of her ear. My eyes upon her, perhaps a little too much. On his part, a retreat. Even though she was our little success, the obvious inheritor of the genetic bounty he'd so carefully sourced. His attention turned to the other. At first I thought it a matter of his nerves. His spine. Of course he would avoid the company of my dote—it meant avoiding me. I thought it must be quite a relief for him, as we emerged from the intimate hothouse that was your infancy, to find a way to distance himself. And then, also, I thought it pragmatism—that having procured a biological material that dwarfed him, he was happy to leave the nurturing and tutelage of that material to a person who dwarfed him. That he knew which side his bread was buttered, in other words. But no.

As he leaned back, I observed him leaning in, to the other. Not a retreat but an embrace, an encircling. Physically too—he would literally lean in, his face so close to hers at times it must have interfered with her breathing, a hand almost always upon her. It was not an entirely comfortable thing to observe, and it wasn't just me who felt the unease. On more than one occasion one of the help, fearing for her job no doubt, would make a passing remark so superficially innocuous and yet so unmistakeable to its intended audience—me—that my skin would tingle with the shame. If these remarks made it as far as my ear then there must a deafening cacophony of them in my absence. An inappropriate relationship with a very young child. An untoward intensity. Obsession. But my shame was not the shame they might have expected. They were right to worry—but they worried about the wrong thing.

My husband's conduct towards his child was not the problem—it was a solution. And I knew it. I knew that he had seen me withdraw. I knew that he knew the child was abandoned. And so he swaddled it. There was nothing indecent in the ferocity of his regard for her. Quite the opposite—he was compensating for my indecency. My inhumanity bound them together. How it enraged me to see in him this capacity for unselfish love. I could perceive precisely nothing self-serving in his inclination towards her. He was responding to a need. Not his need—hers. It filled me with disgust. The realisation that I was his superior and he, in the end, my better. I could have allayed the others' fears. Put them right. Fired them for their insolence. But I let the ugly slur linger in the air. It provided me with cover. His unselfconscious, open-hearted behaviour served to mask the actual problem. Reputationally, he would bear the brunt and so, in a way, would she.

A FINGERTIP ON MY BROW. What happened to my little Übermenschen, *chutki*? Hm? I got four little legs, four hands and feet, twenty fingers and twenty toes. But just the one person, really. And one little monster. What would you have done, I wonder, in my place? One child a plan perfectly executed and one a perfect execution. The end of me. If I had, after that, still been a person, I could have responded in all sorts of ways. Human ways. But it did not seem to me I had that choice. No. I went with Plan A. I devoted myself to the genetically optimal. The other, the errant little other who with every disappointment, every aberration reminded me I could not control everything, I could not love. I could not see then, as I do now, her true gift—that she *did* remind me. No, no.

A TAP. She will go her own way and she must go without me. I'm no more good to a person I don't understand than she is to me. If she'd stuck to the script then we'd have a script. I could guide her through it. I could help. ON MY CHEEK I FELT THE FAINT DISPLACEMENT OF AIR AS SHE GOT UP TO LEAVE. But as it is she'll have to find her own way. I withdraw and wish her luck, because finding one's way is the most difficult thing of all.

The Desert

By the time she had said what she had to say, the driver had returned from town. The two men cleared away the dishes, then busied themselves packing the Jeeps with supplies for what it seemed to Liam was to be another long drive. They stuffed cavities Liam didn't know cars had full of water bottles, fuel canisters, food and, for some reason, air tanks as well as blankets and other items intended to afford a little comfort in places where there wasn't any. He didn't pretend to help, didn't pretend to want to, just wandered in misshapen circles around the tents, waiting for someone to tell him to get into a vehicle and wondering if this was what dissociation was. He'd given up all sense of responsibility for being where he was, wherever he was, or doing what he was doing, whatever that was. Maybe it was delayed shock. He was a ghost. Being a ghost didn't feel good especially, but it felt a lot better than being alive. Eventually one of the guys did indeed beckon him into a Jeep, where he once again found himself sharing the back seat with the heiress. Darius was in front, but in the passenger seat. The other guy was driving. That meant guy number one had the other vehicle all to himself but Liam didn't ask why. It was obvious—there was no way the bodyguard would allow his employer to travel unprotected. That Liam hadn't been packed off to the other Jeep made him edgy—she probably wanted to keep talking.

He needn't have worried. After forty minutes driving across the crunching gravel she hadn't said a word. The flat became uneven and the headlights revealed the jumpy outlines of higher ground ahead. Both vehicles came to a halt and the drivers got out, each of them letting a little air out of his tyres.

"We're going out on the sand," she said.

An hour later she'd added nothing to her observation and both vehicles had settled into a very particular rhythm. It was necessary not only to crest an endless series of dunes, dropping off precipitously on the leeward slipface or hewing to the ridge, but to take each one at a particular angle, to follow its lines where the sand was most likely to harden beneath the tyres and hold. They weren't so far yet from the little town and Liam supposed the men knew these huge formations, maybe even by name—there was no hesitation in the way they turned the Jeeps this way and that, curving into an ascent at just the right spot and speed. In any other setting Liam could think of, the way they were grinding the gears would be considered poor driving, but here it seemed an essential element in navigating the gradients. Ditto acceleration. Progress was effortful. None of the work was Liam's but this was the kind of driving to keep even a passenger busy—door handle gripped, eyes on the ceaseless pitch and yaw of the sliver of horizon that snaked through the sweeping headlights. There probably wasn't a drop of water for miles in any direction but the thought wasn't any help with the seasickness.

He was glad of it though—the baseline of discomfort. Now and then they'd reach some flatter terrain but it wouldn't last. Before long they'd be back at it, revving their way up and down and along and around. It went on like that for a long time and it kept them all quiet—just the way he wanted it. Something was wrong with Liam and he didn't want to talk about it. Didn't want to talk and didn't want to listen. There were more than twenty-four hours between him and the mayor, and who knows how many kilometres, but he wasn't getting over what had happened to him. Every now and then he would get a whiff of the charred meat odour that had made him so hungry and his mouth would water, and that would make him want to puke so that he had to grip the door handle even tighter and try to fight it, and while he tried to do that he would see again what he saw, the incompletely incinerated lovers, the remnants of flesh, the woozy light show of the phone flashlights. He wasn't in a Jeep, with an heiress and her help. He wasn't in the desert, beneath the night sky. He was still on his knees in a cave, head still nuzzling a gun. He had an awful feeling that's where he would always be. That once you'd been there, there was nowhere else. That every change of scenery would be another illusion—coping strategies for a cocked pistol, his mind stretching out the seconds before the trigger was pulled into a fractal eternity.

Shock, then. It suited him fine that the drive didn't allow for conversation, so he was surprised to find it was his own voice, as morning overtook them and the horizon brightened up ahead, that brought an end to the permitted silence.

"I think you're making a serious mistake."

She was so slow to respond he thought for a moment she wouldn't.

"You know a better way?" she said, eventually. "You don't even know where we're going."

They finally hit something that wasn't sand—another flat of fine gravel and, after a little way, a real road where Liam learned the reason for the air tanks: both Jeeps came to a halt on the asphalt and the drivers went around, pumping the tyres back up.

"I meant me," said Liam as the passengers waited for them to finish. He got out and walked about twenty meters away to urinate, then kept his back turned for a minute or two, ostensibly to take in the scenery, but mainly in case in case she was doing the same. There was no scenery. When he got back in she had either been quicker than him or she hadn't moved. The vehicles pulled away.

"I get it, I think," he said, and took a sip from his water bottle. He'd been trying to take it easy on the water—he didn't have the bladder of a twenty-year-old any more. "I think I get it." He waved, in a vague way, at the now speeding car and the desert. "This must all be very exciting for you. Off grid with someone you picked at random from the phone book. The whole Zade apparatus at your disposal. The apparatus you designed so much of. There can't be a person alive with your grasp of tech surveillance. You know things I'll never know. How to do things I'll never understand how to do.

But you've decided you're going to tackle your problem *intuitively*—and here we are." Another little wave. "Maybe you think this is how the little people do things. Ordinary people. But crossing the Sahara desert with a wannabe detective, a bodyguard and a couple of air tanks is not how real people do things, Ms Zade." He was aware he had raised his voice a little and that Darius had tensed up. "It's insane."

"I like to think I'm a real person, Mr Tead. Unusual, perhaps, but real." Her unflappable calm, the beatific serenity of the facial expressions that threatened, in any given moment, to give way to that smirk, made Liam want to jump out of the moving vehicle. He'd liked the smirk at first but he didn't want to see it anymore. "And I didn't pick you out of the phone book." Another expression altered her features, for just a moment, that might have been confusion. "You know, I don't think I've ever seen a phone book."

"The phone book is a metaphor. I meant my ad."

"You have an ad? I've never seen that either."

"You said you'd seen it."

"No I didn't. You jump to conclusions, Mr Tead. That's not good in a detective, is it?"

She turned away, but not quickly enough to conceal the grin she was struggling to suppress. Something was tickling her. When after a moment she spoke again it was without turning back.

"My hiring you may not have been entirely random."

The grin was still there. He could see it through the back of her head.

"What do you mean?"

"You showed up on the Zade radar a while back."

Liam bristled, literally. The hairs on his arm. His neck. The old feeling—trouble.

"Me?"

This was the moment, then, that a comic misunderstanding would be revealed. And perhaps its less than humorous consequences.

She kept her face to the window but her tone told the story—she was enjoying herself.

"My father likes to keep abreast, you know—especially, in regard to anything that might have to do with Zade interests. Tech developments, trends, that kind of thing. Market stuff, potential competition. And of course he has the means to know what's going on. Surveillance is very much the Zade schtick, you're aware. You used to write, didn't you?"

"No," Liam shook his head. Then he remembered. "Oh wait, I did do a few listicle type things, for websites. Not for very long—I couldn't make it pay. But I have nothing to do with tech. I don't know anything about it."

"Yes. I believe that was a great relief to my father." She was determined he not see her face. "But you wrote something that made you very interesting to him."

"Interesting?"

"Briefly, yes. Such a density of key terms in your piece that it set off the big flashing lights in his secret underground lair."

"Again, I think there has been a mistake. I'm not the guy you meant to bring along. I never wrote about tech. Ever. I can barely type."

"You wrote about media."

"No—they were travel sites. I wrote about travel destinations. I—" He cut himself off as a memory surfaced. It couldn't be. It would be ridiculous. He leaned forward as far as he could so that she'd know he was looking at her. "You can't mean '9 Reasons You Should Turn Your Social Media Off Right Now and See Bhutan Before Tourism Ruins it Forever'?".

A snort. "That's the one." She finally turned to him and he was momentarily disarmed and at how sunny and unguarded she looked, as though she was savouring a precious memory. "The cause of some uncharacteristic mirth at the Zade dinner table," she said. "Even my mother cracked a smile."

"I don't believe this." He looked out of his window at the blur of alien landscape.

"Don't worry, Mr Tead, you weren't *really* interesting." Once again, her tone teased. "More of an *amuse-bouche*. It stuck in my memory though. Firstly, seeing my parents laugh together—thanks for *that*. And my father's glee at how intuitively—his word—your piece had alighted on certain patterns. You're quite right about intuition, Mr Tead. But don't be flattered—my father loathed it and we were raised to." She turned away again. "I never quite could after that, though." I've associated your name with intuition ever since, and with my mother's laugh, and with good things that happen in the unlikeliest of ways and places. I trust intuition and because you're *my* intuition, I trust you. I'm going to need you to go ahead and deal with that."

Liam couldn't remember ever dealing with anyone this smug. It was a new level. If she was going to need him to go ahead and deal with it then he was going to need her to go fuck herself. Once he'd been paid. He had a few years on this woman. What kind of rare air had she been breathing all her life that she thought she could talk to him that way? To anyone. He almost felt sorry for her. But not quite.

After a couple of hours the Jeeps stopped and the drivers let the air out of the tyres again before leaving the road.

"How are you getting on without the phone, by the way?"

This time it was him that turned away—so she wouldn't see him redden.

"What do you mean?" *Had Darius searched the hotel room?*

"Withdrawal. How are you getting on?" She shuddered so hard he could feel it through the seat. "I itch all over."

"I'm fine."

He had only half turned back but he was keenly aware she was staring at him. She'd said *the* phone, not *a* phone or *your* phone, but it didn't seem like she'd meant anything by it.

"What?" He really didn't like being looked at.

"Come on, Mr Tead. We all have our addictions. I mean no disrespect but you don't strike me as someone immune to compulsive screen-time behaviours. You don't really seem like you'd be immune to compulsive behaviours in general."

"OK, and how is that not disrespectful?"

"Maybe don't take yourself so seriously."

He reddened again. She cocked her head, a superior life form amused by an insect. Then she sat back and looked out of her window.

"I watch handbag hauls. I don't even know why. The conventional wisdom is they provide a vicarious hit of dopamine to those who could never afford the handbags in question. But I'm way richer than the women who make the reels. I can't explain it. But I watch *a lot* of handbag hauls."

She waited for a response. Liam didn't offer one.

"And Darius," she said, "may not realise I'm on to him but I've seen him plenty of times. He likes watching people cook outdoors." Her hand went to her mouth. Liam could actually see the hairs on the back of the bodyguard's neck stiffen.

"So what's your addiction, Liam?" He didn't like it when she used his first name. Especially since she'd always drop it again and revert to mangling his surname.

"Why is it you want to find your sister? You realise you've never told me?"

"I'm working up to it. It's my thing. All in good time."

He let a couple of kilometres slide by, hoping against hope she'd somehow go away. Instead she slapped her thigh.

"Come on, Mr Tead. You're playing for time. I've shown you mine. I've even shown you Darius's. Show us yours."

She wasn't going to let it go. He took a deep, deep breath.

"Short videos about animals in which, at the outset, said animal is in some terrible state or predicament—trapped in a well or afflicted with hideous mange, for example—but by the end of which it has either been successfully freed from that predicament and reintroduced to the wild or has found its forever home, or at the very least finds itself in some kind of foster situation that constitutes a sufficiently upbeat and hopeful note upon which to end the video."

He expected her to laugh but she didn't. She nodded.

"How short?"

"Never short enough. Once I've identified the predicament, I skip to the uplifting part."

"It's the shorts you have to watch."

He didn't know what she meant and that must have been obvious to her.

"I don't mean you have to watch the shorts. I mean you have to watch *out* for the shorts."

He made the facial expression that, across all known cultures, communicates its owner is lost and losing patience. She narrowed her eyes.

"What is Zade, Mr Tead?"

He narrowed his.

"Shouldn't I be asking you that?"

"I mean to you. What do you think Zade is?"

In the moment it took him to fail to come up with a snappy answer he realised it was a pretty good question. He didn't know what Zade was.

"I don't know," he said. "A large company?"

"Oh dear." Again with the persistent, unflinching eye contact. The silence was his to fill, apparently but he wasn't in the mood to play games. She seemed to notice, and although she turned her visual attention to the desert, she spoke first.

"Zade is a thief."

Liam couldn't tell if she was being cryptic or profound, or both. Or neither.

"And what is it you steal?"

"Valuables." *Cryptic, then.* "What is most valuable to you, Mr Tead?"

"You want me to say family? I don't know what you want me to say. I haven't got a car."

"Family wasn't the answer I was expecting, no," she said. "And as for car. Wow. Tell me, are you mortal?"

"What?"

"Are you mortal? Are you going to die?"

Liam let out a sigh that was full, he hoped, of both sarcasm and fatigue.

"You want me to say time. You steal time."

"Very good."

It would have been the right moment, as far as Liam was concerned, to stop talking and watch the world go by. She had some nerve taking this tone. Talking down to him, like he was child. But there wasn't enough out there for the eye to get a purchase on, only so much mileage in trying to distinguish between sand and dust, dirt and dirty sky.

"Can we maybe reel in the poetry a little? What do you do with all this time?"

It was her turn to sigh.

"We don't do anything with it. We don't rob you of your time because we want it, Mr Tead. We steal it because we don't want you to have it."

There was nothing for it but to play along.

"And why don't you want me to have it?"

"Because of what you might do with it. If you're reading brain has time on its hands, it might just prove capable of novel, analytic and deeper forms of thought. That doesn't suit Zade. It needs your attention where it can see it and therefore direct it towards desirable outcomes. Scrolling, mainly, where it can keep an eye, and a hand, on what you think about, what you buy, how you vote and so on."

"So there is a political agenda."

"No *political* agenda." She took a deep breath, as if calling upon reserves of patience. "Nothing as facile as ideology. Zade has no interest in who governs as long as whoever governs doesn't get in Zade's way."

"And what *is* in Zade's way? What does it want?"

She shrugged, but with her face.

"More Zade."

She was obviously very clear on what she meant but if she'd wanted to share it with him she hadn't done a very good job. Maybe she didn't want to. The exchange made him both angry and sad. It all sounded so done and dusted. So hopeless. And deep down he knew it *was* hopeless—not necessarily for the world, or humanity or anything so grand. Hopeless for him. He was into this latest elsewhere so deep now—in the Sahara, for heaven's sake, in a Jeep with a princess prodigy—and it had been the weirdest elsewhere yet, no question about it, but it already wasn't really elsewhere at all. Despite the trappings, it was same old same old. Again. The trauma in the underground chamber had broken the spell. Liam was back in his resting state. Ruined. Because it wasn't the depth he was in, in the end—it was the depth, or lack of it, in him. There was nowhere he could go back or forward to where it wouldn't be like this anymore, no previous or prospective state. He couldn't doggy paddle his way to the shallow end. The out-of-depthness he felt now he would always feel, had always felt. It was in him. Not a drop of water for miles in any direction and he was drowning. There wasn't a shallow end. There wasn't a puddle or petri dish in all the world shallow enough to rid him of the drowning feeling.

"What did you mean, 'my thing'?"

Her silence wasn't evasive—it was an enquiry.

"You said finding your sister was your thing."

"Ah. Yes, it is."

"But what does that mean?"

"Don't you have a thing, Mr Tead? I didn't find it when I looked into you. If I had I'd have leveraged it. But you must. Everybody does." She checked his face, presumably for any sign of comprehension. "Something they carry with them—a burden they long to put down. What drives me to find my sister is mine." She kept herself turned slightly towards him and clasped her hands, signalling it was his turn to speak.

"What's yours?"

The Petrified Forest

By the time Liam had said what he had to say, the sun was climbing high and the Jeeps were pulling into a compound that had appeared out of nowhere, in the middle of nowhere—a squat, one-story building surrounded on all sides by a low wall about twenty metres from the house. Liam wondered what purpose a wall like that would serve out here on this vast flat. It didn't hide the house and just about any four-legged creature would jump it. Not that he could imagine anything with fur surviving in this place. Things that crawled, maybe. Slithered.

"We need to stay out of the light as much as we can." She hadn't said anything about his story—just listened. "At sundown we'll get going again."

It was the bare bones of a house—just a few beds distributed among the rooms. Liam found one and slept a dreamless sleep. When darkness fell they rose from their beds and the drivers retrieved the Jeeps from a sunken ramp at the side of the house where they'd been concealed beneath tarpaulins.

"I *will* tell you why I'm looking for my sister." They were moving at speed over ground that crunched beneath the wheels and made for a bumpy ride. Liam was getting used to it. His whereabouts had become so unlikely they barely registered anymore. At least in the dark he didn't have to deal with the stupefying desolation. "But first there is a lot you need to understand."

Sure.

No food had been prepared in the house. Not even a kettle boiled. They'd all just slept, so Liam sipped from a bottle of water before tearing the wrapper off a dubious-looking cookie.

"My parents each had a favourite. From word go. It was never explained, never justified. There were no apologetics. It was just the way it was. I got all of my mother's attention. My sister got none.

She was my father's little pet. Not that I'm complaining—I feel no resentment towards him and felt no lack of love, no hostility. It has always been my sense that he *had to* dote on her or she would effectively have been an orphan. If it's like that from the very beginning a child will just accept it. It wasn't until I got a little older, when I began—to my mother's horror—interacting with other children and from time to time with their families, that I realized how strange we were. I'd occasionally hear talk of favourites in those other families, of course. All families do that, don't they?"

Liam was paying more attention to the cookie than to her, trying to guess its ingredients without resorting to the long list on the cellophane. But in the corner of his eye he caught her shooting him a look as she asked the question, as though it wasn't rhetorical for her. As though other families, maybe even other people, were a foreign country. But it was surreptitious and she didn't wait for an answer.

"Daddy's girl, Mommy's boy, all that. But it's always sort of innuendo, right? It's acceptable to say those things, as long as you keep it surfacey. As long as it's all underpinned, you know?" She was tackling her own cellophane-wrapped product with the air of someone who had never done it before. Likewise family talk—it was achingly clear to Liam that this was uncomfortable territory for her and part of him was enjoying that. The beatific complacency was dialled down a little for the moment. "We weren't like that. We weren't a family at all, really. We were two single-parent families that shared a breakfast table."

Poor thing.

She finally managed to pull the wrapper apart but in doing so broke the product—some sort of cake simulacrum—into pieces. She picked at a couple of them and then set the packet aside in disgust.

"You've probably seen online speculation about my father's relationship with my sister. It was getting traction a few years ago to the point where we felt the need to intervene. That's where the retreat-from-public-life narrative came in. The Zade machine generated a nice little happy ending—settling down in the countryside to a horsey life, stables, an estate in the Cape Winelands. A retirement of sorts. It brought the *enfant terrible* chapter to an end and that was important. It was that behaviour that fuelled the gossips. Poor little rich girl, poor little traumatised thing. Acting out and what have you. But it isn't true and anybody who'd been there would know it couldn't be true—those tendencies, the delinquency, started early. Right from the beginning."

"I never really paid any attention to that stuff," said Liam.

"Fake news. You knew about it. People are funny." She shook her head. "Really, it makes me laugh that at this point people still claim their attention is something they can pay out or withhold at will. It's a joke."

Liam wasn't in the mood for her mind games. He wanted to hear more about the sister.

"I'm interested in what delinquency would look like that early on."

"Oh, a thousand little things. You name it. Tantrums. Not holding a parent's hand when asked to. Not eating this, not eating that. Wilfulness. Waywardness. A thousand things, but they all added up to not having read the script. Those two little girls, they were princesses really. Born and bred to run an empire. But one of them hadn't read the script."

That was it for conversation, apparently. Liam had never worn a watch and now he didn't have a phone so keeping track of time was impossible. They might have driven on in silence like that for an hour or for three. He dozed a little which didn't help. Eventually, the other Jeep came to a stop and they pulled up beside it. The drivers got out to top up the tanks from jerry cans. The three passengers stayed where they were. Liam opened his door to look around. In the distance he could make out two lights, one white and one bluish— the only evidence of human life. Beyond the reach of the headlights and their incidental glow, he could see nothing—no foreground, just blackness. The lights in the distance might have been a mile away or twenty miles away. Space as well as time was an undifferentiated expanse.

"Maybe they could have changed that narrative too," she said when they were on the move again. "Rewritten the story. Early intervention and all that. Maybe they could have turned their little rogue around. But there was an additional issue. I wouldn't call it neglect exactly. Well, maybe I would. Their attention was elsewhere, let's put it that way. They had another daughter, after all, and she too was showing early signs of what her future held. Rather remarkable signs."

"The great Sherry Zade."

It was intended as a thought but the words came out of his mouth before he could stop them or tone down the sarcasm. It was too dark to bother with eye contact but he could see her well enough to know she was looking at him hard.

"The great Sherry Zade." It didn't sound any less sarcastic when she said it. It occurred to Liam that he hadn't taken the chance to empty his bladder when they'd stopped and that he'd almost certainly regret it. He needed a shower and he wanted a drink.

"You can hardly blame them," she said. The Jeeps had found a stretch of paved road and were moving at a speed Liam didn't want to think about. "It wasn't exactly a normal childhood."

"Well, no—"

"I'm not talking about wealth, or seclusion. I suppose I'm talking about education. We were experiments."

"I don't follow."

"I'm speaking to you in the strictest confidence, you understand."

"Sure." They hadn't made him sign anything but he doubted they relied on such niceties.

"I don't suppose it should surprise anyone that my parents didn't go about having a family in the normal way. Why would they leave anything to chance? They never told us as much but I've always assumed we were genome-edited. And while in one case it didn't really take, in the other it exceeded expectations. So that is where their attention went.

"Even as young children, it was abundantly clear to us that we were a project. That there was something to be achieved, criteria to be measured against. We underwent testing all the time. Physical, cognitive. All very expensive, no doubt. Results and outcomes were discussed in our presence and unabashedly—when we grew old enough to follow their conversations, to a degree anyway, there was no attempt on their part at diplomacy, no effort to soften the blow of the differences they observed. Even where the content exceeded our understanding there was no mistaking the tone. You can imagine, I think, how awful that was for the fifty percent of their investment that was underperforming," she pursed her lips, "and how excruciating, actually, for the other half."

Jesus. Liam could imagine neither.

"It was no recipe for sibling harmony." She was looking out of her window but she couldn't have been able to see anything except her own reflection. "On the one hand, poor performance indicators could be seen as a blessing to the problem child. They bestowed a certain freedom, a release from the maniacal levels of pressure my parents applied either directly or through all the specialists they hired. There are perks to inattention. On the other—"

"On the other," said Liam, "with all their hopes turned on you, it must have seemed that all the love was flowing that way too." He was getting the hang of this. She sighed.

"I won't blame a child for its talents, Mr Tead. As I've told you, I had one parent and my sister another. So I suppose you could say the love was evenly divided. But there are different types of love. I don't even know why I should blame them—what is a good way to handle the reality that one of your children is a gift and the other a liability? One a repository of your success and the other a testament to your failings. Except that the whole predicament had arisen from their vanity. They quite literally engineered it. So I do blame them."

She fell silent. After a while, on the horizon ahead of them, faint light glimmered. They were driving into yet another day and, as the brightening skyline revealed, different country. As the vehicles neared the change in terrain, it might have been taken for a forest. In the murk, Liam could make out what could be tree trunks, blossoming out into rounded crowns. When they got closer still—it was impossible to judge the distance—that illusion swapped out for another. Because the formations were colourless they stopped resembling trees and became mushrooms—an enormous field of vast white mushrooms in the pre-dawn gloom, varying in size but otherwise conspicuously uniform. Of course it couldn't be a forest and of course it couldn't be mushrooms, much less giant ones. Desert didn't become plant life, or any kind of life, so suddenly. Unless it was artificial—some kind of commercial plantation.

"The oasis?"

The sun broke the horizon, throwing razor sharp rays over and between the crooked shapes, instantly revealing their true nature. It was unlike any forest Liam had seen. The rock formations spread out in both directions as far he could see. He was reminded again of the eroded forms he'd first seen in the panoramas of old Westerns. But where those landscapes had become a familiar fixture in those movies, this was anything but familiar. A minute later they passed the first of them and found themselves surrounded. The Jeeps had to abandon their straight trajectories to avoid the smaller examples which were more numerous and densely spaced, though still separated by sand. At larger intervals all around, the mushroom shapes reached heights that dwarfed the vehicles, that would have dwarfed a house. Back on sand the Jeeps were struggling and the drivers grinding gears. Darius inclined his head and when his boss leaned forward whispered something to her as they pulled up in the shadow of one of the giants.

"Not the oasis," she said to Liam, sitting back. "They need to let some air out, and we might as well have breakfast here—where we sleep today is just some shack, I'm told."

It was surprisingly cool in the rock's shade—the temperature jarred with the scenery—but there was warmth already in the sun's first rays. The three passengers wandered away from each other a little to attend to personal business, the bodyguard minimizing the discreet distance he kept from the heiress. Liam walked among the formations till he reached the next really big one. The sand that separated them was conspicuously fine. He wanted to take his shoes and socks off to walk on it but he didn't know what might be alive around here. There was no break in the scenery in any direction. Aside from a forest or a field of giant fungi, it might also have been an alien city. Over the worn curves and ballooning mushroom caps the low, split sunlight threw a different architecture, made of straight lines, stamping its astronomical timeline on the wind-worn sculpture. It occurred to Liam how easy it would be to become disoriented here. He made his way back to the others while he still could.

One of the drivers had a fire going of dried palm fronds and wood shavings that had evidently been brought along in one of the Jeeps—there was nothing to burn anywhere around. The other was kneading dough which he then flattened onto a metal disc. He placed the disc on the fire and brushed some embers over the dough, then busied himself with making tea and boiling some eggs, which must have been packed with great care to have made it this far. They all had to wait a little while for that bread but the waiting smelled good and when it came it was soft and crispy at just the right ratio, steamed and charred. The eggs were chopped up and tossed with onions and tomatoes and there was a bean stew, bitter but good. Nobody spoke or needed to—the place, the moment, was to be taken in, like the fired bread and the potent tea. With every minute that passed beyond the confines of conversation, every spoonful of stew, Liam was taking medicine. For the first time since Tangier he didn't feel like his intestines were still back there. As the drivers, who had eaten a little distance away, squatted by the Jeeps rinsing dishes with the least water possible, he thought he might have the stomach for more of her obscenely privileged self-pity shtick.

"Tell me more about your sister. What do you think it all looked like from her point of view? Disappointing, falling short . . ."

How do you think it felt?

She looked oddly at home in a desert—sitting on the ground, elbows on her knees. She poured sand from one hand, slowly enough to let a slight breeze catch it, and watched it fan out in the air. At least, he assumed she watched—he couldn't see her eyes beneath the brim of her hat. No doubt the safari-style outfit she wore, same colour as the sand, cost more than three months' salary back at Flynn Insurance.

"Well," she said, "we're twins, right? Each is reflected, has her story told, in the other. To understand what it is to fall short you need to have a grasp of the measures met by the other. Or in this case, far exceeded. So let's begin there."

Good grief. She was clearly her own favourite topic of conversation.

"You might have read about how abstemious tech people can be when it comes to screen time for their children. How they protect their loved ones from the habits and compulsions they spend their working days designing. It's a truism and, in as much as I was allowed to mix with other children and get a first-hand look, it's true." She ran out of sand and picked up another handful. It was more like dust, really. "But it wasn't like that in our house. You might have read about that too but the details, I can assure you, go way beyond anything that's been made public."

One of the drivers came over to pour more tea. Liam's glass was tiny. Its resemblance to a shot glass made him wish it was one. He nursed it as if it was.

"Maybe it was because we were pretty much the first family to exist in that scenario," she said. "More likely it was ego. Exceptionalism was the order of the day in our household. And as protective as they were, my parents can't be said to have been protecting out of love alone. They were, each in their own way, protecting an asset.

"No, for us it was all about exposure. Organised sessions at first. Long sessions, sweetened with the kind of entertainments a two- or three-year-old might find attractive, but tinctured with . . . other content. Once we reached an age where we could, literally, be left to our own devices, we were. The one option we weren't given was not to consume content. Observation continued, into adulthood, but the content was neither filtered for us nor in any way controlled. No censorship, no curation of any kind. The journey turned out to be a very different one for each sister. I'll tell you more in the car."

They went to their Jeep where the drivers had packed up and were waiting. Darius was already in his seat. Liam got in, pulled his door shut and waited for her to do the same.

"So what's with the names?"

She seemed, for a moment, inclined to disregard the question, instead concentrating on fastening her seatbelt for the rougher terrain.

"What do you mean?"

What do you think I mean? A lot had been made of the names, little of it kind.

"Oh, you know."

She gave no in indication that she knew. She knew, all right.

"Well, the names are . . . unusual," said Liam. This now seemed like something it would have been better not to bring up. "They don't reflect your parents' origins, for example, so there isn't that connection. People say they wanted American-sounding names. But also wonder why they chose those two specifically, you know? That maybe it was a misfire. I mean, Doonah . . ."

Making it about her sister, and not Sherry, might alleviate some of the awkwardness Liam had clearly introduced.

"What about it?"

"Well . . . it's just . . . unusual, you know? Maybe a little . . . goofy? Not necessarily a popular choice, these days, is what I'm saying."

But she insisted on receiving the insult as a direct hit.

"People have said the same about Sherry," she said through her teeth. "It's tiresome."

It only took them an hour to reach the aforementioned shack. It was a long hour.

The White Mountain

"Bᴇᴛ ʏᴏᴜ never expected to see quite this much of Morocco." Liam didn't answer right away. Just about everything had been unexpected in the last couple of days, but nothing quite as surprising as this. The sun would be up any minute—they'd driven through another night, having slept long in a crumbling, two-room shack, into the evening, then taken up where they'd left off—in tense silence. Hours of being lightly tossed about in the back of a Jeep had turned the tension, gradually, into mere silence. Although there seemed to be an unspoken understanding that the mood had lifted a little, neither had ventured to resume their conversation until now.

"We're not in Morocco," he said.

This would be their third day in the desert, much of that time spent moving at speed. Thirty hours? More? Each morning the sky had brightened directly ahead of them as it was doing now. They were going east and had been all along. Liam's grasp of North African geography was rudimentary, but there was no way they were still in Morocco. She was testing him. It was irritating but he answered anyway.

"We're in Algeria."

Not a country he'd ever expected to see. He didn't think much of it, although he didn't have a lot to go on. Unless this was where the drivers were from, he hadn't spotted a single Algerian. Apart from a couple of distant glints in the night, he hadn't seen a house, let alone a town or village. Nothing but the waste. Driving at night for the most part had meant much of the terrain remained a mystery to Liam, but although the ground was uneven here and there he knew they hadn't made any dramatic ascents or descents. It had been one huge flat. Country like that will lull a person into believing they've bottomed out. For whatever reason, such an expanse of level ground seemed like it had to be low ground. So when the Jeeps pulled up and they all followed the drivers a little way off to the side, it had caught Liam by surprise when torches had been directed at their feet so they could take care. So they could stop, in other words, before stepping off the edge of a high cliff that ran unevenly towards the dawn. Liam couldn't take his eyes off the scene, but he knew she was smirking when she spoke.

"Didn't want to get caught out again, huh?" She was very close, just over his shoulder. "Been paying more attention."

A low bank of cloud in the east obscured a sun just clear of the horizon—its light burned through diffusely to colour the panorama a murk the purple of bluebottle's egg. The depression extended beyond the reach of Liam's sight, east into the light and south into an ocean of sand, of such enormous proportions it was difficult for his eye to credit. When the sun broke free of the cloud bank the cliffs that marked the northern limit glowed like molten lava. Some of the distances were punctuated by rocky forms like the one under which they'd breakfasted the previous morning, but solitary or in small clusters. When direct sunlight hit them they threw long, long shadows, shadows the length of an Irish county, which proceeded to sweep, at a solar crawl, the surface of the earth. Further south the same rays made a sundial of the dune fields. Not so far from the base of the cliffs, at what in this immensity might be described as the middle distance, was . . . something. Even before the sun cleared the cloud it had attracted the eye—nothing more than a lighter, colourless patch, an uninformative shape that, when the sun finally broke cover, gave itself away in a glint.

"I'm afraid to ask," said Liam.

She came level with him.

"The oasis."

Darius was a few steps away, right on the edge, training what looked like a military-grade monocular in that direction. He lowered the device and shook his head, then handed it to his employer. When she had taken a look she gave it to Liam.

"Find the lower edge of the water, then move left till you see a table mountain the colour of chalk."

He did as she said.

"Got it."

"At the base of the mountain, on the right."

At first he couldn't see anything. The ferrous striations of rock that ringed the base of the mountain were interrupted there by some boulders, but otherwise nothing stood out. He scanned the base all the way along and it wasn't till he returned the sights to bottom right that he realised the boulders there were incredibly well-camouflaged buildings—an irregular little complex of seven asymmetrical structures, varying in size and height, a rather haphazard appearance to them but at the same time seeming as ancient and unchanging as the mountain itself. Or more so. No lights, no parked vehicles, no signs of activity or occupation.

"No one home," she said. She didn't sound happy but she didn't sound very surprised either. "We'll be down there in a couple of hours. See how warm the trail is. Oh," she said, turning towards the vehicles but pausing before she walked away, "we're in Libya."

They got back into the Jeeps and headed further east along the escarpment, close enough at times to make Liam nervous, later veering away from it and onto terrain that rolled and dipped where prehistoric floods, he supposed, had created gullies and slopes between the sculpted outcrops and where an asphalt road had been built that took them gently down into the depression. By the time it bottomed out they were clearly approaching something like civilisation—a neglected building here and there by the roadside that might have been a school, or mosque, or municipal something-or-other, many unused and no way to tell if long abandoned or yet to be occupied. At a fork in the road, one way led evidently towards town—the buildings were more densely clustered that way and there was even some traffic consisting of scooters and donkey carts. The riders, men and boys, resembled the two men who'd driven the little party here from Morocco. A surprising number of them were blue-eyed. Also trucks—the oasis wasn't small.

They took the other road. Soon they were driving on a raised causeway over muddy ground, obviously managed in some way Liam couldn't fathom, churned up into channels and pools in which long grasses leaned. Palm trees were abundant until the ground became much harder looking, crystalline and near white, and suddenly the causeway took them out over water on both sides. The lake wasn't quite so enormous that Liam couldn't see the far shore, but he had to squint. To be surrounded all at once by so much water was shocking—it took his brain the whole time they were out on it to process. Half an hour later the table mountain they'd observed from above sat in full view—now back on land, the road once again forked, and the drivers headed for it. Distance didn't make any sense out here, stripped of the kind of reference points Liam could work with. The mountain was right there but it would be another half hour before the Jeeps pulled up and they walked the remaining few yards into the compound.

Up close the buildings looked like the work of a child's imagination—no straight lines or sharp edges, a Teletubby charm, in a way not unlike the kasbahs he'd seen in Morocco, but plainer, less ornamented. The view of them from afar, up on the cliffs, hadn't granted him an appreciation of scale—they varied wildly in size, from low huts to sizeable, multi-story buildings. They could have been made of mud for all he knew. He stepped up close to one of them, a rounded tower—the surface was rough and fibrous and when he placed the palm of his hand on it, harder and sharper on his skin than he expected. He pulled a crumb of the material away between his finger and thumb and, without knowing why, put it to his tongue. Salt.

He followed the others into the cool gloom of one of the larger houses and a series of rooms furnished with low benches and cushions, and striped rugs the manufacture of which he couldn't account for when he bent to feel a corner—something he almost always did with a rug. They might have been wool and then again they might have been woven from some kind of vegetal yarn. The windows were tiny, few and shuttered, and most of the shutters were closed—one of the drivers went around opening them which added to the light, but only a little. The smell of cooking perfumed the air. They stepped into a small chamber where one wall was made of a different material—a brickwork in various shades of pink and white that glowed with light from the outside. She put a hand to it and so did Liam. It was brushed smooth, like the *tadelakt* he'd found so attractive in Tangier.

"Salt crystal," she said. "Why don't you take a look around, see if you find anything?"

The near-white sand and rock, the merciless sun and mirroring water were an assault on the eye—stepping into and then back out of the murky spaces meant the retina could never stop adjusting. He'd have to stop at the threshold and wait every time. The next building along consisted of bedrooms and bathrooms and the one after that, beside a pristine swimming pool, of a dining area. Both bore signs of recent use—crumpled bedclothes, chairs set at odd angles from tables, an open toothpaste tube. Not to mention the pool itself, which was well maintained and smelled of chlorine. There might have been people here half an hour ago. Apart from some pretty fancy carpets, the interiors were as spartan as the buildings were from the outside, punctuated with nooks and niches, many of which held half-melted candles. Although the walls were smoother than outside they retained a fibrous patina and the lintels over the low doors were bound tightly with wound rope. Some of the little windows were just inches from the floor, so that someone sitting on it could benefit from the light and air.

A long low structure on the other side of the pool advertised its difference in the size of its glazed, reflective windows and the number of aircon units clinging to its upper walls. Inside, it turned out to be a single space, more or less. Elsewhere the dusty floors had seemed as though they'd been patted gently flat over time by the soles of bare feet, but the polished concrete here seemed designed more than anything else for wheels, and indeed there were a few wheeled trolleys and shelving units around, along with reels of cable and any number of power points. It was jarring to look up and, where he might have expected wooden beams, see instead the foam tiles and aluminium grid of a drop ceiling. On one wall the kind of large, mirrored window he associated with interrogation indicated that whatever took place in here was observed from in there. Sherry stepped in behind him and Darius behind her, taking up a position by the door, and the penny dropped.

"You've been here before," he said.

"Many times."

"And *this* is where you'd set up shop," he said. "Where the magic happened."

She nodded. He was through the looking-glass now. Zade dominance had bred all sorts of rumours, of course, ranging from the licentious to full-blown political conspiracy theory. He assumed it was mostly bullshit, but also that Zade nurtured the bullshit because it was a useful distraction from that-which-was-not-bullshit. A conspiracy theorist was someone convinced they knew what was going on, but everybody knew *something* was going on. They knew about data mines and troll farms and all the rest of it, but one of the theories that hovered most persistently around Zade was that there was something else at work. Something no competitor had. Something not accounted for by algorithms or AI. Something proprietary. Liam looked at the heiress. Something cooked up by his prodigy of a daughter.

"Wherever he is," she said, "he needs somewhere to set up." She seemed dejected but even in her dejection there was that untouchability, the detached invincibility that infuriated him. "Time for you to do your thing again, Mr Tead. We'll stay out here but you need to get into town and ask around."

He pushed open a metal door on one of the other walls and walked along a narrow corridor, around to the room on the other side of the mirror. She followed.

"You read Tarot, Ms Zade?"

"Excuse me?"

"Horoscopes? I'm just struck—I continue to be struck—by your approach."

If he'd been expecting to see some sort of console or server bank in there then he was disappointed. There was an electric kettle, a jar of instant coffee, a mini fridge and a leather armchair and, along the base of the one-way mirror, a bed. Suddenly he wasn't struck at all. It made perfect sense. They were all mad. That's what happened to such rarified people, wasn't it?

"What do you mean?"

They went back out.

"This gift of yours," he said. "It's for numbers, right? Mathematical, basically. I don't understand it but it's basically numbers, right? Or code, or whatever. Patterns. But here you are, having basically stuck a pin in the phonebook, asking me to do my thing, when I'm pretty sure you have no idea what my thing is. I'm not sure you really believe I have a thing. To you, I'm voodoo. It makes you seem awfully vulnerable and you don't come across as the vulnerable type. Where's this gift of yours? Why can't you push a few buttons and fix this?"

"Go up against Zade with Zade methods? That sounds like a better idea to you?"

"I don't know," said Liam. "Yes? What do I know? I have no idea what Zade methods are." He waved at the room. "What happens here. Nobody does, do they? Apart from you."

She laughed.

"I could have a stab at explaining it, but if it will seem impossibly complicated to you, and it will, why don't we just agree to call it what you just did—magic?"

Jesus.

She made for the door, no doubt assuming he would follow. Despite himself, he did. At the threshold, she took a last look back at the room and seemed to him, for just a moment, inexpressibly sad.

"A gift can also be a burden, Mr Tead."

Here we go.

"This particular gift," she patted the doorframe and stepped outside, "comes with a certain isolation." Liam followed her and Darius followed Liam. They all walked towards the largest building of the seven. "To be so exceptional in such a specific area might even be considered a disability. It implies neglect of other areas. It pretty much guarantees a host of deficits and pretty much all of those, if the excellence belongs in the digital world, will be real-world deficits."

One area in which she definitely excelled was this tone she always struck, that so delicately balanced arrogance with victimhood. He might have felt bad for her, if only she was nicer.

"Very good with computers," she smiled and gave him a faux salute, waving him through a door and into an impressively equipped kitchen, "but not so much at solving real world problems."

"Like finding your sister."

"For example. Or cooking."

Liam had opened one half of a huge fridge.

"There's *guanciale* in here."

For the first time since they'd left Tangier, he observed his own reflection slide into view on the bodyguard's aviators.

"What do you mean, isolation?"

She pulled open the fridge's other door and shrugged.

"Problems with people," she said. The fridge was stocked to bursting point. Under her breath, "They didn't know they were leaving until they left." Then, to Liam. "The work entails inordinately high levels of focus and concentration. People don't help, so there's always been this need to have them go away. To really hear the digital noise requires human silence."

"Security details under instruction not to speak, for example." He glanced at Darius.

"For example. It isn't hostility, or misanthropy. You must believe that. In fact, the curiosity about people can be almost overwhelming." She sounded defensive, peevish. "But that curiosity has had to be explored at a remove. On screen. To spend so much time, in fact, alone and literally surrounded by screens—it's self-perpetuating. An aversion to physical company sets in. The life of a caged bird." The smirk. "Poor little rich girl, right? But the claustrophobia of the cage is preferable to that of human proximity."

"Driving across the desert for three days stuck in a Jeep with me must have been excruciating for you."

"Driving across the desert for three days stuck in a Jeep with you was necessary, Mr Tead. Anyway, time for you to do your thing. One of the drivers will drop you at the edge of town. Darius has put some cash in your bag, more than you'll need. For accommodation and for Ali, who has a date shop on the square. He knows everything and everyone and will help you. Find out what's been happening here. They call it the house at White Mountain. Just don't tell him I'm here. He'll find out sooner or later but let's buy whatever time we can. Be generous with him but judicious. And with yourself, take care. I wonder if you had rather too good a time in Tangier, and we saw the consequences of that."

Liam's skin flushed in anger, which must have been visible.

"You're telling me to stay out of bars."

"There are no bars in the oasis. I'm afraid you'll find it rather dry for your palate."

"Are you hungry?" His eyes were back on the shelves. "I could knock up an *Amatriciana*." There was probably wine here. "Darius looks hungry."

"We're fine," she said. "You should go. We'll expect you when we see you." Even in her dejection, there was that breezy confidence. "Please focus. I've yet to tell you the rest of the story but you can rest assured my sister's situation is grave."

He might have been imagining it, but there was something in the bodyguard's bearing as he retrieved Liam's bag from one Jeep and threw it on the back seat of the other that spoke to Liam of cruel disappointment. He couldn't assess the quantity of cash very well because he had no idea about the exchange rate but there was no world in which it wasn't a lot of money. Back out on the causeway over the lake and sitting up front, the water dazzling because the Jeep was speeding back towards the sun, the windows down and the whipping air saline sweet, it dawned on him that when he'd used the word *excruciating* he'd been projecting. Those days cooped up in the Jeep with her *had* been excruciating, but for him, not her, and he could only really feel it now that he was free of her. The unearthly strangeness of her. He was becoming rather fond of a very specific scenario—putting distance between himself and the great Sherry Zade with a bag of cash in hand. It wasn't his fault she was crazy. It wasn't his responsibility. And what a spot for distance: this was the ultimate elsewhere, surely—even the limits of his sight, the faraway sand banks and rock cliffs, merely heralded more of the same beyond. Nowhere, it occurred to him, was his favourite place, and here he was in the middle of it.

The Oasis

BELLYSPRAWLING the stout bough panther fashion, chin on a church of woven fingers, one bare foot hooked over the heel of the other, Liam waited lazily on the third day and the lowest limb of one of the very, very few trees in this, a land of trees, that wasn't a date palm, the sturdy branch hanging over a garden wall to give him a look at the within, face dappled in evening light, skin sundarkened, he waiting in repose, lazily for his prey, the posture eased by the straddle of his dress, a bran-new *jalabiya*, plain and pale blue, in which he thought himself rather magnificent even if some local reaction, that of Ali's friends for example, had been jocular and even if, from a fray on the collar, it could be deduced that Ali had sold it to him, freshly laundered, off his own back, still it wasn't as bad as the incredulous looks the sports gear had earned him, even from a distance, in the town at the centre of the swathe of lakes and palm groves that was the oasis.

Ali wasn't as easily found as *date shop on the square* might have suggested. The town was small but not tiny and the square was broad and long, consisting not only of shops around its perimeter but also of an inner arcade, a square within a square. Most of the shops were date shops. The walk to the square was short and unlike anything Liam had ever experienced. He liked to think he'd been around but he hadn't been here. While traffic was heavy it consisted of donkey carts and bicycles—motor vehicles, apart from the few scooters and trucks, were few and far between and invariably looked as if they were passing through, laden with whatever cargo: dates going out and almost everything else coming in. The street was unpaved, packed earth. There were blackened workshops, coffee houses, a garishly-decorated travel agency devoted to the *hajj*, a telecoms outlet emblazoned with every logo Liam could think of but here hand-painted. The largest of course was the Zade plume. As he neared the square the call to prayer went up, giving a sonic account of the size of the oasis—no fewer than half a dozen *muezzins* megaphoning from near and very far, the same words sung at varying pitches, separated by seconds, syncopating a jumble of sound, a scrambled and splendid aural mess.

He saw almost no women. It set him on edge. The few he did see were sitting cross-legged on donkey carts and covered up by long, blue-grey shawls. Black gauze obscured their faces. They gave so ghostly an impression that Liam imagined for a second only he could see them, that the little boys who piloted the carts were unaware of their passengers. When he got to the square he did a couple of circuits, the crumpled sports-casual aesthetic attracting unwanted stares. The second pass was intense. It wasn't hostility exactly but clearly none of these guys was going to fall over himself trying to help the stranger. They seemed happy to indulge a disinterested curiosity, leaving the matter of what happened next entirely to Liam, who didn't know where to start. He had one word to work with—Ali—and a large number of shopkeepers around here, it would transpire, went by that name.

On its first deployment, the man Liam addressed stood up from the stool he'd occupied at the front of his store, smiled and offered his hand. Liam took it, unable to believe it had been so easy and reaching the conclusion very quickly that it hadn't—this guy didn't speak a word of English. It made him an unlikely guide. When he eventually released Liam's hand he proceeded to pat his own chest at short intervals, repeating the name with every pat, his broad smile narrowing a little each time as Liam shook his head, till the shopkeeper's lips were pursed in something like offence. Then he raised a decisive finger and beckoned for Liam to follow. They walked a few feet into the adjacent store where the first shopkeeper presented a second. Things didn't go any better there. By the time he was introduced to the fourth Ali, Ali number one was clearly struggling to maintain his positive attitude and numbers two and three looked like their moods were spiralling also.

"*Ali esfeech oore donbi bisi.*"

Liam looked behind him, where a crowd had materialised. It was a small crowd but it wasn't small enough for his liking. The interjection had come from a tiny boy of indeterminate age. He looked like the last person around here who was going to clear up the confusion. On the other hand his words had an obvious impact on the grown-ups, a number of whom were nodding in agreement.

"*Ali esfeech oore donbi bisi.*"

The first Ali shoved Liam towards the boy, dismissing them both with an impatient wave of his hand. The crowd melted away almost instantaneously, the matter evidently resolved and all interest therefore lost. Liam was glad for the scene change and to follow the boy as the latter darted ahead along one side of the square, then waited for him to catch up. He took his time, a little less intimidated by a small child than he had been by a clutch of increasingly irate men, and allowed himself to take in the square's main feature. It wasn't a feature of the square, really, but towered over it—a huge fortification, maybe eight stories at its highest point, built from that same fibrous, muddy material that had surprised his touch out at the White Mountain house, but on an altogether different scale. The massive walls were curved, forming towers and turrets, and only one stretch of them reached full height—to either side the structure fell away in ruins, the upper reaches either eroded or cannibalised for the same building materials that went into the houses down here. The thing was obviously ancient and obviously abandoned, a conundrum of human ingenuity and natural decay—it gave the impression of having been both built and destroyed by termites.

The stacked fruits of the date vendors were punctuated by general stores, grocers and mountainous bundles of something like clover that probably fed the donkeys. The boy stopped outside a shop that sold dates but also pottery and woven fabrics. A hand-painted sign read, in English, *Ali's Shop. Dates, Handicrafts and Desert Safaris. As featured on BBC.*

"Ali esfeech oore donbi bisi."

A small photo, much the worse for wear, was taped to the sign and in it a slight man in local dress posed in front of a 4x4 with a recognisable BBC journalist, though Liam couldn't recall the name. The local was certainly Ali, because the same man emerged from the shop, beckoned by the boy who was yelling at an unnecessarily high volume and pointing at Liam.

"You are looking for me?"

"I think so," said Liam. "I was told to find Ali, that he was the man to help a stranger out around here. But so far I've met four of them and they haven't helped at all."

"It is absolutely no doubt that your friend spoke of me and he did very well in doing. We will have a meeting. Pay the boy."

Liam hesitated.

"He brought you to me did he not? This is excellent work he did very well in doing," said Ali, ruffling the boy's tight, curly hair, "so pay him. You are not a thief I hope. If you are a thief I shouldn't know you."

Liam pulled a note from the stuffed envelope in his shoulder bag and held it out to the boy. He was quite an appealing little boy, really, and Liam thought he might also ruffle his hair, but by the time he had formulated the thought the child had snatched the note and disappeared.

"You are insane?" said Ali. "Do you know how much money? He could feed his whole family on that for a month if so inclined."

"I don't really care about the money," said Liam. "It isn't mine."

"I am very happy to meet you," said Ali. "Here." The shopkeeper had taken a string bracelet from a shelf and handed it to Liam. "Put it on your wrist if you are sick. Are you hungry?"

"I'm starving. I suppose the chances of a pizza are slim round here."

"You joke? This is Little Italy, my friend. Come."

Just off the square, at the base of the giant fortification, was a tiny restaurant, if you could call it a restaurant, open on to the street, if you could call it a street, where Ali invited Liam to sit and did the ordering for them.

"You will pay of course. What do you need from Ali?"

Liam's eyes were roving over the rambling, ruinous construction opposite. There was a breach here in the outer walls and something of the interior could be seen—more of a town than a castle, a hive of alleyways and steps, towers that Liam supposed had been minarets, houses piled upon houses, all the way up to the raw, ragged top.

"Doesn't look like Italy to me," he said. A man put two mugs of juice on the table. Liam didn't know what type of juice it was but it wasn't date juice and he was glad of that. The smell of the things filled the square. It was a heavy smell. It had weight.

"My grandfather used to tell us stories about the Italians," said Ali. "He found them crazy but he liked them well. The oasis has changed hands many times over the years—it has usually made little difference to us. These days it's Alexandrians. The Italians took their turn during your war."

"My war?"

"The one with Hitler. Here is your food."

Ali hadn't ordered anything for himself and would not accept any of Liam's. It wasn't a pizza, exactly, but it was close enough and very good—the same size and shape as a pizza but stuffed rather than topped and made of layered, flaky pastry instead of bread dough.

"The Italians taught you guys how to make these?"

"The Italians, one way or another, have been visiting this land for centuries. There is no doubt at all that we teached them. That's the reality. Please let me pick the note when you pay."

When the time came, Liam held out the envelope and Ali chose a note for the restaurant owner, taking another, a larger denomination, for himself.

"Retainer. Come, I will show you my garden."

Liam didn't like the sound of that. They walked back through the square and away from it on the far side, on a sandy path that cut through the date palms till they left the sounds of the market behind them. The food had had a calming effect but Liam was on edge again. Ali came recommended but it didn't seem like a good idea to follow a man into a forest, a man perfectly aware of the cash Liam was carrying. A significantly smaller man, admittedly, but he could be working with accomplices. Ali had led them off the main path and there was nothing now to distinguish one direction from another.

"Where's your garden?"

"You are in it."

They had reached a small clearing where a fire had regularly been lit beside a felled palm that served as a curved bench.

"You like tea?"

From beneath a lid of palm fronds at one end of the trunk, Ali produced a pot, a bottle of water, a pouch of tea and a tin of sugar, and set about lighting the fire.

"Why don't you tell me what you want?" he said. "Desert safari?"

Liam sat on the tree trunk.

"I've had my fill of desert," he said. "I'm here to write a story."

"Story?"

"I'm a journalist."

"Not BBC."

"How do you know?"

"If they are BBC they open with that. You are CNN? Zade?"

"Freelance."

"Hm. And what is the story?"

"I'd rather not say, exactly. But one place to start would be I'm interested in any movements there might have been at the White Mountain house. Do you know it?"

"You are not Zade then. Zade is the story, yes?"

"No, no. The story is really the oasis. I just think that the Zades have a house here is an interesting place to start."

"Hm."

In a few minutes the water boiled and, several times, Ali filled two small glasses and poured their contents back into the pot. Finally he filled them for the last time, from a theatrical height, and passed one to Liam. Once it was cool enough to drink, it was stronger than Liam had thought tea could be.

"I don't know anything about movings," said Ali. "I can ask people. But if the story is the oasis it is no doubt I can help. That's the reality."

He was to demonstrate the latter point over the next two days, finding Liam a room at the foot of the *Shali*—the name Ali gave the ancient fortification—in a place whose construction made it difficult to distinguish it from the ruins that sprawled above it but where the service was surprisingly smart, and proving himself to be an assiduous dispenser of small, monetarily insignificant gifts—a clay cup, a multi-coloured fly swat, fragments of salt crystal—in return for regular top-ups of his retainer. Out of the shaded density of the date groves and over the glittering eastern lake on a donkey cart, the shock of transition to that open vastness, the quick colouring of the skin, the salt excavators, the salty pools they left with their Dead Sea buoyancy—Ali gave Liam, who he called Lim, a very thorough introduction to the oasis, to its many hot and cold springs, Roman-walled, to the temple where he said Alexander consulted the oracle. Together they climbed the defunct minaret there and alone Liam climbed the mountain of the dead, a Swiss cheese of rock tombs that Ali refused to scale with him because night was falling.

On the second day they climbed another small mountain, the highest in the oasis, and from its summit Liam could take in the whole depression, ringed in every direction by higher ground, the mountain at its centre like the iris of an eye. Ali sold Liam the *jalabiya*. They explored the *Shali*, its incomprehensible mess of stairs and alleys, and in the evening he showed Liam how they tapped the trees for palm wine and scoffed at Liam's surprise.

"Lim, there are angels, there are people and there are jinn," he said. "I am no angel."

They drank wine and Liam found its effect very agreeable, a warm fuzzy buzz that could be maintained with regular replenishment from the large plastic bottle Ali gave him, and a hangover the following morning so mild as to be almost pleasant, just a little nudge to take another sip and keep it all going, the warmth, the soft focus, the sensation of having travelled back and far in time and space, a sensation upon which not even Ali's compulsive checking of his WhatsApp, or his incessant posting to Facebook, could intrude. They ate roast goat, that second afternoon, and later Ali took him to a rocky height outside town from where they could look back at the rambling ruins of the *Shali* as the sun set, and how they burned so red it was as if they didn't reflect its light but glowed, like the embers of a forgotten fire, with their own. It occurred to him more than once that he was making a poor show of pretending to be a journalist and an even worse one of doing his real job, that how he was passing time here was really more akin to tourism. But it did not occur to him to admonish himself.

Why should he? If the whole thing was a matter of faith, based entirely on her intuition, why shouldn't he just go with the flow? Why direct events, or try to? Time would pass and something would happen. It was enough. The palm wine eased the passage. He did try, now and then, to revisit the subject of the Zades and their house but Ali had not been forthcoming. If anything he seemed to clam up. The only morsel Liam had from him was on that first afternoon, when they had left the garden and were walking along the sandy path towards the square, and Ali had pointed out a donkey cart pulling into a walled property bearing three of those ghostly, shrouded women, and Ali had said that one of them was the White Mountain housekeeper whenever Zade was in town and that she lived there with her two sisters.

And so here was Liam, up a tree, having shaken Ali off with a flimsy excuse and a more convincing banknote, waiting at the same time of day he'd seen the women arrive, having nothing more to go on and not at all anxious he'd gotten it right or concerned about what might happen next, or when, bellyflesh separating bough from palm wine, the sun soothing, the breeze a breathy tune played on leaves, when the donkey cart pulled in through the front gate. Liam had seen two types of house in the oasis—those made of *karshif*, as Ali called the salty, fibrous, hardened mud, and a few newer-built brick and concrete homes, walled and painted brightly, that wouldn't have looked out of place in a Spanish suburb. This two-story house was of the latter sort, the gardens that surrounded it lovingly tended and comprised of fruit trees, damsons and cherries, almonds and fig, beds of roses, eglantine, violets and chamomile. The little boy who drove the cart was paid and dismissed and the gate shut behind him. The two women who had shut it pulled the veils from their faces, revealing instantly that they were sisters, almost identical, jet black hair braided and oiled and pulled back tightly from dark, fine-featured, blue-eyed faces. They were dutiful towards the third, who, rather than remove her own veil, waited for them to attend her. This they did with some ceremony, removing the embroidered, blue-grey outer shawl first and folding it with great care before lifting the black gauze from her face. When they did this, Liam's wits left him. The face revealed glowed pale as a full moon trespassing upon the day, rosiclear cheeks framed by golden tresses, and two gleaming green eyes fit to exchange glances with a gazelle.

At that moment, a commotion in the tree. A little black bird that, unseen, had been keeping Liam company, now took wing from its perch, fluttering upwards and disturbing a sprig of leaves directly overhead. They cost it a single plume which, to Liam's astonishment, and though he was certain the bird had been black, was pure bright white. As he fixed his eyes on it, its sashaying descent, its shimmying saunter towards the earth, he quite forgot that a feather might have anything to do with a bird, that an origin was even necessary for such irreducible beauty, such pure expression of form and function. His passion overcame his reason. He knew he must have it, so getting to his feet and straightening carefully upon the branch, he reached as far as he dared, hoping to intercept it. Just when he thought he might lose his balance, it came easily to the palm of his hand and, steadying himself, he examined it more closely.

His holding diminished it. Pinched between his thumb and forefinger it seemed a more ordinary thing than it had in the air, in the neither-here-nor-there between its previous existence and Liam's grip, flashing in the odd shaft of sunlight. But it was still beautiful. He wondered at the change written between the rachis—the supreme, high definition geometries of the centre—and the blur of its outer extremities, the vague down at its coast as feather gave way, fuzzily, to that-which-is-not-feather. Then he remembered his attention had been elsewhere and returned it there. When he did this, his judgement was confounded and his mind lost. Love exceeded all limits. It had always been this way with women. The sisters had continued to disrobe the lady until there was no garment left to remove. In doing so they had unveiled a wonder of the world and a miracle for the ages. The sight was enough to befuddle the wise and make any coward courageous. So demented with lust was he that he fainted away and fell to the ground on the inside of the wall, the bough meeting with his head on the way down and granting him the mercy, before her annihilating splendour, of unconsciousness.

The American Tourist

Liam had only had his eyes open for a minute, but already he'd reached a couple of reasonably solid conclusions. The flicker on the inside of his eyelids that had ushered him into consciousness remained almost unchanged when he lifted them—a blackness that quivered, that trembled with something not black. He was on his back, looking at the ceiling of a very dark room and this was his first conclusion—that in some distant corner of it, a single candle burned. In the moments it took him to reach it, an automatic inventory was performed, the old brain survey that accompanies all awakenings. He was not at home, whatever that was; he did not know this place; he could not detect any pain or problem in any part of his body, though he did feel a curious detachment from it. The prospect of moving was impossibly distant. He had stumbled into wakefulness but felt no compunction whatever to step into physicality. A delicious sensation, a contentment to accept the stuttering gloom, to take it for the whole world and forever. And somewhere, deep and yet to be revealed in this unfamiliar state, something familiar.

The second conclusion concerned a circumstance closer to hand. As his brain ticked through its limbic list, another part of it had observed the room's quiet not to be silence. It was in fact a hurried, animated and respiratory quiet. What distinguished it from silence spoke wordlessly of bulk. Of taut muscle and loose tongue. Of patience and purpose. Of presence. And it stank. This new world existed in a miasma of bad breath. Quick, shallow breaths, punctuated now and then with the swill of tongue over teeth, the clap of a closed jaw. It came to Liam, as if from very far away and long ago, that he had a serious problem with big dogs. This felt true to him—an abstraction in the moment, but true. The only thing for it was to look. But looking meant movement and movement meant inhabiting his body, once again taking control of it, accepting responsibility for it, and he didn't want that.

And yet the breathing was insistent as only a dog's breath can be. *Do something*, it said. *Move*. It took a long time for Liam to remember that he had a neck and that there were muscles there, and ligaments that he could call upon, and so he did call upon them and, after a couple of failed attempts, he lifted a trembling head and looked to his side.

A black mastiff, a couple of feet away at most, teeth bared, had begun, on noticing this tiny movement, to emit a growl Liam could feel though the mattress beneath him.

"Hello."

The thing lunged and the whole room quivered as its chain snapped tight. Its fury was deafening, the rage of ten dogs. A pack of rabid dogs. A dog demon. It took just moments for its fur to glisten with sweat, its mouth to fill with foam, just inches from Liam's turned head. Again and again it coiled back to lunge again, straining at the chain which, now Liam looked at it, seemed inappropriately slender. When his eyes followed the line of it to the metal loop on the far wall where it was fastened, they found another dog there, identical, unchained, sitting sphinx-like, still and perfectly content, it seemed to Liam, notably unaffected by its associate's frenzy. But then, he supposed, he didn't seem all that affected himself, and that was when he realised what it was that seemed so familiar about the situation. He was heavily drugged. As if the realisation itself had a sedative effect, his head fell back, and even as the beast raged and spattered Liam with its saliva, sleep returned.

When he came to, the room was quiet and it was daylight that played across the ceiling, reflected from a rippling surface somewhere outside. He could tell from the warmth of the light and the heat in the room that it wasn't morning and that he had therefore slept long, deep into another afternoon. That the observation occurred to him so quickly brought with it the realisation he once again had his wits about him. He lifted his head effortlessly. Both dogs were gone. Looking down, he saw that he lay uncovered and naked and, rather startlingly, that he had been shaved clean from the neck down. Bathed too—there was no bad smell, nothing of the canine spittle that must have drenched him. He knew he hadn't dreamt that—the chain lay loose and limp on the floor. When he sat up he saw that a crisp white *jalabiya* had been left by the bed for him, and a pair of slippers.

The bedroom door led directly outside, into a courtyard at the centre of which was a fountain, surrounded by a plunge pool. On the other three sides the courtyard was lined with arched compartments and niches, those in turn lined with cupboards and cabinets in carved wood, partly covered by curtains. In the niche opposite stood a couch of black wood upholstered in white silk and inset with gems and pearls, over which hung a mosquito net of red silk with fastenings of pearls the size of hazelnuts—a delicate hand undid them and from beneath the net emerged a woman he felt he remembered. How could it be possible to forget this woman? Her hair was a dome of gold. It vaulted over golden eyebrows arched like raised longbows to protect a pair of gleaming green eyes, fit to return the gaze of a gazelle. Whoever she was, she was, like Liam, a foreigner here, as pale as a lily petal. Around her wafted the scent of ambergris and the radiance of her face put the sinking sun to shame—she brought to mind a star more distant and more magnificent, or a morsel of luscious fat in a bowl of milk soup.

"There you are, lazy boy," she said in an American accent. "I'd offer you a seat but you've been on your back so long maybe you prefer to stand. Are you thirsty?"

As if the question was an instruction, another woman emerged from some corner of the yard and busied herself at a cabinet, retrieving cups, decanters and utensils of silver and gold, and laying them out on a low table beneath the silken net.

"A little," he said. When Green Eyes beckoned for him to take a place at the table, he sat on a cushion there. "How did I get here?"

She herself sat opposite him on a couch so that she could recline there and look down upon him, resting her cheek in the palm of her hand.

"You fell out of the sky," she said. "You'd think you'd remember something like that."

She wore a simple white robe so fine Liam could make out the contours of her body beneath it. The other woman smelled good as she leaned over to fill his cup with red wine. When she had filled three cups she began to bring all kinds of food to the table—candied fruits and nuts, salads of pomegranate seeds and onion, bowls of aromatic soup and platters of roasted goat and grilled chickens, as well as many delicious-looking dishes that Liam couldn't name. Delighted at the sight of wine, he took a deep draught. The other woman joined them. She sat as Liam did on a cushion and crossed her legs. She passed Green Eyes' cup to her and took it when it had been drunk from, so the latter never had to reach.

"I've been manscaped," said Liam.

"Hair is so disagreeable," said Green Eyes. "We left you some on your head."

Liam's hand instinctively went to his scalp. He hadn't thought of it till now and hadn't seen any mirrors. His hair had been neatly cut. His face was smooth-shaven. He was perfumed. His toe and fingernails were filed and his hands and feet had been moisturized with rich creams.

"Drink," said Green Eyes.

He emptied his cup and the other woman filled it. The wine was sweet and strong.

"There were three of you, I think."

"Ah, so you do remember something." The other woman got up to fetch a little wooden box from a cabinet and brought it to Green Eyes, who lifted the lid and took out a white feather. "The other sister isn't happy with you and won't show herself. She thinks we should have thrown you out. Do you remember this?"

She waved the feather in the air.

"I . . . think so," said Liam.

"The oasis is a superstitious place. We ain't exactly from around here," said Green Eyes with a comic twang, "but the youngest of us has rather taken its beliefs to heart. She was just a pup when she came here, after all. Do you know what this is?"

Again she waved the feather.

"A feather?"

She rolled her eyes. "The plume of the *Haj Mawly*. A spirit of the oasis. To harm one is forbidden. When you fell to the ground you were clutching it. How did you come by it?"

"I do remember," said Liam. He described seeing the little bird take off through the canopy and how the feather had blinked in the light, dropping into his hand. When he finished telling his tale, the third woman had already approached the table as though she had been listening from behind one of the many curtains.

"This is the truth?" She was comely like the others. Compared with her, the moon was a toenail clipping, the sun a spent ember. Her jet black eyes were fit to return the gaze of a gazelle. Liam nodded, transfixed. She went to a cabinet and fetched another little box. Then she took the feather from Green Eyes and from the box a needle and thread and, sitting at Liam's feet, sewed the feather into the hem of his robe.

"If it is the truth then you are blesséd. The plume is a gift from the *Haj Mawly* and you will know success in your quest. If you are lying then it is a curse and you will know sorrow."

Liam caught the other sister rolling her eyes, but nobody questioned the behaviour or tried to stop it. Liam became aware that as the woman worked his hem, he was exposed to her. But then it had already been established that these three had their own ideas when it came to personal space.

"There were dogs."

"My guards. They watch over me each night," said Green Eyes. "In the daytime, as you see, I have better company."

Cups were refilled and emptied, and again refilled until Liam felt as drunk as he was bewitched. One of the sisters played on the lute as the other danced provocatively, and they all of them shed their inhibitions, carousing and cavorting long into the evening as they kissed and bit and rubbed, playing jokes on each other, biting, groping and fingering. When they were all thoroughly drunk, the sister who had laid the table got up, raised her robe over her head and discarded it. She got into the pool and standing under one of the fountain spouts, washed herself between her legs. When she got out she sat in Liam's lap and pointed at her slit.

"What is this?" she asked.

"Your pussy," said Liam.

"So lame. Try again."

"Your crack?"

She hit him on the back of his neck with a force that cut right through the wine.

"Show some respect," she said. Liam hoped that might be that, but she persisted.

"Look at it. Tell me what it is."

He looked and answered her reluctantly, expecting another blow.

"Your vulva."

The blow came, and another, and another, and a blow from her sister, and many more blows, with increasing force till, in a wild panic, Liam shouted "The Aromatic Slipway!"

They fell about laughing. Liam didn't mind—he didn't know where the words had come from but they'd stopped hitting him.

"Eh, no—it is not The Aromatic Slipway," said the owner of the body part. Her sister was topping them up with wine.

"Why don't you just tell me what it is?" said Liam, rubbing his neck.

"Why couldn't you have said The Salty Marina? I prefer that."

Having poured the wine, the other woman lifted her robe over her head and washed herself in the pool. Then she shooed her sister out of Liam's lap and sat there herself, pointing at her crotch.

"And what is this?" she said.

Liam braced. "The Salty Marina?'

She didn't hit him but she shook her head.

"Too easy," she said. "Try again."

"Well, if it isn't The Salty Marina," said Liam, "then I'm pretty sure it's your cunt."

She slapped him in the face, hard enough that he checked his lip for blood.

"Guess again. And be nice."

It was time to play it for laughs again. His last quip had earned him a little respite. This was an incredibly difficult room to read. They were hurting him but on the other hand they weren't wearing any underwear.

"The Husked Sesame."

"The Husked Sesame?" she asked, and punched him in the gut. He bent over her lap, winded.

"The fuck is a husked sesame?" said Green Eyes.

"Please," said Liam when he could take a breath. "It's anything you want . . . what do you want . . ."

"Why couldn't you have said The Shucked Oyster?" said the sister on his knee. "That would have been better."

Wine was poured and Liam was relieved to see that Green Eyes made no move to go to the pool and wash herself, instead remaining on her couch as she had all along. However, on emptying his cup and lowering it, he saw that she had pulled her robe up to her waist.

"And what is this?" she said.

"No offence," said Liam, "but I'm not sure I want to know."

"You must guess."

Liam guessed. And guessed again. And again, and again, and all the while the blows and slaps and pokes and pinches rained down upon him till, in real pain, he cried out "Stop! Please stop!" and they did.

"Tell me what it is," he said, "and I promise I'll never get it wrong again."

"Why couldn't you have said The Holiday Hotel?" said Green Eyes, lowering her robe. "I would have liked that."

Liam drank the wine he was offered. The erection that had been denied him during his beatings came now and, standing to pull his robe over his head, he washed himself in the pool. When he got out he stood in front of the three women and pointed at his member.

"What is this?" he said.

"Your dick."

"Your testicles."

"Your thing."

Not thinking it wise to reciprocate their violence, Liam saw to it that each wrong guess earned a tickle.

"Your penis."

"Your stick."

"Your cock."

He tickled each of them till they could take no more and begged him to stop.

"Why don't you just tell us what it is?" said the sister who had sewn the feather into the hem of his robe.

Liam stood back to once again display himself.

"It is The American Tourist," he said.

Green Eyes snotlaughed into her wine. The feather sewer spat hers out. From the table-setter, who had covered her face with a hand, emanated a series of choking noises. The first to recover was the sewer.

"Why is it The American Tourist?" she asked.

"Well," said Liam, hands on hips, "you can hardly miss it, can you?"

As they laughed, he expounded.

"It is the hull of the cruise ship that slides along The Aromatic Slipway. It docks in The Salty Marina. It is the bibbed glutton who shucks oysters in the seafood restaurant there, and the most demanding guest at The Holiday Hotel."

He returned to the cushions and to the embrace of the two black-eyed sisters and they continued to play and fuck. Green Eyes contented herself with a spectating role from her couch. Night drew in. Liam was either deep in his element or way out of his depth, but probably both. Perhaps they were the same thing.

"Hey, what are your names?"

He was on his back and the table setter was grinding upon him, but the moment he asked the question she got off and the other two fell silent from their talk.

"It is time for the two of you to go," said Green Eyes.

The two sisters gathered up their robes and left the courtyard without a word.

"Have you enjoyed yourself?" she asked Liam, who had propped himself up with his hands on the floor behind him.

"Yes," he said. "It's been a lovely evening." He had drunk far more wine than he'd expect to be able for, but although he felt he neared the edge of consciousness, his heart raced. Something buzzed in him that had laced the drink.

"You can come here every day and enjoy us as we enjoy you," said Green Eyes. "You can eat and drink your fill and frolic with us. Would you like that?"

He nodded.

"On one condition," she said, with the slowly-enunciated patience of a primary school teacher. She smiled at him with her temple resting on her fist and there was warmth in the smile but a warning in her eyes. "We have no need of names here. Have we asked for yours?

You must not ask us ours. In fact you must not ask us anything. No what is this or what is that. No questions of any kind. Can you do that? It is not as easy as it sounds."

"I can do it," said Liam. The change in mood and circumstance had had a physical effect. He was dizzy.

"Good," she said. "Then we have a deal. And I suppose since they have gone it's my turn."

But Liam couldn't focus his eyes. Everything wobbled. Laying his head on a cushion to close them for a moment, he blacked out.

The Guessing Game

ANOTHER AWAKENING. This time, Liam did not feel rested. His eyeballs hurt and their lids remained shut—if he tried to lift them the pain intensified, so it was through his nose that the world reintroduced itself. It smelled of warm earth. Many hours must have passed, since it was bright and already hot. He became aware of sound, of the occasional hushed voice, the turning of a cartwheel, soft footsteps. The earth that smelled so good was coarse—he knew this because it dug in to his cheek. He opened one eye and groaned, the closed gate of the house resolving from an initial blur. When he had taken a few more breaths, he lifted himself into a seated position and sat panting, exhausted by the move. His vision vibrated and his ears buzzed with whatever had laced the wine. He was, of course, attracting attention—looks that ranged from disapproval to disgust—so, despite the seeming impossibility, he got to his feet and set out in the direction of the market square.

Something was going on there, judging by the noise levels as he approached. As the palm-lined path gave way to the outermost buildings of the town and then the market itself, it wasn't the same place Liam had known for the last few days. The air was dirty, filled with dust kicked up by the trucks that passed through at speed on the far side. All around the square, donkey carts were outnumbered by noisy tuk-tuks. If the vehicle had changed the use hadn't—many of them were driven, wildly, by the same small boys he'd seen chauffeuring the shrouded women about town, the latter now holding on to the metal frame of the tuk-tuks for dear life. The square was roaring. Apparently the date market was irregular, because most of the stalls had been replaced with other goods—everything from cosmetics to kitchen goods, carpets and USB sticks. In his current state, Liam didn't feel confident about getting through the traffic to his hotel alive so he headed for Ali's shop, closer by, blinking in the airborne dust. What had happened to this place, apparently overnight?

As he approached Ali's an SUV pulled up, blocking it from view. The passenger door was pushed open and Liam recognised one of Zade's drivers. He experienced a strong urge to run—she was the last thing he wanted to deal with—but there was no way his body was going to respond to it, so he got in the car. Out on the causeway, he had to ask the guy to stop so he could spend a good ten minutes retching on his hands and knees in the gravel, depositing his debauched filth on the pristine landscape. He was still cold-sweating and contemplating the possibility of further evacuations via a furiously watering mouth when they got to the house and he stepped out into fierce heat, walking unsteadily up the path between the *karshif* structures. His employer was poolside, in a deck chair beneath a parasol, a magazine in her lap and a jug of iced juice at her side. It was all very Hockney.

"You're alive," she said, lowering her sunglasses unnecessarily and making a piece of theatre out of looking him all the way up and down, "if by a narrow margin."

There was another deck chair, also shaded, and Liam didn't wait to be invited to sit there. Darius was at the far end of the pool, immaculately turned out in suit and tie. The only concession the giant had made to the blazing heat was to remove his shoes and socks, roll up his trouser legs, and sit with his feet in the pool. Liam wondered how much water they were displacing.

"Progress?"

"I should have something today." The same guy who'd driven him out here appeared with a tall glass of water and Liam downed it in one, hoping it would stay down.

"Then I won't keep you too long. At least while you're here we can hydrate you." She waved a hand, presumably at the driver. "I must say you make some interesting wardrobe choices. It's almost as if you're a fucking clown."

It was the first time he'd heard her use a profanity. He shivered involuntarily—the mood had changed. He might be in proper trouble. This would be the time to say something clever, some demonstration of the sharpness of his wit, but that possibility had rarely been so remote. A second glass of water was placed at his side. His stomach wasn't ready for it yet but he picked it up, just for something to do. She sighed.

"If, in spite of appearances, you're to help me find my sister, it may help if in some way, at some intuitive level, you understand us. A sibling of course can only explain the other to you in terms of the relationship. Of what unites and what divides us." She hadn't closed the magazine but was clearly about to embark on one of her monologues. Or was that soliloquies? "You're not that much older than me. You must have been looking at pictures of me in the media most of your life. Stories about me. Special gifts, child prodigy, alleged superhuman abilities."

So that was what she meant by *terms of the relationship*. She was going to talk about herself again. Liam had to fight hard to suppress a noxious belch. He badly needed painkillers but some unnamable resentment stopped him from asking. Anyway, they probably didn't have any—these people didn't seem like they were familiar with the concept of pain. He missed Reynolds.

"Are you familiar with the term *logosyllabary*, Mr Tead?"

"No."

"I don't have time to explain it to you. Let's go with alphabet. I take it you know your alphabet.

"The truth is," she went on, "that despite all the nonsensical media speculation, there *is* something exceptional—something that made itself known at the onset of my adolescence. Bear in mind that my sister and I were studied and assessed continuously—it never let up. It wasn't until I left the household that I got a break and I suspect my father tracks the same performance indicators remotely now. He can't help himself."

He wanted her to stop saying words. He wanted the sun to stop shining and his stomach to stop turning. A stop to the arrogance and self-satisfaction and the patronising tone. The pool pump had started up and he wanted that to stop too.

"I'm not claiming these aptitudes were unprecedented in all of human history, you understand. That would be maniacal. But something in the combination of extraordinary ability and the tsunami of exposure to the digital world effected brain changes significant enough to show up in imaging. This is where the alphabet comes in. Think of a letter."

The pump had agitated the water and the little waves and eddies on the pool's surface were making Liam seasick. Was she going to guess the letter? He settled on F.

"The transition to the alphabet from previous writing systems was not a trivial thing. A letter is a human artifice, a technology, that has itself engendered human evolution. Real brain changes leading to novel forms of thought. These brain changes can be observed in any learning child and certainly were in our case. Are you with me?"

He wasn't, but at least he knew it wasn't a guessing game.

"It doesn't really matter," she said. "What matters is that by combining these simple data we get not only words but poems, novels, fake news. When one of us began to exhibit novel brain activity, nobody could have been better placed to detect it than our parents and their people. The activity in question had nothing to do with learning to read, at least ostensibly, but it was unquestionably analogous."

Wow.

"The formation of entirely new pathways and the apparent, later evident, ability to process complex data—memes, narratives, stories—as though they were themselves the basic building blocks of larger patterns we have yet to name. Algorithms would be a serviceable metaphor but remember I'm talking here about a human mind and—if you can believe it, Mr Tead—a human heart. And at that age these abilities arose just in time to serve my father's business very well indeed. Ever since then Zade has had an asset unlike any other. It trumps everything else because it's unique and unprecedented. It can't be replicated, or at least it hasn't yet. We can't even explain it—it has nothing to do with troll farms, data mining or any other ridiculous theories you've seen printed below my photo."

She raised her palms. "The great Sherry Zade," she said, flicking her hair away from her forehead. "Are you getting my good side? People would be unsettled way beyond any of the nonsense you've read online if they knew the real nature of the Zade advantage. It isn't technology, and even if was technology it wouldn't matter that it was, because we don't know how it works. It's thaumaturgy." She made a faux sympathetic expression. "Magic, Mr Tead."

In truth, Liam *was* having a problem with the human heart part. How could there be room in there with an ego bloated enough to burst her ribcage? He took a sip of water before he spoke because it meant he didn't say what came to mind first.

"I know this is all meant to help Ms Zade, but since it's your sister I've been employed to find, maybe you could tell me something about Doonah."

"Ah yes, Doonah." She brushed the magazine off her lap and stretched. "We need to talk about Doonah. You'll have to forgive me, Mr Tead—I've quite fallen out of the habit. The whole family has." She drank some juice and winced—it apparently fell short of some standard.

"Where should I start?" she said. "You'll be aware of the 'early retirement' of Doonah Zade. It's more of a containment measure. It has been sensible, expedient, for the family to use one sister to represent the two for some time now. Although the differences—the deficits, shall we say—were detected very early on, the real problems began at around the same time I've been talking about. Adolescence. That much we have in common, my sister and I—radical developments at that age that would set us on very different paths. But the contrast could not have been greater. You look pale. Can we get you anything?"

"No. What contrast?"

She sighed. "To be honest, a lot of it is too sordid to go into. On the one hand you have this blossoming gift, that none of us understood—myself included—that made this one daughter, little more than a child, suddenly a material asset, an integral part of the Zade machine. The most important part, even. On the other," she sipped her juice and put it back down, "her sibling, whose deficits had always been mere measurements but now became serious problems."

"Problems how?" he had noticed, since she had been steered away from talking about herself, a certain reticence, an awkwardness, and he was enjoying it.

"Reputational, for one thing. Scandal and so on. For a few years there, it seemed like as much work went into concealing the various behaviours as into anything else at Zade."

"Behaviours?"

"Behaviours. A compendium of them on legs, that Doonah."

"Yes but *what* behaviours?" He had arrived here this morning with very much depleted reserves of patience and they'd been draining away ever since. He needed to go to the toilet. She seemed to squirm and he liked that.

"Is your imagination failing you this morning?" she said. "An adolescent girl? There were boys." She put her juice down. "Also men. In school, pupils and teachers, at home with the staff, pickups in bars because sometimes an underage girl looks old enough to pass. Street hookups. It was pretty disgusting."

She sat back in the deckchair.

"Interventions, of course, made everything worse. Where one outlet was denied, even if only temporarily, another was sought. So to sexual transgression was added substance abuse and to substance abuse was added petty crime. On a few occasions, crime that wasn't so petty." She pursed her lips. "But there is nothing to be gained by retelling all of this."

The conversation had taken a turn that Liam, for reasons he didn't care to examine, was more comfortable with. He felt a simmering anger—maybe that was it. This was really the first time this woman had spoken so directly of her sister and she evidently had nothing nice to say. Why was she even looking for her? Did she just miss the opportunity to sneer?

"How awful for the family," he said, just about suppressing his sarcasm. "You must all have been so shocked." Doonah seemed much more his type than this one, who was beginning to make his skin crawl. Actually she seemed exactly his type. He liked her already.

She snorted.

"Oh dear. Public scandal was to be avoided, Mr Tead, because it would more than likely be expensive, both materially and strategically. If you think the *family* was scandalized then you've understood nothing I've told you about it. We members may have our differences but we are quite united in our sociopathy."

"You sure about that?" Now he really was angry. So what if he didn't know why? She didn't seem to have registered his question.

"The family wasn't shocked. It was disgusted. We have our own delusions, you know, in addition to the myths we've peddled for public consumption. Behind them, we might be this and we might be that—it's all up for grabs. What *isn't* negotiable is that we are rare air. If we aren't that, we aren't anything. So this stuff was unacceptable. It was just so . . . *ordinary*."

"Do you ever listen to yourself?" It occurred to Liam that he was, all of a sudden, on his feet, and that the bodyguard's spine had straightened a little. He took a couple of steps backward to defuse that particular tension.

"Excuse me?"

"Has it occurred to you that your sister was the odd one out because she *wasn't* a fucking sociopath? Because that's how it's coming across to me." All of a sudden he knew this Doonah and he knew her well. He knew he'd like her and he thought that if he found her he just might try to get her away from all of this. What must it have been like to grow up around these freaks?

"It's funny," he said, "you've said nothing good about her, and yet I've somehow figured out she's worth ten of you."

He'd stepped in to deliver the line, forgetting about the bodyguard. For his part, Darius was giving a masterclass in confidence—bolt upright and directing the aviators at Liam, but not making a move. He hadn't even taken his feet out of the water.

"Maybe she's just aimless. People get like that because they have nothing to aim *for*. Nothing to devote themselves to. Did any of you try to help her with that? Do you think maybe she did all those things because she just didn't know *what* to do?"

His voiced cracked on the last couple of words and he took a breath.

"Some people don't know what to do." He slapped his chest. "I don't know what to do."

She got to her feet.

"Perhaps this wasn't a good time for one of our little talks." He couldn't read her. He never could. "I don't need you to know what to do, Mr Tead," she said, "but I do need you to do it. The driver will take you back to town. It's sweet of you to think you've got Doonah Zade figured out. But as is so often the case with sweetness, hopelessly naive. She always had one devotion.'

"Oh, and what was that?"

The shrug. The smug grin.

"Her sister."

She picked her magazine up and turned away.

"Nice of you to acknowledge it, anyway," said Liam to her back, and this time he did not intend to suppress his sarcasm. He wanted his words to drip with it. But his voice cracked again and to his disgust it sounded like genuine gratitude.

Out on the causeway he had to get the driver to stop again, this time to empty his bladder. It took an age—he had plenty of time to take in the beauty he was once again desecrating: the salt lake, the distant cliffs that ringed the depression, the emptiness, the light. Last night's edibles were still there, attracting flies. On the square there'd been no let up—it was still crazy with noise and traffic. He ducked into Ali's shop and through it into the dim cave of a back room where he was used to finding the owner. There were two sources of faint light—a flickering candle and the screen of a smart phone that illuminated the shopkeeper's face.

"Lim. Welcome." He was sitting beside the candle on a rug and Liam joined him there.

"You would like tea?" Then, reacting to Liam's hesitation, "Wine?"

Liam assented to the latter and when a coconut shell (he had not seen a single coconut tree in this ocean of trees) full of it was put in his hand he downed half, then looked at it and around, wondering how you put a coconut shell down.

"You are in the confusion."

"Excuse me?"

"You are in the confusion that follows upon a revelry. I envy you your good fortune."

Liam resolved his issue by emptying the shell. "I am not to be envied today, Ali. And the confusion runs deeper."

"Tell me."

"I wouldn't know where to start." He couldn't get comfortable, uncrossing and recrossing his legs. "Nothing stays still. The only thing I ever knew about oases was from the movies, and that they were basically always mirages. Turns out this one's no different."

Ali tutted.

"No, no Lim. Quite incorrect. I don't know how have you reached at this conclusion but it is absolutely ass backwards. This is an expression. Have I not told you so much of the oasis these past days. Of culture and history, of its magic and so on and what have you? But it makes no sense to speak of history in the oasis."

He put the coconut shell back in Liam's hand and filled it, and one for himself.

"This is the Land of Palms. The island of truth. It is eternal. The *world* is the mirage. Everything you remember before you came here and everything that happens after you leave—for you must leave—is all a dream. Not to be trusted."

"Why must I leave?"

"You must. There are those who defy this. They linger here and we watch as their own story drains out of them. They become transparent. They die and nobody mourns."

"But why is it better to leave? To exist only in the dream?"

That put a smile on Ali's face.

"Best question, Lim! Perhaps you are a worthy student after all. I doubt it though. Do you like ink?"

Ali had been introducing his little Socratic interludes with questions like that for days so Liam knew he didn't have to answer. The shopkeeper went to a shelf in the dimmest corner of the room and returned to the candle, beside which he placed a sheet of paper.

"Look closely at this and tell me what it is. Don't say paper."

He proceeded to unscrew one half of a fat old fountain pen from the other, dip its nib in a bottle of ink and twist an interior mechanism to fill the reservoir. Liam scrutinized the sheet. The paper wasn't white, instead an untreated off-white, getting on for brown, but it was the texture that captured the attention, especially thrown into relief as it was by the candle. He was instantly reminded of the oasis town—the *karshif* constructions and all their rope-bound lintels, the old minarets, the baked pathways between the palm gardens, carpeted with sand and desiccated fronds, every fibrous surface waiting to soak up moisture that never came.

"Blotting paper," he said.

"Good." Ali held the pen's nib over the centre of the page.

"A metaphor," said Liam. "The oasis."

In his mind's eye he saw a giant nib over the town and a huge inky drop, pendulous in the moment before falling to impregnate the earth, there to blacken the soil and spread.

"Let's see," said Ali. "But of course you are a clever man and you understand by now the oasis is itself a metaphor."

He squeezed a drop from the nib. They both watched as the paper quickly absorbed it and the ink began to race along capillary fibres.

"I do this often," said Ali. "It is very nice. Do you like it?"

"I do." It was a soothing thing to see. The first thing today that had soothed. The ink, and the wine. There was something in the irregular growth of the ink blob's outer limit that reminded him of watching a flame.

"Perhaps the page is the whole world, Lim, or time itself, or mere emptiness. What do you think? What would that make the ink?"

"I think I'm not having a very nice day, Ali," said Liam. "Maybe just talk me through this one."

"The ink would be the oasis, would it not? Or perhaps it is you," said Ali, "or perhaps it is knowing." He added a second drop to the same spot and the blot's outline bloomed. "To be ink is to be what is. To be paper is to be what is not, or what is not yet, or what is not yet known."

A third drop.

"I don't understand."

"Of course not. You are ink. Look at the edges—how they resemble the cliffs that circle us here, or the beaches and bays of an island. How they move. This is knowledge. What lies within is forgetfulness, without is a dream. Only at the edge of a cliff, on the coast of everything, is it possible to know yourself."

"Good to know," said Liam. "How do I get there?"

Ali grinned. It had seemed to Liam over these last few days that this guy, in addition to requiring funds, liked him. Seemed to find him funny at least.

"You have always been there," said the older man, barely visible at the edge of the candle's glow, "but always forgetting, always dreaming. To be ink is to be blind to paper. You think you move, you think you push. But look, Lim, at what is happening before your very eyes. The ink is powerless—it is the paper that pulls. That which is not charms that which is. You see yourself as on a quest, but you move only because something is pulling you. Something that is everywhere, in every direction, and that therefore lies in no particular direction, and is nowhere, draws you towards it."

"I think this lesson is lost on me, Ali."

"No matter. A lesson can be repeated. Perhaps then. Or," Ali winked, "perhaps you will learn something later, with the woman."

"What makes you think I'm going there?" said Liam, who had no intention of going there.

"Ha!" The shopkeeper got to his feet. Apparently it was time for Liam to go. He could see the front door and through it the failing light, and wondered where the day had gone. "It is no doubt at all that she has ensorcelled you," said Ali. "That's the reality."

The Question

WHEN LIAM knocked at the gate that night, Green Eyes opened it herself, invited him in, closed it behind him and led him into the courtyard which had been prepared as though in expectation of an honoured guest. Various low tables had silken cushions strewn all around them, and around the cushions water bowls and vases had been set and filled with daisies and daffodils, Damascus lilies, gillyflowers and mignonettes, as well as pomegranate blossoms, anemones, myrtle berries and Aleppo jasmine. This profusion filled the little courtyard with its many fragrances and they in turn mingled in the air with the scents that rose from each table.

One was laden with fruit bowls, overflowing with fresh seacoast lemons, red and yellow apples, baby cucumbers, Turkish quinces, Hebron peaches and oranges, as well as dried fruits and nuts such as shelled pistachios, pressed Ba'albak figs, roasted chickpeas, raisins, almonds and hazelnuts. On another, fresh mutton sizzled over a charcoal brazier and sent up its aroma to fill the lungs of the hungry, along with the scents of the spices in which it had sat—saffron and powdered lime, cinnamon, za'atar, cumin, galangal and sumac.

Wordlessly, she lifted his robe over his head and bade him lower himself into the pool. The cool water was welcome to his flesh, refreshing his spirits after a perplexing day. She washed him in silence, filling a jug from the pool to pour over him, and he too was silent—the other sisters were nowhere to be seen but, mindful of her strict injunction, he knew better than to ask after them. When she had washed him she had him step out of the pool and before drying him, poured water from ten little jugs over him, one scented with rose, another with aloe wood, one with musk, another with lily, ambergris, rosemary and so on. She patted him gently dry and applied rich, perfumed unguents to his hands, feet and member, causing him to swell.

They left his dirty robe on the floor where it lay and she led him to the cushions and had him recline there, with his head on her lap as she sat cross-legged. She filled a cup of wine for him and lifted it frequently to his lips where also she placed morsels of delicious meat and fruits, and into his ears she poured tales of distant lands and days long past, of love and grief and magic, and all the while Liam had never to lift a hand, his every need anticipated—when he craved meat, he would find it on his tongue; when he longed for something sweet, she would drop a raisin there, or slice him a peach and feed it to him a piece at a time, regaling him as she went with stories, sometimes of herself and sometimes of her sisters, and sometimes they were *her* sisters and sometimes they were *the* sisters, which Liam found curious but resisted the temptation to question as this was an evening he wished never to end. It occurred to him that his friend Ali had undoubtedly spoken the truth in the gloomy back room of his little shop earlier but also, on the other hand, that if this was what being ensorcelled was like, he didn't really have a problem with it.

When they had eaten and drunk their fill, she cleared a table, taking the things from it to a curtained cabinet. Then she lit a long, waxed wand and went around the courtyard lighting the many little candles she had arranged on the floor, so that by the time she had lit them all a carpet of fire burned hot enough to warm Liam's face. With so little room to step between the candles, she removed her own robe lest its hem catch a flame, but instead of coming back to Liam she disappeared into a shadowy corner. Anxious to see her leave, Liam wondered if he should follow, but it seemed so long since he had had a will of his own that instead he lay where he was. The candles served as a mirror to the other square of splendid lights that hung over them. Stars so numerous they seemed to thicken in waves and eddies as though some animating force, some tide, were moving through them. He recalled the night sky in Woodview, Lucan, County Dublin and how he had looked up at it as a child and done well to find it, let alone stars within it—everything below the height of two stories was veiled in the yellow taint of suburban nightlight. The roofs marked the boundary between two types of time—below them, human hours scuttled; above them aeons crept so slowly as to seem the purest form of stillness. The purest form a human could know. Cloud cover was normally complete and usually low, low enough for a giant to need to bow his head, but once in a while, in Winter especially, it would be clear and Liam would make out a few indistinct stars through the corruption. He would count them until he lost track and start again but, given the fact the night was usually young when he was awake, and the poor visibility, his tally would rarely exceed ten.

Here it would also be difficult to reach a count of ten but for a different reason. There was little darkness in the night sky over the oasis. It pulsated with a thousand points of light. A million. The abundance of stars was so overwhelming it became necessary for Liam to withdraw his attention from the entirety of the sky revealed by the walls of the courtyard, applying it instead to a chosen sector till the rest drained away from his consciousness and then, finding this new patch just as overwhelming, isolate an area smaller still and concentrate on that. No matter how many times he repeated this, training his eye on successively smaller quadrants till his mind was focussed on an area so infinitesimally small he wouldn't have believed it possible at the outset, he never reached a point at which he could not count ten stars and in fact many more. Just as he gave up, she returned to the candles' glow carrying a large silver tray which she set on the low table, taking her place beside him and his head onto her lap once more. The tray was heaped with every kind of pastry—widow's bread and almond pudding, Turkish rolls and ladyfingers, date rolls, sweet rolls, Balkan biscuits and barley rolls, eat-and-thanks, amber combs and musk-scented *kataifs*. Each delicacy found its way to Liam's palate without his having to reach for it as they feasted and frolicked and filled their cups repeatedly. When they were done with the sweets they rolled on the cushions playing with each other, sometimes pinching and sometimes fondling, rubbing and sucking but when he went to enter her she cupped herself, saying:

"I am not as the other two, an animal to be mounted on the floor."

She stood and bade him do so and when he had, shakily, she led him carefully through the sea of flames, to the far side of the courtyard where she had earlier disappeared and through a doorway there, into a bedroom also lit with many candles and where incense burned, filling the air with sweet musk. A large bed was strewn with fine silks and overhung with curtains of satin and lace. She sat on the edge of it and waited for him to approach her, but as he leaned over her she pushed him gently away, then pressed on his shoulders until he was kneeling on the floor at her feet. Once he was on his knees she raised her legs and opened them and, gripping his head by his hair, she held his face very close to her sex. There was enough heat there to warm his face as the candles had done in the courtyard.

"Now," she said, "what is this?"

He held his tongue a moment, afraid that he might answer incorrectly, that the night would end here, on his knees, in failure, banished from her bedchamber, or that she would again beat him without mercy—but Ali, his guide, came unbidden to the rescue.

"It is the 'Ayn al-Gubah," he said, and let his lips brush it as he went on. "The Spring of the Sun. Alexander swam here. It is mentioned in the histories of Herodotus, who wrote of how in the high heat of noon its waters are cool to the hand." She had lain back so he paused until she raised her head to look down at him through the valley of her breasts, then held her eye as he kissed it. "And how it boils at midnight."

She laughed and let her head fall back once again, evidently pleased with his answer, and continued to voice her pleasure as Liam attended to her, first with his lips and when she wettened with his tongue, quickly and slowly, lightly and deeply, and he found that as he probed a tremendous appetite was awakened in him, and his attention became less that of a lover than that of a greedy mutt, that he was lapping at her hungrily, a hunger that only increased until he was pressing his whole head into her, pleasuring her with his lips, tongue, nose and face. Still, he could not be sated, becoming more ravenous still. In, in, in—he had lost his wits but not so entirely that he couldn't take a moment to wonder to himself what it was he was trying to achieve, worming his way into this stranger's vagina. What awaited him in there? What did he hope to find? But of course he knew. He wasn't trying to get into anything. He was trying to get out. And this seemed like it might be as good a way as any. His escape route, his getaway—away from fear, from guilt, away from the world, from the Zade woman, away from desire and away from himself. Out, out, out. This was the route to the last elsewhere, an escape from that-which-is into that-which-is-yet-to-be, the dream world, everything beyond the ink blot. Paradise lost—to the mind that can conceive of such a thing, what could be more alluring than the way back? It was the spring, the fountain of myth. He wanted to breach the current, to swim upstream, away from entropy and contamination towards . . . towards the beginning. Towards the truth. Whatever that was—but as long as he had his face buried, he didn't have to ask the question. So he buried it till he was spent and sleep overtook them both.

    When he woke it was into silence but with the certainty he'd heard something—an echo resounded, not in the darkness but in the dissipating sleep state from which he emerged. He had no memory of rising from his knees and getting into bed but he was in it now, covered and warm, warm and alone. So profound was the quiet and so complete the darkness, his certainty wavered and he wondered if he'd imagined the sound, and just as he concluded he had, heard it again and shivered in the sheets. He sat up and stayed still, waiting to hear it again as he knew he would, and when after a moment he did was on his feet before the sound, brief as it was, had come to an end. A cry. He thought he recognised her voice. She was somewhere else in the house, weeping so wretchedly it verged on the inhuman, racked by an unfathomable grief. He heard it again and it reached into him like a talon to pull his heart out of his chest. Full of fear, he knew nevertheless that he must go to her. Following the faint light that came through the cracks in the doorframe, he went cautiously out into the courtyard and to the pool there so that, the next time he heard her, he might know from which direction. Some candles still burned, though only a few. In their weak light, smoke rose from the spent wicks of others, the twisted pillars of a temple to the stars, still dazzling and numberless overhead.

When he heard her again, the very last thing he wanted to do was follow. He wanted to flee, to run to the gate and through it, never to return to this house. A sound so excruciating he knew he could never be adequate to its cause—a suffering deeper than any he had known certainly, a pain that made a pampered child of him in its presence. And yet he knew he must go, that to slink away like a coward was to be a coward forever, a fate he yet hoped to avoid. He went towards the shadowy corner he thought her voice had come from but didn't find a room there. Edging along to his right, past the cabinets of crockery and crystal, he, terrified, turned the handle of the first door he came to and pushed it open. It gave on to an unoccupied space, unlit, in which he could just make out the fixtures of another bedroom in the shaft of starlight that entered. At the next door, the same thing. At the next, a dim kitchen. Before he reached the next, her cry again—a howl—freezing him to the spot, where he remained until it came yet again. When it did he returned to the pool to await the next. When *that* came he was none the wiser—the appalling cries echoed from every side of the courtyard. One by one, he tried each door he could find, finding nothing behind them and returning to the pool each time, until there was only one door left.

Up close, he couldn't be sure if it was his imagination, but he thought his eye detected a weak light around the hinges. There was no keyhole—just a heavy latch, unchained. He put his ear to the door.

Nothing. He tried the other ear. When the scream came, he jumped back like a spooked cat—it had vibrated in the wood. Not wanting to know, but knowing he must, he took a breath, stepped forward and put his hand to the latch. Despite its size, it released easily and he pushed the door open a crack without making a sound. With his eye to the gap he could see within.

She stood in the centre of a large room, naked as he was, her back to him. In her right hand she held a braided whip. At the far wall, the two mastiffs cowered. To the ripples of lighter hair that variegated their black coats here and there were added raised and bloody welts. All three of the room's occupants were breathing heavily, as though from recent exertion. Liam held his own breath as their chests slowed and they quietened. When a certain calm had descended, she stepped towards the dog to her left. It whined. Raising the whip, she brought it down heavily, drawing more blood. As she did so again, the animal was mute, submitting in silence to the savage beating that followed. When the woman's arm must surely be tired and the dog could withstand no more, it let out a cry—the same cry, Liam now knew, that he had heard—and fainted. Only then did Green Eyes relent, dropping to her knees and taking the beast's head in her arms to smother it in kisses. Together they cried, the dog lapping hungrily at her face and she kissing it a thousand times till finally its whimpers and her sobbing subsided. When she had quieted it she stood, once again taking up the whip.

She beat the other dog as viciously as she had the first, and again, when it cried out and fainted away, she embraced it and together they cried and kissed, till one had comforted the other. She then took the whip and stood back from them to wait as their laboured breathing, and hers, abated. It was clear to Liam she would beat them again. He urged himself to intervene but did not have the courage. She had the whip and they were all three formidable. As he pondered the matter he saw that one of the mastiffs looked directly at him. As, when he checked, did the other. In his amazement, he had pushed the door open wider and stepped inside. Now a real terror entered him—neither dog was chained. He felt his legs weaken, beyond even the capacity to retreat. The paralysis of terror. But they did not attack. Nor did they distinguish themselves, one from the other, as they had done in their demeanour when he first encountered them. In unison they crawled to him, never lifting their bellies from the packed dirt floor, pushing themselves over it with their hind legs, whimpering all the way. When they reached his feet they laid paws upon them and licked at them, now and then looking up at him piteously, begging him for his intercession. He did not know what to do. When he looked up Green Eyes had turned to face him. He shrugged at her, palms up, a question mark in human form. That he had not yet voiced the question meant he had not yet disobeyed her, but she shook her head slowly and in her disappointment she said "Oh, Liam," knowing before he did that he would, and though he heard her and knew what it meant, he could not stop his lips from moving.

"What *is* this?"

The Last Voyage

The first thought to cross Liam's mind was that it must be possible to pass through life's scenes, from one chapter to the next, without an involuntary loss and recovery of consciousness. But for now, the possibility eluded him. The second thought to cross his mind was that he was burning. He was on his back, on soft ground in some very quiet place where the light glared and, when he opened one eye, blinded. He flinched and turned over. Sand. Not the dirty, dusty mix of sand and clay that donkey carts and scooters had packed down in the oasis, but pure, clean, bone dry sand. The kind he would first have encountered on Poulshone beach in County Wexford—what brought that to mind, now?—but that here left him in no doubt he'd been dumped in the desert. Out on the sand, as his employer had put it. He sat up and waited for his stinging eyes to adjust, for his surroundings to resolve out of the bleached-out brilliance.

He was on a slope, the lower reaches of a big dune, facing into a kind of valley, a dip at the confluence of this with other dunes, so that he couldn't see very far in any direction. He hadn't imagined the burning—when he looked down at himself, his skin was in bad shape, livid and beginning to blister. Whoever had left him here had left him with nothing to wear. A very particular urgency asserted itself, leaving no room for other considerations: wherever this story was going, it wasn't going anywhere good if he didn't find shade and quickly. He got to his feet and made his way along an ascending ridge of sand, towards the highest point he could identify. It was hard going, much harder than he expected. With every step his feet sank deep, and slipped often, and progress was slow and laborious.

When he reached the top, there was no apparent reward for him there. The sun was so high in the sky it was impossible to tell north from south, and there was little differentiation to the views. In one direction it perhaps looked as if the terrain got rockier, and therefore maybe shadier, but only at a distance he'd be dead before he covered. Days away. In the opposite direction, lower country and, knowing the oasis was in a depression, he considered it, but not for more than a moment. It was a dune field—a vast and uniform swathe of giant, crab-shaped dunes, all facing the same way, all on the move, he knew, but at so invisible a pace they seemed the perfect picture of stillness itself. They spoke of eternity, or at least of time beyond human measure. They spoke of death. The one shred of potential he could latch on to was that in another direction, some hours away for sure, there was some higher ground and therefore the possibility of a more informative view. He started moving automatically because there was nothing else to think about. It was a certainty he would find neither shade nor water before he got there. This was real trouble. Move or die, and maybe die anyway, but *move*.

All because he'd asked a question. An overreaction, surely? Though he couldn't say she hadn't warned him. He put a hand to the back of his head. No bump, no tender spot, no evidence of a blow. But somebody must have knocked him out—the scene break was too clean a cut. And the absence of a head injury didn't mean there wasn't any pain—his skin, head to toe, everything in front, was practically sizzling. The sun on it was unbearable but must for now be borne. It wasn't as if it would feel any better if he lay down. He trudged on for an hour, two, his condition worsening. At some point he stopped thinking straight, stopped thinking at all—what was happening in his mind wasn't thought, it was time. In the incandescent nothing of his surroundings, there was nothing for a mind to hang on to, nothing upon which to conjure his will. He was a vessel, a channel, a frequency, through which flowed nothing but memory: Lucan and Dad and drugs and madness, failure, the vanities, Mum, money, Jewel, the desert, the music of time, its rhythms, the jazz of it, the bum notes, the lies and let downs, the waste, the miserable, awful, risible waste of it all, Madrid and Chapelizod, the hiding places, the hiding, the debts and losses, the invertebrate cowardice, the courage. He did, just, have the presence of mind to remember he should at least be *walking* straight and so after however long he schlepped his way up the ridge of a dune to take a look.

At the top he sat down in something like despair, though the feeling was too weak, too dissociated, to be called that. If he was still headed towards the higher ground he wouldn't know it—there wasn't a level stretch of horizon against which to gauge such comforting notions as up or down. He'd lost the reference point. Swinging his legs over the apex he scanned the other direction. Nothing to help him. He swung back—facing that way gave him a vestigial sense of resting position—that he might not know where he was or where he ought to be going but that he wasn't yet *quite* lost, that as unlikely as it seemed he might be just where he was supposed to be. Maybe everybody was. Everybody and everything, always. Even things that hurt. Maybe everything was just where and as it was supposed to be, as awful and cruel as that might be. He considered not getting to his feet again. It seemed like it would be an effort and the idea of effort was losing its currency. Why struggle against this when it made so much sense? This was the end he'd spent his life earning. He'd lived in hiding—why would the universe grant him the chance now to show himself? To connect. In the end as it was in the beginning. And so forth. Whenever he'd read news about some poor soul's body found in a wilderness, he'd always thought how terrible that must have been, how harrowing their final hours. But the scenario turned out to be a rather unemotional one. Beyond the physical pain there was even a kind of comfort. At least there was a bit of poetry to it. Hadn't he always managed at least that? A bit of poetry?

Except he could see something, and it bothered him. Middle distance. In the v made by the slopes of two dunes, a patch of something lighter, almost white. It might just be the way the sun was catching it but Liam didn't think so. Something out there was a different colour. Since it was the one and only thing he could see that wasn't exactly the same as everything else he could see, he made for it. Back on the lower ground between dunes he had to hope he was moving in the right direction. A matter of faith. Probably he should never have sat down—his legs were notably less cooperative than they'd been before he did, and when he went for higher ground again to check his progress they hurt like hell. It turned out he hadn't been walking towards the patch of white he'd seen with anything like precision. On the other hand he hadn't done too badly—it still existed. And it was closer.

Not too much closer, but closer. In his mind, he drew a straight line that stretched away from his feet and walked it, retracing it over and over, repeating it, reciting, making a prayer of it, inscribing it in the sand, imposing his own, human architecture on the senseless, epochal, drifts and curves that lay along it, his eye all the time on the furthest available point of reference. That his feet could find the line again whenever he had to deviate from it was by no means assured. His knees were weak and so was his capacity to concentrate.

"When to come."

He was pretty sure he'd said the words out loud. A knee buckled and he had to twist to brace himself, momentarily losing the line. The shock of that, the panic, was more intense than any feeling he could remember. He scanned what passed for a horizon, long and hard, till he believed he had found the reference point and till his heart stopped thumping against his ribs, and walked on. The moment had drained the last of his physical reserves. It was as though the only part of him that could defy gravity, that could stay clear of the sand, was his mind—it moved along the line and dragged the rest of him with it.

"Spring or Autumn, ideally, as overnighting on the dunes in winter can be quite chilly and visitors are likely to find the summer months," he fell, eating sand and dry spitting it, "a little uncomfortable."

He surprised himself with how quickly he righted himself into a sitting position. If he stayed down now he was never getting up again. He would probably accept that soon enough. But not yet. He'd fallen just short of a little ridge, the tapering end of a dune he couldn't see beyond. The least he could do was get up there and take a look at the last thing he'd ever lay eyes upon. He crawled, having lost all faith in his legs, but crawling proved as arduous as walking—the sand was agony on the burned flesh of his knees. When he reached the top, the leeward slip face was far steeper and higher than he'd imagined—another way down would have to be found. But at least he had something to try for. There it was, the patch of whiter ground. It squeezed between two dunes and into an expanse, an open flat, beyond them. He could see only a sliver of it from here but it was unmistakable. What it meant, if anything, he wouldn't know till he was down there. And getting down there was a lot easier than anticipated—as he rose to his feet to make his way along the ridge, he slipped and tumbled.

Even on the loose sand of the slope, it hurt to fall, but didn't take long to land face down on flat ground, coarse and hard against his cheek. One eye was too close to focus, but with the other, while he waited to regain some equilibrium, he examined a little white shard that, like the thousands of other little white shards here, gave the place its colour. It was a broken piece of something larger. The first thing that came to mind was bone, that this was some kind of killing ground, but even as he thought it he knew it wasn't true. It wasn't pottery because it wasn't manmade. Its nature, in fact, was as unmistakable as its colour had been from a distance. The scalloped edges, the ridges along one surface, the pearly convex of the other.

A sea shell.

He lifted himself onto all fours and crawled along the narrow gap between the two dunes. It wasn't long before his hands and knees were bleeding. Whatever he'd expected of the tiny, far away patch of white, it wasn't the sea. Ali had peppered his daily lectures with some geographical nuggets but had never mentioned it. In fact he'd told Liam that before the advent of the motor car it had taken people weeks, days minimum, to reach the oasis from any direction. A momentary anxiety arose that he might be hallucinating. Finally experiencing a real mirage. But the shells were everywhere and they were real enough to cut him. He wasn't so far gone he thought salt water would save him, but he was elated—a coastline was something you could walk. It had a shape. It attracted settlement. It would be a reason to keep going. He didn't need to interrogate any of it too closely. He was grateful to be here, if only because it marked a boundary between sand and that-which-is-not-sand. But where was here? If he'd been taken far enough to be dumped near the coast, in which direction? The coast of what? When his hands and knees couldn't take any more he stood and walked, clear of the dunes and into the open.

A few meters out, he stopped dead. From here the nature of this place was as clear as it was impossible. The marine flooring, the crunching expanse of sea shells and shards, spread out in every direction including, now, behind him. The size of two football fields, maybe three. But in every direction the crisp white tapered out into the sands. He was in the open, but surrounded by the dunes, by the desert. No sign of sea, no saline scent. A sharp pain in both his knees alerted him to the fact that he had fallen on them. Presented with a visual field he could not comprehend, his mind simply shut down. He fell forward, and blacked out.

On coming to, some part of him was already aware of how surprisingly cool and soft the ground now felt against his cheek. And of a gentle wind and fresher air and of the receding silence, replaced by a pillowy breeze against the drum of his ear, and of another sound, more regular and rhythmic. Accustomed by now to these face-down reintroductions to reality, he open his uppermost eye. The day was overcast. Low cloud filled the sky. The sand under his head was damp. The rhythm was of the sea that dampened it. The waterline was not so far from Liam and must have been closer while he slept.

It must have lapped at him. He let himself lie there and took it all in, running through his senses to check on each one—the sounds, the salty air, his fingers in wet sand, the gunmetal sea. He could hear the call of seabirds. When he rolled over he could see them, and see also the figure that stood over him, upside down from that perspective but recognisable.

"Hello, Ali."

"Greetings, Lim."

The distinct possibility occurred that he was dying a slow, dry death on sharp shells and that all these more agreeable sensations were his mind's way of easing his passage. But he dismissed the thought. Nothing about his surroundings admitted of the possibility. Every faculty delivered hard evidence. This was real all right—it was the baking dunes that had seemed to surround the beach that were imaginary. Feverish artefacts of his burned body and burned-out brain. He was still parched and no doubt still in some trouble. But his friend was here. And that was where, in fact, one problem—a problem of perspective—presented itself. He sat up.

Ali didn't disappear, thankfully. Nothing did. The whole scene, everything around him, was underpinned by a reassuring sense of object permanence. Of solidity. But the shopkeeper's head was bowed a little and from his seated position, Liam could see it was to avoid the blanket of cloud that distant birds flew beneath. He let his eyes run down his friend's body, dressed in splendid robes as if for some celebration or ceremony, to where his legs should have been, and found there instead a mighty water spout that twisted and buckled between Ali's beltline and the sea.

"You've changed," said Liam.

Ali smiled.

"Were I not to bring myself to my full height, Lim," he said, "it is no doubt at all your friends would never find you. That's the reality. Look."

Liam followed Ali's outstretched finger. Over the grassy dunes that backed the beach appeared three tiny figures. When they hit the open sand, two of them ran along it and one of them turned to run out towards Liam. Not until it had reached him and bent low to scoop him up in its arms did he register the unexpected identity of its owner.

"Hello, Dr Reynolds."

"We must hurry," she said as she carried him off. "Al-Rhukh is near!"

Liam raised an arm to wave to Ali but there was no sign of the shopkeeper apart from the spent wisp of a water spout out at sea. Reynolds wasn't quite as she had been the last time Liam had seen her. In place of her tight bun and buttoned-up attire, she wore a magnificent turban of silver lamé at least four times the size of her head. Pinned to the front was a peacock feather, a not-quite-welcome reminder of the Zade plume. Her long blue satin robe, open fronted, revealed a billowing blouse and baggy trousers in the same silver lamé and on her feet she wore golden slippers, finely embroidered, which curled up at the toes.

"Look!" she said.

Liam peered ahead to where the other two were nearing something in the sand among the dunes, something that from here was small, but tall enough to dwarf the figures that approached it. A resplendent white dome. The doctor hastened, bounding over the sand, taking great, gravity-defying strides—and all this with a grown man in her arms.

"You're very fit for someone your age, Doctor!"

He had to raise his voice as they rushed through the sea breeze. She laughed and smiled down at him indulgently, though he couldn't think of anything he'd said that was funny.

"I'm actually a vegetarian," she yelled, leaping across the outermost dunes to where Sherry and Darius stood by the white dome. They were dressed in similar fashion—Darius wore a short pony tail, high on his otherwise bald head and was bare chested beneath a small, sleeveless vest with ornate trimmings of golden thread. Sherry wore a turban similar to the doctor's and her red, bejewelled robes sparkled. The dome was smooth as alabaster, nowhere upon it could be seen a seam or feature or mark of any kind.

"What is that? A tomb?"

Reynolds placed Liam in the bodyguard's arms.

"The opposite. An egg."

She launched herself to the top of the thing, as high as a house, and from her belt retrieved a small axe, and with it she began to strike the white surface. She inflicted no damage that the others could see, no matter how many times she struck and no matter her fantastic strength. But with every blow she sounded the great egg like a bell, a bell that made a drum of the sand, so that even Liam could feel it through the soles of Darius's feet. Soon enough, to bell and drum, was added wind—a distant call came from above, beyond the blanket of cloud, and then came a second time, less distant. The doctor increased her efforts, striking all the more and all the harder. When the call came a third time, it was close enough to send a chill through poor, burned Liam, who shivered in Darius's arms. It was not a harmonious sound, no choir of trumpeting angels, but an animal shriek, the fury of a mother come to protect her child. A colossal bird descended through the cloud, her great wings parting it effortlessly so that sunlight burst through, its sudden warmth a horror to Liam's skin, soothed a little at terrifying intervals as the circling bird's shadow passed over.

"Al-Rhukh!" Reynolds was unravelling her silver turban. "Be ready!"

Once unwound, she formed a loop at one end of the long, silver lamé ribbon, all the while continuing with her blows to the egg, and all the while the bird circled lower and lower, till its caterwaul assaulted the ear, each of them covering theirs save Darius, who held Liam. The doctor tucked the hand axe back into her belt and stood, swinging the glittering lasso around her head. When the bird was low enough that its final sweep displaced sand, making it painful for Liam to keep his eyes open, and stretched a talon out towards Reynolds that might easily enclose a horse, let alone a diminutive doctor, the latter lassoed it, pulled the silver cord tight, and slid down the shell's curve to the ground. There she pulled at the protesting creature till it sat upon the egg, wings flapping violently, pummelling the earth.

"Quickly!"

Sherry pulled herself onto the bird's tail and made her way quickly along its back, to where it could not turn its head to peck at her. Darius did the same, with Liam now held under one arm. Once there, he set Liam down.

"Hold on!" said the doctor. "For your life!"

"What about you?" cried the heiress.

"I will bind myself to its leg," Reynolds shouted. "Hold on!"

Liam could hear all this but see nothing. His hands had found two feather shafts to grip, thick as human legs and slippery smooth, and he was too terrified to lift his head and look, instead burying it in a mass of downy afterfeather, but he knew perfectly well, on account of the immense forces acting upon his body, that Al-Rhukh had left the ground and was twisting angrily in the air. How high he could not tell, but if the breeze on the beach had been loud, the wind up here was a hammer in the ear. The bodyguard and his employer were calling to each other, and he could hear the doctor's voice, but if they were saying something to him it was pointless. The only two things he could conceive of were the imperative to grip and the terror, as even that gave way to an oblivion made not of the blackness to which he had become accustomed, but of pure light.

The Mother of the World

AND AGAIN. The whiteness faltered first at the periphery, receding there to expose a greenish gloom. The darkness was hardly complete, but a light bulb, high overhead, was too weak to properly illuminate an obviously large room. He couldn't focus his eyes. There was that familiar sensation of a receding sedative. Just the one bulb and a ceiling fan—he could feel no effect but he could hear its rhythm and make out the ill-defined swirl. There were people in the room but he didn't want to investigate that just yet, just to note that the acoustic of their muttering testified also to the size of the space. He could no more make out the words than he could blink his way to clear sight. He lay in a single bed, covers pulled neatly into his armpits. Looking down, it wasn't a very homely-looking bed, even through his fuzzy eyes. More like a camp bed, or an army bed, or a . . . and there were other beds, one on each side of his, but he couldn't turn his head enough to get a look at the occupants. That, or he didn't want to. He had the beginnings of an idea who, or at least what, they were, and the idea was awful.

One of the people in the room was unnervingly close. At his left, sitting, in fact, at his bedside. A familiar figure, fussing with something which stood on the floor at the level of his head. He wrestled with the familiarity a moment. Reynolds? The figure was a similar, slight size, moved in a similar, meticulous, business-like way, wore similarly dull colours. But the setting gave it away. Not Reynolds.

Düssel. And come to think of it, hadn't she done just this before? Sat at his side as he came to? It would no doubt read as diligent to others in the room. Staff, family members. Protective, even. But a point of pride with Liam was that he had come to understand the doctor rather better than she had ever understood him. She wanted to be the first thing he saw in his new world. It was dominance, then and now.

It had happened again. His faculties, such as they were, lined up in defence formation. He knew how this went and he would need a strategy. What might he say to her, when she asked, as she inevitably would, what his understanding of his situation was. *What is the case, Liam?* The world is all that is the case, he had allowed his stupid, smart mouth to reply, that first time. *Very well, tell me about your world.* Something in the *your* had put a fear into him that never left. It hadn't returned today—it was merely reasserting itself. Sometimes it was an undercurrent and sometimes—now, for example—it was all there was.

The oasis stuff was obvious. Giant birds and nympho princesses. *Christ.* His breath quickened, along with his heart rate, and he noted a faint, institutional smell of disinfectant soap. People continued to murmur. He set out on the mental walk that any psychotic must take, back to when things last made sense, to when his version of events might conceivably match up with someone else's. Anyone else's. It was going to be a long walk. None of it seemed all that plausible now. Who traversed deserts with billionaires? Stowed away on shipping containers? In Tangier he had seen, or believed he had seen, a perfect, pitch-black underground orchard. Beautiful, incestuous siblings had set themselves alight. He'd seen genies and giant birds that laid eggs the size of trucks. A cartoon mayor had bought him a suit.

But none of that was the point, it dawned on him. He felt suddenly cold. The fear was a funny thing—when it hit hard, it always allowed you think, momentarily, that that was it. That was the gut punch. But then came the real wave. The one that drowned you. Düssel at his side meant he wasn't in any of those places, and it meant he wasn't in the States. Had he returned? Or had he never gone to California? Had he met Sherry Zade? Been to Jewel? Was there such a place? If the truth of it was as he feared then he hadn't lost mere days this time. There were months of delusion he would have to learn to unremember. A long, long walk.

"His mind should be clearing now," said a familiar voice at his side. Something plastic, shiny was suspended over his head. A drip. He didn't want to move his head, didn't want to see the face, but he wasn't given a choice. She got to her feet and in doing so leaned in close, so that her features came into sharp focus.

"All relative, of course," she said. Not Düssel.

Reynolds. She stepped away from the bed, into a still blurry middle distance, while into the closer, higher definition stepped the heiress. Liam wanted to yell but he barely croaked.

"For fuck *sake*."

There was no immediate relief at madness's apparent retreat. Also, all things considered, it hadn't retreated very far.

"Delighted to see you too, I'm sure."

She sat. A door clicked shut—Reynolds had left. No doubt Darius remained on this side of it. Liam let his head turn briefly in both directions. He'd been right about the other beds, but this was no ward. A triple room in a decidedly downscale hotel. It was the furnishings that gave the latter away—the building had obviously known better times. High ceiling, decorative mouldings stained by damp and cigarette smoke, elaborate, egg-and-tongue cornices—a distinct *fin de siècle* feel to the place. Automatically, he lifted his head to check out the flooring, but there wasn't any—time had long since stripped the floor boards of their varnish, let alone a carpet. He let his head fall back and kept his eyes on the dirty ceiling.

"Where are we?"

"Cairo." She had taken the doctor's chair.

Now that he wasn't straining to make out muttered words, other sounds made themselves known. The noise of a street and of traffic outside—an incessant clamour of car horns over a tuneless drone of mixed musics. It was quiet, so they were some stories up, but it sounded busy down there.

"How did we get here?"

"We flew." There was something a little off about her. Something pinched, that reminded him more of the photos he'd seen than of the person he'd met. She'd been in the habit of holding his gaze more than was comfortable for him, but now she avoided his eyes.

In a plane? he wanted to ask, but something stopped him. He was asking questions but he didn't really want answers. Answers contained the fear. They were where it lived. The wrong answers, anyway. The wrong question from him now and everything might fall apart. He noticed the drip again.

"How long have I been out?"

"A few days, I'm afraid. It was the easiest way to manage the pain, and you were . . . somewhat agitated. Your skin is still in rough shape but it has healed up a lot. You'll be able to get around. Maybe avoid mirrors for a while."

Is that why she wouldn't look at him? He could see for himself, now, when he looked down at where the drip was bandaged to his arm, that his skin was raw and greasy with whatever had been applied to it. No, there was something else.

"How did you find me?"

"I told you. Ali knows everything."

Ali. So *he* existed. Maybe. So then did Green Eyes? The sisters? What had happened? What hadn't? These were the ones, he was pretty sure—these were the questions he didn't want answered.

"She seems pretty handy to have around," he said. "Reynolds, I mean. I've never travelled with my own private doctor before."

She snorted.

"What's funny? Did I say something funny?" Liam didn't think he'd said anything funny.

"She's actually a veterinarian," she said, "but yes, useful. She knows what she's doing."

He still hadn't spotted Darius. Was it possible the bodyguard had left him in here alone with her? He supposed it was—he had never felt less threatening than he did now.

"So what happens?" he said.

"Excuse me?"

"What happens now? What do I do?"

"Your job, Mr Tead. I'm going to need you to go ahead and do your job."

For once. She didn't say it but he didn't doubt she meant it. She was losing patience with him. Good.

"No," he said. "No more. This stops now. I can't do it."

"You must do it. There's no alternative."

"I nearly died."

"Nearly died is just another way of saying still alive. There are so many catastrophising ways of making the point, but I would say it's a good thing, wouldn't you?"

"You're insane."

She laughed. It was more of a bark. The loudest sound he'd heard from her.

"Really? *I'm* insane?"

"I can't do it. I don't know why we're in Cairo. The trail is cold." He shook his head, exasperated. "I never *had* a trail."

"Reynolds needed medicines. If we're in Cairo, it's because we're meant to be in Cairo. They must be here."

"Fuck *sake*." He shifted himself into a slightly less prone position—the skin on his back screamed at him but it felt it too weird to talk with her sitting over him. "You can't seriously believe that."

"Can't I? I'm out of options, Mr Tead. So you see, the imperative to hope, despite . . . everything . . . is stronger than ever."

"Coming here wasn't my decision. I was out of it."

"Your situation brought us here. We're here because of you."

"You really are insane."

"You're freaking out because someone is showing faith in you. This is how faith works. It's what makes it faith. It might help if you had some in yourself. To maintain your composure, at least."

"There isn't a hope in hell of that unless I get the explanation I've been waiting for. What are we doing here, Ms Zade?" He wanted to shake her. "What's *happening*?"

She stood and went to a pair of french doors at one end of the room. One of her little pieces of theatre. He waited for the dramatic turn but instead she opened them and stepped onto a balcony. The city flooded in, not quiet at all. But even if the activity that made these sounds was frenetic, the overall effect wasn't—it was positively soporific, scored on the Arabic scale. Liam had always loved and longed for that sound. The city. A place for disappearing. While her back was turned, he grabbed the dressing gown that hung from the chair and joined her on the balcony. It was the closest he'd ever been to her but intimate it wasn't. Below them cars honked with an inexplicable frequency—a mysterious language that didn't necessarily limit itself to traffic offences.

"The time for you to know everything is coming very soon. You're so close." She took the balcony railing in both hands and scanned the street below. "My mother—"

"Please, Ms Zade, not another one of your run-a-rounds. No more stories. I need the truth." His fists found the gown's pockets. "I'm scared, if you want *my* truth, and I don't care if you know it. I don't understand any of this, not the first thing. I don't know what to do."

In both directions, Cairo stretched away—dusty, Italianate, somewhat past its best, signs and billboards everywhere rendered in another mysterious language, an alien script, some of it in the neon that blinked on here and there. To the unfamiliar, it might as well have been the moon. If he hadn't been in pain, afraid he was losing his mind, it would have been delicious to Liam. But as it was, he just wanted to go home. He might not know what that was but he had an idea of how it should feel and he wanted to feel it now.

"Oh, I think you can put up with another story or two. Like I say, we're very close. Besides, what are you going to do, at this point? In a strange city? No papers. *Cairo?* You wouldn't last a morning."

One of her hands went to a pocket in the jacket she wore and patted it, then returned to the rail. It was a nothing, but Liam noticed it—a smoker's motion. He'd never seen her smoke. But then he couldn't tell what he knew from what he imagined any more.

"I'm glad you're scared, if you want the truth, Mr Tead, because I am too. This way I feel like I have some company."

"What do you have to be scared of?"

"You'll see."

She was still withholding eye contact, in a way that made her seem newly vulnerable. That pinched look. He just couldn't read it—like she was annoyed with him, specifically him, about something, but also annoyed about being annoyed. Maybe he was projecting.

"My mother may have recoiled from my sister first but the truth is that, with time, she withdrew from all of us. From the family, from my father. Even from our home, most of it. She moved into the uppermost lodge of our compound, the one hidden among the trees. She rarely leaves it now."

At least she wasn't talking about herself. It was a hot evening in Cairo but she hugged herself as if to suppress a shiver.

"From me. I couldn't tell you the last time she said anything, asked a question, that had anything to do with me. With any of us. Until now."

So the mother had something to do with all this?

"She disappeared, retreated not only uphill but from the personal. From the particular. She allowed herself—no, she willed herself—to be wholly subsumed by Zade. She is all machination now. All machine. Her pursuits are corporate—that's her ecosystem. Her children are data and they are countless."

She jerked her head in irritation at the noise and stepped back into the room. Liam followed.

"Her reclusiveness created a very particular problem for my father—me. With less of my mother's attention I had more time on my hands, and an appetite to spend it with my sister. He didn't like that at all. He was not unkind to me, you understand. Not cruel. But his assumption was that I was a ward, first and foremost, of my mother—even when that was no longer really the case. His ward was the other one, and he thought me a bad influence. I didn't *do* anything to her—I never would—but my presence was enough."

She sat on the edge of one of the vacant beds and Liam sat on his own, facing her.

"Actually, he wasn't wrong," she said. One advantage of her averted eyes was that Liam could watch her face intently. There was an absence there—she was more present in her past than in this hotel room. "The contrast. Our abilities, the differences—that was very, very hard on her. Not being able to help her was very hard on me, but that's not what my father saw. He saw her torment and he wanted to protect her from it." This time the shiver was real. "From me. There wasn't even the sham of a marriage any more to tie him to the compound. He saw a chance to get her away and I think he saw the same chance for himself. My mother would barely notice. My feelings were not taken into account."

The door to the room opened quietly and Darius poked his head around it. Liam was surprised it had taken him this long.

"I'll be out in a minute," she said, and the bodyguard shut the door.

"Nothing is more important to me, Mr Tead, than what we are doing now. Not myself. Not Zade. Nothing. If you can find a compliment in that you're welcome to it. From the day my father and sister left, they've basically been on the run. He sets up in a variety of locations—some I know about, some I don't. Communication is remote. I haven't set eyes on either of them, physically, since they left."

"The place in South Africa. The horsey stuff? She spends a lot of time there, doesn't she?"

"The place in South Africa is for photo ops. You can take enough photos in a morning to spin a yarn months or years long. Besides, we've leaned more and more into AI. What we've been able to deploy in that respect is more sophisticated than anything known on the open market. Smoke and mirrors, remember."

She stood.

"When we knew the day of our parting was close, we made a promise to each other. I'm going to keep it."

"But what promise? Forgive me, Ms Zade, but you talk a lot—and I still don't know why you want to find your sister."

"I don't want to find her. I have to find her. There's a difference." She was at the door. "There is plenty of cash in the cabinet by your bed. Cream for your skin in the bathroom. Some clothes in the wardrobe. Adil will make you as much sweet tea as you can stomach. He's positively fervent in that respect. Reynolds says your appetite should return quickly. I'm staying elsewhere."

Of course.

"But I'll check in with you in a day or two. I think it's best we handle it that way this time, don't you? Left to your own devices, who knows when we'd see you again?"

"For the love of all that's holy, would you just tell me what the promise was?"

She seemed genuinely amused by his frustration.

"Isn't it obvious? I promised her I would find her when the time was right. The right time was always hers to choose." She opened the door. "And now she has."

Smart Village

THEY WERE RIGHT about his appetite. As Liam took the unlit stairs the following morning—he'd spent a futile minute in the antique lift first—he was famished. He was back in sports gear and pleased about it. It seemed to him a cap, a hoody and some sweatpants would provide anonymity in the city and the fabric was suitably soft. One glance in the bathroom mirror had been enough—he'd avoided it since, and applied a lot of cream. He had some doubts about Reynolds' work this time—there was a hardened bump on his arm where the drip had been attached. It was the sort of bump a horse might not notice but Liam did. It itched.

But they weren't right about everything. It was a comfort to know that, for all her resources and whatever her gifts, she was fallible. It was a human failing, to see what you wanted to see, find what it suited you to find. Their homework had been extensive but not exhaustive, it would seem—Liam had known the second he'd stepped onto the balcony that he was on Talaat Harb, and therefore a couple of blocks away from a fast food place that happened to be a favourite. As he walked those blocks, little had changed. Street-level Cairo was a succession of cities that had been built in the same place without clearing out the old to make room for the new. Storefronts, entryways, mailboxes—they were all encrusted with placards announcing not just what they were but what they had been in every previous iteration—too many meanings to mean anything in particular, a mess of signals signifying nothing except maybe the passing of human life and the signing over of leases. Time didn't march here—it was an unceremonious tumble. Every square inch of real estate was not only occupied but usually shared—street vendors setting up on the pavement but also in the lobbies and on the stairwells that could be seen from there. All of it threatening to burst through the ubiquitous scaffolding.

Felfela's was a hole-in-the-wall that opened early to dole out *ta'amiya* and *fuul*—broad bean patties and paste in pockets of granular *baladi* bread. It was the first place Liam had ever eaten either, the first place in the city he'd ever negotiated the language barrier and incomprehensible menu board and gotten himself something good. This morning, it was also closed and, by the looks of it, permanently. He took a couple of corners onto Moustafa Abou and found what he was looking for—a street cart serving the same thing. *Ta'amiya* was as good as he remembered, better than any chickpea falafel*. His mood was good—not even the loss of Felfela's could dampen it. It

* Ta'amiya for two.

Ingredients:

    125 dried split broad beans
    2 minced garlic cloves
    1 small onion
    2 spring onions, finely chopped
    ¼tsp bicarbonate of soda
    1 tbsp chopped cilantro
    1 tbsp chopped parsley
    1 tsp ground cumin
    A pinch of chilli powder (optional)
    Salt and black pepper
    Sesame seeds
    Sunflower oil

Method:

1. Having soaked the broad beans overnight, drain them well and add them to a food processor along with the garlic, onion, spring onion, bicarbonate of soda, cilantro, parsley, cumin, chilli powder (if using), salt and pepper.
2. Process to a rough consistency.
3. On a work surface, divide to taste—not fewer than 6 patties or they will be too big. 8-10 is about right.
4. Pour sesame seeds into a small bowl and roll or flip each piece in them to coat. Refrigerate the patties for half an hour.
5. Heat the oil till a crumb of bread sizzles when dropped in, then cook the patties for two minutes on either side. Depending on how wide your pan is, you may prefer to cook them in two batches.
6. Serve with flatbreads and a minty yoghurt or tahini sauce.

wasn't that his familiarity with Cairo would make his so-called job any easier. It wouldn't. He knew Cairo just well enough to know the job couldn't be done. That it was hopeless. He could only claim, in fact, to know certain neighbourhoods right at the heart of the city. Greater Cairo wasn't a city at all—it was a concrete country, too huge and teeming to be contemplated. Twenty million souls. Of course he didn't know Cairo. Nobody did.

But he had a plan. It wasn't a plan that would help him find anybody, or anything, but it was an elegant solution. It didn't solve her problem but it did solve his, and she was the unwitting inspiration. He was done with her faith, done with being the object of it. It repulsed him. He'd lain awake thinking about it and finally recognised it for what it was. There was nothing mystical about it. There was nothing special about it, except that it was probably necessary to have had a very special life if you were going to fall so hard for such bullshit. It was irresponsible, nothing more. A complete abdication of responsibility. It was pure narcissism. It was pathetic, and if she could do it then why shouldn't he? He had his breakfast standing at the cart and when he finished headed for the Midan Tahrir. He was still hungry but more food could wait. He was going to find his own stooge and he was going to invest that stooge with absolute responsibility for whatever happened next.

On Tahrir, he walked past the old museum, the cap's peak helping him avoid unwanted stares, and along the Nile Corniche, where taxis lined up outside the Ritz. It had to be a taxi driver. They were a particular breed, here as elsewhere, and he needed a stooge with wheels. He knocked on the window of the first car in the rank and when its occupant gestured for him to do so, he got in.

"I'm just going to assume you speak English. How much to drive me around for the day?"

It was difficult to tell who was the more startled. Liam knew that up close he was a sorry sight but the driver, in his own way, was next level. He wore a full length *jalabiya*, a pair of knock-off baseball shoes, silk socks, a silk scarf around his neck and a turban. Whatever the cultural differences in play, there was no context in which, for a man in middle life, mauve was not a bold choice—and the only thing on this guy that *wasn't* mauve, shoes included, was an enormous, white, walrus moustache.

"What happened to you?" he asked in unbroken English.

"Long story," said Liam. "So how much for the morning?"

"You said day."

"OK, how much for the day?"

The guy looked him up and down.

"Three hundred US." He visibly winced as he said it, as if he thought he might have overshot the mark.

"And for the morning?"

A shrug. "Three hundred US."

"OK. I have a question. I'm the head of the world's largest tech company. I—"

"I'm going to need to see some cash, please."

"I'm not talking about myself. It's a scenario. I'm the head of the world's largest tech company. I'm in Cairo but I don't want anyone to know. I need to get work done so I need facilities, but I also need to hide. Where?"

"Smart Village."

Liam cocked an eyebrow.

"That was quick. All right, tell me about Smart Village."

"Technological park out in 6th of October. New enough and still growing but already very big. That's where."

"I definitely want to check that out. Anywhere else?"

"No."

"No? *No* other ideas?"

"You gave me a scenario, I gave you my answer. Smart Village is where."

"Look, I like confidence as much as the next man. It's an attractive quality. But in a city of twenty million people I think we may need to look in more than one place."

Another shrug. It occurred to Liam that from this point on none of it was his responsibility.

"Fine. Smart Village it is."

"You want to stop at a chemist? For sunblock?"

"I think that horse has bolted."

The driver pulled out, performed an illegal u-turn and drove north along the river.

"My name's Liam."

He didn't get a response. Driving here was a demanding activity. Nobody was paying any discernable attention to lane markings and the other cars were getting very close. The majority of the honks were intended to communicate a very simple and necessary message—*I am here*. They took an exit ramp that curled around onto a wide bridge. There was a kind of shock in the transition from the claustrophobia of Downtown Cairo to the vastness over the open water. No wonder the ancients had used the same word for the river as they had for the sea. The billboards that capped the taller buildings on the other side were still too far away to read, and Liam knew that the bridge didn't even cross the Nile—that was an island over there.

"The name's Zack."

It took a distracted Liam a second to register the words.

"Seriously?"

The driver bristled. Every part of his body communicated his offence, but none more so than the moustache.

"Sorry, it just doesn't seem—"

"It's short for Zaccaria."

"OK. That sounds a little more Egyptian, I suppose."

"It isn't Egyptian. It's Italian."

"You're Italian?"

"I'm Egyptian."

Liam rolled his window down, expecting fresh air but getting exhaust fumes.

"So how come you have an Italian name?"

The driver sighed.

"Actually, it isn't Italian. Zaccaria Pagani. It's Venetian."

"Isn't Venice in Italy?"

"Have you ever considered reading a book? Venice is older than Italy."

"You've read a book or three. Your English is flawless."

"An Oxford education will do that."

"Don't tell me. Oxford Polytechnic."

The moustache could have *written* books.

"I went to Balliol."

"To study taxi driving?"

"Yes, well, I've had my issues." He looked at Liam. "I'm guessing you have yours."

The island of Zamalek would have given most cities a run for their money in terms of busyness and bustle, but compared to Downtown it had a laid back feel to it. It was leafier, and a good smattering of the houses that could be seen in their walled gardens would qualify as mansions. A lot of the businesses, whether the offer was food or furniture, looked upscale. Before long they'd crossed another strip of water and therefore the Nile. The highway descended slightly into a sunken channel that cut through a different type of jumble—residential blocks squeezed together so tight it made him wonder just how any of them could be built in such confined spaces. They presented a notably uniform aspect—the same joyless, utilitarian construction, the same patina of dust and pollution, the same colour: a muddy, pinkish yellow as if to precurse the approaching desert. After a little while the views opened up, though the grasslands and palm groves gave it away they hadn't yet left the delta. It was less residential but hardly rural—the place was a mess of development, half-finished infrastructure projects on a massive scale all around. The sky was dirty, barely blue at all, veiled by the city's miasma, the effluvia of overpopulation.

The highway widened and the parklands and palm groves became more extensive. Liam noticed some apartment buildings, a distance from the road, had been left without any rendering. Whole swathes of them, towns in their own right, exposed, in the cavities of their rudimentary concrete gridwork, mud red bricks made of delta clay. They were clearly occupied—laundry hung from every balcony. Maybe they weren't expected to last long enough to bother finishing. There was no great sense of solidity to them. One or two appeared to lean.

The extra lanes attracted as little respect from drivers here as elsewhere, but as the distance from the city centre increased, so did the quality of the cars. Reconditioned, antique Peugeots and decrepit minivans gave way to Chevrolets and brand new SUVs. They were in traffic now that hadn't originated in the old city and would probably never go there—this was the Cairo of gated communities and business parks, the Dandy Mega Mall, the Mazar Mall, the Mall of Arabia, the international schools. Sandier ground, but only in small patches, the last remnants of virgin territory. Liam was reminded of the sidewalks downtown—any real estate, even a square meter, was or would be exploited. The difference out here was the scale. Instead of someone hawking tissues, a new train station. Instead of a hole-in-the-wall luggage shop, a power plant.

"This is Smart Village."

Zack left the highway and drove along a wide boulevard lined with neatly planted palms, then through a security checkpoint where a guard waved them on. There was no sign for Smart Village but there was no doubt. This was a different country—a magical land of gleaming glass pyramids, blue-tinted window-walls, cantilevered architectural improbabilities, manicured gardens and, above all, space. It was huge. No crowding or overpopulation here—every glossy edifice had its own large plot, plenty of room on all sides for carparks, park benches, rose beds. Even the sky was bluer. The desert had not so much been reclaimed as erased. What kind of resources—water alone—would need to be pumped into a place like this, just to stop it getting eaten by sand? It stank of money, but not of the kind of money someone like Liam would understand. Big money. Incomprehensibly big, permanently unavailable money. No coincidence that everything here had a hard gloss to it and sharp edges—if you weren't already in then you weren't welcome.

"Is there a newer part to this? Where they're still building?" An unclaimed building would probably be the way to go.

"How would I know? You seem to have mistaken me for Wikipedia."

"OK, just drive around."

About ten minutes later they found themselves among scaffolded, unglazed buildings that would no doubt someday sparkle but were, for the time being, grey hulks. Most of them looked unsuitable for any type of occupation, even temporary, but one or two of them were further along and potential candidates. As they drove by the mesh fence that surrounded one of these, Liam could see that in what would probably be its carpark, a little row of six or seven temporary, prefabricated buildings had been installed. On the one hand they made a rather motley impression, varying in size and shape and looking a little unloved. On the other, there was something about them—they drew his eye more than the enormous concrete structures that dwarfed them. Wouldn't this be just the kind of thing? Liam had worked on sites and there was something about the set up that didn't say site office to him—the separate structures were joined by enclosed walkways so that a person could move through all of them without having to go outside. He'd never seen that kind of trouble taken over a site office.

"Can we stop?"

"Of course. If you want to attract security. Most security are ex-police. Would you like to attract some former Egyptian policemen?"

"Trouble is," said Liam, "it isn't much good being here if I can't take a closer look. To be fair to you, it could very well be some place like this, but—"

"Not some place like this. This place."

"—I'd need to sniff around."

"I have no expertise in bypassing corporate security. I hope you can forgive me. But if I were you I'd come out here on a Friday. Skeleton crews, mostly napping. And even if they were awake, without the boss around they'd be easier to bribe."

Zack had made an executive decision—they were once again approaching the security checkpoint.

"What day is today?"

"You don't know what day it is? Where's your phone?"

"I don't have a phone."

"You don't have a phone? We should get something to eat. There's no way you don't have an interesting tale to tell."

They got back on to the highway and headed for town.

"Today is Thursday," said Zack. "What do you want to eat?"

"I've been trying to get hold of some pizza for a while," said Liam.

"Perfect. Little Italy then."

"There's a Little Italy in Cairo? I didn't know."

"Of course there is. The Venetian Quarter, really. I need to refuel anyway."

That was it for chat. Traffic was heavier in this direction and it took around an hour. Liam could see the attraction this bullshit had for the heiress. In anointing Zack, he'd unburdened himself. This first foray had seemed surprisingly promising, it had to be said. Amusingly so. But that way of thinking was a trap, a good glug of the Kool Aid—that Zade was even in Cairo was a wild assumption, a throw of the dice. All of this was batshit. But the plausibility of Smart Village was enough that Liam could say he was doing his job. He'd take a second look there and elsewhere tomorrow, no matter how dismissive Zack was of other options. He glanced at the driver—

a difficult man not to stare at and, even if neither knew it, the new repository of Sherry Zade's faith.

On the way back, Liam could appreciate the extent of those teetering redbrick cantons. If they were all around the city, they must have housed millions. There was no way they were properly planned or permissioned—nobody in their right minds would green-light building like that, so densely and shoddily. And there was a subcategory of these things that underscored the point. Liam got a good look at one as they neared the Nile, where the settlements lined the road. Further out, it had been hard to tell whether these particular buildings, lacking the red bricks of their neighbours, were going up or coming down, but here it was clear. They were coming down. The more horrifying possibility was that the blocks collapsed so regularly that the remaining husks were a feature of the urban landscape. More likely, he supposed, these were slow demolitions.

Either way, interior walls could be seen through the concrete frame. On them, colour choices, paper patterns, light fixtures—Liam could see a coil-bound calendar hanging from a hook on one of the lower floors and wondered about the appointments that might still be pencilled on it. Had they happened yet? Had they been missed? All these remnants, these traces of story, eccentricities of taste, were stamps of the human on an inhuman canvas. They threw out, from the right angles and straight lines of the concrete, an architecture of other spaces—memory, family, connection and loss, kindnesses, cruelties, the possibility of love and the certainty of grief.

El Horryia

"The Mousky."

Zack said it as if by apology, but there was also a note of pride. He'd left the taxi in a parking garage and they'd made their way beneath tangled overpasses that shaded a street-level melee of microbuses and market stalls, into a neighbourhood of narrow streets where the only wheeled vehicles were the handcarts pushed or pulled by porters.

The street would have been wide enough for one-way traffic if the space in front of every shop hadn't been colonised by the owners. The channel left between their stalls was barely wide enough for foot traffic, and every Cairene alive seemed to be shopping here today. It was a place where you could be pressed up against someone and still fearful you were going to lose them in the crowd. Liam and Zack squeezed past giant rolls of fabric, stacks of cheap stationery, homeware, lighting shops like Aladdin's caves, a basket weaver frowning over his crossword, until the busy traffic of a wide avenue cut across them. The snaking market continued on the other side, but Zack led him instead to the left.

"Over there it's all minarets and mausoleums," he said. "This is where *we* have always lived."

They walked for a minute to a quieter street with a church on it that ran parallel to the congested avenue, a line of trees dividing the two.

"Hazelnut Street," said Zack, cracking his first smile of the day. "I was born here. But the shop is around the corner."

"You have a shop?"

"The family."

They turned away from the traffic again, into streets lined with suppliers of the same wares—decoration, lighting, fabrics. That it was an area for cloth merchants was a potential mitigation of Zack's assertive wardrobe choices—Liam guessed he was in the business. The streets were tidy enough but it must have been a hundred years since anyone had cleaned them. The paving, the shop fronts, the walls to a height of several stories, were blackened with grime. It made the place seem that much darker on a sunny day, the slit of sky above them bright and clear blue. On the ground they might as well have been under it.

"This is our *baret*," said Zack.

Liam followed him into a side alley where in an instant all was transformed. Somewhere at the end of it there must have been an open place because a brilliant shaft of sunlight there reached the ground. The effect was less of a cave and more of a magical grotto or indeed of an enchanted glade—for surely that was what awaited them in the light. To reach it, they stepped through a garden of unlimited delights. All around and before them the way was shaded by fronds of palm, sprays and bouquets of silk acacia blossoms, acanthus, blue iris, enchanter's nightshade, vervains, thorn apples, white cherry blossoms, snapdragons and white orchids, each of these adding their hue to the sunlight they filtered. Birdsong filled the air and ladies sauntered with their baskets. The very ground, to either side of the path, was strewn with precious stones and metals that glinted from where they nestled in the undergrowth. A man could make himself rich in minutes, but Liam's imagination was alight with what awaited them in the glade. Ali turned to him and spoke.

"You were expecting trattorias and checkered tablecloths," he said, and it came back to Liam that Ali was Zack now.

The taxi driver indicated a pair of stools next to a shop doorway. Liam hesitated, trying to make sense of things—shouldn't he be overcome by the perfume from all these blooms? Intoxicated? He reached out and touched a palm frond, then overhead to stroke a willowherb, a rainflower. Plastic. The glade was indeed just a widening of the alley where the rooftops were low enough to admit light. Zack was not a cloth merchant.

"Are you all right, Liam?"

His shop was filled with homeware, lamps, decorative objects. The goods were downscale but the shop itself was smart enough, like it did business. There was a rack of faux-distressed, wooden wall hangings that said things like *Live, Laugh, Love* and *Your First Instinct is Usually Right*.

"Please sit. You've gone pale."

Liam looked back the way they'd come. The birds were real enough, mostly obscured by the fake foliage. Maybe they were also for sale. Caged birds set him on edge. What he had taken for the glint of precious gems in the undergrowth came from displays, behind the fake plants, of out-of-season Christmas tat—baubles, tree decorations and tinsel. He sat.

"You look like you've seen a ghost," said Zack. "Time for that refuel."

He went inside and quickly returned with two clay beakers, handing one of them to Liam. Liam put it to his nose and its contents smelled strong. Nothing ever smelled so good. He'd never in his life been so grateful for the vapours of alcohol in his nostrils.

"I appreciate it, Zack," he said and held the beaker out, "but not now."

"Really? You look like you need it. I'll send for pizza."

The taxi driver hid the beaker behind a plant pot. Liam almost asked for it back. But he didn't want anything in him, anything near him, that might further loosen his grip. He couldn't blame it on the meds this time—the painkillers that had been left for him were standard. Something was wrong. Again.

"Wait a minute. *Refuel?* This isn't your first of the day? You've been driving me around."

Zack shrugged.

"Issues. You're alive, aren't you?"

His demeanour was different when he wasn't behind the wheel. It was understandable—driving in Cairo was high-stakes stuff, and doing it drunk would only add to the challenge. Outside his shop, there was an affability to him. Indeed, with more refuels, he became more and more amiable, enthusiastically providing unsolicited historical context on the neighbourhood, a Christian quarter for Copts and Franks, whatever Franks were. Liam half listened as Zack recounted centuries-old vendettas as if expecting to finally do something about them later today, his voice rising here in rancour, there in gleeful schadenfreude, the odd word slurred. Evidently, he felt he had earned his dollars and wouldn't be driving again today. The pizza came in a proper pizza box and the dough was proper pizza dough. The toppings were another matter—döner kebab meat slathered in ranch dressing—but as Zack reminded him, there weren't any Italians around to disapprove, just Venetians. Liam was supplied with a cola to go with the pizza and sweet tea thereafter. It suited him fine that Zack carried the conversation through the afternoon but eventually the other man ran out of historical factoids.

"So, Liam. I know *you* have a story. What brings you to Cairo?"

A giant bird.

"No can do," said Liam. "Sworn to secrecy."

The bristling. The moustache.

"Sorry Zack, I really can't. But the story isn't so different from the one I gave you in the car. I'm working for someone swanky and I'm supposed to help them find some other swanky person. I'm *not* helping but swanky person number one doesn't seem to want to acknowledge that. It's all hush hush. Why I don't have a phone."

In the shop window opposite, more lamps were on display. Liam wondered how so many lamps could possibly be needed in the world and then remembered there were twenty million people nearby. These particular examples sported ceramic stands in the shape and garish colours of Disney princesses.

"Although, if it's my real story you're after—the long version—that's easy. My long story is a short story playing on repeat. It's no different right now. I find myself working for the richest person I've ever met. Possibly the richest person anyone's ever met. It is without doubt the greatest opportunity, completely unearned, that has ever come my way. All I want to do is wriggle out. Get away."

"Away from what?"

"From whatever keeps me here. Whatever makes me squirm. Whatever's messing with my head, getting in my way."

He had done this with Ali, too—made a therapist of him. The Great White Saviour act in reverse.

"Your way to where?"

"I don't know. Somewhere. Somewhere else."

"And what will you find there?"

It was a good question—really the only question.

"I don't know. Something that doesn't feel like how I feel now. Something that feels like . . . freedom."

Zack doubled over on his stool, spitting a little of his liquor. Liam had felt his blush rising even as he'd said the word, but it intensified as the taxi driver guffawed. The guy could hold his drink but he was getting good and loose.

"Happy to entertain."

The Venetian made an effort to suppress his mirth. It took a while.

"No insult intended, Liam. But if you'd just told me it was freedom you were looking for, I'd have taken you there. It opens at half five." He checked his phone. "It's nearly that now." He yelled into the shop, got to his feet, waited for Liam to do the same, and set off.

Freedom, it turned out, was to be found on Muhammad Mazloum Street in the Bab El-Louk district. The sun hadn't quite set but it was gloomy in the urban canyons of Downtown and lights were coming on.

"There we are," said Zack, patting the sign as they entered. "Freedom."

El Horryia was a cavernous space, faithful in design and decor to that same faded, *fin de siècle* glory that characterized this part of Cairo.

To the left of the entrance, men of a certain age, some in *jalabiyas* and turbans, smoked shisha and drank coffee. At one or two of the marble-topped, cast iron tables a game of dominoes was underway. The large windows had been swung wide open in the warm evening. To the right, a younger crowd, mixed, not all of the women in *hijab*, a few foreigners. The smoke that settled in layers on that side, all the way to the high ceiling above the suspended strip lights, came from cigarettes—a blend of cheap Cleopatras and foreign imports. The tabletops were crowded with beer bottles. The place rattled with chat, much of it centred around a young man there who seemed to be holding court. Zack found them a table beneath an old etched mirror—*Vimto, vous boisson préférée.*

Sitting with his back to the room, Liam could use the mirror to take it in. El Horryia, strip-lit and colourless—the walls were a beige that might have been white before a million cigarettes were smoked here—nevertheless had a warmth to it. Mirrors everywhere, most plain but some etched—*Lipton, Bière Stella*—meant the curious eye could wander unintrusively. The windows at this end were kept closed, frosted in faux *zellig* to the height of a seated patron lest the disgraceful business of beer drinking offend passersby. A bottle was popped open and put in front of him. A moment later the waiter brought a bowl of lupin beans. Liam took a swig—it was getting late in the day and he'd keep it to just the one. There was a rhythm to whatever the young man was saying—the laughs were coordinated. People were pulling chairs up.

"What's his story?"

The taxi driver snorted.

"The question is well put," he said. "He's telling the Tale of the Eloquent Peasant. Do you know it?"

"No." Liam's beer was going down well. The guy had the crowd rapt.

"Storytelling is popular here?"

"Sure," said Zack, "if you happen to live in the 19th fucking century." He squeezed a lupin bean from its skin. "Those days are long gone. But this guy is different, I've seen him before. Puts a topical spin on it. Political satire and what have you. I think he's been on TV." He put his empty bottle down. "Doing his tamest material, no doubt. You want another?"

"Not yet," said Liam. He passed a wad of cash across the table in a closed fist.

"Much obliged," said Zack, waving for the waiter. "If he passes a hat around he'll have to be quiet about it or they'll throw him out. This place attracts trouble from time to time. Freedom has to watch its back, you know?"

Another beer was plonked on the table.

"But he's probably doing it for content. Tic Tac or whatever."

Liam turned so he wasn't watching via the mirror. Several phones were held up, and one expensive-looking camera on a handheld rig. He emptied his bottle and set about calculating the possible repercussions of a second. The story must have been reaching some kind of climax—the pace was picking up and the laughs coming thick and fast. There was something in the percussive power of it, the laughter, decoupled from any sense of understanding—a sadness, a sound that signified nothing, that a narrative was unfolding that he could not access. He could sit here among all these people but he was not among them. He wasn't really here. Not really. The laughs were coming so close together he felt physically crowded by them. Because he wasn't privy to what prompted them, they seemed shocking, and almost a little aggressive—a woozy music, a soundtrack to claustrophobia and maybe the beginnings of panic.

"Where's the toilet?"

Zack pointed back to the other part of the café. The toilet smelled like a hundred unwashed toilets—it was bracing, like smelling salts. He had to steady himself against the wall as he pissed. There wasn't anything fishy going on—his beer bottle had been opened in front of him. He didn't suspect Zack of anything. But he shouldn't feel like this. Maybe an aftereffect of the sedatives. He made his way back towards the storyteller as slowly as he could because he didn't really want to get there. The noise level hadn't abated and the guy was still in full swing. When Liam reached the table and looked down at Zack, he froze and put a hand to the back of his chair to steady himself.

"What are you doing, Zack?"

"Hm?" The taxi driver looked up.

A ripple of cold electricity passed over Liam—through every hair on every part of his body. On the table in front of Zack was a sheet of blotting paper and beside it a bottle of black ink. In his hand he held the bottle's lid, a pipette, with which he had been impregnating the paper with drops.

"*What is this?*"

Liam didn't sit.

"A habit," said Zack. "Something I like to do. I find it—"

But Liam's attention was on something else. Someone else—behind the teller of this seemingly interminable story, a young man sat, listening intently, who stood out from the others. He was the only one at this end of the café who wore a *jabaliya* and turban, both in an awful, unwashed state, as was their wearer, who would have looked out of place in just about any indoor setting—like a beggar, like someone who couldn't pay the price of a beer. It was always tricky not to take a second look at someone with an eye patch, but that is not why Liam stared. The face was emaciated, skeletal, but it still carried traces of a ruined beauty. A Moroccan beauty. How a face could have been *so* ruined in so short a time, Liam didn't know, but there was no doubt in his mind as to whose it was.

"Ahmed!"

More than one head turned at the interruption, but none of them as instantly as that one eye turned on Liam. The owner of it looked to a window, where peeping over the *zellig* frosting was a young woman, equally wretched, equally one-eyed, head covered in a dirty rag. *Hayat.* The young man bolted for the door. Liam ran after him but by the time he was on the street, he couldn't see either. He went to the window where she had been. The street was crammed in both directions. He ran a little one way, then the other. He could see four or five streets leading off Muhammad Mazloum. There must have been thousands of people in his field of view, none of them the ones he was looking for. He paced up and down a few more times, his legs refusing to accept what his mind already had—they were gone.

When he returned to the table, Zack was gone too. He wasn't in the toilet and when Liam offered a note to the waiter it was waved away with a shrug. He stood outside again for a minute. The crowd was thickening and he was getting jostled. Something was wrong—a familiar feeling to which he had a standard response. He headed for the hotel.

He'd seen Ahmed and Hayat. Or he hadn't. But if he hadn't, why had the two run from him? He had yelled at the youth. Both of them had looked so derelict they were almost certainly in trouble with someone, somewhere. A lot of people were called Ahmed. They probably spent half their time running away. But he'd *recognised* them. Hadn't he?

He'd spent the day with a Venetian called Zack. Or he hadn't. He tried to visualise the taxi driver. It wasn't a very convincing image. If he hadn't . . . it was time to stop thinking. On Talaat Harb, at the top of the stairs a short man with a combover was manning reception.

"Good evening Mr Tead. Would you like some tea?"

"It's Téad," said Liam, "actually . . . but yes. Yes, please."

"I'll bring it to your room."

When Adil brought a tray to the door, Liam asked him to bring another in a couple of hours, to the evident approval of the beaming hotelier. He put the tray on his bedside cabinet and sat on the edge of the bed, resonating like a piano string. In front of him, another bed and beyond that the wall. He let his eyes defocus a little, withheld his gaze from anything in particular, letting it hang in the air between him and the other bed. The bedclothes were green like the walls, the pillow white, the floorboards at his feet more grey than brown. Now there was no one in his field of view and it contained precisely who he was looking for—no one. This little space—the grey boards and green blanket, the pillow, the bedside cabinet, the green wall, was of a type he had sought often. It was still and so was he. He not so much occupied it as allowed it to occupy him. He let it in, as he had let in so many small, still, unpeopled spaces. He carried them with him. To sit here was to revisit them all. Once Adil had brought more tea and he had drunk it, the sugar had the desired effect. The beer wooze gave way to a more pleasing tiredness and Liam felt well enough to undress, fold his clothes and put himself to bed as night traffic beeped sleepily.

By the time the heiress knocked on his door, early the following morning, Liam was showered, shaved and dressed in clean clothes—when he opened it, she didn't quite manage to conceal her surprise. Adil had provided her with a tray of tea which she set down on the room's only chest of drawers. She looked different. She'd looked a little different every time he'd set eyes on her these past days, as though something unseen was evolving, some private thing of hers. But this was *different* different. She looked like she'd had the wind knocked out of her sails. She looked like he pretty much always felt—like someone in trouble, someone sitting outside the headmaster's office. She looked afraid.

"I should have something for you later today," he said.

She was pouring tea.

"You found her, you idiot. Darius is getting a car. He'll be downstairs shortly."

She might almost have been accused of imbuing the word *idiot* with a hint of affection, although his imagination was the last thing Liam was inclined to trust just now.

"News to me." He accepted the glass she held out.

"Yesterday. Smart Village. Darius checked it out. She's there."

He put his glass down on the tray, aware that he was about to become angry.

"You had me followed?"

"We've been keeping tabs." Her eyes went to his arm, just where that bump had been bothering him. "Reynolds will take it out." As Liam put a thumb to the bump, she took a step towards him. "I knew you'd find her. I told you, didn't I?" There was no triumph in it, none of the self-satisfaction. It was like she was sorry.

"You told me you had faith in me. That you trusted me."

"I also told you that nothing was as important to me as finding my sister. Your behaviour has been somewhat erratic. I needed to eliminate that variable." Her eyes went to his arm again. "We all have our frailties. You have yours. But I did believe in you. And despite your best efforts, you came through."

Liam was surprised at the anger. He'd thought her faith schtick was bullshit. But if he felt like this now it must have meant something to him.

"You think better of me now." It was true and it was novel. Maybe it was because she'd found him sober. He wanted her to agree, and then to say something to her that was as mean as he could make it.

"I've thought well of you for a little while, you might be surprised to hear."

"Since when?"

She was fidgeting, if not quite wilting, beneath his gaze, clearly sensing his annoyance. She thought about her answer for a second, pouring herself a second glass of tea.

"Since you told me about your mother, I think."

"Fuck off."

"It's true."

"I tell you about the worst thing I've ever done." He was going to well up. He didn't understand where any of it was coming from. Fuck tears, fuck her and fuck Liam Těad. Fuck it all. "The absolute shittiest thing. And you think more of me."

"You looked me right in the eye," she said. "I remember you didn't blink. I think it took guts, that's all."

"I had a gun to my head."

She frowned, gave him a sidelong look. Then the strangest thing—she went into a bit. She stepped forward, fluffing up some imaginary hair and pretending to chew gum.

"We all have a gun to our head, Mr Těad," she said, in the voice of a gangster's moll.

It was the nicest she had ever been to him. The most human. To look for a laugh from someone, after all, is the act of an equal. A supplicant, even. She'd come down off her perch. In other circumstances, this might have been the exchange that made him warm to her again. But the only sources of heat in the room were his anger and, if his imagination wasn't playing more tricks on him, her blush.

"Anyway," she said, "we should wait downstairs."

"Knock yourselves out." He said it through his teeth as she went to the door. "I've played my part. Let me know when your vet can remove my chip."

She turned.

"Come on, Liam," she said from the doorway. "You've come this far. Are you really going to skip the last chapter?"

Doonah

Darius turned up in a car he was wearing like an outgrown prom suit—an old Lancia and a former taxi, judging by the state of the fake leather. Maybe it still was a taxi—Liam didn't suppose it mattered where or how the colossus had gotten hold of it. Reynolds was sitting behind him. Liam got in beside her. The heiress got in beside Darius. It was cosy. They'd be inconspicuous on the way out of town, at least to anyone who didn't look in the windows. Liam could think of a few choice words on the ridiculousness of it all but he never got to deliver them—the mood in the car was in no way conducive to conversation. There was a tension but it was one he, yet again, couldn't read. Anticipation for sure, but also something like dread. According to the boss, his job was done. Mission accomplished. But she was not OK.

In Smart Village Darius stopped the car near the irregular cluster of prefabs that had caught Liam's attention. The bodyguard had laid some groundwork—the gate in the perimeter fence was unlocked and unmanned. They walked briskly across the open ground to the first of the prefabs. Two of them carried shoulder bags—Reynolds had her medical kit and, when they got to the door, Darius took something from his that could have been a soldering iron or a voltage tester except that it looked more sophisticated than either. Whatever it was, it had the door open in no time—a much heavier door than Liam would have expected in such an apparently flimsy structure. Once it was closed behind them, Darius reapplied the instrument to the interior control panel. They crossed an empty space to a second, similar door, where Darius repeated the process.

Five more times, Darius got them through a heavy door and tampered with it afterwards, presumably disabling the electronics to slow a security detail down. They passed servers and office desks, cleaning supplies and a kitchen. At the last door it seemed to Liam he was stepping into the room for the second time. The first time, it had been at the base of White Mountain, outside the oasis. Now it was in a technology park on the outskirts of Cairo—but it was the same room: the same size and shape, the same drop ceiling, the same one-way mirror, the same bright lighting. On second thought, he noticed differences—the brushed concrete flooring was gone, replaced by a mean-looking carpet that had no discernible characteristics, not even a distinct colour. The only thing that could be said about it, really, was that it was on the floor. The set-up was still windowless but towards one corner, in the ceiling, a roof window had been installed that admitted a near-vertical shaft of light. If the intention had been to cheer the place up, the installation was a failure. The slender column of natural light served only to highlight the joylessness in the rest of the room. In comparison, the bright strip lighting felt like gloom. The main difference, though, was that this room was occupied.

A tall gurney stood alongside the mirror, level with its bottom edge. The occupant in question was obscured from view by all sorts of equipment set up on this side of the gurney. Some of the equipment was clearly medical but much of it wasn't—there were multiple screens and keyboards on rigs that made them mobile, so that they might be pulled in or pushed away. One of the screens displayed a convoluted array of scrolling data, another code, another was split across a large number of social media feeds. Not sure if he should, Liam pulled it aside and his first good view of the woman he'd crossed ocean and desert to find was her reflection in the one-way mirror. It was the same profile he'd first seen in the creased photograph he'd been handed in the Granada Hotel. This woman was not so young. Her face was drawn, bone prominent. She was clearly very ill, but apart from that she was identical. Identical to the photo and identical to her sister, but what he saw reflected in the mirror was not identical to what Liam saw when he looked down, at the side of her that faced him.

"Hello," she said, in that one word communicating to Liam a burning intelligence he knew might overwhelm him. Then she looked past him, and said "Hello, Doonah."

And from the woman who had crossed that ocean, that desert, with him, came the words "Hello, Sherry." When Liam turned to look, she bore little resemblance to the heiress he knew, her face contorted in a failing attempt not to cry.

"You took your time," said Sherry Zade. "I see you're still picking up strays."

The left side of her face was an unsuccessful approximation of the right. The eye there was milky and misshapen—sightless, it did not move in unison with its counterpart. Her mouth drooped in a way that should have affected her speech but didn't seem to, and her withered left arm hung uselessly. It felt intrusive to look at her so long but Liam couldn't stop. He couldn't *not* look at her.

"This is Liam. He found you for me."

The way she said it. Liam felt his chest swell.

"And that's Darius."

Sherry smiled at that.

"Oh, I know about that one. I sent him your way."

"And that's Reynolds."

His employer was having some trouble getting her words out.

"Cry baby," said Sherry. "You're supposed to be the big sister."

Liam noticed, awkwardly, that he was standing between the two. He stepped aside and Doonah came to the gurney's hand rail.

"I *am* the big sister."

Reynolds was at the head of the bed, investigating the innumerable lines and tubes that met in a hub there. Darius was tampering with some sort of console at the side of the one-way mirror. Despite the words and whatever the technicalities, Liam knew it was the other way around with these women. Sherry wore the mantle. It was the bedded sister that took care of the other. With her single eye she strained to look above and behind her.

"Hello Doctor."

"She's actually a vet." There was a tinge of something like mischief in her sister's voice.

"She's a doctor," said Sherry. "I have standards."

The mirror shuddered in its frame. On the other side, someone was beating it in a fury.

"There's Dad," said Sherry. "He must have been napping. He does that more and more."

"Darius has killed his mike," said Doonah. "He can hear us but he can't interrupt."

"Good," said Sherry. "He'll simmer down." She projected a little more to be sure he would hear.

"Interrupt what?" said Liam. Reynolds was carefully removing the lines, which made sense of course if they were to get out of here, but this woman was on a gurney and he was mindful they'd arrived in a Lancia. A tiny noise, a tormented sound, came out of Doonah.

"This will go awfully hard on him," said Sherry. "It's cruel. Sometimes that's the choice we're left with—between two cruelties." She was speaking to Liam, not to Doonah. She was explaining something to him that Doonah already understood. "I am ready and he isn't."

She searched Liam's face for some sign of understanding.

"It is time for me to go, Liam. But not with you."

Doonah had taken her hand, the near one, the one that didn't work. That was how Liam knew what she meant.

"Hang on." He was looking at Doonah. He waited till she looked back.

"I'm sorry," he said. "I know I've given you headaches. I don't mean to give you more. But I didn't sign up for this. I can't—" He shook his head, trailing off.

She squeezed his upper arm. The first time she'd touched him.

"I didn't sign up for it either," she said.

"Actually, *you* did," said Sherry. Their father was still banging on the mirror, now with the flats of his hands. "It's cruellest of all for you."

"I'm sorry." This time Liam was talking to Sherry. "I can't—"

A lifetime in a body she couldn't use to embrace, to comfort, had taught her to do it with her eye.

"You can," she said. "You are. This isn't your responsibility. I'm sick and there's too much pain." She scanned the screens they'd pulled away. "Anyway, my time is over. The AI can take it from here."

Doonah's hand went to an inside pocket and took an envelope from it.

"Mum wrote you a note."

The crumpled envelope had a single word written on it—*chutki*.

"Read it to me, will you?"

Doonah tore it open. As she unfolded the letter, she looked at Liam.

"Is it OK . . . would it be OK if you—"

He retreated to the other side of the room, where Darius sat on a sideboard and, for want of anything else to do, sat next to him. A noise, muffled but violent, came from beyond the door they'd entered by. Somebody was making their way through the prefabs. Liam should probably have been more concerned about that, but he was busy thinking about every word Doonah had said to him since they'd met in the Granada.

As Reynolds worked quietly, Doonah leaned in and read the letter. She was able to read it in the hushed tone they needed for privacy— Zade's hammering on the mirror had stopped. It wasn't a short letter. As Doonah read, a desk lamp was lit on the other side of the mirror, next to the glass. It was enough that Zade's figure, if not his features, could be made out. He too was right up against the mirror, a slighter figure than Liam had imagined from the rare photos he'd seen online. Zade was kneeling on what must have been a bed, level with the base of the mirror, as the one at White Mountain had been. As Doonah read to her, Sherry reached out towards the glass and pressed the palm of her hand to it, fingers splayed. On the other side, Zade put his hand there too, lining his fingers up with hers. Doonah laid the letter down on Sherry's chest, where she could still read it, and leaned over her sister to put her own hand to the glass. It took a moment, but Zade did the same for her.

And there they were. The sultan on his divan and the two sisters, but not quite like it had been in Doonah's book. Now she was the teller. The little lamp could only outline Zade—the bright light on this side of the glass overpowered it. From Liam's point of view, the mogul's face was replaced with the bodyguard's reflection, moving the silent man, the attendant, from the periphery to the centre. He realised with a start that Darius had removed the aviators but resisted the temptation to look directly. It seemed to him of the utmost importance he remain perfectly still and silent. Instead, he kept his eyes on the mirror, on the sisters, Zade and Darius commingled between them. He could see now why the shades never came off—those eyes were capable of striking terror. The grey eyes of a wolf—not cruel exactly but no trace of mercy in them. Reynolds had finished her work and stepped away from the gurney. They all waited for Doonah to finish the letter, and when she did, stayed quiet.

"Why don't you tell us a story?" said Doonah, breaking the silence. "It might help pass the time." Her voice cracked on the last word, like the last thing she wanted was for time to pass.

"I don't know that I have another story in me," said Sherry. "I don't know that I can."

"Of course you can. Don't you remember? When we were little?" Her voice trembled. "You would tell me all sorts of stories at night. You'd make them up on the spot. It was like *I Spy*—you'd just pick something in the room and start with that, and make up the most wonderful stories. Nothing could stop you. I should have appreciated them more."

She'd just about kept it together to read the letter, but now she was crying again.

"But all I did was complain. You were so fascinating you'd keep me awake, sometimes all night, and I'd be grumpy and tell on you in the morning. But I was so young then and didn't know the difference between *awake* and *alive*, and I'd complain to Mum that you were keeping me alive, and so everyone would just laugh at me and you'd get away with it, and do it again the next night."

Another sound from beyond the door. Louder. They were using cutting machinery. Darius put his hand on the back of Liam's neck. It was large enough to get a good hold there, and it was a message—it said *don't interfere, do nothing, say nothing*. But somehow, after all this time, it also said *hello*.

"Do that now, Sherry." Doonah leaned in, tears streaming, squeezing her sister's hand. "Please. Pick something and tell me one of your tales. Keep me alive."

It seemed for a moment that Sherry might refuse. She hesitated a long time.

"Very well," she said, eventually, and fell silent again. Liam supposed she was looking around for something to start with. For someone flat on her back, there was really only one direction to look in.

"Ceilings."

They were cutting again. Two doors away? Three? Sherry was quiet. She'd made her choice but nothing followed. No tale came. Maybe she was exhausted. She certainly looked it. Maybe she didn't want to tell tales anymore. Maybe she couldn't. The possibility was terrifying to Liam. His eyes were on Doonah. She needed this and Liam needed it for her. She must have it. Then he looked up and understood Sherry's problem.

What an awful place, this and all the other, identical rooms there must have been, for a person to spend her life. She probably hadn't noticed—apart from the basic needs of her broken body, her existence had essentially been digital, unencumbered by the strictures of the physical. It may not have mattered to her where she was, or may not have seemed to matter. But it mattered to Liam. This was not a place where a human being should find themselves for long, let alone live. And yet so many human beings everywhere found themselves in rooms exactly like it. There was something wrong in these rooms. The drop ceiling was the same as any other drop ceiling anywhere in the world—squares of white foam in an aluminium grid. Like everything else in the place that wasn't breathing it was mean and miserly, no one square differing from another in any way. No differences, no variation. Nothing from which a story might spring. Even if he isolated a single square and then honed his attention on a particular quadrant of it, and, once he had done so, honed it on a still smaller quadrant of that quadrant, Liam found nothing. This is what it was—nothing. Death.

Up above it would be all the ducts, the wiring, all the behind-the-scenes stuff. Except it was really *behind-behind-the-scenes*, wasn't it? Wasn't down here behind the scenes already? Nobody in their right mind, with a human heart, would ever design a space like this for show, for front-of-house. The pathologically bland colour schemes, the windowlessness, carpets that were hard-wearing to the point of hostility. Even when there were windows, there weren't. There had been some, now and then, in places where Liam had worked. But they were unlooking. Installed at chest height so as not to distract, presumably, from a seated position. The true definition of a window had to encompass more than a pane of glass in a wall. The true definition had to include the view and the looker. But it was never the intention that anyone would look through those office windows. Their inclusion in the architecture was probably just habit, or maybe prompted by some psychologist's input on natural light and productivity. Nobody ever stood at them, looking. They were glass in a wall. They weren't windows.

And as for the carpet. The carpet was beneath contempt. Rough and coarse and ugly. The opposite of everything a carpet should be.

Because it wasn't really a carpet. The true definition of a carpet ought to encompass more than some fabric on the floor. It ought to encompass the feel of it on the sole of a foot, the way it changed a room's acoustics, a room's light. But this carpet was never meant to be stepped upon barefoot. And if a carpet was never to be stepped upon barefoot, what even *was* a carpet? Something was wrong with all of it. With this place and others like it, where so many people wasted so much of their time. Backstage crews in a back-end world. In Liam's language, it was the polar opposite of elsewhere. It was that most fatal of things—it was *exactly here*. The ultimate deception. Because when the crew went home, weren't they all subjected to messaging, an awful lot of messaging it seemed to him, *around-the-clock* messaging, to the effect that *they* were the audience? That this was their very nature? That fulfilment meant shipping fulfilment? That their function was to receive deliveries—goods, services, entertainments? They were to be told stories, not to tell them. Even though everyone knew, somewhere under their skin, that this couldn't be their nature. That they weren't audience. How could they be? Hadn't they just come from backstage? Didn't they have a story of their own?

What is this?

Like sitting between two boundaries, one above and one below, beyond which lay nothing. Death. And here, between them, all life. Everything. Liam had never been more certain of anything—everything he'd done and everything he hadn't, everything he was, had led him here. He was home and home happened to be, among other things, a prefab in a technology park outside Cairo. It was having his neck squeezed by a giant. It was waiting quietly for someone to die. It was, after all, listening to a story. Except something was wrong. There was no story. She couldn't *tell*. Now, when it was more important than ever, when her sister needed this parting gift from her. Something to keep her alive. Liam took his eyes off the carpet to look at Sherry but found it was impossible—they locked on instead to Doonah's. She was looking at him.

One door away, the cutting.

Why would she look at him now? Of all people? And why would she look at him *like that*? How could she, knowing what she knew of him, having seen what she saw, look at him like that? Her eyes, her lips, trembling. Lost. She was nothing but an I-don't-know-what-to-do. A node of not knowing in a network of question marks. She *was* a question mark, in human form, and she was the answer to every question Liam had ever asked or ever would.

And she was looking at him. He got up and Darius let him. He didn't know what to do either but he didn't want her ever to stop looking at him like that, impaling him on her faith. Maybe it was hope. He didn't really understand the difference and it didn't really matter. He was worthy of neither but here they were. He was going to do *something*.

"Take the other end," he said to her, "and follow me."

He flipped the brakes off the gurney's wheels and waited for Doonah to do the same, and then he pulled Sherry towards the sunny rhombus beneath the skylight. Once her head was illumined, he locked the brakes again and stepped back. That was it. That was his something. The cutting began at the last door. It was loud but it wasn't enough to disturb Sherry's joy, looking up at the patch of pure blue. Liam looked too—it was just as undifferentiated as a square of foam, and yet it wasn't. It was everything and it was forever. Every story ever told. The greatest game of *I Spy*. He looked back at Sherry and knew that it had worked. She was grinning like a child, her eye darting from from one quadrant of the blue square to another. With a single word she broke her awful silence, and her story could begin.

"Skies."

THE LITTLE PARTY had come to a standstill, as if by some unspoken agreement, and Clara fell silent from what she had been able, what with the quease and the worrying weather, and the constant swaying of the litter and the occasional stumbles, to say.

"What an astonishing and lovely tale!" said Jordi.

"Pfft," said Clara. "It is nothing compared to what comes next." She was afraid her friends were wavering. "Do please carry on, Jordi! Rolf! And I'll tell you what happened to the inhabitants of the Isle of Truth."

And so I filled a while with more beautiful lies. I don't think she could quite believe I was sharing content with her. Stroking her head, I told the tale and she leaned into my hand. Forgive me for the description, Lita, but she really was like some poor mistreated animal who had finally found sanctuary, some tenderness. Her breathing slowed and became less labored, and she closed her eyes as she listened.

And then a fear got into me. I hadn't really thought—I'd just plucked a story from my head, from the materials I'd been reading, but now I didn't want to tell her the ending. About the sisters and the promise. About that parting. I didn't want to tell her about any parting, about anything that was sad or final, or that would remind her of parting from you, and I readied myself to make something up—to introduce some frivolous change into the ancient story, to make something different of it. An alternative ending. A content creator now—heaping new lies upon old ones.

I wanted to give her a bit of happiness. It had been so long since I'd made her smile and I wanted to do that for her now, one little act of kindness for her before she had to go. And so I took a breath and looked down at her to say something that might buy me a minute to think, and I saw that it didn't matter—she was already smiling, and she was already gone.

"That was long," says Mr Cyre, when the audio stopped.

"Very," says Mrs Cyre.

"*Very*," says Fafl, as though the word had waited a century to escape him.

"I don't know what all of it was about," says Wigbert, "but—"

"But," says Simon, "we may be sure, now."

"Sure of what?" says Mrs Cyre.

"It is a certainty we are observed," says Mr Bull. "It must be so."

"A hasty conclusion, Mr Bull," says Fafl, who nevertheless appears rather ill at ease. "But we should see these two off with all possible dispatch, I think. Preparations have been made?"

Mr Bull, the Stationmaster, Simon and his parents, Wigbert and the boy—all don oilskins and file out into the night and, observing that no victuals are to be produced, Heft and Pack follow. The storm makes too much noise in the trees, and more again down at the water, for any to make conversation—they each pull their hood tight and cower against the gusts.

"This is madness," yells Fafl when they reach the jetty. "You should not have waited so long."

"P-perhaps we should wait yet?" returns Simon, "For the storm to p-pass?"

"For *goodness sake*, Simon!" says Mr Cyre. He takes his son's face in both hands. In the darkness it isn't possible to tell whether the drops of moisture on the older gentleman's cheek have fallen from the sky or from elsewhere. "Just go, son."

The yellow pod bashes wildly against the jetty. The voyagers are helped aboard, Wigbert silently thanking the storm for removing any possibility of a protracted exchange between him and the boy. Fafl pulls a metal box from his waterproofs.

"You know how to use this, Mr Grim?"

"I do."

They climb aboard and duck beneath the tarp that covers the bow. Fafl watches as Wigbert, unsteady on his feet and having to weave about to remain upright, fixes the device to a board at the helm.

"Enter these coordinates," says Fafl, and calls out a series of numbers.

Wigbert complies. "It is activated," he says.

"Simon," says Fafl, "do you see the display?"

Simon nods.

"When the outer rim breaks your horizon," continues the Stationmaster, "you must approach on this line. Do you understand?"

A second nod.

As Wigbert clambers back on to the jetty, the Stationmaster clutches at Simon's coat. "Do you hear me?" he yells over the weather's roar. "It must be that precise coordinate." His voice would be shrill enough to pierce the storm even if not raised so. "Or all is lost. Tell me you understand!"

A third nod. "I understand," shouts the younger man and Fafl, with some apparent reluctance, lets go of him and takes a helping hand from Heft to get back on the jetty.

"Pappy!"

"You get along there," Wigbert shouts, untying the pod, "and look after Simon." He throws the coiled line into the pod's uncovered stern. "And don't go milling through those supplies, d'you 'ear me? You'll be on that thing for days."

"Yes, Pappy."

Simon starts the motor and, despite the wild water, gets the pod moving. Wigbert steps to the end of the jetty. Sheltered on the lower lip of his hood, Mouse takes his leave of the boy also, who has insisted he stay to keep the old man company.

"You're a good boy, d'you 'ear me?" Wigbert shouts.

"Yes, Pappy," comes the hollered reply.

The pod works hard, its engine moaning, yet manages little more than to tread water. Even this close to shore, it tilts with every wave as though it might go over at any moment. In time though, as the others look on, it puts some distance between itself and the island.

"You're a good boy," says Wig, but it is only a murmur, and no one but Mouse hears it. When he turns, the Marshal is watching him. Mrs Cyre weeps in Mr Cyre's arms. Man and wife have not been seen to treat one another with such affection as they do now in the gale, lashed by rain, their only child lost to them, carried away on the swell.

Fafl is already uphill of them all, his lantern blinking between the trees.

---

perfection   I have never been this close   I take this last step towards it   and cannot even describe the feeling   he came to me   he to *me*   put himself on a plate for me   dropped it in my lap a leather notebook   and bade me look   a fellow aetiologist   a colleague   perhaps he taunted me   perhaps he flattered me   either way I couldn't see it   could not decipher the contents   so he told me   and I could not believe it   till he told me again   the paradigm   the look on his face   something like desperation   or fervour   I had never seen it in him at least   it must go to the magistracy   he said   and lil with it   he said   with *you* he said   but she will not go while I live   he said   and somebody   after all   must pay for the breaches   he said   and I saw where he was going with it   and the very thought was transport   his words filled me up like nectar wine   perfection   *after* all my long suffering   was mine   of course there was the small matter   of the magistracy's not actually wanting the paradigm   that they in fact reviled such a thing   feared it   and if I had it   I suppose   feared *me*   I wouldn't tell *him* that   of course   might make him think himself important and besides I now could see him as he was finally and share their revulsion as he with a temerity I hadn't suspected even in him outlined his heresy to me a magistracy stationmaster that he would see his precious izzy again that he hoped to join her more than hoped believed he would on the hearing of which the death of him became less a nuisance and more a relished duty and so I went along with it why wouldn't I how much greater a leverage was this than that which I'd had in the boy who could now live out his oblivious days on the Warburg for all I cared I had so much more the man his life his paradigm his *girl*

Despite the storm that holds sway without, the silence in the dome is so thick it can be heard to murmur in the ear. It hangs so heavy its weight can be felt in the upturned hand, on the slumped shoulder, over the bowed head. It heaves and roils about the place as cold waters do about the lonely island.

Here, too, it is cold. The vaulted cavity is barely lit. A small, mean desk lamp seems almost to begrudge its light where the Stationmaster sits—head bowed and shoulders slumped, one hand upturned carelessly on his desk—and a single bulb hangs over the sick bay that gives the sepulchral gloom its full justification. The place is become a tomb, and the two sick beds mortuary slabs. One of them is for the great aetiologist, Arenaceous Nell; the visionary, the heretic, the broken heart, the drunkard—the other is for his poor daughter. Jasper Fafl is wrapped up good and warm against the icy breath of the refrigeration unit. He has donned his ceremonial uniform, replete with heavy greatcoat. His own expirations trumpet visibly in the air about him before they dissipate into the gloom. For some hours now, he has not moved in his seat. From it, chin to chest, he regards her.

He is conscious that there has been a knocking at the metal door, more than once, but not even as it became so ringing and insistent a cacophony, this last time, was he moved to stir. It is as though his eyes have found their way home at long last and will not willingly give it up again. She can no longer return his gaze and cause him to avert it in shame. Therefore he can take this time to luxuriate in the looking, to suck with the eye on what it sees, and does so.

The eye sucks; it seeks; but it does not hunt—this new gaze is not that of a predator. This is no prey: no, not even a bird trapped. Instead, the pale flesh seems to him a break in the murk: a chink of light in the darkness, a breach in a trap of his own making and in which he is the trapped. He is not the pursuer; instead he feels himself drawn in by a force he has not felt before and dare not name.

She is naked. The tarpaulin they wrapped her in to carry her here has fallen open beneath her. It drapes the bed, its red folds tumbling to the floor like a shroud. He has covered her modesty with a little towel, but otherwise allows his eyes to rove about her body.

His princess. The lips are parted and the eyes not quite shut, the hair just long enough for the ends of it to hang with the tarpaulin. Rather thin, he thinks—the ribs are visible, marked with a laceration that the buoy's metal rivets must have administered. That, or some creature of the sea in the time she spent adrift. He cleansed it himself when they first brought her. The fingers are long and curl over the bed's edge. The toes too are long, and the feet bony. The body is not emaciated, though; the musculature in the legs and arms is well defined—wiry—and he supposes the young woman must have been deceptively strong all these years. Physical strength is not a quality he has associated with her till now.

He stands, and his old legs, still and bent these past hours, complain as he shuffles to the bed to look down upon her. From this angle, with the pupils just showing between the lids, it is suddenly as though she looks back at him. Involuntarily, he lowers his eyes.

 forgive me lil forgive me

 He puts a hand on hers. The cold flesh cannot quell the rush of warmth that envelops him. It surges through him, spilling over in the hot tears that bathe his cheeks, dropping from his chin to sound a slow patter on the tarpaulin. He shuts his eyes tight to stem the flow, but the flood must find egress, and escapes his mouth instead—an almost inhuman, tortured growl comes from there.

 you look free lil and what I would not do to join you would give my life to be with you you look so free to me at this moment is the credit mine do you think did I set you free can I make the claim do you think but we both know I cannot don't we forgive me lil I hope you can I have preyed upon you and what a poor hunter have I been what a swathe have I left in my chase what an untidy kill

 In his other hand, something glints.

 do you know that I love you lil I do I know it that is the name after all is it not of this of this torment I love you I who have loved nothing and nobody not since but never mind it I find myself the recipient of this wonderful gift this torture and am grateful for it really truly I am and having been a killer of you of yours would kill for you again kill to have you or kill at your command whichever and I would die for you oh yes that too in an instant I would lil know it

 He takes the hand and gently rotates the arm, lets his eye roam over softer, paler flesh.

 and yet even now loving you so completely I know too that I must fail you isn't that lovely lil isn't it just right but I am locked into this course and have no choice I cannot do what I ought and leave you free making you my salvation but must trap you once more making you my prey

"Forgive me, Lil," he says aloud. "I hope you can. I thought they'd go this morning. But that young fool hung on and on. It was nearly the undoing of me. We're still in time, though, still in time." He has bent down and rubs the pad of his thumb along the inside of her elbow. When he finds what he seeks he raises the glinting object in his other hand—a syringe—and breaks her skin with the needle. Emptying its contents into the limp body, he dares a glance at what is visible of the pupils between those lids, withdraws the needle, and turns away.

And now there is a change in the old man. He mutters to himself, hums a little ditty, fairly bounces along on those old legs to replace the syringe in a case on his desk and pick up a ring of keys there. The curved wall behind the desk is lined with lockers from waist height up, and below them several columns of long, slender drawers—it is to one of these that the Stationmaster, dropping to his knees like a youth, applies one of the keys. The drawer slides out smoothly on its rollers, revealing a layer of tissue paper, browned by time. Gently, the old man lifts the tissue, to reveal a more brilliant white beneath. He reaches towards it, then checks himself, turning his hands over to examine them. They are dirty, grime packed under the nails and grease smeared over the pads and palms. He pulls a handkerchief from his pocket and wipes them, tongue between his discoloured teeth as he gives the task his most assiduous attention. When it is done, he parts the tissue paper once again, with all the caution of an archaeologist.

this was to be for your mother

He places one hand on the white material and strokes it.

my queen

Now he lifts it from the drawer, sitting back on his heels to lay it upon his lap. A white dress.

but it will do just as well for you

He pushes the drawer and hears its satisfying click behind him as he shuffles around on his knees to get up, and bring the dress to

Lil—but, astounded, he has not the strength to lift himself to his feet.

She is on hers. The towel has fallen away and there is nothing to cover her, but he hesitates to go to her, to offer her the dress or, for the moment, to speak a word; she has taken one of the harpoon guns from the fishing tackle rack. She aims it directly at him but, though the sight is momentarily startling, he can see that it is not loaded. She blinks down at him, as if to clear her vision. The poor thing has yet to emerge from her stasis daze. She must think him an abductor. It is natural, and he has so much to explain, so many reassurances to offer, so much forgiveness to beg.

Her line of sight appears to follow his to the muzzle of the gun and, seeing no harpoon there, she drops it to the floor and turns, walking towards the locker where the medical scrubs and overalls are kept. Of course, as a child of the Warburg, tutored in this dome, she knows where everything is. She takes a pair of orange-and-green overalls and steps into them.

but no   wait   take this   it is yours now lil

He goes to get to his feet and, finding that his legs will not comply, looks down. See there! The resplendent whiteness corrupted. From a point between the two hands that cradle it, a red flower blooms. The petals spread outward through the fabric, racing along each capillary fibre. And in the centre, like a stamen, the shaft of a fishing harpoon protrudes from his chest. Fixed and immobile, it pins him to the wall behind. He looks up.

Lil has fastened the overalls. Walking back towards him, she stops at the little trolley of medical implements that stands between the sick beds. She seems not to notice her father's body. But something in the trolley has caught her eye. She reaches into the top tray and lifts it out—a rubber band. Pulling her hair back tightly, she uses it for a tie and, taking a chair and placing it before the Stationmaster, she sits and crosses her legs.

The storm is at its height—trees will be felled before morning and damage done to the compound that Heft and Pack will be busy repairing for weeks. The night lamps creak urgently on their metal posts, their halos illuminating mad flurries of rain. The wooden walkways are slippy underfoot, loose shutters bang open and closed over them. Here and there an awning flaps wildly. It is not a night to be out but to be crouched over a heater or curled in a bed, and that is precisely where everybody is, with the solitary exception of Reginald Bull. Not once in his long tenure at the Warburg has the Marshal failed to make this nightly patrol. Never, it must also be said, has the perambulation served any discernible purpose. Until now.

He stops at the door of a hut and looks quickly up and down the walkway, though there isn't a chance that anyone can be watching him in this weather. When he has satisfied himself of it, he puts a hand to the knob and a shoulder to the door, sways back and forth twice, and on the third effects a forcible entry.

Inside, he pauses for his eyes to adjust to the darkness, and makes his way to the window. He lifts the lid of a box that sits on the sill. Something inside reflects the scant light from a lamp outside. He pockets the thing.

At the door, he looks both ways again and closes it behind him. It may not stay closed in this wind, with a damaged lock, but that, it seems, does not concern him—without pushing it to check, he walks, fondling the object in his pocket, in the direction of his own quarters.

Out on the water, a dreadful scene. A yellow pod thrown about like some plastic bauble, like a ball for ping-pong in a vat of boiling water. A silly anomaly in the great maelstrom—how could such a thing hew to any line when every wave threatens to hurl it over, and consign its contents to the deep? A boy and a man not much more than a boy. The former clings to a handrail with one hand and the food box, for all his life, with the other. He has not spoken since the unlikely pair embarked, has not had the courage to. The tarp overhead holds, for now.

Simon has been bent over the navigational instrument for some time, a man possessed. He has hung on to the wheel with both hands except when momentarily raising one of them to pull at his hair in panic. Fafl's coordinates are a cruel joke in these conditions. They lost the line before the island was out of sight. Ever since he has been toiling, and failing, to return to it. His arms ache. He doesn't know how long the storm is to last. They could wait it out, drifting. But there is no telling how quickly the Magistracy, alerted to their escape, could deploy a perfectly storm-proof craft to intercept them—there is nothing to do but go on. And there is some hope; although the exact line still eludes him, he is mastering a new art, that of erring from it ever less extremely. The task calms him, and he tacks a weaving line that closes in each time on their true path. He is an empty man, an automaton. All that gave him his humanity is gone. And so, he makes of himself a machine for navigation. And he has his coordinates.

What a curious thing it is that he feels no pain. The dome must still be cold for he can see his laboured breaths as he puffs them out towards her, but he does not feel that either. His mind, it seems to him, is clear as glass. He is in a shock, no doubt, and it shields him for the moment from any ill effects. They will doubtless come.

"It will take time," she says, as if reading his thoughts. "That's good. We can talk."

She leans forward. His eyes go to the Magistracy insignia, back at her breast as it always has been. "Beauty is Utility"—it bothers him that, a Magistracy man through and through, and long convinced of the absolute truth and universality of Magistracy values, he finds himself at a loss as to how the maxim might be applied to his current situation. The emblem, though—the feather—is apt. As his gaze goes from it to her wide, unblinking eyes it comes to him that there is something of the avian about her. Something that does not seem human to him.

I the prey now

"When was the Warburg shut down?"

the downed prey

He does not immediately reply. Let the sharpshooter worry a moment that she has missed her mark, that the wound will drain him too quickly and that even now, the power of speech has left him. But only a moment—the truth is, he wants to speak to her. He has wanted nothing else.

"Oh," he says in the end, "many a year ago, Lil my dear."

She nods. It was the answer she expected.

"When you had my father's work reassigned?"

His silence is affirmative.

"Then you executed him," says Lil. "You alone."

That cold gaze again. It reminds him of the goonies and the satisfaction of trapping them. Then it occurs to him: she may yet be his caged bird, though she doesn't seem to realize it. He bears it for just a moment, and then must lower his eyes.

"Arenaceous and I," he says, then loses his train of thought, then takes it up again. "Our fates were tangled long ago, Lil. If one of us were culpable in his end, we both were. If he was a victim, so were we both." He looks around the dome's interior, searching for something, not knowing what it might be, then looks back at Lil, eyes narrowing. "How did you know, my dear?" In response to the interrogative rippling of her brow, he goes on. "That the buoys induce stasis, not death."

She uncrosses her legs and leans forward, elbows resting on her knees. Those eyes. "I can't say that I did know. Not with certainty. Your lack of concern for the boy's safety out there on the water, for one thing. It is obvious you care for him, though not why. You might say it was an article of faith. A little fiction to render death palatable." A joyless smile briefly disrupts the impassive features. "I have learned at first hand how plausible faith becomes when nothing else is left."

She sits back.

"But I thought it just as well, in case fiction were to prove fact, to have a plan."

this is not my lil

Breathing is a little harder now. He wheezes. Life has already fled his extremities. He can see the hands that had held the dress but they have released it, leaving it to hang from the harpoon and almost entirely red now, soaked in his spirit—he cannot feel or move them. The moment nears, he supposes. But she is not done with him.

"Knowing now that I was right," she says, "I know, too, that you might have saved my mother."

He lets silence speak for him again, since it always does so with such eloquence—and always of his guilt.

"The remaining nanos were given to Simon and the boy?" Her voice is raised a little, more urgent. It seems she does not like the mute replies. She must be worried he will fade away, leave her here in the dome alone before she has asked all of her questions. His lip curls: the old smirk.

this creature   it is not my lil

Alone in the dome and trapped there. "They have a half day on you, dear," he says weakly. "I waited to make sure it was so."

"I don't need to catch them—just to know where they are going."

"And if I refuse to tell you?"

"I don't need that either. Wig will tell me. You'll have needed him to set the coordinates."

For the first time, it seems to the Stationmaster, the eyes reveal something of what lies behind them. The sparkle of triumph. She straightens, leans forward, and her gaze intensifies.

you would like to see me wilt wouldn't you   see me break   before you watch me die   a pity   a pity for you

"Clever girl, Lil, but I'm afraid you *do* need to catch them, if you're to save them." What begins as a bark of laughter turns into a coughing fit. He is, at last, becoming acquainted with the pain.

"Save them?" She is rattled—he can see it—but does not want him to see it—he can see that too. "They have their nanos."

ha

"Oh, they do, they do indeed," says the old man, "and more besides."

His visage must be a fearful shade of grey by now; any colour that had been his is hers—it drips from her dress. He lets his eyes wander around the dome, as if seeing the place anew. It is dark and he cannot focus properly; there are only a few points of blurred light and the blackness overhead. For just a moment, a bliss fills him up. His mouth hangs open as he looks into what may as well be the night sky—he cannot tell whether he is indoors or out, whether the distances he perceives are cosy and close, or vast and beyond his comprehension.

He looks to her, to ask if she sees it too—this wondrous universe that envelops them, neither large nor small, neither friendly nor threatening—but the expression on her face pulls him out of the moment. He laughs, an easy laugh she will not have heard before, since neither has he. He is amused. He can see her fear of him. No—not of him, but of his imminent demise. She needs more, before he takes his leave. He wonders what it might be. Perhaps he will give it, perhaps not. The strangest, most intriguing sensation introduces itself: that none of this really matters, after all. That nothing that ever seemed to matter ever did. The realisation is the deepest joy and the profoundest sadness of his waning life. He would weep if his old body didn't want for the fluid with which to perform the act.

Lil's eyes are suddenly in motion. Then they stop still and wherever it is they rest, they find the salve there. She takes more steady breaths and he can see a calm spread bodily through her. He follows her gaze—there, on the desk, sits her father's notebook.

"Ah yes," he says. "The rub. You have your nano now, Lil, and your father's work would have been mine. My leverage. *Our* leverage. You could have enlightened me. Let me in on this wisdom of your father's. Let me tell you something you do not know, dear. They don't want it. They *fear* it. If they knew I . . . we . . . had it, they would fear *us*."

"But the Magistracy does not know," says Lil. She blinks. "What do you mean—*save* them?"

He smiles again, though his lips tremble—pain picks them like a plectrum. "The Magistracy will know soon enough," he says, and almost laughs but, thinking better of it, grimaces to suppress another coughing fit.

"What do you *mean*, save them?" presses Lil. "And what do you mean, they have *more besides?*" Her alarm can be read in the downy hair that stands erect on her forearm, where she has nervously pulled a sleeve of the Stationmaster's tunic up.

"The boy," he says, and there is the bubbling of fluid in his throat now, "has been something of a project for me, dear, as his tutor and his doctor. The latter, of course, involves regular use of the syringe." He looks at her intently, to see if she understands his meaning. "The boy's nano was merely the latest of many. I've been filling him up with 'em since he was small, you know. Infoplants, the archive artefacts. The boy *is* the archive, Lil. And now, a message for the Magistracy too." The pleasure he takes in the revelation proves too much, and a fit ensues. When it abates, he takes a few breaths and groans with the effort.

"They believe themselves bound for a resistance outpost," he says. "But to reach the resistance they need only have pointed the pod anywhere south west of here—that whole quadrant is lost to the Magistracy. I, however, gave them a very precise coordinate indeed, to the east. Magistracy. They will execute Simon, of course. Before he disembarks from the pod, in all likelihood. But a minor they will not execute. He'll be sent to camp, and will therefore be traceable to any Magistracy operative. Me, for example. The archive will be out there, Lil. And so too would you and I have been. Think of it. Whoever has the child has the lock, but not the key. He who holds the notebook in his hand has the key, but not the lock. We could have had both."

She is on her feet.

in a hurry now are we   you'll never catch up lil   you've been one step behind all along   you and your father   and that's where you'll remain   here with him and me

She however makes no attempt to leave, instead approaching him. Kneeling in the pool of his blood, she puts her face close to his.

"You are a monster, Jasper Fafl. A wounded, sickly beast, and a broken thing. But I never took you for a fool."

Even now, at such close quarters, the eyes are cold and communicate nothing. He cannot make out her meaning. She shakes her head slowly.

"I could never have deciphered my father's work for you. I do not understand it. I never did. I never could. But there is one who does, Jasper," she leans closer still, until he can almost imagine she intends to kiss him, "and you have sent him to his death."

As her words hit their mark, it must be revealed in his face—for the first time an expression, a slow smile, shows itself on hers, then quickly fades. She gets to her feet, walks back to the little trolley by the sick bay beds and peers into it.

well   you surprise me   I didn't think there would be any more surprises   but it hardly matters now   I will not be the last piece left on the board   and neither will you

"How can you know anything of a resistance? Or its locations?" She has come back to him, but remains on her feet. "You've been using the emergency frequency. *You're* responsible for the security breaches."

He nods. "I'm afraid the Magistracy cannot be said to be quite in control, dear. No more than I have been of events on the Warburg, it seems." His voice is very faint now, and he must separate his words with long, deliberate breaths. "It still astonishes me that, in the vastness of the archive, you came across these new artefacts almost immediately. Confound them." He raises his eyes up to hers. "And confound you."

Another shake of the bird-like head. "And you the dyed-in-the-wool Magistracy man, Jasper. What have all these machinations of yours been about, really?"

His head drops. It is not so easy to hold it upright. "At first I truly believed we were an observatory," he says. "A flagship. We were, at first, I still believe. Then, later, an archive. I could live with that. When they cut us off, I had a glimpse at last of what we really were. What we really are. And now I know it." The red pool on the floor is spreading—smoothly, slowly and beautifully. "A dump." These last words are voiced so feebly, he cannot be sure she has heard them. She has taken something from the trolley, but his vision is failing and he cannot make it out.

"What is that, Lil?"

There is no reply.

"No matter," he says. "Take what you will." With the greatest of efforts he lifts his head. His eyes narrow. "You look so hard at me, Lil," he gasps. "What is it you want? Take it, whatever it is—but that which you need above all, in this moment, cannot be held in the hand." His old throat produces what might, once upon a time, have been his signature bark of self-satisfied laughter. Now it is the weakest of sighs.

"You may be right, Jasper. We will have to see." She takes a step towards him. "You've told me so little. Nothing I did not already suspect. Nothing of yourself, Jasper—no making a case for yourself, no argument for the defence. This could be your only opportunity to tell your story. Will you not take it?"

She takes a handful of his hair in one hand and with the other raises the metallic object—a scalpel.

no

He moves his lips, but makes no sound. Without words, he can only appeal to her in the language of the wide, watery eye. Even as he does so, he sees the impassivity—that it may as well be the crab's appeal to the albatross.

She nods. "Then the story must go untold," she says. The blade nears. "No matter. Perhaps it's as well. This will be uncomfortable. What I need from you, I need to take while you live."

A feeble shaft of light is thrown onto the walkway when the dome's door opens. The slight figure that steps out into it seems feeble too—in the sudden violence of the storm, which is anything but feeble—as it drops to its knees. It raises a hand in which is revealed a human eye, and casts it away, then falls forward onto that same hand, and empties the scant contents of its stomach onto the wooden slats.

I live.

When she has done, though the cruel elements would surely have her hurry away, she remains quite still.

I have my father's work.

In her other hand, she clutches the leather notebook to her chest, away from the rain. Faint light is visible over the treetops to the east, auguring the dawn. As the metal door slides shut behind her, snuffing out the light, she feels a pang of regret for this final separation from Arenaceous Nell. From everything, in fact—all of her past, of her world, is separated from her in the clink of the closing door and, she now perceives, anything of what might have been a future.

This is no triumph. The old monster has his victory, and it is complete.

A little way off, illumined upon the ground beneath one of the walkway lamps, the Stationmaster's eye has come to rest, and looks coldly at her.

Even now. The eye that soiled me all my life soils me still. The owner of it, who destroyed my mother and took her life, destroyed my father and took his, has destroyed me and condemned me to live.

Simon and the boy are doomed. The man navigates their way to his certain death, the boy's destruction. It is the one variable she hadn't seen coming, the one possible outcome that would have changed her course of action. As much as Fafl, she is responsible for their fate. She curses herself and gets up, tucks the notebook into her overalls, and makes for the beach.

Down at the jetty, the red pod pulls violently at its mooring. The tarpaulin that would provide some shelter on her mad, useless voyage, she remembers, lies where she left it on the sick bed in the dome. She pauses before stepping on to the jetty and approaching the boat—huddled beneath the standing shelter at the wheel are not one figure, but two. She recognises the outline of the Marshal. Wig is first on his feet to clasp her to him when she steps on board.

"I didn't think it had worked!" He has to shout to be heard, even as he holds on to her. "You've been so long."

"It worked," she shouts back. "He has delayed me, nothing more!" She hugs him tightly, thinking to herself that rain makes the best weather for false farewells—it washes the lie away. Then she pulls back. For entirely different reasons, she must see this through. "Did you bring it?"

Wigbert looks to the Marshal. "Mr Bull?"

The latter pulls an object from his pocket and places it in Lil's hand. Her compass.

"If I wasn't looking right at you, Lil," he yells, "I'd think old Wig here had lost his marbles!"

She manages a smile. "Do you have the coordinates, Wig?"

He gives them to her, and takes her by the shoulders. "Lil, it's not Magistracy! Fafl, has sent them the way of the resistance!" His face is full of hope, not entirely void of mischief. Gleeful, even. She hasn't seen him like it before—of all the Warburg's inhabitants, he has always been the least devout. For as long as she can remember, this old man has infuriated the Stationmaster—and delighted her father—with his cynicism and heretical pronouncements. Now, glimpsing some future for his child that exceeds the boundaries of his fantasy, he is as a child himself.

"I know," she nods. "He told me." She grits her teeth and puts a hand to his old back as Mr Bull, already on the jetty, helps him off the pod. Then she starts the motor.

"There's food and water in the locker beneath the wheel," Wig yells as the pod begins to move away. "You look after my boy, Lil, and yourself. D'you 'ear me?"

"I hear you," she shouts, but does not look back—does not do so, indeed, until she is sure they will have left off watching, and the island is a mere black strip in the enormity of the storm, the churning sky above it barely lighter, the frenzied sea below barely blacker. It is bitterly cold, the Stationmaster's uniform was wet through even before she reached the jetty, and waves toss her about like a rag doll. She holds to the wheel and to the coordinates Wig gave her, as best she can with the little antique compass, until she can no longer be seen from the shore. Now, she must choose, and there is only one choice that makes any sense—to skirt the island and head south west. To deliver her father's work into the hands of the resistance. To resume her search for that final audio fragment.

She cannot do it, cannot let go of the coordinates that Simon and the boy were given. She is too late to help them, yet they are out there somewhere and while they live—while Simon lives—she cannot turn away.

Forgive me, father.

For how many hours does she ply that hopeless course? She cannot tell. It is but a gesture—a desperate analgesic to her torment, a transitory opiate to her grief. She hews to the line through the morning and long into the afternoon, seeing nothing but storm. The murky, dirty light changes not with the passing of time. There is nothing but the wind, the wild water and a body approaching exhaustion. Until the pretence can sustain her no longer and the shutters of her mind, that have blocked out the truth, drop all in a moment and so too does she, to the floor of the pod where she despairs of the wheel. The compass falls from her hand and rolls away and she has neither the energy to leap for it nor the nerve to let go of the wheel post. The storm will not relent—indeed, it grows more violent still and out here, far from any land, lightning strikes at the water.

It doesn't matter. None of it matters now.

She weeps. For her doomed love, for the boy, for her father, for herself—she weeps and cares not whether she will rise to her feet again. Let the tumult cast her about as it sees fit. No meaning lies in any direction, in any course of action. She weeps for Wig, and for those who remain on the Warburg. She weeps for the lie they will live now, that she has left them to live—that she has saved Simon and the boy. And yet she knows the lie will be kinder to them than the truth. The three united, and under the protection of the resistance, the continuation of Arenaceous Nell's work, the boy growing, Lil and Simon wed, the possibility of looking out over the water one day and seeing a craft approach that the Magistracy has not sent—let that be the story for them. Let it sustain them.

She is startled. An albatross has made an awkward landing on the gunwale. Briefly, this new animal presence frightens her. The gooney is huge, threatens the stability of the pod, already precarious. Whence did it come, in this savage weather? Wings extended to maintain its balance, till it drops down onto the deck, at the opposite end to Lil, folds the wings, tucks its bill in, and huddles. Now she takes pity on the wretched thing—scared to madness, it no more belongs out here in this tempest than does she. It must be lost. Its predicament is not much less hopeless than Simon's. Let it shelter here, if you can call it shelter. No storm—no, not even this—can blow forever. If the bird does not take fright and launch itself anew, if it can wait out the worst of it here, with her, then at least *it* has a chance. As the universe tumbles around her, and swings and lurches, feinting this way and that like an errant merry-go-round, she keeps her eyes open and on the poor, bedraggled thing. To do so steadies her stomach. The albatross blends into her visual field, becomes a motif in the awful tapestry—just another thing in a perfect storm of things.

But not for you, Reader. For you, a flicker of recognition has resolved into certainty. This is the very bird that brought you here, the creature upon whose airborne wings this narrative had its beginning. Join with it once more, for you are certainly of no use to Lil, and must take your leave of her now. She will be left here at the mercy of her world and you will return to the mercies of yours—to the little comforts that keep you warm, and fed, and hopeful. Why would you linger here? In what is nothing more than a foolish story? Return to your world, to real things; to matters of import; to matters that *matter*.

Your world—how much more clearly would you perceive it, if you could but cleanse your mind of these follies, these heroes and villains and their fanciful tales? What of any value could you hope to find in these fictions? Wherefore place your faith in them? Are they not mere trinkets? Cheap baubles? Dirt on the lens? *Muscae volitantes*? Yes, see through the eyes of this albatross a last time.

How the scene contrasts with what you last saw from here! In place of the open sky, a wretched, drenched little boat. Where before there was such lofty peace, now roar the waves around you. The stillness of altitude is become the heaving depths beneath. And instead of your fellows, contentedly hovering about the decks of fishing vessels, here is this pitiable human creature, alone where no human ought to be. Sobs escape it, deep and harrowing enough to alarm your old maritime friend.

But the bird knows nothing of human pity. Its eye has been caught by something that rolls towards its feet—a little object, round and reflective. The only bright thing, it seems, in all the world. How it glitters! In a single movement, the gooney has grabbed it up in its bill and taken to the air. The human cries out and reaches for it in vain. Below, as the great bird wheels, battling the gusts which threaten to blow it out of the air, the pod spins and swirls in your sight. Smaller and smaller—for the bird has espied a small break in the cloud, and sets a course for it—with each ascending spiral, the little pod becomes a tiny red dot on an ink black ocean. From this distance, that which seemed so chaotic, close up, takes on order—the dot, despite the harrying swells, makes its slow way in a more or less straight, more or less meaningless line.

Your view of it becomes misted by low cloud as the bird makes its bid for brighter skies and somewhere to stow its new treasure. You have but this moment to bid Lil a mute farewell, before the gooney turns itself and its gaze upwards for the ascent into light. Momentarily, it levels out, dips a wingtip towards the water and circles, and eyes the scene below once more. Then, it flips, launches itself upward through the electric murk and you, even with the boon of an albatross's eye to peer with, do not even know what you've seen till you've turned away forever and have had a moment to process the bird's superior sense data.

At first it seemed the bird was taking a last look at Lil, to bid its own farewell perhaps, or merely to service a cold avian curiosity. But now your slow, human, perception grasps what to it was immediate—that the little red dot that bobs about down there is not quite alone on the vast ocean, that there is second speck of colour; that it follows its own course; that the two courses are certain to converge; that from this vantage, exalted by height and distance, there is little to distinguish the other dot from Lil's, save for its colour: the same hue as the Goldilocks shrubs that grow in the dunes up at the end of the beach on the Warburg, or a hornet, or light bouncing from the crystalline surfaces of a lump of orpiment.

Lemon yellow.

THE MORNING wore on and Clara lapsed into silence, and cursed herself for doing so because Jordi and Rolf reacted by stopping again.

"Melon!" said Lia.

"A truly remarkable story," said Jordi. He was breathing heavily.

"Really?" said Clara. "I though it rather ordinary. But perhaps that's because I know what became of the poor porter."

"What? What happened to him?"

"Keep going won't you? Find your strength, and I'll tell you all about it."

FOR THE SECOND TIME in as many days, I woke in my bed with no memory of getting there—just some acid reflux I could have fried an egg in, a violent headache and a broken heart. Charles Dickens's story swirled around in my mind. I couldn't quite remember it, couldn't quite forget it. This then, had been the purpose of his visitation—my paltry efforts had been but a prompt. A literary colossus was once again on the march; it was his work we were to disseminate, not mine. What vanity to have thought so, if only for a moment.

On the upside, I was back in business. So were you.

I left Charles Dickens in an uncharacteristically conscious state when I went down to work. He'd even made the coffee, though he'd done an awful job of it. He was to spend the day revising his first draft and we were to talk that evening about a copy for you. I was excited to have something new, something *really* new, to pass on to you, but I was also one link in the chain away from being detained, or worse.

How could it be coincidence that that morning, of all mornings, you would throw a pebble against the little frosted window at the bellhop station to tell me you needed to see me? We arranged it for six in the evening—I was on a double shift—and I got on with the first runs of the day, mainly early checkouts by guests who had airport transfers booked. Early morning checkouts were notoriously poor tippers and this morning's first two were no exception, despite my charm offensives. I was curt with the rest—expecting, and getting, nothing.

The day staff came on at eight and the place livened up. Jacob, the night porter, sauntered over to the station, grinning.

"There you go," he said, and dropped a pack of mints in front of me.

"Eh . . . thanks, Jacob," I said. "What are these in aid of?"

He cackled. "Don't bother, man. Don't even bother. I saw you."

He winked at me. I must have looked blank because he stepped closer and lowered his voice.

"I saw you, man. I saw you throw up out the window."

"Ah, I see," I said. "No, you've got the wrong end of the stick, Jacob. I was talking to someone down there."

"Yeah, right," he said. "That's a private yard, buddy. Ain't nobody down there."

"No, I have this—" I was suddenly aware I was discussing our rendezvous arrangement, and the skin at my hairline prickled beneath my cap, "—friend, and he comes there sometimes, if he has something to tell me . . ."

Jacob smirked and I didn't blame him. I wouldn't have believed me either.

"Jumps the fence, does he?" He went to the window, opened it and looked down into the yard. "Hey, Vince," he said, pulling his head back in, eyes wide, "I think your friend is still there."

"What?" He stepped back from the sill and I poked my head out. It was daylight now and I could see the yard clearly. The window was around fifteen feet above the ground. Directly below it was an irregular star shape—the unmistakeable splat of stomach content. Just as I recognized it, Jacob gave my back an almighty slap.

"He must have melted!"

I shut the window. Jacob was already walking away.

"You suck on those mints, before Reynolds gets a smell of you."

I didn't know what to make of it. You'd seemed alright when we spoke. It was dark, though. Perhaps I hadn't appreciated how afraid you were. Too busy with my own fear.

"Vince?"

It was Jeffreys, the assistant manager who ran the restaurant and bar. I didn't like Jeffreys.

"Yes, Mr Jeffreys?"

"You OK, Vince?"

"Yes, Mr Jeffreys. Did you want something?"

He put his hands to his hips. He didn't like me either.

"Stocktake this morning—we'll need your help. Hand any runs over to reception at nine-thirty and come through. I want it done by lunch."

He walked away and I liked him less than ever. Stocktakes were always a couple days after payday and I was into the bar for a few bottles. Everybody knew that's how it worked. At least, I assumed they did. It wouldn't matter—my money was always in my account well before lunch, but it made me nervous. Since one of those bottles had been a Luis Felipe, the likelihood of covering my bill with tips this morning was non-existent. At nine, I checked my account on the station screen. There was nothing there. Not all that unusual, but annoying. At nine-thirty I went through to the bar. It was me and Larry the bartender.

"How come we're doing this today, Larry? Wouldn't it normally be after the weekend?" I wanted to sound nonchalant.

"Dunno," said Larry. He was on his knees behind the bar, counting bottles of soda. "But he wasn't taking questions, put it that way." He stood up and arched his back. "Must have Reynolds on his case," he said and got back down again, groaning. Larry wasn't young.

"I'll do liquor," I said and picked up the inventory tab.

" 'Course," said Larry.

By ten-thirty I was almost finished with the liquor list. I couldn't close it off without paying for my bottles, or accounting for them, so I slipped back to the bellhop station screen to check my account. It was empty.

"I've done sodas and beers," said Larry when I got back to the bar. "How are you doing?"

"Almost finished with liquor," I said, through clenched teeth.

"Really? Help me out here, would you, Vince? You on a go slow?"

"Hey," I said, "as long as we're doing this, we don't have to deal with guests, right? We stretch it out into the afternoon and that's one of my shifts taken care of. Easy life."

"No way, Vince. My knees are screaming at me. Get snacks done as quick as you can."

I left the liquor list open and started on snacks. That meant toing and fro-ing from the bar to the cold and dry stores. Maybe it was stepping in and out of the fridge and maybe it was anxiety—either way, I felt sick. At eleven I checked my balance again, then again at eleven-thirty. Nothing. There was definitely some kind of problem. When I returned to the cold store, Jeffreys was sitting at the little work station outside it.

"Where have you been?" he said. "Larry's complaining about you."

I know my voice wavered when I spoke. I wanted to sit down.

"Do you know anything about the wages, Mr Jeffreys? Mine don't seem to have gone through."

He arched his eyebrows. "Didn't I tell you?" he said, standing. "Gosh, I really thought I told everyone. Oh well, my bad." He shrugged. "There won't be any wages today, Vince. Administrative error. Sorry about that. Again," he grinned, "my bad. I've made sure they'll clear first thing in the morning."

Before he walked away, he squeezed my shoulder. He'd never done that before. "Right now, I need you to finish the stocktake."

I had never lied to Reynolds—nothing major anyway—and never stolen from anyone. Apart from Mother's purse but I was a child then. I am a good person. I am a decent person. My parents, though I reject so much about them and they, apparently, so much about me, brought me up decent. This I know. I am decent.

But I was cornered. I had to buy myself twenty-four hours. So I went back to the liquor list and closed it, and that was that. All stock accounted for. There was no reason I could think of why anyone would ask questions. Jeffreys made me uneasy though. I finished the food inventory as slowly as possible. Larry could complain all he liked—I didn't want to see him or anyone else so the stores suited me just fine. By the time I closed my list it was lunchtime. I left the tab on the bar and made for the elevator. I would hide for an hour. Jeffreys would be gone for the day by two—he never worked lates—and I'd be able to get on with my shift in peace. Just one overnight and the money would be in the bank. He probably wouldn't even look at the lists today—he was always telling everyone else to hurry up while he dragged his heels. He was that type.

As I crossed the lobby, Kacey beckoned me over to reception. "Jeffreys wants to see you in his office with the stocktake inventories."

"Oh," I said. I put a hand on the desk and swallowed. "After lunch? I'm on lunch now." I looked over at the elevators. "It's lunch."

"I think you better just go, Vince. He doesn't look like he's taking any prisoners today, if you know what I mean."

"OK." I tapped the desk a couple of times and when I noticed Kacey's quizzical expression, attempted a smile and made my way back to the bar to get the tab. Then I went to Jeffreys' office. Larry was there too.

"You got snacks and liquor, Vince?" said Jeffreys.

"Yes, sir," I said, putting the tab on his desk.

"Any discrepancies?"

"No, Mr Jeffreys. Everything squares."

He picked up the tab without taking his eyes off me.

I swallowed. "Is that everything, Mr Jeffreys? I'm on my lunch now."

"Yes, Vince. That's all I needed." He glanced at Larry, who wore a smirk I didn't like. Jeffreys stood up.

"Vince, I'm going to step over to Mr Reynolds' office now and show him this," he said, waving the tab. "I'm also going to show him some security footage I have that I believe will interest him. After that, if I'm not very much mistaken, he's going to want to talk to you. You get yourself upstairs and enjoy your lunch." He winked. "Maybe make a start on packing."

Jeffreys left. I looked at Larry. Then I left too. I went to the bar and took a bottle of single malt. Then I made for the elevator, grinding my teeth till the door closed behind me. Gripping the waist-level hand rail, I doubled over, trying to breath. Instead, just as the bell pinged and the doors slid open on some floor that wasn't mine, I threw up. Somebody shrieked and I stumbled out into the corridor, then followed it round to the stairwell door. Nobody ever used the stairwell. I sat on a step and wiped my mouth with a sleeve. I tried to think about my next move until I realized there was no need. There was no next move. There was only going upstairs. I was going upstairs. That was it.

It turned out to be a long walk. By the time I reached my floor, my lunch break was over. It didn't matter; I had no intention of going back down there. My legs ached and it felt good—the only sensation at my disposal I could properly account for. Soaked in sweat, I'd tried to vomit another couple of times but there was only retching, nothing left inside me. Some fluid: I was tearing up as I pressed my doorbell.

The door swung inwards. Charles Dickens held it open for me. He seemed taller. For the first time since he'd moved in he was fully clothed. He had groomed his hair and beard. Trousers, waistcoat, overcoat—all immaculately pressed and brushed. The chain of his pocket watch gleamed. There was the same silken sheen to his cravat and to the handkerchief that protruded from his breast pocket. It didn't seem real to me, as though he were a monument to himself. He was magnificent. I was appalled. He reeked of the grave, of dirt and flesh, of soil and stone, bone and blood.

"You look . . . well," I said.

He stepped aside to let me in. "You don't."

I stepped into the kitchen, put the whiskey on the side.

"I'm not well," I said. He'd followed me in and I looked at him. Tears wobbled on my lower lids. "I'm not well, Charles Dickens."

"What has happened?"

"We're moving out, that's what's happened. I don't know where we're going but we need to get out of here."

"We . . . ? You seem to think . . ." He consulted his pocket watch and put it away. "Let's leave that aside for now. What has happened, Vinny?"

"I very strongly suspect that as of today I am no longer an employee of the De Nuys hotel," I said, unscrewing the cap from the whiskey bottle and pointing the neck at Charles Dickens. He shook his head. "Also, I may soon be a person of interest to local law enforcement agencies. I think that about covers it. You and I need to talk about how—"

Somebody knocked at the front door. Not the rap of a knuckle, but the repeated thud of the soft flesh on the side of a fist. The knock of a visitor who has been rehearsing what they are going to say and who is keen to say it. I put a finger to my lips. We stood in silence for a few moments—twenty seconds, thirty—then whoever it was started pounding again, hard enough for the door to rattle in its frame.

I tiptoed into the hallway to take a look through the peephole. I don't know what difference it would have made—whether it was Reynolds, or Jeffreys, or whether one of them had sent somebody else up—but I wanted to see. When this second burst came to an end, there was another sickly, throbbing silence. I was close to the door and afraid to take the last couple of steps in case I made a sound—a squeak on the parquet or an involuntary noise from my throat. But there was no need to put my eye to the lens.

"Vince?" It was Reynolds' voice, followed by another round of thuds. "Vince, are you in there? I need to talk with you."

I let another nauseating quiet descend. Frozen in the last step that I'd been taking, I stretched my hand out, put my fingertips to the wall for balance and waited for the next volley. I could see the shifting shadows of Reynolds' feet in the gap under the door. I noticed the paper cup on the side table. It had been there for days. Not like me, to leave things lying around like that. But then I hadn't been myself lately.

"I know you're in there, Vince," he said, finally. "You were seen coming up."

Turning, I saw that I wasn't alone in the hallway. I shook my head and put the forefinger of my free hand to my lips again. The last thing I needed now was Charles Dickens mouthing off. What I needed was for Reynolds to go away. He had to go away. Then I'd be able to think.

"This is all a bit strange isn't it, Vince?" said Reynolds. He spoke softly; his mouth must almost have been touching the door. "I thought we'd had our chat about strange." There was an audible sigh. "OK, Vince. Have it your way."

It occurred to me that Reynolds, unlike Jeffreys, might not actually despise me. But that didn't matter now. I just needed him to go, and a second later he did—the two shadows under the door slid away. I dared to step up to the peephole. There was nobody there. I held one hand up, fingers splayed as a sign to Charles Dickens that he should stay quiet. The lights out there were activated by a motion sensor. When they went out, I knew Reynolds was gone. I emptied my lungs, leaning my forehead against the door, not remembering when I'd last taken a breath. Then I went into the bedroom and got into bed.

A few moments later, I heard Charles Dickens step into my room. I turned around. He'd brought the whiskey. There was chair beside my bed and he sat on it.

"What's happened, Vince?"

I couldn't look at him. I didn't want to look at anything. But with my eyes closed, all I could see were my accusers. Jeffreys, Reynolds, you, my sister, my mother, those men who'd picked my contact up— I opened them and let them rest, unfocussed, on the folds of the pillow.

"The same thing as always," I said. "I've happened. Things would work out fine, probably, if it wasn't for me. I keep happening." I pulled the blanket up to my chin. "Could you do something for me?'

"Of course."

"Could you switch the light off?"

He got up and went to the door, closed it and switched off the light, throwing the windowless room into murk, enough light penetrating from beneath the door that I could watch the shape of him return to the chair. For the moment I was where I wanted to be—in a dark room with a closed door. I was still for a little while. He was too.

"So," I said. "What do you think of me now, Charles Dickens?"

There was a pause and then he said, "You haven't told me what's happened, Vince."

"Yes I have," I said. I sat up. I didn't want to move but I couldn't stay still. "Not interested in the whiskey? It's the good stuff."

He lifted the bottle from the floor at his feet. "One of us needs a drink," he said, "and it isn't me."

He passed it to me and I took a slug—a long one and then another. It was honey and warmth and happiness. I didn't pass it back.

"I'm not like you," I said. "I don't make beautiful things." I waved the bottle at the darkness, though I doubt he could see the gesture. "I make this."

My eyes acclimatized a little. I took another slug and watched him check his pocket watch again—its glint disappeared when he put it away. He said nothing. Another slug. I kept my eyes on Charles Dickens, not knowing if he was looking back at me.

"We can't all be literary giants, I suppose," I said.

"No."

Another slug.

"But I wanted to do something. I wanted to make something. Something that didn't break. That didn't fail." I snorted. "Listen to me. I'm getting maudlin. That's a good sign—I'll be asleep soon."

Another slug.

"Maybe you should sleep," said Charles Dickens. "We can talk later."

I reached out to clasp his wrist. It was bony and cold and the cold shot up my own arm. I shivered.

"Don't leave. Please. Stay here."

My head was lolling. I rested it against the headboard. I couldn't hold my eyes still either, so I let them roll back and close.

It wasn't easy to tell if I was coming round or not. I couldn't see or hear anything so it didn't seem to make any difference. For a few moments though, I was aware of a transition—from the black nothing of my unconsciousness to that of the room.

"Charles Dickens?"

There was no whiskey bottle in my hand. I patted the blanket. It was dry, so I hadn't spilled anything. Perhaps Charles Dickens had taken it. He liked a drop.

"Charles Dickens? Are you there?"

I went to swing my feet onto the floor, but they were caught up in the blanket. I struggled with it.

"Are you there, Charles Dickens?"

The blanket wouldn't give my legs up. I slumped back against the headboard and tried to keep my breathing steady.

"I'm here, Vincent." His voice came from right beside me, from the chair.

"You didn't answer."

"Excuse me. I was asleep. When you slept, I did too. When you woke, so did I. It takes me a minute though. I'm getting on, you know."

He patted my forearm and my breathing slowed. Then I remembered about Reynolds and it quickened.

"Did you finish the whiskey?" I said.

"I took it from you when you fell asleep. Here."

He passed the bottle and I sucked on it. It tasted like a deep hole. Warm and dry.

"I just wanted to do something," I said. I didn't know what I meant.

"Yes."

"Something. Anything." I was losing my train of thought. "All I got was nothing. All I am is—" I couldn't remember what I was talking about.

"What do you think?" I said. I tried to find his eyes in the dark, but holding my own steady was too much of an effort. I blinked hard but they wouldn't stay still.

"About what?"

"About . . . about . . . nothing."

I took another long drink.

"You know, you've got something no one else has, Vincent," said Charles Dickens.

"I do?"

"Yes. You can make a real difference now."

"I can?" I shook my head. This I wanted to hear, so I needed to stay conscious, even if I had closed my eyes. "What have I got?"

"My story, of course. How many people can claim to have a story by Charles Dickens? A new one?"

I smiled in the dark. "That's true," I said.

"It's a masterpiece. You'll be responsible for getting it out into the world."

They were nice words. The smile lingered on my lips and I opened my eyes to answer him, but the strip of light under the door distracted me.

"Is it morning?"

"What? Oh." He had turned to look at it too—I could see his profile faintly. For a moment he just looked. Then he checked his watch and pocketed it.

"The first ray of light," he said, as if in a reverie, "that illumines the gloom."

If he said anything else, I'll never know. Consciousness slipped away again.

And again, the melting away of one darkness to reveal another, till my eyes soaked up some of the light that leaked in from the hallway.

"Charles Dickens?" I whispered.

I didn't know how I knew, but I knew; someone had been knocking at the front door. Insistently, angrily, I pulled the blanket back and swung my legs over the side of the bed, grateful it didn't creak.

"Charles Dickens?" I hissed.

I planted my feet on the carpet and tiptoed to the door, using a hand on the wall to steady myself. Once there I rotated the door knob, slowly, to minimize the click. I almost groaned aloud when the hall light hit my eyes, squeezing them shut till I'd gotten used to the brightness from behind my eyelids. My head hurt. I stepped out into the hall and then into the kitchen. He wasn't there. I wobbled across to the living room and on the way, I glanced at the front door—there had been no further knocking.

I didn't switch the living room light on. Instead I whispered into the room.

"Charles Dickens?"

I took a couple of steps into the room and looked around. With the door to the hallway open, it was bright enough. The armchair was unoccupied. He was gone.

Somebody pounded at the door—the loudest noise I've ever heard. I could physically feel the fist that made it, could have fallen over under those blows. I sat on the floor, wet with sweat.

When the pounding stopped, the quiet spun around me like a whirlpool. I wanted to puke. To cry. I wanted a witness. I wanted Charles Dickens back. I got myself on all fours and crawled into the hall. Stopping there I raised my eyes to the door. There was no sound, no knocking or yelling, from the other side. Unsteadily, I got to my feet. I had no idea how long I'd been out but it couldn't have been that long because I was still drunk. Using both hands held out to either wall to keep myself upright, I made my way to the door. With every step, I expected more thunder, but it never came. When I was close enough, I place both palms on the wood and put my eye to the peephole. Whoever it was had gone. I felt something against my foot.

An envelope. I recoiled as though I'd stepped on a snake, took two steps back and stood shuddering. The envelope was a breach, a brown paper intrusion into my safe space. There was no need to pick it up. I don't think I could have. But I didn't need to look inside. The message was clear to me: *We will open the door, Vince. The next time, we will open your door and come in.*

They would, too. They had the right. At least I knew what I had to do now. I had to get out of there. This was my one, final chance to take control of things. I could wait here like a trapped animal till they came for me or I could show some spine, sneak out of the hotel and run away. I'd take Charles Dickens's story with me, hole up somewhere and consider my next move.

All this made me think of you. I made my way back to the kitchen to check the wall clock there and had to wait a little for it to resolve itself in my double vision. Five-thirty. I could still make it to see you. I had one thing to focus on—getting myself to that diner. I could talk to you there, tell you the story. I knew you would help me.

You will help me, won't you?

In the bedroom I put my off-duty clothes on and my own boots, struggling with the laces. Then I got down on my knees beside the bed and pulled Charles Dickens's manuscript out from under the floorboard. Then my tab went. The ringtone was deafening—I took the call as quickly as I could.

"Mother?"

"Do not hang up on me, Vincent."

"No, no of course not. But I—"

"We need to talk. You missed another dinner and we're all so worried. Your father–"

"No problem, Mom. I'll be there next time, I promise. Right now, I need to—"

"What's happening to you, Vincent? You're slurring your words, are you OK? Why won't you let us help you?"

I didn't answer. She waited. I could hear her breathe.

"Maybe I will, Mom." I thought I might be able to get some money out of them. Not out of him, but out of her, maybe.

"One of the managers here has it in for me," I said. "Framed me for something. Had me under surveillance. Do you believe that?"

She didn't answer for a moment and when she did it was a deep moan.

"Oh, Vincent." I knew she was shaking her head. "Vincent. Is it happening again? This is what Dr Düssel . . ." She trailed off then and left a long silence. When she spoke again she was more controlled, her words spoken softly down the line as if she wanted to put her arms around me but the words were all she had. "Didn't we say, Vincent? We can't talk properly, we can't get anywhere when you tell us these stories. Didn't we say? No more stories, please, baby, please . . . why don't you come—"

"Yes," I said. I needed to stop the call. I needed it to stop. "I'll come there, Mom. Later. Got to go now."

I hung up. The books I left—if the hotel people found them, there was a chance they wouldn't shop me. They were just as likely to cover up. I doubted counter-terrorism was a concern for Reynolds. He was more the quiet life type. Either way, I was going into hiding. It didn't make a difference any more.

I stashed the manuscript under my belt and straightened myself up as best I could in front of the mirror in the hall.

As I approached the door the envelope on the floor caught my eye again. The revulsion was strong enough to stop me in my tracks. That's what made me notice the paper cup. I couldn't bring myself to leave without taking care of it. They could burst in here and discover my links to a terrorist organization, but I'd be damned if they were going to call me a slob. I keep a tidy home.

I brought it back to the kitchen. It didn't feel empty so I held it over the sink and pulled the plastic lid off. It wasn't empty—there was some coffee left in the bottom, which I poured into the sink, and a colony of mould. And there was a clear plastic, ziplock bag. I fished it out and rinsed it under the tap, wincing at the noise the water made. Then I dried my hands and opened it to pull out the little slip of paper it contained—a tiny, hand-written note. Once again, double vision proved to be a problem. I sat in one of the kitchen chairs, blinked and waited. On the third or fourth attempt, I managed to read the thing.

compromised — u may b 2 — tel ur contact

So she'd known. I crept towards the door. Her note didn't do me any good now. But she hadn't known about Charles Dickens. About his story. I was back in business. I was getting out of here, out of this cage, out there into the world. I was going to mean something. I had a mission. I had you. I had a masterpiece in my pants. I looked through the peephole. There was nobody there so I put my hand to the latch, and pulled.

THE MORNING became dark as night, Clara was quiet once again, and once again Rolf and Jordi came to a halt.

"One last push, boys! If you can get me up this hill, I'll tell you the secret of the Enchanted Road."

It took Vince eight minutes to tell his story. Two minutes in, Billy knew he was in even more trouble than he'd thought. At the four-minute mark he decided he wouldn't be leaving the little plastic bag with anyone.

He spent the remaining four minutes trying to think. Nothing that Vince was saying made a blind bit of sense. He was talking about something in his apartment. There was mention of a haunting. Listening to it made Billy feel queasy, so he stopped listening to it. It didn't matter what Vince said now. It just didn't matter any more—the point was he couldn't be relied on. The guy wasn't well.

At around the six-minute mark it dawned on Billy that not only would Vince be unable to help—he was now a liability. In a day very generously populated with problems, Jane's kid brother was Billy's newest. There was no time to figure out what had happened to Vince. But Billy needed to deal with it.

When the eight minutes were up, Vince went quiet and looked at him expectantly. Billy lowered his eyes. Presumably, this was the part where he said something helpful about the ghost. He needed to get away from here and he needed to get Vince somewhere he couldn't talk to the wrong people. But he couldn't even look at him, couldn't look up from his coffee. Billy didn't know what to say, how to begin, but it just so happened he didn't need to. A few seconds later, Vince was dead.

The latest generation of D-Energy™ handguns were noiseless, so nobody heard the shot. A couple of people near the front window might have heard the ping when a tiny hole appeared in the glass. If they did, they took it for the toaster or something else that Benny was doing. A moment later, the pane began to craze around the entry point.

The perfectly circular opening became the epicenter of a sprawling mosaic. It was slow and there was a sound to it—the irregular, inexorable morse of ice between the feet and water, or of a hangman's rope swinging with a heavy load. Now every head, or so Billy thought, turned to watch it spread. It travelled up and sideways, around the curve of the corner. There was no other movement in the place and apart from the arhythmic snapping of glass, a perfect hush. Before long the window all around the diner was opaque and the street outside hidden from view. Eyes went up as the maze of fractures reached the top of the window and disappeared into the frame. When no clear glass was left the cracking sound slowed. It didn't stop, but the noises became sporadic. When it seemed as though it *had* stopped, it seemed that time had too. Billy realized he wasn't breathing. One last snap that made a lady at the counter squeal, then nothing. Nothing but a diner full of silent people standing still and a giant window that had turned to frost. An odd feeling of safety came over Billy, as if he were cocooned.

Then it fell.

It dropped like a stone. Quietly in the first instant, then noisily as a hundred thousand glass nuggets hit the floor and the pavement outside. For a few seconds it sounded like rushing water, and then sunlight sparkled on a crystal carpet. It was quiet again, but not *as* quiet; the sounds of traffic blew in on the breeze. Alphonse was sitting in a car outside the bookstore.

"Vince, we have to—"

Billy stopped when he saw the hole in his friend's head. Vince had an elbow on the table and leaned against the wall—neatly, eyes open. It was a shame he was dead; for the first time that day he looked relaxed, a lot better than he had a few moments before. Billy couldn't help noting what an excellent shot it had been. And then he corrected himself—it wasn't good at all. Alphonse had missed. To put that right, the giant was squeezing himself out of a car that fitted him like a wetsuit. Once on his feet, he raised the pistol.

Billy bolted. Through the door and out onto De Nuys, then down the street and into an alley before Alphonse could round the corner and get a shot. It wasn't the alley he used to meet Vince at the back of the hotel and he didn't know it, but he'd struck lucky. It was long and straight and it gave him options. Open at the far end, it gave off at regular intervals onto side passages. Two choices, then—run to the end and a chance to disappear. Maybe make for the car. Or he could duck down one of the side alleys. There were half a dozen at least so that might buy him time to get into the back of a building.

He chose neither—next to him, at the beginning of the alley, were a couple of dumpsters. He would easily fit inside one of them. Opposite was a pile of cardboard boxes, some broken down and some not. The pile was barely three feet high and ran along the wall for less than six. It would be a ridiculous place to hide. He hid there. Once behind them he pulled Phillips's gun out and tried to control his breathing. Then he noticed he had absolutely no overhead cover. All Alphonse would have to do was lean slightly and he'd be exposed. It would have to be the dumpsters. He raised himself on his elbows to go, then dropped back. There were footsteps at the entrance to the alley.

And then there weren't; their owner had stopped. And then there were: coming toward him. They stopped again, right by the dumpsters. Billy could hear a lid lifted and dropped. And another. Then nothing—nothing but the cold calm that filled him. He gripped the gun. In the next few seconds he was going to kill for the second time that day or, more likely, be killed. Either way, he was through the looking-glass now, to borrow a term from one of the books. It felt fine. More footsteps, moving away this time. They stopped a little way up the alley.

"Mr Stringer?"

There was no mistaking the voice. It would register nicely on the Richter scale.

"You OK, Mr Stringer? You seem kinda . . . agitated."

Billy could hear him chuckle but then, presumably, so could the people on the eighth floor.

"I don't really want to shoot you, Mr Stringer," said Alphonse. The footsteps moved further away. "I'd much prefer to cut you. But I gotta get up close for that."

Billy put one eye above the boxes. Alphonse had his back to him. The big man had put the gun away and had the knife in his hand. This was his chance. In one movement he'd made it to the corner of the alley and back onto De Nuys. He was quick but he wasn't quiet—Alphonse was after him. As he ran past the steps at the front of the De Nuys Hotel, one of the columns that held up the hotel's porch splintered into shards of marble. There were screams in the street. Billy began to weave in and out of the trees that lined it. He heard, or rather felt, a couple of thuds as tree trunks behind him took a blast. At the corner of Linley he went right and zig-zagged through traffic to the far pavement, then left onto Wert.

He hadn't moved this fast in a long time. The screaming behind him was constant now. Being shot at in the street was a lot of bad things but, it turned out, was also liberating. You knew where you stood. These people had no interest in taking him in, in any kind of process. Billy's story wasn't going to involve any more surprises—there was only the one plausible ending. In that light the persistence of his flight response surprised him, but he went with it.

Wert was a short street, just a single block, and where it came to an end so did downtown. This was where a swathe of the city had been leveled to make way for the Harrison interchange—a mammoth array of raised junctions and circling off-ramps where the ninety-one met the three-oh-five, the Express Toll and various urban arteries. Now the Litera-Track™, too, picked its way on slim columns, perfectly straight as it cut through the elevated tangle around it. Its outer edge was almost flush with the last buildings.

In the middle of the street, where a narrow traffic island split it, there was an oblong podium. About nine or ten feet above it the steps to a Litera-Track™ access point stopped in mid air, the final section of them stowed until needed. The thing was designed to be out of reach. He wondered if they'd accounted for medal-winning high jumpers.

Of course, there were twelve intervening years and a bottle of scotch to take into account, but options were scarce. As Billy ran past a blue Oldsmobile its windscreen shattered. That would mean that Alphonse had made it around the corner, onto Wert. It was now or never. He sprinted for the podium, got a foot on the edge of it and launched himself, reaching for the bottom rung. For the first time that day something went right. He got it, and soon had it with both hands. He felt the heat of a D-Energy™ shot close to his legs but he was swinging too wildly to make an easy target. Adrenalin still had enough of a grip on him to get his hands up a few rungs and his feet onto the bottom one. He kept his body tight now and was hidden from Alphonse by the concrete support struts. He climbed.

At the top he stepped out onto a studded metal walkway that ran along the track. He could hear the sweep of traffic on the other roadways but there were no voices up here, none of the hubbub of a city street. It was peaceful. The far side of the track was a long way away. He could see an off-ramp over there which, as it sloped to ground level, passed within feet of the Litera-Track™. It might be jumpable—he wouldn't know till he got closer. He stepped toward the edge of the track and was immediately blown back against the railing behind him. A Litera-Truck™ convoy sped by. The separate units formed a train and the speed of the thing made it a blur. It was long. Billy could do nothing but wait for the several minutes it took to pass. There must have been hundreds of them. He'd been lucky—the convoy made almost no sound. If he had taken the first step he'd be dead.

The convoy had emerged from a covered stretch of the track about a hundred and fifty feet away from him, where the whole thing seemed to dip. A tunnel, and there had been a little red light over it that blinked out now that they'd passed. A lane indicator, maybe. Just as he made the observation another light came on, about halfway across the track, and another train emerged from the tunnel under it. Yes, lane indicators. He timed this one—it took almost exactly two minutes to pass. The same as the last one, he guessed, so they were probably a standard length. The speed of the things was incredible—he'd have to watch those lights. Something made him look behind, over the railing. Down on the street, Alphonse had his gun drawn but it hung from a lowered hand. The giant looked up at him and smiled, then walked calmly beneath the track and out of sight.

He'd been right, up on the skyway—there were eight lane indicators. Near the far side another one came on and there was the whoosh of displaced air as a train passed. He got to his feet and stepped to the edge. It felt like a starting line and that made him snort. The end of everything was back at the beginning. He breathed, filled his lungs a few times, kept his eye moving between that off-ramp across the track and the lights over the tunnel. Then he felt the metal vibrate beneath his feet and looked toward the tunnel. Alphonse was running along the walkway. Of course, the lummox would have access. He'd holstered his weapon and he wasn't alone. Billy could see two security types running along behind him. They were no doubt armed but none of them had drawn. It seemed to him he therefore had an advantage, so he pulled Phillips's pistol from his suit pocket and pointed it at them. That stopped them dead. Slowly, and much to Billy's surprise, Alphonse showed him the palms of his hands and the others did the same. But the big man kept walking. He was only fifty feet away.

Billy checked the tunnel. None of the lights were on. He shrugged, pocketed the pistol and ran. Somebody yelled at him but there were no shots. As soon as he'd cleared the first lane, its light came on and a convoy blocked him from their sight. He kept going but it wasn't like he'd expected. The gooey surface was thicker than he'd thought. His feet were sinking into it. After just two lanes he wasn't running at all, but planting one foot as far ahead as he could and then pulling the other out of the sticky mess.

He started to panic—if the light over his lane came on he wouldn't be able to get out of the way in time. A couple of minutes later the train behind him had passed and he was in the third lane. Maybe the fourth, it was difficult to tell. He looked back, carefully so as not to lose his balance. Alphonse and the others were standing at the side of the track. They hadn't drawn their weapons. He looked at them, and they looked at him. They didn't seem particularly hostile. It was more like they were intrigued.

He kept going. Progress was absurdly slow now. It would be so easy to pick him off. Why they didn't was beyond him. The sounds of rush hour had abated. He didn't like how quiet it was.

"You OK, Mr Stringer?"

He stopped and stooped for a moment with his hands on his knees and laughed.

"That's funny, Alphonse." He was running out of adrenalin and starting to feel drunk again. "You're pretty angry with me, huh?"

"Not really, Mr Stringer. Not right now. I just want to see what happens next."

Billy straightened up. With great effort he released a foot and planted it ahead of him.

"Well, keep watching, Alphonse," he said. He was breathless and he felt a little giddy. There was no point watching the lights, nothing he could do about them anyway. He kept his eyes on the off ramp ahead. "Should be interesting."

He couldn't understand the track surface—it was as if it was getting deeper. He was wading now, unable to remove his feet. Maybe he made another lane, maybe not even that, before he fell. He went down on one knee and put a hand out to stop himself. Then he couldn't get up. He couldn't get his hand out of whatever it was. It was in up to the wrist. He was pinned. He checked the tunnel and there were no lights, and he wondered how long it would be. The convoys seemed to come about every five minutes. There were eight lanes. So that might give him a maximum of forty minutes before he was flattened. Except he'd already seen two. So that meant thirty minutes, maximum. Was that the way it worked? Had he figured it right?

It didn't matter. Thirty minutes would be too long. He felt nothing. It was what it was. He couldn't turn his head enough to get a look behind him anymore, so Alphonse and the others no longer mattered. All that crazy stuff was over. Just like him.

He laughed. Murphy had been right about one thing—they'd messed his shoes up pretty bad. And as he laughed, he remembered he wasn't a fly on paper but a person, and that there was a girl he loved and a friend he'd gotten killed and a mother waiting for him at home and so he stopped laughing and cried. He cried like a baby.

Where was Jane? Were they hurting her? He could feel himself sinking into this stuff and there was no way he was getting free of it now. Nobody was going to do anything about it either. This was it. His tears bobbled about on the track like drops of mercury. The sobs came up from the pit of him, from his belly, and were the only sound to cut through the silence. The only sound made by the nothing he'd become. In the corner of his eye he caught a red light and it looked to be over the lane he was in. He braced himself, but then the thing passed behind him, inches from his foot, hiding him from Alphonse and the others.

Two minutes. There was one thing he could still do, for whatever it was worth. He took his hat off and laid it upside-down on the track.

As it started to sink with him, he fished out the little plastic bag and fumbled one-handed to get it open and remove the contents. His stuff. He held the thing in his hand for a moment and then he arched his back and threw it as far as he could. It seemed to him it cleared the track. Maybe it was on that off-ramp now, maybe it had fallen into the space between it and the Litera-Track™. What did it matter? Even if somebody found it, the chances that they would recognize a replica First Era stick drive were remote. Even if they did they wouldn't know how to access the files. It all amounted to nothing, everything he'd put on it.

One last laugh escaped him, bitter and spiked with salt tears. The little stick drive was his risible contribution to a world he would be leaving very soon. The only real thing he'd ever done, now that Jane was gone, and any minute now it would probably be wiped in a maglev field. It only existed at all because he was such a coward. Because he never had found anyone to pass the books on to. He'd been too afraid.

He'd betrayed Vince this whole time, Vince and everyone further up the chain. With him, their efforts had come to a full stop. Another nothing. Instead he'd spent night after night up on the laundry terrace, face lit by the screen of the oldest machine he'd been able to get hold of and hook up to a home-made USB adaptor, and he'd typed each of them out. Page by page, word by word. It had been his way of telling himself he would do something. Sometime. Well, this apparently was it—he'd thrown it under traffic.

And that wasn't all—there was another file on the drive. Something had happened to Billy up on the terrace. The act of reproducing the books one by one had become about much more than reading. He'd begun to write. It was a selfish act—Vince had talked once or twice about his own efforts, but had written them off as irresponsible. The role of the organization was to save what there was, he'd said. That had to be the focus. New production would be for those who came next.

Once he'd started, he'd been shocked by how it had flowed from him. Effortlessly, as if carried along by something larger than himself, he'd written his own little book. He'd called it *Literature* because that was its subject. What else would you write about? What else could you? A betrayal to add to the others—at least it too would be lost or destroyed.

He was brought back into the moment—something was wrong. He was still sinking. His trapped arm was in up to the elbow. His knees had sunk to the point where his belly was on the surface. Only his upper torso and his one free arm were clear. He looked closely at where his arm disappeared into the track. Up close, the stuff wasn't quite jet black. It was dark but not opaque and he could see a stretch of his forearm under there. Not all of it, and he couldn't see his hand any more—where it ought to be, there was nothing.

It might have been the lack of light, or it might be ... he blinked—there was a texture to the stuff. A crystalline movement. There was something familiar about it but he couldn't focus properly. He was drunk and his eyes were full of tears and he was tired. He blinked again. And again, trying to clear his vision. He put his face as close to the surface as he dared.

Letters. A sea of them, swirling, glinting as they eddied and flipped. The thing was a mass of bioluminescent typeset. Something vibrated against his breast. He pulled his tab out.

luk up bili

He looked up. A car had come to a stop on the off-ramp. The driver window was down. From it, a woman looked at him. He rubbed his eyes—the last useful thing his free arm would ever do—till he could make her out. She gradually resolved in his vision. The woman from *The Standard*. What was her name? She looked at him and nodded. He didn't know what that meant.

Then somebody lowered the rear window to look at him from the back seat. She looked at him and he looked at her and it was enough. It was all, suddenly, enough. He felt his chin touch the surface and so, while he still had a mouth to do it with, he mouthed the last three syllables of his life.

i—luv—u

Jane nodded as her own tears fell and raised a hand to wave him goodbye and in it, pinned between her thumb and palm, was the stick drive. As the car pulled away there was just time to mouth her own three syllables.

gil—ga—mesh

And she was gone. In the same moment, the Litera-Truck™ convoy behind him passed and he was alone on the track. As his head sank he turned it in the direction of the tunnel. Though he knew now he wasn't sinking. He was melting. Letters swirled across his eyes. The stuff was getting into him, or he into it, or both. He found that he could bend the floating symbols to his will, as though they were *muscae volitantes*, tamed and obedient. He could discern the programmed texts. He could alter them at will. He could reproduce passages from the books he'd typed up. From his own. He could do it all instantly.

Just one eye remained clear and he trained it on the tunnel, though he had nothing left to fear. He'd be gone in a moment and nothing and nobody would be able to hurt him. Jane was safe. There was no pain—it seemed to him his capacity to feel anything at all was melting away with his body.

Perhaps there was one last feeling. He felt grateful. He felt a deep gratitude. That she'd come. That she'd seen him do something. That she hadn't seen him in the prom suit. That she would read his book and the parts of it that were about her. That he didn't seem to be dying. Only changing. That the books he'd saved were inside him and so, now, inside the Litera-Track™. That he was taking his book with him too. That this thing would never be wholly controlled by them. Yes, he was grateful. He was becoming . . . *something*. He didn't know what, but he didn't feel like nothing anymore.

A red light came on.

𝓐 SADNESS overcame Clara as she lapsed into silence, having said all she was able to say. There was no more story and their little party had not yet made it to the top of the hill. She closed her eyes and stayed quiet, hoping with all her might that Jordi and Rolf could get her there now with their own strength, and that Lia would spot any rocks. The stories she had told, their aftereffects, must now be enough. All she had was hope.

Running on fumes, just like poor Liam.

𝄐ourbaki. His baritone. Frau Pfafl could hear it but, muffled by rows of assorted merchandise, not what it was saying. She'd been the last to enter the store and consequently found herself at the rear of a snaking conga that consisted of Öttinger, Doctor Amstutz, Gloor; all three members of the school board who had attached themselves to the enterprise as soon as they'd gotten wind of it; Rorschach from the post office; Ümmel and herself. She was more accustomed to being out in front but one didn't always get one's way.

Not even Bourbaki—if he'd been able to squirrel every item in the shop into one of the hundreds of drawers that Manni Lustenberger patrolled, he would have. Loved a bit of mystery, did Bourbaki. Always the theatrical flourish with that one. In thrall to the sense of dominion that secrecy gave him. Probably. Mr One-Step-Ahead. But of course there were goods that were simply too large, or long, or awkwardly shaped and so the floor space on this side of the counter was crammed with them—a small yet disorientating maze of stuff.

She could hear Öttinger and Doctor Amstutz taking turns to speak to him. Their words, too, were beyond the reach of her hearing, especially since old Manni was barking away at someone at the counter, but she could make out the tone—obsequious, supplicatory.

Wheedling, if one was given to coming straight out with it, as she was. In his replies, Bourbaki played a tune of benevolent magnanimity.

"What did he say?" she asked Ümmel.

"What did he say?" asked Ümmel of Rorschach.

"What did he say?" asked Rorschach of Mrs Rennels, one of the three school governors.

The question was relayed to the front of the line and an answer passed back. Rorschach muttered something to Ümmel who nodded and turned to Frau Pfafl, solemn-faced.

"Doctor Amstutz says he didn't quite catch it," he said.

"Oh, for heaven's *sake*."

They'd shuffled forward a little and turned a corner—Bourbaki must have been on the move—and were now in the *Heimwerken* aisle. There was no doubt whatsoever in Frau Pfafl's mind that squeezed between a carefully stacked tower of wood varnish tins and a barrel from which leant out a spindly array of hoes and rakes, and stuck behind the unforthcoming Ümmel, was absolutely the worst place in the entire country to be.

"Do we know anything," she said, "or not? It's a perfectly simple question!"

There was a peculiar acoustic to the crammed space and it was impossible to tell whether the muttering came from left or right, one aisle away or two. She briefly entertained the notion of climbing up on the tower of varnish tins but it looked awfully precarious and she did have her standing in the community to think of. Besides, there were all those pots and pans hanging so low from the ceiling. The delegation shuffled forward again, around another corner, and it wasn't paint anymore but a wall of flour sacks on one side and equestrian paraphernalia on the other. She suppressed the urge to grab a whip.

"Would someone please ask him," she said, rapping on Ümmel's shoulder as though it were an office door, "what it is he's building on the Wahrberg? Or is that too gargantuan a task?"

Ümmel consulted with Rorschach and the sentiment was passed along, but no message was returned for the time being as they found themselves on the move again, rather more quickly. Bourbaki on the run, she didn't doubt. Another opportunity lost! But then his unmistakable low tones again—all schmaltz and soothing music. Rorschach whispered something, at length, to Ümmel, who turned again.

"Well," he said, "This is awkward. It seems your remarks have rather put the doctor out. He asks for patience, and reminds you he knows perfectly well our business here."

The constable withheld eye contact and spoke in an almost inaudible whisper. If he hadn't been studying the floorboards he'd have seen Frau Pfafl redden. His message delivered, a horrible silence filled the aisle. He kept his eyes down. Bourbaki's voice could be heard, still too muffled to make out his words but clearly pontificating, and pompous with it.

"Please tell the doctor," said the organist, her speech slow and controlled, "that Frau Pfafl feels she has been supremely patient. Congratulate him on knowing our business." She tapped the fingertips of one hand with those of the other. "Ask him why he hasn't got to it."

Ümmel continued to contemplate the dark wood beneath his feet, silently rehearsing his next communication with Rorschach. Bourbaki's unctuous discourse was beginning to make Frau Pfafl feel seasick. The smell of turpentine and an open sack of dried pig's ears didn't help.

"Right," she said, and turned away from Ümmel to find another route to the shopkeeper. At the end of the aisle she turned to the left and found herself in *Heimwerken* once again—she could see nobody at the far end so she retraced her steps and tried the aisle to the other side of Ümmel's. The little party had edged forward and the policeman was at the end of it. Bourbaki's voice was louder here. At the end of the next aisle, Mrs Rennels. At the next, of wicker baskets and enormous candy jars, the shopkeeper's voice was less muddy. "Gentlemen, gentlemen . . ." At the end of the next, Gloor. Then Amstutz in a clutter of ironmongery. "Gentlemen, all . . ." And then the tiny little patch of floor that passed for the shop's only open space, encroached by sacks of grain and spice, and old Manni up a ladder with his back to her.

". . . revealed."

On this side of the counter, Öttinger, and now Amstutz peering over his shoulder, the counter flap up and the door behind it, which led to Bourbaki's apartments, clicking shut. No Bourbaki.

"Wonderful," said Frau Pfafl. "Well done, gentlemen." She smiled at them. "Pathetic."

"On the contrary, Frau Pfafl," said Öttinger. "Why, just a moment ago, I got exactly what we came here for."

"We came for Bourbaki," said Frau Pfafl. "We came for the truth. What is it that you have got?"

The innkeeper and the doctor both looked very pleased with themselves as Öttinger replied.

"An appointment."

News of the unveiling spread through Einpferd that same morning and formally arrived in the house a few days later, in the form of an embossed invitation card addressed to Clara's mother. As the widow of the town's only dentist she was considered a notable and invited to most functions, though she rarely accepted. In this case she made an exception, being as curious about the goings-on up the Wahrberg as anybody else in town. The details on the card, as it happened, did not quite comprise an appointment in the usual sense:

> *Herr Benjamin Bourbaki*
> *begs of the*
> **Noble Burghers of Einpferd**
> *that they ready themselves for a*
> **Magnificent Revelation**
> *on*
> **The Wahrberg.**
> *Time & date to be announced*
> *with perhaps as little as*
> *some hours notice,*
> *but almost certainly in*
> **June.**

"How like him," the invitee had said. "Melodrama. Brazen hintery."

Mila had been livid. She wouldn't say so, of course, but the renewed vigour with which she undertook her various tasks on the day the invitation came had bordered on aggression. She didn't appear to have calmed down much the following morning as she'd helped Clara with her toilet.

"I grew up playing on that mountain. Belongs to all of us, if you ask me, noble or not."

She'd been half talking to her ward and half muttering to herself as she'd pottered between the wardrobe and the chest of drawers.

"Not right fencing it like that. What's he up to, anyway? If it isn't something sinful why keep it a secret?"

Her voice had broken a little as she turned her back to look out of the window for a moment.

"I wonder if I'll ever again sit on the curvy old stone bench up there, and look down here, like me and Noah used to. Noble townspeople indeed!" The almost artificially perfect profile of the Wahrberg had been framed in the window. She'd dabbed at an eye with the hem of her apron and gone to the top drawer for a toothbrush.

Clara knew who Noah was. Mila mentioned him often. He'd been her beau, a childhood playmate become sweetheart, long before Clara was born. A proscribed union: Noah was the eldest boy in the familie Heffelfinger—the wealthiest in town—and he was considered too good for the likes of her, the daughter of a coal merchant's labourer. The Heffelfingers had gone to great lengths to put an end to it and, once they'd realised the futility of their efforts, had sent Noah to a military academy. In doing so, the romance was rewritten as tragedy—Mila had heard, second-hand and years later, that he'd died in a war with the French.

"I don't fancy your chances either," she'd said, taking the brush to Clara's teeth. "I didn't see a plus-one on the invitation and you know how your mother hates to have you out of the house. She doesn't even like it that you go to the school." There was a break in the rhythm of the brush. "Wants you safe and sound, no doubt," the cook had continued in a quieter tone. "Such a worrier." She removed the brush from Clara's mouth and brought her some water. "I don't know what's going on with these teeth of yours. Browner and browner, and mine just as bad. Anyone would think we smoked."

It had taken every bit of Clara's guile that morning to calm Mila down. Heaven only knew what would become of the poor creature, the girl had thought to herself, and not for the first time, if she weren't there to look after her. Now it was June. Bourbaki hadn't been joking; as the first storm of the summer began to work itself up late one Wednesday morning, notice had come that the unveiling was to take place that afternoon.

Einpferd had ruffled like a roused aviary. In no time at all the town's great and good were preened and plucked and on their way up the mountain. As soon as mother was out of the way, Rolf had come and Mila had left for her father's house with the box of eggs. With the housekeeper gone, Jordi and Lia had come to the back gate as arranged and they'd all set off.

Since Clara's little expedition had to stay out of sight, away from the track, the ascent was made more difficult—a fact brought home to her now as Jordi had clearly encountered an obstacle.

"That hurt," he said. "Quite a bit."

"What is it, Jordi?" said Clara.

"A rock," said the blind boy. "A big one. Did you see the rock, Lia?"

"Yes," said Lia.

"Shall we back up a little, Jordi?" said Clara. "Can you do that, Rolf?"

Rolf made his end of the litter nod.

"No, I've fallen on top of it," said Jordi. "I might drop you if I go backwards. Best to soldier on. Once I'm on the other side I should be able to hold you up high enough to keep you straight, for a little while anyway. Rolf will have to be as quick as he can getting himself over so that we can lower you again. I should be alright. Hopefully there aren't any more rocks."

Silence.

"Lia? Did you hear that, Lia?"

"What?" said Lia.

"I said, I hope there aren't any more rocks."

"Yes."

Clara felt a drop of rain on her cheek. Just the one, but it could only be a matter of time now. She could hear a low rumbling already, out over the plain in the direction of the Schleierhorn. Jordi was off the rock—she could feel the underside of her litter drag along it a little, though he held the handles as high as he could, arms extended. When Rolf got to it he had to straddle it like a rider, and inch himself along on his thighs. It was slow work. Every shimmy drew a grunt from the dwarf. At last she felt the beanpole of a boy at her feet come away from the rock and lower the litter, allowing Jordi to do the same and let out a slow sob with the relief of it.

"Bigger upper!" said Lia.

"Don't drink the water."

"It's gin, darling. I drink nothing else when I travel. Nothing. I believe poor Öttinger's stocks are quite depleted."

"Where *is* Öttinger? I should like a tincture."

"In the pantry. He hides from us there. I'm afraid we've scandalised him."

"Excuse me, did you say don't drink the water? You don't think Herr Bourbaki was telling the truth, do you?"

"I wouldn't put it past him."

"Neither would I. The man's a menace. Or a visionary. It really depends on how you look at it."

"But to do such a thing! A whole town! Wouldn't it be a felony? Or something?"

"Sedition?"

"Perfidy."

"Ah! Language is fugitive, is it not? We fail to describe the machinations of genius, my friends, precisely because *they* describe *us*. Anyone for a top up? Bourbaki's been good to his word—this one's a Château-Chalon from the Jura."

"Mine's a gin. I do hope this isn't the only bottle left."

"Not to worry. Bourbaki's last consignment is due today. It'll come with victuals and refreshment, no doubt. He *does* look after us."

Öttinger was indeed in the pantry—a troubled man. Bourbaki had filled his gasthaus with an entirely different type of cargo and the innkeeper didn't know what to make of it. The yard next door had been emptying out that month—most of the materials were already up on the mountain and the constant deliveries had tapered off. Instead, carriages had been arriving from the city carrying people. But not people as Öttinger had previously known them.

The first had been Yoder, who had arrived on the late coach one night, waking Öttinger and Adelheid, his wife, and bearing a letter of introduction from Bourbaki, as well as a substantial credit note. It had been raining and so they'd lit a fire to warm the travellers—Yoder had an entourage of two—and relieved the surprise guests of wet hats, cowls and overcoats. What this kindness revealed thoroughly unsettled the hotelier and his wife—Adelheid instantly made her excuses and retreated to the kitchen on the pretext of preparing sandwiches, leaving the man of the house alone with their guests. Yoder was a fashionably-dressed man, his age nevertheless betrayed on the back of his hands, in the curve of his dowager's hump, on his throat once released from a damp cravat, across a deeply-lined face and in a seemingly permanent, toothless smirk. He had such a full head of perfectly motionless hair that it could only be a wig—a speculation reinforced for Öttinger by its mauve colouring and propensity to sparkle. It was past midnight and the room was dim in the half-hearted light of a single lamp. The fire's flickering seemed to throw each corner into a deeper gloom. None of this prompted the old man to remove his dark eyeglasses.

One of his companions was diminutive, all frilled foppery—an olive green velvet suit on a slight frame, a hand on a hip, pursed red lips and the complexion of a Russian doll. Rouge, or simply colour in the cheeks? Man or woman, boy or girl—it bothered Öttinger that he couldn't tell. Yoder declined to introduce this person, instead gesturing towards the third.

"My colleague, Eschmann."

Eschmann, on the surface of it, was the least bizarre of the three. Elderly, though not as ancient as Yoder, he wore a tattered old cardigan from the pocket of which he now retrieved a pipe. The little hair he had left was longish and yellowing grey, the same colour as his neatly trimmed beard. Amiable eyes squinted through thick spectacles. He smiled and nodded. Öttinger, for some reason that he would never pin down, felt an unnameable horror. He looked at the note he held in his hand.

"You are an artist, Mr Yoder?"

Yoder put an open hand to his breast.

"You know me not," he said. "A dreadful crime. An outrage, I should say. Beauty itself is violated. Oh! But I forgive you, I forgive you." With the other hand he waved a black handkerchief around him as if to fend off his surroundings. His speech was a little difficult to follow for the want of teeth. "Had I been called upon to conjure up, in my mind's eye, some corner of the Earth where my name were not revered, it would be just such an outpost as this. Little Poppet, steady me."

The diminutive person took Yoder by the elbow and glared at Öttinger.

"My good man," said Yoder to the innkeeper, having taken a few recuperative breaths. "I am the greatest artist who ever lived."

"Oh," said Öttinger, his face flushing. "You'll have to forgive me, Mr Yoder. We don't get many—"

"Not another word. I do. I do forgive you." Once again, he swatted at the room with his handkerchief. "It's to be expected. You won't have seen my name sullied, for example, by inclusion in any of the dailies. I do not permit daguerrotype reproductions. I'm afraid celebrity would bore me.

"The decoration of trinkets," he continued, "the jotting down of ditties, low manipulations of clay—I leave all that to others. It is not of interest. I am subsumed—*subsumed*, I tell you—by an altogether more serious concern."

He had taken a step forward and, for all Öttinger knew, was looking right at him from behind those glasses.

"I forge reality itself."

"Oh," said Öttinger. "Well, that does sound—"

"The Vistorium at Schliebnitz! The legendary Look-A-Rama at Platzograd! To name but two."

"Very good." There was no sign of Adelheid or the sandwiches. "Perhaps I could show you to your rooms? The three on the top floor should do very nicely."

"Nonsense," said Yoder. "We are one—Eschmann, The Little Poppet and I. A single being. We shall bunk." Two crooked fingers had gone to The Little Poppet's chin. "We are delighted to do so. Besides," he said, without looking at Öttinger, "you are to expect more guests, my good fellow. A clutch of 'em!"

They had been arriving ever since, not a single one any less alarming to the innkeeper and his wife. He sat now in his own pantry to avoid eye contact with any of them. It only seemed to make things worse. Outside, in a dining room where no burgher would ordinarily have put an elbow on a table or chewed with their mouth open, they lounged and frolicked. It was noisy—the air brimmed with their ostentatious tributes to Bourbaki, whom they referred to as The Impresario.

"Such stature!"

"The vim of him!"

There was something in the tone, though, that didn't seem quite right.

There was dancing at two o'clock. Liqueurs had been ordered at breakfast. Despite his repeatedly telling them he didn't have any, they would enquire for laudanum. They were here, of course, for whatever was up there on the Wahrberg, but few of them had any obvious profession. Among them, Yoder was revered. Some of the women might have been dancers—they were certainly very good at it. One remarkable young man, dressed from head to toe in white linen, who never sat down, had introduced himself as a *papetier*. It was all a bit much. Adelheid had gone to stay with her sister and here he was in the pantry, eavesdropping.

"But you don't mean to say they haven't cottoned on?"

"Watch your words though, eh, Zaugg. We promised to be discreet. And we wouldn't want to imperil our little jolly now, would we?"

"The audacity of the man!"

"A genius."

"Or a menace. Though, in fairness, to get away with such a thing—"

"And for so long."

"Not an inkling in the bedchambers? Surely—"

"The deformities—"

"Zaugg!"

The thunderclaps were more frequent, separated from lightning flashes by umbilical seconds. The storm was still out there, over the plain, but it was coming—the odd, heavy drop spattered Clara's forehead and face. She kept her eye closed against them but otherwise found them pleasant, cooling and salty between her parted lips. At a brief tug from Rolf at the rear, Jordi stopped. Clara could see that they were in a gateway—two tall wooden posts and a chain-link gate that swung open between them. The smell of fresh timber and overturned earth. She could hear horses snort and champ in their bridles; Bourbaki had built the entrance where the Wahrbergweg, the only track that zigzagged its way up this mountain, petered out. No carriage could go further. The way ahead would be a muddy mess of footprints and pocked with the divots made by walking canes.

"I don't want anyone to see us," said Clara.

"I know where I am now," said Jordi. "I can take us round the other side, up along the gully. You know it, Rolf?"

Rolf's end of the litter nodded.

"But they'll see us eventually, Clara," said Jordi. "There's no avoiding it."

"We'll wait for the storm," said Clara. "For the heavy rain. They won't turn us away then—they'll be stuck with us."

Lia and Rolf could see something sparkle between the pines, though Rolf couldn't tell anyone and Lia didn't know the word for sparkle. Jordi was confident here and their progress quicker—he knew the woodsman's path that predated the fence and ran along the inside of it. He led them through half a circumnavigation and then turned uphill, the noise of trickling water to his right. At the top, they emerged from trees where Bourbaki's secret erection rose suddenly, almost filling the clearing that had been made for it. It was tall—tall enough for Clara to get a look.

"It *is* a greenhouse!" she said.

It was made of glass and iron—huge panes of the former to a height of perhaps eight metres, housed in slender frames of the latter. It curved away from them in both directions to form a circle, Clara supposed, of between thirty and forty metres in diameter. At the top, it tapered inwards and there was a second circle sitting on the first, this upper tier just two metres or so in height and, on top of that, right at the centre of the whole thing, a little glassless gazebo. The rain began to pelt the sides of the thing, washing down the panes of glass. Through them, nothing—white window blinds obscured the interior.

"It's time," said Clara, and they set off along the sweep of the glasshouse. As they rounded it, a melee of raised voices came within earshot. None of the several dozen guests, it seemed, had yet been let inside and they had congregated as near to the entrance as they could, though there was no porch and it did them no good in the heavy rain. Gentlemen were gallantly holding umbrellas aloft over the ladies' heads. The storm was tumbling in overhead and the wind was up, the odd gust blowing the rain horizontally and wetting the indignant little crowd. Darkness had fallen suddenly, as if dropped upon them. One or two of the gentlemen were using the handles of their canes to rap on the door. Nobody noticed the newly arrived children.

Then the little gaggle began to shrink, as if breathed in by the building, and the children found themselves at the threshold and an opened door, and were inhaled in their turn. Once inside Clara was surprised to discover not some high open space but a low, dark corridor, its walls and ceiling lined with black fabric. A row of flickering gas lamps, high along one side, lit the way till at the end a set of steps was faintly lit from above. The staircase presented an obvious challenge and they were a while at it. At the top they emerged through a double door lined with the same black felt, onto the edge of a round, raised platform in the middle of the glasshouse. The door clicked shut behind them. There were two circular rails on the platform—one at the centre around a little hatch in the floor and a second around the edge. At this outer rail, the guests had fanned out along one side of the circumference, standing or sitting on chairs with their backs to the children, looking at whatever lay beyond. Their chatter thrummed with expectation.

"Oh, look," someone said.

Heads turned—at first a few, then all—to see the new arrivals: the blind dwarf boy bearing a stretcher on his shoulders, the gangly mute at the other end of it with arms down, the quadriplegic on it and the slow girl, who had obviously been at her mother's make-up, all of whom were sodden.

"Who brought *them* here?"

The initial, perplexed silence became a rising hubbub.

"Ghastly."

"Someone should deal with this."

"They'll be ill from the wet."

"And catching, do you think?"

When nobody approached the children—both the burghers and Bourbaki's entourage stayed where they were—silence fell again, heavy and impotent.

"Lia," said Clara, "can you see my mother? Has she seen us?"

Lia looked around till she saw Clara's mother, who was in a chair and had the back of one hand to her forehead while two other ladies leaned over her, fussing and fanning.

"Pretty!" said Lia.

"Can you tilt me, boys?" said Clara. "I can't see anything."

Hanging over them was a shallow black dome, no more than three metres from the floor and also lined with the black fabric. It seemed to suck the light in; Clara had never seen such darkness, such negative space, anything so opposite of her notion of a *good* ceiling. It was just . . . nothing. There were no words in it. No stories. She shivered. It extended a little further out than the platform, blocking any view of the building's upper reaches, obligating the eye to the horizontal. The boys tipped her slightly. The straps held. Behind them was the entrance they'd come through—Clara noted distractedly that the doors didn't have handles—and to the left was an unoccupied stretch of railing. Rolf steered Jordi till they had the litter alongside it. Then they laid it on the floor and tipped her some more so that she could have a good look.

Below them and all around the platform, filling the entire floor space of the great glasshouse, were treetops. Real treetops—the perfume of a pine forest wafted up from them—but cut from their trunks to sit below the level of the platform. A few birds had either been set free in the glasshouse or found their way in—they flitted about, adding to the realism. The treetops closest to the inner platform had been left taller—any of the guests might have crouched to reach out and touch one—but as the eye moved towards the outer wall they gradually got shorter, as if the hill were falling away in here just as it did out there. Now Clara could see that it wasn't blinds that blocked the view from outside, but a huge canvas wrapped around the interior of the glass circle.

On it, where the shortest treetops lined the edge of the floor space, painted pines seemed to continue the wood's orderly descent: above those, a great panorama.

"Jordi!" she said. "It's the Siebenköpfe!"

The seven heads of the massif peered down at the Wahrberg from the north. The scene perfectly replicated the stormy weather outside, the peaks only just visible in the murk of low cloud. Bolts of lightning in bright white wound themselves around the upper reaches, forked and seeming to fizzle with electricity, the effect intensified by the real storm outside, louder and louder. From time to time, the whole canvas was backlit for an instant. The artist had made the mountains look just as they normally did at this time of year—only the scantest snowcaps—and had rendered the rain in such a way as curtains of it could be seen here and there, thicker and darker where it fell in sheets, the inconsistencies of violent weather racing over the earth.

"They look so real," said Clara.

At the opposite rail, pride straightened Yoder's spine a little. Like everybody else, he was listening intently to the peculiar children.

"They are real, Clara," said Jordi.

"No, Jordi. This is a painting of them. Herr Bourbaki has covered all the windows with a great big painting of everything outside."

"Oh," said the boy, and was quiet for a moment. "Why?"

Clara's eye moved up in its socket to follow the scene as it bent away to their right, where the foothills of the Siebensköpfe were depicted and then the gap between that range and the Lügenspitze. At the nadir she could make out the box-like shapes of the pit heads and the smoke stacks from the steelworks. There was some light left in this sky, just as there had been outside, but Yoder's storm threw the industrial scene below it into gloom. Dots of bright red and orange paint expertly evoked street lamps, distant and smeared a little in the painted rain. Only the air in the glasshouse—perfectly still—betrayed the artist's handiwork for what it was.

"A masterpiece?" said Yoder. The children could just hear him speak at the other side of the platform, since the noise of the deluge against the glass was tremendous now—surges of sound that rose and fell in volume as gusts beat down upon the structure. "Certainly, certainly. My opus magnum? Oh! You mustn't ask. You can't."

But none of the party were admiring his masterpiece. Neither, in fact, was he; all eyes were on the children. Rolf and Jordi had pulled Clara a little further along the floor and tilted her right up against the railings where she could look through, watched by all.

Einpferd. From here the little town seemed tiny indeed, looked down upon not only by the Wahrberg but also from the Dreischwestern in the distance behind it, the three white peaks a part of the ring of mountains which surrounded the town, lowering only where the coal mines clustered. It occurred to Clara as her eye moved over Yoder's scene that the oval thus created was like an eye itself, with the Wahrberg for a dark pupil at its centre and Einpferd a fleck in the green iris of orchard and farmland that surrounded it. The rain drummed a quickening rhythm.

"Look," said somebody behind them. It was Frau Pfafl.

Between the gathering of local dignitaries and the children, who continued to look out over the panorama, the circular hatch opened in the middle of the platform. Light shot up out of it, along with theatrical smoke, and a voice.

"Since the dawn of time—"

The church organist rolled her eyes. *That* voice. As Bourbaki ascended, it was evident that he did so on a spiral staircase—his head and shoulders emerged, circling. He wore a top hat and a dark burgundy suit. Illumination from below made a burlesque of his features. An unseen string quartet had embarked upon a suspenseful tune.

"Unnecessary," muttered constable Ümmel.

"Yes," said Dr Amstutz, beside him. "This part is heavy-handed."

"Man has felt—" continued Bourbaki.

As he made his last round of the staircase and turned away from the guests, he saw the children and stopped, then ascended the few remaining steps in silence till he once again faced the crowd. He jabbed a thumb over his shoulder.

"Who brought *them* here?"

Nobody replied.

"This is no place for . . ." he said. "It's meant to be . . ."

His tone was irritable.

"Right. Well, time is against us. From the dawn of time, my friends, Man has felt—" he paused to emit a crestfallen sigh, "the desire to deceive."

Flourishing an ivory-handled cane, he emerged from the railed circle at the top of the stairs and stood before the assembled townspeople. Behind him, the children—Clara transfixed by the panorama, supported by Rolf and Jordi, Lia practising hopscotch—were the only ones to pay him no heed.

"Well," he planted the tip of the cane on the floor before him with a metallic thud and rested both hands on the handle. "Not I."

He had to raise his voice to be heard—that and the racket of heavy rain accentuated his natural theatricality. Raising a hand, he waved it, as if to provide a cue. When no one responded, he waved again.

"Zaugg? Why is nothing happening, confound you? We rehearsed this."

The reply came from beneath their feet.

"I don't think the mechanism is sparking, Herr Bourbaki. Some rain might have gotten in."

"Damnation!" Bourbaki had flushed to the colour of a bruise as he returned to the hatch. "How much have I spent on this contraption?" He wound his way back down the staircase, pulling the trap door closed behind him. Muffled remonstrations could be heard.

"Mechanism?" said Yoder, to no one in particular.

"There's no time! I'll do it myself, damn you!" Bourbaki's voice was clear again, though it still came from below. A door was slammed shut.

"There he is," said Adelheid Öttinger. She leant over the rail and pointed downwards. Everyone apart from the children spread out on either side of her to get a better look. Bourbaki was making his way between the truncated treetops, muttering to himself. As he got further away from the platform and found himself among the shorter ones, he seemed to be growing, becoming gigantic against the painted forest and distant mountain ranges. The effect dumbfounded them all and positively dizzied one or two of the ladies, especially when he reached the canvas and turned to address them; some acoustic quirk of the glasshouse amplified him—though they could barely hear each other for the thunder, Bourbaki's voice filled the space with ease.

"This would have been better," he said, "if the mechanism had worked."

"*What* mechanism?" said Yoder. Whenever agitated, he would produce the black handkerchief and wave it about. Behind him, the children were oblivious—Lia because she always was, the boys because they were supporting Clara and Clara because she had drawn an imaginary square around the image of Einpferd and was pouring her attention into it, blocking out the rest.

"As it is," said Bourbaki to the burghers, "I'll have to do it myself. You'll excuse me, Yoder," he shrugged. "The mechanism . . ."

He turned to the canvas and took a pocket knife from his waistcoat.

"What is this?" Yoder, who was usually scrupulous in his avoidance of touch, had elbowed his way to the railing. But Bourbaki had already begun to unpick the stitches of a seam, enough to work his hand into it, whereupon he turned to face them again.

"Not I!"

He pulled at the canvas and it parted at the seam from top to bottom. Another tug and a section of the panorama, identical in size to one of the huge panes that formed the glasshouse, fell to the artificial forest floor.

"Stop it!" said Yoder. The view through the exposed glass was obscured by the rain, and darker than its painted counterpart—illuminated from within—had been, and without the paper to diffuse it, the lightning blinded them. The flashes had lengthened into dazzling seconds, as if some deity were flicking an electric light and leaving it on for a moment. They could hear it, *feel* it fizzle with current, still lit when its thunder struck with the violence of a bomb, causing several of the gathering to duck and cower. Even Clara registered it, pulled out of her trance for a moment.

"I can see your house, Rolf," she said. "The parlour window is lit."

Lia giggled, loving the pandemonium.

"Can you see mine, Clara?" said Jordi.

On the other side of the glasshouse, Bourbaki ripped his way through the panorama. Some of the sheets came down neatly in his hands, others tore unevenly and he would flail about for the scraps left up. Unreachable tatters dangled here and there.

"*Please* don't," Yoder whimpered. It wasn't immediately obvious that Bourbaki even heard him, so intent was the shopkeeper on his labour. But after a moment he stopped to address the occupants of the platform.

"Oh, do stop snivelling, Yoder. Didn't you wonder why I'd have you recreate the very scene that anyone who stood on this spot would already see? In every pointless detail? Or did vanity blunt your wit?"

"I did think it odd," said the artist, applying the handkerchief to his wet cheeks—though Bourbaki, having resumed, paid no attention. Nor did anyone else; the whole structure was rattling in the wind and the newly-revealed glass seemed to expose them all to the storm. "But you are country people, I supposed. Simple folk. I accept commissions. Oh!"

He covered his face and sobbed. At the circumference, Bourbaki had torn his way through the arc of a quadrant. He stepped back to admire his work and turned once more to the little crowd, arms outstretched.

"Look at it!" he said. "Look at what I give to you. No deception, this. No mere trick!"

To everyone gathered, bar the distracted children, his voice was as clear as if he whispered in each ear.

"Did you really think I'd content myself with a glasshouse?" he said. "A folly?" He doubled over so suddenly it was as if something invisible had dealt him a body blow and as he straightened, the grimace of pain that twisted his face became a rictus of joyless laughter, till he gripped his hips and spoke. "Look at it! I give you the world! The world itself!"

He set off again on his way around the circle, ripping at the panorama.

"And why such magnanimity?" he said as he went. "How could I possible be so generous as to give you—my disappointing burghers—the very *world*?" He doubled over again—another silence followed by another cackle. "So that you see it's mine to give!" he roared. "So that you know it's mine!" He made his way through another section of the canvas, towards the spot upon which Clara had set her eye—Einpferd.

"I can see it, yes, Jordi," she said. "There's a figure in the kitchen window. Perhaps it's you!"

Jordi snorted.

"I don't think so," he said. "I can't reach that window. Oh, what a playground for you Clara! Is it better than your father's ceiling? We could bring you up here to look at it, often. Imagine all the stories you could tell!"

Clara tried to imagine. She let her eye rove over the tableau of the town. Hauptstrasse and the general store. The church and graveyard on the low hill behind the wood mill. The neat crescents of the nicer houses. The pond.

"Is it even better than the sky, Clara?"

But she couldn't. Something was wrong. Her gaze moved from place to place, painted thing to painted thing, with increasing unease. It darted, desperately now, from the weathervane to the old well, to the copse of chestnuts and the coach house.

"I . . . I can't see any at all, Jordi," she said, unable to stop the acceleration of her breath. "I don't see any stories at all. The world like this," she shuddered, "is a story told."

Rolf squeezed her.

"Everything is done," she said.

Somewhere above them, glass shattered and showered the metal dome that hung over the central platform. Bourbaki too, at the outer rim, was pelted with shards—he grabbed a discarded swathe of the panorama and crouched beneath it. Once the glass had fallen, he stood and kept it wound around him, against the rain. He sheltered his eyes against the downpour to squint up at the roof, then again at the platform, the swaggering showmanship gone from his expression, it seemed to Frau Pfafl, and replaced by a bewilderment. He almost seemed to appeal to them to say something. To do something. For someone else to decide what happened next.

"Isn't this all getting a little out of hand, Bourbaki?"

Yoder's demeanour, too, had changed. He had stopped snivelling. He had his hands on the rail—the dark eyeglasses dangled from one of them, his exposed eyes watery slits. Predatory, pinhole irises peered from them. His high-collared cape had dropped from his shoulders to reveal his stoop and his chin jutted forward, head low and mantis-like.

"A little out of control?" His voice, though raised, was perfectly steady. "It all seems to be falling apart around you, sir, this creation of yours. Oh! How it unsettles when affairs don't proceed according to our designs. Horror!" He smiled. "But we mustn't upset the little ones, must we?"

The question went through Bourbaki like a harpoon. He took an instinctive step towards the platform.

"Yoder," he said, scowling.

"Oh!" One hand went to Yoder's breast. "Have I said it? Could I?" Now both hands cupped his face. "Didn't I promise you? Promise you! But I know not what I say on this mountaintop—I am at sea, sir—all at sea." He dabbed at an eye with his handkerchief. "I don't know myself like this, I'm sure. My nadir, certainly! To have betrayed so beloved a patron. And in earshot of his own!"

The great artist sobbed, and continued to apply the handkerchief, and smirked behind it.

"His own what?" said Frau Pfafl. "What are you talking about, man?"

"Goodness!" Yoder wailed. "The cat's out of the bag! Oh!"

"Yoder!" Bourbaki took a few more steps towards the platform, but it was too late. Yoder pressed his chin to his chest, shut his eyes and reached out with one hand in the direction of Clara and the others.

"His children," he said. "His *own children*."

More sobbing.

"Ridiculous," said Frau Pfafl. "You are confused. Bourbaki is childless. Why, that is Clara. And Rolf, and—"

"No, wait." Öttinger stepped forward. He stood now between the oblivious children and the others. "There is something about the children," he said. "I was listening to this lot," he waved his hand at Yoder and The Little Poppet, the quiet *papetier*, Eschmann and presumably Zaugg—a balding and bespectacled man who had emerged from the trap door—who stood together looking at once very pleased with themselves for having a secret to tell and somewhat apprehensive about telling it, "jabbering in the gasthaus. There *is* something."

"Öttinger, I—"

"Quiet, Bourbaki!" Öttinger raised his voice. He hadn't taken his eyes from Yoder's. "This isn't your show anymore."

Bourbaki stood in the rain looking up at the platform and a line of backs, the owners of which had turned their attention elsewhere. He pulled the shawl of canvas tighter, covered his eyes from the rain, flinched at another lightning strike.

"Go on, then," said Frau Pfafl. "Out with it!" Despite the tumult and the clear signs of stress to the structure in which they all stood, she was beginning to enjoy herself.

"I?" Yoder's bony fingers were splayed over his heart, his narrow eyes widening just a touch. "Yoder? *Yoder* is asked to speak? Now? Here?" He waved his hanky. "With his work in tatters? Oh! You want his integrity too? Beast! No! He mustn't . . . he can't . . ." He buried his face in the velveteen folds of The Little Poppet's blazer and issued a muffled "He don't!"

Eschmann stepped forward.

"I believe I can be of some help in clarifying the matter," he said, taking his pipe out of the pocket of his cardigan and thumbing some tobacco into it. With some difficulty—gusts were finding their way in through the broken roof—he lit up and puffed on it a few times, his gaze in the middle distance, the picture of a shabby academic mentally preparing some opening remarks to a lecture. Every burgher, to a man and woman, felt the hair on their arms stand up.

"Since he claims to have no interest in deceiving us, I can only surmise that Mr Bourbaki has undergone something of a Damascene conversion," he began. "His has been quite the deception, I can assure you. Quite the deception." He spoke softly and was therefore almost inaudible above the storm. All heads bent forward and bowed under the strain of hearing him.

"You are mocked, Einpferd!" Yoder had separated himself from the The Little Poppet's bosom. "Cuckolded!"

"Yoder!" came Bourbaki's voice from behind them. "Eschmann!" The threat was gone from it—it was supplicatory now. A plea.

"Oh, do be quiet, Bourbaki!" said Frau Pfafl. She and the others had crowded around Eschmann. "Get to it man! What are you talking about?"

"Who are these people anyway?" said Adelheid Öttinger, fidgeting. "Why should we believe—"

Clara's mother let out a cry and fainted into one of the vacant chairs, where a companion fanned her.

"It's got something to do with the water," said the Öttinger.

Lightning hit the turret. A cascade of sparks bounced from the dome over the platform and showered Bourbaki. He didn't cower this time. He didn't flinch. He looked up at the congregation and waited. They too were still and silent, intent on Eschmann.

"Indeed," said that gentleman. "Indeed it does, indeed it does."

He took another puff and was about to continue when a second roof pane gave in and fell in one piece to the floor, where it broke on the treetops.

"Can't this nonsense wait?" said Adelheid Öttinger. "We must all go!"

But Eschmann didn't hesitate.

"The water indeed," he muttered round the stem of his pipe, "is the very matter. The very matter."

"For heaven's *sake*, man—" said Frau Pfafl.

"Tell me, Dr Amstutz," said Eschmann, ignoring her, "are you familiar with a compound called hexafluorosilicic acid?"

"I am not," said the doctor.

"No, indeed. No, indeed," said Eschmann. "We are in the provinces. It's a wonderful little compound, Doctor. Very good for the teeth, you know. You must have noticed how the town's teeth have become so strong and shapely? If a little stained. Why, your late dentist has never been replaced for the want of demand."

He shrugged.

"A town without a dentist? How should one account for such a circumstance?"

"Mountain air," said Doctor Amstutz. "Diet. Modern—"

"Hexafluorosilicic acid, doctor," said Eschmann. "Nothing more. I must say, I do find it surprising that a town would hand control of its water supply to one with so pronounced an appetite for power and influence as Mr Bourbaki." He smiled. "Really very surprising indeed. And yet, there it is."

"I don't understand," said constable Ümmel. "Why are we talking about teeth?"

Eschmann chuckled.

"We aren't," he said. "In considerably larger concentrations than would be necessary for the aforementioned benefits, hexafluorosilicic acid has a quite distinct effect. Quite distinct." He brushed some ash from his paunch. "I'm afraid I must risk offending the sensibilities of ladies present," he said, "in pointing out to you all that Mr Bourbaki's interest has not been primarily orthodontical."

"Please—" A faint voice from the back of the little crowd. It was Clara's mother.

"Oh no. No, no. Not orthodontical," said Eschmann. "No, indeed. It was with regard to the town's procreational activities that Mr Bourbaki sought my advice, in response to which I offered my recommendation. Your water supply has been heavily contaminated, and your menfolk quite sterile, ever since."

"Ever since? Ever since *when*?" said Frau Pfafl.

"Oh, some years. Some years now," said Eschmann. He had stepped towards the central rail to tap his pipe out on it. Embers dropped harmlessly to the metal floor, and some fell over the edge to smoulder, less harmfully, below. Little wisps of smoke rose where they settled on the dry pine needles. Other wisps, further out where the sparks had landed, already had the look of a large fire in the miniature forest. "Good twenty of 'em, I should think."

"That can't be," said Frau Pfafl. "Rolf there can only be fifteen. And the others are younger."

"I think you're missing the point, Frau Pfafl," said Öttinger. His gaze had settled on his wife, who would not return it.

"Leo . . ." she whispered.

"And all of them," his eyes were back on Eschmann, "during that time, have been *his*?"

He pointed to Bourbaki, below them, mute and unmoving.

"Yes," said Eschmann.

"*All* of them?" said Frau Pfafle. "Little Aldo Blosch with the cleft palate?"

"Yes," said Eschmann.

"And Gertie, the baker's daughter, who has no feet?"

"Yes," said Eschmann. "And narcoleptic Agatha Huber. Pieter, Vitus and Clement, the asthmatic triplets. And—"

"And my Lia," said Öttinger. He too had come to the inner rail. He looked over at the children and began to descend the spiral stair.

"Well!" said Frau Pfafl. "The cheeky badger!"

"Behold!" said Yoder, waving his handkerchief in the direction of Clara and the others. "The poor suffering souls he spawned! The issue of his poisonous seed. His twisted drive made manifest! The, eh . . . waste product . . . the, eh . . ."

"Detritus?" said the young *papetier*.

"Effluvia?" said Eschmann.

"Oh!" said Yoder. "Language!" A flourish of the handkerchief. "How it escapes us!"

He turned back to the outer rail and once again gripped it, leering down at Bourbaki.

"But not our progeny, eh maestro? Hm? Not our sins. Oh no. No, no—*we* are the prey. *They* stalk *us*. Hm? Through our nights, our days. The years. Even," he said, replacing his eyeglasses, "if my eyes do not deceive me, unto the grave."

Bourbaki had doubled over again, straightened again. Once the grimace had faded he was perfectly expressionless. He returned to the canvas and began to pull it down, bit by bit, without passion now—as if he could think of nothing else to do.

Another lightening strike to the iron frame of the glass house. Clara felt the surge of it in her. She'd heard them talking, half paid attention with her eye on the painted scene and her ears on them, but she hadn't understood. Something about father, and teeth. She didn't feel as though she suffered, all that much. Perhaps in school, in maths. She didn't know what 'effluvia' meant but she knew 'detritus', and 'waste'. How could that be her, though, when so many depended on her? Rolf and the boys for the stories, and Mila. And father.

Her eye had closed in on the house and the garden, and now on the pear tree, painted from above. She isolated an area of the upper branches and concentrated, and now a gap among them, and concentrated on that. And now a . . . and now . . .

She blinked in disbelief. In a space between the branches where the little grass verge was visible, the artist had painted a girl in a chair. In *her* chair, in a green dress that was her green dress, the girl looked back up at her. For a moment she saw herself as others did—the bent frame, the misshapen features, the broken little body. But it wasn't her. She wasn't that. How could she be, when that Clara sat there looking up at her? She must be a bird in the air. She must be the air. Somebody screamed. There was the sound of smashing glass and, even as she felt the rain on her face, her nose filled with the smell of burning.

"We shall all die here!" said Frau Pfafl, watching Öttinger from the platform as he picked his way between the little fires in the fake forest, towards Bourbaki, whose oil-painted cloak was also aflame. Oblivious, the shopkeeper pulled methodically at successive swathes of the panorama.

The girl. The dress. Her face. And now the eye—there was nothing but the green eye of her doppelgänger and its flecked iris and Clara, *real* Clara, had no body. She was the storm, and at last the scene matched the sounds around her—the noise and the gusting rain that had been so strangely absent. The thunder that sounded as if it was ripping through the world and then the real rip of paper and the painted eye was torn. Where half of it had been was now the blackness of reality—the waves and rivulets of water that drenched the glass house, so that she couldn't see a thing outside. As the paint, so artfully deployed, yielded nothing to her imagination, so the world outside deformed, rippled ceaselessly, refused to reveal itself. She focussed on the strip of torn paper that divided the two—an irregular border, raw and fibrous, it seemed to Clara the only safe place to hold her gaze, the only reliable spot. The only way to tell that one was one and the other the other. The edge of everything.

A scream.

"We shall die!" someone yelled. It wasn't Frau Pfafl.

Clara felt the storm's electricity enter her and, as it did, Jordi's voice as if from far away.

"Is she going to fit, Rolf?"

Lia giggling.

Rolf's arm around her, reminding her once again that she was Clara.

And now she was the storm. And now, for just a moment, Clara again. And now a bird over the pear tree. Her eye closed and she was Clara, opened and she was the bird. Closed, Clara. Open, the storm. Closed—now she was someone called Lita. Open—and she was Sharazad. And now, the bird again. Now Clara, now not. Sharazad. Lita. Clara. And Rolf's arm was tight, and began to lift her and there was still the smell of burning, despite the wet and the wind. Someone screamed. And someone else. And no, she wouldn't die. She would live. Because they needed her. The boys for the stories. Lia. Because

Mila was so utterly dependent on her, and was waiting for her. Clara. Sharazad. The bird. The storm. And now she was.

Lita on the observation deck. Break from stasis. Forty-eight hours to eat and shit, then fast, then stasis. Real sleep, vitals, psych eval, gym. Some down time. She always came here. But this time it was a disappointment. The last time, and the time before that, the window wall had been awash with nebulae. Ablaze.

The scale of it. Later, she would want to call it interplanetary. Not least because it literally was. When she reached for words, longed for them, the literal was the only poetry available to her. Finding exactly the right word. The true word. The news.

The colors. Impossible. No words.

Stars so numerous they seemed to thicken in waves and eddies as though some animating force, some tide, were moving through them. A thousand points of light. A million. She'd spent precious hours there, hours the others spent on their mail, letting her eyes fix upon a certain spot in space and pouring her attention into it, letting it drain from elsewhere, till that tiny quadrant was all there was, and then pouring her attention into a tiny quadrant of that quadrant and then another, then another, never reaching a point where the area thus isolated was not incandescent with suns and worlds.

This time, nothing. An undifferentiated expanse that bore no tidings. No news. And even though she knew this could not be true, that the nothing was not made of absence but merely of distance, still there was nothing she could do with it, no journey to take. No destination. No destiny.

A ping, a blue square engraved in the corner of her eye. Notification. Another file, from him. She'd woken up to a glut of them this time. Had opened none. Had never once opened his files. Send to bin. Empty bin. Are you sure? Yes, she was sure. But she paused now, not knowing why. Maybe it was just boredom, that there was nothing to look at out there. Maybe because this file was tagged 'end transmission'. Endings are terrifying. But beautiful. They make a story of what came before.

Open file.

Scans of its surface revealed nothing, either from below the step or above it. The little party had vacated and we could see them further up, hiking towards an opening in the crater wall. I contemplated the blank grey slab, an intrusion of form into the undifferentiated expanse of white.

I'd get to the bottom of this—I always did—but I had to admit I was running out of options. No bodies were falling. Whatever happened here happened in the cloud that hovered just below the rim. The angel's breath. I instructed Evans to ease us in. It was like looking out of the porthole into a glass of milk.

"Readings?"

"No," said Zwickl. "The instruments don't like it."

"Get us a physical sample, will you?"

I got up and leaned against the back of his seat. He was peering through the sloped cockpit window at the ship's nose, from which a slender robotic arm now extended. At its tip was a spherical container for the sample.

"Look," he said.

I leaned over further and followed his finger. The top hemisphere of the little container had flipped open. The cloud around it, however, and also around the robotic arm, seemed to have fallen back. I saw that all along the hull as well, the whiteness seemed not to touch the ship but to hover close—the angle of the cockpit window revealed a clear gap, of maybe a centimetre.

"How fast can you move that thing? Maybe try to scoop?"

"Let's see."

Zwickl retracted the arm, leaving the receptacle open, then extended it again at speed, holding down a lever with his thumb to make it arc. Instantaneously, the gas retracted, leaving a large and perfectly neat absence of cloud.

"Ever see anything like this?"

"No."

"Artificial?" I was asking for the doctor's opinion but I was looking at the old man.

"Could be, yes," said Zwickl.

"Scan the edge. Look for any openings, irregularities. Anything that might be man-made."

"Not going to happen," said Evans. "Nothing works in here."

"How interesting," I said, my eyes still on our host's. The sensation of closing in on the truth is unmistakeable. I have experienced it many times.

"We'll do it the old-fashioned way," I said. "Return the ship. Get back up here on foot with rope and ladders."

And so here I am, Lita. He wasn't joking about the hike and I'm not as young as I used to be. Half a day, up through an old vent, lugging oxygen tanks and equipment. Me out ahead, no one talking. The old man bringing up the rear. The security detail stayed with the ship and didn't like letting us go, but I had to get here. This place is where the answer is.

Place. The word isn't enough. This place only begins in the physical. It stretches out from that mundane coordinate into us, tracing in us a different architecture. The very deepest currents in all of the literatures we've suppressed flow from right here. They cascade over the rock face of a history the contaminated tell themselves is immutable. But is it? Where it isn't eroding under the flow, it's encrusted with their prayer—a great mossy mess of meaning, slow and old but strong with its own life, and always changing. They no longer distinguish—how could they?—between the stories about it and stories about the stories. They can't see rock any more so they talk—and write, and sing and chant—about the moss. Well, I can see rock. I'm standing on it.

Once we were out into the crater and between the two layers of cloud, I was able to lift my visor. It was as though two boundaries, one above and one below, separated us from death. From nothing. And here, in between, all life. I knew the moment I took my first unaided breath that everything I'd ever done or been had led here. I've kept the helmet on for the audio. Forgive all the heavy breathing, won't you?

Can you hear that? Is the mike picking it up? Perhaps not—the water is deafening. They're yelling at me. I'm the first onto the platform and I've laid out the rope and climbing gear.

I have to tell you about the scent, Lita. When my visor went up, for a moment I was back in the garden, in the perfume of the azalea. I haven't smelled that for so long. Evans is bringing some sampling equipment and Zwickl has all his usual gizmos. Keep an eye out for the findings, won't you? They'll be up on the Neb soon, no doubt.

I'm glad I've told you everything. It's your story too. Forgive me for taking so long. They're still a hundred meters or so uphill of me, Evans and Zwickl, waving frantically. The old man is too, but he's smiling. He looks a lot happier than he was in the ship. Perhaps, at last, he understands me.

Those two are fretting because they don't like me off the safety line—I unclipped myself for a bit of mobility when laying out the gear. They think I'll walk too close to the edge, no doubt. I won't. Forgive me, Lita, but I'm not walking anywhere.

I'm running.

END

Acknowledgements

Deepest thanks to Jacob Smullyan, the second-most fortuitous encounter of my life, and to Katja Spindler, the first. To David Collard and Christopher Boucher for their Exacting contributions and to John Patrick Higgins for the same, but above all for the good company as I found my way. To Bill Spencer and Brad Turner for their indispensable advice. To the nameless authors of the Nights and their numerous translators, to Mr Werner for his Nomenclature, and to my family for their love and support.

Guillermo Stitch is the author of *Lake of Urine* and executive editor at *Exacting Clam*.